continued . . .

SHIFTER'S WOLF

MASQUES AND *WOLFSBANE* IN ONE VOLUME

PATRICIA BRIGGS

ACE BOOKS, NEW YORK

THE BERKLEY PUBLISHING GROUP
Published by the Penguin Group
Penguin Group (USA) Inc.
375 Hudson Street, New York, New York 10014, USA

Penguin Group (Canada), 90 Eglinton Avenue East, Suite 700, Toronto, Ontario M4P 2Y3, Canada
(a division of Pearson Penguin Canada Inc.) • Penguin Books Ltd., 80 Strand, London WC2R 0RL,
England • Penguin Ireland, 25 St. Stephen's Green, Dublin 2, Ireland (a division of Penguin
Books Ltd.) • Penguin Group (Australia), 707 Collins Street, Melbourne, Victoria 3008, Australia
(a division of Pearson Australia Group Pty. Ltd.) • Penguin Books India Pvt. Ltd., 11 Community
Centre, Panchsheel Park, New Delhi—110 017, India • Penguin Group (NZ), 67 Apollo Drive,
Rosedale, Auckland 0632, New Zealand (a division of Pearson New Zealand Ltd.) • Penguin Books,
Rosebank Office Park, 181 Jan Smuts Avenue, Parktown North 2193, South Africa • Penguin China,
B7 Jaiming Center, 27 East Third Ring Road North, Chaoyang District, Beijing 100020, China

Penguin Books Ltd., Registered Offices: 80 Strand, London WC2R 0RL, England

SHIFTER'S WOLF

Previously published as *Masques* and *Wolfsbane*.

Masques copyright © 1993 by Patricia Briggs, copyright © 2010 by Hurog, Inc.
Wolfsbane copyright © 2010 by Hurog, Inc.
Map by Michael Enzweiler.
Cover art by Larry Rostant.
Cover design by Jason Gill.
Text design by Kristin del Rosario.

PUBLISHING HISTORY
Ace trade paperback edition / January 2013

Ace trade paperback ISBN: 978-0-425-26421-8

An application to register this book for cataloging has been submitted to the Library of Congress.

PRINTED IN THE UNITED STATES OF AMERICA

10   9   8   7   6   5   4   3   2   1

CONTENTS

MASQUES

WOLFSBANE

MASQUES

With love to my parents:

Harvey C. Rowland
1917–1989

Betty J. Rowland
1920–1992

INTRODUCTION

ONE DAY, IN THE MIDDLE OF MY SENIOR YEAR OF COLLEGE, I DECIDED to write a book. I'd written a few things before. Nothing so complex as an actual short story (aside from a few five-hundred-word shorts for various high-school assignments and one memorably bad story I'd written in German in lieu of a report), but scenes and scraps of dialogue. I'd never met an author, never gone to an SF convention, when I set out to write this book. And for the next few years I wrote, and rewrote, the first ten pages of my novel. Those ten pages, I might add, are the first thing I cut for this edition. Sometimes I wake up in the middle of the night and find myself muttering those lines: *The great hall of the castle was his favorite room . . .*

With our newly minted degrees, my husband and I set out for the wilds of Chicago, where Mike had taken a job as an aquarist with the John G. Shedd Aquarium (we do seem to have had a lot of interesting if not lucrative careers, my husband and I) and I began working at an insurance office. The Greater Chicago area had seven and a half million people. My home state of Montana (in the 1990s) had eight hundred thousand people—in the whole state. Suddenly my manuscript represented more than a challenge—it was an escape. Don't get me wrong, I loved Chicago—I just didn't love living with seven and a half freaking million people.

We stayed a full year before culture shock sent us racing homeward, and about that time, somewhat to my surprise, I had finished the book.

I knew that I knew nothing about writing a book when I started it. So I took those things I did know and stuck with them. The plot, my patient husband pointed out, had been done before—but I was okay with that. The important thing to me was that I'd actually finished the book. It shocked and amazed me when the book actually sold.

Masques, when it came out, was what my husband likes to call an extremely limited edition. That's husband speak for "It sold very poorly." Fortunately, before my publisher figured out just how poorly it had done, they'd bought *Steal the Dragon* as well. My second book, blessed by a terrific Royo cover and a writer who had figured out a little more about writing, did a lot better than the first. *Masques* went out of print the month *Steal the Dragon* came out back in 1995, and hasn't been in print since.

Years passed by, my career started to pick up, and *Masques* started to command higher prices on the secondary market. If I had a box of twenty-four copies left, I could sell them on eBay for more than I sold the publication rights for the original novel.

With that in mind, I took out the unpublished sequel, *Wolfsbane*, blew off the dust, and did an extensive polishing run. I sent the result to my editor and asked about reprinting *Masques* and publishing *Wolfsbane*. She agreed and asked me if I wanted to revise *Masques* before they released it. Absolutely, I said. Please. And that was about the time I got a call asking me if I'd like to try my hand at an urban fantasy first. With the subsequent success of the Mercy Thompson and Alpha and Omega novels, *Masques* and *Wolfsbane* got put on the back burner for a few years.

Finally, I had a bit of breathing room and sat down for the first time in a decade or so to start reading *Masques*. I had intended to do a brief polishing run. I read the first chapter (squirming uncomfortably all the way through) and turned to my husband. "By golly," I said (or words to that effect). "Why didn't someone tell me I needed to use a few descriptions?"

When I wrote *Masques*, I was in my twenties and hadn't even finished a short story worthy of the name. I knew nothing about writing. The only tool I had in my craftbox was that I loved the fantasy genre and had read a lot of books. Twenty years later, I've written more than fifteen books, discussed/argued writing with a number of enormously skilled craftspeople—and learned a lot in the process. But that same experience also means I could not write *Masques* now.

Thus, fixing the book and still allowing it to be the same story, my first story, became quite a problem.

In the end, *Masques* and I have come to a compromise. Though I have added a bit to the beginning, I have not taken away any of the original pieces of the story (much as it sometimes pained me). I just fit those pieces together a little better. I left in most of the clichés and the oddities that, if I were editing an unpublished work, I would have removed. Thus, I hope that those few of you who read the original and remember it fondly will feel as though this is an expanded version of the same story. And that those of you who are only familiar with my later, more polished work won't be disappointed.

PROLOGUE

THE WOLF STUMBLED FROM THE CAVE, KNOWING THAT SOMEONE WAS searching for him and he couldn't protect himself this time. Feverish and ill, his head throbbing so hard that it hurt to move, he couldn't pull his thoughts together.

After all this time, after all of his preparations, he was going to be brought down by an illness.

The searcher's tendrils spread out again, brushing across him without recognition or pause. The Northlands were rife with wild magic—which is why other magic couldn't work correctly here. The searcher looked for a wizard and would never notice the wolf who concealed the man in its shape unless the fever betrayed him.

He should lie low, it was the best defense . . . but he was so afraid, and his illness clogged his thoughts.

Death didn't frighten him; he sometimes thought he had come here seeking it. He was more afraid he wouldn't die, afraid of what he would become. Perhaps the one who looked for him was just idly hunting—but when he felt a third sweep, he knew it was unlikely. He must have given himself away somehow. He'd always known that he would be found one day. He'd just never thought it would be when he was so weak.

He fought to blend better with the form he'd taken, to lose himself in the wolf. He succeeded.

The fourth sizzle of magic, the searcher's magic, was too much for the wolf. The wolf was a simpler creature than the mage who hid within him. If he was frightened, he attacked or ran. There was no one here to attack, so he ran.

It wasn't until the wolf was tired that he could gather his humanity—
that was a laugh, *his* humanity—well then, he gathered *himself* together
and stopped running. His ribs ached with the force of his breath and the
tough pads of his feet were cut by stones and an occasional crystal of
ice from a land where the sun would never completely melt winter's gift.
He was shivering though he felt hot, feverish. He was sick.

He couldn't keep running—and it wasn't only the wolf who craved
escape—because running wasn't escape, not from what he fled.

He closed his eyes, but that didn't keep his head from throbbing in
time with his pounding pulse. If he wasn't going to die out here, he would
have to find shelter. Someplace warm, where he could wait and recover.
He was lucky he'd come south, and it was high summer. If it had been
winter, his only chance would have been to return to the caves he'd run
from.

A pile of leaves under a thicket of aspen caught his attention. If they
were deep enough to be dry underneath, they would do for shelter. He
headed downhill and started for the trees.

There was no warning. The ground simply gave out from under him
so fast he was lying ten feet down on a pile of rotted stakes before he
realized what had happened.

It was an old pit trap. He started to get up and realized that he hadn't
been as lucky as he thought. The stakes had snapped when he hit them,
but so had his rear leg.

Perhaps if he hadn't already been so sick, so tired, he could have done
something. He'd long ago learned how to set pain aside while he used
his magic. But, though he tried, he couldn't distance himself from it this
time, not while his body shivered with fever. Without magic, with a
broken leg, he was trapped. The rotting stakes meant no one was watching the pit—no one to free him or kill him quickly. So he would die slowly.

That was all right because he didn't want to be free so much as he
didn't want to be caught.

This was a trap, but it wasn't *His* trap.

Perhaps, the wolf thought, as his good legs collapsed again, perhaps it would be good not to run anymore. The ground was cold and wet underneath him, and the flush of heat from fever and the frantic journey drained into the chill of his surroundings. He shivered with cold and pain and waited patiently . . . even happily, for death to come and take him.

"IF YOU GO to the Northlands in the summer you might avoid snowstorms, but you get mud." Aralorn, Staff Page, Runner, and Scout for the Sixth Field Hundred, kicked a rock, which arced into the air and landed with an unsatisfactory splut just ahead of her on the mucky trail.

It wasn't a real trail. If it hadn't led from the village directly to the well-used camping spot her unit was currently stopped at, she'd have called it a deer trail and suspected that human feet had never trod it.

"*I* could have told them that," she said. "But no one asked me."

She took another step, and her left boot sank six inches down into a patch that looked just like the bit before it that had held her weight just fine. She pulled her foot out and shook it, trying unsuccessfully to get the thick mud off. When she started walking again, her mud-coated boot weighed twice what her right boot did.

"I suppose," she said in resigned tones as she squelched along, "training isn't supposed to be fun, and sometimes we have to fight in the mud. But there's mud in warmer places. We could go hunting Uriah in the old Great Swamp. That would be good training and *useful*, but no one would pay us. Mercenaries can't possibly be useful without someone paying us. So we're stuck—literally in the case of our supply wagons—practicing maneuvers in the cold mud."

Her sympathetic audience sighed and butted her with his head. She rubbed her horse's gray cheekbone under the leather straps of his bridle. "I know, Sheen. We could get there in an hour if we hurry—but I see no sense in encouraging stupid behavior."

One of the supply wagons was so bogged down in mud that it had broken an axle when they tried to pull it out. Aralorn had been sent out to the nearest village to have a smith repair the damage because the smith they'd brought with them had broken his arm trying to help get the wagon out.

That there had *been* a nearby village was something of a surprise out in the Northlands—though they weren't very deep into them. That village had probably been why the mercenary troops had been sent to practice where they were instead of twenty miles east or west.

The mended axle was tied lengthwise onto the left side of Sheen's saddle, with a weighted bag tied to the opposite stirrup to balance the load. It made riding awkward, which was why Aralorn was walking. Part of the reason, anyway.

"If we get to camp too early, our glorious and inexperienced captain will be ordering the wagon repaired right away. He'll send us out from a fairly good campsite to march for another few miles until the sun sets— and we'll be looking for another reasonable place to camp all night." The captain was a good sort, and would be a fine leader—eventually. But right now he was pretty set on proving his mettle and so lost to common sense. He needed to be managed properly by someone with a little more experience.

"If I don't arrive with the axle until it's dark, then he'll have to wait to move out until dawn," she told Sheen. "With daylight, it won't take long to fix the wagon, and we'll all get a good night's sleep. You and I can trot the last half mile or so, just enough to raise a light sweat and claim it was the smith who took so long."

Her warhorse jerked his head up abruptly. He snorted, his nostrils fluttering as he sucked air and flattened his ears at whatever his nose was telling him.

Aralorn thumbed off the thong that kept her sword in its sheath and looked around carefully. It wasn't just a person—he'd have alerted her to that with a twitch of his ear.

The scent of blood might have called her horse's battle training to the fore, she thought, or maybe he sensed some sort of predator. This was the Northlands, after all; there were bear, wolves, and a few other things large enough to cause Sheen's upset.

The gray stallion whinnied a shrill challenge that was likely to be heard for miles around. She could only hope that her captain didn't hear it. Whatever Sheen sensed, it was in the aspen grove just uphill from where they stood. It was also, apparently, in no hurry to attack them since nothing answered Sheen's call: no return challenge, not even a rustle.

She could go on past. Likely, if it hadn't come out yet, it wasn't going to. But what was the fun in that?

She dropped Sheen's reins on the ground. He'd stand until she came back—at least until he got hungry. Aralorn drew her knife and crept into the thicket of aspen.

HE HEARD HER talking and smelled the horse without moving. He'd heard them come by earlier, too—or he thought so anyway. The horse put up a fuss this time because the wind that ruffled the leaves of the aspen would have brought him the wolf's scent.

He waited for them to leave. Tonight, he thought hopefully. Tonight would be the third night he'd spent here, maybe it would be the last. But part of him knew better, knew just how long it took for a body to die of thirst or of hunger. He was too strong yet. It would be tomorrow, at the soonest.

He'd distracted himself with the hope of death, and only the sound of the woman's feet told him that she'd approached. He opened his eyes to see a sturdily built woman, plain of face except for her large sea-green eyes, leaning over the edge of the pit. She wore the uniform of the mercenaries, and there were calluses and mud on her hands.

He didn't want to see her eyes, didn't want to feel interest in her at all. He only wanted her to leave him alone so he could die.

"Plague them all," she said, her voice tight and angry. Then her voice softened to a croon. "How long have you been here, love?"

The wolf recognized the threat of the knife she held as she slid down the far side of the pit to stand, one foot on either side of his hips. He growled, rolling off his side in preparation to get up—because he'd forgotten he wanted to die. Just for a moment. He shook from exertion, sickness, and from the pain of moving his leg. He lay back down again and flattened his ears.

"Shh," she crooned, inexplicably sheathing her knife in the face of his aggression. "Not so long as all that, apparently. Now what shall I do about you?"

Go away, he thought. He growled at her with as much threat as he could, feeling his lips peel back from his fangs and the hair rise along his spine.

The expression on her face was not the one that he'd expected. Certainly not one any sane person would turn on a threatening wolf she was standing over. She should fear him.

Instead . . . "Poor thing," she said in that same crooning tone. "Let's get you out of this, shall we?"

She dropped her gaze away from his and knelt to examine his hips, humming softly as she moved closer.

She didn't stink of fear, was all he could think. Everyone feared him. Everyone. Even *Him*, even the one who searched. She smelled of horse, sweat, and something sweet. No fear.

He snarled, and she wrapped one hand over his muzzle. Sheer astonishment stopped his growls. Just how stupid was she?

"Shh." Her voice blended into the music she was making, and he realized that her humming was pulling magic out of the ground around and beneath them. "Let me look."

He was as surprised at himself as he was at her when he let her do just that. He could have torn out her throat or broken her neck while she examined every inch of him. But he didn't—and he wasn't quite certain why not.

It wasn't that killing her would bother him. He'd killed a lot of people. But that was before. He didn't want to do that anymore. So perhaps that was part of it.

He knew she was trying to help him—but he didn't want help. He wanted to die.

Her magic swept over and around him, cushioning him. The wolf whined softly and relaxed, leaving the mage in him fully in charge for the first time since the illness had hit. Maybe even longer ago than that.

Her magic didn't work on the mage because he knew what it was—and, he admitted to himself, because it wasn't coercive magic. He was mage enough to read her intent. She didn't want the wolf to become a lapdog but only to relax.

But the woman's helpful intent wasn't why he didn't kill her. Not the real reason. He hadn't been interested in anything in longer than he could remember, but she made him curious. He'd only ever met a practitioner of green magic, wild magic, once before. They hid from the humans in the land—if there were any still left. But here was one wearing the clothes of a mercenary.

She could pick him up—which surprised him because she didn't weigh much more than he did. But she couldn't hoist him high enough to reach the edge of the trap, so she set him down again.

"Going to need some help," she told him, and clambered to the top. She almost didn't make it out of the pit herself; if it had been round, she wouldn't have.

When she departed and took her magic with her, it left him bereaved—as if someone had covered him with a blanket, then removed it. And only when she left did he realize that her music had deadened his pain and soothed him, despite his being a mage on his guard against it.

He heard the horse move and the sound of leather and something heavy hitting the ground. The horse approached the pit and stopped.

When the mercenary who could do green magic hopped back into his almost grave, she had a rope in her hand.

He waited for the wolf to stir as she tied him in a makeshift harness that somehow managed to brace his bad leg. But the wolf waited as meekly as a lamb while she worked. When he was trussed up to her satisfaction, she climbed back out.

"Come on, Sheen," she told someone. Possibly, he thought, it was the horse.

The trip out of the hole was not pleasant. He closed his eyes and let the pain take him where it would. When he lay on the ground at last, she untied him.

Freed at last, he lay where he had fallen, too weak to run. Maybe too curious as well.

ONE

———— ༺ ————

ARALORN PACED, HER HEART BEATING WITH NERVOUS ENERGY.

It had seemed like a good idea at the time. She intended to sneak in as a servant—she was good at being a servant, and people talked in front of servants as if they weren't there at all. But then there had been that slave girl, freshly sold to the very Geoffrey ae'Magi whose court Aralorn was supposed to infiltrate and observe . . .

Maybe if the slave girl hadn't had the gray-green eyes of the old races, eyes Aralorn shared, she wouldn't have given in to impulse. But it had been easy to free the girl and send her off with connections who would see her safely back to her home—proof that though she had lived in Sianim all these years, Aralorn was still Rethian enough to despise slavery. It was even easier to use the magic of her mother's people to rearrange her body and her features to mimic the girl and take her place.

She hadn't realized that slaves could be locked away until they were needed; she'd assumed she'd have work to do. It was well-known that the Archmage's passions were reserved for magic, and he seldom indulged in more fleshly pleasures. She'd figured that the girl had been purchased to *do* something—not sit locked in a room for weeks.

Aralorn had been just about ready to escape and try again using a different identity when she'd been brought up to the great hall of the ae'Magi's castle four days ago and put into the huge silver cage.

"She's to be decoration for the ball," said the servant who put her in the cage, in response to another servant's question. "It won't be for a week yet, but he wanted her here so he could see the decorations and her at the same time."

Decoration. The ae'Magi had purchased a slave to decorate his great hall.

It had seemed out of character for the Archmage, Aralorn had thought. It took more than power to become the ae'Magi. The man or woman who wore that mantle of authority was, in his peers' eyes, a person of unassailable virtue. Only such a one could be allowed the reins to control all of the mages—at least all those west of the Great Swamp—so there was never again a wizard war. Purchasing a person in order to use her as decoration seemed . . . petty for such a one as the ae'Magi. Or so she'd thought.

Four days ago.

Aralorn shivered. Her shoes made no sound on the marble beneath her feet, not that anyone would have been able to hear them over the music.

Beyond the silver bars of her cage, the great hall of the ae'Magi's castle was resplendent. By reputation, if not fact, the room was nearly a thousand years old, kept beautiful by good maintenance and judicious replacement rather than magic.

Though this room was the heart of the ae'Magi's home, by tradition no magic was to be done here. This was the place the rulers of men conducted business with the ae'Magi, and the lack of magic proved to one and all that there was no magical coercion taking place. Aralorn now knew that the current ae'Magi didn't particularly care about following tradition, and coercion was something he used . . . on everyone.

That first day, she'd been shocked when the stone beneath her feet vibrated with magic. She looked out at the room. Ten centuries old, or at least ten centuries of care and careful preservation by the finest craftsmen available. And the ae'Magi had saturated the stone with magic. No one would think to check, would they? And if they did, they'd just suspect another ae'Magi, an earlier one, because Geoffrey ae'Magi would never defy tradition.

This evening it was lavishly decorated for the pleasure of the people who danced lightly across the floor. Late-afternoon rays of sunlight streamed through the tear-shaped crystal skylights etched on the soaring ceilings. Pale pillars dripped down to the highly polished ivory-colored marble floor that reflected the jewel-like colors of the dancers' clothing.

Aralorn's cage sat on a raised platform on the only wall of the room that lacked a doorway. From that perch, she could observe the whole room and be observed in return. Or rather they could see the illusion that the ae'Magi had placed on the cage.

Instead of the tall, white-blond woman that the ae'Magi had purchased to decorate his great hall with her extraordinary beauty, observers would see a snowfalcon as rare and beautiful, the ae'Magi had told her, as his slave, but not so controversial. Some people, he'd told her, licking blood off his hands, disliked slavery, and he disliked controversy.

He'd decorated the room around his slave for his own amusement. Disguising her as a rare predator was simply a joke played upon the people who'd come here for entertainment.

A chime sounded, announcing new visitors. Aralorn hugged herself as the ae'Magi greeted his guests with a warm smile. He'd smiled that same smile last night while he'd killed a young boy and stolen his magic.

The stone floor had been red with blood, but it wiped up cleanly, and only someone able to sense magic might notice the pall that unclean death had left. Or not. The ae'Magi was the lord of mages, after all, and they could only use their powers to the extent he allowed.

She was scaring herself again—that was really not useful at all. Biting her lip, Aralorn gazed at the dancing nobles in an effort to distract herself. She matched names and countries to the dancers' faces with the ease that made her the valuable spy she was.

The ae'Magi had killed an old man, an old man without a spark of magic—human or green—about him and used the power of the death to turn the walls of the great hall a sparkling white. "An illusion," he'd told her. "It takes some power, and I don't like to use my own when I might need it at any time."

That had been the first night. On the second, he'd brought a man— one of his own guardsmen. With that blood, the ae'Magi had worked some magic so foul that the taste of it lingered on Aralorn's skin still.

The boy had been the worst. Only a child, and . . .

Dozens of the rulers of the kingdoms of the Anthran Alliance were present. Some of them had been members of the Alliance for centuries, others were newer than that. The Empress of the Alliance wasn't here, but she was six, and her guardians kept a sharp eye on her lest any of her subjects decided to make her cousin the new empress instead. Just because they were allied didn't mean they were loyal subjects. The squabbles among the Alliance helped keep the coffers of Sianim full.

Gradually, she managed to replace the boy's dead eyes with dates and politics, but she still paced her cage restlessly. It wasn't just the horror of her discovery of exactly what kind of man held the power of the ae'Magi that kept her from sitting down—it was fear. The ae'Magi scared her to death.

There was a kaleidoscopic quality to the dance: the brilliant colors of the rich fabrics twisting around and around only to stop, rearrange themselves, and swirl into motion once again. More like a clockwork than a dance populated by real people. Perhaps it was a side effect of all the magic. Or maybe it was deliberate, the ae'Magi amusing himself. He liked to make people unwittingly do his bidding.

She saw the Duchess of Ti and the Envoy of the Anthran Alliance dancing cordially with each other. Ten years ago, the Envoy had had the Duchess's youngest son assassinated, sparking a bloody feud that left bodies littering the Alliance like a plague.

The Envoy said something and patted the Duchess's shoulder. She laughed gaily in return as if she hadn't had the Envoy's third wife killed in a particularly nasty manner only a month ago. She might have thought it a clever ruse designed to put the other off guard, but the Envoy was not particularly politic or clever. Aralorn wondered if the effect of whatever spell the ae'Magi had apparently cast upon his guests was specific to them and whether it would last beyond this evening. Just how powerful was he?

When the musicians paused for a break, people crowded around the Archmage, Geoffrey ae'Magi, drawn to his twinkling eyes and mischievous grin the way butterflies surround the flowering coralis tree. When a butterfly landed on the sweet-smelling scarlet flower of the coralis, the petals closed, and the flower digested its hapless prey over a period of weeks.

There were some times when her penchant for collecting trivia wasn't an asset.

Like the coralis, Geoffrey ae'Magi was extraordinarily beautiful, with blue-black hair, high cheekbones, and the smile of a child with his hand caught in the cookie jar.

Aralorn had been in his presence before. The Spymaster liked to use her in the rarefied society of which the ae'Magi was a part because she knew how to negotiate it without betraying herself. She'd attributed the wave of magic that surrounded him to his being the most powerful mage in the world. His beauty had stunned her at first, but it hadn't taken her long to decide that the attraction lay in his gentle warmth and his self-deprecating humor. Four days ago, Aralorn, like every other woman who'd ever laid eyes upon him, had been more than half-enamored of him.

Aralorn turned her gaze away from the ae'Magi and back to the room. While she'd been watching the Archmage, someone had stopped next to the pillar nearest her cage.

Leaning lazily against the polished pillar, a short, square-built young man wearing the colors of the royal house of Reth also observed the throng: Myr, Prince—no—King now, of Reth. His face was strong-featured, even handsome in other company. There was a stubborn tilt to his chin that he'd inherited from his paternal grandfather, a formidable warrior and king.

It wasn't his appearance that caught her attention; she'd expected that he was the person from whom the ae'Magi had been hiding his slave. It was the expression of distaste that briefly crossed his face as he looked at the crowd, remarkably different from the vacuous smiles that everyone else wore.

He shifted unexpectedly and met her gaze. He looked quickly down, but then began to make his way through the edges of the crowd toward her cage. When he reached the platform, he tilted his head down so that no one could read his lips, and asked in a low tone, "Do you need help, Lady?"

Shocked, she glanced quickly at the mirror that covered the back of the cage. The ae'Magi's illusion of a snowfalcon stared back at her indifferently.

She knew that Myr was no mage—he wouldn't have been able to conceal that from her, not with her mother's blood in her veins. Green magic could usually hide from the tamed stuff that the more human mages used, but the reverse was not true. Still, there was no doubt that he saw a woman and not the rare bird the ae'Magi showed his guests.

Rethians believed they were the descendants of an enslaved people who had risen up to kill their masters. They were taught at their mother's knee that to take another human and own him was evil beyond comprehension.

Even so, even for the King of Reth, it was a bold move to offer to help one of the ae'Magi's slaves to escape. There were a lot of mages in Reth who owed obedience first to the ae'Magi and second to the king— obedience enforced by their own magic. To move against the ae'Magi could spark a civil war in Myr's kingdom. His offer was heartfelt and showed just how young this new king was.

Perhaps it was his rash offer that appealed to her or that she had been born Rethian and part of her still thought of Myr as her king. In any case, she answered him as herself, and not the slave that she played for the ae'Magi.

"No," she answered. "I'm here as an observer."

There were rumors that the ruling family of Reth had occasionally produced offspring who were immune to magic. There were stories, and Aralorn was a collector of stories.

"A spy." It wasn't a question. "You must be from either Sianim or Jetaine. They are the only ones who would employ women to spy in as delicate a position as this." Women were important in Reth, and they were far from powerless politically. But they didn't go to battle, didn't put themselves in danger.

With a half smile, Aralorn clarified, "I get paid for my work."

"Sianim mercenary."

She nodded. "Pardon me for asking, but how did you see past the illusion of the snowfalcon that the ae'Magi placed on the cage?"

"Is that what you're disguised as?" His smile made him look even younger than he really was. "I wondered why no one said anything about the beautiful woman he had in the cage."

Interesting. He saw through the ae'Magi's illusion but not her altered shape. No one had ever called Aralorn beautiful. Not in those tones. Maybe it wasn't only altruism on his part that had him offering to free her. That made sense, though; when she'd taken the likeness of the slave girl, magic had altered her—not just other people's perceptions of her as the ae'Magi's illusion did.

She felt eyes on her and glanced up under her lashes to see the ae'Magi not ten paces away, staring at Myr in fascination.

Myr might have been young and impetuous, but he wasn't dumb. He caught the subtle tension of her body.

"Aren't you a pretty thing," he murmured softly, though a little louder than he'd been speaking before. "I wonder if you are trained to glove and jess?"

"Ah, I see you admire my falcon, Lord." The deep, resonant voice of the ae'Magi could have belonged to a musician. Not only was the Archmage physically beautiful; he even sounded beautiful.

Myr straightened abruptly, as if taken by surprise, and turned to look at the ae'Magi, who strolled up to stand next to him in front of the ornate cage.

"She is extraordinary, isn't she?" the ae'Magi continued. "I purchased her a month or more ago from a traveling merchant—she was captured somewhere in the Northlands, I believe . . . I thought she would go well with this room." He waved a casual hand that managed to indicate the rest of the hall.

Aralorn had grown adept at reading the ae'Magi's voice, and his tone was just a little too casual. She wondered if he'd also heard the stories of the odd talent said to crop up in the Rethian royal family.

Reth was a small country in size but rich in minerals and agriculture.

It also had a well-trained army, left as the legacy of Myr's grandfather. Its army had served to keep Reth independent every time the Anthran Alliance had periodically tried to swallow it over the past few centuries. Myr was a very new king, and certain conservative political factions would have been happier had he been the same kind of puppet as his father. But there were enough houses who would support him against all comers that Myr should be safe even from the Archmage. She didn't know why she thought the ae'Magi might harm Myr. Maybe it was because part of her still believed she owed fealty to the royal house of Reth, and it made her overprotective. Maybe it was the way the ae'Magi reminded her of a cat watching a mouse hole.

The sweet interest in the ae'Magi's face gave Aralorn cold chills. *Be careful,* she silently urged Myr.

Myr turned to the magician with a smile and more confidence than a boy his age should have had. "Yes, the ivory tinge is the same as the color in the marble here. It's unusual to see a snowfalcon this far south; you must have paid a great deal for her."

The two men talked at length about falconry, something that Aralorn happened to know interested neither of them. When they had exhausted the subject, the ae'Magi abruptly changed topics.

"My dear Myr," said the ae'Magi, "please accept my condolences upon the untimely death of your parents. I had no opportunity to talk to you at the funeral. I sent a note, of course, but I wanted to speak to you face-to-face."

Myr started to speak, but the ae'Magi laid a long-fingered hand on Myr's shoulder, effectively forestalling what the younger man might have said.

"If you have need of anything, feel free to turn to me. I have connections and substantial power as the ae'Magi, and you may need what aid I can offer. It has never been easy to ascend the throne, especially now with the Uriah restless in the eastern forests. Not to mention that there are always opposing factions or"—he hesitated, waving his hand expressively—"other enemies."

With professional interest, Aralorn heard the slight edge of guilt in his voice. It was masterfully done and reminded her that the former rulers of Reth had been killed after leaving one of the ae'Magi's elaborate parties. No one had ever implied that the accident might have had more sinister causes. She wouldn't have thought about it on her own—but, given what she now knew, Aralorn would have been astonished to discover the Archmage *didn't* have something to do with the king's death.

She wondered if Myr knew why the ae'Magi apparently had such interest in him. She could all but smell the wizard's intent. She just couldn't tell why he was so intent. Myr suspected something; his distrust was obvious from his little charade.

Myr bowed his head quickly to acknowledge the offer without accepting it. "I know my parents counted you their friend. I appreciate your offer." He smiled apologetically. "I have enjoyed our conversation, but I must excuse myself. You see"—he leaned in closer, as if confessing an embarrassing secret—"I just bought a new stallion, and I'm not sure I trust him on the trails after dark." His face lost its eagerness for a moment. "After what happened to my parents, sir, I feel a need to be overly cautious."

Had that been a dig? *Don't bait him,* she thought urgently. *Don't bait him.*

The magician smiled understandingly. "I'll summon your servants for you."

Myr shook his head. "I left them outside with orders to meet me an hour before dark."

"The gods follow you, then." The Archmage paused. "I hope you know that your father was so proud of your courage and strength—you do credit to your lineage. I wish that my own son had been more like you."

To Aralorn's sensitive ears, the magician's voice held just the right amount of pain. She wondered why she hadn't noticed before she'd been assigned here that his emotions were always perfectly calculated.

"Lord Cain could not be termed a coward or weak, sir." Myr's voice held a matching amount of sympathy, as false as the ae'Magi's. He should have just thanked him and left, gotten out of his sight and hoped the ae'Magi forgot all about Reth and its young king.

"No," the ae'Magi agreed, "I think that it would have been better for all of us if he were a coward. He would have done less harm."

The ae'Magi kept his dark magics secret, but his son had performed them in the broad light of day.

Aralorn had never met Cain: He'd disappeared before she'd become involved in her present occupation. She'd heard the rumors, though— they got worse with each telling. But Myr would have known him; the ae'Magi and his son had been frequent visitors to his grandfather's court.

The stories put the ae'Magi in the role of a grieving father, forced to strip his son of magic and exile him. Aralorn suspected that the boy had died rather than been exiled. It would have been inconvenient if someone had questioned where the ae'Magi's son had learned so much about forbidden magic. As he'd told her himself, the ae'Magi preferred to avoid controversy.

"Be that as it may"—with apparent effort the ae'Magi dismissed the thought of his son—"your servants will probably be awaiting you even now."

"Yes, I should go. You may be sure I shall remember your gracious offer of assistance if ever I need help." With that, Myr bowed once more and left.

Watching Myr's broad back as he strode through the room, the ae'Magi smiled—the slight imperfection of one crooked eyetooth lending charm to the more perfect curve of his lips. "What a clever, clever child you have grown to be, Myr." His voice purred with approval. "More like your grandfather every day."

It was late before the crowd began to thin and later still before everyone had gone. Aralorn couldn't control her apprehension as each person left, knowing that the meager protection their presence offered would soon be gone. After seeing the last couple out, the ae'Magi walked slowly over to the cage.

"So," he said, swaying gently back on his heels, "the Rethian doesn't see my lovely Northland bird."

"My lord?" she said neutrally. Having had most of the night to reflect upon the incident, she'd been pretty sure that the ae'Magi had figured that much out. She'd also had time to come to the conclusion that if he thought Myr was immune to magic, the ae'Magi's primary power, Myr would die.

The Archmage smiled and flicked a silver bar of her cage with his forefinger chidingly. "When he looked at you, he looked where your eyes are, not where the eyes of the falcon would have been."

Plague it, Aralorn thought. The ae'Magi put one hand through the bars and caressed her neck. She leaned against him and rubbed her cheek on his hand, forcing herself to obey the vague compulsion of the charismatic spell that had kept his guests happy instead of throwing herself backward and huddling in the far corner of the cage.

The ae'Magi tilted her face so that her eyes met his, and said in a leading tone, "I wonder how he broke through my illusion."

He couldn't expect a slave to understand what had happened, he was talking to himself. But he'd given her an opening—this was going to hurt.

"But he didn't break through your spell, Master," she answered in bewildered tones.

He looked down at her expressionlessly, and she quit fighting the urge to curl into a ball on the floor of the cage. He made a small motion with a finger, and she screamed as her body twisted helplessly under the fire of his magic.

Each time he did this to her was worse than the time before. Aralorn watched as the tendons pulled and stretched, protesting the sensations they endured. When it finally stopped, she didn't fight the tremors that shook her, telling herself that she was playing her part—but wondering deep inside whether she could have stopped had she tried.

After she lay still, the ae'Magi said softly, "I don't like to be contradicted, child. He knew you were not a falcon."

It was over. Over. He probably wouldn't do that again tonight. Or if he did, he'd at least give her some time to recover. She could tell herself that anyway.

"Yes, my lord," she said hoarsely, from her position on the floor of the cage. "Of course he knew, I didn't mean to contradict you—how could I? I misunderstood what you meant. You knew his magician broke the spell for him, how else would he have known?"

"What magician?" The ae'Magi's voice was sharp, almost worried.

"He was standing over behind that pillar." She pointed to someplace vaguely on the far side of the room, and the mage turned swiftly as if to look for someone still there.

"What made you think that he was a magician?"

"He made gestures like you do sometimes. He left with the young king." Aralorn kept her voice to a whisper such as a frightened girl might use. No anger. No protest. People in his thrall felt pain all right, but they adored him even while they shuddered in fear of what he could do. She'd seen them.

"What did he look like?"

"I don't know, he stayed in the shadows. He was dressed all in blue, my lord." Blue was the ae'Magi's favorite color—a good third of the people in the room had been wearing some shade of blue.

"What did the boy say to you?" He held the word "boy" just a little longer than necessary, apparently liking it better than "king."

"I don't remember . . ."

Whatever he did with his spell didn't work only on her body—though her muscles cramped hard enough that she thought she could hear the bones begin to break. The pain weakened Aralorn's natural resistance to his other spells and gradually the newly familiar feeling of shame crept over her. *She should try harder to please him. Why wasn't she more obedient? Look at what she made him do to her.* As suddenly as it had begun, it stopped, leaving her shuddering and crying helplessly.

"When I ask you something, I expect an answer." The ae'Magi's voice was gentle.

"He asked if I wanted to be freed. I told him I wanted to be here. I live only to serve you, my lord. It is my honor to serve the ae'Magi . . ." She let her voice trail off. *That's it,* she cheered herself silently, placate him, stay in character; the gasps as she fought against crying and the whimper at the end were a nice touch; artistic really—it was too bad that she hadn't thought to do them on purpose.

He reached a hand out to her, and she pressed against it, getting as close to him as she could though the pain had gone and, with it, the full effect of his magic. She almost wished that the magic he used to increase his charisma stayed as effective on her as it was when he hurt her. Instead, she experienced an overwhelming desire to bite the manicured fingers— or throw up. The cold, metal edge of the cage dug into her side.

"What else did you say to him, little one?"

Aralorn pulled back from him and gave him a wide-eyed, somewhat confused look, even as she felt herself regain some clarity of thought. "Did you want me to say something else to him? I didn't because I wasn't sure if you would want me to." She deliberately widened her eyes as if she were pleading with him to be pleased with her, trying to keep herself from tensing in anticipation of the wild, twisting pain.

"No. You did well." He absently patted her cheek. "I've been working on other things lately and haven't had the time to do more with you. Tomorrow, when I've completed this spell, I've got a use for you."

If she were in any doubt about what he was talking about, the hand that ran lightly down her breast would have clarified it for her. The ae'Magi seemed satisfied that the shudder that ran through her at his touch was in response to desire. He smiled warmly at her and, humming a sweet tune, walked lightly through an archway.

Aralorn stared at herself in the mirror at the back of her cage. The ae'Magi must have dispelled his illusion, because she didn't see a bird anymore. The flickering light from the torches gave a dancing appearance to the fine, blond hair. The fragile face that stared expressionlessly back at her was extraordinarily beautiful. A thin sheen of sweat glistened on her forehead, and the misty, sea-green eyes looked dazed and vulnerable.

Abruptly irritated with that vulnerability, Aralorn stuck her tongue out at her reflection. It didn't make her feel any better.

She wrapped both arms tightly around her legs. Head bowed on her knees, she listened to the sounds the servants made as they banked the fireplaces and snuffed the torches, trying to think over the uncontrollable panic that the thought of his intimate touch brought on.

"Patience, Aralorn, patience," she warned herself, speaking almost soundlessly. "If you leave now—granting that you *can* leave—he is going to doubt what you told him about Myr, which may not matter in the long run anyway." She tilted her head back and addressed her words to the reflection, summoning up a tone of bleak humor. "But if I don't get out of here, I'm going to break and tell him everything I know, from the name of my first pony to the bald spot on the top of Audreas the Vain's head."

It was the truth. Four days—she didn't count the time she'd spent locked up alone. A fifth day here would break her. And someone needed to let the Spymaster know what dwelled in the ae'Magi's castle.

Decision made, she waited while the sounds of the castle diminished and the moon hung high in the sky, revealed by the clear panels in the ceiling.

When she was more or less satisfied that the people who were going to sleep were asleep, she knelt in front of the cage door. Grasping each edge, she began to mutter quietly, sometimes breaking briefly into song or chant to help focus her magic. She pushed aside the doubt that kept trying to sneak in: Doubt would cripple the small gift that she had. She was grateful to the ae'Magi's vanity that her cage was made of precious silver rather than the iron that would have kept her prisoner until her bones crumbled to dust.

First her fingers, then her hands, began to glow a phosphorescent green. Gradually, the light spread to the metal between her hands. When all the metal of the gate held the soft, flickering glow, she stepped through, leaving the spells on the locks intact. Her body ached from the ae'Magi's magic, but nothing that wouldn't fade in a day or two. It wouldn't slow her down much, and that was all she was worried about.

The light of her magic died, leaving the great hall black as pitch. She stood still and waited for her eyes to start adjusting before venturing out into the room.

The only light in the room came from the skylights high above, only

a faint reflection of the moon, which made it difficult to find the doorways. She took the first doorway that she could find, hoping that it was
one of the two that traversed the outer wall of the castle.

She bent low, occasionally putting a hand on the ground to help keep
her balance. It was awkward, but people generally look at eye level, so
from her lower vantage point she should be able to see any guards before
they saw her. Her position also had the secondary benefit of making her
a smaller target if she was seen.

The corridor was lighter than the great hall had been, although not
by much. The stone of the floor was dry and cool, and she ran a hand
lightly over the walls. It took her longer than she thought that it should
to find the small opening she was searching for.

Panic clawed at her, and the temptation to run blindly down the
hallway was almost overwhelming. *This,* she thought with wry humor,
*must be how a pheasant feels just before it jumps out of hiding and into
the path of the arrow.* She bottled up the panic and stored it away where
it wouldn't get out until this was all over.

She had almost decided to look for another way to leave when she
found what she was looking for. Just above the bottom row of blocks, her
fingers scraped over one end of a pipe cut flush with the wall. Silently,
Aralorn blessed the old man she'd met at a bar one night who told her
the story.

Centuries ago, an apprentice to one of the ae'Magis discovered an old
rain spell in a book he was reading while the master was away. Three
weeks later, when the Archmage came back, the castle was flooded, and
the apprentice was camped outside. The Archmage drained the castle
expediently by placing a drainpipe every sixteen stones in the outer
corridors.

One such drainage pipe was under her fingers. It was bigger than
she'd hoped for; being about four fingers in diameter. It cut directly
through the thick stone wall of the castle to the outside. The air coming through it smelled like a moat. Like freedom.

She took a deep breath and concentrated. The familiar tingle spread
though her body until it was all the sensation she could absorb, leaving

no room for any of her other senses. Unable to see or feel, Aralorn focused on each part of her body shifting into one part of the mouse at a time; nose first, then whiskers. It took her only as long as it took to breathe deeply three times before a very small mouse crouched where she had stood.

The mouse who was Aralorn shrank against the wall underneath the pipe for a minute and waited for the ae'Magi to investigate the magic she'd used—but he didn't come. Human magicians weren't usually sensitive enough to detect someone else using magic, but the ae'Magi was a law unto himself.

The mouse shook herself briskly, twitched her whiskers, and scratched an itchy spot where the tingle hadn't quite worn off yet; then she climbed up into the pipe.

It was dark, which didn't bother her much, and smelly, which did. Centuries of sludge had built up in the opening, and if several other bold rodents hadn't foraged through (perhaps to escape a castle cat), she wouldn't have made it. As it was, she was belly deep in slimy stuff. Busy not thinking about the composition of the muck, she almost fell out of the pipe and into the moat some distance below—only saving herself by some ungraceful but highly athletic scrambling.

Poised on the edge of the old copper pipe, Aralorn shivered with nervous energy. Almost. Almost out. Just this one hurdle, and she would be away.

The little slime-coated mouse leapt. The air blurred, and a white goose flapped awkwardly over the water, one wing dripping goo from the moat. There were plenty of birds who could fly better than a domestic goose—most birds, actually, since the goose could manage little better than a rough glide. But the goose was the only bird Aralorn knew how to become.

Hampered by the wet wing, Aralorn was unable to gain any altitude and came to a flapping halt several hundred yards beyond the moat, in front of the bushes that signaled the beginning of the woodland surrounding the castle. She straightened her feathers and waddled toward the woods, carefully leaving the ooze-covered wing stretched away from the rest of her body.

A black form erupted from the shadows, its ivory fangs catching the light of the moon as it halted directly in Aralorn's path. The goose squawked and dodged backward, resuming a human form just in time for Aralorn to fall on her rump rather than her tail.

Her own rump, too. She was back in her own skin: short, brown-haired, and plain-faced. Her anger fueled the speed of her transformation.

"Allyn's blessed toadflax!" she sputtered, using her father's favorite oath. There had been no need for drama, and she'd been scared enough for ten lifetimes in the past few days. "Wolf, what are you trying to do to me?" Mindful of the proximity of the castle, she lowered her voice to a soft tone that didn't carry but did not lack for force either. But anger faded into sheer relief, and the abrupt transition left her giddy.

"I could have died of shock"—she put her hand theatrically over her heart—"then what would you have done? Why didn't you warn me you were here?"

The wolf stood over her, fey and feral, with the stillness of a wild thing. The snarl had disappeared at her furious whispers, and he waited for a moment after she finished, as if he wanted to make certain she was done.

His macabre voice, dry and hoarse, was passionless when he spoke—he didn't answer her question. "You should have told me that you intended to spy on the ae'Magi—if I had known that you were contemplating suicide, I would have killed you myself. At least it would be a cleaner death than any *he* would bestow." Fathomless golden eyes gazed at her coolly.

A green mage could speak in animal form—though it required practice and a great deal of uncomfortable effort. Wolf wasn't a green mage, though, not as far as she could figure him out. And those few human mages who could transform themselves to animals were lucky if they remembered to transform themselves back again. Wolf was an endlessly fascinating puzzle who didn't fit into any category she could find for him.

A reassuring puzzle, though.

She watched him for a moment.

"Do you know," she said, after weighing his words, "that is the first time I have ever heard anyone say anything against him? I even asked why I was being sent to spy there—and none of it struck me as strange at all."

She nodded at the dark shape of the castle where it stood on the top of the mountain, its silhouette almost blacking out the sky to the east. "The Mouse said that there were rumors of an assassination plot, and I was to investigate it and warn the ae'Magi if necessary." Her customary grin restored itself, and if it felt a little stiff, that was all right.

Safe. She was out, Wolf was with her, and she was safe. "If there is such a plot, I can only wish them luck in their endeavors."

"It has always amazed me how well he can blind people, even when he is not using magic to do it," replied the wolf. He glanced at the castle, then away. His yellow eyes glistened, glowing with a light that might not all have been a reflection of the moon. He looked back again, as if he could not resist the impulse. A growl rose low in his throat, and the hair on his neck and back stiffened.

Aralorn cautiously set a hand on his fur, smoothing it down. In all the time she'd known him, he'd always been slow to warm from his customary reserve, and though she'd seen him kill several times, she'd never seen him quite this upset. "What's wrong?"

The wolf quieted and lowered his head for a moment. Then he shook himself, and said softly, "Nothing. Perhaps it is the moon. I find that it sometimes has this effect on me."

"The moon." She nodded solemnly. "That must be it." She caught his gaze and raised one eyebrow. The wolf stared back at her. Aralorn gave up the contest without a fight, knowing that he was perfectly capable of continuing the stare-down all night. "Shall we go, or do you want to wait for the ae'Magi so we can destroy him and win the world back for goodness and light?"

The wolf grinned ferally. "If we killed him, the world would be more likely to draw and quarter us than praise us as saviors. So by all means, let us make haste so as not to be forced to destroy the ae'Magi." The sarcasm in his voice clearly dismissed any chance he thought they'd have of destroying the Archmage.

He turned and made his way back through the brush, leaving Aralorn to follow.

Several hundred yards from the edge of the woods, her gray stallion was tied to the trees. At their approach, he whickered a greeting. Aralorn laughed as the animal lipped the plain tunic she wore, then drew back in obvious disgust at the taste.

"Why how did you find your way here, Sheen?" She slanted a look at the wolf, and said to him, "Thanks, I wasn't looking forward to walking back."

Over the years, she'd learned not to question him too closely—mostly because he wouldn't answer her. If he wanted to be a wolf, who was she of all people to question it? Still, the knot that attached the colorful cloth reins to the tree would have been difficult for someone with no fingers to tie.

Aralorn untied the reins and mounted, only to dismount and shorten the stirrups. She sighed loudly as she untied the leather strings that were woven into the saddle to keep the stirrups at one length. Someone with much longer legs than hers had ridden the horse last.

"Sheen, how many times have I told you not to give strangers a ride? You never know where they might take you."

She might not question him out loud, but she liked to make it obvious that it was cooperation and not stupidity.

The wolf tilted his head to one side, and there was a hint of amusement in his eyes. She laughed and continued to unweave the strings. He'd even remembered to bring her sword and knives.

Sometimes she thought that he might be a renegade shapeshifter, one of her mother's people—though he lacked the gray-green eyes that were characteristic of the race. Someone more skilled than she and able to hide what he was from her. It shouldn't be possible, but nothing he was should have been possible.

That he was a human magician was very unlikely because human magic didn't lend itself well to shapeshifting. Instead of blending in with the forces of nature, it sought to control them and required immense concentration that was impossible to maintain for extended periods of time. To turn oneself into an animal for a prolonged period would require the strength of the ae'Magi . . . or his son.

Her normally deft hands faltered at their familiar task, so she stopped and gazed almost impersonally at her hands, which trembled without her consent. The mindless babbling fear threatened her as she worked her way through her suspicion. It was very unlikely that Wolf was a human mage, she reminded herself again. She glanced at the wolf and then back to her saddle. The ae'Magi's son had disappeared six years ago. There were other green-magic users than her own people, and she'd never heard of a human mage who could take and keep an animal's shape so long, not in all the stories she'd ever collected, ae'Magi or not. Still, her body would not release the panic it insisted on; terror was a difficult emotion to reason with. She'd noticed that before.

She looked at him again, and he caught her gaze and held it, his gold eyes no more readable than a pair of amber gemstones. She remembered the fever-bright agony that had been in them when she first met the wolf.

It had taken only a week for her to heal his leg, but he'd fought the fever for almost a month. He'd left as soon as he could stand up, at least for a while. One day she'd looked up to find him watching her with his uncomfortably canny eyes. After that, he came and went, sometimes staying away for months at a time, then appearing as suddenly as he had left.

She remembered how long she'd worked to gain his trust. It had taken time to get him to let her touch him, more time before he would eat food she gave him, and almost a year before he trusted her enough to reveal for certain that he was more than just a wild animal. She compared his remoteness to the ae'Magi's easy smile and beautiful voice. If she ever met a corpse that talked, she imagined that its voice would be similar to her wolf's.

THE WOLF WATCHED her and saw the wear of her time with the ae'Magi. He saw the tremor of her hands and smelled the sweat of her fear. He saw that she'd used the cheerful demeanor that was her habit as a mask, and he lost the hope that she had by some miracle escaped unscathed from the ae'Magi's games. The desire to kill the Archmage rose in his throat and was set aside for future use. He saw the fear in her eyes, but until he stepped closer to comfort her, he didn't realize that she was afraid of him.

Instantly, he halted. This was the one thing that he hadn't expected. Four years, and never had he seen the fear that he'd inspired in everyone else he'd ever met. Not even when she'd had reason to fear.

The old ache of bitterness urged him to flee. If they had been somewhere else, he would have left without a backward glance, but here, near the castle, she was still in desperate danger; already he could smell the excitement of the ae'Magi's "pets." She wouldn't be able to lose them on her own despite her training and surprisingly formidable combat skills—she wasn't very big to be so dangerous. After three weeks in confinement, she was hardly at her best, so he waited.

WHOEVER HE WAS, whatever he was—he was not anything like the ae'Magi. She was jumping at shadows. But that certainty had come too late; she could see it in the stillness of Wolf's body.

She crouched down to look him in the eye; she didn't have to lower herself far—he was tall and she wasn't. "I'm sorry. I'm . . . just a little shaky"—she gave a half laugh and held up an unsteady hand—"as you can see. He's got me doubting everything I know." She moved the hand to touch him, and he quietly moved just out of reach.

She knew that she had hurt him, but before she could fix it, the stallion snorted softly. She turned back to him and saw that he was twitching his ears back and forth and shifting his weight uneasily.

"Uriah," commented the wolf, looking away from her. "If they are getting close enough that even Sheen can smell them, we'd best be on our way. There are riding clothes in the saddlebags. Put them on, we may have a long ride ahead."

She wiped herself off as best she could on the simple cotton slave tunic she wore. Ten years of being a mercenary had destroyed any vestige of ladylike modesty she might once have felt, but she hurried into the clean clothes anyway, as they could use every second to avoid a confrontation with the Uriah.

She swung into the saddle and let the wolf lead the way at the brisk trot dictated by the rough country and the dark. Had the Uriah been closer, she would have risked a fall with a faster gait, but for now there was no need for panic.

When she had scrounged for her clothes, Aralorn found that the saddlebags also contained oatcakes. She pulled a couple out and ate one as she rode, feeding the other to the horse, who knew how to eat and move at the same time. When she offered one to the wolf, he refused. She let him pick the way, trusting him to do his best to rid themselves of the Uriah.

The Uriah were vaguely human-looking creatures that appeared more dead than alive though they were almost impossible to kill. The insatiable hunger that drove them gave them a berserker's ferocity. They were normally found only in the far eastern regions that bordered the impassable Marshlands, but in the last decade or so they'd begun to turn up in unexpected places. But to find them this far west was almost unheard of. Especially since the ae'Magi could certainly . . .

"Stupid!" she exclaimed out loud. The warhorse, slightly spooked by the nasty smell behind them and miffed by the slow pace they were taking, took exception to the sudden sound and bucked hard. She didn't fall off, but it was a near thing, and it took a while to stop the curvetting completely. "The sudden upswing in Uriah attacks, their appearance in places where there have never been Uriah before—that's all him, isn't it?"

The wolf waited until the show stopped, then said, "They belong to him." Without commenting further, he continued on, leaving Aralorn to follow as she could.

The sun began to rise on the silent travelers. Aralorn was quiet at first because she didn't know how to undo the damage she'd done to him with her distrust; after a while, it was fatigue that kept her silent. Three weeks with no exercise left her feeling as if she were recovering from a prolonged illness. Despite her tiredness, when the wolf halted and told her they were stopping for the afternoon, she protested.

"If we don't stop and let the horse graze and get some rest, you'll be walking tomorrow." He spoke slowly and clearly, and his voice managed to pierce through her exhaustion.

She nodded, knowing he was right, but the urge to run away from the castle was stronger than her common sense, so she didn't dismount. The horse arched his neck and blew, as if ready for battle, responding to the invisible signals of his rider.

Wolf was silent until he saw her sway in the saddle from sheer tiredness. "I will stay on watch, Lady. I know when the ae'Magi or his playthings are near, and I won't let them take you back." His voice softened.

Again she nodded, but this time she dismounted and, with more instinct than willpower, began to untack the horse. The light saddle seemed to weigh more than she remembered, and it was an effort to reach high enough to get the bridle off—but she managed. Sheen needed no restraint to keep him close.

She untied the sleeping roll and climbed in it without even dusting off her clothes. The wolf stretched out beside her, his big warm body warding off the chill of lingering fear even better than her blankets. The last thing she noticed before sleep claimed her was the comforting sound of the stallion munching grass.

TWO

ARALORN BREATHED IN RAGGED GASPS AND RUBBED A SHAKY HAND across the wetness on her cheeks. Sweating, and still half-caught in her nightmare, she curled under her blanket and covered her ears with her hands to shut out the soft seductive voice of the ae'Magi.

She'd fought in the regular troops and knew that nightmares were part of the territory. They'd get better, but for right now, every time she drifted to sleep, her dreams all led back to the Archmage's fine-boned hand holding the ornate silver dagger he used to butcher his sacrifices. The young brown-eyed boy, no older than some of her brothers the last time she'd seen them, was so caught by the spell that he smiled as the ae'Magi drew his knife. At least it was daylight when she opened her eyes—and the dirt under the leather comprising the outer layer of her bedroll felt a lot different from marble.

She sat up abruptly and wiped at her wet cheeks. Sheen stood nearby, dozing with one hind foot cocked and his convex nose lowered almost to knee level. Near Sheen, Wolf lay still, his muzzle on his paws. He was looking away from her. Aralorn knew that he must have heard her when she woke up, so his inattention was deliberate. Her momentary fear had hurt him—she hadn't realized he worried about her opinion. She hadn't thought he worried much about anyone's opinion of him.

She addressed his back. "That place—it . . . twists everything. There is so much magic in the castle, it makes the air heavy, and when I breathed it . . . He loves it, you know—playing games and making people into his puppets. Power."

She shuddered slightly, and continued, "I watched him drink the blood of a child he'd just killed, and I found myself thinking how beautifully the light of the candles reflected off his hair. It's . . . not pleasant not to know whether your feelings are your own." She brought her legs up until she could wrap her arms around them.

She'd begun in an attempt to explain herself to Wolf—to show him that it wasn't him she'd distrusted but her own perceptions. Once she'd started talking, she couldn't stop. "I have never been so frightened in my entire life," she whispered. "I always thought that I was strong-willed, but even with my mother's blood to help me resist the spells, I couldn't completely block the feeling that I wanted to please him." Her voice died.

For a long time there were only the sounds of the forest—the wind in the trees, a creek nearby, and a cricket singing.

She sighed. "I might have been able to block it entirely toward the last—when I knew what the spells were and how he worked them; but I couldn't, because I had to act as if the spell were having its effect on me. Sometimes I think . . . that maybe I didn't want to block the spell because it made me feel so much better . . ." She knew that she would have bruises in the morning from gripping herself so hard. She took a shuddering breath and put her forehead down on her knees. "I can't get him out of my mind. I think some of it is still his magic, but I see his face every time I close my eyes."

Slowly, Wolf stood up and left his place. He sat down and leaned against her. She loosed her grip on her legs and ran a hand in the thick pelt.

A cold nose worked its way under her arm, and his warm, wet tongue licked at her chin until she squealed and pulled away with a quavering laugh, wiping at her face with her sleeves.

The wolf smiled, as wolves do, and rolled over against her on his back. She rubbed his stomach (something that he *didn't* allow in public) and one back leg snapped rapidly back and forth as she caught just the right spot.

After he felt he had cheered her up, he said in his usual cool voice that sounded wrong coming out of a wolf getting his stomach rubbed, "Don't worry about it, Lady. Living in that place for any length of time will twist your thoughts and feelings until what you feel and what he wants you to feel are tangled together in a knot that would baffle a sailor." His voice was gentler, sounding like velvet on gravel. "Time will help."

"I know," replied Aralorn, then continued in a lighter tone, "but I'm not looking forward to the next decade or so."

Wolf rolled over with improbable quickness and nipped her lightly on the hand in response to her quip, tacitly agreeing with her unspoken decision that the discussion was too serious.

Aralorn tilted her head to the side, a slow grin twisting her lips. "So you want to fight, do you?" She tackled him and began a wrestling match that left them both flat on the ground and panting.

"Will you be able to sleep now?" he asked, rather hoarsely, even for him. "I'll wake you up when it's time to go."

She nodded and rolled over until she was on the bedding, unwilling to use enough energy to get up and walk. She mumbled a good night that lost most of its consonants. He touched his nose to her cheek and woofed softly before curling up against her.

In the end, it was the stallion that woke them both. The high-pitched whistle split the night.

Aralorn leapt to her feet and had the bed rolled up almost before she opened her eyes. Bridling and saddling took somewhat longer as the obstinate beast wouldn't stand still. As she worked, she kept an eye on the wolf as he stared into the night. At his signal, she left what was not already attached to the saddle and mounted the stallion, who was already trotting. Although not built for running, Sheen managed a very credible speed as he followed the wolf's lead. The Uriah were close enough behind them that they could hear the howls the beasts made when they found their camp.

Aralorn had fought the Uriah before, and she knew that they were faster than any horse—certainly faster than Sheen. The creatures were too close behind and gaining quickly. She drew her sword and slowed the stallion in preparation for facing them.

Noticing that Sheen was slowing, the wolf darted back and nipped at the stallion's heels, nimbly dodging the war-trained horse's well-placed kick.

"No," Wolf snarled at her. "You don't stand a chance against the number that we have behind us. If you keep going, I can lure them away." With that, he began to veer off, but Aralorn guided Sheen to block his path.

She shook her head and shouted over the sounds of the Uriah, "It's me that they want. They won't follow you, and even if they did, it would mean that you would have to face them alone. Together, we might stand a chance."

"You know better than that, Lady." His tones rang with impatience. "Against two or three maybe, but there are many more than that. You needn't worry about me, I can keep ahead of them on my own." Here the wolf paused a moment, as if he were choosing his words carefully. "They will follow me if given a choice between the two of us."

"What do you mean by that?" Then, before he could answer, she said, "Cursed obscure Wolf. Never mind. We don't have time to argue." It was getting difficult to talk and keep Sheen from bolting as the howls grew nearer.

He flashed his fangs at her in a mock smile as only a wolf can do. "Lady, this isn't the first time I've dealt with them. Nor will it be the last."

She didn't want to leave him. If she hadn't known he was no ordinary wolf, she wouldn't have even considered leaving. But, against so many Uriah, she would have been more of a hindrance than a help. She heard the wails of the Uriah increase exponentially as they sighted their prey.

"Right," she said abruptly. "I'll see you in Sianim. But, plague it, Wolf, take care not to let them ruin your fur coat." With that, she turned Sheen in their original direction and urged him on. The wolf stayed in the path of the Uriah and watched with yellow eyes as they came closer. When the tone of their calls changed and became even more frantic, he broke into a swift run, leading them away from the path taken by his companions. Aralorn, looking back, saw that Wolf had been correct: All of the grotesque, humanoid forms followed the wolf's trail, ignoring her entirely.

She wondered, this time without last night's panic, exactly who Wolf really was. It wasn't a new puzzle, by any means. She had a list somewhere of possible identities for Wolf. Some of them were vague, others were names of specific people—today she added another name to it: Cain, the ae'Magi's son. Cain was younger than she'd placed Wolf's age, and she'd never caught a whiff of human magic off Wolf. She'd be surprised if Cain wasn't buried with the other people the ae'Magi had been killing, whose magic he had been stealing to use for himself. But wasn't it interesting the way the ae'Magi's creatures took off after the wolf?

ARALORN TRAVELED DURING the dark and slept, or at least tried to rest, during the day—not because it was safer that way but because she couldn't stand to wake from her nightmares alone in the dark. Sometimes she traveled for miles without seeing anything. Being alone didn't bother her; she'd done a lot of traveling on her own.

She had nothing of value except her warhorse and her sword—and both were as much a deterrent as a prize. On the evening of the third day, she left the forested mountains behind for the gentler hills and valleys of the lowlands. Traveling was faster, and it was only another day until she caught sight of Sianim.

The fortressed city stood on the top of an artificial plateau in the middle of a large valley. Nothing but grass was allowed to grow within a half mile of the hill, and even that was kept short. The plateau itself was steep-sided, and the road that led to the only gate into the city was narrow and walled, so that only three people could ride side by side through it. Although it was good for defense, the narrow path made it a nightmare to get large groups of soldiers in and out of Sianim.

The origins of the city were buried in the dust of ages past: Even the oldest known manuscripts mentioned it as a thriving city. Originally it had been a center of trade, but the small armies hired by the merchants to accompany their wagon trains drew mercenaries from all over. People looking for groups of mercenaries to hire began to go to Sianim. Gradually, the mercenaries themselves became the center of Sianim's economy.

A school for teaching the arts of war was founded, and eventually Sianim became a city of professional warriors.

Mercenaries of Sianim were some of the finest fighters in the world. With the only other military school at Jetaine, which had the minor drawback of allowing no males entrance within its walls, Sianim had little competition. In addition to training its own mercenary troops, Sianim also trained fighters for various kingdoms and principalities for a healthy fee. The elite guard for most of the rulers were Sianim-trained.

Because politics and war go hand in hand, Sianim also had a spy network that would have amazed an outsider. It was run by a slender, short academian. It was to his small office tucked away in the rabbit warren that was the back of the government building in the center of town that Aralorn went after stabling Sheen.

Someone needed to know as soon as possible the danger that Geoffrey ae'Magi presented.

Stairs and narrow hallways connected little rooms occupied by bureaucrats necessary to the successful and profitable running of the mercenary city: taxes and licenses and all. And buried away down a stairway behind a worn door that nonetheless opened and closed tightly and soundlessly was a large, airy room with a window (she'd never managed to figure out which window it was from the outside) that housed the man whose fingers dipped into the well of rumors and politics that drove the world.

She slipped through the worn door without knocking—if the Spymaster had wanted privacy, the door would have been locked. She closed the door, sat on a ratty-looking chair, and waited patiently for Ren, known semiaffectionately as the Mouse, to acknowledge her.

He was perched on top of his battered-but-sturdy desk, leaning back against a bookshelf and reading aloud from a collection of poems by Thyre. He was only a little older than Aralorn, but he appeared as though someone had put him out to dry and forgotten to take him back in again.

His hair had faded and thinned until it no longer concealed the scalp beneath. His hands were ink-stained and soft, free of calluses, though she knew he was an excellent swordsman and for a time, before he came to Sianim, had made a living as a duelist in several of the Alliance cities. Only his sharp eyes distracted from the impression of vagueness, and at that moment they were hidden from her as he kept his attention on the lines he read.

Thyre wasn't one of her favorites; he reached too hard for his rhyme. Usually, she would have fished out a book from Ren's impressive library and read until he decided to question her; but today she just sat quietly, listening, finally stretching out on the padded bench and closing her eyes. Since Thyre was notoriously long-winded, she had plenty of time to rest.

When Ren finished, she was snoozing peacefully, and the soft sound the book made as Ren stuffed it into one of the many bookcases made her jump to her feet. He offered her a glass he filled from the bottle on his desk.

Aralorn accepted it but sipped cautiously. Bottles on Ren's desk could contain anything from water to Wyth, more affectionately known as Dragonslayer. This time it was *fehlta* juice, only a mildly alcoholic drink, but she set it down on the end of his desk. She had the rueful feeling that it would be a long time before she would take anything that could cloud her thoughts. She sat back down on the bench and waited . . . and waited.

When Ren finally spoke he sounded almost nervous to her sensitive ears. "I trust that everything went smoothly as usual, hmm? Got in, got out, came here."

"Yes. I—" He cut her off before she could speak.

"Did you talk to him about the assassination attempt?" Ren strolled around his desk and resumed his seat.

"No, the—"

"Good," he said, breaking in once again before she could continue. "I would hate to have him upset with us, or think that we were spying on him—although I doubt that he would mind. I'm sure he would have understood that we gather information whenever we can. I trust that you were either able to put a halt to the assassins or discovered that the rumor I sent you to investigate was just a rumor."

Aralorn tapped her fingers on the arm of the chair and contemplated

Ren. His babbling didn't bother her, he always talked like that. He once told her that it distracted people, and they said things that they wouldn't normally have said—just to get him to shut up. She'd used the technique herself upon occasion and found it effective.

What did bother her was that he wasn't listening. Usually, he listened carefully to everything she said, then quizzed her for hours about what she'd heard and seen. It just wasn't like him to gloss over anything or stop anyone from speaking. He never, not ever, interrupted. The bright black, somewhat beady eyes shifted restlessly.

She had never seen him embarrassed before, so it took her a while to identify the emotion that brought a red tinge to his face. Ren was ashamed that he had sent her to spy on the ae'Magi—the same Ren who had once sent her to spy on his own brother.

None of her disquiet showed on her face. She didn't want to heed the intuition that was hinting that something was awry. She wanted to give her report with no more than the usual lies: Not even Ren knew that she could alter her shape. Shapeshifters used wild magic—and this was a world that had learned to fear magic used without strict limits.

She wanted to ignore the insistent disquiet that the Mouse's unusual reactions spawned, but she couldn't. With visions of the docile people in the ae'Magi's ballroom in her head, she bowed her head and waited.

She'd never heard anyone say anything against the ae'Magi—only Wolf. The people the ae'Magi had brought out to sacrifice to his magic had come willingly. Only Wolf knew what he was—and he hadn't really told her until he was certain she knew what she'd gotten herself into.

While Ren talked, she carefully edited what she was going to tell him, waiting as he drifted from topic to topic until he got around to asking her about her mission.

Aralorn gave him a brief description of her method of entry, incorrect, of course. Someday Ren would find out just how poor she was at picking iron locks and would be deeply disappointed.

Ren needed to know about the ae'Magi, but somehow she found herself rattling on at length about the various heads of state at the dance the ae'Magi had held and obligingly going into as much detail as she could when Ren requested it. Evidently, he was only upset about her spying on the ae'Magi—otherwise, he wanted to know everything. He could pull surprising conclusions out of the smallest thing.

"Wearing a red cape?" he said, after she'd described what one of the Anthran demiprinces was wearing. "It was a gift from his sister's husband—looks like peace talks between their territories might be on again. We'll be able to pull those troops out and use them elsewhere."

She hedged when he asked her about Myr, saying only that she'd seen him talk with the ae'Magi but hadn't been near enough to hear what was said. Time enough to inform Ren of the young king's interesting talent after she discovered what was making the Spymaster behave so out of character.

To distract him from Myr, Aralorn continued to the main reason for her mission and said with some caution, "I couldn't find any information on an assassination attempt. If there is a plot, it doesn't originate from within the castle. I did get the impression that if there was such an attempt, the ae'Magi would be perfectly capable of handling it without need for our aid."

She paused, to give herself time to choose just the right words. "I left early, I know. But I felt so *uncomfortable*." Uncomfortable was true, uncomfortable enough to curl into a quivering ball of jelly at the bottom of that cage. "I thought that I had better get out before he figured out who I was and took offense. If it were widely known that Sianim spied upon the ae'Magi, half the world would be angry at us."

"Ah yes, I quite understand." Ren nodded and picked up another book—his habitual method of dismissal.

If she needed confirmation that something was awry, she had it then. Ren would never, ever accept "uncomfortable" as a reason for leaving an assignment early without picking the vague term into pieces. Unhappy, and baffled by what to do about it, she exited the room.

ALONE, REN PUT his book down and rubbed his hands together with great satisfaction. If that performance didn't cause Aralorn to start thinking, then nothing would. He needed her to be suspicious and questioning, but also cautious.

He'd had a feeling about her—she got out of too many situations that should have been fatal—and those eyes. He'd seen that color of eyes before. He had wizards who worked for him, but they'd have been useless. The office of ae'Magi existed to control them.

She'd come right to him, and she was well and truly spooked, he thought, though he flattered himself that no one else would have been able to read that in her.

He couldn't afford to come out and warn her; the ae'Magi had his own ways of learning things . . . and if anyone would be subject to the Archmage's watchful eye, it would be the Spymaster of Sianim.

He rubbed his chest, pressing into his skin the charm he wore on a thong. A gift from a friend, another mage, it was supposed to be able to dispel magic aimed at its wearer. It dated from sometime around the old Wizard Wars and, his friend had told him, was unlikely to still have the power to block a spell directed specifically at him. It had been given as a curiosity—from one collector to another.

He still wasn't absolutely sure it worked, but he'd been wearing it day and night for the past few months. So far he seemed to be immune to the odd fervor that had taken most of the usually sensible people he reported to when he chose. He patted his chest again and worried, though his ma had taught him that worry did no one any good.

IF ARALORN'S FOOTSTEPS were quiet, it was out of habit rather than intent: She was deep in thought as she wandered down the cobbled street. She absently waved at acquaintances but didn't stop to talk. She shivered a little, though it was warm enough out. Why was Ren acting as if he'd never had a suspicious thought about the ae'Magi? Ren was suspicious of *everybody*.

More by chance than design, she found the dormitory where she stored her few possessions, and retreated through the halls to her room.

It was musty after her prolonged absence and in desperate need of dusting. There were only a few pieces of worn furniture placed here and there, but the room was small enough that it still seemed cluttered. She spent so little time in it that size and clutter didn't matter.

Aralorn sneezed once, then, ignoring the much-abused chair, she sat on the rough stone floor that was unrelieved by carpet or fur.

Never before had Ren seemed worried about where he sent her to spy. He cared little for politics, leaving that to the statesmen to whom he gave selected bits of information. Instead, he thirsted for knowledge the way that some men thirst for food or sex. It was from him that she had gleaned many of the folkstories she collected.

He was no respecter of persons, not ever. When she had protested her assignment with the ae'Magi, he had laughed at her and quoted her his favorite saying: "He who does no wrong need not fear perusal." He used it so often and said it with such pride that she suspected that he had made it up himself.

When he sent her to the castle, he'd made it clear that although nominally she was investigating the "assassination attempt," her main objective would be to gather information on Geoffrey ae'Magi. Why else would he send her when a simple note of warning would have done the same thing? She had, even at the time, suspected that there was no assassination plot except in the Mouse's busy labyrinthian mind.

All of which led her back to her original question: Why was Ren troubled about her spying on the ae'Magi? Had the ae'Magi bespelled Ren? If so, why? And worse, who else had he taken?

Aralorn sat for a while and came to no brilliant conclusions. It was better than worrying about the wolf—though she did that as well. Fretting about one was about as useful as fretting about the other—so she, being a believer in using her resources properly, gave equal time to each.

Finally, tired in mind and body, she stripped off her clothes and threw them on the floor. She stretched out carefully, slowly working each muscle until it was relatively limber. She pulled off the top covering of her cot, careful to leave most of the dust on it. Then she collapsed onto the bed and slept.

The nightmare came back—it wasn't as bad as it had been the first few days, but it was bad enough. She was only half-awake when she touched the wall that her cot sat against and thought for a minute that she was back in the cage.

She rolled away from it quickly and landed with a thump, fully awake and surrounded by a cloud of dust from the blanket on the floor.

She sneezed several times, swore, and wiped her watering eyes. It was obvious that she wasn't going to get any more sleep for a while, so she lit a small lamp and dressed, pulling on her practice garments—knee-length leather boots, loose breeches, and tunic.

Night had fallen, but the nice thing about being home in Sianim was that even in the busy summer season, there were always people in the practice arenas willing to go a few rounds; mercenaries tended to keep strange hours. She strapped on sword and daggers and slipped out the window and onto the narrow ledge just below.

Gingerly, she traversed the narrow pathway until it was possible to drop onto the roof of the building next door. From there it was only a short jump to the ground. It would have been easier to exit by normal means, but she took opportunities to practice wherever she could get them.

Outside, the street torches were already lit for the night, but people were still wandering around. There was a friendly brawl going on at one of the pubs, with bystanders betting on the outcome.

She inhaled deeply. The smell of Sianim was a fusion of sweat, horse, dust, and . . . freedom.

Aralorn had grown up stifled by the restraints placed on women of the high aristocracy, even bastards like her. Reth might have outlawed slavery, but women of high estate were surrounded by a wall of rules strong enough to confine any drudge. If it hadn't been for her father, she might have been forced into a traditional role.

When the Lyon of Lambshold's illegitimate daughter came to him and stated her objections to the constant needlepoint and etiquette lessons that his wife imposed on his daughters, he'd laughed—then taught her to ride like a man. He also taught her to fight with sword and staff. When she left home, he sent her off with his favorite warhorse.

She had tried Jetaine but found that the women there were enslaved to their hatred of men. Aralorn had never hated men, she just hadn't wanted to sit and sew all her life. She'd often wondered what it would have been like for her if she'd been born a merchant's daughter, or someone who had to work for a living, instead of an aristocrat, who was expected to be decorative.

The thought of herself as decoration was absurd. Even before she'd become battle-scarred, she'd been short, plain, and too willing to speak her own mind.

Two big men in the rough, hooded garb favored by the farmers who serviced the town had been following her for the past few blocks, and now they were getting close enough to be worth paying attention to. Sianim might be used to women in its ranks, but outsiders could be bothersome, expecting a woman wearing pants and a sword to be a woman of loose morals who would sleep with any man who asked. A simple refusal could end in a nasty fight.

Out of the corner of her eye, she noticed the pair slink behind a cart she'd just passed. Her left hand went automatically to her sword. Her right already held a dagger. One of the thugs said to the other in a stage whisper meant to carry to her, "Squelch you, Talor, you lumbering ox. She saw us again. I told you to change those shoes. They make too much noise."

She laughed and spun around to face them, her dagger tucked invisibly back into her sleeve sheath. "You're getting better, though. This time I honestly thought that you were just a couple of outsiders looking for prey."

The second one pushed the first sideways with a playful punch. "See, Kai? I told you that we'd do better blending in with the environment. Who pays attention to a couple of hog lovers in this place?"

Kai twitched one eyebrow upward, managing, despite the dirt on his clothes, to look aristocratic. "However, if you had worn the shoes I told you to . . ." He let his voice trail off and flashed the wicked grin he shared with his twin brother.

With practiced ease, he slipped out of his assumed character and flung an arm around Aralorn's neck. "Well, my dear, it looks like I have you at my mercy." Or at least that's what he meant to say. Actually, thought Aralorn, the last word sounded more like "eyah" than "mercy."

She turned to Talor, and said, "I need to bathe in muck more often. It seems to work better than throwing him on the ground and making him look silly like I did the last time he tried to kiss me, don't you think?"

Old friends—the perfect answer to the frightening feeling that she was all alone. She'd served with both of them right up until the Spymaster had pulled her to his office and informed her she was changing jobs. Her gift of manipulating her superior officers had been noted as well as her ability to act without direct orders. Ren had been right—she was far better suited to spying than to warfare. Still, it was a lonely profession and she treasured her friends from the old days. Especially the ones smart enough that she didn't have to lie. Talor and Kai were sharp and knew how not to ask questions.

Talor assumed a serious demeanor, but before he could say whatever he intended to, Kai broke in. "Tell me, Lady, what villain gave you that perfume? Surely it must be cursed. Let me slay him for you that you may once again be your sweet-smelling self."

"I'd almost gotten used to smelling like this," she said truthfully. She'd slept like this on her bed, she remembered. She'd have to pull off all the bedding and take it to the laundry for cleaning. "I was going to go to the practice ring, but I think that I'll head to the baths first. Interested in a little fun?" Kai brightened comically until she added, "In the ring."

Kai bowed low. "To my sorrow, I have a previous engagement." He slanted her a grin. "Do you remember that redhead in the Thirty-second?"

"Uhm-hmm." She raised an eyebrow, shook her head, and in an exaggeratedly sorrowful tone said, "Poor girl, doomed to a broken heart." She grinned, and added, "Have a good time, Kai." He waved and sauntered away.

Aralorn looked at Talor, and inquired, "Does he really have a date with Sera?"

He laughed. "Probably not, but he will. Mostly, I think, his skin is still too thin from the last time you put him down. The whole squad ribbed him about being beaten by a woman for weeks. I, on the other hand, have no pride and, after you rid yourself of the unfair advantage you now hold"—he grabbed his nose with a hand to show her what he meant—"I will be awaiting you at the Hawk and Hound."

"Done." She gave him a mock salute and headed for the baths.

IN ONE OF the sparring rings that, like many of the taverns around town, the Hawk and Hound provided, Aralorn faced Talor warily with a single body-length staff held lightly in her hands.

Normally, they were evenly matched with the long staff, Talor being a better fighter than his brother, but Aralorn was still stiff. They fought together often because no one else wanted to face either of them with staves, long or short, in serious sparring.

As a warm-up, they played with variations on the training dances, and rather than aiming for body shots, the object was to hit a small metal plate, which dangled from a belt. Normally, there would be a third to call shots fair or foul and award points at the sound of wood striking metal, but she and Talor were veterans and cared more for the sport than for the winning or losing.

The ring that they had chosen was in the basement of the tavern rather than the one on the main floor, so they had no spectators. By mutual consent, they stopped for a bit to rest before they proceeded out of the standard patterns for some real sparring.

"So, what was that smell anyway? It seems somewhat familiar, but I just can't place it. Something like a cross between an outhouse and a pig barn." Talor's voice was a bit unsteady because he was stretching out as he talked.

Breathing ridiculously hard from such light exertion, Aralorn leaned unashamedly against one of the waist-high walls that surrounded the ring. She was paying for her confinement and the long ride home with her lack of stamina.

She started to think up a reason for the moat smell but decided that there was no harm in letting him know what she'd been doing. Kai and Talor didn't ask questions, and they also knew when to keep their mouths shut. There was nothing secret about what she had done, now that she was out of there. And it would be good to talk to Talor about what she'd found. She wouldn't go so far as to tell him about Ren, though. She needed to think about what had happened.

"Unless you've been visiting the ae'Magi's castle lately," she said, "it probably wouldn't be too familiar. I only wish the ae'Magi was half as honest and sweet-smelling as his moat . . ." Conditioned reflexes were the only thing that brought her staff up to deflect his from her face. The sheer force of the blow numbed her hands, as she hadn't been holding the staff in a proper grip.

She ducked underneath his arm to come to the center of the arena and give herself some room for maneuvering. The move also gave her a chance to talk. "What are you doing?"

Talor's face twisted with wrath as he came after her. "How dare you, worthless bitch? How dare you sharpen your tongue on the ae'Magi?"

It was his rage that saved her, interfering with the timing and precision of his attacks. Time and time again, she was able to block or turn aside his furious blows.

This unchecked anger was unlike him: A good warrior strives above all for control. She knew something was terribly wrong, but his ruthless barrage left no more time for speculation or analysis. She cleared her mind and concentrated on staying alive.

Finally, one of his swings caught her hard behind the back of her knees and she fell backward, letting his staff carry her legs up with it. She turned the fall into a roll, going over onto her shoulders and coming up on her feet. As soon as she was upright, she raised her staff to guard position, trying to protect her face and torso.

The roll had forced her to take her eyes from her opponent, and she barely saw the flicker of movement as his staff came under her defenses. Rather than the standard sweep-strike, Talor had chosen to thrust. The end of the staff caught her low in the chest and drove the breath out of her body. Without the protective padding she wore, it would have broken ribs. Had his staff struck just a few finger-widths higher, it would have been fatal, padding or not.

She twisted frantically to the side, trying to dive out of striking range. It was a desperate maneuver, exposing her vulnerable back to her opponent, and after the blow she'd just received, she knew she was moving far too slowly. Even as she moved, she waited for his strike—knowing that there was no way for her to evade the impact of the metal-shod staff.

The blow didn't come. She completed the diving roll and snapped to her feet, staff poised and lungs working desperately for air.

Talor stood in the middle of the ring, leaning against his staff. He shook his head like a wet dog, then looked up at her in dazed bewilderment. "I don't know what came over . . . Are you all right, Aralorn?"

"Fine." She gasped the word out, her diaphragm not operating quite correctly yet. "Don't . . . worry about it. No harm done, and I . . . needed a workout. Your stick work has improved, but you're still a little slow on your returns . . . Watch your hands. You hold on too tightly when you're mad, and it makes it easier for your opponent to force you to drop your staff."

As she got her breath back, she made her tone more baiting, trying to get him to forget what had happened. If she was correct about the cause, then it would do him more harm than good to worry about it. It scared her that the ae'Magi's magic was able to do what it was doing. It was just possible that he would have chosen to turn Ren into one of his puppets—but Talor had no political power. If he was affected, then she had to believe that most people in Sianim would be touched by the ae'Magi's magic: They all belonged to him. The thought of how much power that would take terrified her.

Talor took the refuge she offered. "You need to pay more attention to your opponent's eyes. You watch the body too much, and that doesn't give you much advance warning. If you'd been watching more closely, you could have avoided that last hit."

She dropped her staff and waved her hands out in the traditional surrender, and said, "Okay, you beat me. My reputation is in tatters. Just do me one favor and don't tell your brother about it. Last time you beat me, he challenged me, then I had to put up with his sulks for a week." It was important to act naturally.

"You only got it for a week because we had to go out on maneuvers. He sulked for almost a month. Okay, I won't tell him. Besides"—here he struck up an obviously false pose and looked down his nose at her—"it ill becomes a man to brag about beating a woman."

For all of his humor, Aralorn could tell that he was feeling uncomfortable. She wished she was only uncomfortable. She wasn't surprised when Talor excused himself though they generally would have drunk a couple of rounds before they left. When she turned to watch him leave, she noticed the wolf lying just inside the doorway, his head on his front paws. Talor stooped and patted him on the back, which Wolf answered with a small movement of his tail, but his clear yellow eyes never wavered from Aralorn's face.

Aralorn waited until Talor was gone before dropping exhausted to the floor, her back against the barrier. She patted the space beside her in invitation. The wolf obligingly got up, trotted over, and resumed his relaxed pose, substituting Aralorn's shins as his chin rest.

They sat like that for a while, Aralorn running her hand through the thick fur—separating the coarse dark hair from the softer, lighter-colored undercoat. When her breathing had returned almost to normal, she broke the silence.

"It's good to have you back," she commented. "I take it that they didn't kill you."

"I think that is a safe assumption to make." His voice was more noncommittal than it usually was.

She gave him a halfhearted grin.

"How long had you been watching?"

"Long enough to see you put your foot in it and almost let that clumsy young fool remove you from this life."

She obligingly rose to his bait. "Clumsy? I'll have you know that he is the second-best staffsman in Sianim."

"You being the first?" Amusement touched his voice.

She cuffed him lightly. "And you know it, too."

"It looked to me as if he had you beaten. You might have to step into second place." He paused, and said in a quieter voice, "Finally noticed that people are a bit touchy concerning the ae'Magi, have you?"

She gave him an assessing look. "Has it been going on for a long time?"

He grunted an affirmative. "I first saw it about a year ago, but recently it has gotten much more intense."

"It seems to be some sort of variation of the spells that he had at his castle, but I didn't think that anyone could create a spell of this magnitude alone." Aralorn's tone was questioning.

"He's not doing it alone," replied the wolf. "He started small. The villages near the ae'Magi's castle have quite a few inhabitants who are strong in magic. The side effect of having so many young virile magicians apprenticing at the castle for several hundred generations." His tone was ironic. "The adults that he couldn't subdue he killed because their deaths provide more of a kick to his power than people with no magic at all. But the ones he craves are the children, who have raw power and no training . . ."

Aralorn shuddered and rubbed her arms as if chilled.

"You've seen what he does with the children." Wolf's tone gentled. "Fifteen years ago, if you made a negative remark about the ae'Magi, only the reaction of the villagers just outside the castle would be as strong as Talor's. Now the streets of that village are empty of all but old men and women because the rest are dead. He has taken them and used them. As far away as Sianim, people are affected by the ae'Magi's spell. He needs still more prey to continue to increase the strength of his magic, so he's looking elsewhere. Sianim, I think, is merely getting the backlash of the main focus."

"What is the main focus?" she asked.

"Where is magic at its strongest? Where do many of the common villagers have the ability to work charms? Where has magic flourished, protected by strong rulers from the persecution that magic-users were subject to after the great wars?"

"Reth," she answered.

"Reth," he agreed.

"Crud," she said with feeling.

THREE

—⟋⟍—

THE INN LAY ABOUT HALFWAY BETWEEN THE SMALL VILLAGE OF TORIN and the smaller village of Kestral. It had been built snugly to keep out the bitter cold of the northern winters. When the snow lay thick on the ground, the inn would have been picturesque, nestled cozily in a small valley between the impressive mountains of northern Reth. Without the masking snow, the building showed the onset of neglect.

The inn had had many prosperous years because the trappers of the Northlands were bringing down the thick pelts of the various animals that inhabited the northern mountain wilds. For many years, merchants from all over flocked to Kestral each summer because it was as far south as the reclusive trappers would travel. However, over the last several years, the trappers had gradually grown fewer, and what furs they now brought to trade were hardly worth owning—and the inn, like the villages, suffered.

The Northlands had always been uncanny: the kind of place that a sensible person stayed away from. The trappers who came to stay at the inn had always brought with them stories of the howlaas that screamed unseen in front of the winter winds to drive men mad. They told of the Old Man of the Mountain, a being who was not a man, no matter what he was called, who could make a man rich or turn him into a beast with no more than a whisper.

But now there were new stories, though the storytellers were fewer. One man's partner disappeared one night, leaving his bedding and clothes behind although the snow lay thick and trackless on the ground. A giant bird hovered over a campsite where four frozen bodies sat in front of a blazing fire. One trapper swore that he'd seen a dragon, though everyone knew that the dragons had been gone since the last of the Wizard Wars.

Without the trappers or the merchants who came to buy the furs, the inn depended more heavily on the local farmers' night out and less on overnight guests. The once-tidy yard was overgrown and covered with muck from horses and other beasts, some of them two-legged.

Inside, greasy tallow candles sputtered fitfully, illuminating rough-hewn walls that would have lent a soiled air to a far-more-presentable crowd than the one that occupied the inn. The chipped, wooden pitchers adorning the tables were filled with some unidentifiable but highly alcoholic brew. The tabletops themselves were black with grease and other less savory substances.

Rushing here and there amid the customers, a woman trotted blithely between tables refilling pitchers and obviously enjoying the fondles that were part of any good barmaid's job. She wasn't as clean as she could have been, but then neither was anyone else. She also wasn't as young as she claimed to be, but the dim light was kind to her graying hair, and much was forgiven because of her wholehearted approval of the male species.

The only other woman in the room was wielding a mop across the uneven floor. It might have done more good if both the water and the rag mop she used weren't dirtier than the floor. The wet bottom of her skirt did as much to remove the accumulated muck as the mop.

As she passed close to the tables, she deftly avoided the casual hands that came her way. Not that many did. Most of the customers were regulars and were aware that if someone got too pushy, he was liable to end up with the bucket over his head for his troubles.

Dishwater blond hair was pulled into an irregular bun at the back of her neck. Her plain face was not improved by the discontented expression that held sway on her thin lips as she swung the mop. "Discontented" was a mild word for how Aralorn was feeling.

A month after she'd returned from the ae'Magi's castle, Ren had called her into his office and told her that he was sending her to the middle of nowhere to keep an eye on the local inhabitants. The only reason that she'd been able to think of for her demotion to this kind of assignment was that Ren no longer trusted her; something that he had in common with most of the rest of Sianim. The story of what she had said to Talor had somehow become common knowledge, and even her closest friends avoided her as if she had a case of the pox. Ren hadn't been interested in discussing it one way or the other.

She had spent almost a full month cleaning floors, scrubbing tables, and serving poor man's ale. Profits might be down, but business at the inn was still fairly brisk because of a high rate of alcoholism and infidelity among the people of both villages. If the tavern had been located in the middle of a busy town, she might have picked up some useful bits of information for Ren. However, the inn was mostly frequented by tinkers, drunken "family men," and occasionally by one very impoverished highwayman—the more skilled and ruthless of his kind having left for richer pastures.

The most monumental thing that had happened since Aralorn started there was when the daughter of the Headman of Kestral ran off with somebody named Harold the Rat. When the highwayman came in next time looking more miserable than usual, accompanied by a female who was taller than he by a good six inches and harangued him from the time they sat down until they left, Aralorn concluded that he was the mysterious Harold and offered him her silent condolences.

Normally, she'd have been relatively content with the assignment, especially since she'd added a few new tales to her collection of stories—courtesy of the few trappers she'd seen. But she had the doubtful privilege of knowing that the ae'Magi was striving to re-create the power the wizards had held before the Wizard Wars—and hold that power all by himself.

She *should* be doing something, but for the life of her she couldn't think what. If she left without orders or extreme necessity, being banished from Sianim was the very least of the punishments she was likely to suffer. It was more likely she'd be hung if they caught her.

Tonight, her restlessness was particularly bad. It might have had something to do with the innkeeper's wife being sick, leaving the inn-keeper doing all of the cooking—rendering the food even less edible than it usually was. That led to more than the average number of customers getting sick on the floor—because the only thing left to do at the inn was drink, and the alcohol that they served was none of the best and quite probably mildly poisonous judging by the state of the poor fools who drank it.

As the newest barmaid, the task of cleaning up fell to Aralorn. With the tools she'd been handed, this consisted mostly of moving the mess around until it blended with the rest of the grime on the floor. The lye in the water ate at the skin on her hands almost as badly as the smell of the inn ate at her nose.

She dipped the foul-smelling mop into the fouler-smelling water in her bucket and occupied herself with the thought of what she would do to Ren the next time she saw him. As she was scrubbing, humming a merry accompaniment to her thoughts, a sudden hush fell into the room.

Aralorn looked up to see the cause of the unusual quiet. Against the grime and darkness of the inn, the brilliant clothing of the two men in court attire was more than a little incongruous.

Not nobles surely, but pages or messengers from the royal court. They were usually used to run messages from the court to a noble's estate. What they were doing at this little pedestrian inn was anyone's guess. Unobtrusively, Aralorn worked her way to a better observation post and watched the proceedings carefully.

One of the messengers stayed near the door. The other walked to the center of the room. He spoke slowly so that his strange court accent wouldn't keep the northerners from understanding his memorized message.

"Greetings, people. We bring you tragic news. Two weeks ago, Myr, your king, overset by the deaths of his parents, attacked and killed several of his own palace guard. Overwrought by what he had done, His Majesty seized a horse and left the royal castle. Geoffrey ae'Magi has consented to the Assembly's request to accept the Regency of Reth until such time as King Myr is found and restored to his senses. The ae'Magi has asked that the people of Reth look for their king so that a cure may be effected. As he is not right in his mind, it may, regrettably, be necessary to restrain the king by force. As this is a crime punishable by death, the Regent has issued a pardon. If the king can be brought to the ae'Magi, there is every possibility that he can be cured. As loyal subjects, it is your duty to find Myr.

"It is understood that a journey to the royal castle will be a financial hardship, thus you will have just recompense for your service to your king. A thousand marks will be paid to the party that brings King Myr to the capital or restrains him and sends a message to the court. I have been authorized to repeat this message to the citizens of Reth by the Regent, Geoffrey ae'Magi." He repeated his message twice, word for word each time, then he bowed and left the inn with his companion.

A thousand marks was more than a farmer or innkeeper would make in a lifetime of hard work. *Recompense, my aching rump,* thought Aralorn, it was merely a legal way to put a bounty on Myr's head.

Wandering between tables, she caught bits and pieces of conversation and found that most people seemed to feel the ae'Magi had done them a great service by taking the throne. They didn't all agree on what ought to be done for the king. She heard an old farmer announce that everything should be done to see that Myr was captured and taken to be cured, poor lad. He was answered by agreeable muttering from his table.

Olin, the tanner from Torin (and more than slightly drunk), spoke up loudly. "Anyone who cares about Reth should kill Myr and ask for Geoffrey ae'Magi to take the kingship of us. Who needs a king what is going to attack his own folk out of the blue like that? Just think what'd be like havin' the Archmage for a king. We'd not worry 'bout those Darranians, who're claiming our mines over in the west borderlands." He paused to belch. "'N with the most powerful magician in the world, we could even drive those Uriah spooks outta the wilds. We could claim the Northlands altogether. Then we could be rich again."

The patrons of the inn shifted uncomfortably and chose another topic to speak on; but they didn't disagree with what he'd said.

Proof, if she'd needed it, that what Wolf had warned her of was actually taking place. The whole of Reth had adored their handsome prince, who was promising both as a warrior and a statesman—and it didn't hurt that he was the spitting image of his grandfather, who had been a great king by any reckoning. Two years ago, the last time Aralorn had worked a job in Reth, Olin's words would have gotten him into a rough argument or even a beating.

Moving unobtrusively, Aralorn took the slop bucket outside to dump it. That done, she strolled to the stables, where Sheen was.

She received a lot of harassment from Ren when she took the warhorse with her on assignments, because he was too valuable to go unremarked. Talor carried an old coin for luck when he went into battle: It must be much more convenient than a horse.

She did what she could to disguise his worth. He'd long ago learned to limp on command, which helped somewhat. She also left him ungroomed, but anyone with an eye for horses could see that he was no farmer's plug.

At the inn, she'd let it be known that he was the only legacy left to her when her elderly protector died. The innkeeper didn't ask her too many questions—just retained the better part of her weekly salary in payment and half the stud fees Sheen had been earning.

Aralorn scuffed her foot lightly in the dirt as she leaned against the stall door. Sheen moved over to her and shoved his head against her shoulder. Obligingly, she rubbed his jaw.

"The last time I saw Myr, he was hardly distraught enough to go berserk," she confided. "Convenient that the Assembly decided to place the ae'Magi as Regent. I wonder how he managed that—only in Reth would a mage of any sort be welcome to help himself to the throne. But there are some really strong mages in the Assembly. Hard to believe he could use his magic on them, and no one even noticed."

The stallion whickered softly, and Aralorn fed him the carrot she'd taken before it would have gone to its death in some greasy pot of stew. She tangled her hand in Sheen's coarse gray-black mane as he munched. "I could go to Ren with this, but given his present attitude toward the ae'Magi, I don't know what he would do—and doubtless he knows about it anyway. Probably supports it the same way those fools in the inn do— and for the same reason." She tightened her hands in the horsehair, and whispered, "I think we should go looking for Myr, don't you? Myr is immune to magic—he's the ideal hero to stand against the ae'Magi. An outcast spy from Sianim isn't enough to make a difference, but maybe I can help with strategy. At the very least, I can tell Myr why everyone is suddenly against him."

There was a noise—she froze for a moment, but it was only the wind rattling a broken board on one of the stall doors.

Even so, she lowered her voice further. "I only wish I had some way of contacting Wolf. Knowing him, he probably could tell us exactly where Myr went." Wolf was full of useful information when he chose to share it. "It could take us quite a while to find Myr." She paused, then smiled. "But if I'm going out to engage in hopeless tasks, I'd rather look for Myr than struggle to clean that floor another day. We'll start with those messengers and see what they know."

Finished with the carrot, Sheen bumped her impatiently—asking for more. "Well, Sheen, what do you say? Should we abandon our post and go missing-monarch hunting?" The gray head moved enthusiastically against her hand when she caught a particularly itchy spot: It looked for all the world as if he were nodding in agreement.

The restlessness that had been plaguing her was gone. Like a hunting dog let off the leash, she had a purpose at last. She snuck into the kitchen and blessed her luck because no one was there—she could hear the inn-keeper arguing with someone in the common room. It sounded as though he might be occupied for a long time, which suited her just fine.

She located a large cloth that was almost clean and folded it to hold such provisions as would keep on a journey: bread, cheese, dried salt meat.

Cautiously, she made her way upstairs without meeting anyone and snuck into the room that had belonged to the only son of the innkeeper. He'd died last winter of some disease or the other, and no one had yet had the heart to clean out his room. Everything in the room was neat and tidy—and she had the sudden thought that perhaps it hadn't been the change in customs that caused the inn to fall on harder times. She murmured a soft explanation of what she was doing and why in case the young man's spirit lingered nearby.

She opened the chest at the foot of the bed and found a cloak, a pair of leather trousers, and a tunic: tough, unremarkable clothes well suited to traveling. At the bottom of the trunk, she found a pair of sturdy riding boots and a set of riding gloves. She wrapped all of her ill-gotten goods in the cloak and hurried out of the room and up the ladder to her attic room.

She retrieved her sword from its hiding place inside the straw mattress (she generally slept on the floor, it being less likely to be infested by miscellaneous vermin). Before sliding the sheath onto her belt, she drew the sword from habit—to make sure that the blade needed neither sharpening nor cleaning. It was a sword she'd found hidden in one of the many cubbyholes of her father's castle—the odd pinkish gold luster of the metal had intrigued her. It was also the only sword in the place that fit her, her father's blood tending toward large and muscle-bound, which she was not. Aside from Sheen, it was the only thing she'd taken from her home when she left.

She wasn't a swordswoman by any means. Practice and more practice had made her competent enough to make it useful against things like the Uriah, creatures too big to be killed quickly with a dagger and not easily downed with a staff—creatures not holding swords of their own.

She gratefully rid herself of the filthy maidservant's dress and dropped it on the floor, donning instead the stolen garments and found that, as she expected, they were very tight in the hips and chest and ridiculously big everywhere else. The boots, in particular, were huge. If the innkeeper's son had lived to grow up, he would have been a big man.

Her mother's people could switch their sex as easily as most people changed shoes, but Aralorn had never been able to take on a male's shape. Perhaps it was her human blood, or perhaps she'd never tried hard enough. Fortunately, the boy whose clothes she'd appropriated had been slender, so that it was an easy thing to become a tall, angular, and androgynous woman—with big feet—who could pass as a man.

Once dressed, she was satisfied she looked enough like a young man neither rich nor poor, a farmer's son . . . or an innkeeper's. Someone who wouldn't seem out of place on a sturdy draft horse.

Most of the items in the room she left behind, though she took the copper pieces that she'd earned as well as the small number of coins that she always kept with her as an emergency fund.

She shut the door to her room and made sure that the bundle that she was carrying wasn't awkward-looking. As she made her way down the stairs, she was met by the other barmaid. Aralorn gave the woman a healthy grin and swept past her unchallenged.

In the stable, Aralorn saddled Sheen. The cloak and the food she packed into her copious saddlebags. She filched an empty grain sack from a stack of the same and filled it with oats, tying it to the saddle. From one of the saddlebags, she took out a small jar of white paste. Carefully, she painted the horse's shoulders with white patches such as a heavy work collar tends to leave with time. Farmer's plug no, but he could well pass for a squire's prize draft horse.

On the road, she hesitated before turning north toward Kestral. That was the direction that the messengers had been traveling. If she could find them, in the guise of a young farmer, she could question them without anyone's taking too much notice—as the barmaid could not have. A second reason for looking north was that the mountains were the best place for someone seeking to hide from a human magician. Human magic didn't work as well in the Northland mountains as it did elsewhere. She knew stories of places in the mountains where human magic wouldn't function at all. Conversely, green-magic users, her mother's brother had told her, found that magic was easier to work in the north. She'd experienced that herself.

As Myr was from Reth, Aralorn felt that it was safe to assume that he was aware of the partial protection the Northlands offered. There were very few other places as easily accessible that offered any protection from the ae'Magi. Unfortunately, the ae'Magi would also be aware that the Northlands were the most likely place for Myr to go, hence the messengers to the otherwise-unimportant villages that dotted the border of Reth.

Although it was still late summer, the air was brisk with the chill winds. They retained their bite this far north year-round, making Aralorn grateful for the soft leather gloves and warm cloak she wore.

Several miles down the road, she turned off to take a trail she'd heard the highwayman describe when, half-drunk, he bragged about getting away from an angry merchant. The shortcut traversed the mountain rather than wandering around its base. With luck and the powerful animal under her, she could cut more than an hour off her travel time.

Sheen snorted and willingly took on the climb, his powerful hindquarters easily pushing his bulk and hers up the treacherously steep grade. His weight and large hooves worked against him on the rocky, uncertain ground, though, and Aralorn held him to a slow trot that left Sheen snorting and tossing his head in impatience.

"Easy now, sweetheart. What's your hurry? We may have a long way to go yet this evening. Save it for later." Always mindful that someone could overhear, she kept her voice low and boyish.

One dark-tipped ear twitched back. After a small crow hop of protest, Sheen settled into stride, only occasionally breaking gait to bounce over an obstacle in his way.

As evening wore on, the light began to fade, and Aralorn slowed him into a walk. In full dark, his eyesight was better than hers, but in the twilight, he couldn't see the rocks and roots hidden by shadows. They had a few miles before the sun went down completely, then they could pick up the pace again.

Being unable to see clearly made the seasoned campaigner nervous, and he began to snort and dance at every sound. There was a sudden burst of magic nearby—she didn't have time to locate it because that was the last straw for Sheen, who plunged off the trail and down the steep, tree-covered side of the mountain.

She sank her butt into the saddle and stayed with him as he dodged trees and leapt over brush. "Just you behave, you old worrywart, you. It's all right. Nothing's going to get us but ghosts and ghoulies and other nice things that feed on stupid people who ride in the woods after dark."

The dark mountainside was too treacherous to allow her to pull him up hard, especially at the pace he was going, so she crooned to him and bumped him lightly with the reins—a request rather than an order.

He sank back on his haunches to slide down a steep bit instead of charging down it, and stopped when the ground leveled some. He took advantage of the loose rein to snatch a bit of grass as if he hadn't been snorting and charging a minute before.

Aralorn stretched and looked around to catch her bearings. As she did so, she heard something, a murmur that she just barely caught. Sheen's ears twitched toward the sound as well. Following the direction of the stallion's ears, she moved him toward the sound. When she could pick up the direction herself, she dismounted and dropped his reins.

She crept closer, moving as slowly as she could so as not to make any noise. Several yards from Sheen, she picked up the smell of a campfire and the residue of magic—it tasted flat and dull: magic shaped by human hands despite the nearness of the Northlands. Probably the remnant of the spell that had startled Sheen into charging down the hill, toward danger, just as any good warhorse would have done.

She followed the sound of men's voices and the smell of smoke through a thicket of bushes—she had to use a tendril of magic to keep quiet going through that—and around a huge boulder that had tumbled down from a cliff above. Peeking around the side of the boulder, she saw a cave mouth, the walls of the entrance reflecting light from a fire deeper inside.

The voices were louder, but still too far away to be distinguishable.

The wonderful thing about mice, Aralorn reflected as she shifted forms, was that they were everywhere and never looked out of place. A mouse was the first shape she'd ever managed—and she'd since worked hard on a dozen different varieties and their nearest kin. Shrew, vole, field mouse, she could manage any of them. The medium-sized northern-type mouse was just the right mouse to look perfectly at home as she scampered into the cave.

Two men stood by a large pile of goods that ranged from swords to flour, but consisted mainly of tarps and furs. The scent of fear drifted clearly to her rodent-sharp nose from the more massive (at least in bulk) man as he cowered away from the other. He bore the ornate facial tattooing of the merchant's guild of Hernal, a larger city of Ynstrah, a country that lay several weeks' travel to the south on the west side of the Anthran Alliance. He was wearing nothing but a nightshirt.

The second man had his back to her. He was tall and slender, but something about the way he moved told her that this man knew how to fight. He wore a hooded cloak that flickered red and gold in the light. Underneath the hood of the cloak he wore a smoothly wrought silver mask in the shape of a stylized face.

Traveling players used such masks when they acted out skits, allowing one player to take on many roles in a single play without confusion to the audience. Usually, these masks were made out of inexpensive materials like clay or wood. She'd never seen one made of silver, not even in high-court productions.

Each mask's face was formed with a different expression denoting an explicit emotion that mostly bore only a slight resemblance to any expression found on a real face. As a girl from a noble house, Aralorn had spent many a dreary hour memorizing the slight differences between concern and sympathy, weariness and suffering, sorrow and defeat. She found it interesting that the mask this man wore displayed the curled lips and furrowed brow of rage.

In one hand the slender man held a staff made of some kind of very dark wood. On the lower end was the clawed foot of a bird of prey molded in brass, and its outspread talons glowed softly orange in the darkness of the cave as if it had been held in hot coals. The upper end of the staff was encrusted with crystals that lit the cave with their blue-white light.

The staff made it obvious that this man was the mage responsible for the magic that had so startled Sheen. If he had spirited the merchant and his goods from wherever he'd been to here—she assumed the man hadn't been traveling in his nightshirt—then he was a sorcerer of no little power.

Hmm, she thought, *maybe this mouse idea wasn't such a good one.* A powerful mage on alert might find a nearby mouse that wasn't really a mouse, and he wasn't likely to be very pleasant about it. Even as she started to back away, the mage looked over his shoulder and gestured impatiently. She didn't even have time to fight the spell before she was stuffed into a leather bag that smelled strongly of magic.

She tried once to shift back into her human shape, but nothing happened. He'd trapped her, and until she figured a way out, she was stuck.

"How much, merchant?" the mage asked in Rethian. His voice was distorted with a strange accent—or maybe it was just the leather bag.

"Fourteen kiben." The merchant, too, spoke good Rethian, but his voice was hoarse and trembling. Still, Aralorn noticed, the price he'd quoted was at least twice what the items were worth, unless there was something extremely valuable among them.

"Six." The magician's voice may have had an odd slur to it, but it was still effective in striking terror into the heart of the merchant—who squeaked in a most unmanly fashion. Aralorn had the feeling that it wouldn't take much to achieve that result.

"Six, I accept," he gasped. There was the sound of money changing hands, then a distinctive pop and an immense surge of magic, which Aralorn decided signaled that the merchant had been sent back to wherever he'd come from in the first place.

There was a moment's pause, then a third person's voice spoke.

"It worked." He sounded as if he hadn't expected it to. He also sounded young and aristocratic, probably because Myr was both.

She hadn't planned on finding him quite so soon, not a half day's ride from the inn. It was too convenient. Had Ren known that something was going on here? Was that why he'd sent her out to the backside of nowhere? She might have to take back months of heartfelt curses if that was so.

"Hopefully our mutual enemy will not think to question all of the merchants traveling in Reth." There was something about the tone of the magician's voice that was familiar, but the odd accent kept throwing her. She should be able to figure out what kind of an accent it was, she *knew* languages—which was why Ren had pulled her out of the rank and file in the first place.

"He wouldn't learn much even if he did. The merchant doesn't know where you brought him to."

The magician grunted. "He knows that it was in the north because of the cold. He knows that it was in the mountains because of the cave. That is more than we can afford to have the ae'Magi know."

Myr gave no vocal reply; but he must have nodded, because when he spoke again, it was on a different topic. "What was that you grabbed off the floor?"

"Ah yes. Just a . . . spy. Small but effective nonetheless." Was that amusement she picked up in his tone?

The bag was opened, and she found herself hanging by her tail for the perusal of the two men. She twisted around and bit the hand that held her, hard. The mage laughed, but moved his hand so that she sat comfortably on his palm.

"My lord, may I present to you the Lady Aralorn, sometime spy of Sianim."

She was so shocked she almost fell off her perch. How did he know who she was? It wasn't as if she were one of the famous generals that everyone knew. In fact, as a spy, she'd worked pretty hard to keep her name out of the spotlight. And no one, *no one* knew that Aralorn could become a mouse.

Then it hit her. Without the additional muffling of the bag she recognized the voice. It was altered through the mask, a human throat, and that odd accent—but she knew it anyway. No one else could have that particularly macabre timbre. It was Wolf.

"So"—Myr's voice was quiet—"Sianim spies on me now." Aralorn turned her attention to Myr. In the short time since she'd seen him, he'd aged years. He was thinner, his mouth held taut, and his eyes belonged to the harsh old warrior who had been his grandfather instead of the boy she'd met. He wore clothing that a rough trapper or a traveling merchant might wear, patched here and there with neat stitches.

Deciding that the mouse was no longer useful—and it was easier to talk as a human—Aralorn jumped nimbly off her perch and resumed her normal shape, which was not the one that he would recognize. "No, my lord," she answered. "Or at least that wasn't my assignment. Sianim has spies on *everyone*. In fact, this is a rather fortunate meeting; I was looking for you to tell you that the ae'Magi's messengers have reported your fit of madness to all the nearby townsfolk." She spoke slowly and formally to give him a chance to adjust to her altered state.

Rethians were not less prejudiced against shapeshifters, just more likely to admit their existence. Since her mother's people lived in the northern mountains of Reth and paid tribute yearly to the King of Reth in the form of exquisite tapestries and well-crafted tools delivered in the night by unseen persons, the Rethians had a tougher time dismissing them as hearsay.

Folktales warned villagers to stay out of the forests at night, or they would be fodder of the shapeshifters or other green-magic users who might still be lurking in the impenetrable depths of the trees. Given the antagonism that the shapeshifters felt toward invading humans, Aralorn was afraid that the stories might not have it all wrong. But the royal family tended not to be as wary, probably the result of the yearly tribute they received—and the fact that they lived in southern Reth, far from any possible outpost of shapeshifters.

Myr glanced at the mage, who nodded and spoke. "That she means you no harm, I will vouch for." The slurred quality was not a product of the muffling of the pouch; if anything it was stronger than it had been. Maybe it was the mask.

"She has a gift for languages," Wolf continued. "I need someone to help me in my research. If she is not occupied with other things, it would do no harm to bring her to camp with us. She can fight, and the gods know we have need of fighters. Also, she stands in danger from the ae'Magi if he should discover who it was that spied on him."

"You spied on the Archmage?" Myr raised an eyebrow at her.

Aralorn shrugged. "It wasn't my favorite assignment, but definitely one of the more interesting." She let her face shift quickly to the one he'd seen in the ae'Magi's castle, then went back to normal.

Myr looked a little sick—watching someone's face move around could do that—then he blinked a couple of times. Finally, he smiled. "Yes, I see. Welcome, then, Lady. I invite you to join our small camp."

Myr gave a short bow of his head, which she appreciated as exactly the correct height for a male sovereign to give in polite invitation or acceptance to a female who was neither his subject nor fellow royalty.

She in her turn, dressed in the clothes of the dead son of the innkeeper, gave him the exact curtsy she would have given him as her father's daughter. Rethian nobility overdid manners, so she knew he'd catch the subtle difference.

He did. "*Who* are you?"

She gave him an apologetic smile as she pulled at the uncomfortably tight front of the tunic. "Lady Aralorn of Lambshold, at your service."

"One of Henrick's daughters." Myr's voice carried a hint of incredulity.

Aralorn nodded, smiling apologetically. "I know, I don't look much like him, do I? He didn't think so either. I was quite a disappointment to him." She rolled up the sleeves until she could see her hands again.

"No, that's not what I mean," said Myr. "I've seen you in court—a long time ago. You're his oldest child?"

She laughed. "You must have been all of ten. I'm the oldest daughter, but I have a brother a year older than I am. We two are the illegitimate get of youthful folly. My older brother's mother was a household maid, and my mother was a shapeshifter who seduced poor Father in the nearby woods. With fourteen of us, I can see where you could have trouble keeping us straight. My siblings are all copies of our father, rather unfortunate for my sisters, but my brothers are all considered quite handsome."

She startled a laugh out of Myr at her descriptions of her family. Her sisters were all quite beautiful, golden like their father—and like their father, they overtopped most men by a good handspan.

"How did you end up in Sianim?"

She tilted her head, thinking about how best to frame a reply. "I am too much my father's daughter to be content with sewing a dress or learning how to converse. He taught me swordplay with my brothers because I asked him. When it came time for me to go to court, it was obvious to both him and me that as a Lady I was hopeless. He gave me his own horse and sent me on my way."

It had been a lot more complicated than that, but that had been the heart of the matter. The rest of it wouldn't matter to the King of Reth. As she talked, she worked at rolling up her pant legs. Finally, she cut the bottom off with her dagger. There was nothing to be done for the boots.

"Somehow that sounds like the Lyon of Lambshold. He's the only man I know who is unconventional enough to do that." Myr shook his head.

Straightening up to her unimpressive height, Aralorn continued, "He said, if memory serves, that if no one had the nerve to laugh in his face when he was addressed as the 'Lyon of Lambshold,' no one would say anything about an absent daughter."

"If you are through talking, it might be best if we left for camp." The harsh voice was distracted, and Wolf's eyes focused on some distant point.

"Someone coming?" Myr changed in an instant from courtier to warrior.

Wolf grunted, then said, "Not here, but near enough that we ought to move out. So much magic was bound to attract attention."

Aralorn left them to their packing and ducked through the trees to grab her horse. As she checked the girth, she muttered to Sheen, "I wonder what mischief our friend Wolf has been up to?"

FOUR

WHEN ARALORN AWOKE TO FACE HER FIRST FULL DAY AT MYR'S CAMP, it was still dark. She slipped out through the tent opening, moving quietly to avoid disturbing the two women who had shared their quarters with her. She retied the crude flap so the cold early-morning air would stay outside.

Most of the tents in the camp were makeshift. Several were little more than a rug stretched over a stick or rope in true field-soldier style. The only tent she'd seen that had been worthy of the name belonged to Myr, who shared it uncomplaining with a number of the smaller children.

As she passed Myr's tent, near the fire pit, she gave the royal dragon embroidered on the side a respectful nod, but it glared balefully at her anyway. The flickering light of the fire gave the illusion of life to the green-gold eyes.

Also near the fire pit was one of the few wooden structures in the camp. The kitchen was little more than a three-sided shed, but it kept the food dry. The camp cook was already up, chopping something by lantern light, but he stopped long enough to give Aralorn a look no more friendly than the dragon's had been. Aralorn grinned cheerfully at him and kept on her way.

The camp was located in a small dale, no bigger than the largest of the riding arenas in Sianim, that lay half a day's ride north of the Rethian border. It was long and narrow, with a stream in the middle that she suspected would cover a much larger area in the spring, when the top layer of snow melted off the mountain peaks. As it was, the ground near the stream was marshy and made soft, slurping sounds when she walked over to take a drink and throw water on her face.

The tents were all in the eastern end of the valley near the only obvious trail down the steep, almost clifflike sides. Those sides, heavily covered with brush on the top, were the strongest defense the camp could have, rendering it almost invisible to anyone not already in the valley.

By the simple expedient of running a split-rail fence across the valley the narrow way, the western end had been turned into a pasture for most of the livestock—two goats, four donkeys, several horses, and a scrawny cow. It was toward this part of the valley that Aralorn headed.

Knowing how well Wolf liked people, she thought that he would be as far from the tents as he could get—although she couldn't see him anywhere in the dale. As she neared the pasture, she was welcomed with a soft whinny. Sheen, only slightly inconvenienced by the soft leather hobble that bound his front legs, bounced up to her to get his nose rubbed. She'd hobbled him outside the pasture so that the owners of the two mares didn't end up with unwanted foals. He followed her for a while before wandering off to forage.

It took her a little time to find the faint trail running up the steep slope near the fence. The terrain was rough and treacherous with loose stones, and she thought ruefully that a person would have to be part mountain goat to try this very often—or part wolf.

Grabbing a ragged piece of brush, she pulled herself up a particularly steep area and found herself unexpectedly in a hollow that hadn't been visible from below. A small smokeless fire burned near a bedroll. The rather large, lank wolf turned amber eyes to her and swayed his tail in casual welcome.

Since he wasn't using it, she seated herself on the bedroll and rested her chin on her raised knees. Casually, she threw a few more sticks onto the fire, leaving it for him to break the silence. Typically, he explained nothing but questioned her instead.

"Tell me about the camp." His voice was mildly curious.

"Why? You've been here much longer than I have."

He shook his head. "I just want to know what you see—how much I need to explain to you."

"Well," she began, "there has been a camp here for several months, probably starting in the spring. Originally, the person or people who started it didn't know much about camping in the woods, so I'd guess that they weren't locals. It looks like someone is in the process of reorganizing camp. If I were a gamester, I would place gold that Myr is the reorganizer—since I suspect you wouldn't bother." She looked to the wolf for confirmation.

Wolf nodded, and Aralorn continued to speak.

"From what I can tell, most of these people came with not much more than the clothes on their backs. There are what, maybe fifty people here?"

"Fifty-four with you," Wolf replied.

"Then over a third of them are children. There is no common class among them. I've seen peasants, townsfolk, and several aristocrats. The children are, as far as I've seen, without family. They are almost all Rethian." Aralorn lay back and made herself comfortable. "They have all the earmarks of refugees, and I'd lay my last gold that they are running from the ae'Magi."

Wolf grunted an affirmative.

"How did they all get here, though? I could see northerners finding this valley, but I heard southern Reth accents, too."

"You, of all people, should know the reputation of the northern mountains," replied Wolf.

Aralorn frowned at him. "I saw you transport the merchant, and my understanding is that teleportation is a difficult, high-level spell. And you managed it in the Northlands."

Wolf shook his head. "I wouldn't have tried it this far north even if we weren't worried about the ae'Magi finding the valley. Small spells seem unhampered here, but more delicate spells are harder to control. Some people it affects more than others—the ae'Magi won't travel even as far as the northern lands in Reth. It doesn't seem to have much effect on my magic"—he nodded at the fire, which flared up, dancing wildly with purple and gold flames—"but I wouldn't have bet even the merchant's life on it; so we traveled south."

"The stories about that aspect of the Northlands are common enough, even in southern Reth," agreed Aralorn. She gave him a look. "I suppose that this area would be a good place to run to if you were trying to hide from a human magician."

"I"—he hesitated a minute, and Aralorn got the distinct feeling that he changed what he was going to say—"previously located this valley as a possible refuge although I never intended to set up a camp of this size here."

He gazed with an air of bemusement over the camp. "I don't know how these people found this valley in particular. You can ask, but everyone has a different story. It is unreasonable that fifty people, most of whom have never been a mile away from their own front doors, would wander blithely into a hanging valley that would be hard for a forester or trapper to find."

After a slight pause, he continued, "As you speculated, they are all running from the ae'Magi in a manner of speaking—the way that you would have been fleeing from Sianim if you had made a few more negative comments about the ae'Magi. Most of them were driven from their villages by the townspeople.

"Except for Myr, everyone in camp can work a little magic. The adults didn't have enough ability to be trained as magicians and escaped the ae'Magi's control that way. The children are young enough that they had not yet been sent for training."

"How far does that control go?" she asked him. "Are they his puppets?"

"No more than Ren or any of the other nonmages who do as he wants. He just takes away the advantage their magic gives them, and so they only see what he wants them to see."

Aralorn turned until she faced him. "Why aren't you under his control?" She expected him to avoid answering as he usually did when her questions became too pointed.

But Wolf moved in a lupine version of a shrug. "I either broke the ties of the binding, or I wasn't in training long enough. I am not sure which."

Aralorn and Wolf sat in silence, watching the camp stir in the valley below them. Aralorn stretched her feet out to the fire, which still flared uneasily, as if waiting for another command.

Watching the red play of flame reflected on her feet in the dim light, she ventured another question. "How long have you been helping Myr?"

She noticed with self-directed amusement that her tone was disinterested, revealing none of the jealousy she felt. It had surprised her to feel resentful of Myr, but Wolf was hers. When she found out that not only was there someone else close to him but that Wolf had revealed himself as a human mage to him—it bothered her.

Wolf spoke slowly. "I have been looking for a way to move against the ae'Magi for a long time. It came to my attention that Myr didn't hold the ae'Magi in the same esteem that most people do: Apparently, Myr is not susceptible to magic. I am still not sure what use he will be against the ae'Magi, but it seemed prudent to watch him. At first I did little more than observe, but after Myr's parents were killed, I introduced myself and offered my help. For the most part, all that I did was offer advice and block a few spells that might have resulted in fatal accidents."

"Accidents like a carriage overturning unexpectedly," offered Aralorn, remembering Myr's parents.

Wolf nodded. "Or an archer's arrow going astray, things that immunity to magic does not shield against. I am not sure if I helped much in the end. The last attack that the ae'Magi set against Myr was more subtle. Did you hear what happened?"

Aralorn shook her head. "The first thing that I heard about it was back at the inn, when some messengers from the capital rode in and spouted nonsense. Myr was supposedly crazed with grief and attacked one of his own men."

Wolf snorted. "Myr was in his private courtyard in the palace when he was attacked by an elemental—a lucky choice for Myr, as most of an elemental's ability to harm is magical." So maybe she'd convinced the ae'Magi that Myr wasn't immune to magic, or maybe he was testing it.

Wolf continued with the story. "They made enough noise that I went out to investigate. I think that Myr would have won even if I hadn't been there." Wolf shrugged. "When it was dead, the demon transformed into a more mundane creature—one of Myr's personal guards. We were still standing over the body when the better part of the castle guard ran into the courtyard. They attacked, and we managed to flee. Here is where we've been ever since."

"What now?" asked Aralorn, drawing pictures in the dirt near the blankets.

Wolf let out a sound that passed as a laugh. "Now, Myr is trying desperately to prepare this camp for winter, and I am trying to find a way that I can move against the ae'Magi." He paused, then said in a tone that reeked of frustration, "It's not that I don't have the power. It is the training I lack. Most of what little I do know I've learned myself, and it's not enough. If I could find just one of the old magicians not under his spell, I could find something to use against him. Instead, I have to wade through piles of books that may be utterly useless."

"I will help with the books," offered Aralorn. He wasn't worried about power? Against a mage strong enough to turn Sianim into his worshipping congregation? "But this *is* the ae'Magi you're going up against, Wolf. He's not just some hedgewitch."

He ignored her worries about the ae'Magi. Instead, he said, "If I have to read through the dusty old relics, you might as well suffer, too." He was teasing her; she could tell by his tone of voice. He knew she would devour every time-scarred tome with a zealot's passion—she loved old books. "How many languages do you read? I've heard you speak three or four."

Aralorn shrugged. "Including dialects? Ten, maybe twelve. Sometimes I can pick out the essentials in a related language. Father was a fanatic about it—he got caught in a battle one time trying to negotiate a surrender, and the only person who spoke both languages had been killed. So he started us all when we were children. After I came to Sianim, I learned a lot of others. Anything very old, though, will be in the Ancients' tongue. I can pick my way through that, but I'm not fluent."

He gave her a wolfish grin. "And they always said that collecting folktales was a useless hobby." He continued more seriously, "The two of us can get through more material than I can alone. If I even had the name of a magician with a spell that could stop him, I could save time. I have a library near here, and if you can go through the secular books, it would leave me free to work with the grimoires."

Aralorn made a point of looking around at the mountain wilderness that surrounded them. "You have a library nearby?"

"Yes."

"Yes," she repeated.

Gravely, he met her eyes. If she hadn't known him as well as she did, she might not have seen the faint humor in the amber depths.

"I did notice that you ignored me earlier," she said. "This is the ae'Magi you are talking about facing. Do you really think you can take him?"

"No," Wolf answered softly. "But I'm the only chance we have, aren't I?"

From the valley rose the distant sound of a metal spoon hitting a cooking pot—the time-honored call to gather for a meal.

Wolf rolled lithely to his paws, changing almost as he moved into the tall, masked figure that was his human form. Courteously, he extended a hand to help her to her feet.

Aralorn accepted the hand a little warily, finding that Wolf in his human form was somewhat more intimidating than the wolf was. As a human, he maintained the grace that he had as a wolf. She watched with envy as he easily negotiated the slope that she scrambled and slid down.

A stray thought caught her. At the valley bottom, she touched his arm to stop him.

"Wolf, I think that I may have caused a problem for you." Anxiously, she bit her lip.

"What's that?" he asked.

"During the ball at the ae'Magi's castle the night I left, Myr saw me in the cage where he should have seen only a bird. The ae'Magi saw him talking to me and questioned me about it. I told him that I'd seen a magician help Myr break the illusion spell, hoping to keep Myr's immunity to magic from the ae'Magi." She kept her eye on the contrast her hand made against the black silk of his sleeve: It was hard to remember that the masked figure was Wolf. "Did I cause you any trouble?"

He shook his head. "I don't think so. That was probably why he progressed beyond straying arrows to an elemental—the timing is about right. But since we survived it, there was no harm done."

Myr was up and arranging breakfast with a dexterity that Aralorn, who liked to arrange people as well, found fascinating to watch. She let herself be organized with a bowl of cooked grain that made up in amount what it lacked in flavor. After the food she'd eaten at the inn, she felt no inclination to complain. Wolf neither ate nor removed the mask, a situation that seemed an established pattern since no one commented on it.

As she ate, Aralorn took the time to observe the people. The introductions she'd received the night before had been needfully brief, and many of the people had been asleep. She could only place the names to a few of the faces.

The sour-faced cook was a smith from a province in southern Reth. A large snake tattoo wrapped itself around one massive forearm, disappearing into his sleeve. She noticed that for all of his gruffness, his voice softened remarkably when he was talking with the children. His name was Haris.

Edom sat a little apart from the rest. He had the dark straight hair and sallow skin typical of parts of western Reth, the legacy of interbreeding with the dark Darranians. His hands were the soft, well-cared-for hands of an aristocrat. He was an oddity in the camp. Too old to be a child, yet younger than any of the adults. He was a recent arrival and still looked as if he felt a little out of place.

All but two of the children had been sleeping when she'd arrived at the valley. Those two who she'd met were now seated as close to Myr as they could get. Stanis had the red hair and freckles of the Southern Traders and the flamboyant personality to go with it. The second boy, Tobin, was a quiet shadow of his friend. Stanis tugged impatiently at Myr's shirt until he had the young king's attention. Then he settled back on his knees and started talking with grand gestures of his arms that looked a little odd on a boy of ten or eleven summers.

Aralorn was just about to look away when she saw Myr's expression sharpen with alert interest. He looked around for Wolf and waved him over. Aralorn followed.

"Stanis, tell Wolf what you just told me."

Stanis hesitated for a moment, but the enjoyment of being the object of attention manifestly won out over any shyness that he felt around the intimidating magician.

"Yesterday afternoon, when it was time to eat lunch, nobody could find Astrid. Me and Tobin thought that she might have been playing up near the old caves. So we all went up there to see if she still was. Edom was too scairt to go in, but I wasn't. We looked for hours and hours. Then when we all got back out together, she was waiting with Edom.

"She said that she was lost in the dark. She cried and a nice man who knew her name found her and took her out of the caves. Edom says that he didn't see no one with her when she came out. And Haris said that he thinks that she wandered into the mouth of one of the caves and fell asleep and dreamed about the man. But I think that she met a shape-shifter, and Tobin does, too. Only he thinks that it could have been a ghost."

Aralorn suppressed a smile at the boy's delivery—he'd gotten most of that out in one breath.

"What do think, Wolf? Astrid doesn't tell stories, for all that she's but a child. Who do you think she saw?" Myr's tone was quiet, but it was evident that the thought of someone living in the caves (wherever they were) bothered him.

Wolf said, "It's entirely possible that she did meet someone. Those caves interconnect with cave systems that run throughout the mountain chain. I have seen many strange things in these mountains and heard stories of more. I know for a fact that there are shapeshifters in this area."

He didn't even look at Aralorn as he said that, nor did Myr, though the young king twitched. "I'll keep an eye out—but if he were going to harm us, I'd think he'd have already done so."

Myr relaxed a little, relying on the older man's judgment. Stanis looked pleased with himself—Wolf had agreed with *him*.

AFTER BREAKFAST, ARALORN found herself cornered by Myr, and before she knew it, she was agreeing to give lessons in swordsmanship. Myr divided the adults into four groups to be taught by Aralorn, Myr, Wolf, and a one-armed ex-guardsman with an evil smile and the unlikely name of Pussywillow. The other three teachers were, in Aralorn's estimation, all much better with a sword than Aralorn was, but luckily none of her students were good enough to realize how badly outclassed she was.

The first part of any low-level lesson was a drill in basic moves. Haris Smith-Turned-Cook handled the sword with the same strength and sureness that a good smith uses in swinging a hammer. He learned rapidly from a word or a touch. Edom had the normal flaws of adolescence—all elbows and awkwardness. The others were in the middle range. Given three or four years of steady sword work, they would be passable, maybe.

It didn't really matter, she thought. If it came down to hand-to-hand fighting, they were all doomed anyway. But it was something to keep the people busy and make them feel as though they were working toward a common goal.

She fought her first bout with Haris, deciding to face the best fighter first—when she was fresh. It was a good idea. He might not have had much experience with a sword, but he had been in more than one dirty fight. If she'd had to rely on only her swordsmanship to fight him, she might have lost, but she'd been in a few dirty fights herself.

When she finally pinned him, Haris gave her the first genuine smile she'd seen on his face. "For a little bit of a thing, you fight pretty well."

"For a hulking brute, you're not too bad yourself," she said, letting him up. She turned to the observers. "And that is how you fight on a battlefield. But not in a training session on swordsmanship. The sword got in his way more than it helped him. If he were fighting in a battle today, he'd be better off with a club than with a sword. That will not be true in a month, for any of you—I hope."

The others were easier, so she lectured as she fought. By the time she was facing the last student, Edom, she was short on breath. Cleaning the inn had been good for keeping in shape, but a two-hour workout with a sword was enough to test her powers of endurance.

She opened with the same move that she'd used in all the other fights—a simple sidesweep that all the others had been able to meet. Edom fell, which should have shown him to be an utter idiot with a sword. She heard a few suppressed sniggers from the audience. But something about the fall struck her as a little off; if he had fallen from the force of the blow, he shouldn't have fallen quite as far as he had. She wasn't big enough to push him that distance without more leverage than a sidesweep allowed for.

She helped him up and handed him his sword. Grasping his wrist, she showed him the proper block and swung again. He met it that time, clumsily. She worked slowly with him at first, gradually speeding up. He progressed slowly, with nothing more odd than ineptness showing in his fighting.

She worked with him on three blocks, aiming different attacks at him and showing how each block could be used. She was getting tired, and made a mistake that a better swordsman would never have made. She used a complex swing, difficult to execute as well as counter, and mis-judged it. Horrified, she waited for her sword to cut into his leg.

He blocked it.

He shouldn't have been able to, not at his level. She wasn't sure that she could have blocked it. She certainly couldn't have executed the com-bination that he used. She stepped back and met his eyes. Softly, so that no one but she could hear, he said, "Can I explain in private?"

She considered a minute and nodded. Turning back to the others, she dismissed them, sending them to watch Myr, still fighting nearby.

Alone, Edom met her gaze. He shuffled a foot in the dirt. "You . . ." His voice cracked, and he cleared his throat and tried again. "You know that I'm not quite what I appear to be. I'm not even Rethian; I'm from Darran. I don't know if you know it, but Darran is under the ae'Magi's influence, too."

"Darran?" Darranians hated magic. People who could work magic left, or risked being killed. Impossible to imagine Darranians approving of the ae'Magi.

He saw her expression.

"Yes. It was pretty obvious when it happened," he said. "Scary. I said the wrong thing, and I had to run for my life." He shrugged. "I don't know why I came here. Something . . . drew me here, I guess. It seemed as good a place to go as any. I found the valley full of people like me, hiding from the ae'Magi. But they were all Rethians. Given current feelings between Darran and Reth, I could hardly tell them that I was a noble-born Darranian.

"So I told them that I was the son of a Rethian merchant. I thought that it was a good idea, I speak Rethian with a faint enough accent that I could pass for any number of western provinces—and it explained the richness of my clothes.

"Then Myr came and started this swordsmanship training. Where would a merchant's son get trained in Darranian-style swordsmanship? So I faked it."

Aralorn looked him over. "Quite a problem, I agree. What you will do is tell this all to Myr. You do it, or I will." She put a bite into her last sentence. She'd trained her share of new recruits before she became a spy—some of them needed orders that sounded like orders.

Edom balked; she saw it in his eyes. Whether it was the order, the idea of telling Myr his secret, being told what to do by a woman, who was also obviously Rethian (prejudice went both ways between Reth and Darran), or all of the above, she didn't know. Though she suspected all three. She waited while he worked it out, saw him swallow his pride with an effort.

"I've heard he's not as prejudiced as most Rethians." She waved a hand in the vague direction of the rest of the camp. "And with the lack of trained fighters here, Myr can't afford to be too picky."

Edom stared at her a moment. "I guess I'll go do that now, then." He gave her a small smile, took a deep breath, and seemed to relax. "If he doesn't kick me out, I guess it might be nice to be useful, instead of sitting on the sidelines all the time." After a brief bow to her, student to teacher, he ran off to where Myr was fighting.

Aralorn stretched wearily. Tired as she was, it had felt good to work out with a sword rather than a mop—it was almost as good as playing at staff.

The exercise had made her hot and itchy, so she wandered over to the creek. It took her a while, but she found a place deep enough to wash in, with a large flat rock that she could kneel on and avoid the worst of the mud. She ducked her head under the water—its icy temperature welcome on her overheated skin.

As she was coming up for air, she heard a newly familiar voice say, "See, I told'ja she had a funny-looking sword. Look, the handle's made out of metal."

Aralorn took her time wiping her face on her sleeve and smoothing her dripping hair away from her face. Stanis and his silent-but-grinning companion, Tobin, stood observing her. She hid a smile when she recognized Stanis's solemn-faced, feet-apart, hands-behind-his-back pose. She'd noticed that Myr did that when he was thinking.

"Have you killed anyone?" Stanis's voice was filled with gruesome interest.

She nodded solemnly as she rolled up the long sleeves of the innkeeper's son's tunic again. Maybe she should cut them, too. The boots were giving her blisters.

"You're not supposed to fight with swords that don't have wooden handles," said Stanis worriedly. "If you kill a magician with your sword, his magic will kill you."

She could have explained that any mage powerful enough to be problematical that way would certainly not need a sword to kill her. But she didn't want to scare them any worse than they already were.

"That's why I only *wound* magicians with my sword," she explained. "When I kill magicians, I always use my knife. It has a wooden grip."

"Oh," said Stanis, apparently satisfied with her answer.

They were silent for a moment, then Stanis said, "Tobin wanted to know if you would tell us about killing someone?"

"All right," agreed Aralorn. Far be it from her to give up the chance to tell stories. Her friends rolled their eyes when she started one, but children were always a good audience. She looked around for a good place. She settled on a grassy area, far enough away from the stream so that the ground was relatively dry, and sat down cross-legged. When her audience joined her, she cleared her throat and began the story.

THAT WAS WHERE Wolf found her. Her audience had grown to include most of the camp, Myr's raggle-taggle army as enthralled as any bunch of hardened mercenaries at her favorite tavern. He walked quietly closer until he could hear what she was saying.

". . . so we snuck past the dragon's nose a second time. We had to be careful to avoid the puddles of poison that dripped from the old beast's fangs as it slept."

She had just thrown away her career and her home—no matter what the outcome of this, she had disobeyed orders. If she returned to Sianim, it would be as a criminal and a deserter. She knew that. Knew that Myr's little band of refugees was doomed unless they had the luck of the gods— and he didn't believe in luck, not good luck, anyway. Yet here she was, entertaining this grim and hopeless bunch with her relentless cheer.

"Dragon's ears"—she spoke in such serious tones that several people in her audience nodded, including, to Wolf's private amusement, Myr— "though you can't see them at all, are very acute. There we were, the four of us, loaded down with all sorts of treasures, sneaking past this huge beast that could swallow us all in one gulp. We held our very breath when we neared it. Not a sound did we make, we stepped so soft." Her voice dropped to a carrying whisper. "Now you remember those bejeweled golden goblets Wikker'd liked so well? Just as we crossed in front of the dragon . . . that great beast, he breathed out, and it was as if we were caught in a spring storm the wind was so bad. It grabbed one of Wikker's

goblets, and it landed right on that giant fiend's scale-covered muzzle."
She closed her eyes and looked sorrowful for a moment, waiting . . .

"What happened?" asked a hushed voice from the crowd.

Aralorn shook her head and spread her arms. "What do you expect
happened? It ate us."

There was a short silence, then sheepish laughter as they realized that
she'd been telling them a tall tale from the beginning. Wolf was close
enough to hear Stanis's disgruntled, "*That's* not how it should have ended.
You're supposed to kill the dragon."

Aralorn laughed, hopped to her feet, and ruffled the boy's hair as she
passed by him. "There is another ending to the story. I'll tell you it later.
Now, though, I think that I hear someone calling us for lunch."

ARALORN ATE THE last of the bread and cheese that was lunch, and Wolf
touched her on the shoulder. She dusted off her hands and followed
him without a word. They slipped out of camp and scaled one side of the
valley. Once on the top, they followed a faint trail through the trees
that led to a cliff with several dark openings, including a large, shallow-
looking cave.

Wolf walked past that and took her into a smaller opening twenty
paces farther along. As he entered the dark tunnel, the crystals on his
staff began emitting a pale blue light. Aralorn hadn't noticed that he
was carrying the staff while they were walking, but she supposed that it
was just part of being a mysterious mage . . . or maybe it was just Wolf.

"These caves would make a much better shelter than the tents. Why
aren't you using them?"

Wolf motioned to a small branch and halted her with a hand on her
arm. He tilted the staff slightly until she realized that directly in front of
them was a dark hole. "Aside from the problem of lighting them—which
could be managed—there are several of these pits. That one goes down
far enough to kill someone, and there are some holes deeper than that.
If there were no children, you might risk it, but it's too difficult to keep
them from wandering. We are storing a lot of the supplies in a few caves

near the surface, and I drew up a map for Myr of a section that is pretty isolated from the main cave system. If it becomes necessary to move the camp into the caves, we can. But it is safer in the valley."

Aralorn looked at the blackness in front of them and nodded. She also stayed close to Wolf the rest of the way through the caves.

They came to a large chamber that he illuminated with a flick of a hand. The chamber was easily as spacious as the great hall in the ae'Magi's castle. Carved into all the walls were shelves covered with books. Wooden bookcases were packed tightly with more books and stacked in rows with only a narrow walkway between them. Here and there were careful stacks of volumes waiting to find places on the crowded shelves.

Aralorn whistled softly. "I thought that Ren's library was impressive. We're going to read all of these?"

Wolf shrugged. "Unless we find something before we have to read them all." As he spoke, he led her through one of the narrow pathways between bookcases to an open area occupied by a flat table that held an assortment of quills, ink, and paper. On either side of the table were small, padded benches.

Aralorn looked around, and asked, "Where do you want me to start?"

"I'll take the grimoires. Normally, I know, you can tell if something is magic, but for your safety let me look at the books before you open them. There are spells to disguise the presence of magic, and some of the grimoires are set with traps for the unwary. I'd prefer not to spend valuable time trying to resurrect you," he said.

"*Can* you resurrect people?" She kept her voice mildly curious, though she'd never heard of such a thing actually happening. He'd brought all of this here from somewhere, just as he'd transported that merchant and the supplies. She was ready to believe he might bring people back from the dead.

"Let's not find out," he said dryly.

"So, what do I look for, I mean other than a book titled *Twenty-five Foolproof Ways to Destroy a Powerful and Evil Mage*?"

He gave a short laugh before he answered. "Look for the name of a mage who fought other mages. Some of these books go back a long ways, when dueling was allowed between mages. If I have a name, I might be able to find his grimoire. You also might note down any object that could be of use. Magical items are notoriously hard to find—even if they're not the creation of some bard's overactive imagination—and we don't have the leisure time to go on a quest."

She could go though the books methodically. Doubtless that was what Wolf was doing. But sometimes . . . She blew on her fingers and thought hard on how much a little luck right now would be of use. She didn't pull more than a breath of magic for it—luck magic could backfire in unexpected ways. It was best to keep such things small. Then she walked to a random shelf and took out the first book that caught her eye. She ran her fingers lightly over the metallic binding of the book. Originally, it had been silver, but it had tarnished to a dull black.

She could read the title only because she once coaxed Ren into teaching her the words inscribed on the old wall mosaics in some of the older places in Sianim. Reluctantly, she put it away without opening it, knowing that it wouldn't have anything of use. The people who used that language had disliked magic to such an extent that they burned the practitioners of it. They had been a trading people, and merchants in general were not overly fond of mages. She thought about the chubby merchant she'd seen in another cave and smiled; maybe merchants had good reason to dislike magic.

It took several more tries before she found a book that suited her and passed it by Wolf for inspection. He handed it back to her with a perfunctory nod and went back to his work.

This book was, in her estimation, about three hundred years old and told the history of a tribe of tinkers that used to roam the lands in great numbers. They were scarcer now and tended to keep to themselves. Whoever wrote the book she was reading still believed in the powers of the old gods, and he intermixed history and myth with a cynicism that she thoroughly enjoyed. Taking a piece of blank paper, she kept careful note of anything that might be potentially useful.

Her favorite was the story of the jealous chieftain whose wife was unfaithful. Frustrated, he visited the local hedgewitch, who gave him a fist-sized bronze statue of the demigod Kinez the Faithful. When his wife kissed a man in its presence, it would come to life and kill the unlucky suitor. The chieftain had the statue placed in his wife's wagon, and after several of her favorites died, she sinned no more. Or, noted the author of the book, at least she found another place to sin.

At last satisfied that his wife would be faithful, the chieftain entered her wagon to engage in his husbandly duties. He forgot to remove the statue first. His widow became chieftain, enjoyed her widowhood, and ruled for many prosperous years.

WOLF WONDERED WHY it was that mages had such wretched handwriting. The fine motor skills prerequisite to spellcasting should be reflected in decent writing: His own was very nearly flawless. He painstakingly cross-checked the word he was trying to decipher with several others to compare the letters. As he was writing the actual word neatly in the space above the original in case he ever had to read the book again, he heard Aralorn laugh softly.

Safe behind the mask, he smiled at the picture she made with her quill scritching frantically along the paper. Her handwriting wasn't any better than what he'd just been attempting to read. The hand moving the quill was callused and ink-spattered. Ink also resided in blotchy patterns across her face where she'd pushed back her hair.

Reluctantly, he returned to his reading.

ARALORN FINISHED HER book and replaced the slender volume on its shelf. When she found another likely-looking candidate, Wolf was deeply engrossed in his grimoire, so she sat to wait.

"Wolf," she said suddenly, startled by a strange thought.

He held up a hand to ask her to wait while he finished, which she did with some impatience. Finally, he looked up.

"What is the difference between standard and green magic to you? I have always been told that human mages draw the magic from themselves while green-magic users draw power from the outside world, but didn't you say that the ae'Magi had found a way to link to outside power? That that's how he manages to push his influence all the way out to Reth and Sianim? Does that make him a green mage, too? His magic doesn't feel like green magic to me."

In typical Wolf fashion, he started his answer with a question. "How much training have you had in magic?"

She grinned at him. "Not much. You mages are not especially open to sharing knowledge even among yourselves, and the shapeshifters are not exactly fascinated by intellectual pursuits. The only thing I know even about green magic is how to use it, and in that I'm by no means an expert. I spent enough time with my mother's people to learn how to shapeshift and a few minor magics. I can feel the difference between the types of magic"—she put a fist against her heart—"here, but I don't know exactly what it means."

He grunted in acknowledgment and paused to choose his words. "I've heard that explanation, too. I would even venture that most mages believe it. That human magic is more powerful than green magic." He tapped his fingers on the table a couple of times, which surprised her. He was so shut down, so self-controlled, that to see him make a movement for no other reason than that he was collecting his thoughts was unusual.

Finally, he said, "The Ancients believed magic existed in a secret pool in the castle of the goddess of nature, and she used this magic to make the seasons change and the grass grow. One day, a clever man found a way to steal some water out of the pool without the goddess's knowing about it. He was the first human magician.

"Picture magic as a pool of raw, unshaped power that gradually seeps into the natural world to act as nature would have it—making the trees grow and the sun rise. My understanding of green magic is that it is the magic already harnessed by nature the green magician uses, persuading it with nudges here and there to take a different course. The magic that he uses is nature's magic already shaped to a purpose. It is safer and perhaps easier to use, but it is not as flexible as the raw stuff.

"If you accept that story—even just as imagery—then normal . . .

human magic . . ." He hesitated. "At least for most magicians, it works in steps. First, the human magician must tap into the magical pool. It is like drinking through a straw—when one runs out of breath, the liquid stops flowing. The magician then takes the raw power he has gathered and uses it to form a spell or pattern that he shapes himself. The more magic the magician can pull, the stronger he is, but he needs to know the patterns into which to shape the magic and begin the shaping immediately, while he is still drawing it out, so it doesn't overwhelm him."

He looked over her head. Aralorn took a quick look, too, but didn't see anything that would hold his attention.

"If he cannot shape the magic, he must release it as raw power. Raw magic let loose in the world will take the form of fire and burn itself out. Few mages can call enough power that their uncontrolled magic will do much more than start a campfire. Because for most mages, it is the gathering of magic that is the most difficult. Containing it and making it follow one's will is generally a matter of memorizing a spell or two, although a large amount of raw magic is more difficult to shape than a smaller amount."

"Are you going to get kicked out of the secret society of mages for telling me all of this?" asked Aralorn, feeling a little breathless at the amount of knowledge he'd just given her.

"Secret society of mages?" His voice was amused, but it wasn't happy. "If there were such a society, I ripped myself free of that a long time ago. Trust me, sharing a few stories is the least of my crimes."

He looked down at the book in front of him, but she didn't think he was reading it.

"The ae'Magi, powerful as he is, could not do *this*—" His whole body was tight, and he flung a hand outward—she supposed toward outside, though she'd have to think about it for a minute before she could be sure which direction was "outside." "Could not take over the minds of a whole people without turning to older ways."

"Older ways?"

He slumped, his hands petting the book as if it gave him comfort.

"There is a lot of knowledge stored in the ae'Magi's castle. They brought the things—books, artifacts, and the like—that could not be destroyed there, where they would be safely guarded against misuse. In the forbidden books, the ae'Magi found a way to leach energy so that he could use it to hold open the magical channels longer than he otherwise could have. He has greatly increased the amount of power that he can capture at any one time, making him stronger than any wizard living."

She looked at him and thought again about Cain, the ae'Magi's son. But the ae'Magi, by his actions, betrayed a lot of people. The personal knowledge that Wolf had could have come from any of the wizards who'd been close to the ae'Magi. One of his apprentices maybe. There were several who had "died" or disappeared five years or more ago—the study of magic at the higher levels wasn't any safer than being a mercenary.

"Earlier, you said that human magic works this way for most magicians, not for you?" asked Aralorn carefully.

His yellow eyes caught hers like a bird of prey's. He seemed a stranger to her, hostile almost.

Aralorn set her chin and stubbornly refused to let herself feel threatened. "How does it work for you?" she rephrased her question.

Suddenly, he relaxed and loosened his shoulders. Mildly he said, "I forget sometimes, how difficult it is to intimidate you. Very well, then; yes, it is different for me. When I started working magic, it wasn't obvious just how different I was. Not until I started working the more powerful spells did the difference make itself felt. Most magicians are limited by the magic they can draw into themselves; I am limited more by the amount of magic I can shape into a spell."

A lot, Aralorn thought, remembering the merchant he'd transported.

"I suspect that the ae'Magi"—he paused and touched her hand lightly—"who was my teacher, as you suspect"—he'd learned to read her, too, over the past few years—"knew long before I did, and separated me from the rest of his apprentices. From then on, I lacked anyone with whom to compare myself. When I was fifteen, the ae'Magi decided to try to use me to gather more power. He had me gather all the magic that I could so that he could use it."

Wolf fell silent. Aralorn waited for a minute, then asked, "Something happened?"

Wolf made a sound that could have been a laugh. "Yes, something happened. Either the method that he was trying to use wasn't successful, or he wasn't ready for the amount of power I drew; but before he could do anything, I destroyed most of the tower we were in. The stones were melted. I don't know how he managed to keep us alive, but he did. It was three months before I could bring myself to collect enough magic to light a candle." He paused for a minute, collecting his thoughts or dealing with the memory.

Aralorn waited patiently for him to continue or not, as it suited him. He had told her more about himself in the last five minutes than he'd told her in the four years she'd known him. If he chose to stop, she wasn't going to push him.

In time, he began again. "That was when he turned to the older texts. He began to experiment with drawing power from others. Not with me, because that first experiment had proved such a disaster. It was during these experiments that he found that with the aid of certain rituals—rituals forbidden even before the Wizard Wars, if you can imagine anything those wizards would have forbidden—he could use the power of untrained magic-users, especially children. They don't have the defenses that others do." He stopped again, his golden eyes bleak.

I should stop here, he thought. She knew what he did now about the ae'Magi. If something happened to him, she might be about to find another mage—surely some of the more powerful mages could work themselves free, if the half-trained wreck that he'd been had managed it. But he was consumed by the desire, the *need* to let her glimpse the monster that he was, to destroy her belief that Wolf, her wolf, was some kind of paladin for right and justice.

"For a long time, I helped him," he continued. To his surprise his voice was still its sepulchral self, cool tones that gave no hint of the volcano of emotion that seethed within him. It sounded as though he were telling the story about someone else. "You need to know that." *I need you to know that.* "Even though I knew what he was. I used dark magic, knowing it was evil. I worked his will and gloried in the power and the madness of it. Knowing what he was, I tried to please him."

His hands gripped the table until they were white-knuckled, he noticed, but he couldn't force them loose. Maybe she wouldn't see them. Maybe he didn't care if she did.

"What happened?" she asked. As if she were pulling information for an assignment, something that had nothing to do with her.

When he didn't speak, she did. "What happened? What changed?"

Didn't she understand what he'd told her? Where was her fear? Her disgust? Then he remembered—she was a green mage, not a real one. She wouldn't know exactly how bad it was, how evil the things he'd done. The screams of the innocent and the not-so-innocent—he could still hear them sometimes when he permitted himself to.

He released his grip on the table abruptly. He didn't want to hurt her, he reminded himself, and if he let himself get . . . She wanted a story, something pleasing, something hopeful. Something he could talk about without touching on things best left alone.

He started almost at random. "When I was young, the passages of the ae'Magi's castle fascinated me." That was good, he could feel something settle down. "I wandered through them for hours, sometimes days." When he could. While the ae'Magi traveled, or had to attend to others who couldn't know what he did. "There are places in the passages that haven't seen human hands for generations." The discovery of those safe, dark ways had saved him, he thought. "About a year before I left the castle, I found an abandoned library. A whole library that no one but me had been in for a very long time." A private library, he thought later. Some ae'Magi had picked out favorite books and tucked them away where he could keep them to himself.

"It fascinated me. Almost everything that I had read before I found the library was grimoires and the like. Books I had been told to study." Endless lists, useless, weak, or broken spells, he figured out later. Things to keep him busy without really educating him. "There were books in the little room of another ilk entirely. Someone had collected books about people—histories, biographies, myths, and legends. I learned from what I read." He hesitated, understanding for the first time that he'd actually been answering her question—what had happened to change his path. He looked at her, but her face was still, intent on picking through every word he gave her. Impossible to tell what she was thinking, when she was just listening.

"What I learned made my current occupation . . . more distasteful. So I left." Those were Aralorn's words when she told people why she was no longer filling the role of daughter to one of the best-loved heroes in Reth. He wondered if those words covered up as much for her as they did for him.

She smiled at him and touched her finger to her temple in salute. She'd heard the echo.

The smile let him end his story as lightly as he'd tried to begin it. "Departing the castle was easy enough; but changing what I am has proven to be more challenging."

"If you change into one of those zealots who give everything they have to the poor and go around all the time telling everyone else to do the same, I will feed you to the Uriah myself."

She startled a laugh out of him, and he shook his head in mock reproof. "*You* ought to watch what you say around me. I might forget that I have repented of my evil ways and turn you into something really nasty."

FIVE

Myr, Aralorn decided approvingly, had the soul of a sergeant where a king's should have been. Sometime during the night, he had apparently decided that the camp needed improvement more than the refugees' weapons skills did.

After breakfast, anyone who could ply a needle was sent to turn yards of fabric into a tent. The design of the tent was Myr's own, based loosely on tents used by the northern trappers.

When the project was finished, there would be three large tents that could house the population of the camp through the winter. The tents would be stretched over sturdy frames, designed to withstand the weight of the snow. The exterior of the tent was sewn with a double wall so it could be stuffed with dry grass that would serve as insulation in the winter. A simple, ingenious flap system would make it possible to keep a fire inside the tent.

Those who could not sew, or who were too slow to grab the needles Myr had also procured, were put to work building what Myr termed "the first priority of any good camp"—the lavatories.

The risk of disease was very real in any winter camp, and any military man knew stories of regiments destroyed by plagues because of the lack of adequate waste facilities. Myr's grandfather had been a fanatic on the subject. Myr, thought Aralorn with private amusement, was more like his grandfather than some people in the camp could appreciate.

Aralorn, needleless and worried that Myr would notice, searched futilely for Wolf and noticed Edom looking frustrated as he was trying to stop the tears of a little girl in a ragged purple dress.

"I want Mummy. She always knows how to fix it so her hat doesn't come off." Clutched in the child's grubby hand was an equally grubby doll.

"Astrid, you know that your mum isn't here and can't help you," said Edom impatiently. This was the child who'd been rescued by a stranger in Wolf's caves. Aralorn looked at her with interest. How had a girl as young as Astrid made it to the camp safely without kin? Maybe someone had brought her—she'd ask Wolf. In the meantime, she couldn't leave Edom so obviously in over his head.

"Hello, Astrid," Aralorn said, and got a suspicious look in return.

After a wary second, the girl said, "Hullo."

"Boys don't know how to dress dolls," said Aralorn, squatting down until she was at eye level.

Astrid looked at her distrustfully for a minute before slowly holding out doll and hat.

Years of being the oldest daughter of fourteen gave Aralorn the experience to twist the hat on at just the right angle so that it slipped firmly over the doll's wooden head and caught on the notch that had been carved to hold it in place. Astrid took the doll in one hand and smeared her tear-wet cheeks with the other.

"Can you see if you can get all of you young ones over here?" asked Aralorn. Astrid nodded and ran off.

Turning to Edom, Aralorn said, "I take it that you are supposed to be keeping an eye on the children?"

Edom rolled his eyes. "Always."

"I can relieve you for a while if you like."

He nodded and took off with a grin before she could take it back. She wondered if he'd be as pleased when Myr cornered him for latrine duty.

She had the children sit in a semicircle around her. Some of them did it with a sort of hopelessness that broke her heart. Astrid was the youngest by several years. Most of them were ten or eleven, with a few older and a few more younger. There were more girls than boys. Wary eyes, eager eyes, restless eyes, children were a much more difficult audience than adults because no one had yet had a chance to teach them that it was better to be polite than honest.

Before she began, she looked at their faces to help her select a story. At breakfast, Stanis had told her that most of them hadn't been there much over a month. None of them had any family at the camp, and judging by Astrid's tears, they were all feeling lost.

She sat cross-legged and looked at them. "Do you have a favorite story? I won't claim to know every story anywhere, but I know most of the common ones."

"'Kern's Bog'?" suggested one girl. "Kern's Bog" was a romantic story about a boy and his frog.

"'The Smith,'" said Tobin in a rusty little voice. Everyone looked at him, so Aralorn guessed that it wasn't just in her company that he was mute. "My pa, he told me it. Right before I had to leave."

It wasn't a gentle story, or, really, a children's story. But, she supposed, sometimes a story isn't about entertaining.

"All right," she agreed. "But you will have to help me if I get parts wrong or forget things. Can you do that?"

She waited until they agreed.

"Very well," she said, sitting back and settling into the proper frame of mind. "Once upon a time, when the old gods walked the earth and interested themselves with the affairs of men, there lived a smith in a small village. The smith was skilled, and his name was known far and wide. Although he was a gentle man, he lived in a time of war and so spent most of his day shoeing the great warhorses of the nobility, mending their weapons, and creating and repairing their armor."

A hand went up.

She stopped and tilted her head, inviting a dirty girl with two mismatched braids to speak.

"He didn't do it to get rich," she said. "It was because the war made food expensive. And if he didn't make swords and stuff, his family would have starved."

Aralorn nodded. "These things he did so that he would have money to live, for food was scarce and dear. But at night, in the privacy of the forge, he created other things. Sometimes they were practical, like rakes and hoes or buckles. Sometimes, though, he made things whose only purpose was to be beautiful."

"The war god," said a boy, one of the younger ones, jumping to his feet. "The war god comed. He comed and tried to take the beautiful thing for himself."

"Hands, please," said Aralorn.

The boy's hand shot up.

"Yes?"

"The war god comed," he said in a much more polite voice.

"So he did," she agreed. "Temris, the god of war, broke his favorite sword in battle. He heard of the smith's skill and came to the village one night and knocked upon the smithy door.

"The smith had been working on a piece of singular beauty—a small intricately wrought tree of beaten iron and silver wire bearing upon each branch a single, golden fruit." It had always sounded to her like something a goldsmith or silversmith might make, but it was an old story. Maybe back then a smith did all those things: shod horses, made armor and jewelry. "Temris saw it and coveted it and, as was the custom of the gods when they wanted something from a mortal, demanded it."

"'Cause he was greedy," someone said.

She looked around, but no hands went up, so she ignored the comment. They were all old enough to know proper protocol for storytelling. "The smith refused. He said, 'You who are creator of war cannot have something that is rooted in the hope of peace.'"

Stanis raised his hand. "How come a tree with fruit is rooted in the hope of peace?"

Tobin said, "My father said it was because during a war there aren't any fruits on any trees."

Aralorn looked at the solemn little faces and wished Tobin had chosen a happier story. "The smith cast the statue to the ground, and such was his anger, he shattered it into a thousand thousand pieces. Temris was angered that a lowly smith would deny him anything." Aralorn dropped her voice as low as she could and spoke slowly, as befitted a god of war. "'I say now, smith, that you will forge only three more pieces, and these will be weapons of destruction such as the world has never before seen. Your name will be forever tied to them, and you will be known forever as the Smith.'

"The smith was horrified, and for many days he sat alone in the forge, not daring to work for fear of Temris's words. During this time, he prayed to Mehan, the god of love, asking that he not be forced to build the instruments of another man's destruction. It may be that his prayer was answered, for one day he was seized by a fit of energy that left all the village amazed. For three fortnights he labored, day and night, neither eating nor sleeping until his work was done."

"My ma said that if you spent six weeks not eating, you'd starve to death," said one of the older girls.

"Not if the gods don't want them to," said Tobin fiercely. "Not if they have things to do that are important."

"Quiet, please," Aralorn told them. "Raise your hand if you have something to help me."

They settled down, so she resumed the story. "The weapons he created could only be used by humans, not gods. He made them to protect the weak from the strong. He built Nekris the Flame, which was a lance made of a strange material: a red metal that shimmered like fire."

A hand was raised. "It kills sea monsters," Aralorn's newest helper informed her.

Aralorn nodded. "It was Nekris that King Taris used to drive the sea monster back into the depths when it would have destroyed his city.

"The second weapon was the mace, Sothris the Black. The weapon that, according to legend, was responsible for one of the nine deaths of Temris himself. It was used during the Wizard Wars to destroy some of the abominations created in the desperate final days.

"The last weapon was the sword, Ambris, called also the Golden Rose. There are no stories about Ambris. Some say that it was lost or that the gods hid it away for fear of its power. But others, and I think they are right, say it was hidden until a time of great need."

"Donkey warts!" exclaimed Stanis wide-eyed. "Your sword is a rosy color and kind of gold."

She raised her eyebrows and pulled it out so all the children could see it. "Well, so it is."

"It's kinda puny, though," said one young boy a year or two older than Stanis, after careful inspection.

She nodded seriously. "I think you're right. Ambris is big enough that only a strong warrior could hold her. This sword was built for a small person—like me or you."

The boy gave her a little grin of solidarity.

"A big strong warrior like our King Myr?" asked someone else.

She sheathed her sword before someone decided to touch it and got cut. "Exactly like our King Myr."

Stanis, evidently deciding the topic of Ambris had been covered enough, said, "Do you know any other stories? Other ones about swords an' gods an' stuff? I like 'em with blood an' fight'n, but Tobin says that it might scare the young'uns."

Aralorn grinned and started to reply, but noticed that Wolf was waiting nearby. Beside him was Edom. "It looks like I'll have to wait and tell you a story another time. Remind me to tell you the one about a boy, his dog, and a monster named Taddy."

Edom came up to her. "Thank you for the break," he said with a short bow. "I am most grateful. But Wolf says he needs you more than Myr needs another hand at the trenches."

"Watching the children is better than digging?" she asked.

He grinned. "Absolutely. Hey, Stanis, how about you help me get a game of Hide the Stone going?"

And a moment later they were all running for the bushes to search for just the right stone.

"So you wield Ambris now?" Wolf commented, walking toward her when Edom and the children were gone.

She hopped to her feet. "Of course. I am Aralorn, Hero of Sianim and Reth, didn't you know?"

"No." She heard the smile in his voice. "I hadn't heard."

She shook her head and started for the caves. "You need to get out more, have a few drinks in a tavern, and catch up on the news."

"I think," he said, "even as isolated as we are here, I should have heard of the woman who wields Ambris."

Aralorn laughed. "Half the young men in Sianim paint their maces black. And at the Red Lance Inn of the Fortieth's favor, just a few blocks from the government building, there's a bronze ceremonial lance on the wall that the innkeeper swears is Nekris. I guess we don't have to worry about the ae'Magi, you and I. We'll just take Nekris and Ambris to destroy him."

After a few silent steps, she said, "I will admit, though, that when I found it in the old weapons hall at Lambshold, when I was a kid not much older than these, I used to pretend I'd found Ambris."

She drew the sword and held it up for his inspection. It gleamed pinkish gold in the sunlight, but aside from the admittedly unusual color, it was plain and unadorned. "It was probably made for a woman or young boy, see how slender it is?" She turned the blade edgewise. "The color is probably the result of a smith mixing metals to make it strong enough not to break even if it is small enough for a woman. Even the metal hilt isn't unusual. Before the population of magic-users began to recover from the Wizard Wars, there were many swords made with a metal grip. It has only been in the last two hundred years that metal hilts have become rare." As if he needed her to tell him that. "Sorry," she said sheepishly. "That's what happens when I've been storytelling to the children."

"How long did you pretend she was Ambris?" asked Wolf.

"Not long," she said. "No magic in her. Not human, not green, not any. And I was forced to concede that the Smith's Weapons would be rife with magic." She gave him a rueful smile. "Not to mention bigger, as is fitting for a weapon built to slay gods.

"She might not be Ambris, but"—Aralorn executed a few quick moves—"she's light and well balanced and takes a good edge. Who can ask anything more than that? I don't need a sword for anything else, so she suits my purposes. I don't use a sword when a knife or staff will do, so I don't have to worry about accidentally killing a magician." She sheathed the sword and gave it a fond pat.

THE ROUTE THAT they took from the cave mouth to the library was different this time. Aralorn wasn't sure whether it was deliberate or just habit. Wolf traversed the twisted passages without hesitating, ducking the cave formations as they appeared in the light from the crystals in his staff, but she had the feeling that if she weren't there, he wouldn't need the light at all.

The library was as they had left it. Aralorn soon started skimming books rather than reading them—even so, the sheer volume of the library was daunting. Once or twice, she found that the book that she arrived at the table with wasn't the one that she thought she had picked up. The fourth time that it happened, she was certain that it wasn't just that she had picked up a different book by mistake: The book that she had taken off the shelf was unwieldy. The one that she set in front of Wolf to look over was little more than a pamphlet.

Intrigued, she returned to the shelf where she'd gotten the book and found the massive tome she thought she'd taken sitting where she'd found it. She tapped it thoughtfully, then smiled to herself—wizards' libraries, it seemed, had a few idiosyncrasies. It certainly wasn't her luck spell—that had dissipated a few minutes after she cast it.

Wolf had taken no notice of her odd actions but set the thin, harmless book on her side of the table and returned to what he termed "the unreadable scribbles of a mediocre and half-mad warlock who passed away into much-deserved obscurity several centuries before: safe from the curses of an untrained magician, however powerful."

Aralorn, returning to the table, listened to his half-voiced mutterings with interest. The mercenaries of Sianim were possessed of a wide variety of curses, mostly vulgar, but Wolf definitely had a creative touch.

Still smiling, Aralorn opened the little book and began reading. Like most of the books *she* chose, this one was a collection of tales. It was written in an old Rethian dialect that wasn't too difficult to read. The first story was a version of the tale of the Smith's Weapons that she hadn't read before. Guiltily, because she knew that it wasn't going to be of any help defeating the ae'Magi, she took quick notes of the differences before continuing to another story.

The writer wasn't half-bad, and Aralorn quit skimming the stories and read them instead, noting down a particularly interesting turn of phrase here and a detail there. She was a third of the way through the last story in the book before she realized just what she was reading. She stopped and went back to the beginning, reading it for information rather than entertainment.

Apparently, the ae'Magi (the one ruling at the time that the book was written, whenever that was) had, as an apprentice, designed a new spell. He presented it to his master to that worthy's misfortune. The spell was one that nullified magic, an effect that the apprentice's two-hundred-year-old master would have appreciated more had he been out of the area of the spell's effect.

Aralorn hunted futilely for the name of the apprentice-turned-ae'Magi or even any indication when the book was written. Unfortunately, during most of Rethian history, it had not been the custom to note the date a book was written or even who wrote it. With a collection of stories, most of which were folktales, it was virtually impossible to date the book reliably within two hundred years, especially one that was probably a copy of another book.

With a sigh, Aralorn set the book down and started to ask Wolf if he had any suggestions. Luckily she glanced at him before a sound left her mouth. He was in the midst of unraveling a spell worked into a lock on a mildewed book as thick as her hand. She'd grown so used to the magic feel of the lighting, she hadn't noticed when the amount of magic had increased.

He didn't seem to be having an easy time with it, although it was difficult to judge from his masked face. She frowned at his mask resentfully.

"Doesn't that thing ever bother you?" she asked in an I-am-only-making-conversation tone as soon as the lock popped open with a theatrical puff of blue smoke.

"What thing?" He brushed the remaining blue dust off the cover of the book and opened it to a random page.

"The mask. Doesn't it itch when you sweat?"

"Wolves don't sweat." His tone was so uninterested that she knew that it was a safe topic to push even though he was deliberately avoiding her point. And he did, too, sweat—when he was in human form, anyway.

"You know," she said, running a finger over a dust pattern on a leather book cover, "when my father took me to visit the shapeshifters, I thought that it would be really fun to be able to be someone else whenever I wanted. So I learned and worked at it until I could look like almost any person I wanted. My father, though, had an uncanny knack of finding me out, and he was a creative genius when it came to punishments. Eventually, I got out of the habit of shapechanging at all.

"The second time that I visited with my mother's people, I was several years older. I noticed something that time that I'd missed the first time. If a shapeshifter doesn't like something about himself, she can just change it. If her nose is too long or her eyes aren't the right color, it is easily altered. If she did something that she wasn't proud of, then she could be someone else for a while until everyone forgot about it. They, all of them, hide from themselves behind their shapes until there isn't anything left to hide from."

"I assure you," commented Wolf dryly, "that as much as I would like to hide from myself, it would take more than a mask to do it."

"Then why do you wear it?" she asked. "I don't mean out there." She waved impatiently in the general direction of camp.

"It's that way," Wolf said, moving her hand until it pointed in a different direction.

"You know what I mean," she huffed. "I am sure that you have your reasons for wearing a mask out there. But why do you use it to hide from me, too? I am hardly likely to tell everyone who you are if that is what you're hiding."

He tensed but answered with the same directness that she had shown. "I have reasons for the mask that have nothing to do with trust or the lack of it."

She held his eyes. "Don't they? There are only the two of us in this room."

"Cave," he interjected mildly.

She conceded his correction but not the change of subject. " 'Cave,' then. A mask is something to hide behind. If I am the only one here to look at your face, then you are hiding from me. You don't trust me."

"Plague take it, Aralorn," he said in a low voice, stealing her favorite oath. "I have reasons to wear this mask." He tapped it. There was enough temper in his eyes, if not his voice, that a prudent person would have backed down.

Not even her enemies had ever called Aralorn prudent.

"Not with me." She wouldn't retreat.

He closed his eyes and took a deep breath and opened them again. The glitter of temper had been replaced by something that she couldn't read. "The mask is more honest than what is beneath it." There was emotion coloring his voice, but it was disguised so it could have been as mild as sorrow or as wild as the rage portrayed by the mask.

She waited, knowing that if she commented on his obscure statement, he was fully capable of sidetracking her into his peculiar philosophical mishmash until she forgot her purpose.

When he saw that she wasn't going to speak, he said softly, "I find that trust is hard for me to learn, Lady."

There was nothing obvious holding the mask on his face, no hidden straps to hinder him when he put his hands up and undid the simple spell. He gripped the mask and took it off smoothly. She probably only imagined the slight hesitation before his face was revealed.

She'd been certain it was his identity that he hid. If she had been another person she might have gasped. But she had seen burn victims before, even a few who were worse—most of those had been dead. The area around the golden eyes was unscarred, as if he'd protected them with an arm. The rest of his face matched his voice: It could have belonged to a corpse. It had that same peculiar tight look as if the skin was too small. His mouth was drawn so tightly that he must have trouble eating. She knew now why his voice had sounded muffled, the words less clearly enunciated than they had been when he took wolf shape.

She looked for a long time, longer than she needed to so that she could think of the best way to react. Then she stood up and walked around the table, bent over, and kissed him lightly on the lips.

Returning to her seat, she said quietly, her eyes on his face, "Leave your mask off when we are here alone, if you will. I would rather look at you than a mask."

He smiled warmly at her, with his eyes. Then he answered what she didn't feel free to ask. "It was that spell of which I lost control. I told you that uncontrolled magic takes the shape of flame." As he spoke, he clenched his fist, then opened it to show her the fire it held. "Human flesh burns easier than stone, and the ae'Magi wasn't able to extend his shield to me fast enough."

When he was fifteen, he'd said. It took effort, but she sensed that he was still uncertain, so she grinned at him and playfully knocked his hand aside. "Get that out of here. You, of all people, should know better than to play with fire." She knew by his laugh that she had taken the right tack, and she was glad for the years of acting that allowed her to lighten the mood.

Obediently, he extinguished the flame, and with no more ceremony than he usually exhibited, he turned back to his book. Aralorn went to the nearest bookcase and picked out another book.

After it had been duly inspected for traps and pitfalls, she opened it and pretended to read as she pondered several other questions that popped up. Things like: Why couldn't a magician, who could take on the form of a wolf indefinitely, alter his face until it was scarless? The most likely answer to that was that he didn't want to. *That* led to a whole new set of questions.

She was so engrossed in thought that she jumped at the sound of Wolf's voice as he announced that it was time to leave. She set the book she'd opened on the table, on top of the book she'd forgotten to tell Wolf about. Tomorrow was soon enough for both books. As she started after Wolf, she caught a motion out of the corner of her eye; but when she turned, there was nothing there. Nonetheless, she felt the itch of being watched by unseen eyes all the way through the caverns. Places where magic was worked often felt like that, so she didn't say anything.

As they left the caves, Aralorn noted that there were faded markings just inside the entrance. Some sort of warding was her guess because they had been drawn around the cave mouth. There had been people here long before them, she thought while touching the faint pattern lightly. Under her fingertips, she felt a sweet pulse of green magic.

Outside, the gray skies carried the dimness of early evening. Reluctant drops of rain fell here and there, icy and cold on her skin. There was no wind near the caves but Aralorn could hear its relentless spirit weaving its way through the nearby trees. She looked apprehensively at the sky. It was still too early for snow, but the mountains were renowned for their freak storms, and the icy rain boded ill.

Seeing her glance, Wolf said, "There will be no snow tonight at least. Tomorrow, maybe. If it hits too soon, we might have to move them into the caves. I would rather not do it; it's too easy to get lost, as has already been demonstrated. Next time there might not be a rescue." She saw that he had replaced the mask without her noticing when he did it.

THOUGH IT DID not snow, it might as well have. The storm that hit that night was violent and cold. The wind carelessly shredded the makeshift tents that still comprised most of the camp. Everybody huddled in the tents that leaked the least and waited out the storm. It left as abruptly as it had struck. With the wind gone, the body heat from the huddled people warmed the remaining overpopulated tents. Tired as they were, everyone, with the exception of the second-shift night watch, was soon fast asleep.

Aralorn woke to the sound of a stallion's whistle. There was probably a mare in heat. She swore softly, but when Sheen whistled again, she knew she had to go quiet him before he woke the camp. It probably would be a good idea to check on the horses after the storm anyway.

She reached under the furs she slept on—not an easy feat with so many others sleeping on the furs, too—and strapped on her knife. Carefully, she stepped over the slumbering bodies and threaded her way to the door.

Once outside, she jogged toward the corral. Sheen's light gray underbelly was easy to see against the darkness. Just as he was about to cry out again, he saw her and came toward her, hopping because of the hobble. She looked him over, but saw nothing unusual.

He shifted abruptly, as if the wind brought a scent to his nose. His attention was focused high on the ridge surrounding the valley. Every muscle tensed, and only a quick word from Aralorn kept him quiet.

It could have been only the scent of one of the two guards Myr posted every night in shifts or, more probably, a wild animal of some sort. For her own peace of mind, Aralorn decided to trek up the side of the valley and see if she could locate whatever was disturbing the stallion. She commanded him to silence again, told him to wait, and started the climb.

The terrain was more cliff than anything else. There was an easier trail over more-exposed ground, but she chose to stay in the sparse cover of the tough brush that grew here and there. Once on the crest, crouched in the dense thicket of young willows that surrounded the valley, she glanced back down to see if Sheen was still upset.

His attention was still focused, but he could have just been watching her. Swearing softly to herself, she crept through the brush. If it had been a wild animal, it was probably long gone, or waiting for a nice tasty human to join it for its evening meal—wasn't it dragons that were supposed to enjoy feasting on young women?

She tripped over it before she saw it—or rather him. He was very dead. She called a dim light ball that would allow her to get a better look at the corpse without drawing attention to herself.

It was one of the guards—Pussywillow, the one-armed veteran. He had been killed recently, because the body was still warm, even in the chill of the wet foliage. What really bothered Aralorn was the way he'd been killed. He'd probably been knocked out, judging by the lump on his head. With him unconscious and unable to struggle, it had been an easy matter to cut his heart out of his chest and carve the skin of his chest with runes. The same runes she'd seen the ae'Magi cut into living skin.

Impulsively, she traced a symbol over one of the bloody runes. She knew that certain symbols and runes held a power of their own, independent of green or human designation. Once when she and Wolf had been traveling, she had seen him trace the symbol with a stick held in his jaws (he'd been in his wolf guise). Curious, as always, she asked him the meaning of it. Wolf told her that it was a symbol that simply promoted good rest and taught it to her at her request. She hoped it would help.

She started to run around the edge of the valley without worrying about cover. She almost hoped to draw the attention of the killer; she was able to take care of herself better than almost anyone else in the camp. From the signs around the body, there had been only one person, but he was skillful.

Heart pounding, and not from effort, she searched the darkness for some clue as to his whereabouts. Less than halfway around the camp, she found the other guard. The woman's heart lay, still hot, on the grass that was too dark even in the night.

She had probably been killed after Aralorn found the first body. The killer, safe in his knowledge that there was no second guard to worry about, had taken his time and done the ritual more properly, though still without active magic use that might have alerted Wolf (or anyone else in the camp, for that matter). The guard had been awake for the ceremony, gagged so that she could make no sound. A small pewter drinking glass lay near the body, stained dark with blood.

Gently, Aralorn closed the open eyes.

Taking stock of her position, Aralorn realized that she was no more than a hundred yards from Wolf's camp. It would be wiser to have two people looking for the killer. Finding the camp from her position on top of the rim was not as easy as finding it from the bottom, though; there were no trails to lead her to it.

Just as she decided that her time would be better spent trying to locate the enemy, she saw the light from the meager campfire Wolf preferred.

With a sigh of relief, she made her way down the steep slope, taking the path slowly to avoid twisting an ankle.

Without warning, a violent surge of magical backlash drove her to her knees. She waited until the wash of magic dulled to a point that it was no longer painful before struggling back to her feet. Forgetting caution, she grabbed a stick and used it for balance as she slid down the hill, announcing her presence with a modest avalanche of stones and dirt.

She slid to a stop just above the small, flat area that Wolf had appropriated as his camp. Wolf, in human form, lay unmoving on his back, eyes glistening with rage. Narrow luminous white ropes lay across his legs, chest, and neck.

Edom stood over him, his attention momentarily diverted to Aralorn. Half-raised in his right hand, he held a sword that was *not* the sword he'd been using in the sparring match. It glowed gently, with a pulsating lavender light.

The sight of it sent a cold chill up Aralorn's back as she recognized the weapon for what it was: a souleater. The last of them was supposed to have been destroyed centuries ago—but, she reminded herself grimly, that was storytelling for you: You could only trust it so far.

Even minor wounds from a souleater could be mortal.

The section of the ledge that she stood on was just far enough above Edom to be out of the sword's reach. Crying out an alarm to the camp, she drew her knife and shifted it lightly by the blade in a thrower's grip. At this distance she didn't even need to aim, so she had it in the air before he would have been able to see what it was she threw. He certainly shouldn't have been able to dodge it, but her blade landed harmlessly on the ground behind him.

The speed of his move told her that he was a much better fighter than he had shown himself to be. Easily good enough that he could have fooled her into thinking him unskilled if he'd wanted to. Darranians being singularly prejudiced against women, she thought, Edom probably simply hadn't bothered.

His face, revealed more by the light of the souleater than the modest campfire, appeared older—although that could simply have been an effect of the light. He smiled at her.

She was unarmed against him. Normally that wouldn't have worried her, but the souleater made the situation anything but normal. She could only hope to hold out until someone from the camp got there. Preferably lots of someones.

All the shapes that she could take quickly were suited to her chosen trade as a spy: the mouse, several types of birds, a few insects. Nothing that would hold off an experienced swordsman for long enough to keep both her and Wolf alive.

She took an apparently involuntary step sideways, away from Edom, and lost her footing. She made sure that the fall carried her past Wolf's ledge and on down the hill into some brush.

Edom had two options, either he would follow her down, getting more distance between that sword and Wolf, or he would turn to finish Wolf off—giving her the extra few seconds that she needed. She planned for either—and he turned back to finish his business with Wolf.

She chose the first form that she could think of; it was deadly, though small. The icelynx had no trouble with the steep climb and launched herself at Edom's back before he even had his sword raised at Wolf.

Warned by the brief shadow she caused when she ran in front of the fire, Edom turned—sweeping aside her rush with his sword arm, but not before she raked his back with her formidable claws. Hissing, she faced him as she crouched between him and Wolf, still held captive on the ground.

Pale sword and paler cat feinted back and forth: she, just out of reach of the lethal blade; he, careful not to expose himself to the poisonous fangs of the icelynx.

Suddenly, Edom spoke softly as if not to antagonize the cat, though his tone carried anxious desperation. "It's Aralorn. She's a shapeshifter, don't you see it? She's here to destroy us, betray us. I came up to ask Wolf about something, and I found her here, with Wolf like that. You've all heard of the arcane practices of shapeshifters. Help me before she kills him. Quick now."

Aralorn didn't have to look to see what her nose had belatedly informed her. A half dozen armed people from camp had just shown up to rescue the wrong person. They were too far to do anything—yet. It wouldn't take them long to reach her.

She couldn't speak when in animal form without more preparation—which she was too busy to do—and so was without her most formidable weapon.

Edom continued, even as he tried to maneuver closer to Wolf. "I've heard that shapeshifters need to kill when the moon is full. I guess that Wolf, out here alone, seemed an easy victim. I found this sword near, it must be Wolf's. She seems afraid of it."

Aralorn knew that she had to do something before the time to act was gone entirely. If he succeeded, Wolf would be dead. Disregarding the sword, she leapt at his throat while Edom was still distracted by the sound of his own voice.

She missed as he threw himself flat on the ground. However, Edom managed to nick her with the sword as she passed him. Her rear leg became icily numb and folded underneath her, but worse was the strange sucking sensation that consumed her. The sword was alive, and it was hungry.

Edom quickly regained his feet. On three legs, fighting the pull of the sword, she didn't have much of a chance. Aralorn watched as the sword descended.

Abruptly, it was jerked out of its intended path. Aralorn could feel the sword's intense disappointment as Edom was suddenly consumed in flames. The smell of burning flesh offended her feline-sensitive nose almost as much as the light bothered her nocturnal eyes.

Apparently, someone—she found out later that it was Stanis—had finally thought to remove the ropes holding Wolf down. The spells that allowed the ropes to hold him unable to move or work magic didn't keep someone from simply pulling them off.

Wolf did a more thorough job of burning Edom than was absolutely necessary, but then it must have been maddening to lie there and know what was going on without being able to do anything about it.

She yowled at him demandingly. With her leg numb and the odd dizziness that accompanied the wound, she was stuck where she was—too close to the flames. He also made her nervous, putting so much effort into burning a dead body. He needed a distraction. When the yowl didn't do it, she rolled until she could bite him on the ankle, hard enough that he could feel it, but not hard enough to release the venom in the glands underneath her fangs.

Abruptly, she was gathered up and set gently down on his bedroll. Wolf grabbed his staff from wherever he put it when he wasn't using it and balanced it on its feet so that he could examine her wound in more certain light. She noticed with interest that the rest of the camp was staying well away from them. Well, Wolf's pyrotechnics had been pretty impressive.

Wolf traced a quick design over the wound with a finger; Aralorn decided that it was to break the sword's hold rather than close the wound, since human magic-users were not the best healers. Nothing seemed to change. He frowned and traced it again, and this time she could feel the power that he used. Still nothing happened. She meowed at him nervously. He ignored her and chanted a few words.

Abruptly he stood and looked toward the crispy skeleton that was all that was left of Edom. Aralorn rolled to stand shakily on her three good legs to see what he was looking at. At first she didn't see it, but a flicker of movement caught her eye. It was the sword. Edom, or the thing that was Edom, had kept its grip on the sword. Now it lay a good foot away from the body. Except for the flicker that caught her eye at first, she hadn't seen it move again—but it was undeniably closer to her than it had been when she'd first seen it.

The coldness that numbed her leg seemed abruptly to be spreading. It could have been her imagination, spurred by the thought that the sword was coming for her. Aralorn lost her precarious balance and fell, missing exactly what Wolf did.

With a harsh, almost human cry of anguish that she heard only partly though her ears, the sword broke. Abruptly, the numbness ceased, and for a brief moment the pain made her wish it back; then it was only a small cut that bled a little.

The icelynx twitched its stubby tail and exploded to its feet with legendary speed. When she was sure all her legs were working, Aralorn arched purring against Wolf, who was still kneeling beside the blankets.

When she'd stood, she heard someone cry out, reminding her that there was an audience. Looking at all the fear and hostility in the surrounding faces, Aralorn decided that it might defuse matters if they weren't being reminded that she was a shapeshifter. She transformed herself into her usual shape and dusted off the innkeeper's son's tunic that was looking the worse from her roll down the wet hillside. Surreptitiously, she kept a close eye on the others. She'd expected them to be worried about her, but they were all staring at Wolf.

He had furnished an excellent display of what happens when a wizard with his strength lost his temper. They all must have known that he was powerful, but knowing something and seeing it were different matters.

Most people also lacked the casual acceptance of gore that mercenaries had. It didn't help that Wolf didn't wear his mask to sleep in, and his horribly scarred visage had been clearly revealed in the flaring light. He wore his mask now, but the knowledge of what lay underneath it was with them all. What was really needed at that moment was someone to take control.

Aralorn looked around to see if she could find Myr, but he was conspicuous by his absence. There was always the possibility that he was still asleep, unaffected by the magic disturbance that had waked the rest of the camp; but, given what she knew about him, Aralorn thought that unlikely. The noise alone should have brought him out.

As the thought crossed her mind, Myr—his clothes covered with bits of brush and blood—took the same path down the side of the hill that she had. *Plague it.* She must have woken him up when she went to check on the horses. If he'd been following her around, there was a good chance that he thought that she'd been the one who murdered the guards. As she had not been trying to hide anything, her footprints would be much more conspicuous than Edom's.

Myr ignored the commotion in favor of investigating the blackened corpse. Aralorn wondered how much he hoped to learn from the scorched, skeletal remains, and suspected he was using the time to think. When he stood up, he seemed slightly paler, though it could have been a trick of the light.

Composedly, he directed his question at Wolf. "Who was it?"

"Edom," answered Wolf, his chilling voice even rougher than usual. If Wolf's hand hadn't been locked on her shoulder with a bruising grip, Aralorn would have thought him unaffected by the events of the night. It was obvious from the incredulous looks they directed at Wolf that most in the little gathering were disturbed by his calmness.

"Is he the victim or the attacker?" asked Myr, voicing the question that was on almost everyone's mind.

"The attacker and the victim, though he didn't intend to be the latter," answered Aralorn, deciding to take part in her defense. Myr, at least, had already known what she was. She continued to tell them what she had done and the discovery of the dead guards. "I came to see if Wolf wanted to help track him down and found Edom with his nasty little sword drawn, standing over Wolf."

An unfamiliar voice asked, "How do we know she's telling the truth? She could have laid a spell on Master Wolf so that he thinks that she has the right of it. Shapeshifters can do things like that. Edom was just a boy. Why would he attack Wolf? As for magic rituals, I spent three days teaching him how to move a stick without touching it. He didn't have hardly any magic at all."

Wolf spoke, and even the most unobservant could see that he was not in control of his temper yet. "I assure you"—he looked at the man who'd spoken, and the man took a quick step back and stumbled over a rock—"I am certain of what took place tonight."

Silence fell.

Wolf's gaze found the ropes that had been left tangled on the ground.

He gestured and the ropes burst into flame so hot it was blue and white rather than orange. The three or four people nearest them flinched, even Myr.

"Also," growled Wolf in a voice like a coffin dragged over rock, "the sword Edom fought with was a souleater. It did not belong to me. Aralorn, with her shapeshifter blood, could not have held anything so unnatural for long enough to draw it."

Good to know, Aralorn thought. In the unlikely event of her running into another one.

Myr said, "Our guards were dead before Aralorn found them."

Tobin spoke up from his position as Stanis's shadow, his eyes on the blackened bones. "Edom had a lot of books in his tent written in Darranian."

There was a brief silence. Aralorn almost smiled as she saw the meaning of Tobin's words echo in the minds of all present. It was Tobin's testimony that bore the most weight. A shapeshifter, being, after all, native to the Rethian mountains, was better than a Darranian. If Edom was a Darranian, it put an entirely different light on the events of the night.

All the same, nobody but Myr met her eyes as they left to collect the bodies.

They buried the guards in rough graves dug in the night, as Wolf said that it was the best. He had counteracted the runespell as best he could, but the runes enacted on the living flesh of dying people were stronger than they might otherwise be. He never made clear the exact purpose of Edom's runes, but he said that burying the bodies would give strength to his own spells.

When the last shovelful of dirt had been spread Wolf raised his hands and spoke words of power and binding. It was coincidence, Aralorn knew if no one else did, that it started pouring rain at the moment Wolf finished speaking.

The huddled group of people stood uneasily for a minute under the rain. The sting of death was no new thing to any of them, but that didn't make it any more pleasant. They all shared guard duty, and it could have been any of them. None held any illusions that they would have escaped better than Pussywillow had. The magic they had witnessed this night had its effect as well. Most of them were not quite comfortable with magic even though they could work a touch of it themselves.

Gradually, they drifted back to their tents until Aralorn, Myr, and Wolf were the only ones left by the new graves.

Myr hit the stone he was standing near with a clenched fist, hard enough to break the skin. He spoke with quiet force. "I am tired of feeling like a cow waiting for slaughter. If we didn't realize before this that the ae'Magi is just biding his time until there isn't something more interesting to turn his attention to, we know that now. Edom is . . . was too young to be anything but a minor servant, and we almost didn't stop him in time. When we face the ae'Magi, we don't stand a chance."

"Edom was older than he looked, and more than a minor servant if he worked the runes that were on the bodies," commented Wolf calmly, having recovered most of his usual control. "Carrying and hiding a soul-eater from me is not much easier. Don't make the same mistake that the ae'Magi is: He is not invincible."

"You think that we have a chance against the ae'Magi?" Myr's tone was doubtful.

"No, but we can bother him for longer than he thinks that we can," said Aralorn briskly. "Now, children, I think that it is time for us to go to sleep. Don't forget that we have the sanitary facilities to dig in the morning. Wolf, if you don't mind, I think that everyone would be a little more comfortable if I sleep in your camp rather than the tent I've been sharing." *Me, too,* she thought, *I'll be much happier here.* "Let them meet their shapeshifter in the light of day."

SIX

Somewhere in the darkness, a nighthawk cried out in defeat, and the mouse escaped for another night. Aralorn sympathized with the mouse, as she knew exactly how it felt.

Edom's remains had been gone when she'd arrived back at Wolf's camp with her belongings. Nothing remained of the blackened body except a slight scorched smell, as if someone had left the stew on the fire too long. She supposed that Wolf had disposed of the body somewhere; she hadn't been inclined to ask.

Now that the excitement was over, it was time to rest, but she couldn't do it. When she closed her eyes, she could all but feel the not-quite-cold metal cutting her and tearing at more than the flesh of her thigh. Every time she managed to doze off, she had nightmares about arriving too late to help Wolf or the sword's bite cutting all the way to her soul and leaving her bleeding to death from a wound that no bandage could stem.

As she lay awake in the chill air of early morning, the blankets she used seemed too thin to protect her from the cold and damp. She pulled her legs up and wrapped her arms around them in an effort to get warm, but even that didn't seem to help. She shivered convulsively and knew that some of it was due to fear rather than the night air.

She sat up and rested her forehead on her knees. She closed her eyes, but that didn't stop the jumbled images from presenting themselves to her.

If she hadn't decided to find out what was bothering Sheen, or Edom had been just a little swifter in his work, Wolf would be dead. Not only would that have meant the end of any chance of defeating the ae'Magi, but she would have lost her enigmatic companion. Some part of her was amused that of the two results, it was the second that bothered her the most. Ren would not approve.

She was so intent on her thoughts that she didn't notice that Wolf had gotten up until he sat down beside her.

"Are you all right?" he asked softly.

She started to nod, then abruptly shook her head—without lifting it from her knees. "No. I am not all right. If I were all right, I would be asleep." As she spoke, still without looking up, she scooted nearer to him, until she was leaning against his shoulder.

There was a pause, and then he slid an arm around her shoulder. "What's wrong, Lady?"

He was so warm. She shrugged.

"Is there something I can do?"

She let go of her legs and snuggled closer until she was almost sitting in his lap. "You're already doing it, thanks. I'm sorry. Just jittery after the fight."

"I don't mind." He sat still, holding her almost awkwardly—but his warmth seeped in and alleviated the cold that blankets hadn't been able to dispel.

Aralorn relaxed but felt no pressing need to move away. "I must be turning into one of those women who moan and wail at the first chance they get—just so a handsome man will take them into his arms." Yes, she was flirting. It didn't seem to bother him.

"Hmm," he said, apparently considering what she had said. "Is that why they do it? I have always wondered."

"Yup," she said wisely, noticing that he wasn't holding her as stiffly. As if he wasn't used to someone so close. She'd snuggled down with the wolf sometimes—although rarely. He seldom invited touch. "Then," Aralorn continued, keeping it light, "she has her way with him, and he has to marry her. It's nice to know that I haven't fallen to that level . . . yet."

"So that's not why you're here?" He seemed intrigued rather than unhappy, she decided.

She paused, then said, "I was just getting a little chilled and thought to myself, 'Aralorn, what is the easiest way to get warm?' 'Well,' I said, 'the fire is nice, but moving requires *so* much effort.' 'Ah yes,' I answered, 'why didn't I think of it before? There is all of that heat going to waste on the other side of the fire.' All it took was a few broad hints, and, presto, you're here: instant heat with very little effort upon my part."

"Yes," he said, tightening his grip and releasing it a moment later. "I can see how that works. Nicely underhanded of you."

She nodded happily: The tension caused by the nightmare dissipated with the familiar banter. "I thought so, too. It's Ren's fault—he teaches us how to be sneaky." She yawned sleepily, closing her eyes. "Oh, I meant to ask—who is keeping watch on the camp?"

"Myr took care of it," he answered her. "The ae'Magi won't have planned two attacks in the same evening, and he won't find out about Edom's failure until he doesn't report. Magical communication isn't all that it could be in these mountains."

"Report." She sat up a little straighter. "Wolf, if Edom was his creature, the ae'Magi knows where we are. Are you sure Edom wasn't acting on his own?" It was unlikely, but it was possible.

"Edom belonged to the ae'Magi," Wolf answered. "I recognized the sword. As far as the ae'Magi knowing where we are . . . Aralorn, there are only so many places we could hide from the ae'Magi. Eventually, he'll find us, whether or not Edom had a chance to tell him." He shrugged. "If it helps any, I would have noticed anything Edom could do magically to communicate. He'd have had to use mundane means."

It did make her feel better. Her temporary alertness faded into exhaustion. As she wiggled into the generous warmth of him, she decided that Wolf was more comfortable to sleep on when he was wearing human shape; he smelled better, too.

WOLF WAITED UNTIL she was asleep before he set her back down on her blankets. He added his blankets to hers and tucked them carefully around her. He brushed a hand against her cheek. "Sleep, Lady." He hesitated, but she was truly asleep. "My Lady," he whispered.

He shifted into his wolf shape and stretched out beside her and stared into the night. Being human so much made him nervous after all the time he'd spent as a wolf. The wolf would have heard Edom coming.

The wolf wouldn't have felt so awkward taking what she'd given him.

As she had expected, Aralorn was alone when she woke up. Wolf's longest absences were the result of a display of affection on his part, as if it was something with which he was not comfortable or, in light of what she'd been learning about him, felt he didn't deserve.

To her surprise, her reception at camp was cordial. She collected a few wary looks, and that was all. Mostly, she thought, Myr was keeping them too busy sewing and digging to worry about her one way or another.

If the adults showed little reaction, the children were fascinated by the shapechanger in their midst. They wanted to know if she could change into a rock (no) or a bird (they liked the goose, but would have preferred an eagle or, better yet, a vulture), and if shapeshifters really had to drink blood once a year, and . . . She was grateful when Wolf came to get her. For once she was tired of telling stories.

"I hope," she said, as they reached the caves, "that they don't believe half of what I tell them."

"They probably don't," Wolf replied. "Your problem is that they will believe the wrong half."

She laughed and ducked into the opening in the limestone wall.

When they reached the library, she noticed that her notes had been scattered around. One of the pages that she had been writing on the previous day was conspicuously situated in the space where Wolf worked. Looking closer at it she saw that it was the one that she'd been using to jot down the stories she'd found in the last book she'd read the day before. She never had gotten around to telling Wolf about the apprentice's spell that negated magic.

Wolf took up the paper and read her closely written scribblings with interest—or maybe, she thought guiltily, her handwriting was bad enough it required his whole attention. Aralorn straightened the rest of her papers, then glanced around the library. What kind of a breeze could pull a sheet of paper out from under the books that were still neatly stacked where she had left them? If she hadn't been here with Wolf, she'd have been worried; as it was, she was merely curious.

"I assume that if the apprentice who developed a way to negate magic were given a name, you would have told me." Wolf set down the paper.

She nodded. "I don't remember ever seeing that story before, so it can't be very well-known."

Wolf tapped the paper impatiently with a finger. "I *have* read that story somewhere else, a long time ago. I know that the one that I read gave his name. I just need to remember which book I read it in." Wolf stood silently a minute before shaking his head in disgust. "Let's work on this mess"—he waved his hand vaguely at the bookcases—"and hopefully I will remember later."

They sat in their respective chairs and read. Aralorn waded through three rather boring histories before she found anything of note. As she was reading the last page of the history of the Zorantra family (who were known for developing a second-rate wine) the spine of the poorly preserved book gave way.

While inspecting the damage, she noticed that the back cover consisted of two pieces of leather that were carefully stitched together to hide a small space inside—just big enough for the folded pages it contained. Slipping the sheets out of their resting place, she examined them cautiously.

BY THIS TIME Wolf was used to Aralorn laughing at odd moments, but he had just finished deciphering a particularly useless spell and so was ready to relax for a minute.

"What is it?"

She grinned at him and waved the frail cluster of parchment in his general direction. "Look at this. I found it hidden in a book and thought that it might be a spell or something interesting, but it looks as though someone who had the book before you acquired it was quite an artist."

He took the sheets from her. They were covered with scenes of improbably endowed nude figures in even more improbable positions. He was about to give it back to her when he stopped and took a closer look.

He crumpled the pages and flamed them. Someone had set protection and hide-me spells, doubtless the reason Aralorn hadn't felt its power, but the old magic wasn't up to withstanding his will. The drawings—on sheets of human skin, though he wasn't about to tell Aralorn—flared deep purple and silver before settling into gold-and-red fire. He dropped the flaming bits, and they fluttered to the table, burning to ash before touching down. If it smelled like burning flesh, she'd probably just assume they had been made of goatskin.

"Wolf?"

"You were right on your first guess." He couldn't look at her. "It is a spell. It's a rather crude representation on how to summon a demon."

"Demon?" asked Aralorn, sounding interested without being eager. "I didn't think that there was any such thing, or do you mean an elemental, like the one that tried to kill Myr?"

Wolf tilted his head and laughed without humor. He should just drop it, but felt the self-destructive urge that had been such a huge part of who he'd once been take hold of his tongue. "This from a shapeshifter? Yes, there are demons, I've summoned them myself. Not many magicians are willing to try it. Mistakes in the spellcasting can be dangerous, and it's getting difficult to find a virgin who can be forced to submit to the process. The ae'Magi never had a problem with it, though; his villagers could always produce some sort of victim.

"The depiction was not entirely accurate. It isn't necessary for the magician to participate in the sexual activities unless he wishes to. He can use a proxy if he wishes."

WOLF CONTINUED TO outline the practices of summoning demons. It wasn't something she'd want to listen to on a full stomach, and if Aralorn hadn't been a mercenary, she wouldn't have been able to sit coolly through it all—but a reaction was what he wanted, and she'd be plague-stricken before she gave it to him. So she maintained a remote facade while she listened. This, she decided, was his way of driving her away after the closeness of last night.

". . . so afterward, it is necessary to dispose of the focus, or the demon will be able to use her again to return without summoning. The blood of a woman used in such a fashion is valuable, as are the hair and several other body parts. The most useful method of killing the girl is to slit her throat." His voice was clinically precise. His glittering eyes never left hers.

She listened to his detached description of the horrors he'd committed and decided that she must be in love because what she really heard was the self-directed hatred that initiated his lecture. Doubtless he'd participated in the twisted ceremony of demon summoning and probably worse. Aralorn was even more certain that it now revolted him as much as he intended it to appall her. Possibly it had revolted him even then.

She waited until he was starting to run out of details, cupping her hand under her chin in feigned boredom. When he stopped speaking, she said, "Fine. I understand. You've done things that a normal human being would find abhorrent. All right. You've stopped doing them . . . I hope. Now can we get back to work?"

There was a long pause, then Wolf commented in the same dry tones he'd been using before. "You are frustrating at times, aren't you?"

She grinned at him. "Sorry, Wolf. I can't help it; melodrama has that effect on me."

"Pest," he said, his tone not at all affectionate, but then his voice seldom showed what he thought.

"I try," she said modestly, and was pleased when his eyes warmed with humor.

Deciding that the crisis was over, she bounced up and strolled to a bookcase several rows away from the table, out of sight of Wolf to give them both time to calm down and sort things out. Absently, she plucked a book from a nearby shelf. She had started to open it when it whisked itself out of her hands and leapt back on the shelf with a loud thud.

She stared at it for a minute, then took two quiet steps backward until she could see Wolf, seated half of the room away with his back toward her, muttering to himself as he wrote. There was no one else in the library.

Carefully, without opening it, she picked up the book again and examined it. Now that she was paying attention, she could see the faint magical aura that was just barely visible woven into the cotton that covered the thin wood that lent the cover its hardness.

Just to be sure, she took the book to Wolf for inspection.

"Trapped," he confirmed, and sent a flash of magic toward the book. A pop, a sharp scent, and a bit of dust floated up and returned to the surface of the book. He opened it and glanced through. "Not a grimoire. Looks like it might be a diary."

She sat down with the book—for lack of anything better to do. Rather than a diary, it contained the autobiographical history (exaggerated) of a mediocre king of a long-forgotten realm. As a distraction from the gory details of Wolf's discourse that kept trying to play themselves out in her head, it ranked right up there with sewing and digging holes in the dirt. She had no idea why anyone would have thought it valuable enough to trap.

"Wolf," she said, staring at open pages. Time to ask him rather than trying to figure out what was going on herself.

"Hmm?"

"Is there someone besides us in your library?" She kept her tone carefully nonchalant.

"Hmm," he said again, and there was a quiet thump as he set his book on the table. Aralorn did the same. "What prompted you to ask?"

She told him of her odd experiences, leaving out the last incident to spare herself his censure. When she was through, he nodded.

"These mountains have a reputation for odd happenings, like Astrid's guide through the cave. A ghost or spirit of some sort would not be out of place." He paused. "Though I brought these with me from the ae'Magi's castle, I suppose something could have come over with them."

It didn't sound like it bothered him too much.

He looked over at her, read her face, and shrugged. "So far whatever is here has been relatively helpful. It could just as easily have hidden your papers or led Astrid to fall into one of the pits. With the ae'Magi to deal with, it is surely the least of evils."

WHEN THEY LEFT the caves it was still light outside. The skies were slightly overcast, but the wind was from the south, so it was warm enough.

Aralorn took a deep breath of air and Wolf's arm at the same time. "Have I thanked you yet for rescuing me from the tedium of mopping the floor of the inn for another six months or however long Ren decided to leave me there?" she said to distract him from her touch.

His stride broke when she took his arm, and he stiffened a little. She'd have backed off, but he put his hand on hers where it hooked into his elbow.

"I am certain"—he said gravely—"I will find the proper way for you to express your gratitude. I noticed just today that the library floors are starting to get a bit dusty."

Aralorn gave an appreciative snort and quickened her pace a bit to keep up with him. He noticed what she was doing and slowed his stride until her shorter legs could keep up.

They were traveling in comfortable silence until Wolf stopped abruptly and snapped his fingers.

"I just remembered where I read that story about the apprentice who killed his master. It will take me a few days to get the book. Tell Myr that I've gone seeking a clue. Between the two of you, you should be able to handle anything that happens." He stepped away from her, then turned back. "Don't go to the library without me, I'd rather lose a few days' work than have you turned into a rock if you opened the wrong book."

Aralorn nodded. "Take care of yourself."

He took the wolf's shape and disappeared into the woods with all the stealth of a real wolf. It wasn't until he was gone that she thought to wonder how the camp would take the fact that she was returning without Wolf after the events of last night. Edom's death would not have vindicated her of all suspicion. With a wry smile, she resumed her course.

At the camp, Aralorn skulked around until she found Myr organizing a hunt for the next day, as the camp supplies were getting low. She caught his attention and waited for him to finish. Listening to him work was unexpectedly fascinating.

He reassured and soothed and organized until he had a small, skilled party who knew where to go and how to get back—without any of those who were not chosen feeling slighted or overlooked. With everybody as edgy as they were, this was a major accomplishment. If Myr survived to regain his throne, he would be a ruler that Reth would not soon forget.

"What did you need, Aralorn?" Myr asked, approaching her after he sent the others to their appointed tasks.

"Wolf is going to be absent for a few days. He is looking for a book that might be able to help us fight the ae'Magi."

She kept her voice neutral, not certain how he would take it. He had no reason to trust her except that Wolf did—and Wolf was gone.

"All right," he said. When she didn't take that as a dismissal, he paused and considered what she'd said again. "I see your problem. You think people are going to wonder if you were really the villain last night and have completed your nefarious plot today."

Aralorn nodded, relieved that he seemed not the least bit leery of her. "I didn't think of it until Wolf was already gone, or I would have made him come back to camp before he left. I thought that you might want to break the news."

Myr nodded. "I'll tell them that he left and leave out the details. There are enough things to worry about—we don't need a lynching."

Abruptly, like an extinguished candle, the taut energy that generally characterized him was gone. He just looked very tired. He needed to pace himself better.

"You need to let them look after themselves for a while," she told him. "They don't really need you to tell them what shoe they should put on which foot or how to make stew."

Myr laughed involuntarily. "You saw that one, huh? How should I know how much salt to put in? I've never cooked anything in my life— that was edible, at any rate."

"I wish I could help you more; but even if they aren't terrified of me, I'm not someone they can trust. You have my sympathy—for what it's worth."

"Thanks, anyway." He glanced up at the cloudless evening sky. "I wish all the tents were done and we had twice as much food. The winter comes in the blink of an eye this far north. My old groom could predict the weather. He told me that the air had a tartness to it before a snowstorm, but I could never smell it." He was talking to himself more than Aralorn. Abruptly, he turned on his heel and headed toward the center of activity.

Aralorn watched as he stopped and laid a hand on the shoulder of an older woman plying a needle. Whatever he said made her smile.

He looked as if he'd seen ten years more than she knew he had, and she wondered if he would live to see the year out. He'd probably wondered about that, too.

Since Wolf had asked her to stay out of the library, Aralorn did her best to keep busy. It wasn't difficult. Without Pussywillow or Wolf, only she and Myr had the training to teach the motley band of rebels how to fight.

Haris was easily the best student. The muscles he'd developed swinging a smith's hammer lent an impressive strength to his blows. Like most big men he was a little slow, but he knew how to compensate for it. In unarmed combat, he could take Aralorn but not Myr.

The rest of the camp varied from bad to pathetic. There was a squire's son who had at one time been quite an archer, but he was old, and his eyesight wasn't what it had been. One of the farmers could swing a scythe but not a sword. Then there was the big carpenter whose greatest asset as a fighter was his size, which he more than made up for by his gentleness.

"Okay now." With an effort, Aralorn kept her voice from getting snappy. "Keep your sword a bit lower and watch my eyes to see where I'll move. Now, in slow motion, I'm going to swing at you. I want you to block overhanded, then underhanded, then thrust."

The carpenter would have been a lot better off if he could have forgotten she was a woman. The only way that she could get him to strike at her was if she did it in slow motion. But when they sped things up, he wouldn't use his full strength. She was about to change that if she could.

"Good," she said when he had completed the maneuvers. "Now at full speed."

He blocked just fine, but his strike was slow and careful, lacking the power that he should have been able to put behind the blow.

Aralorn stepped into it and inside. With a deft grip and twist she tossed him over her head and into the grass. Before he had a chance to move, she had her knee on his chest and his sword arm twisted so that it would hurt him; maybe enough that he would fight her when she let him up.

There had been a collective gasp from her audience when she tossed the big man on his back. The move looked more impressive than it was, especially since he easily outweighed her by a hundred pounds.

Stanis, who was watching with his faithful shadow and a couple of other children, said, "I wouldn't pin 'em that way, Aralorn. Two coughs from a cat, and I'd be out of it if it'd been me you caught."

Aralorn raised an eyebrow and let her victim up. Stanis, she'd learned, had been born to a group of Traders, traveling clans no better than they should be. It was very possible that he had a few good tricks up his sleeve.

"Right, then. Come on, Stanis," she invited.

He did. She must have pinned him a dozen times, but he kept slipping out of her grasp. Drawn by the noise, Myr quit his bout to come and watch, too. Soon the whole crowd was cheering for Stanis as he broke away again and again. Aralorn quit finally and raised her hands in surrender.

"You're using magic to do that," she said quietly as she shook his hand. No one but Stanis could hear her—she wouldn't give away his tricks without permission. "I've never seen anyone do that."

Stanis shook his head, gave her a wary look, then grinned and nodded. "Most of 'em are easier with magic, but there's a few tricks that the Clansmen know if ya wanna learn 'em."

So Stanis took a turn at teaching. He must have been a very good thief, and doubtless there were a few magistrates who were looking for him. They'd have had a hard time keeping him.

When it was time to dig latrines, sew, or hunt, Aralorn watched over the children. It was nice to have a ready audience who believed every word that came out of her mouth—at least until they got to know her better. Keeping the mischievous, magic-toting hellions out of trouble kept her from getting restless while Wolf was away. It also kept her from latrine duty.

THE STORM STRUCK without warning two nights later. Within moments, the temperature dropped below freezing. Without a tent to cover her, since she was still sleeping in Wolf's camp, Aralorn woke as the first few flakes fell. Instincts developed from years of camping had her gathering her bedding before she was really awake. Even so, by the time she left Wolf's chosen spot and made it into the main camp, most of what she carried was already covered with snow.

At the camp, Aralorn found that Myr, efficient as ever, was shuffling people who had occupied inadequate tents to the few that looked like they would hold up in the storm. Seeing her trudge in, Myr motioned her toward his own.

She found it full of frightened people. The storms of the Northlands were rightfully legendary for their fierceness. Although their camp was protected from the brunt of the storm by the steep walls of the valley, the angry howl of the wind was so loud that it made it difficult to hear when someone spoke.

Evaluating the situation, Aralorn casually found a place for her blankets, lay down, and closed her eyes, ignoring the slight dampness left on her bedroll after she had brushed the snow off. Her nonchalance seemed to work because everyone settled down and were mostly asleep when Myr returned to his bed.

By morning the worst of the storm was over. The snow was knee deep everywhere, and in places it had drifted nearly waist high.

Aralorn was helping with the fire when Myr found her and pulled her aside. "I'm no mage, but I do know that this is a freak storm. Feel the air. It's already getting warm, the snow is starting to melt. The storms come suddenly here, I know—but this is more like the spring storms. The winter storms hit and don't ease for weeks. Did you notice anything unnatural about it?"

Aralorn shook her head and sneezed—sleeping in damp bedding wasn't the best thing for one's health. She wasn't the only one coughing. "No, I wondered about that myself so I tried to check. I couldn't find any trace of magic"—human magic, anyway; there was always green magic in a storm—"in the storm, although there was something strange about it, I'll grant you." She shrugged. "If the ae'Magi was causing that storm, he was trying to hide it, which is something he could probably do—at least from me. Weather isn't something that mages like him are generally good with. The trappers who hunt these parts for furs would tell you that it was the Old Man of the Mountains who caused the storm."

There was a brief silence, then Myr, who was beginning to know her, smiled slowly. "I'll take my cue, storyteller. Who is the Old Man of the Mountain?"

She grinned cheerfully at him. "The trappers like to tell a lot of stories about him. Sometimes he is a monster who drives men mad and eats them. Other times he is a kindly old man who does things that kindly old men can't do—like change the weather." *Maybe he might guide a child to safety,* she thought. *Given that there's a thread of truth in any story. Sometimes just a piece as big as spider silk.* She'd run it past Wolf when he returned. "The Old Man of the Mountain is invited to every trapper's wedding or gathering, and a ceremonial place is laid for him when the trapping clans meet in their enclave each year to decide which trapper goes where."

"Which mountain?" he asked.

Aralorn shrugged. "'The Mountain,'" she said. "I don't know. I've met trappers who swear that they have met him. But I've never seen the story in any book."

"Do you think he could be one of the shapeshifters?"

"The Old Man who drives men mad and eats them, certainly," she said. "But I've never met a full-blood shapeshifter who'd help a human find water in the middle of a river."

"Could one of them have brought the storm?"

Impossible to explain fully how taboo it was for a green mage to mess with the greater weather patterns. Taboo implied ability, and she didn't want the King of Reth to know that her mother's kin had that kind of power. Eyes as clear and innocent as she could manage, she said, "Absolutely not." Truth, but not quite the truth he'd think it.

His curiosity satisfied, Myr changed the subject. "I wish I knew how long this weather was going to last. We need to get more meat, and I can't send the hunters out in this. They don't have the skills to hunt in the snow. Only two or three of them have the skills to hunt at all, and none are experienced with northern weather." As he spoke, he paced back and forth restlessly. "And mud. We're going to have mud everywhere, then we'll have ice."

"Don't borrow trouble." Aralorn's tone was brisk. "If we starve, there is nothing that you can do about it. However, Sheen's not been getting much exercise lately, and I'm not too bad with a bow. I also know how to set traps if we need to. Keep your hunters home, and I'll see what I can do for our larder."

Myr's face cleared. "Are you sure? This isn't good riding."

"Sheen's no stranger to snow, and he's big enough to break through this with no trouble."

She hadn't intended to leave just then, but the relief on his face kept her from putting it off until afternoon. She recovered her gear from the storage tent, commandeered a pair of boots, and borrowed a crossbow and arrows from one of the erstwhile hunters.

Sheen snorted and danced while she saddled him, and took off at a dead run when she was only half in the saddle; a dramatic departure that was met with ragged cheers and good-natured laughter. When she was able to pull him up and scold, they were already headed up the main trail out of the valley.

It wasn't as difficult to travel once they were out of the valley as the harsh winds had swept the snow away from many places. As long as she stayed out of the gullies and valleys, the deep snow was usually avoidable.

There were few tracks in the snow. Hunting usually wasn't her job; she didn't know the habits of deer after the first good snowfall. She'd have expected them out once the snow started to melt—on the sun-exposed slopes if not the valleys—to eat the revealed greenery before winter came for good. But perhaps they were just staying sheltered. Maybe they knew something about the weather she didn't.

She stumbled upon tracks that she'd never seen before. The prints were several hours old and smeared hopelessly by the melting snow. Whatever had made them was big—she found a branch as big around as her leg that the animal had snapped off a tree. She looked at the branch a minute and guided her nervous mount away from the thing's trail.

"Anything that big, Sheen, is bound to be too tough and stringy to make good eating. Besides, it would be a pain to drag the body back to camp." Sounded like a good excuse to her. The big horse snorted at her and increased his speed.

Several hours later, Aralorn wiped a gloved hand across her nose and squinted against the glare of the sunny snow-covered meadow. The oiled boots that she'd found in Myr's stockpile worked well to keep out the water. She appreciated them all the more for the fact that all of the rest of her was wet.

The brush was so laden with heavy wet snow that even riding she got drenched. There was a lot of undergrowth on the steep slope behind them. The sun had melted enough of the snow that water ran down everywhere, making the ground muddy and slick. The light sneezes of the morning had turned into a full-blown plaguing cold.

"You know, Sheen"—she patted his glossy neck, also somewhat damp—"I think that I would prefer it if it were really cold. At least that way we would be just chilly and not wet, too."

She pushed a soggy strand of hair out of her face with a sigh. The sun was starting the trek toward its evening rest, and they hadn't seen so much as a rabbit. It was unusually bad luck. The camp was far enough off from commonly hunted areas that the game animals were unafraid of people. Just on the walk from the camp to the caves, Aralorn generally saw traces of deer. Today, even the birds were scarce.

Maybe whatever large beastie left its traces for her to find had scared off all of the prey. She hoped not. That would mean that it was probably something that people should be running from, too. She wished Wolf were here to tell her what it was.

A grin caught her lip as she thought about what his response to being viewed as a rescuer of Ladies in distress would be. The picture of herself as a Lady in distress caused her smile to widen a bit. She still wished for his comforting presence.

Absently she looked at the meadow and admired the pristine beauty of the untouched snow that gleamed subtly with all the colors of a rainbow, more startling because of the dark, dense forest surrounding it. She was deciding whether it was worth crossing the meadow to the river that ran on the other side or if she ought to head up the steep and muddy side hill and circle around back to camp when she noticed that there was something odd about the peaceful meadow.

She stiffened at the same time that Sheen noticed them.

"*Yawan,*" she whispered.

The filthy word described exactly the way she felt. Stupid, stupid to have missed them when in front of her the whole meadow was moving slowly. The covering of deep snow completely masked their scent, or maybe the cold kept them from rotting. Whatever the case, not two feet in front of her a Uriah rose from its snowy bed. It wasn't the only one. There must have been at least a hundred of the defiled things, and though none of them was on its feet, their heads were turning toward her. She had never in her life seen so many in one place—or even heard of such a thing.

The path behind was no escape. The slick mud would slow Sheen much more than it would the Uriah. Cold slowed them, but not enough. The best ways to stop them were fire and running water. There were no fires around that she could see, but running water there was aplenty.

All this took less than a second to run through her head. She squeezed Sheen with her knees, and bless his warrior's heart, he plowed right into the meadow filled with moving mounds of snow. The Uriah howled, and Sheen redoubled his speed, leaping and dodging the creatures. One of them stood up reaching for the reins. Aralorn shot it in the eye with a bolt from the crossbow. It reeled back but recovered enough to catch Aralorn's stirrup. Desperately she hit it hard with the butt of the crossbow, breaking the arm off the body at the shoulder. Sheen struck it with his hind feet as it fell.

The cold must have had a greater effect on their speed than she thought it would, because—much to her surprise—Aralorn made it to the ice-edged river while the Uriah were still sluggish. Sheen protested the cold water with a grunt when he hit, but struck out strongly for the other side. Aralorn took a good grip on Sheen's mane and lay flat on the fast-running surface, letting the water take most of her weight.

The river was deep and swift, but narrow. The horse towed Aralorn to the far bank without mishap. The current had swept them far enough downstream that the Uriah were no longer in sight, but she thought that she could hear them above the rush of the water. When she turned back to mount again, she noticed that the arm she'd severed from the Uriah still held fast to her stirrup.

There was a story about a man who kept a finger from a Uriah's hand for a trophy of war. Ten years later the Uriah who owned the finger showed up on the man's doorstep. Aralorn didn't believe that story, she told herself. Not really. She just wasn't enthusiastic about riding around with a hand attached to her saddle.

Aralorn pried at it with grim haste. The thing was strangely stubborn, so she finally used an arrow as a lever to pull it away. As she worked she noticed that it wore a ring of heavy gold on a raggedly clawed finger—stolen from some poor victim, she supposed. Ren would be fascinated—Uriah were not generally looters; their primary interest was food.

She threw the arm and its ring in the river and watched in some satisfaction as it disappeared in the depths. She reloaded the crossbow from habit; it obviously wasn't much good against Uriah. Mounting Sheen, she headed in the general direction of camp, hoping that there would be a good ford over the river between here and there.

Uriah, normal Uriah, never came where it was cold. Never. But the ae'Magi had Uriah who were—how had Wolf phrased it?—pets. A hundred of them? Ren was fond of saying that it was futile to argue with your own eyes. A hundred of them, then.

The only thing that Uriah who were the ae'Magi's pets could be after was Myr—assuming that Wolf was correct in labeling them servants of the ae'Magi. They had obviously been caught by the storm and incapacitated by the sudden cold. Given when the storm had hit, if the snow hadn't stopped them, they would have reached the camp early this past morning. The storm gave her a chance to bring warning.

Shaking with cold, she urged the stallion to a trot that he could maintain until they made it back to camp. As they went, she sawed at the girth and dumped the heavy saddle and bags to the ground—staying on Sheen while she did so with a trick her old troop's first scout had taught her. The less he had to carry, the better time he could make. She retained her grip on the loaded crossbow.

The Uriah's ring nagged at her more as she rode. That, and how to turn whatever time they had before the Uriah came into a way to survive.

The river was between the Uriah and Aralorn, but it stood between her and the camp as well. She rode as far as she could, looking for a shallow place to ford across, but there was none. The only choice was to swim again. When they came out of the water the second time, Aralorn was blue with cold, and Sheen stumbled twice before he resumed trotting. Warming was one of the easier magics she knew, but, cold and exhausted, it took her three times to get it right.

She rode right into the camp, scattering people as she went. She stopped finally in front of Myr's tent. Drawn by the sound of horse's hooves, Myr ducked outside just as Aralorn slipped off the stallion's back.

"What's wrong?" he asked, taking in her appearance.

"Uriah . . . about a hundred of them. They're coming." Aralorn panted heavily, her voice hoarse with what was turning into the grandfather of all colds. Winter river crossings will do that. "Caves. We can defend the entrance. Leave the tents behind, but take all the food, blankets, and weapons that you can."

He was acting before she finished speaking. The children, under the leadership of Stanis, were sent ahead with such things as they could carry. Myr had the majority of the camp packed and on the trail to the caves before anyone had time to panic.

Aralorn and Myr brought up the rear of the procession. Aralorn, listening for the Uriah behind them, chafed at the slow pace they were forced to take because most people were on foot—but then again, even a dead run would have been too slow. She walked beside her exhausted horse and hoped that Sheen wasn't so tired that he wouldn't give warning if the Uriah got too close.

By the time they arrived at the caves, Aralorn found herself mildly surprised that they had beaten the Uriah there. Light wasn't a problem— light, like fire, was easy magic. Even the children could form the small balls of light that mages used in place of torches.

Myr followed Aralorn as she led Sheen into a solitary cave a hundred feet from the entrance—one big enough to hold the animals they had. "I've been told they can track a man as well as a hunting dog and travel faster than a man on horseback." Myr spoke in a soft voice designed not to carry to anyone but Aralorn. "I don't have much experience with Uriah. All that I know is that they are very hard to kill and are almost as immune to magic as I am."

Aralorn nodded. "They don't like fire, so make sure that there are torches ready. This lot"—she swung a hand in the general direction of the others in the cavern—"will fight better with torches than swords."

Myr gave her a tired smile. "And no worries about how to light the torches either, with this assortment of amateur magic-users. I think that the only one who can't light a torch with magic is I. Haris!" He caught the attention of the smith, who was organizing the storage of supplies. "I want a bonfire laid in the entrance and someone who can light it from a distance stationed somewhere safe to watch for the Uriah."

Haris waved an acknowledgment, and Myr returned his attention to

Aralorn. "There are three or four here who should be able to light the fire from a good distance. I'll station them in relays."

Aralorn shivered in her still-damp clothes. "We could be lucky. There is some kind of warding near the entrance. You can see the markings if you want to look. I suspect that the warding was the reason that Edom wouldn't enter the caves. Do you remember? When he lost Astrid?" She'd given it a lot of thought and decided they'd have to plan as if the warding wasn't there. But still, a little hope couldn't hurt.

Myr nodded.

Aralorn continued, "If it works like the shapechangers' spells do, the Uriah won't even see the caves unless we are lighting fires and running in and out to attract their attention. The trail that we took up here is virtually a stream from the melting snow, so in a little while there will be no sign that we came this way. With luck, we'll have that time. The cold makes them slower than usual. That's the reason Sheen and I beat them here."

"I'll see that everyone stays inside." Myr started to go—someone was calling his name—then turned around. "Aralorn?"

She pulled off Sheen's bridle and vainly patted her clothing in search of something she could use to dry him off. But he was dryer than her clothing. "Yes?"

"I'll send a couple of the older children in with toweling to dry your horse. You change your clothes, before you catch lung fever. My packs are marked over against the far wall; find something in them."

It made sense. "Thanks."

She made her way to his packs, unmistakable because of the embroidered dragon that glared at her as she riffled through his belongings. A true shapeshifter could probably alter the clothes that she was wearing, but Aralorn had no idea how to go about it. She pulled out a pair of plain trousers and a tunic of a dark hue and, best of all, a pair of dry cotton stockings. With clothes in hand she hunted down an unoccupied cranny and exchanged the wet clothes for the dry ones.

The oil coating on the boots worked better in snow than in rivers. The water had run in from the top and been prevented from leaving by the oil on the outside so that they were marshy inside. Aralorn dried them out as best she could and pulled them on over her newly acquired socks. She had hoped for better results.

She surveyed herself wryly when she was done. Myr was not tall—for a man—which left him only a head or so taller than she. He was, however, built like a stone wall.

Well, she thought, tugging at the front of the tunic, at least she wouldn't have to worry about its being too tight.

The camp was starting to look organized again. Aralorn went back to check and found Sheen had been dried. He stood quietly with head lowered and one hind foot cocked up—a sure sign that he was as tired as she was.

Stanis found her there, her head resting against the horse's neck, more asleep than awake.

"Aralorn, I think Astrid went back to camp."

It was enough to wake her up. "What?"

"I can't find her anywhere, an' neither can Tobin, we searched an' searched. She was crying all of the way up here because she left the doll her mother made her at camp. We tried to tell her that it would be all right, everyone knows that Uriah don't eat dolls, just people. But I haven't seen her since you came in, and neither has anyone else."

"How many people have you told this to?" She fitted her bridle to the fastest of the camp horses. Sheen was too tired to run.

"Lots of people know I'm looking for her, but you're the only one I told what I thought happened to her. I tried to tell Myr, but Haris was talking to him and lots of other people."

"Here's what we're going to do. I'm going to sneak out of here and go look for her. I don't want you to tell anyone that I've gone." There was no use sending out more than one person. She was more than enough to bring back one little girl if the Uriah hadn't found her yet. If they had made it to camp, then there was no sense in sending more people to die. "Keep looking for her here. She was pretty excited about the man who helped her find her way out of the caves. She may have just wandered deeper into the cave to see if she could find him. Wait until Myr isn't busy, then tell him where I've gone. That should take long enough that I'll either be back or I'm not coming back. Tell him that I said not to send anyone else after me. There aren't enough people to spare. I'm just going to sneak down to our camp and see if I can spot her. If I don't see her, I'll ride right back up."

She paused only long enough to get her sword. As she belted it on, the thought occurred to her that if she were going to have to keep using it against Uriah, it would behoove her to get more proficient at using the plaguing thing.

It wasn't easy, with her limited magical powers, to sneak through a cave filled with magic-users, albeit weak ones. The gelding, sulky at leaving the other horses munching dinner, didn't make matters any easier. She almost left him behind, but although he made it a little bit more difficult to escape undetected, he also gave her an edge if the Uriah were there.

Once out of the occupied caves, she gave up trying to remain unseen. The guards didn't challenge her as she took the horse past them. They were looking for Uriah coming in, not people going out.

The camp gelding was a lot skinnier than Sheen and not so well trained. She stayed off the trails and followed a creek bed to the far side of the valley near Wolf's camp, so the Uriah couldn't easily follow her back trail to the caves. It wasn't until she got to the valley that she realized that Astrid would have followed the main trail down and back.

Tired and cold and stupid.

It was quiet and peaceful, so she turned the horse directly toward camp. He took three strides forward, stiffened, and spooked wildly. She clung to his back, cursing silently, as the animal's distressed cry and crashing branches gave whatever had scared him no doubt that there was someone riding on the mountainside above them.

Apparently the ae'Magi's pets were capable of stealth.

She'd just gotten the horse under control when she heard a whistle from down below.

She would have known it anywhere. Talor had always been tone deaf—giving his signals a peculiar flat sound all their own, as well as making it unclear exactly what he was signaling. In this case it could have been either "all clear" or "help." Given the circumstance, Aralorn picked the latter.

Without hesitation, she urged the horse down the slope. The only excuse that she had for her action was that she was exhausted and reacting from instinct. Gods bless them, was all she could think, somehow Ren had known. Somehow he'd sent them help from Sianim.

Her borrowed horse was not as sure-footed as Sheen and fought her all the way down. The horse made a lot of noise and ended up sliding most of the way on a small avalanche of his own making.

The gelding was still sliding uncontrollably when she ran into a small group of Uriah. As they easily pulled down her mount, Aralorn jumped clear, hoping that the horse, poor thing, would distract most of them and give her a chance to find either Talor or Astrid.

Her jump took her clear of the feeding frenzy and earned her only a scraped shin and modest bruises. By the time she regained her feet, there were two Uriah nearly upon her. She used the split second before they attacked to search for a possible escape, but everywhere she looked there were more of them converging.

Bleakly, she thought of another of Ren's homilies—rashness eventually exacts a full, fell price. She used her sword in a useless attempt to defend herself and waited to die.

It seemed like it took forever. She swung, and limbs fell, still writhing as if unwilling to accede to death with somber dignity. She swung until her arms were heavy and her tendons burned like slow acid in her shoulders. Her body was covered with myriad scrapes.

Surprisingly, none of her wounds was in itself serious; but collectively, they sapped her strength and dulled her reflexes. The Uriah just kept coming. The horse's screams had stopped, for which she was profoundly thankful. It had been stupid of her to come running; any human who had been here was beyond anyone's ability to help. The gelding had died for her foolishness, and she would soon follow.

She had little talent as a mindspeaker, but she sent a distress cry on a thread of magic to Wolf or any gods who happened to be listening anyway. Then she bit her lip and grimly hacked away.

Her arms were numb by the time that it dawned on her what was going on. She timed her strokes to the refrain in her head: *stupid, stupid, silly bitch.*

They could have killed her anytime they wanted to, but they didn't want to. They were trying to capture her to take back to the ae'Magi for questioning. The thought of that redoubled her efforts. If she could win herself enough space, she could draw her knife and eliminate the chance of being questioned by the ae'Magi again. Her sword, although shorter than normal, was still too awkward to kill herself with before they stopped her.

She spun around, slicing a creature open across the belly when she heard some disturbance behind her, more a lack of attackers than a noise. She caught a quick glimpse of Talor's face before she struck. Frantically, she avoided hitting him by a narrow margin, leaving her sword in an awkward place for defense. But that was all right, because it was Talor.

She blinked sweat out of her eyes. Something was wrong with him. Bile rose in her throat as she brought the sword back up again, but before she could strike she was caught from behind and held helpless.

What happened next was enough to top her worst nightmares. Talor smiled—and it was Talor despite the rotting flesh—and it said in Talor's teasing voice, "I told you to always follow through on your strokes, or you would never make a swordmaster."

She thought that she screamed then, but it might have been just the sound of a Uriah lucky enough to feast on the horse.

SEVEN

THE WOLF LEAPT NEATLY OVER THE SMALL STREAM THAT HADN'T BEEN there the week before, and landed in the soft mud on the other side. The moon's light revealed other evidence of the recent storm—branches bent and broken from the weight of a heavy snowfall, long grass lying flattened on the ground. The air smelled sweet and clean, washed free of heavy scents.

Knowing that the camp was near, Wolf increased his speed to a swift lope despite his tiredness. He reached the edge of the valley and found it barren of people. He felt no alarm. Even if the storm hadn't driven them to the caves, the meltwater from the heavy snow that turned most of the valley bottom to marsh would have.

With a snort, he started down the valley side nearest where he had made his private camp. He decided to stop there and get his things before going on to the caves. Aralorn's bedroll was gone, but his was neatly folded and dry under its oilcloth cover.

He muttered a few words that he wouldn't have employed had there been anyone to hear and took on his human form. Wearily, he stretched, more than half-inclined to stay where he was for the night and join the others in the morning.

He'd always been solitary. As a boy and while an apprentice, he'd spent time alone as often as he could manage. He had become adept at finding places where no one would look.

When he left his apprenticeship behind him, he'd taken wolf shape and run into the wilds of the Northlands, escaping from himself more than the ae'Magi. He had avoided contact with people at all costs. People made him uncomfortable, and he frightened them—even Myr, though that one hid it better than most. He had a grudging respect for the Rethian king but nothing that approached friendship.

For Wolf, the only person who mattered was Aralorn.

Absently, Wolf moved his bedroll with the toe of his boot. He made a sound that was not humorous enough to be a laugh. He'd been running away from and back to Aralorn for a long time. She had caught him in a spell, and he hadn't even known that she was weaving one.

Four years ago, he'd told himself that he followed her because he was bored and tired of hiding. Maybe it had even been true at first. She was always *doing* something. But then he'd heard her laugh. Until then, laughter had never made Wolf feel anything but repulsed (the ae'Magi laughed so easily).

He needed to see her.

Needing someone made him *very* uncomfortable. He didn't remember ever needing anyone before, and he hated the vulnerability of it almost as much as he . . . as he loved her.

It wasn't until he'd found out that Aralorn was spying on the ae'Magi that he knew how much she meant to him. Even the thought of her there made him shake with remembered rage and fear.

He wasn't quite certain when his interest had turned to need. He needed her to let him laugh, to be human and not a flawed creation of the ae'Magi. He needed her trust so that he could trust himself. Most of all, he needed her touch. Even more than laughter—he associated touch with the ae'Magi—a warm hand on his shoulder (cut it so, child), an affectionate hug (it won't hurt so much next time . . .).

Aralorn was a tactile person, too, but her touch didn't lie. It still made him uncomfortable to feel her hands on him, but he craved it anyway. He picked up the bedroll and went down into the valley since it was the shortest way to the caves. When he arrived at the valley floor, even his dulled human nose caught the scent.

Uriah.

Not panicking, he took a good look around him and noticed the signs of hasty packing as well as the fact that the tents (including the one that

Myr had worked so hard to get finished) had been torn into pieces by something other than the wind. He also noticed that there were no obvious bones.

He walked briskly though the camp to get a closer look. Here the scent was stronger, and everywhere were signs of anger vented on inanimate objects. That was good, he assured himself. Anger meant they had missed their prey.

There was a small bone—chicken. Haris would be unhappy about that. Human bones were conspicuously absent, and he felt a faint sense of relief. Myr must have had enough warning to get the camp into the caves. As long as the Uriah hadn't been within sight when the people entered the caves, the wards would keep the entrances hidden from them.

Wolf had started once more for the caves when he saw something white in the drying mud: a horse's skeleton. Too small to be Sheen.

It was picked clean, with only a wisp of mane to distinguish it. The leg bones had been cracked so that all the marrow could be sucked out. It wasn't until he noticed the distinctive patterns on the silver bit that lay nearby that he knew that Aralorn had been riding the horse.

He found another pile of bones, also picked clean, fifteen or twenty paces away. They all had the peculiar twists of the Uriah. He found several skulls—she'd accounted for three of them. He had hoped that he would find her among the dead—something inside him howled with mocking laughter at the thought. But dead would be . . .

He could have followed her there easily.

He left his bedroll forgotten among the ruins of the camp and took wolf shape to run toward the caves because it was faster. On the way there he found the pitiful remains of a small child—a dirty battered doll lay nearby. Astrid—he remembered the doll. He knew then why Aralorn had confronted the Uriah.

Rage sang in his blood. He restrained it with a pale sense of hope that Myr would know something to help his search. If he let the rage take him, there was no telling who would die. If everyone was dead, he reminded himself, no one could tell him if a search had been made. And Aralorn wouldn't want him to kill her friends.

He planned quickly as he ran so that he wouldn't think too much about the wrong things. He was conscious of a numbness that crept over him, covering hot rage with a thin coating of ice.

The furious arguments were audible even before he entered the darkness of the cave.

"Silence!" Myr's voice cracked with tiredness but its power was still enough that it stopped the bickering. "There is nothing that we can do. Aralorn and Astrid are gone. I will not send out parties to be picked off two at a time by the Uriah. We will wait here until I am satisfied that they are gone. Even if Aralorn and Astrid were still alive, even if our whole party went down to the camp and found them prisoners of the Uriah, it wouldn't matter. We could not take them. A hundred, she said, and she didn't strike me as a person who exaggerated."

Only in her stories, Wolf thought. *Not when it mattered.*

He stopped in the shadows of the entrance to one of the great caverns. Myr stood in front of him, facing the main room so that Wolf had a clear view of his profile. The light from the torch revealed the tired lines of his face. "It wouldn't matter because twenty Uriah could destroy all of us, however we were armed. They would kill us, and we'd be lucky if we killed ten of them. Aralorn knew that when she went out looking for Astrid. She stood a better chance than any of us because she has dealt with them before. Had I known what she was doing, I would have stopped her, but I didn't. I will, however, stop any of you who try to leave now. When the sun comes up, I will look."

"Afraid of the dark, princeling?" A swarthy man stepped out of the crowd. His face was unfamiliar, so he must have arrived after Wolf left. He was an aristocrat, from his clothes—less impressed with the king than the peasants were.

Wolf spoke then from the darkness of the entryway, almost not recognizing his own voice. "As you should be," he said. "If I were he, I would send you out on your own to find out what happens to fools in the dark."

Wolf stepped to the left of Myr, clearly revealing himself in the light of Myr's torch. When he was sure that all eyes were upon him, he took his human form with all the theatrics that even the ae'Magi could have used. Masked and cloaked, he stood with a hand on his glowing staff that made Myr's torch look like a candle.

"As it happens, though, it is unnecessary for anyone to go out. Astrid is dead." Wolf pitched his voice so that it carried to everyone in the room without echoing. "I found her remains as well as those of the horse that Aralorn was riding. I found no trace of Aralorn's body. I suspect that she is a prisoner of the ae'Magi."

He had to quit speaking after those words left his throat. From the reaction of the people facing him, he could tell that they hadn't realized that this attack, too, had been engineered by the ae'Magi. He couldn't work up the effort to care. As long as the ae'Magi didn't know that Wolf was here helping Myr and as long as he didn't know what Aralorn was to him, the Archmage probably wouldn't torture Aralorn himself—he wouldn't consider any information she had to be vital. She had to be important enough that he didn't just kill her for the power he might gain, but not so important that he concentrated on her himself. That would buy Wolf time. It would keep her alive for him to find. It all rested upon how independent Edom had been.

The ae'Magi tended to give his tools more autonomy because he could trust that they had his best interests at heart. So Wolf would believe that he had time to find Aralorn. He had to believe he had time.

Wolf continued in a voice that sounded disinterested even to his own ears, this time speaking directly to Myr. "My advice is for you to stay here for now. It is probably quite safe for you to go out for a while yet. The ae'Magi won't expect you to be this close to the original camp. If I am not back in a fortnight, it would be best for you to move on." Wolf started to leave but turned back. He might not care for them, but Aralorn would want them safe.

"I would find a way to block off the paths that I didn't map for you so that no one is hurt or lost. You could follow these caves for a hundred miles if you wanted to." He left then, as quietly as he had come in.

————————

HE KNEW ALL the ae'Magi's holdings, even those acquired after he'd left. He had made a point of exploring each of them, partially to see if he could do it without getting caught, but also because he might find that he needed the knowledge. Even as he had done so, he'd been amused that Aralorn's passion for information had passed on to him. Now he was grateful for the habit.

First, he went, traveling by magic, as soon as he was far enough south that his spells worked, to the ae'Magi's castle since it was the ae'Magi's preferred residence as well as the closest one to the camp. He took the time to see if the ae'Magi was in residence, not that it would have kept Wolf out if he had been. He searched the dungeon twice, certain that she would be there—but he didn't see her among the pitiful captives. He looked through the castle, even the stables, but saw no sign of her anywhere. Then he continued to the next hold.

HE SEARCHED THROUGH the night and all the next day, even the royal palace of Reth and the small cottage in which the ae'Magi had been born. Finally, he had to admit defeat. He hoped that she had been able to kill herself because he found no trace of her anywhere with which the ae'Magi was remotely connected. For lack of anything better to do, he returned to the caves.

ARALORN TRAVELED OUT of the Northlands flopped over the back of the Uriah who had captured her (she would *not* think of it as Talor). The smell of the thing at such close range was debilitating, and she was glad enough for the cold that stuffed up her nose. She had been stripped of her weapons with ruthless efficiency and bound hand and foot. The constant jostling of the thing's shoulder in her midriff was giving her a headache that made it difficult to think clearly.

They stopped when they were out of the mountains and dumped her ignominiously facedown on the ground. By turning her head to the side, she could see them moving about restlessly, snarling irritably at each other. For the most part they ignored her, but she received enough hungry looks that she tried to make herself as inconspicuous as possible. She tried shapechanging once when nothing was paying attention to her, but the pain in her head kept distracting her.

She was concentrating for another attempt, but this time the distraction came in the form of a thud originating just out of her field of view. One by one the Uriah dropped to the ground; only the glitter of their eyes gave indication that they were not asleep—or dead.

"Sst. Filthy things. Why he uses them I cannot imagine." The voice was a light tenor, speaking Rethian with a high-court accent. Her position on the ground limited her field of view, but she could see the elegant shoes topped by the embroidered stockings of a true dandy.

"So," the soft voice continued, "you are the prisoner the ae'Magi is so anxious to get."

She was pushed over on her side by a magical shove and got her first full look at the mage. His face was handsome enough although overpowered by the purple wig he affected. She didn't know him by sight, but his ability to immobilize an army of Uriah and his dress let her put a name to him: Lord Kisrah, a minor noble whose abilities had been invaluable to Myr's grandfather in the last war.

Her father told her once that he was a competent tactician and diplomat, high praises from a man who despised the courtier type.

"Not very much of you, is there? From all the fuss the ae'Magi is putting up over you, I had expected more—although you would clean up well enough, I suppose. It is too bad that you chose to attack the ae'Magi in such treasonous fashion." He shook his head sadly at her, and she noticed with shock that his eyes were kind. "Get set now. I'm going to transport you to the ae'Magi's castle. I don't like transporting humans, it's too hard on them. But the ae'Magi is concerned about Myr. It's not right to take advantage of a man whose mind is turned by grief, and we need to get to him as soon as possible."

He rubbed his hands together a minute in preparation. "The ae'Magi is much better at this than I am; but he is busy with other matters, so I will have to do."

His magic hit her body with enough force that she almost passed out. She hit a hard stone floor sweating and coughing. If she wasn't careful, she was going to die of lung fever before the Archmage could get his hands on her. She laughed at the thought, bringing on another fit of coughing.

Ungentle hands grabbed her upper arms with bruising strength, but the man grunted as he picked her up—she was a lot heavier than she looked. Muscle would do that.

It had been daylight outside, so the gloominess of the torchlit stone walls and her hair, which had come undone from its customary braid and hung over her face, rendered her effectively blind.

She was stripped with ruthless efficiency. To take her mind off what *that* meant, she tried to recapture a stray thought she'd had just before Lord Kisrah had sent her over. She had a vague notion that it might be important. Her aching head didn't want to cooperate.

"Look here, Garogue, she ain't as small as she looks!" Rough laughter and comments she would have felt better not hearing as a second guard neared.

Think, Aralorn. I was relieved that . . . that I had not met Lord Kisrah before. Her face felt hot and tight, in spite of the coolness of the stone under her feet. *Lord Kisrah would not recognize me as the Lyon's daughter.* She waited a minute before the significance of that thought hit her. *I have, however, met the ae'Magi as the Lyon's daughter. He was intrigued with the color of my eyes—my shapeshifter blood.*

Gods, she thought bleakly. *If he realizes who I am, he can use my father against me.*

While the guards were preoccupied, she tried again to change. Not a drastic change this time, just an adjustment to her face and eyes. Her features sharpened until they were as common to Rethian peasant stock as her medium brown eyes. The eyes were always the hardest part, for some reason, and she didn't usually bother. But she didn't want the ae'Magi to think that she had even the slightest touch of green magic. It might be important in her escape. With a bit more effort, her skin darkened to add authenticity.

"Too bad we can't do nothin' with her but look." A callused hand ran over her hip.

"Yup, don' you ever think of nothing else. Just you remember what happened to Len. He thought the ae'Magi wouldn't ever know. Besides, we usually get a turn at 'em."

Goody. Something to look forward to.

She was dragged forward again, her exhaustion making her more of a deadweight than before. Her head contacted the stone wall when she was swung over a broad shoulder.

"They sure grow these Northerners heavy!" More laughter, but by then Aralorn was beyond caring.

IT WAS LATE at night when Wolf returned to the camp. He expected everyone to be asleep. Instead, he came upon Myr seated on a rock in front of the caves and polishing Aralorn's sword by the light of the moon.

"Where did you find it?" Wolf asked.

Startled, Myr leapt to his feet, holding the sword at ready. Seeing Wolf, Myr resumed his former position on the rock.

"Oh, it's you, Wolf. No luck? Damn." Myr held the blade up to the light. "I found it in a small cave off the entranceway this evening. Someone had made an attempt to clean it but didn't do a very good job. I suppose that one of the children found it and left it there when he realized what it was. I couldn't sleep, so I thought I'd clean it—no sense letting a good sword rust."

"No," agreed Wolf, lying down facing Myr with his muzzle on his paws.

Myr wasn't his friend. But Aralorn had liked him.

After a while, Myr asked, "Where did you look?"

So Wolf told him. It took some time. Myr listened, running the soft cloth over the odd-colored blade. When Wolf was done, Myr thought for a minute.

"How did you look for her? I mean did you just look? Couldn't a shapeshifter change her shape and escape?"

Wolf shook his head. "Once she was imprisoned, she wouldn't be able to change. Too much iron in the bars." And she'd have been chained.

"Iron does suppress magic?" Myr said, only half asking.

"Shapeshifter's magic."

The night was still except for the noise the soft cloth made on the sword. Then Myr said, "I'd met her once before, did you know that? It took me a while before I could pin down just where, because I was only a child. A more pompous, self-centered, proper little brat than I was you'd be hard-pressed to find. She was younger then, too, but she had the same mannerisms. Equal with anybody and observing protocol only because it suited her. I was offended, but my grandfather laughed and kissed her hands and said something about counting on her to liven up a dull reception."

There was a brief pause before he continued with his story. "You have to understand that I've been raised reading people's faces all my life. I saw that she really respected the tough old man, and the lack of sincerity in her manners was—dislike for the untruths that protocol demanded. It was a lesson that I took to heart." Myr paused, examining the gleaming blade.

With a sigh, he set it aside. "What I'm getting to is this: The ae'Magi was at court a lot in those days. My grandfather thought the world of him. If I met Aralorn at court, wouldn't he have? She's not . . . pretty, but she is memorable. And if she wasn't, her father certainly is. If I were going to break someone, the easiest way would be to go after her family. You might check out Lambshold and see if all of the Lyon's family are accounted for."

Wolf caught his breath sharply. "She would be much more conscious of that than you. With that in mind, she would do her best to make herself unrecognizable. How long is it since she was taken?" He'd lost track of time.

"Four days."

Finally, the wolf spoke again. "She's in one of the dungeons obviously—or she's escaped, though that is extremely unlikely." She'd escaped once, but the ae'Magi hadn't been expecting it. "I think she may be in the first place I looked—in the Archmage's castle. When I searched the last few castles I was thorough, and I think that she would have had to hide herself really well—better than she probably could by then. She doesn't have much time, the dungeon masters in the ae'Magi's keeps are not renowned for their gentle treatment of the prisoners—to say nothing of the ae'Magi himself. She should be safe from him, though; he's got other concerns that are more important." Wolf hadn't been subtle the last two places he'd been, and the ae'Magi would know he'd been inside. Three dead men would have told him that someone had been there, and the method of their deaths would have told the Archmage who.

Wolf paused to think before he continued. "If she's not there, I'll come back here to check in with you. If she escapes, this is the only sanctuary that she has to come to." On those words, the wolf melted into the forest shadows, leaving the young king sitting alone on his rock.

"MYR HAS A mage with him. What does he look like?"

The ae'Magi's voice was really extraordinary, thought Aralorn. Soft and warm, it offered sanctuary—but she knew those tones, and terror cat-footed toward her.

But not even that fear combined with the cuts he was making on her arm was enough to hold her attention for long. The pain from the recoil of centuries of magic woven tightly into the stones of the dungeons made what he was doing to her body seem secondary.

She wondered if she ought to tell him that if he used iron manacles in the torture chamber as well as in the cell, she would be much more aware of what he was doing. The iron effectively blocked her meager talents from picking up on the twisted magic that a thousand years of magicians had left in the stone of the dungeon.

A bucket of cold water brought her attention back to her body. It felt good against her hot skin at first, but then the chill made her shake helplessly. In a rational moment, she smiled; the lung fever would take her soon—in a few days—if she could just hide it from him so that he wouldn't turn her into one of the dead things that hung restlessly in her cell. She'd been grateful when she didn't have to look at them anymore—if only she could do something about hearing them.

He wasn't using magic on her as he had the first time she'd visited his castle. Maybe the dungeon inhibited his magic as well—or maybe he was using all his magic for something else.

BAFFLED, THE AE'MAGI looked at the pathetic figure hanging in front of him. He had seen her smile while he was cutting her, and it bothered him. She wasn't one of those who enjoyed pain, but she didn't seem to even feel it. Torture wasn't working on her.

She seemed confused sometimes, though. Perhaps stealth could get him what pain could not.

"Sweetheart, sweetheart, listen to me," said the ae'Magi in Myr's voice, his tones gentle, like a young man courting a mate.

Aralorn jerked in reflex at the voice.

"Sweetheart, I know that you hurt. I've come to get you out of here, but you need to tell me where Cain is. We need him to get you out."

She frowned, and said in a puzzled voice, "Cain?"

"Yes," asked Myr again, and she heard a touch of anger in the voice now, "where is Cain? Where is Myr's mage?"

MYR WOULDN'T BE angry with her—even though it sounded like Myr, it wasn't him. The certainty came from somewhere. She should know who Cain was, though, and it bothered her that she didn't. That didn't mean that she wanted the person who stole Myr's voice to know that.

"Dead," she said then, with utter certainty in her voice. Somewhere a part of her applauded the edge of melancholy she gave to her voice. "He is dead and gone."

THAT HADN'T OCCURRED to him; it simply hadn't occurred to him. The ae'Magi paced the length of the chamber. It wasn't possible. Angrily, he stripped off the gloves he'd fastidiously donned to separate him from her filthy flesh.

It would ruin everything if his son was dead. All his efforts would be for nothing. He raised the knife to her throat, then thought better of it. She still had information for him; he wouldn't kill her for spite.

Turning on his heel, the ae'Magi stalked out of the chamber. As he passed through the guardroom, he left orders to have her moved back into her cell and, as an afterthought, told the dungeon master that if he could find out where the rebels were hiding, he would give him a silver piece.

THE DUNGEONS WERE among the parts of the ae'Magi's castle that were very old—the result of those years was not lovely. The smell made Wolf choke as he snuck into them from the hidden entrance. Magic had taken him to the castle, but he'd been forced to use mundane methods to enter. The ae'Magi was in residence, which gave him hope that Aralorn would be, too—but it meant he had to be very careful about the magic he used.

No one saw him as he emerged into the walkway between the cells. The night guards were in the room that was the only passageway from the main dungeon, other than the hidden ones, of course. There was no need for their presence in the actual dungeon at this time of night, unless they were escorting a captive in or out—or someone was being tortured.

He stood on a wide stone walkway, in human shape. On one side were seven cells, sunken the depth of a grave, in the old style. On the other side was the torture chamber, also so sunken. It was unoccupied at the moment. The only hint of life came from the smoldering coals in the raised hearth in the center of the cell.

There was no light in the dungeon other than Wolf's staff, but it was sufficient. The ring of keys was still kept on its holder near the guardroom door—for convenience's sake.

He slid the nearest door open and climbed down the steep, narrow stairs. The prisoners chained to the wall were too far gone to notice him.

He took wolf shape because of the wolf's sharper senses and regretted the necessity. The smells of a dungeon were bad enough to the human nose, but the wolf's eyes were watering as he backed out of the cell. Returning to his human form, he closed the cell back up. She wasn't in there. He found the same at the second cell.

In the third cell, chained corpses littered the floor and hung on the wall like broken dolls, but they moaned and breathed with the pseudolife that animated Uriah. They watched him with glittering eyes as he shifted again to wolf shape to sample the air. But they were too new, too heavily controlled by the ae'Magi's spells, to give alarm.

More people in the fourth cell. When he'd lived here, there had seldom been more than one or two people in the whole dungeon. He shifted to wolf, took a breath—and stopped breathing altogether.

She's here.

He pushed the fierce joy of that aside. Time enough to celebrate when he had her safe.

He found her in the corner of the cell. Her face was different, but she was muttering to herself, and it was her voice, her scent under the filth. Her breathing was hoarse and difficult, breaking into heavy coughing when he shifted her against him to take off the irons—the dungeons held so much magic that short of melting the stone, the ae'Magi wouldn't feel what he did unless he was in the next room. That didn't mean they could afford to stay here long. Wolf swore at the wounds the cuffs left on her ankles and wrists.

No time to look for further wounds. He had to get out of here.

Gently, he picked her up, ignoring the smell of dungeon that clung to her. He stepped over the huddled bodies of her fellow inmates with no more attention than if they had been bundles of straw. Although he had no hands free to carry it, the staff followed him like an obedient dog.

It wasn't until he stood outside the cell that he realized he had a problem. The secret door he'd entered through was a crawl space, too narrow to get through with Aralorn unable to move on her own.

He didn't have time to dawdle.

A touch to the mask with his staff and both disappeared. A brief moment of concentration, and the scars followed. He was no shapeshifter. The face he wore beneath the scars was the one he was born with: It was his as much as the scars were also his.

Trying to avoid causing her any further hurt, he positioned Aralorn on his shoulder, holding her in place with one hand and letting the other hang carelessly free. A ball of light formed over his left shoulder and followed him to the guardroom door.

As he opened the door, the guards scrambled for their weapons until they saw his face. Wolf carelessly tossed the keys on the rough-hewn table, where they left a track in the greasy buildup as they slid. When he spoke, it was with the ae'Magi's hated voice, soft and warm with music. The illusion was simple—he didn't need much to make his face look so near to the ae'Magi's that in the dark they would not be able to tell him from his father.

"I think that it would be wiser from now on," he told them, "for the guard in charge to keep the keys on his person. It is too easy for someone to enter the dungeon by other paths. There is no reason that we should make it any easier to get into the cells than it already is."

Without looking at the men again, he walked to the far door, which obediently opened to let him through and closed after him. The wide staircase that led to the upper floors stretched in front of him, leaving but a narrow space against the wall, supposedly to allow access to the area under the stairs that was sometimes used for storage. It was this path that he took, ducking as he moved under the stairway.

Unerringly, he touched the exact spot that triggered the hidden door. As he stepped through, he whispered a soft spell, and the dust under the stairs rearranged itself until it looked as it had before he walked there.

He put out the light as the stone door shut behind him. The passage was as dark as pitch, and there was little light for even his mage-sensitive eyes to pick out. Tiny flecks of illumination that found their way through openings in the mortar made the towering walls glitter like the night sky. Their presence was the reason he'd put out the light—lest someone in a dark room on the other side of the wall witness the same phenomenon.

. Wolf kept one hand against a wall and the other securely around

Aralorn and felt the ground ahead with his feet. He slowed his progress when a pile of refuse he kicked with his foot bounced down an unseen stairway. With a grim smile that no one could see, he continued blindly down the stairs.

There were shuffling noises as rats and other less savory creatures scrambled anonymously out of his way. Once he almost lost his footing as he stepped on something not long dead. A growling hiss protested his encroachment on someone's dinner.

Only when they reached the last of the long flight of steps did he decide they were far enough down that he dared a light. The floor was thick with dust; only faint outlines showed where he had disturbed the dust the last time he'd been here several years before, raiding one of the hidden libraries—there were more than the one he'd made off with completely.

Content that the passage had remained undiscovered, Wolf walked to a blank wall and sketched symbols in the air before it. The symbols hung glowing orange in the shadows until he was finished; then they shimmered and moved until they were touching the wall. The wall glittered in its turn, before abruptly disappearing—opening the way to still another obscure passage, deep in the rock under the castle. He continued for some time, his path twisting this way and that, through passages once discovered by a boy seeking sanctuary.

Twice he had to change his route because the way he remembered was too small for him to take carrying Aralorn. Once, the passage was blocked by a recent cave-in. Several of the corridors showed signs of recent use, and he avoided them as well. They surfaced finally from the labyrinth, several miles east and well out of easy view of the castle.

He shifted her from his shoulder then, cradling her in his arms, though she was harder to carry that way. There was nothing that he could do until they reached safer ground, so he trod swift of foot through the night-dark forest, listening intently for sounds that shouldn't be there.

He wished that he hadn't had to show himself, because now—after all of his caution—it was going to be obvious that he was mixed up with Myr's group. The ae'Magi had been seeking him for a long time. So the attacks on Myr's camp were going to intensify. It was possible that the guards wouldn't mention the incident to the ae'Magi—but it was always better to be prepared for the worst. He was going to have to stage his confrontation with the Archmage soon.

He wasn't looking forward to the coming battle. Old stories of the Wizard Wars—Aralorn could tell them by the hour—spoke of battles of pure power between one magician and another, and the great glass desert, more than a hundred square miles of blackened glass, gave mute evidence of the costs of such battles. If he, with his strange mutations of magic, ever got involved in a battle on those terms, the results could be far worse.

It might be better by far to let the magician extend his power. Even the best magicians live only three to four hundred years, and the ae'Magi was well into his second century. Expending his power the way that he was now, even taking into account the energy he stole, would take years off his life. A hundred years of tyranny was better than the destruction of the earth.

The glass desert had been fertile soil once.

HE WALKED UNTIL well after the sun rose, following no visible trail—losing the two of them in the wilds as best he might. He stopped when they reached the cache he'd set up on his way to the castle, far enough off the trails that they should be safe for a while. Not safe enough to use magic to transport them—that the ae'Magi might follow. But he could hide them from this distance—he'd found some spells that worked for that since his time hiding in the Northlands. Spells that had allowed him to follow Aralorn around without worrying the ae'Magi would find him.

He opened the bedroll awkwardly, unwilling to set her on the hard ground, and gently placed her on the soft blankets. His arms were cramping and sore from carrying her, so he had to stretch a bit before he did anything else.

Her darker skin hid the flush of fever, but it was hot and dry to his touch. Her breathing was hoarse, and he could hear the fluid in her lungs. He rolled the second blanket up and stuffed it under her head to help her breathe. Efficiently, gently, he cleaned her with spell-warmed water.

On the dark skin it should have been more difficult to see the bruises, but her skin was gray from illness, revealing the darker patches. Some were obviously old, probably from her initial capture. But fresh bruises overlay the old ones.

Three ribs were either broken or cracked, he wasn't well enough trained in healing to tell the difference. The ribs and a large lump on the back of her head seemed the worst of her wounds—both were more likely the result of her initial capture than any torture.

Her fingernails had been removed, swollen knuckles revealed the violence of the method used to pull them. The toes on her right foot were broken, the smallest torn off completely. She had been whipped with efficiency from the top of her shoulders to the backs of her knees. But those wounds would heal in a few weeks (except, of course, for the misplaced toe). A woman could live without a toe.

He pulled out the bag of simples that he had brought with him. He wasn't a healer, by any means, but he'd picked up enough to bind her wounds.

When he was through cleaning her back, he covered it with a mold paste and wrapped the bandage around tight enough to help immobilize her ribs. He splinted the toes and cleaned and bandaged her ankles, hands, and wrists.

It was while he was working on her wrists that he noticed the large sore where the inner side of her arm had been skinned. He stilled, then very gently covered the sore with ointment and wrapped it as if it hadn't sent chills down his spine.

It was one of the ae'Magi's favorite games. The inner arm was tender, and a man who was skilled with a skinning knife could cause significant pain without incapacitating his victim. The ae'Magi usually did something extremely nasty first to soften his victim.

Carefully, Wolf opened Aralorn's mouth and examined the inside of her cheek, the roof of her mouth, under her tongue, and her teeth. Nothing. He looked inside her ear and said a few soft words of magic. Nothing. As he turned her head to look at her other ear, something sparkled in the sun. Her eyelids.

Carefully Wolf held her face where the sunlight fell on it fully. Both of her eyelids, on careful examination, were slightly swollen, but it was the seepage that told the real story.

He held his open hand several inches over her eye and murmured another spell. When he took his hand away, he held four long, slender, steel needles, each barbed on the end like a fisherman's hook. The needles were sharp enough that they slid in with little pain, but every time the eye moved, the sharpened edges of the needle cut a little more. They were not the expensive silver needles, but the cheaper iron-based steel— made primarily for coarser work.

He looked at them for a minute and they melted, leaving his hand undamaged. As he removed four more from her other eye, he wished passionately, and not for the first time in his life, that he knew more.

True healing was one of the first things taught to a shapeshifter; but for a human magic-user, it was one of the last arts learned. Increasing the efficacy of herbs was the best he knew. He doubted that in this case even a shapeshifter could heal her eyes—he seemed to remember something about wounds made with cold iron being more difficult than others.

He put her in a soft cotton shirt that reached to her thighs. When he was finished, he put a cold-spelled compress over her eyes and bound it tightly in place.

He had reached the end of his expertise. Tiredly, he covered her with another blanket and lay down next to her, not quite touching. He slept.

HER WORLD CONSISTED of vague impressions of vision and sound. She saw people she knew, strangely altered. Sometimes they filled her with horror, other times they drew no emotion from her at all. There was Talor as he'd been the last time she'd seen him in Sianim—then something happened to him, and he was dead, only he was talking to her and telling her things that she didn't want to hear.

Sometimes she floated in a great nothingness that scared her, but not as much as the pain. Her body was a great distance away, and she would pull back as far as she could because she was afraid of what she would find when she returned. Then, like the stretchy tubris rope that children played with, something would snap, and she would find herself back in the midst of the pain and heat and terror. Someone screamed, it hurt her ears, and she wished the sound would stop.

THIS TIME HER return was different. Besides being hot, she was also wet and sticky. The pain was dimmed to bearable levels; even the ache in her side was less. There was something that attracted her attention and she concentrated—trying to figure out what it was. It had called her back from her nothingness into a place she'd much rather not be. She decided in a moment of pseudorationality that she needed to find it and kill it so she could be free to go away.

She looked for it in her dreams and fragments of impressions touched her. There was something terribly wrong with her eyes. Cold iron whose wounds were permanent. It had bitten and chewed and . . .

She shied away and found another piece of memory. Magic horribly distorted and twisted, making dead men breathe. It frightened her. There was no safety in death here, and she wanted the sanctuary that death should offer. Then the cold iron cut off her awareness of the dead things that shared her space. She had never felt so helpless; it gave her a dispirited claustrophobia that made her strain repeatedly against the bonds, until she exhausted herself. Bonds that most well-trained, full-blooded shape-shifters might have gotten out of, but she had all the weaknesses and too little power.

There . . . while she was fighting . . . she almost had it. The thing that had pulled her back and made her hurt again. It was sound, familiar sound. Why should that bother her?

She was so tired. She was losing her concentration, and pictures came more rapidly until she was lost in her nightmare memories again.

THEY'D BEEN CAMPED in the same place for three days. It worried him because they were much too close to the ae'Magi's castle, but the thought of moving her worried him more. Instead of getting better since being out of the cell, she seemed worse. Her eyes were seeping with the pus of infection. Her fever was no higher, but it was no lower either. Her breathing was more difficult, and when she coughed, he could tell that it hurt her ribs.

As he watched her, he tormented himself with guilt. Had he been quicker to find her, she would have stood a better chance. The needles had been used on her eyes only recently. He could have found her in his first search if he'd only remembered that she might be wearing someone else's face.

As it did when he was angered, the other magic in him flickered fey—nudging him, tempting him. Usually he used it, twisting it toward his own ends, but this time he was tired with worry, guilt, and sleeplessness. The magic whispered, seducing him with visions of healing.

His eyes closed, without conscious thought he stretched out carefully beside Aralorn. Gently, he touched her face, seeing the wrongness there— the slight fracture in the skull that he hadn't been aware of.

As he gave control away to the seductive whispers of his magic, he found that he could feel her pulse, almost her thoughts. Sex notwithstanding, this was closer than he'd ever been to another human being. With anyone else, he would have lashed out, done anything just to get away—to be safe alone.

But this was Aralorn, and he had to heal her, or . . . He caught a flick of the desperation of that thought, but was soon lost in the peace of his magic. He floated with it for what could have been a hundred years or a single instant. Gradually, his fear of the loss of control, so well learned when his searing magic had leapt out burning, hurting, scarring, crept upon him—breaking the trance he'd fallen into.

He opened his eyes and gasped for air. His heart was pounding, and sweat poured off his body. Great shudders racked him. He turned his head enough to look at Aralorn.

The first thing that hit him was that he *was* looking at Aralorn. The guise she'd donned was gone. The bruises on her legs looked much worse on her own relatively pale skin. Fever had brought unnatural color to her pale cheeks.

When he could, he bent over and removed the bandage from her eyes. The swelling had almost completely gone and her eyes appeared normal when he carefully lifted her eyelids. He hadn't looked before—he knew what those needles had done. He felt carefully with his fingertips where he'd seen the break in her skull and could locate nothing.

Almost too tired to move, he pulled her head onto his shoulder and drew blankets neatly around them. He knew he should stay up and keep watch—there was no warhorse to share guard duty with—but he hadn't been this tired since his early apprentice days.

IT WAS MORNING when Aralorn awoke, still slightly delirious. She'd had dreams of the quiet sounds of the forest before, and she let herself take that comfort now. She knew that all too soon she would have to face reality again. The nice thing was that the times reality crept in were getting further and further apart.

She thought about that for a minute before she realized that there was a man beside her. Delirium took over then, and she was drowning slowly. It was very hard to breathe, and she lost track of the forest while she strangled.

The soft sounds of a familiar voice lent her comfort and strength, but there was something wrong with the voice. It was too soft, it should be cold and rough, harsher. She associated unpleasant things with the warmer tones. The voice she wanted to hear should be dead like the Uriah, like Talor. She could hear someone whimpering and wondered who it was.

She ate and it tasted very good, salty and warm on her sore throat. She drank something else and a part of her tasted the bitter herb with approval, knowing that it would help her breathe. *Wasn't there some reason that she didn't want to get better?*—but she couldn't decide why she wouldn't want to get well, and while she thought about it, she drifted back to sleep.

WOLF WATCHED HER and waited. Without the unquenchable energy that characterized her, she looked fragile, breakable. Awake, she had a tendency to make him forget how small she was.

He gritted his teeth and controlled his rage when she cried out in terror. Although she babbled out loud, she said nothing that would have been any use to the ae'Magi were he listening.

She was quiet finally, and Wolf sat propped up against a tree, near enough to keep an eye on her but far enough away that he wouldn't disturb her slumbers.

He should never have been able to heal her. Indisputably, he had. Even if he did nothing more than eliminate the paths the needles had cut into her eyes, it was more than human magic allowed for. Less dramatic but even further outside the bounds of magic, as he understood it, was the fact that she now wore the appearance that was hers by birth.

He'd always had the ability to do things beyond the generally accepted bounds of human magic—taking wolf shape for extended periods of time was one of those. Always before he could have attributed this to the enormous power he wielded. Human magic could heal, but it required a more detailed knowledge of the human body than he had acquired— killing required much less precision. Human magic could not recognize a shapeshifter's natural shape and restore her to it . . . as he had done.

His magic had blithely crashed through the laws of magic established for thousands of years. What *was* he that he could do such things?

He found no answers. He'd seen the woman who bore him only once that he could remember. She'd seemed ordinary enough—for a woman who had spent a decade in the ae'Magi's dungeon. But the ae'Magi had got a son on her and kept her alive afterward. She must have been more than she seemed.

Wolf had been the result of an . . . experiment perhaps: one that had gotten out of hand.

Aralorn stirred, catching his attention. He got to his feet with relief at being drawn from his thoughts, and went to her.

EIGHT

ARALORN WAS IN THE HABIT OF WAITING UNTIL SHE KNEW WHERE SHE was and who she was supposed to be before she opened her eyes—a habit developed from frequently being someone other than herself. For some reason, it seemed more difficult than usual. The warm sun on her face seemed as much out of place as the sound of a jay squeaking from its perch somewhere above her.

She moved restlessly and felt a warning twinge from her side that was instantly echoed from various other parts of her body. As a memory aid, she found it effective—if crude.

The problem was, she had no idea how she had gotten from the ae'Magi's dungeon to where she was.

Deciding that it was unlikely that she would come to any earth-shattering conclusions lying around feigning sleep, she opened her eyes and sat up—an action that she had immediate cause to regret. The abrupt change in position caused her to start coughing—no pleasant thing with cracked ribs. She collapsed slowly back into her prone position and waited for her eyes to quit watering.

Breathing shallowly, she restricted herself to turning her head to examine her current environment. She was alone in a small clearing, surrounded by thick shrubs that quickly gave way to broad-leafed trees. She could hear a brook running somewhere nearby. The sun was high and edging toward afternoon. Mountains rose, not far away, on at least three sides. They were smaller than their Northland counterparts, but impressive enough. Also unfamiliar, at least from her angle.

The blankets in which Aralorn was more or less cocooned were of a fine intricate weave and finer wool. She whistled softly at the extravagance. Just one of them would cost a mercenary two months' salary, and she was wrapped in two of them, with her head pillowed on a third. She should have been too warm, bundled up so heavily—but it felt good.

The bandaging on her hands and wrists was neatly tied and just snug enough to give support without being too tight. Whoever had tied it was better at binding wounds than she was—not a great feat. She didn't bother to examine the other bandages that covered her here and there, preferring not to scrutinize her wounds in case too many body parts were missing or nonfunctional.

It occurred to her then that her eyes should belong to the category of missing and nonfunctional items. The method the ae'Magi had used to blind her had been . . . thorough. Enough so that she had not thought that even shapeshifter magic could heal her.

She shivered in her blankets. She had the unwelcome thought that it might be possible for a strong magician to create the illusion of this meadow. She didn't know for sure, but from her stories . . . Much more likely than someone breaking her out of the ae'Magi's dungeons. Much easier, she was certain, than it would be to heal her eyes.

She looked around, but she was still the only occupant of the clearing.

Deciding that if it were the ae'Magi who was going to show up, she didn't want to face him lying on her back, she found a slender tree growing near her head. She pushed herself back until she bumped into it—the effort it took was not reassuring. Gradually, so as not to trigger another fit of coughing, she raised herself with the tree's support until she was sitting up with her back against it. She waited for a minute. When she didn't start coughing, she slid herself up the tree, the bark scraping her back despite the wrapping job someone had done—that felt real enough. Finally, she was standing—at least leaning.

She didn't hear him until he spoke from some distance behind her. His voice was without its usual sardonic overtones, but it was still blessedly Wolf's. "Welcome back, Lady."

Sheer dumb relief almost sent her crashing to the ground. Wolf. It was Wolf. He, she was willing to believe, could rescue her and heal whatever needed healing. Safe.

She swallowed and schooled her face—he wouldn't enjoy having her jump on him and sob all over him any more than she'd have enjoyed the memory of it once she got her feet safely under her again.

When she was sure she could pull off nonchalant, she turned her head with a smile of greeting that left her when she saw his face. Only years of training kept her from giving her fear voice, even that couldn't stop the involuntary step backward that she took. Unfortunately, her feet tangled in one of the blankets, she lost the support of the tree, and fell.

Definitely cracked ribs, but not even pain could penetrate her despair. The Archmage.

Unwilling to let her enemy out of her sight, she rolled until she could see him, which set off a coughing fit. Eyes watering from pain, she saw that he, too, had stepped back, albeit more gracefully. He raised a hand to his face and then dropped it abruptly. He waited until she finished coughing and could talk—and there was no expression on his face at all.

Aralorn found herself grateful that she was unable to speak for a minute because it gave her a chance to think. The ae'Magi's face it might be, but Wolf's yellow eyes glittered at her—as volatile as the face was not.

It was Wolf, her Wolf. The still, almost flight of his body told her that more than his eyes. Illusion could reproduce anyone's eyes, but she was unwilling to believe that anyone but her knew Wolf's body language that well.

Cain was the ae'Magi's son, but no one had ever told her how much the son resembled the father. If the ae'Magi's son had shown the world his magic-scarred face, the one she knew best, surely someone would have mentioned the scars. Perhaps the ae'Magi didn't want people to remember how much he looked like his demonized son. She could believe that if he didn't want people to comment, they wouldn't. Her next thought was that Wolf didn't look like a man only a few years older than Myr—a few years younger than she was. Her third thought, as her coughing slowed down, was that she'd better figure out a way to handle this—she didn't want to hurt him again.

Before she could say anything, Wolf spoke. "If I thought that you could make it to safety alone, I would leave you in peace. Unfortunately, that is not possible. I assure you that I will leave as soon as you are back . . ."

She ended his speech with a rude word and assumed as much dignity as she could muster while lying awkwardly on the ground amid a tangle of blankets. "Idiot!" she told him. "Of course I knew who you were." She hadn't been certain—he'd just made her short list, but she didn't need to tell him that. "Just how many apprentices do you think the ae'Magi has had? I know the name of every one of them, thanks to Ren. He seemed to think that information might be valuable someday. How many mages do you think would have the power to do what you did to Edom?" Two or three, she thought, but one of those was Kisrah—who had not been on her list. "Just how stupid do you think I am?" She had to pause to keep from coughing again—but he didn't attempt to answer her question with any of his usual sarcasm, and that worried her. So she turned her defense into an attack. "Why did you hide from me again? First the wolf shape, then the mask and the scars." She let her voice quiver and didn't give in to the temptation to make it just a little too much. "Do you distrust me so much?"

"No," said Wolf, and the hint of a smile played around his mouth—more importantly, he no longer looked like he'd rather be anywhere than there. "I forgot." He waved a hand in the general direction of his face. "The scars are legitimate. I acquired them as I told you. It wasn't until I left there . . ." Left his father, she thought. "I realized that I could get rid of them the same way that I could take wolf shape. But for a long time, it didn't matter because I was the wolf. When I decided to act against him instead of continuing to run—all things considered, I preferred to keep the scars."

Aralorn certainly understood why that would be. "So why change now?"

"When I got you out of the dungeon, it was necessary to appear to be the ae'Magi in order to get past the guards. I was . . . I forgot to resume the scars, the mask." He sat beside her. "I didn't mean to startle you."

Startle. Yes, that was one way to put it.

With an expression that didn't quite make it to being the smile she intended, Aralorn told him, "When I die of heart failure the next time you frighten me like that, you can put that on my gravestone—'I didn't mean to startle her.'"

As she talked, she looked at him carefully. Seeing things that hadn't been apparent at first. His face was without the laugh lines around the eyes and mouth that characterized the ae'Magi's. There was no gray in the black hair, but the expression in his eyes made him look much older than his father had. Wolf eyes, Wolf's eyes they were—with a hunter's cold, amoral gaze.

"So why didn't I know that Cain was scarred?" she asked him.

"My father kept them hidden."

"Does Myr know who you are?" She found that was important to her—which told her that she'd never given up Reth, being Rethian, the way she'd given up Sianim. Myr was her king, and she wouldn't have him lied to.

He nodded. "I told him before I offered my assistance. It was only fair that he knew what he was getting into. And with whom."

There was a slight pause, then Aralorn said, "The ae'Magi asked me about you, about Cain." That much she could remember.

"Did he?" Wolf raised an eyebrow, but he wasn't as calm as he appeared. If he had been in his wolf shape, the hairs along his spine would have been raised: She recognized that soft tone of voice. "What did you say?"

Aralorn raised her eyebrow in return. "I told him that you were dead."

"Did he believe you?" he asked.

She shrugged and started to tug discreetly at the heap of blankets that intermingled with her feet. "At the time he did, but since you chose to rescue me, he'll probably come to the conclusion that I lied to him."

"Let's get you into a more comfortable position"—he indicated her troublesome hobble with a careless hand—"and back under the covers with you before you catch your death, shall we?" His voice was a wicked imitation of one of the healers at Sianim.

Even as he untangled her and restored her makeshift bed to its previous order, she could feel an imp of a headache coming on. "Wolf," she said softly, catching his hand and stilling it, "don't use the scars. You are not the ae'Magi—you don't have to prove it."

He tapped her on the nose and shook his head with mock despair. "Did anyone ever tell you that you are overbearing, Lady?" That "Lady" told her that things were all right between the two of them.

That knowledge meant that the crisis was over, and she was suddenly exhausted. He resumed his efforts and tucked a pillow behind her head.

"Where are we, and how long have we been here?" It was an effort to keep her eyes open any longer, and her voice slurred as she finished the sentence, ending in a racking cough. As she hacked and gasped for breath, he lifted her upright. She didn't notice that it helped any, but the feel of his arms around her was pleasant.

The hazy thought occurred to her that the greater part of the reason she'd left Reth to go to Sianim in the first place was to get away from the feeling of being protected. Now she was grateful for it. She didn't think that he'd notice that the last few coughs were suppressed sounds of self-directed amusement.

"We're about a day's brisk walk away from the Master Magician's castle. We've been here for three days. As soon as you wake up, we'll start on our way."

He said something more, she thought, but she couldn't be bothered to stay awake for it.

He bent down and whispered it again. This time she heard it. "Sleep. I have you safe."

THE NEXT TIME Aralorn regained consciousness, she was ruthlessly fed and dressed in a tunic and trousers she recognized as her own before she had a chance to do any more than open her eyes. She was propped up with brisk efficiency beside a tree and told to "stay there." Wolf then piled all of the blankets, clothes, and utensils together and sent them on their way with a brisk wave of his staff.

"Where did you get my clothes?" Aralorn asked with idle curiosity from where she sat leaning against a tree. Her tree.

"From Sianim, where you left them." With efficient motions, he was cleaning the area they had occupied until only the remains of the fire would give any indication that someone had camped there.

She'd known that. Had just needed him to admit it to her.

She raised an eyebrow at him, crossed her arms over her chest, and said in a deceptively mild tone, "You mean the whole time that I was all but bursting out of the innkeeper's son's clothes, wearing blisters on my feet with his boots—you could have gotten mine for me?"

He grunted without looking at her, but she could see a hint of a smile in his flawless profile. He was, she decided, without it soothing her ire in the least, more beautiful than his sire.

"I asked you a question," she said in a dangerously soft tone she'd learned from him.

"I was waiting for the tunic seams to finally give way . . ." He paused to dodge the handful of grass she threw at him, then shrugged. "I am sorry, Lady. It just never occurred to me."

Aralorn tried to look stern, but the effort turned into a laugh.

Wolf brushed the grass from his shoulders and went back to packing. Aralorn leaned back against her tree and watched him as he worked, trying to get used to the face he now wore.

In an odd sort of way, he looked more like his father than his father did. The ae'Magi's face was touched with innocence and compassion. Wolf's visage had neither. His was the face of a man who could do anything, and had.

"Can you ride?" he asked, calling her back from her thoughts.

Aralorn considered the state of her body. Everything functioned—sort of, anyway. Riding was certainly better than any alternative she could think of. She nodded. "If we don't go any faster than a walk. I don't think that I could sit a trot for very long."

He nodded and said three or four brisk words in a language she didn't know. He didn't bother with the theatrics in front of her. The air merely shimmered around him strangely. Not unpleasant—just difficult to look at, much nicer than when she changed shape. The black horse who had replaced Wolf snorted at her, then shook himself as if he were wet. His eyes were as black as his hide, and she found herself wishing he'd kept his own eyes no matter how odd it would have seemed for a horse to have yellow eyes.

She stood up stiffly, trying not to stagger—or start coughing again. When she could, she walked shakily up to him, grateful to reach the support of his neck.

Unfortunately, although Wolf-as-a-Horse wasn't as massive as Sheen, he was as tall, and she couldn't climb up. After her third attempt, he knelt in the dust so that she could slip onto his back.

He took them down an old trail that had fallen into disuse. The only tracks on it were from the local wildlife. The woods around them were too dense to allow easy travel, but Wolf appeared to know them—when the trail disappeared into a lush meadow, he picked it up again on the other side without having to take a step to the left or right. Wolf's gaits, she found, were much smoother than Sheen's; but the motion still hurt her ribs.

To distract herself when it started to get unbearable, she thought up a question almost at random. "Where did you find a healer?"

A green magic-user would never be anywhere near the ae'Magi's castle. Other than her, she supposed, but she was no healer—green magic or not.

Speaking had been a mistake. The dust of the road set her coughing. He stopped, turning his head so he could watch her out of one dark eye.

When she could talk again she met his gaze and didn't like the worry in it. She was fine. "You got rooked if you paid very much; any healer worth his fee would have taken care of the ribs and cough, too."

Wolf twitched his ears and said in an odd tone, even for him, "He didn't have enough time to do much. Even if there had been the time, I wouldn't have trusted him to do more than what was absolutely necessary—he . . . didn't have the training."

Aralorn had an inkling that she should be paying more attention to the way he phrased his explanation, but she was in too much misery between her ribs and her cough to do much more than feel sorry for herself.

Then she had it. The conviction when she'd first heard his voice after waking alone in the little camp he'd set up. Of course Wolf had gotten her out and fixed her eyes so she could see.

But Wolf was a human mage. Son of the ae'Magi. And human mages might be okay at some aspects of healing—like putting broken bones together. But no human mage could have dealt with what had been done to her eyes.

WOLF KEPT TO a walk, trying to make the ride as smooth as possible for her. He could discern that she was in a lot of pain by the way her hands shook in his mane when she coughed, but she made light of it when he questioned her. As the day progressed, she leaned wearily against his neck and coughed more often.

Worse, after that one, brief conversation, she'd quit talking. Aralorn always talked.

He continued until he could stand it no more, then he called a halt at a likely camping area, far from the main thoroughfares and out of sight of the trail they'd been following. As soon as he stopped, before he could kneel to make things easier, Aralorn slid off him, then kept sliding until her rump hit the ground. She waved off his concern, breathing through her nose, her mouth pinched.

Wolf regained his human form, then turned his attention to making a cushion of evergreen boughs and covering the result with the blankets, keeping a weather eye on his charge. By the time he finished, Aralorn was on her feet again—though, he thought, not for long.

"I'm moving like an old woman," she complained, walking toward the bed he'd made. "All I need is a cane."

She let him help her lie down and was asleep, he judged, before her eyes had a chance to close.

While Aralorn slept, Wolf stood watch.

THE NIGHT WAS peaceful, she thought, except for when she was coughing. It got so bad toward the morning that she finally gave up resting and stood up. When she would have reached for the blankets to start folding them, Wolf set her firmly down on the ground with a growl that would have done credit to his wolf form and finished erasing all traces of their presence.

Dawn's light had barely begun to show before they were on their way.

Once she was sitting up rather than lying down, Aralorn's coughing mercifully eased. It helped that today they were cutting directly through the woods, which were thinned by the higher altitude. There was no trail dust to exacerbate the problem. When her modest herb lore identified some beggersblessing on the side of the road, she made Wolf stop so she could pick a bunch. With a double handful of the leaves stuffed in her pocket and a wad of them under her tongue, she could even look at the day's journey with some equanimity.

The narcotic alleviated the pain of her ribs and some of the coughing, although it did make it a little more difficult to stay on Wolf's back as it interfered with her equilibrium. Several times, only Wolf's quick foot-work kept her from falling off.

WOLF DECIDED THAT the giggling was something he could do without but found that, on the whole, he preferred it to her silent pain. When they stopped, Wolf took a good look at Aralorn, pale and dark-eyed from the drug she'd been using. She'd refused food, because beggersblessing would make her sick if she ate while under its influence.

The end result, he judged, was that she was weaker than she'd been when they started that morning. He had not transported them by magic because he was afraid that his father would be able to track them and find where they went. But if they continued at this donkey's pace, it was even odds whether his father would find them before she got too sick to ride at all.

He donned his human form once again, with his scars, and after a moment's thought added the silver mask. It was a difficult spell, and without the mask and scars, he was uneasy. He didn't need anything distracting him.

"Wolf?" she asked.

"We're taking another way back," he told her, lifting her into his arms—and took them into the Northlands.

Transporting people by magic was difficult enough that most mages preferred travel on horseback or coach rather than by magic, even in the spring, when the roads were nothing more than a giant mud puddle. Transporting someone into the Northlands, where human magic had a tendency to go awry, was madness, but he aimed for the cave where he had brought the merchant the day Aralorn had joined them. That would leave them with only one day's ride to the camp and only a few miles to travel before the ae'Magi's magic would be hampered if he found out where they had gone.

Concentrating on the shallow cave, he pulled them to it, but *something* caught them and jerked them on with enough force to stun Wolf momentarily . . .

He landed on his knees in darkness on a hard stone floor. His instinctive light spell was too bright, and he had to tone it down.

He was in the cave that housed his library.

Warily, he stood up and looked around—with his eyes and his magic. Aside from the irregular oddness that had become a familiar part of working his magic in the Northlands, nothing seemed wrong.

He laid her on the padded couch and pulled his cloak over her. It would only take him a minute to let Myr know he was back.

IN THE CASTLE of the Archmage, the ae'Magi sat gently drumming his fingers on the burled wood of his desk. He was not in the best of moods, having tracked an intruder from castle to hold trying to discover who would be foolhardy enough to trespass and powerful enough to get away with it.

And now he knew who it had been—and what he'd been looking for.

The room that he occupied was covered in finely woven carpets. Great beveled windows lined the outside wall behind the desk, bathing the room with a warm golden glow. On the opposite wall was a large, ornate fireplace that sat empty in deference to the warmth of late summer. In front of the fireplace, the pretty blond girl who was his newest pet combed her hair and looked at the floor.

She trembled a bit. A month as his leman had made her sensitive to his mood, which was, he admitted, quite vile at the moment.

FACING THE DESK was one of the dungeon guards, who held his cap deferentially in his hand. He spoke in the low tones that were correct for addressing someone in a position so much higher than his own. Though he was properly motionless, the ae'Magi could tell that his continued silence was making the man nervous. As it should. As it should.

Finally, the ae'Magi felt he could control himself enough to speak. "You saw Cain take one of the female prisoners? Several nights ago."

"Yes, Lord." The guardsman relaxed as soon as the ae'Magi spoke. "I remembered him from when he lived here, but I didn't realize who it was until he'd already gone. Last time I saw him, he were all scarred up, but I 'membered meself when he were a tyke he looked a lot like you, sire."

"And why did it take you so long to report this?"

"You weren't here, sire."

"I see." The ae'Magi felt uncouth rage coil in his belly. Cain had been here, *here*. "Which prisoner did he take?"

As if he had to ask. Dead, she'd told him. Cain was dead. And he'd believed her—so much so that when he found someone sneaking around in his territories, he'd never even considered it might be Cain.

"That woman Lord Kisrah brought in, sir."

There was a darned patch on the guardsman's shoulder. It had been so well done that the ae'Magi hadn't noticed it until he got closer. He would see to it that the guardsmen's uniforms were inspected and replaced when necessary. No one in his employ should wear a darned uniform.

This guardsman, the ae'Magi thought, enjoying himself despite his anger, wouldn't be needing a new uniform ever again. He took his time.

"Clean up the dust and leave me."

Shuddering, the sixteen-year-old silk merchant's daughter swept the ashes of the guard into the little shovel that was kept near the fireplace. She did a thorough job of it but wasted no time.

After she had gone, he sat and ran his finger around one of the burls on his desk.

"I had him," he said out loud. "I had the bait, and he came—but I lost my chance. I should have felt it, should have known she was something more." He thought about the woman. What had been so special about her that would attract his son?

Moodily, he took the stopper off the crystal decanter that sat on a corner of his desk and poured amber wine in a glass. He held it up to the light and swirled the liquid, admiring the fine gold color—the same shade as Cain's eyes. He tipped the glass and drank it dry, wiping his mouth with his wrist.

"There are, however, some compensations, my son. I know that you are actively working against me. You cannot remain invisible if you want to move to attack, and I will find you. The woman is the key."

He whispered a minor summoning spell and waited only a short time before he was answered by a knock on the door. At his call, the Uriah who had once been a Sianim mercenary entered the study. The mercenaries had made fine Uriah. They were lasting longer than the ones he made from peasants. This one might last years rather than months. The old wizards had done better—theirs were still functioning though they had been created in the Wizard Wars.

He wished the second half of that book hadn't been destroyed. He'd been looking for another copy of it for years, but he feared that there were no more.

"You're that one who told me that you were familiar with the woman you took from Myr's campsite?" the ae'Magi asked.

The Uriah bowed his head in assent.

"Tell me about her. What is her name? Where do you know her from?"

Another problem with the Uriah, besides longevity, the ae'Magi had found, was that communication was not all that it could be. Information could only be gotten with detailed questions, and even then a vital fact could be left out. They were good soldiers but not good scouts or spies.

"Aralorn. I knew her in Sianim," it replied.

Sianim. Had his problem spread beyond Reth?

"What did she do in Sianim?"

The Uriah shrugged carelessly. "She taught quarterstaff and halfstaff. She did some work for Ren, the Spymaster, I don't know how much."

"She worked as a spy?" The ae'Magi pounced on it.

"Ren the Mouse doesn't formalize much. He assigns whoever he thinks will be useful. From the number of her unexplained comings and goings, she worked for him more often than most."

"Tell me more about her."

"She is good with disguises and with languages. She can blend in anywhere, but I think she used to be Rethian." The Uriah smiled. "Not much use with a sword."

He'd liked her, the ae'Magi thought. *The man had liked her.* The Uriah was nothing more than a hungry beast, but he remembered what the man had known.

And then the Uriah said, "Ran around with a damned big wolf. Found him in the Northlands and took him home."

"A wolf?" The ae'Magi frowned.

"Those yellow eyes made everyone jumpy," the Uriah said.

The ae'Magi remembered abruptly that he'd recently had another escape from his castle. The girl had been aided by a wolf—or wolf pack—that had killed a handful of the ae'Magi's Uriah, who had inexplicably gone after it rather than after the girl they'd been ordered to chase.

He tried to remember what this Aralorn had looked like—surely he'd have noticed if she were as exotic as his Northland beauty.

"Describe her to me."

"She is short and pale-skinned even with a tan. Brown hair, blue-green eyes. Sturdily built. She moves fast."

Not her, then, but still . . . green eyes. He'd bought that slave because she had gray-green eyes, shapeshifter eyes. Blue-green, gray-green—two names for the same color.

"You say she was good with disguises?"

ARALORN WAS TOO tired to wake up when the covering was pulled back, letting the cool air sweep over her warm body. She moaned when gentle hands probed her ribs, but felt no urgent need to open her eyes. She heard a soft sound of dismay as her hands were unwrapped. A touch on her forehead sent her back into sleep.

It was the sound of voices that woke her the second time, a few minutes later, much more alert. The nausea that was the usual companion to beggersblessing use had dissipated.

She noticed that she was in the library, covered with a brightly colored quilt. A familiar cloak, Wolf's, lay carelessly tossed over the back of the sofa. Men's voices were approaching.

She wondered how she'd slept through the trip to camp—because he'd said that he couldn't have brought the merchant all the way here.

She started to sit up, only to realize that the clothing scattered on the floor was what she had been wearing. Hastily, she pulled the blankets up to her neck to protect her dignity just as Myr came around a bookcase.

"So," said Myr with a wide smile, "I see that you're more or less intact after your experience with the ae'Magi's hospitality. I must say, though, that it will be a long time before I loan you any of my clothes again. I didn't bring many with me." The pleasure and relief in his voice was real, and she was surprised and not a little flattered that he cared so much about someone he'd known such a short time.

Aralorn smiled back at him and started to say something, but noticed that Wolf, who had followed Myr, was focusing intently on her hands. She followed his gaze to where her hands gripped the top of the blanket. Ten healthy nails dug into the cloth. The beggersblessing had left her wits begging, too; she hadn't even noticed that she didn't hurt at all.

Aralorn answered Myr absently. "Yes. Though he wasn't the best of hosts. I only saw him once or twice the whole time I was there."

Myr perched on the end of the sofa near Aralorn's feet and looked, for once, as young as he was. "And he prides himself on his treatment of guests," he said with a mournful shake of his head. "It doesn't even look like he left you any mementoes."

"Well," said Aralorn, looking at her hands again, very conscious of Wolf's doing the same thing. "You know he did, but I seem to have lost them. The last time I looked, my hands were missing the fingernails."

"How is your breathing?" asked Wolf.

Aralorn took a deep breath. "Fine. Is this your healer's work?" She wouldn't have asked, would have assumed that it had been Wolf, but he was looking particularly blank.

Wolf shook his head. "No, I told you that he was not experienced enough to do more than he did."

Wolf glanced at Myr. "I saw a few new people here, are any of them healers?"

"No," replied Myr, disgust rich in his voice. "Nor are they hunters, tanners, or cooks. We have six more children, two nobles, and a bard. The only one who is of any help is the bard, who is passably good with his knives. The two nobles sit around watching everyone else work or decide to wander out in the main cave system so that a search party has to be sent after them."

"You might try just letting them wander next time," commented Wolf, whose attention was back on Aralorn's healed hands.

Myr smiled. "Now there's an idea." Then he sighed. "No, it wouldn't work. With my luck, they'd run into the dragon and lead it back here."

"Dragon?" asked Aralorn in a startled tone, almost dropping her blanket.

"Or something that looks an awful lot like one. It's been seen by two or three of the hunting parties although it hasn't seen them, yet," replied Myr.

Dragons were even more interesting than her healed hands. She remembered something. "That day I went out"—she glanced at Wolf and away again, not wanting to set him off—"I found some tracks. Tracks of something big. It was about six miles away and traveling fast. Where have you sighted it?"

"East and north, never closer than ten miles. Do you know anything about dragons? Something along the lines of whether or not they eat people would be helpful," asked Myr in a hopeful tone, sitting down on one arm of the couch. "Some of my people are inclined to panic."

"'Fraid not," she answered. "The only ones that I've heard of are in stories. They do eat people in stories, but for some reason, they seem to confine themselves to virgins chained to rocks. Since I haven't heard of anyplace nearby where there is a steady supply of virgins chained to rocks, I would suppose that it is a safe bet that this one has differing dietary requirements." She nodded at Wolf. "Why don't you ask the magical expert around here?"

Wolf shrugged. "The closest that I've ever gotten to one was the one asleep in the cave underneath the ae'Magi's castle. Since it had been asleep for several centuries, I didn't learn much. I thought, though, that it was supposed to be the last of its kind—the reason that it was ensorcelled rather than killed."

"Well," said Myr, with a lifted eyebrow, "if this creature isn't a dragon, then it is closely related."

"Wyverns are supposed to resemble dragons," Aralorn suggested. "Smaller, dumpy dragons."

"Wyvern or dragon, I'm not too sure that I'm comfortable with its being so close," Myr said.

"Maybe it'll eat the nobles that are giving you such a bad time," suggested Aralorn. "You might try chaining them to a rock."

She found that she was starting to get tired, so she leaned back against a cushion and closed her eyes. She didn't sleep but drifted quietly, listening to the other two talk. She found it comforting. There was something she wanted to ask. She sat up abruptly when she remembered what it was.

"Astrid," she said, interrupting them in the middle of a discussion on the best method of drying meat—something neither of them seemed to be too sure of—"did someone find her?"

"Yes," said Wolf.

"The Uriah got her," answered Myr at the same time.

Aralorn swallowed, and in a hoarse voice not at all like her own she asked, "Will she . . . ?"

"Will she what?" asked Myr.

Aralorn watched her hand as it traced patterns in the quilt, and asked in a low voice, "Will she become one of them now?"

Myr started as if to say something, but held back, wanting to hear Wolf's answer first.

"No," answered the ae'Magi's son, "there is a ritual that must be followed to turn men into Uriah. She was simply eaten."

Myr looked at him sharply.

"I'd always heard that they were the creation of some long-forgotten magician who left them to infest the Eastern Swamp," Aralorn said. "Maybe protecting something hidden there, long forgotten. I assumed that the ae'Magi just found some way of controlling them."

"He found out how to control them, yes. He also found out how to make them—it was in the same book"—Wolf reached casually to a shelf near Myr's head and pulled out a thin, ratty volume—"this book, as a matter of fact. His version has only the first half of the book."

Myr said, "That's why you spelled the graves of the two people Edom killed."

Wolf nodded, replacing the book on the shelf. "The runes that Aralorn traced over the bodies, and the fact that Edom hadn't completed the ritual—the heart must be consumed—should ensure that they rest quietly. I just didn't want to take chances."

"Talor was one of them," Aralorn told Wolf. "I was starting to head back to camp that day when I heard Talor's signal."

"He always was a little off pitch," said Wolf.

"I thought that he was caught by the Uriah and needed help." Her agitated hands gripped the quilt with white knuckles although her voice was calm. "I guess that was more or less the case, but there was no way that I could help him."

There had been more than just Talor, she realized. She hadn't even noticed at the time—or she'd been too dazed from the blow to the head to realize what she had been seeing: the features of friends in the faces of the Uriah.

A sharp sting on her cheek brought her back shaking and gasping. Wolf sat on the couch beside her, and she buried her head against his shoulder and shuddered dry-eyed, grateful for the firm arms wrapped around her back.

"He knew me, too," she whispered. "It was still Talor, but he was one of *them*. He talked to me, sounded just like himself—but he looked at me like a farmer looks at dinner after a hard day's work. I didn't even know that Uriah could talk."

Then, with difficulty, because she didn't have much practice, she cried.

MYR TOOK WOLF's cloak and covered her back where the quilt left her exposed. He touched her hair a little awkwardly, and said quietly to Wolf, "She won't appreciate my presence when she recovers. I'll tell the others that she's well. Stanis has been blaming himself for her capture—he won't eat. It will be a weight off his back to find out that she's been rescued and is here unhurt."

Wolf nodded and watched him go. He rocked Aralorn gently and whispered soft reassurances. He was concentrating on her so that the voice took him by surprise.

"Tell her to stop that."

Wolf brought his head up, alarmed at the strange voice. It was heavily accented and firmly masculine if a bit fussy. It also didn't seem to come from anywhere, or rather there was no one where the voice came from.

"Tell her to stop that, I said. She's driven my Lys away, and I simply won't abide that. I have allowed her here because Lys likes her—but now she's made Lys go away by thinking of all of those bad things. Tell her to stop it, or I will have to ask her to leave no matter what Lys says." The voice lost a little of its firmness and became sulky.

The sound of someone else in the room distracted Aralorn, and she pushed herself up away from Wolf's chest. Reaching down, she grabbed her tunic off the floor and used it to wipe her nose and eyes.

She, too, looked at the conspicuously empty space at the end of the sofa near her feet. Magical invisibility consisted of blending into shadows and turning eyes away rather than absolute invisibility; when someone actively *looked*, the invisible person could be seen. Wolf knew what she was doing—but there was nothing at the end of the sofa.

"Can you see him?" she asked Wolf.

When he shook his head, she directed her questioning to the man who wasn't there. "Who are you?"

"That's better," said the voice, and there was a distinct pop of air that accompanies teleportation.

That pop made Wolf confident enough to say, "He's gone."

"What do you think?" asked Aralorn, settling back onto Wolf, her voice husky from crying. "Was that our friend who gives us a hand with the books and healed me?"

"I can't imagine that there is an endless supply of invisible people here."

Wolf knew he should be more concerned, but he'd suddenly become aware that Aralorn was naked under the quilt. It hadn't bothered him before, when she'd been upset.

He started to shift her off him, with the end goal of getting as much distance on his side as possible. But as soon as his hands touched her hip—on top of the blanket—they wanted to pull her toward him, not push her away.

Self-absorbed, he only caught the tail end of Aralorn's question. "Say that again?" he asked.

"I asked how long you left me alone in the library."

"Not more than fifteen minutes. Less probably."

She made a sound of amazement. "I've never heard of anyone who could heal that fast. No wonder I feel like a month-old babe; by all rights I should be comatose now."

"Powerful," Wolf agreed.

Aralorn nodded. "It was odd in a voice that young, but he sounded a bit querulous, maybe even senile." She closed her eyes, and he couldn't make himself shove her away. More asleep than awake, she murmured with a touch of her unquenchable curiosity, "I wonder who Lys is."

When Wolf made no attempt to add to or answer her question, she drifted off to sleep.

Wolf cradled her protectively against him. He thought about shapeshifters, children, and refugees who unerringly found their way to Myr's camp. And he remembered the ae'Magi's half-mad son who wandered into these caves to find solace one night, led by a small gray fox with ageless sea-green eyes.

NINE

───ᘚᘚᘚ───

FROM HER STATION ON THE COUCH, ARALORN WATCHED WOLF DEPOSIT another armload of books on the floor beside the worktable. The table, her chair, and most of the floor space were similarly adorned. He'd been silently moving books since she woke up, even less communicative than usual. He wasn't wearing his mask, but he might as well have been for all she could read on his face.

"Have you given any more thought to our invisible friend?" she asked, just to goad him. They'd worried and speculated for hours last night. During which time, Wolf had spent ten minutes lecturing her about how real invisibility was a myth, impossible to achieve with magic for a variety of reasons laid out in theories proposed over centuries.

She wasn't fishing for answers from him now; she was fishing for a response. Some acknowledgment that he was aware she was in the room.

He grunted without looking her way and went back into the stacks.

She might have been more concerned with their invisible—to all intents and purposes, no matter what Wolf maintained—visitor. But whoever it was had made no move against them; quite the contrary, in her opinion. If their visitor had meant mischief, he'd had plenty of opportunity. This was the Northlands, after all, full of all sorts of odd things.

It was Wolf she worried about.

He'd never allowed her to get as close as they had been last night. But always, whenever he'd opened up to her, let down the barrier that separated him from her, from everyone, he'd abruptly leave for weeks or months at a time. She thought this morning's distance might be the start of his withdrawal.

Having experienced the ae'Magi's touch firsthand, if only for a brief time compared to whatever he'd gone through, she finally understood some of what caused Wolf to be the way he was. It increased her patience with him—but it didn't mean she was going to let him pull away again without a fight.

"Did our apprentice write all of these?" Aralorn made a vague gesture toward the stacks before continuing to put a better edge on her knife.

Wolf turned to survey the piles. He let the silence build, then growled a brief affirmative before stalking back into the forest of bookcases. It was the first word he'd said to her since she'd woken up.

Aralorn grinned, sheathed her knife, and levered herself to her feet, still annoyingly weak. Scanning the nearby shelves, she found a book on shapeshifters and wobbled with it to the table, careful not to fall. Wolf had made it clear that he would rather that she stay put on the couch for a couple of days. She had no intention of giving in; but if she fell, there would be no living with him. So she'd save it for desperate measures if he didn't start talking to her. If she fell deliberately, it wouldn't be as humiliating.

She cleared off her chair and space enough to read. Now that the search had been narrowed to books that were likely to be trapped, Wolf had forbidden her to help. Aralorn decided if she couldn't be useful, at least she could enjoy herself.

Wolf balanced the books he carried on another stack and eyed her narrowly without meeting her eyes. He took her book and looked at it before handing it back.

"I thought human mages were supposed to keep their secrets close—not write down every stray thought that comes into their heads." With a tilt of her head, Aralorn indicated the neat piles of books he'd brought out.

He followed her gesture and sighed. "Most mages restrict their writings to the intricacies of magic. Iveress fancied himself an expert on everything. There are treatises here on everything from butter-making to glassblowing to governmental philosophy. From the four books of his I've already looked through, he is long-winded and brilliant, with the annoying habit of sliding in obscure magic spells in the middle of whatever he was writing when the spell occurred to him."

"Better you than me," said Aralorn, hiding her satisfaction in having gotten him to respond at last.

She must not have hidden it quite well enough. He stared at her from under his lowered brows. "Only because his books were considered subversive a few centuries back, and mages spelled them to keep them safe. Otherwise, I'd make you help me with this mess." He took a stride toward the shelves again, then stopped. "I might as well start with what I have."

"No use discouraging yourself with an endless task," she agreed.

He growled at her without heat.

She grinned at his familiar grumpiness—much better than silence—and settled in to read. It was fascinating, but not, Aralorn fancied, in the fashion the author meant it to be. In the foreword, the author admitted she had never met a shapeshifter. Regardless, she considered herself an expert. The stories she liked best were the ones that represented shapeshifters as a "powerful, possibly mythic race" whose main hobby seemed to be eating innocent young children who lost themselves in the woods.

"If I were one of a powerful, possibly mythic race," muttered Aralorn, "I wouldn't be bothering with eating children. I'd go after pompous asses who sit around passing judgment on things they know nothing about."

"Me, too," agreed Wolf mildly without looking up. Evidently the reading he was doing was more interesting than hers, because even his grumpiness had faded. "Do you have someone in mind?"

"She's been dead for years . . . centuries, I think."

"Ah," he said, turning a page. "I don't eat things that have been dead too long. Bad for even the wolf's digestion."

She snorted and kept reading. Aralorn learned that shapeshifters could only be killed by silver, garlic, or wolfsbane. "And all this time I've been worried about things like arrows, swords, and knives," she told Wolf. "Silly me. I'd better get rid of my silver-handled dagger—it would kill me to touch the grip."

He grunted.

The author of her book was also under the mistaken impression that shapeshifters could take the shape of only one animal. She devoted a section to horrific tales of shapeshifter wolves, lions, and bears. Mice, Aralorn supposed, were too mundane—and unlikely to eat children.

She shared bits and pieces of the better wolf tales with Wolf, as he waded through a volume on pig training. He responded by telling her how to train a pig to count, open gates, and fetch. Pigs were also useful for predicting earthquakes. Iveress had helpfully included three spells to start earthquakes.

Aralorn laughed and returned to her reading. At the end of the book, the author included stories "which my research has proven to be merely folktales" to entertain her readers. After glancing through the first couple, Aralorn decided that the thing that distinguished truth from folktale was whether or not the shapeshifters were evil villains. Most of the tales were ones she'd heard before. Most, but not all.

She read the final story, then thoughtfully closed the book and glanced curiously around the room. Nothing was moving that shouldn't be. Wolf had set the pig book aside and was sorting through a pile near his chair.

"Once long ago, between this time and that, there was a woman cursed by a wizard when she was young, for laughing at his bald head." She didn't need to use the book to help her memory, but kept her eyes on Wolf. "She was married, and her first child was born dead. Her husband died in an unfortunate accident while she gave birth to her second, a daughter. When she was three, it became apparent to one and all that the second child bore a curse worse than death—she was an empath. Upon that discovery, her mother killed herself."

"A useless thing to do," murmured Wolf, pulling a book out of the pile and setting it before him. He made no move to open it. "You'd have gone hunting for the wizard."

Aralorn raised her eyebrow, and said coolly, "I'm not finished."

He smiled and lifted both hands peaceably. "No offense meant, storyteller."

"The girl child was taken to a house outside the village and cared for as best the villagers could. Her empathic nature meant that none of them could get too close without causing her pain."

"I thought your book was about shapeshifters," Wolf said, when Aralorn paused too long.

She nodded. "She grew up and learned to glean herbs from the woods to pay for her keep. When she was sixteen, a passing shapeshifter saw her. He took to following her around in the guise of a crow or squirrel. But whatever shape he took, she knew him."

Wolf's eyes grew reserved. "Indeed?"

Aralorn frowned at him. "This isn't about you and me—and you would have found me the first time though if you'd thought about looking for someone who didn't look like me."

He looked away. She decided to ignore him and continued with the story.

"She knew when he fell in love with her, too. And he was able to guard his touch so she could bear it. When the villagers came to her home, he was her invisible guardian. She loved him and was happy.

"Once a month, the shapeshifter returned to his village to assure his people that he was well. They were not happy with his choice, and eventually his mother decided to solve the problem herself. She saw to it that a Southern slaver became aware of the girl and took her the next time the shapeshifter left her to visit the shapeshifter village. He returned to find the cottage empty, with the door swinging in the wind.

"The Trader was wary and, hearing that she had a magical lover, he took her through the Northlands, where no mage could follow. But her lover was no human mage, and he found them—too late."

A moaning sound echoed through the caves. Wolf tilted his head slightly so she knew that he heard as well.

"When the shapeshifter reached the slavers' camp," she continued, "he found nothing left of the would-be slavers except mindless bodies. The girl, terrified and alone, had evoked an empath's only defense, projecting her terror and pain onto her tormentors. She was alive when the shapeshifter found her, so he took her to a cave, sacred to his kind, where he tried to heal her. The worst of her wounds were of the spirit that even a shapeshifter's magic may not touch; and though her body was whole, she spoke not a word to him but stared through him, as if he were not there. Not entirely sane from his grief, the shapeshifter swore to keep her alive until he could find a way to heal her soul. And so he lives on, an old, old man tending his beloved from that day until this—and that is the story of the Old Man of the Mountain."

The moaning waned to a hesitant sigh that whispered through the library and faded to nothing.

Wolf raised an eyebrow at her. "I have never heard of a shapeshifter with the power that the Old Man is supposed to have."

Aralorn rubbed her cheek thoughtfully, leaving behind a streak of black dust. This was a secret—but she didn't feel like keeping secrets from Wolf. "The older a shapeshifter is, the more powerful he is. Like human mages, it is not unusual for a shapeshifter to live several hundred years. A really powerful shapeshifter can make himself younger constantly and never grow old. The reason that you don't see a shapeshifter much older than several hundred years is that they are constantly changing to new and more difficult things. It's hard to remember that you are supposed to be human when you change into a tree or the wind. An uncle of my mother once told me that sometimes a shapechanger forgets to picture what he is changing himself into, and he changes into nothing. There is no reason why our Old Man of the Mountain couldn't be several thousand years old rather than just a few hundred. That would make him incredibly powerful."

She stopped as something occurred to her. "Wolf, there was a snowstorm the night before the Uriah came. If it hadn't slowed them down, they would have come upon us at night and slaughtered the camp."

Wolf shrugged. "Snowstorms are unpredictable here, but I suppose that it could have been he who caused the storm. I suspect that we'll never know."

Wolf opened his book and went back to reading.

Aralorn found another book and managed not to show Wolf how

unsteady she was. But when he'd checked it for her, and she opened it, it was difficult to concentrate as the little energy she'd regained dissipated. The words blurred in front of her eyes and soon she was turning pages from habit.

She dozed off between one sentence and the next. When Wolf touched her shoulder, she jumped to her feet and had her knife drawn before she opened her eyes.

"Plague it, Wolf!" she sputtered. "One of these days, you are going to do that, and I'll knife you by mistake. Then I'll have to live all my life with the guilt of your death on my hands."

Her threat didn't seem to bother him much as he caught her and lowered her to her chair as her legs collapsed under her. "You are trying to do too much," he said with disapproval. He started to say something else, then lifted his head.

She heard it, too, then, the sound of running feet. Stanis popped into the room at a dead run—he was one of the few people who knew his way to Wolf's private area. He was pale and panting when he stopped, looking as though he'd sprinted the half mile or so of cave tunnels that connected the main camp with Wolf's library. "Uriah," he panted.

Aralorn tangled with her chair when she tried to push it out of the way too fast, but kept from falling with the aid of a hand on her arm. She was firmly sat down on her seat.

Wolf, who had somehow donned his mask again, looked her straight in the eye, and said, "You stay here." His voice left no room for arguments. He shifted into the wolf and melted into the tunnel.

WITH THE SCARY mage gone, the library felt safer than the outer cave to Stanis. But his mates were out there; he wasn't going to stay safely behind.

"Hey now," he said when Aralorn used the table to get to her feet. She looked like she weighed half what she had the first time he'd seen her—all pared down to bone and sinew. But she walked without limping to the little padded bench and shuffled under it until she came up with a sword and scabbard she belted on. He didn't miss that the scabbard was stained with blood—from the Uriah who'd killed Astrid.

"He told you to stay here." Maybe she hadn't heard the mage.

Aralorn glanced up as she sheathed the sword. "It says in my files—I know because Ren showed them to me—'Does not take orders, will occasionally listen to suggestions.' Did Wolf sound like he was suggesting anything to you?"

Stanis shook his head. "No." He shuffled his feet a little. "I don't follow no orders either, but if that one ever told me to do anything in that tone of voice, I can't help but think I'd be sitting where he wanted me until I was covered in dust."

She laughed. "Yes, he's a little intimidating, isn't he?" She checked the draw of the sword, adjusted it a little, and said, "But there's no way I'm sitting here while everyone else gets to fight." She looked at him. "You know your way to the rest of them? I might be able to find my way out, but I don't know how this cave connects into the rest."

Stanis squirmed.

She smiled. "No need to tell *him* that I couldn't find my own way there," she said.

"I'm not afraid of him," Stanis stated belligerently, though his mam had taught him better than that.

"Of course not," she said stoutly. "Nothing to be afraid of."

After about the halfway point, she put her hand on his shoulder. "Sorry, Stanis, we're going to have to slow down."

"No trouble," he said. "Why don't you lean on me a bit?"

She muttered something he didn't catch but put some of her weight on him. For a while that was all she did, but eventually her arm wrapped around his shoulders, and she honestly leaned on him.

"Good thing you're short," he said. "You should have stayed. What would have happened if I weren't here to help you?"

"Then I'd have crawled," she said grimly.

He glanced up at her face, visible in the light of one of those little glowy balls Wolf had shown him how to make.

"Right," he said. She didn't look like a nice Lady right now, she looked like someone who could lick her weight in Uriah and then some. Maybe she was a match for that Wolf after all.

ARALORN SWUNG A leg over the barricade erected to keep people—except for runners like Stanis, whose magic seemed capable of keeping them from getting hopelessly lost—from wandering the tunnels.

She listened for sounds of battle, but the tunnel was suspiciously silent.

"Where were the Uriah when you came running?" she asked, as the passageway floor took a steep upward bend.

"Don't know." Stanis shook his head. "Somebody spotted 'em outside and sprinted to the caves like an idiot. They're sure to have followed 'em here." He paused. "I don't hear nothin'."

"If they were inside our camp when Wolf came, you'd still be hearing things," she told him stoutly, finding that she couldn't quite believe it. What if they'd taken him by surprise? What if he hadn't had a chance?

"What if they took him by surprise?" asked Stanis, echoing her thoughts, his voice a bare whisper as they crept closer to where there should be a bunch of people fighting for their lives.

Her hands were sweating—from effort, she told herself. "No one takes him by surprise," she told Stanis. "He works things the other way."

And that was truth. She could breathe better, doubtless because the floor had flattened out again.

Stanis stopped. "Big cave's just around the corner," he mouthed. "The main one where everyone's camped. We should—"

"*Not* his wards?"

Oh, she recognized that voice. She stood up straight and strode around the corner, where the whole camp—as far as she could tell at a glance—was standing armed and ready. She couldn't see the owner of the loud voice, but she could hear him just fine.

"What does he mean 'not his wards'? Why didn't you ask him more? Do we expect them to come running in?"

She pushed her way through—not hard once people realized where she was going.

"It means that they aren't his wards," said Myr neutrally.

The big nobleman who stood in front of him was used to getting his way—with money or intimidation.

"Boy," he boomed. "You don't let that strippy bugger get away with half-assed answers. He's not in charge here."

She couldn't get there any faster without falling on her face, but . . . Myr hit him. A quick, decisive blow that dropped the ox like a stone.

Aralorn pulled her sword and held it to the downed man's throat, making sure he felt the sharp edge. A foot on his shoulder.

The fear that had held her since she realized that it was too quiet made her testy, and she would have been quite happy to put the sword all the way through the blasted man's neck and take care of the problem. But her father had been a canny politician when it suited him, and she could hear his voice in her ear.

So instead of killing him, she said coolly, "Do you desire this man dead, my king? I assure you it would be a pleasure. We could display his body on a stake just outside for the crows to eat."

"And attract every scavenger in twenty leagues," said Myr regretfully. "No. Not just yet." She couldn't read his voice and wouldn't lift her eyes from her enemy to look at his face.

She grimaced at the triumph in the eyes of the nobleman at her feet. He started to say something, then stopped. Maybe it was the weight of her heel on a nerve just in front of his shoulder, maybe it was that her arm dropped just a bit, letting the sword dig a little deeper.

"Permission to deal with him as my father would?" she asked.

"I recall the stake incident," said Myr dryly. "My grandfather told me about it. No one disobeyed the Lyon's orders for a few years afterward. Effective but extreme, you have to admit. We are a little short of numbers here—so I find myself reluctant to give you my unqualified permission."

The nobleman paled. "The Lyon?" he said.

Aralorn bared her teeth at him, but continued to talk to Myr. "Your Majesty, if you please. Haris?"

"Aye?"

"Haris, I think that you've been working too hard. You need an assistant."

"Don't need no nobleman to help me cook," said Haris grumpily.

"Haris," said Myr in silky tones, "I have no intention of allowing this man to interfere with your efforts. However . . . skinning, turning the spit, or taking out the refuse—how much could he hurt?"

"Oh aye," said Haris, sounding remarkably happier. "That I'll do, sire."

"Aralorn, let him up," Myr said.

She pulled her sword away after wiping the blood off on the idiot's shirt.

"Oras," Myr said. "A week of helping Haris is a gift. Do not make me regret it."

The nobleman swallowed. Perhaps he recognized, as Aralorn did, the old king in his grandson's face.

Myr turned his attention to Aralorn then, ignoring the man on the ground. "I need you to go out and find Wolf. Is this an assault we need to prepare ourselves for—or can I take people off alert?"

"What's going on?" she asked, sheathing her sword.

"The Uriah tried to come into the caves after our hunting party and were stopped by wards on the cave mouth. Wolf says they aren't his wards and sent us all back here to cool our heels and guard the narrow entrance."

Aralorn looked at the opening Myr indicated, where daylight shone through.

"Oras aside," Myr said, "it would be useful to have a bit more information. I'd like an update, and you're likely to get more information out of our wizard than anyone else."

ONCE IN THE tunnel to the outside, she drew her sword and held it in a fighter's grip. Someone had painted signs on the walls of the tunnels to facilitate travel, and it was a simple matter to follow the arrows to the outside by the magelight she held cupped in one hand.

The howls were louder as she turned into a cave marked "Door to Outside" over the top. She smiled at the awkward lettering even as the cold sweat of fear gathered on her forehead. Cautiously, she crept forward through the twisted narrow channel.

The Uriah were there, howling with frustrated rage at the wall of flame that covered the entrance. Someone, Aralorn noted with absent approval, had set up the wood for a bonfire where the tunnel began to narrow—it sat unlit, a good ten feet behind the magical fire that blocked the entrance. Aralorn couldn't feel the heat from the fire, but toasted bodies of Uriah lay twitching feebly just outside the cave as evidence of the effectiveness of the barrier.

Aralorn leaned against the side of the cave and watched as another Uriah, incited by her presence just inside the barrier, dove into the flames. Nausea touched even her hardened stomach as she watched the hungry flames engulf it.

"I told you to stay in the library."

She'd been expecting him, knowing that the situation would mean that she probably wouldn't hear him. She didn't jump, didn't start, just turned to look at him a little faster than strictly necessary. It wouldn't have mattered except for the low spot in the roof of the cave.

"Ow," she said with a hiss of indrawn breath, putting her hand to her head where the rock had cut it.

He came out of the shadows and set his staff down—the crystals on the top blazed as soon as its clawed feet touched the ground. She shut her eyes against the light.

With a hand on her chin, Wolf used the other to explore the damaged area despite the fact that she squirmed and batted at his hand. In clipped tones, he said, "It seems like every time I've turned my back on you lately, you are getting hurt one way or another."

To her surprise, he bent down and pressed his cheek against hers. She hadn't experienced the healing of a green-magic user very often, barring her more recent experience. Generally she hadn't been in any shape to know exactly what it was that they did, but she knew enough to know that this was very different. This was not purely physical, there was an emotional link, too—a meeting on a more primal level.

It was over before she could analyze it further. Wolf stepped back as if bitten, and she could hear him gasping for breath beneath his mask. She looked at him in wonder—she knew enough about human magic to know that he shouldn't have been capable of doing what he had just done.

"Wolf," she said, reaching out to touch him. He backed away, keeping his head away from her and his eyes closed.

"Wolf, what's wrong?" When he said nothing, she took a step back to give him room.

He flung his head up then, and blazing yellow eyes met hers. When he spoke, it was a whisper that his ruined voice made even more effective. "What am I? I should not be able to heal you. The other things—the shapeshifting, the power I wield—they could be explained away. But magic doesn't work this way. It doesn't take over before I can react and do things that I don't ask of it. I swore that I would never . . . never let anything control me the way my father did. In the end, even he could not eat my will entirely. This . . . does."

"It was you who healed my eyes." She wanted to give herself time to think. There was something that she should be grasping, a puzzle solved if she could just figure out how to look at it.

"Yes," he said.

"Were you trying to, then?"

He forced himself to adopt a relaxed posture, leaning against the wall as he spoke. "If you mean did I try to heal you with a spell, no. I just . . . wanted you to quit hurting."

She could almost see the effort he made to open up to her, this man who was so private. It was, she thought, maybe the bravest thing she'd ever seen anyone do.

He continued with his eyes on the mouth of the cave where three Uriah—none of whom resembled anyone she knew—stood motionless, watching them.

"I was so tired," Wolf told her. "I hadn't slept much since I found that you were gone." He looked at her. "You were getting worse, and I couldn't do anything about it. I do not recall what I was thinking, precisely. I had done all that I could for you and knew that it would never be enough and something made me lie beside you and this magic took over." He clenched his hands in what was very near revulsion.

"Who was your mother? Do you know?" asked Aralorn. "I've heard a lot of stories about Cain, the son of the ae'Magi, but none of them ever mentioned his mother."

Wolf shrugged, and his voice had regained its cool tones when he answered. "I only saw her once, when I was very young, maybe five years old. I remember asking Father who she was, or rather who she had been, for she was quite dead, killed by some experiment of his, I suppose. I don't remember being particularly worried about her, so I suspect that it was the only time I saw her."

"Describe her for me," requested Aralorn in a firm voice that refused to condemn or to sympathize with the boy he had been. He wouldn't want that. The Uriah weren't coming in anytime soon, she thought. She folded her legs and sat on the ground—healing or no, her legs had done as much as they were going to for a while, and it was sit down or fall down.

"I was young, I don't remember much," Wolf said. "She looked small next to my father, fragile and lovely—like a butterfly. The only time I ever heard him say anything about her was when some noble asked about my mother. He said she was flawlessly beautiful. I think he was right."

Aralorn nodded, her suspicions confirmed. "I would have been surprised if she had been anything else."

He narrowed his gaze.

"Your mother must have been a shapeshifter, or some other green-magic user—but the 'perfectly beautiful' sounds a lot like a shapeshifter. That feeling that the magic is taking control of you is fairly common when dealing with green magic because you are dealing with magic shaped by nature first, and only then by magician. You need to learn to work with it so that you can modify it. If you fight it, it will prove stronger than you."

He stared at her a bit and joined her on the floor without speaking. Maybe his legs wouldn't hold him up any longer either.

"I suspect," continued Aralorn, as blandly as she could manage, "if you hadn't been taught how magic should work, you would have discovered your half-blooded capabilities long since. You were told that you couldn't heal, so you didn't try."

Two of the Uriah stepped forward at the same time. The wards flared, and they burned. Aralorn caught a brief hint of burnt flesh, like cooking pork, then nothing.

"Your theory fits," said Wolf finally.

"I should have thought about it sooner," apologized Aralorn. "I mean, I am a half-breed. It's just that I've never met another half-breed. I could tell that you weren't a shapeshifter, so I just assumed that you were simply an extraordinarily powerful human magician." She hesitated. "Which you are."

Wolf gave a half laugh with little humor in it. "It sounds just like an experiment the ae'Magi would try. To a Darranian like him, it would be the ultimate form of bestiality. Just the thing to spark his interest."

Aralorn leaned over, pulled down his mask, and bussed him on the unscarred mouth with a kiss that was anything but romantic. "You beast, you," she said, and he made an unpracticed sound that might have been a laugh.

He got to his feet and pulled her to hers, his eyes warmed with relief, humor, and something else. Gripping her shoulders, he kissed her with a passion that left her breathless and shaken. He stepped back and returned the mask to its usual position.

"We'd better get back and tell Myr he can relax. It doesn't appear that the Old Man is going to welcome the Uriah into his cave anytime in the near future," he said, offering her his arm to lean on.

"You think those are his wards?" she asked.

"Someone has powered them up since I looked at them last. It wasn't me and no one else here has the skill or the power."

She caught her breath, smiled, and tucked her arm through his. "Do we tell the whole camp that we are being protected by the Old Man of the Mountain?"

"It might be the best thing, even if it scares a few of them silly. I have the feeling that we shouldn't push his hospitality by wandering around too much. The best way to see that it doesn't happen is to tell them the whole truth—if they'll believe it." Wolf slid though a narrow passage with his usual grace, towing Aralorn beside him.

"We are dealing with people who have some minor magic capabilities; are following a dethroned king who just barely received his coming-of-age spurs; who number among their acquaintances not just one half-breed shapeshifter, but two half-breed shapeshifters—one of whom, incidentally, wears a silly mask. We could tell them that we were in the den of the old gods and that Faris, Empress of the Dead, conceived a sudden passion for Myr and it probably wouldn't faze them," Aralorn told him.

Wolf laughed, and Aralorn pulled him to a halt. "Wait. Did you say that the ae'Magi is Darranian?"

"Peasant stock," he confirmed. "Apparently his master was very surprised to find a magician who was Darranian—used to tell jokes about his Darranian apprentice. My father smiled when he talked about how he killed his teacher."

"Not the first Darranian mage," Aralorn said.

Wolf grunted and started to walk.

Aralorn let her hand drop and followed thoughtfully.

Wolf was first in the tunnel that opened into the main chamber. He hissed and jumped back, narrowly avoiding Myr's sword.

"Sorry," said Myr. "I thought that you were one of the Uriah. You should have said something before you came in. Did you find out why the Uriah aren't coming in?"

"Is there a reason the King of Reth is guarding the doorway instead of someone more expendable?" asked Wolf.

"Best swordsman," said Myr. "Are you going to answer me?"

"Let's do this where everyone can hear," Aralorn said, continuing on so she could do just that. "The Uriah aren't going to be coming in here."

She stepped out into the main cave and saw that most of them had heard her last remark. "Our guardian of the cave doesn't want them in." She was in her element, with a captive audience and a story to tell. She projected her voice and told them the story about the origin of the Old Man of the Mountain and finished with the barrier that was keeping the Uriah out.

SHE MADE THE tale sound as if it were part of shapeshifter history, Wolf decided, rather than a forgotten story in an obscure book. Usually, she did it the other way around—turning an unexciting bit of history into high adventure. He hadn't realized that she could do it backward.

As she had predicted, the refugees seemed reassured by her story, not questioning just how far the Old Man's benign stance would continue. Right then, they wanted a miracle, and Aralorn was giving one to them.

Responding to Wolf's look, Myr joined him just outside the cave, leaving Aralorn to her work.

"We may be locked in here for some time," Wolf informed Myr. "They might not be coming in, but there is no way to determine how long they are going to howl at our door. Do we have enough food to last us a week or so?" He should have been paying attention, but it was an effort to remember that he was supposed to care about these people. He was trying to be . . . something other than what he was. Someone Aralorn could be proud of. When she'd been hurt, he'd lost all interest in the extraneous details.

Myr shrugged. "We have enough grain stored to last us into next summer, feeding animals and people. We're short on meat, which is why I sent out the hunters this morning. They came back with Uriah instead of deer. For a week or two, we can do without. If it turns into a month we can always slaughter a goat or sheep to feed ourselves. Our real problems are going to be morale and sanitation."

Wolf nodded. "We'll have to deal with morale as it comes. I might be able to do something about the sanitation, though. The blocked-off tunnel where you're storing grain leads to a cave with a pit deep enough that you can throw a rock into it and not hear it hit bottom. It's fairly narrow, so you should be able to put some sort of structure over it to keep people from falling into it." Solving logistic problems helped center him.

"That should relieve Aralorn," commented Myr, a smile lighting his tired face for the first time since he'd heard the Uriah. "She was really worried that before this was all over, she'd be pressed into digging latrines."

Myr laughed wearily and pushed his hair out of his face. "I should have asked this right away. Is it possible that the Uriah can find their way in here through another entrance?"

"Maybe," answered Wolf, starting to head toward Aralorn, who was swaying wearily as she finished her story. "The Old Man has been here a lot longer than we have. If this entrance is protected, I suspect that all of them are."

Outside, the Uriah quieted and sank to their knees as a rider came into view. His horse was lathered and sweating, showing the whites of its eyes in fear of the Uriah. But it had learned to trust its rider, and Lord Kisrah was careful to keep the Uriah motionless with the spells of control that the ae'Magi had taught him.

He dismounted at the entrance to the cave. He could see the runes just inside the entrance, but he couldn't touch them to alter their power.

In the air, he sketched a symbol that glowed faintly yellow and passed easily through the entrance. The symbol touched a rune and fizzled as a man walked into the cave and approached the mouth.

"You are not welcome, leave this place," he said. In the light, the man was almost inhumanly beautiful, and Lord Kisrah caught his breath in admiration. Abruptly, the mouth filled with flames, the heat uncomfortably harsh on his face.

Kisrah backed up and tried to push the flames down again, with no effect. The third time he tried it, the Uriah began stirring as his hold on them weakened. With a curse he desisted. He led the horse back through the Uriah until he had some space.

"You will stay here until the ae'Magi releases you," he ordered briskly. "If someone comes out of the cave, you will not harm them. Take them prisoner—you know how to contact me if that happens." He mounted the horse and let it choose its own speed away from the Uriah.

"THANK YOU, LORD Kisrah. I am sure that you did your best with the warding—but the old runes are tricky at best, and in the Northlands, they could easily be the work of one of the races that use green magic." The ae'Magi smiled graciously.

Lord Kisrah looked only a little less miserable in his seat in the ae'Magi's study. "I got a look at some of the runes there, and I'll look them up and see what can be done about them. The magician had no trouble with my magic, though. He's more worrisome than the runes."

"I agree, Kisrah," purred the ae'Magi. "I intend to find out just who he is. Can you describe him for me again?"

Lord Kisrah nodded and set aside the warmed ale he'd been drinking. "No more than medium height. His hair was blond, I think, although it could have been light brown. His eyes were either blue or green—the overall effect was so spectacular, it was difficult to pay attention to the details. He couldn't have been more than twenty-four or -five and could have been younger except that he was so powerful. His voice was oddly accented, but he didn't say enough that I could tell much about the accent other than that the Rethian he spoke was not his native tongue."

"There was no way that his hair could have been darker? His eyes golden? No scars?" queried the ae'Magi softly.

Lord Kisrah shook his head. "No. His eyes, maybe. They were some light color. But his hair was light." He yawned abruptly.

The ae'Magi stood and offered his arm for support to the other mage. "I am sorry, I have kept you up talking, and you are almost dropping from exhaustion." He led him to the door and opened it, clapping his hands lightly. Before he clapped a second time, a pretty young serving girl appeared.

"Take Lord Kisrah to the blue room, Rhidan, and see to his comfort." The ae'Magi turned to his guest. "Pray follow the girl—she will attend to your every need. If you want anything, just ask."

Kisrah brightened visibly and wished him a good night.

Alone in his study, the ae'Magi brooded, disliking the thought of yet another magician in his way. Who could it be? He'd been sure that his son was the last mage of any power who stood against him.

Abruptly, he got to his feet; all this worry could do no good. It was too late at night to try to think, and he was too frustrated to sleep. He motioned abruptly to the pale young girl who had sat in her corner unnoticed by Lord Kisrah. Obedient to his gesture, she dropped the clothes she wore and stood naked and submissive before him.

He cupped her chin in one hand and stroked her body gently with the other. "Tonight," he said, "I have something special in mind for you."

TEN

ARALORN WENT BACK TO WORK TAKING CARE OF THE CHILDREN TO GIVE herself something to do since Wolf didn't need her in the library.

Keeping them entertained was harder than it had been before. There was no place for them to run and play, and they were restless with the Uriah just outside. To distract them, Aralorn taught them the letters of the alphabet and how they fit together to form words. She told stories until she was hoarse.

"So Kai bet the whole troop that he could sneak into camp and steal the pot of coffee on the coals with no one seeing him." Seated on a bump in the floor, Aralorn checked to make sure that most of the children were listening. "He and Talor were raised in a Trader Clan, just like Stanis. When he was little, he had learned how to be very quiet and to sit still in shadows so no one could see him.

"That night, their commander doubled the guard on the camp and assigned a special guard just to follow Kai around. Two men watched the coffeepot. But despite all of that, the next morning the pot was gone. The guard who was supposed to be following Kai around had actually been following Talor, who looked enough like his twin to be mistaken for him in the dark." Aralorn smiled at her intent audience. Stories about the twins were always guaranteed attention holders.

"Kai was not only good enough to get the pot, he also painted a white 'X' on the back of every one of the guards without their knowing it."

"I bet Stanis could do that," said Tobin. "He's sneaky." Stanis, with his inability to get lost, was more often to be found running errands than hanging out with people his own age. It gave him even more cachet among his followers.

"Aralorn." Myr put his hand on her shoulder.

He looked a bit pale. "What's wrong?"

"It's Wolf. Stanis ran a message to him in the library for me and came running back a few minutes ago. He says there's something up—I think perhaps you ought to go check."

THE LIBRARY WAS engulfed in shadows when she cautiously peered into it, and it felt warmer than usual. The only light came from the crystals in Wolf's staff, which were glowing a dull orange. Wolf sat in his usual chair, motionless, his face in the shadows. He didn't move when she came in, that and the scorched smell in the library suggested that the scene wasn't as ordinary as it looked.

Using her own magic, Aralorn lit the chamber. One of the bookcases was missing. Thoughtfully, Aralorn wandered over to where it had been and scuffed a toe in the ashes that had taken its place. The bookcase next to her burst into flames and was reduced to the same state before she even felt the heat. She winced at the destruction of the irreplaceable books.

"Wolf," she asked in calculatedly exasperated tones. "Isn't this hard enough without losing your temper?" She turned to look at him. He wore his mask again.

"I have it, Aralorn," he murmured softly. "I have the power to do anything." Another bookcase followed the first two. "Anything."

Her pulse picked up despite her confidence that he'd never hurt her.

"If I didn't have so much power," he said, "I just might be able to do something with it. You see, I found it. I found the spell to remove the ability to use magic from a magician who is misusing his power. I can't use it. I don't have the skill or the control, and the spell uses too much raw power. If I tried it, we'd have another glass desert on our hands." His eyes glittered with the flickering orange light of his staff.

Aralorn went to him and sat on the floor beside him, resting her head against his knees. "If you had less power, there would be no way to take

the ae'Magi at all. You would never have been able to free yourself from
the binding spells that keep all of the other magicians bound to his will.
There would be no one to resist him. Quit tearing yourself into pieces
and winning the battle for the ae'Magi. You are who you are. No better
certainly, but no worse." It was quiet for a long time in the library. Aralorn
let her light die down and sat in the darkness with Wolf. No more bookcases burned in magic fire. When Wolf's hand touched her hair, Aralorn
knew that it would be all right. This time.

ARALORN TROTTED UP the tunnels at a steady pace, walking now and
again when she ran out of breath—which she felt was far too often. Slowly,
though, her strength was coming back, and she had to stop less frequently
than she had the day before. Morning and night for the past four days,
she had run the tunnels from the library to the entrance, trying to rebuild
the conditioning that she'd lost. Also, not incidentally, building up her
understanding of how to get from one place to another.

Her path was free of people for the most part. The library was quite
a distance from the main caves, and most of the campers respected Wolf's
claims that the Old Man of the Mountain wanted to keep them out of
the tunnels. Aralorn was of the opinion that Wolf didn't want to spend
his time searching for lost wanderers because she'd seen no sign that the
Old Man objected to anyone's presence. Although the path to the library
was carefully marked out and considered part of the occupied caves, in
practice it was seldom that anyone besides Aralorn, Wolf, or Stanis went
there.

Wolf said that they were waiting for the wrath of the Old Man to fall
on them. Myr said that it was Wolf, not the Old Man, that they were
frightened of—Myr was probably right.

Only Oras had ignored the ban on the inner caves. Twice. The first
time Myr brought him back. The second time Wolf went after him. Wolf
wouldn't tell Aralorn what he'd done, and Oras didn't volunteer the information, but he'd come back white-faced and had been remarkably subdued ever since.

As she came to the outer caves, Aralorn slowed to a walk. There were too many people around for her to dodge at a faster speed. When she started down the path that led to the entrance, the first thing that she noticed was the sound of her own footsteps. It took her a minute to realize that the reason she could hear them was because the Uriah weren't howling.

Sure enough, when she reached the entrance, there was no sign of the Uriah. The bonfire Myr had ordered laid near the entrance was still unlit.

She stepped out slowly, moving cautiously in case there were any lying in wait. After so many days in the caves, the sunlight nearly blinded her. The air smelled fresh and pure, without the distinctive odor that accompanied Uriah. Only the smell of burnt grass and other things marred the fragrance of the nearby pine.

It looked as if a ball of fire had been spewed from the cave's mouth. A wide blackened path in the grass and soil began from the entrance and traveled in a straight line a fair distance before disappearing. Within the blackened area were ten or fifteen bodies of Uriah, burnt down to the bone. There were some that were less singed, but something had chewed on them.

Aralorn followed the blackened path up the mountain and found that the trail abruptly stopped on a wide, flat area. She started back and was several lengths down the slope when she realized that she might be thinking backward. What if the fireball hadn't come *from* the cave but had been launched *at* it? Muttering to herself, she trotted back to where the trail stopped.

Tracking wasn't her specialty, but it didn't take her long to find what she sought. When she was looking for them, they were hard to miss—very large, reptilian footprints with marks beside them that could be trailing wings. Just like the ones she'd seen the day she'd been taken by the Uriah.

"Well, Myr," she said thoughtfully, going back to examine one of the half-eaten corpses. She hadn't looked too closely before, assuming that the Uriah had just been practicing their usual cannibalism. Upon closer examination, she could tell that something much bigger than a Uriah had been feeding. "I think I know what dragons eat when there aren't any virgins chained to rocks."

"WELL, THEN," SAID Myr in dry tones after Aralorn related her discovery. The main cave was almost empty. Myr had sent out a party to look for the hunters who'd been missing since just before the Uriah had come, and a second group out to find provisions. He'd sent a few of the remaining people to keep watches from the best lookout stations.

He rubbed his eyes and looked at her. "So what now? We've exchanged the Uriah for a dragon. The question that begs is, of course, is this a good thing?"

"The dragon's quieter and smells better." Aralorn leaned against the cave wall and watched Myr pace.

"At least we knew *something* about the Uriah," Myr complained. "A dragon. There aren't supposed to *be* any more dragons." He broke off when the sounds of ragged cheers echoed into the cave, followed by the missing hunting party and the searchers—all of them looking cold and tired.

When the welcoming was done, Farsi, who'd led the party, told their tale. "We came upon a herd of mountain sheep and got two so we headed back. About halfway here we stumbled upon some tracks, as if an army were wandering around. We followed the trail, and pretty soon we could smell 'em and knew that they were Uriah. Since their path was the same one we were on, it was obvious that the things were coming here.

"Figuring that we were too late to make much difference, we worked our way up the side of the mountain until we could see the Uriah. We couldn't see the cave, but the way they were swarming around showed that you must have found a way to keep them out. We decided that there was nothing we could do but wait. Our vantage point was far enough away that the chance of the Uriah seeing us wasn't considerable."

Farsi cleared his throat. "Late last night—just after the moon had set—I heard a cry like a swan makes, only deeper. I was on watch, and it wasn't loud enough to wake anyone else up. Something big flew over us, but I couldn't quite see it. Afterward, I saw a flash of golden fire down here and heard the Uriah step up their noise. Then it quieted down. I woke up a couple others, and we finally decided that we'd best wait until we had light to see what had happened." He frowned, evidently still unhappy with that decision. "It was just that whatever it was—from the quiet that followed—it had already happened."

Myr nodded at him. "Sensible and smart to wait until you could see, especially with Uriah running around."

Farsi looked like someone had pulled a weight off his shoulders. "This morning, it looked like the Uriah had left, so we started home. The reason it took us so long to get here is that there are still a lot of Uriah scattered about. We were dodging two parties of the things, when we almost ran into a third. It's a good thing that they smell so bad, or we wouldn't have made it back at all."

OVER THE NEXT few days it became obvious that if the Uriah had been held in concert by the will of the ae'Magi, that was no longer true. It didn't make them any less dangerous individually, but it did make it possible to kill them in small groups.

Wolf, when appealed to, produced a detailed map of the area on sheepskin, which was hung on a wall of the central chamber. Aralorn suspected he'd made it himself, either with magic or by hand, because it was accurate, with very specific landmarks. At Myr's command, any sightings of Uriah were recorded on the map, giving them a rough idea where the things were.

Each group of hunters had a copy of the map, and if they ran into a group of Uriah, they would lead them to one of the traps Myr had placed in strategic places. The Uriah were slowed enough by the cold of the deepening fall that the humans could outrun them most of the time, especially since they were careful to go out only when it was coldest.

Haris suggested an adaptation of a traditional castle defense and created a tar trap that was one of the most effective of their traps. The easiest way to kill a Uriah was with fire, so pots of tar were hung here and there, kept warm by magic. Ropes were carefully rigged so that they would not easily be tripped by wild animals. When they were pulled, the pots tipped over, and the motion triggered a secondary spell—something Haris cooked up—that set the tar on fire—dousing the Uriah with flaming tar. The spells on the traps were simple enough that everybody, except for Myr, could do them after a little coaching from Wolf and Haris.

Aralorn watched the small group of refugees become a close-knit community, the grumblers fewer. Every evening, they would all sit down and talk. Complaints and suggestions were heard and decided upon by Myr. Looking at the scruffy bunch of peasants (the nobles, by that time, blended right in with the rest) consulting with their equally scruffy king, Aralorn compared it with the Rethian Grand Council that met once a year, and she hid a grin at the contrast.

Having an enemy they could fight—and defeat—put heart in them all. Even Aralorn, who understood that the Uriah were in truth a minor annoyance. Their real enemy, the ae'Magi, was out there somewhere—and he knew where they were. She suspected he was biding his time. The snow wasn't accumulating yet, but it had become common to see a white coat on the dirt most mornings. A smart general didn't attack the Northlands in the heart of winter but waited for spring.

Only Wolf was excluded from the camaraderie, by his own choice. He made them nervous, with his macabre voice and silver mask. Once he saw that they were intimidated by him, he went out of his way to make them more so. Sleeping somewhere deep in the caverns and spending most of his waking time in the library, he was seldom with the main body of the camp. Usually, he attended the nightly sessions with everyone else, but he kept his own counsel in the shadows of the caves' recesses unless Myr asked him a question directly.

Most mornings Aralorn spent entertaining the children. Occasionally, she went out with a hunting party—or alone to exercise Sheen and check the traps. The afternoons she spent in the library with Wolf, keeping him company and reading as many books as she could.

The nights she spent in the library as well, for she was still having nightmares and didn't want to wake the whole camp. Night after night she woke up screaming, sometimes seeing Talor's face, alive with all that made him Talor, but consumed with a hunger that was inhuman and wholly Uriah. Other times, it was the ae'Magi's face that she saw, a face that changed from father's to son's.

Wolf didn't know about her nightmares, as far as she knew. She had no idea where he was sleeping, but it wasn't the library.

Late in the afternoons, Myr usually joined them, talking quietly with Aralorn while Wolf read through books on rabbit breeding, castle building, and three hundred ways to cook a hedgehog.

After discovering that the spell he'd been looking for wouldn't work for him, Wolf had continued to look through the old mage's books in the hopes of discovering a way to manage the spell more crudely. Most spells, he'd told Aralorn, were refined so they required less power. He had all the power he needed, and an earlier version might work for him. If he could find it.

His temper was biting, and he didn't rein it in for Myr, nor after the first few visits did he bother with his mask. Myr answered Wolf's sarcasm with cool control—and sometimes a hidden grin of appreciation. Aralorn rather thought that Wolf's lack of common courtesy was why Myr liked to visit the library. Here he was a fellow conspirator rather than the King of Reth.

"WHAT'S HE DOING?" asked Myr, setting his torch to sputter on the stone floor, where, with nothing to burn, it would eventually go out.

Instead of reading, Wolf had cleared the table of everything except a collection of clay pots filled with a variety of powders. When Aralorn had gotten there, Wolf had already been grinding various leaves in a mortar.

She waved a lazy hand at Myr, but didn't take her attention off what Wolf was doing. "He thinks he's found a way to manage the spell. We're going to try it outside when he's finished. No telling what would happen if he worked it in here with all of the grimoires, especially since we don't know the range of effect."

She caught Myr's arm when he would have approached the table closer. "He doesn't want us any closer than this," she said.

They both watched, fascinated, though neither she nor Myr could work this kind of magic or probably even understand half of what was going on. Wolf took a small vial from the leather pack on the table. Opening it, he poured a milky liquid into the gray powder mixture, which became red mush and gave off a poof of noxious fumes. He donned his mask and cloak, then, ignoring his audience, he put a lid on the pot and took it and an opaque bottle and strode toward an exit route that would take them directly outside rather than through the lived-in areas, leaving Aralorn and Myr to trail behind.

"Won't the spell be affected by whatever it is that restricts human magic in the Northlands?" asked Myr in a whisper to Aralorn, but it was Wolf who answered.

"No," he said. "It is a very simple spell—its complexity has to do with power management. It should work fine here."

He led them to the old camp in the valley, where they were unlikely to have anyone interrupt them. Aralorn found herself holding the containers while, at Wolf's direction, Myr paced off circles, each bigger than the last until the dirt looked like an archery target. The ground was muddy with last night's melted snowfall and held the marks of Myr's feet well.

Wolf disappeared into the underbrush and reappeared, holding a handful of small stones. He set several of them in each ring Myr had shuffled off, though maybe "set" was the wrong word, because they floated about knee high above the ground.

"This shouldn't be a particularly powerful spell," Wolf said. "If I can get it to work, it doesn't need to be. If he doesn't know that it's coming, then he won't know to block it. All that I need it to do is to throw him off-balance for long enough to turn our battle from magic to more mundane means. Aralorn, stand behind me. It won't hurt Myr, but I don't know what this would do to a shapeshifter."

"If I'm behind you, I can't see what's going on," Aralorn complained. "How about if I stand over by the old fire pit?"

It was well off to the side, a dozen paces away from the target range that Myr had drawn out.

"Fine," he said. "This should be a straight, line-of-sight spell, with a limited range."

He sat on the cold ground in the middle of the innermost circle.

"How old is the ae'Magi?" asked Aralorn from the fire pit.

Wolf shrugged gracefully and gave her a half smile. "You aren't going to kill the ae'Magi the way that Iveress killed his master. His master was ill and near death, kept alive only by magic. As far as I know, the ae'Magi is nowhere near death, unfortunate as that may be—at least not from disease."

"What are our chances if the spell works as it is supposed to?" asked Myr. "Will you be able to kill him? I've seen him fight."

Wolf shrugged. "If the spell takes him by surprise, then the odds are about even. I used to spar with him often, and sometimes I beat him, sometimes not. This spell gives us a chance, but that's all it does. If he recognizes the spell, it is easy enough to counter. That would leave us with only magic."

He looked at Aralorn. "I've learned some things about what I can do that he doesn't know, but even so, he would easily best me that way. Without magic, at least we stand a chance of killing him. Perhaps." No one, not even Aralorn, could have told how he felt about it from his voice.

Aralorn and Myr watched as he emptied the contents of the bottle into the pot. He counted to ten, then poured the mixture onto the ground in front of him, where it gathered into a glowing pool of violet patterned with inky swirls. Dipping a finger into the pool, he used the liquid to draw several symbols in the air. Compliantly, the purple substance hung in the air as if on an invisible wall. Wolf repeated the procedure with his left hand.

He picked up the pool in both hands. It swayed and oozed, never quite escaping the confines of his hands. He held it up in front of his face, then blew on it gently.

Pain hit Aralorn hard enough to knock her to her knees. She fought to maintain consciousness for a moment, but she never felt herself hit the ground.

WHEN SHE RECOVERED, she felt the hard strength of Wolf's thigh underneath her ear.

"I don't know," said Wolf, sounding vicious.

She blinked cautiously, and when her head didn't fall off, she pushed herself up.

"Fine," she told Wolf. "I'm fine. My fault."

Sitting up, she could see what had happened. The spell was directional all right, but mostly in a forward and backward kind of direction rather than the direction of a loosed arrow. It had knocked down the floating stones in a wide "V" pattern, with Wolf at the apex. The stones directly to either side of where he'd been sitting were still floating, but every stone more than two feet in front of him was on the ground.

She had been sitting on the edge of the path of the spell, but apparently the fire pit hadn't been far enough away.

"How long was I out?" she asked, noticing that her ears were buzzing and her balance was off. Even sitting flat on the ground, her upper body wanted to sway.

She was propelled down again with a none-too-gentle hand, as Wolf answered, "Not very."

"How do you feel?" asked Myr, concern evident in his voice.

"Like the entire mercenary army of Sianim just got through marching over my head." She closed her eyes and let herself enjoy their concern. She loved sympathy.

"Not too bad, then," said Myr with evident relief.

"Not horrible, but not fun." Aralorn decided that her headache had subsided enough she could open her eyes again.

"You need to try some magic," Wolf said grimly.

She would have whined at him, but the hand on her shoulder was shaking a little. For Wolf's sake, she called a simple light to her hand, then dismissed it.

"Wolf," asked Myr, "do you think that the ae'Magi will let you complete the spell? It seemed to take a lot of preparation."

"I won't need to," answered Wolf, relaxing against the wall of Haris's former kitchen. His thumb ran over her collarbone, then stilled. "With a spell this simple, it'll be easy enough to re-create the effect."

His relief was more obvious in the amount of words that he was using to explain himself to Myr. "Once I see the pattern to push the magic into," he said, "I don't need the physical parts of the casting anymore. It really is something only a beginning magic-user would have created. Take all of the most common spell components mixed together, add the first five symbols learned in magic, and blow—poof: instant spell. What is really amazing is that it didn't blow up in the apprentice's face. It came uncomfortably close to doing that with me." He tapped Aralorn's nose in emphasis. "Next time I tell you to get behind me, get behind me."

"What's next?" asked Myr.

Wolf took off his mask wearily. In the bright light of the winter sun, Aralorn noticed the strain he'd been under written into the fine lines and dark shadows beneath his golden ambient eyes. "What else? I storm the castle of the ae'Magi and challenge him to a duel. Whereupon he engages me in best Aralorn-story-time fashion. Then either I win, and go down in history as the cruel villain who destroyed the good wizard, his father. Or he wins." Wolf's voice was coolly ironic.

"If he wins, what happens?" Aralorn spoke from her prone position and showed no intention of moving. "I mean, what is he trying to do? Why does he want everyone to love him?"

While he answered, Wolf played with a strand of hair that had worked its way out of her braid. "You asked me about that once before. I think I know the answer now."

Myr sat down beside Wolf. "What? Power?"

"I thought that might be it at first," Wolf said. "Maybe that was even the correct answer at one time. When I was his apprentice, that seemed to be it. He could link with me and use the power that I gathered for his own spells, much, I believe, in the same manner that he now uses the magic released by the deaths of the children he kills. But there was an incident that scared him." For Myr's benefit, Wolf briefly explained his destruction of the tower.

Myr whistled. "That was you? I'd heard a story about that, I've forgotten who told me. They said that the tower looked like a candle that someone forgot to blow out. The stone blocks looked like they melted."

Wolf nodded. "He started to try using control spells on me, after that. I left before he had much success. But what surprised me was that he continued to try and get me back under his control. He's been looking for me for a long time."

He looked down at Aralorn. "If all he wanted was to kill me, he could have done that easily enough. Or at least come close. If it were only my power he wanted, then he's wasted a lot more of it trying to find me than he could ever get from me. I am more powerful than most magicians, but Lord Kisrah is very strong as well, and the ae'Magi never attempted to tap into his magic. The magic that he gets from one of the children he kills is also probably more than he could get from me because my defenses are stronger."

"Revenge, then?" suggested Myr. "Because he thought that he had you under his control and you escaped?"

"So I thought," answered Wolf, "but then Aralorn told me that she thought that I was half shapeshifter and that some of the magic that I am using is green magic."

Myr started. "Are you? That's why you have so little trouble taking the shape of a wolf. I thought it was unusual."

Wolf nodded. "Most of the magic that I use is human magic. Since I found out that I could use it, I've been trying to work with the green magic. It is bound by much stronger rules than what I'm used to; so, except for shapeshifting, I find it much harder to work. Even so, it might give me an edge over the ae'Magi."

Wolf paused, then continued, "The question still remains, what does the ae'Magi want from me? He is a Darranian, and the animalism of having sex with a shapeshifter might appeal to him, but I couldn't conceive that he would raise the resultant offspring as his own. Not until I realized that it might be the green magic that he wanted. Green magic that I didn't use until I left his control."

"But why green magic?" asked Myr. "I can't imagine that he values shapeshifting that highly."

"Healing," said Aralorn softly—for the sake of her throbbing heart. Because the idea that Wolf had been leading them toward was terrifying.

Wolf nodded. "Exactly. As you told me, Aralorn, a shapeshifter can heal himself until he is virtually immortal. What I believe the ae'Magi hopes to do is to reestablish the link that he had with me and use green magic to give himself immortality. Until then, he can use standard magic to defeat the problems of aging, but that doesn't make him young."

"No point in ruling the world unless you have time to do it in," offered Myr.

"Yes," agreed Wolf. "There was another clue as well. Neither of you was particularly well acquainted with the Uriah as they were a few years ago. I was in the ae'Magi's castle when he created the first of his, using his own spell. The Uriah that I knew then were barely able to function. They could not even understand speech as well as a dog can. Now, from what Aralorn says, he has some that even retain the memories of the person that they once were."

"The Uriah in the swamplands were created during the Wizard Wars; they are close to being immortal," commented Aralorn.

Wolf nodded. "They don't die unless they are killed. If he could get them just a bit more pretty, he'd probably turn himself into one."

Soberly, Myr said, "I don't think that he ever intended to turn himself into a Uriah. I've known him for a long time, too. There is no way he would turn himself into something that by its very nature is a slave to its need for food—pretty or not. If a Uriah retains most of its personality, then it is possible that it also retains its ability to work magic. What if he wants to kill you, Wolf, and turn you into one of his Uriah, obedient to his command, but just as powerful as you have always been?"

"Oh, isn't that a lovely thought," said Aralorn.

Blank-faced, Wolf considered Myr's comment. "I hadn't thought of that. I'll have to make sure that it doesn't happen, hmm?"

There was a heavy silence, then Aralorn said in a bright tone, "Speaking of Uriah, do you realize what a mess we are going to have to clean up when the ae'Magi is dead and we have several hundred masterless Uriah roaming the countryside? Sianim is going to be making good money off this."

WOLF WORKED AT the spell for days, until he could direct it better, but the force of the spell varied widely. Wolf muttered and finally even went back to mixing the powders, but the spell still wouldn't stabilize. He told Aralorn he needed to try a few different herbs that might refine the reaction. He didn't have all that he needed, so he left to do some trading in the south.

THE SUN WAS drifting toward evening, turning the peaks of the mountains red. Aralorn shifted contentedly on her rock near the cave entrance. Several days ago someone found a huge patch of berries, and the whole camp had spent the better part of two days harvesting the find. Haris had been adding them into everything and today had managed to cook several pies. Given that the only thing that he had to cook on was a grate over a fire, it was probable that he'd used magic to do it, but no one was complaining.

Licking her fingers clean of the last of the sweet stuff, Aralorn ran an idle gaze up the cliff face and caught something out of the corner of her eye. It was a shadow in the evening sky that was gone almost as soon as she saw it. She got to her feet and backed away from the cliff, trying to figure out just what it was that she saw, calling out an alarm as she did so.

The four or five people who were out milling about doing various chores started for the entrance at a run. Stanis and Tobin were coming up the trail to the valley with a donkey cart laden with firewood. Although they heard the alert, too, they weren't able to increase their pace much because of the donkey, and they weren't about to abandon the results of their labors.

Aralorn distractedly glanced at them, then looked back at the cliff, just in time to see the dragon launch itself. If she hadn't caught the moment of launch, she probably wouldn't have noticed it because it used magic to change the color of its scales until it blended into the evening sky. Aralorn headed for Stanis and Tobin as fast as she could. Seeing her, they abandoned the donkey and began running themselves. As she neared them, the shadow on the ground told her that the dragon was just overhead. She knocked both boys down in a wrestler's tackle and felt the razor-sharp claws run almost gently across her back.

The dragon gave a hiss that could have been either disappointment or amusement, and settled for the donkey, which it killed with a casual swipe of its tail. As it ate, it watched idly as Aralorn drove the two boys into the cave and stood guard at the entrance.

Aralorn met its gaze and knew that her sword was pitifully inadequate for the task, even had she been a better swordswoman. She had some hope that the runes that had kept the Uriah at bay would do the same to the dragon, but dragons were supposed to be creatures of magic and fire.

She heard the sounds of running footsteps behind her, then Myr's exclamation when he saw the dragon. He drew his grandfather's sword and held it in readiness. Aralorn noted with a touch of amusement that his larger sword looked to be a much more potent barrier than her own.

"How big do you think that thing is?" asked Myr in a whisper.

"Not as big as it looked when it was over top of me, but big enough that I don't want to fight it," murmured Aralorn in reply.

The dragon paused in its eating to look over at them and smile, quite an impressive sight—easily as intimidating as Wolf's.

Myr stiffened. "It understands us."

Aralorn nodded reluctantly. "Well, if you have to die, I guess a dragon is an impressive way to go; maybe even worth a song or two. Just think, we are the first people to see a dragon in generations."

"It is beautiful," said Myr. As if in approval of his comment, a ripple of purple traveled through the blue of the dragon's scales.

"Watch that color shift," said Aralorn. "Magic, I think. If it wants to, it can be nearly invisible. Would make it harder to fight."

"It makes you wonder why there aren't more dragons, doesn't it," commented Myr.

Finished with the donkey, the dragon rose and stretched. No longer completely blue, highlights of various colors danced in its scales. Only its teeth and the claws on its feet and the edges of its wings were an unchanging black. When it was done, it started almost casually toward the cave entrance.

Myr stepped out from the meager protection of the entrance into the fading light, and Aralorn followed his lead. Something about Myr appeared to catch the dragon's interest: It stopped and whipped its long, swanlike neck straight, shooting the elegant head forward. Brilliant, gemlike eyes glittered green, then gold. Without warning, it opened its mouth and spat flame at Myr with an aim so exact that Aralorn wasn't even singed although she stood near enough to Myr to reach out and touch him.

Myr, being immune to magic, was untouched (although the same could not be said about his clothes). The hand that held his sword was steady, though his grip was tighter than it needed to be. He was no coward, this King of Reth. Aralorn smiled in grim approval.

The dragon drew its head back, and said, in Rethian that Aralorn felt as much as heard, "Dragon-blessed, this is far from your court. Why do you disturb me here?"

Myr, clothed in little more than the tattered remnants of cloth and leather, somehow managed to look as regal and dignified as the dragon did. "My apologies if we are troubling you. Our quarrel is not with you."

The dragon made an amused sound. "I hardly thought that it was, princeling."

"King," said Aralorn, deciding that the contempt that the dragon was exhibiting could get dangerous.

"What?" said the dragon, its tone softening in a manner designed to send chills up weaker spines.

"He is King of Reth and no princeling." Aralorn kept her voice even and met the dragon's look.

It turned back to Myr, and said in an amused tone, "Apologies, lord King. It seems I have given offense."

Myr inclined his head. "Accepted, dragon. I believe we owe you thanks for driving away the Uriah, sent by my enemy."

The dragon raised its head with a hiss, and its eyes acquired crimson tones. "Your enemy is the ae'Magi?"

"Yes," answered Myr with a wariness Aralorn shared.

The dragon stood silently, obviously thinking, then it said, "The debt dragonkind owes your blood is old and weak, even by dragon standards. Long and long ago, a human saved an egg that held a queen, a feat for which we were most grateful, as we were few even then. For this he and his blood were blessed that magic hold no terrors for them. For this deed of the past, I would have left you and your party alone.

"Several hundred years ago, after the manner of my kind, I chose a cave to sleep—waiting for the coming of my mate. I chose a cave deep under the ae'Magi's castle, where I was unlikely to be discovered. Dragons are magical in a way that no other creature is. We live and breathe magic, and without it, we cannot exist.

"I was awakened by savage pain that drove me out of my cave and into the Northlands. The ae'Magi is twisting magic, binding it to him until there will be nothing left but that which is twisted and dark with the souls of the dead. The castle of the ae'Magi has protections that I cannot cross, and the power that he has over magic is such that if I were to attack him, it is possible that he could control me. That is a risk I cannot take. Except for the egg that lies hidden from all, I am the last of my kind. If I die, there will be no more dragons." It stretched its wings restlessly.

"King," it said finally, "your sword is new, but the hilt is older than your kingdom, and token of our pledge to your line. If ever I can aid you, without directly confronting the ae'Magi, plunge the sword into the soil, run your hands over the ruby eyes of the dragon on the hilt, and say my name."

Aralorn heard nothing but the rushing of the wind as the dragon spoke its name for Myr. Then, in the deepening light of the evening, it reared back on its hind legs and fanned its wings, changing its color to an orange-gold that gave off its own light. Soundlessly, it took flight, disappearing long before it should have been out of sight.

"Beautiful, isn't he?" Wolf's familiar hoarse voice emanated from somewhere behind and between Aralorn and Myr. It comforted Aralorn that Myr jumped, too.

THE HERBS THAT Wolf brought back did work better. Once he got the spell just as he wanted it, he began working it without the props until he could direct it effortlessly. When he could drop the ensorcelled rocks in any pattern he chose, he spoke to Myr over dinner.

"I have what I need to face the ae'Magi. I will leave tomorrow for his castle."

"You aren't going alone," said Myr. "This is my battle as well. He killed my parents to further his plans. You will need someone at your back."

Wolf shook his head. "You are too valuable to your people to risk yourself in such a way. If you are killed, then there is no one to rule Reth. If I am killed, your immunity to magic may be the only weapon left against the ae'Magi."

"Wolf's right," agreed Aralorn, "but so is Myr. Wolf, the ae'Magi is not the only thing that you will have to face. He has quite an assortment of pets in the Uriah. They will tire you out before you even reach the ae'Magi."

Wolf frowned at her. "I know how to avoid most of the monsters. The ae'Magi will see that none of them kill me. Even if he wants me dead, he wants to kill me himself. If there is someone else with me that I have to worry about and guard, they will be more of a liability than an asset. I'll leave at first light." He turned on one heel and walked away, leaving the remnants of his dinner behind—without giving anyone a chance to argue further.

Aralorn finished her roll thoughtfully. If he thought she'd give up so easily, he hadn't been paying attention.

THAT NIGHT, AS Aralorn half dozed on the library couch—she couldn't sleep without the risk of missing Wolf—she heard an unfamiliar woman's voice speaking from somewhere nearby.

"I'm worried," the stranger said. "There are too many things that can go wrong with what they're planning. I wish that they'd paid attention."

"I did what I could." Aralorn recognized the voice of the Old Man. He sounded a little petulant.

"It is up to them." The woman's soft voice soothed agreeably. "She's healed him enough that he might be able to carry it off. Can't you give them a clearer hint, though?"

"No. It isn't our concern. As long as he leaves you alone, I don't care what the ae'Magi does." There was something off about his voice; he sounded more like a child than an adult.

"Of course you do, dear heart." The woman might have been shaking a finger at him from the tone of her voice. "Who was it that brought that young wolf to shelter here? Who gathered all of the people to hide from the human Archmage's wrath? It wasn't I."

"I've interfered too much." The old shapeshifter's voice sounded completely rational for the moment. "My time is past. I should have died with you, Lys. It is not right to be a ghost and not be dead. If I tell them what to do, it might cause more harm than good. I fear that I have let you talk me into too much." There was a pause, then he said in a resigned tone, "Ah well, once more, then. She's listening, isn't she?"

"You know me too well, love," she said. "Yes."

The Old Man's next words were so close to Aralorn's ear that she could feel his breath. "Then daughter of my brother's line, you must go with him to the ae'Magi's castle and take what is yours with you." Aralorn felt a hand on her cheek, then she heard the rush of air that signaled the shapeshifter's exit.

Once they'd left her, she sat up and waved on the lights. "Hearing voices now?" she said. "It is sad to say, Aralorn, but you have definitely lost whatever touch of sanity you once had. That bodes well for the coming adventure though—only an insane person would go to the ae'Magi's castle three times. Once was enough, twice was too many, but my little voices tell me that I'm going to make it three."

She shook her head in mock disgust. Knowing that she wasn't going to get any more sleep, she got up, strapped on her knives, and began stretching. By the time she had warmed up, she knew how she was going to arrange to accompany Wolf.

Before first light hit the mountainside, she snuck out on four feet, following the tracking spell she'd set into the bottom of his left boot a couple of weeks past. It led her to a small cave Wolf occupied. She had never been in it and was distracted from her intended goal by the opportunity to see a different side to her mysterious magician. He kept a small magelight glowing to keep the room from the total darkness that was natural to the cave. Wolf himself was lying with his back to her on a cot against the far end of the room.

Although it was spartan and immaculate, she could tell by the smell that Wolf had occupied it for a long time—longer than the few months Myr had been hiding in the Northlands. Being a mouse had its advantages.

Fascinated, she wandered around, noticing that for all of its surface plainness, there were touches that showed an appreciation of beauty in small things: A small knob of rock reaching up from the floor was polished to a high gloss. A large clear glass vessel was placed in a secure nook; the tiny fractures that spiderwebbed the glass glittered even in the dim light.

Wolf moved restlessly on the bed. Aralorn waited to make sure that he was still sleeping before she crept into the pack that lay out of place near the entrance, trusting that its position signified that it was something he was going to take with him.

She made a place for herself among the various items and sat very still. She didn't have to wait long. Although he had announced that he would leave at first light, she wasn't at all surprised that he was leaving well before that. It had been obvious that neither she nor Myr had been particularly happy with his decision to go and face the ae'Magi alone.

To her relief, he swung the pack up and carried it with him when he departed. She hadn't quite figured out what she would have done if he'd left it.

She felt the roar of dizziness that signaled the magical leap from one place to another. When the sensation passed, she scrambled for a secure position in which the shuffling contents, which seemed to consist of nothing but hard angular objects, were not as likely to squish her. Even in human form, it seemed that Wolf's favorite gait was a ground-eating run.

Apparently he had arrived at a point several miles from the castle, as he ran for a long time. Battered and bruised, Aralorn was beginning to wish she'd figured out a better way to accompany him.

WHEN WOLF OPENED the pack, the first thing that he saw was a bedraggled gray mouse, who looked at him with reproachful eyes, and said, "Would it have hurt to pack something soft, like a shirt or something?"

He should have been surprised. Or angry. He found himself, instead, absurdly grateful.

He picked her up out of the bag and held her at eye level in the palm of his hand. "When one comes along without being invited, one cannot complain about the accommodations."

"Oh dear," said the mouse, in a shocked voice. "I hope I am not intruding."

He took off the silver mask, and sat cross-legged on the ground—careful not to knock her off her perch on the palm of his hand. "I don't suppose that you would go back, would you? I trust it has occurred to you that it would be very easy for the ae'Magi to use you against me."

She ran up his arm and poised for an instant on his shoulder.

"Yes," she replied, cleaning her whiskers, "but it also occurred to me that my wolf was going off alone to kill his father. Granted that he is not the typical father, but—I don't think this is as easy for you as you'd like everyone to believe."

She hesitated for a minute before she continued. "I know how he is. How he can twist things until black seems white. His power is frightening, but it is not as dangerous as his ability to manipulate thoughts with words. I was only there for a short time; you were raised by him. It doesn't seem to me that exposure would make you immune to everyone; the opposite, I think. Perhaps having someone with you might make it easier."

Wolf was still. He didn't want to do this alone, but he wanted even less to have her hurt—or worse. Aralorn abruptly jumped to the ground.

"I couldn't have lived with myself if something happened to you and I was not with you." She shrugged and twitched her whiskers. "Besides, why should you have all the fun? He will see only a mouse, if he looks."

He wanted to send her away, not just for her safety, but because he didn't want her to know what he'd been before, even though he'd done his best to tell her himself. The feelings that she brought out in him were so painful and confusing. It was easier when he had felt nothing, no pain—no guilt. No desire.

His father had taught him how to be that way. When Wolf had understood that he was becoming the monster his father wanted, it had driven him to escape. It was easier when he had cared for nothing, easier when he'd been his father's pet mage. Much easier.

The desire that he felt to return to what he had left behind terrified him. No one who hadn't been raised there would understand the addiction of his father's corruption. Aralorn was right. He needed her to keep him from returning to his old ways, becoming his father's tool once more. The knowledge that she was watching might be enough to strengthen him.

"Stay," was all that he said.

Once he'd made his decision, he ignored her. Kneeling, he emptied the contents of the backpack, a motley collection of jars, which he organized in an overtly random fashion. He stripped himself of his clothes and began a ritual of purification, using the water from a nearby stream.

Aralorn watched for a while, but when he started to meditate, she went for a scurry—mice seldom walk. Once out of sight, where she wouldn't pull his concentration back to her, she shifted into her own form.

She stopped when she had a good view of the castle. It was funny how she always pictured it as black on the outside, the way it had appeared both times she left it. In the sunlight it sparkled a pearly gray, almost white. She could almost visualize the noble knight riding out to face the evil dragon. She hoped in this story the dragon (accompanied by his faithful mouse) would defeat the knight.

She clenched her fingers in the bark of the tree she stood next to and turned her cheek against the rough texture, closing her eyes against the very real possibility that this story would turn out like all the rest—the knight living happily ever after and the dragon slain.

When the shadows lengthened into dusk, Aralorn—once again the mouse—snuck back to where Wolf sat with closed eyes, the last light resting on his clean-shaven unblemished face with loving affection. The sight of his scarless face momentarily distracted her from his nudity.

Aralorn fought the chill that crept over her, knowing that if he looked just then, his all-too-discerning eyes would see her anxiety. It was unsettling to be in love with someone who looked like the face in her nightmares.

Ah well, as her stepmother would have said, at least he was handsome. And his face wasn't the only beautiful thing about him.

She leapt blithely onto his leg and ascended quickly to his bare shoulder, feeling a slight malicious pleasure when he jerked in surprise. When he turned to glare at her, she kissed him on the nose, then began to clean her forepaws with industry. With a sound that might have been a laugh, he ran a finger lightly up her back, rubbing her fur the wrong way. She bit him—but not too hard.

He smoothed her hair and set her down on the ground so that he could regain his clothing. She noticed that it wasn't the same outfit he'd taken off. It wasn't like anything that she'd ever seen him wear. The main color was still black, but it was finely embroidered with silver thread. The shirt was gathered and puffed, hanging down well over his thighs, which was just as well, because the pants were indecently tight, from mouse height anyway. She could see the faint flickering of magic in the fabric and assumed that the clothes he wore were the magician equivalent of armor.

When he was dressed, he put her back on his shoulder and strode out of the clearing like a man who was at last within reach of attaining a much-coveted goal. He talked to her while he walked.

"I thought of confronting him in the castle itself, but it has been the center of so much magic that I really don't know how this spell would affect it. I suspect that at least some of the construction of the older parts of the building was done purely by magic. Without magic, it could collapse on top of us. I don't know about you, but I thought it might be interesting to survive long enough to find out just what the ae'Magi's loyal followers will do to his murderers. That is, if we manage to make it that far."

"I'd forgotten that aspect of it," answered Aralorn in the squeaky-soft voice that was the best her mouse form could manage. "Will his spells still be in effect when he dies?"

"Probably not, but people will still remember how they felt. We will remain the villains of this story." Wolf leapt easily over a small brook.

"Oh good!" she exclaimed, holding on tightly with her forepaws. "I've always wanted to be a villain."

"I am happy to please my lady mouse."

"Uh, Wolf?" she asked.

"Umm?"

"If we're not going to the castle, where are we going?"

"Well," he said, sliding down a steep section of his self-determined path, "when I lived in the castle, he had a habit of going out to meditate every night. He didn't like to do it in the castle because he said that there were too many conflicting auras—too many people steeped in magic had lived and died there in the past thousand years or so. There is a spot just south of the moat that he used to like to use. If he doesn't do it tonight, he probably will tomorrow."

Aralorn sat quietly, thinking of all the things she'd never asked him, might never get a chance to ask. "Wolf?"

"Yes?"

"Has your voice always been the way it is?"

"No." She thought that was all of the answer that she was going to get until he added, "When I woke up after melting the better part of the tower"—he pointed to one of the graceful spires that arched into the evening sky—"I found that I'd screamed so loud that I damaged my voice. It is very useful when I want to intimidate someone."

"Wolf," said Aralorn, setting a paw on his ear since they were on relatively smooth ground, "not to belabor the obvious, but your voice isn't what intimidates people. It could be the possibility that you might immolate anyone who bothers you."

"Do you think that might be it?" he inquired with mock interest. "I had wondered. It has been a while since I immolated anyone, after all."

She laughed and looked at the castle as it rose black against the lighter color of the sky. She had the funny feeling that it was watching them. She knew that it wasn't so, but she was grateful that she was a mouse all the same, and even more grateful that she was a mouse on Wolf's shoulders. She leaned lightly against his neck.

She knew that they were near the place Wolf had spoken of from the tension in the muscles she balanced on. A stray wind brought the smell of the moat to cut through the smell of green things growing. It almost disguised another scent that touched her nose.

"Wolf!" Aralorn said in an urgent whisper. "Uriah. Can you smell them?"

HE STOPPED COMPLETELY, his dark clothes helping him to blend in. His ritual cleansing had left no human scent to betray him, only the sharp/sweet scents of herbs. Even a Uriah couldn't track in the dark, so unless they had already been seen, they were safe for a moment. Wolf scanned with other senses to find where the Uriah were. It wasn't hard. He was surprised that they hadn't run into one before. His father, it seemed, had been busy. There were a lot of the things around, waiting.

Once, he had watched a spider at her web. Fascinated he had tried to see what she thought about, waiting for her prey to become entangled in the airy threads. He got the same feeling from the Uriah. He wondered if he were the victim of this web.

He thought about turning back. If the ae'Magi was aware that he was here, it might be better to return another time. After a brief hesitation, he shrugged and continued on with more caution. The ae'Magi knew his son well enough to know that he would be coming sometime; a surprise appearance would make no difference either way.

ARALORN BURIED HER face in the pathetic shield of Wolf's shirt, trying to block out the smell. For some reason, the smell of the Uriah was worse than the sounds that they had made outside the cave. Hearing Talor's voice, seeing his eyes on that grotesque mockery of a human body, had made her want to retch and cry at the same time. It still did.

By the time she'd gained control, Wolf stopped for a second time and set her on the ground, motioning her to hide herself. He hesitated, then shifted into his familiar lupine form before gliding into the clearing.

The ae'Magi sat motionless on the ground, his legs and arms positioned in the classic meditation form. A small fire danced just between Wolf and the magician. The newly risen moon caught the clear features of the Archmage ruthlessly, revealing the remarkable beauty therein. Character was etched in the slight laugh lines around his eyes and the aquiline nose. His eyes opened, their color appearing black in the darkness, but no less extraordinary than in full light. His lips curved a welcoming smile. The warm tones vocalized the sentiment in the expression on the ae'Magi's face.

"My son," he said, "you have come home."

ELEVEN

—⁓—

IF WOLF WANTED TO BELIEVE THAT SMILE, ARALORN COULD SEE NO sign of it from where she sat hiding under the large leaves of a plant that happened to be growing near the ae'Magi. She hadn't, of course, stayed where Wolf had left her. She wouldn't have been able to see anything.

Wolf lay down and began cleaning the toes of his front feet with a long pink tongue.

The ae'Magi's face froze at the implied insult, then relaxed into a rueful expression. "It was always so with you. Say walk, and you run, stop, and you go. I shouldn't have expected a joyous reunion, but I had hoped. It warms my heart to see you again."

The wolf who was his son looked up, and said, not quite correctly, "We have no audience here. Do you take me for a fool? Should I return as the long-lost son to his loving father? Let me know when you are through making speeches, so that we may talk."

Aralorn marveled at the perfect response the magician made. A hint of tragedy crossed his face, only to be supplanted by a look of stoic cheerfulness. "Let us talk, then, my son. Tell my why you are come if it be not out of love for your father."

Something was wrong, but she couldn't figure out just what it was. Something the ae'Magi said? Something he'd done?

"I pray you be seated." He indicated a spot not too near him with his left hand.

It was a power play, Aralorn saw. By politely offering Wolf a seat, the ae'Magi made him look like an unruly child if he didn't take it. If he did take it, it would give the ae'Magi the upper hand to have Wolf obey his first request. He'd reckoned without Wolf, who looked not at all uncomfortable and made no move to come closer to the ae'Magi.

The entire effect was lost without an audience of some sort, Aralorn thought. Was there someone other than the Uriah watching them?

"I do not play your games," Wolf said impatiently. "I have come to stop you. Everywhere that I go, I see one of your filthy pets. You are annoying me, and I will not put up with it." Wolf put no force behind his words; the grave-gravel tone carried threat enough.

The ae'Magi stood and stepped slightly to his left, so the fire no longer was a barrier between him and the wolf. "I am sorry if I have caused you bother. Had I known that the shapeshifter woman was yours, I would never have taken her. She didn't tell me about you until we were done, and there was nothing I could do about it. Did she tell you that she cried when I . . ." He let his voice drift off.

Wolf rose to his feet with a growl of rage and stalked toward the figure. Abruptly, Aralorn realized what it was that bothered her about the ae'Magi. He cast no shadow from the light of the fire. She noticed something else: Wolf's path would take him directly across the place that the ae'Magi would have had him sit at.

"Wolf, stop!" she yelled as loud as she could in mouse form, hoping that he'd heed her. "He has no shadow. It's an illusion."

WOLF STOPPED, MUTING the feral tones in his throat. Her voice broke into his unexpected rage. He did then what he should have done first. Sniffing the air, he smelled only the taint of moat and Uriah, no fire—no human.

Ignoring the pseudo–ae'Magi, Aralorn the mouse scampered to the space toward which Wolf had been baited. "There's a circle drawn in rosemary and tharmud root here."

"A containment spell of some sort," commented Wolf. She was exploring a little more closely than he was comfortable with. She needed to be more careful of herself. "It's probably best if we don't trigger it." His voice was calm, but his body was still stiff. He sketched a sign in the air, and the image of the ae'Magi froze.

"Is he directing the illusion, do you think?" asked Aralorn, bouncing away from the circle toward Wolf.

"I doubt it. He would not have to. The illusion spell can be given directives, and the trap requires no magic to initialize once it is set." He regained his human form and picked up Aralorn, setting her on his shoulder, where he'd gotten used to having her. "If I had triggered the containment spell, it would probably have alerted him then."

"Like a spider's web," said Aralorn.

"Just so," agreed Wolf.

HE STARED AT the illusion of his father and made no effort to move away. It wasn't a spell; she'd have felt it if something was actually affecting Wolf. Maybe it was something more powerful than magic.

"Where to now?" Aralorn asked. "Do we wait for the Uriah to attack, or do we look for the ae'Magi?"

"For someone who should be scared and cowering, you sound awfully eager." Wolf stood staring at the silhouette of the ae'Magi: His voice wasn't as emotionless as usual.

"Hey," replied Aralorn briskly, "it's better than spending the winter cooped up in the caves."

Wolf made no answer except to run an absentminded hand over the smooth skin of his cheek as if he were looking for something that wasn't there.

Aralorn waited as patiently as she could, then said, "He knew that you were coming."

Wolf nodded. "He's been expecting me for a long time. I knew that. I should have been more alert for something like this." He bowed his head. "I should have asked before. What he said, I have to know. Aralorn, when he had you here, did he . . ." His voice tightened with rage and stopped.

"No," she said instantly. "I'd tell you that before a time like this anyway, so you wouldn't get upset when you need your wits about you. But look here, the first time I was in his castle, he was working on a spell and wanted to save his energy. I was disappointed, but then a slave must wait on the master's convenience."

He was listening. She was taking the right tack, then. "The second time, he was too interested in finding you to worry about it. You shouldn't let him pull your strings so easily." She curled her tail against his neck in a quick caress. "I would have lied under these circumstances, you have to know that. But I wouldn't have hidden something like that when you got me out of there—I don't think I could have." And that was as honest as she was comfortable with—but it did the trick.

The tension eased out of him. "You are right, Lady. Shall we go a-hunting sorcerers in the castle? Perhaps you would prefer a Uriah or two to begin with, or one of my father's other pets. I believe that there are a few that you haven't seen before. Would Milady prefer to be outnumbered a hundred to two or just by three or four to two? This task can accommodate your tastes."

"Then of course," said Aralorn, "once you have attained your goal, we can arrange to have the castle fall on us conveniently. That way we'll escape mutilation from the outraged populace that you have saved from slavery and worse. Sounds interesting—let's get to it." She thought that Wolf might have been smiling as he headed downhill and away from the castle, but it was hard to tell from her vantage point.

THE WOODS GREW increasingly dense as Wolf walked farther from the castle. A hoot from an owl just overhead made Aralorn-the-mouse cringe tighter against his neck. "Lots of nasties in these woods," she said in a mouselike voice devoid of all but a hint of humor.

"And I," announced Wolf in a grim voice that was designed to let Aralorn know that it was time to be serious, "am the nastiest of all."

"Are you really?" asked Aralorn in an interested sort of tone. "Oh, I just adore nasties."

Wolf stopped and looked at the mouse sitting innocently on his shoulder.

Most people cowered under that look. Aralorn began, industriously, to clean her whiskers. When Wolf started to walk again, though, she said in a stage whisper, "I really do, you know."

They emerged from a particularly thick growth of brush into a narrow aisle of grass. In the center of it sat a suggestively shaped altar dedicated to one of the old gods. It was heavily overgrown with moss and lichen until it was almost impossible to tell the original color of the stone. There was nothing unusual about finding the altar, as such remnants dotted the landscape from well before the Wizard Wars. However, the altar itself was flanked by a pair of unusually shaped monoliths.

"Oh dear," said Aralorn drolly, crawling halfway down his arm to get a good look. "Look. Two of them. I suppose that it must have belonged to one of the fertility gods, hmm?"

The southern monolith was broken about halfway up, but the northernmost stood as tall as a man and almost as big around. When Wolf touched it, it slid sideways with a creak and a groan. He slipped inside the dark hole that was revealed and started down the ladder. Aralorn darted off his arm altogether and checked out the ladder.

"The ladder is a lot newer than the altar," she commented, flashing back to her post and tucking a paw inside his collar.

"I put it up myself when I saw that there was some kind of exit from the secret tunnels up here. There was no sign of another one, so I suppose it must have rotted completely away. Plague it, Aralorn, you're going to fall and kill yourself if you don't stay put!"

She'd darted back out to his arm to get a closer look at the tile work on the wall. He picked her off his wrist and set her firmly back on his shoulder. "Just wait until we get down, and you can have a better look."

Once on the floor, he closed the opening with a wave and a thread of magic. As soon as it was shut, he let his staff light the hall in which they stood.

ARALORN SCRAMBLED TO the floor and took her own shape, sneezing a bit from the dust. She scuffed a foot on the floor, revealing a dark, polished surface. The ceiling was as high or higher than the great hall in the castle, and the walls were covered with detailed mosaic patterns of outdoor revelries of times gone by. The ceiling was painted like the night sky, giving the overall impression of being outdoors. Or at least that was what Aralorn assumed. The years had covered the tile on the walls with cracks and knocked down whole sections. The ceiling was badly water-damaged, showing the stonework that held it up through gaps left by fallen plaster.

Reluctant to leave the room without adequate exploration, Aralorn dragged behind Wolf, who'd already ducked through a gap in the wall leading to a drab little tunnel that looked as if a giant mole had dug through the earth. Much less interesting than the room they'd climbed down into, it branched several times. Wolf never hesitated as he chose their way.

"How many times did you get lost exploring this?"

Wolf shot her an amused look. "Several, but I found a book hidden in one of the old libraries that detailed some of the passages, and I found a copy of the master plans in the library—my library. The passages are extensive; it's a wonder the whole thing hasn't collapsed. There are only fifteen or twenty large rooms like the one we started in, most of them about in the same condition. If we make it through the next few days, I'll show you a library that makes the one we have in the Northlands look small. I don't know all of the passages. There are a lot of secret panels and hidden doors, magical and mundane, that make it difficult to find most of the interesting places. Like this one." Wolf waved a hand, and a large section of the tunnel just disappeared into a finished and ornate corridor.

When they stepped through, the opening disappeared—leaving a blank wall in its place. The end of the corridor widened into a huge room with a fountain at its center. The floor had once been wood, which was mostly rotted away, leaving a walkway that was uneven and hazardous.

He wanted to linger and watch her.

Aralorn stumbled and tripped forward instead of walking, because she was too busy staring at the frescoed ceiling and the elaborate stone carvings on the walls to pick her way through the debris that littered the floor. When she started muttering about "where the fourth Lord Protector of Such and Such Port met with the Queen to defeat the Sorcerer What's-His-Face," Wolf put a firm hand on her shoulder and led her patiently around the old traps and pitfalls.

He enjoyed her enthusiasm quietly, as any comment on his part was likely to spark a full-blown story. He led her through several other moldering doorways before they came to one of the stairways that led up to the castle itself. He chose that one to keep their path simple—it would take them to a small closet in the dressing room of the master's suite.

ARALORN DIDN'T NEED Wolf to put his finger to his lips as he opened the secret door that dumped them in a small closet that led to a sumptuously appointed room where hand-carved combs and mirrors sat next to brushes and jewelry of every masculine type. She recognized a piece that the ae'Magi wore and realized that they were in his personal rooms.

The suite consisted of interconnected rooms, all hung with tapestries of great age and richness, preserved through magic that made her fingertips throb when she brushed by them. The rooms were empty except for a girl who was crouched sobbing in a corner.

Her nakedness made her look even younger than she was. The white skin of her back was mottled with bruises and lash marks. An arcane symbol whose meaning eluded Aralorn was etched into one shoulder in bright red.

Wolf grabbed both of Aralorn's arms when she would have reached out to touch the girl. He pushed Aralorn behind him with more speed than gentleness and gripped his staff in one hand. Noiselessly, he drew his sword in the other.

"Child." The word was gentle, his tone sad—for him; but he gripped the sword and held it in readiness. It was fortunate that he did so.

With a chilling cry and uncanny speed, the girl turned and leapt. Once her face had been uncommonly pretty, thought Aralorn, with a small tattoo next to her eye that marked her as belonging to one of the silk-merchant clans. Now the skin was drawn too tightly against the fine bones. Her china-blue eyes were surrounded by pools of bloodred. Her full lips were stretched over pearly teeth, the kind that all of the heroines in the old stories had—with a slight difference. The lower set of teeth were as long as the first two knuckles of Aralorn's ring finger. Her mouth gaped impossibly wide as she launched herself at Wolf.

He knocked her aside easily enough, for her weight was slight, and in the process he cut her deeply in the abdomen. He ended her suffering with a second cut to the back of her neck.

Death was no stranger to Aralorn, so examining the body didn't bother her—much. "One of your father's pets, I assume." It was a comment more than a question.

Wolf grunted an affirmative and touched the symbol on her back. "She'd have been a lot harder to fight if she hadn't been so new at it. She didn't even know how to attack."

Aralorn jerked the embroidered bedspread off the bed and covered the pathetic little body with it before following Wolf out of the room.

The study was a wonder in cultured taste, not that Aralorn expected anything else. Wolf walked to the desk and picked up a sheet of paper. He laughed humorlessly and handed it to Aralorn. It read simply, "I'm in the dungeon. Join me?"

"Apparently," said Wolf, "he *was* monitoring his little trap. He probably knows that you are with me. It is time for you to leave. Now."

She looked at him with due consideration. "I probably should tell you that I will, then just follow you in."

"You would, wouldn't you?" Wolf's voice was soft. He glanced at a decanter on the ae'Magi's polished desk. It imploded loudly enough to make Aralorn jump. "Plague take you, Aralorn, don't you see? He will use you against me. He already has."

Aralorn felt her own temper rise to the surface. "Do you think that I am some weak helpless *female* who can do nothing but stand around while you protect her? I am not helpless against *human* magic or anything else he's likely to throw at us." She made "human" sound like a filthy word. "I can help. Let me help, Wolf."

He was silent for a long moment, then he waved his hand with a haphazard motion and the decanter re-created itself, leaving the desk unblemished. He walked over and pulled the stopper. Taking a token drink from the neck of the bottle, he met Aralorn's glare.

"I owe you an apology, Lady. I'm not used to caring about anything. It's . . . uncomfortable."

She tilted her chin up at him, flags of temper still on her cheeks, then she took the decanter that he was still holding and took a mouthful herself. She set it on the desk and muttered something that he wasn't supposed to hear.

"What?" he whispered. Evidently, he'd heard her.

She put her hands on her hips and glared at him, tapping a foot impatiently on the floor. He didn't have to look like someone had slapped him.

"I said, 'It's a good thing that I love you, or you'd be Uriah bait.' Now that that's settled, why don't we go find ourselves an ae'Magi?" Without waiting for him, she stalked out the door into the hallway.

"Aralorn," he said, his voice a little deeper than usual. "You're going the wrong way if you want to find the dungeons." He sounded . . . almost meek.

She glared at him, and he held out his hand in invitation. So she followed him through the twists and turns of the castle halls that were almost as convoluted as the secret tunnels. The dimly lit passages, which had seemed threatening and huge when she had gone through them alone, were not as intimidating as she remembered them.

Apparently there were no humans in the castle this late at night—at least they didn't see any. The Uriah standing guard here and there paid them no heed. Aralorn was careful to keep her eyes from their faces, but she recognized Talor's boots anyway. Wolf's grip was steady on her shoulder as they went by it. Not him. Never again. It.

When they passed the entrance to the great hall, she couldn't resist the opportunity to look inside. The bars of the cage were discernible in the moonlight, but the light wasn't good enough to see if it was occupied.

The stairway that led down to the lower levels was well lit and smelled of grain and alcohol from the storage rooms on the first sublevel. Each storage room was carefully labeled as to its contents. Most of them contained foodstuffs, but other labels read things like weapons, fabric, and old accounting records. The stairway down to the next level was on another side of the castle.

The second sublevel seemed to be smaller, and here there were several small sleeping quarters intended for the use of apprentices; at least so Aralorn judged them by the traditional sparseness of the cells. The only other rooms were obviously intended for labs, but from the dust that coated the tables, they hadn't seen use for some time.

The dungeon was on the third sublevel, Wolf told her, as they went down another set of stairs. Like the caves, the temperature was consistently chilly but not cold. The smell was overpowering.

Aralorn felt the hair on her arms move with the magic impregnated in the walls of the castle at this level. Countless magicians had bespelled the stones here to prevent the escape of the inmates, and the half of Aralorn that wasn't human told her that the spells had been strong enough to keep some of the prisoners in even after they died. Sick as she had been during her incarceration here, she remembered the feel of the dead weighing down the air.

It occurred to her that she was lucky that she wasn't a full-blooded shapeshifter—they could sense the dead almost as clearly as the living. A shapeshifter wouldn't keep his sanity for very long in a place such as this.

Without the fever that kept her from shielding herself from the human-twisted magic, she could block out enough of the emanations that the pain was nominal. She ignored the discomfort that remained and kept close to Wolf.

The guardroom was empty. By prearranged plan, and it took a strong argument to convince Wolf, she entered the dungeons first—because it was unexpected, and the more off-balance they could throw the ae'Magi, the better off they were.

The first thing that she noticed was the lack of sound. There had never been a cessation of the moaning and coughing—sometimes the noise had almost driven her crazy. Now it was still and silent. The light was dim, and Wolf's staff had stayed in the guardroom with him, so she couldn't see inside the cells. She crept carefully down one side of the path and hid in the shadows. Unlike her, Wolf made a showy entrance. His staff glittered wildly, lighting the room with his power. The illumination slid off the shield of Aralorn's magic and left her hidden.

It didn't slide off the ae'Magi, who stood at the far end of the room. Like Wolf, he, too, carried a staff, massive and elaborately carved, which he tilted as if it were a lance. It wasn't aimed at Wolf, but at her. She dropped instantly to the floor, which vibrated with the force of the explosion of the outside wall of the cell behind her. She was so distracted that she almost missed Wolf's countermove, designed to force the ae'Magi to deal with him.

It caused the ae'Magi to turn to Wolf. While he was watching his son, Aralorn pulled one of her knives and threw it at the ae'Magi. She hit him in the chest. She only had a moment to congratulate herself before the knife passed through him without effect and clattered harmlessly to the floor behind him. The ae'Magi didn't even glance her way.

With a philosophical shrug, she stayed on the floor and prepared to watch the fight. It would have looked odd to someone who was not sensitive to magic and could only see two men gesturing wildly at each other. Aralorn could feel the currents of magic moving back and forth, gaining momentum and power with each countermove, but the only gesture that her limited experience with human magic allowed her to recognize was the deceptively simple spell that Wolf had been working on.

She had a moment to consider the results of an antimagic spell let loose in the dungeon of the ancient seat of the master magicians. A dungeon steeped in the magic of centuries of spells.

Since she was already on the floor, all that she had to do was flatten herself tighter and hope that it was enough. Then the antimagic spell hit, and chaos reigned.

She didn't know if it knocked her out, or just blinded her: Either way, she lost track of time. The first thing she could see clearly was Wolf sitting on the floor and leaning awkwardly against a wall, his staff clenched in his right hand. She crawled to him on hands and knees.

"Are you all right?" She patted his arm anxiously, afraid to touch him without knowing where he was hurt.

"Yes," he said, holding his staff out to her, as if he needed both hands to stand up.

Aralorn heard the noise behind her and twisted her head to see the ae'Magi getting to his feet even as she reached for the staff. She turned back to Wolf to warn him, and noticed something she would have seen right away if she hadn't been so dazed—she'd been in enough fights to know a broken back when she saw it. She saw the same knowledge in Wolf's face.

He smiled at her with a haunting sweetness as she touched the staff. He said something that might have been "I love you, too" but a jolt of magic traveled up her arm, and she blacked out.

When she woke up, the floor she was looking at was bare stone, not cobbled as the floor in the dungeon was. Wolf's staff lay beside her, the crystals in the top smoky dark. The musky smell of the books told her where she was.

"*No!* You stupid son of a . . . Plague take you, Wolf!" Her scream was muffled by the rows of bookshelves in his library. Helplessly, she pounded a fist on the floor, letting rage keep back her tears.

"The sword." She didn't see anyone, but a firm hand pulled her to her feet. The Old Man materialized and shook her by the shoulders. Who else could it have been? His features were the too-perfect features of a shapeshifter.

"The sword, you stupid girl. Where is the sword?"

Aralorn had been through a lot. She had long since outgrown any patience with being manhandled. With a deceptively easy twist recently learned from Stanis, she freed herself and backed away.

With the distance between them, she could see the aura of age that clung to him despite the smooth skin on his face. He was only a few inches taller than she was and far more beautiful to look upon. At another time, she would have been more courteous to the Old Man of the Mountain, but Aralorn wasn't in the mood for politeness.

"What sword are you talking about, old man?" she spat. Hundreds of miles away, Wolf was fighting for his life—she refused to believe that he was dead. She had no patience left.

"The sword! *The* sword!" His arms swung widely in one of the overblown gestures that shapeshifters favored. He dropped into their language, and Aralorn had to struggle to understand the dialect he spoke. "You haven't let the ae'Magi get his hands on it, have you? Where is it? He mustn't have control over it."

"What sword?" Aralorn's voice was harsh with impatience; she needed to travel back to the castle, and a goose wasn't the swiftest of fliers. It would take her days. Too late. She would be too late. "Sir, you will have to explain yourself more clearly."

"Your *sword*, did you leave it there? Didn't . . ." He stopped and looked behind her.

Curious, she looked behind her and saw her short sword, the one that she had left in its usual place under the couch, floating gently in the air behind her. She could almost see the person holding the sword—it was like looking at an image in rough water, impossible to discern any specific features.

"You didn't take it?" The Old Man's voice was filled with disgust. "What is wrong with you? I *told* you. Told *you*. If it weren't for the fact that Lys cares about that Wolf, I would let you stew in your own pot."

He stalked to the sword and took it from the apparition that held it. He unsheathed it and swung it once. "*This* is the third of the Smith's great weapons. Ambris." He gave it another name, but Aralorn was too distracted to translate it. "If the ae'Magi gets his hands on her and realizes what he has, there will be no one who can stand against him. You were supposed to take her with you and use her. I take it that your silly little spell didn't work?"

He didn't wait for her nod, but continued, "I thought that he just might pull it off. Here"—abruptly the shapeshifter's voice lost its force and became querulous like that of a very old man—"take it and go back.

I'm very tired—maintaining this shape is burdensome. Lys?" He shoved the sword at Aralorn and was gone with an abrupt pop.

Aralorn took the sword and looked at it. It looked no more magical than it ever had, but still . . . it did match the description given for the Smith's sword.

And the sword gave her another idea. Sheathing it abruptly, she slipped it onto her belt. With Wolf's staff in one hand, she ran out of the library to find Myr.

TWELVE

———⁓———

MYR WAS NEVER DIFFICULT TO LOCATE. ARALORN SIMPLY HAD TO LOOK for the largest group of people and head in that direction. She found him just outside the cave entrance, giving knife-fighting lessons to a group of the younger refugees. He glanced up and saw her as he was avoiding a crudely wielded blade; the distraction almost cost him a slit throat.

He spoke for just a minute to his former opponent, who was white-faced and shaking. It was no light thing to come so close to killing a king. Aralorn shifted impatiently from one foot to the other as Myr dismissed the class and strode to her.

He took a long look at her, noting the scrape on her cheek that she'd gotten rolling across the floor; the filth that clung to her; and Wolf's staff, which she held clutched in one hand. He didn't demand any explanations, merely asking in a businesslike tone, "What do you need?"

"I need you to call the dragon to take me back to the ae'Magi's castle. I can't get there fast enough by myself." She noticed with detached surprise that her voice was steady.

Myr nodded, gestured for her to wait for him, and ducked back into the caves. He returned carrying his sword in one hand, the belt dangling from its sheath, and led the way through a thicket of brambleberry to a smallish clearing.

Carefully, he unsheathed his sword and gave a rueful look to the blade that years of his grandfather's warring had left unmarred. Then he drove it into the sandy soil, trying not to wince at the grating sound. Another time, Aralorn would have smiled.

When he was done calling the dragon, he stood quietly beside her, not asking her what had happened. It was Aralorn who finally broke the silence.

"We made it into the ae'Magi's castle. He was waiting for us in the dungeons. I think that Wolf's spell would have worked anyplace else. There was too much old magic, and the spell wasn't strong enough and backlashed. I was on the floor already so it didn't hit me very hard. The ae'Magi was knocked out momentarily. Wolf . . ." Her voice cracked and she stopped, swallowed, and tried again. "Wolf's back is broken, he tricked me into touching his staff and sent me back here. I don't know how fast a dragon can fly. Even if it consents to take me to the castle, it will probably be too late."

She laughed then, though it could have been a sob, and clasped the staff tighter. "He may have been right, and it was too late when he sent me back."

Myr didn't say anything, but he put a comforting hand on her shoulder. A cold wind swept down the mountainside, and Aralorn shivered with impatience as much as chill. Even though she was watching intently, she didn't see the dragon until it was overhead. Silver and green and as graceful as a hummingbird, the great reptile landed and eyed them with interest—or perhaps hunger.

"I need you to get me to the ae'Magi's castle as fast as possible." Aralorn knew she was being too abrupt, but she was desperate and couldn't find courtesy when she needed it. The dragon tilted its head back in offense.

Myr's grip tightened warningly on Aralorn's shoulder, as he said, "Dragon, the only one of us who stands a chance of facing down the ae'Magi is hurt and fighting alone at the castle. We need to get there to help him, or the ae'Magi has won. You are our only chance of doing so in time."

Aralorn started at the "we," but decided not to protest as it was likely to offend the dragon even more.

The dragon hesitated a minute, then asked, "Speed is important?"

"Very, sir," Aralorn said carefully, keeping a respectful tone.

It nodded, once. "I can travel much faster than flying, but it means that because of your safeguards against magic, I cannot take you, King Myr. The shapeshifter half-breed I can take."

Myr looked unhappy, but he nodded his acceptance. When the dragon lowered its belly to the ground and folded its wings, Myr helped Aralorn up as she was hampered by the necessity of keeping the sharp claws at the end of Wolf's staff away from the dragon.

The scales on the dragon's back were slick, but otherwise it was no worse than riding a horse bareback—until he began moving. The wings beat steadily until they caught an updraft, then flattened and spread wide—letting the wind pull them south.

Abruptly, the dragon lurched forward, and Aralorn felt a familiar dizziness seize her and clutched the fist-sized scales reflexively. He'd transported them the same way Wolf had sent her back to his library. When she was able to focus her eyes again, the castle of the ae'Magi lay just below.

Shouting, so that the dragon could hear her past the sound of the wind, Aralorn said, "Land wherever you can find a safe place, Lord. I can find my way in." She still had that little follow-me spell on Wolf's boot. He'd changed his clothes preparing to face his father, but not his boots.

In acknowledgment of her words, the dragon changed its angle of flight until it was losing altitude fast. Aralorn's ears popped painfully, and she tightened her grip on the dragon's scales until they cut into her hand. When the dragon landed, the jolt loosened Aralorn's grip, and she landed with a thud next to an impressively armed forepaw.

She rolled to her feet with more speed than grace. She turned to face the dragon and bowed respectfully. "My thanks, sir, and apologies for my clumsiness." Without waiting for a reply, she shifted quickly into a goose and flew as fast as she could to the castle.

The moat didn't smell any better than it had before, and it took her some time to find an intact pipe that was not plugged with grime. Once she found one, maybe the same one she'd used before, she balanced precariously on it until she could turn into a mouse. Even in mouse form, she had trouble negotiating the tricky business of crawling into the pipe from the top, but she managed. All the while, part of her wailed that she was being too slow.

The corridor she entered was only dimly lit by wall sconces, and from what she could see, it was not one that she'd been in before. She considered staying a mouse but decided that she would have a better chance of recognizing something familiar if she were in human form since she'd been in human form while she was following Wolf.

When she took her own shape again, the staff appeared beside her (she hadn't been sure that it would). She wondered if it had changed with her, like the sword and her clothes, or if it was following her on its own. She remembered how Wolf would just reach out and it would be there, under his hand. She'd thought it was something Wolf had done. The idea that it had been the staff all along caused her to pick it up gingerly as she started down the hallway.

There were still Uriah posted in the halls. As before, they allowed her to pass without bothering her though they followed her progress with their eyes. She kept a steady, rapid pace, hoping that she would find a clue to where she was soon enough to be of some help to Wolf. The spell on Wolf's boot was harder to follow in the ae'Magi's castle than it had been in the caves. She could feel it, but it was a faint whisper instead of a call.

The castle was eerily silent, so that when she heard sounds coming from inside a room, she stopped impulsively and opened the door. Kisrah looked up, startled, from where he'd been eating breakfast in bed with a giggling young beauty.

"Lord Kisrah, you wouldn't be interested in showing me the way to the dungeons, I suppose?" asked Aralorn. She wondered if she should draw her sword or knife. She didn't have a chance to act. Something flashed at her out of Lord Kisrah's hands. Instinctively, because it was already in her grip, she moved to block it with the staff. When the flash hit the dark, oiled wood, the crystals on one end of the staff, which up to this point had been dull and lifeless, flared brightly, and Lord Kisrah's magic dissipated without a sound.

Unwilling to let him get another spell off, Aralorn attacked with the staff. Lord Kisrah, unarmed, not to mention unclothed, didn't have much of a chance against Aralorn, who was wielding her favorite type of weapon. Her first blow broke his arm and her second knocked him unconscious on the floor next to the bed.

Aralorn turned to his bedmate with apologies on her lips, but something about the girl made her tighten her grip on the staff instead. Focused intently on the unconscious man, the red-haired woman slithered out of the bedclothes, knocking the bed table with their food onto the floor.

Remembering the harpy that she and Wolf had met earlier, Aralorn tapped the girl's shoulder gingerly with the clawed end of the staff. She hadn't realized how sharp the claws were until they drew blood. She felt bad about it until the girl turned and Aralorn got a good look at her.

The girl snarled, and Aralorn jumped back and seriously considered leaving Lord Kisrah to his fate. As the girl moved, her shape altered rapidly into something vaguely reptilian, with a large spiked tail and impressive fangs, not the same as the silk-merchant girl, though maybe they were at different stages.

The thing, whatever it was, was fast and strong: When its tail hit the post of the bed, the wood cracked. It was also, thankfully, stupid—very stupid. It jumped at Aralorn with a shrill cry and impaled itself on the claws of Wolf's staff.

Dying, it changed back into its former beauty and the woman blinked her green eyes—shapeshifter eyes—and said softly, "Please . . ." before she was unable to say anything.

"Plague it," said Aralorn in an unsteady voice as she retrieved the staff in shaky hands. She backed into the corridor and had started down it when she noticed the hungry gaze of one of the Uriah focused on the bloody end of the staff. She thought of Lord Kisrah lying like an appetizer beside his bedmate's corpse; she went back and shut the door to the bedroom and locked it with a simple spell that Lord Kisrah would have little trouble breaking when he woke up.

Just as she was about to give up hope, Aralorn rounded a corner and found herself in the great hall. From there it was a simple matter to find her way to the dungeon, and the closer she came, the stronger her follow-me spell summoned her. She was concentrating so hard on doing so that the whisper took her by surprise.

"Aralorn," said the Uriah from the shadows near the stairway that led down to the dungeons.

She came to an abrupt halt and spun to face Talor. "What do you want?"

It laughed, sounding for a minute as carefree as he always had, then said in a harsh voice, "You know what I am. What do you think that I want, Aralorn?" It took a step closer to her. "I hunger, just as your companion will shortly. Leave, Aralorn, you can do no good here."

Aralorn shifted her grip on Wolf's staff from her right hand, which was getting stiff and sweaty, to her left. "Talor, where is your brother? I haven't seen him here."

"He didn't make the transition to Uriah," it said softly, and smiled. "Lucky Kai."

Aralorn nodded and turned as if to go down the stairs; instead she continued her turn, drawing the sword as she moved. Smith's weapon or not, the blade cut cleanly through the Uriah's neck, beheading it. The body fell motionless to the stone floor.

"Sweet dreams, Talor," she said soberly. "If I find Wolf in your condition, I will strive to do the same for him."

With the sword in her right hand and the staff in her left, she started down the stairs. The lower levels were darker, but Wolf's staff was emitting a faint glow that allowed her to see where she put her feet. As she started down the third set of steps, it occurred to her that she didn't really know what she planned to do. Alone against the ae'Magi, she had no chance. Not only was he a better magician (by several orders of magnitude), but, if he was Wolf's equal with a sword, he was a much better fighter than Aralorn.

The smells of the dungeon had become strong, and the stench didn't help her stomach, which was already clinched with nerves. In the guardroom, she abandoned the staff because she didn't know how to stop the crystals from glowing.

She sheathed the sword and dropped to her belly, ignoring the filth on the cold stone floor. Slowly, she slid into the dungeon, keeping to one side. The voices that had been indistinct were now intelligible. She heard Wolf speaking, and the huge weight of grief lifted off her shoulders.

". . . why should I make this easier for you than I already have? This is a very easy shield to break through, most third-year magicians could do it. Would you like me to show you how?" Wolf's voice was weaker than she'd ever heard it, but there was no more emotion in it than it ever had. "It does have the unfortunate effect of incinerating whatever the shield is guarding."

"Ah, but I have another method of removing your protection." The ae'Magi's voice was a smooth contrast to his son's. "I have been informed that the girl that you so impetuously sent away has returned all alone. She should be here momentarily if she isn't already."

For an instant, Aralorn plastered herself motionless to the floor before her common sense reasserted itself. It really didn't matter if the ae'Magi knew she was coming, the element of surprise wasn't going to help her much anyway. What did matter was that somehow Wolf had managed to hold the ae'Magi at bay, and no matter how much Wolf cared for her, he knew that it was more important that the ae'Magi not be able to control Wolf's powers. He wouldn't give himself to the ae'Magi just to save her skin . . . she hoped.

She inched forward a few steps more until she could see Wolf revealed by the light of the ae'Magi's staff. He sat in almost the same position that he had been in when she left him. He had drawn a single orange line of power around himself, and there was something different about his position. She looked carefully and saw that he was cautiously moving his toes. She smiled; he had bought enough time with his barrier to heal himself.

Aralorn drew the sword and stepped into the light in front of Wolf. She expected an immediate reaction, but the ae'Magi was pacing back and forth with his back to her.

". . . you should not have crossed me. With your power and my knowledge, you could have become a god with me. That's all that the gods were, did you know it? Mages who had discovered the secret to eternal life, and I have it now. I will be a god, the only god, and you will help me do it."

All of the dictates of honor demanded that she call attention to herself before she attacked. Aralorn, however, was a spy and a rotten swordswoman besides, so she struck him in the back.

Unfortunately the same spell that had rendered her knife useless previously was also effective against the sword, which slid harmlessly through him and knocked Aralorn off-balance. She turned her fall into a roll and kept going until she hit a wall. Although the sword hadn't done the magician any harm, the metal grip had heated enough that she was forced to drop it on the ground.

It had something to do with hitting a magician with metal, she supposed.

"Ah," said the ae'Magi with a smile, "who would think that the son of my flesh would fall for a silly girl who is stupid enough to try the same trick twice."

He turned to Wolf and started to say something else, but Aralorn quit listening. She couldn't believe that the Archmage was just dismissing her. She decided not to question her luck and began to shapechange, trusting that Wolf would see her and keep the ae'Magi's attention long enough that she could complete the transition to icelynx.

"Don't discount Aralorn so lightly, you may be surprised," commented Wolf, stretching the stiff muscles of his neck. "Certainly I never thought that she could get back from the Northlands so quickly. Perhaps the Old Man of the Mountain sent her back."

The ae'Magi snorted in disbelief. "You could not have sent her so far; the Northlands would have blocked such transportation. I do not care where she was. As for the Old Man of the Mountain myth, there is no such person, or I would have run into him long since."

Wolf curved his lips in the dim light of the ae'Magi's staff. "If you are so sure that the old gods are real, why not a folktale as well?"

The keener senses of the icelynx made the smell of the dungeon worse, and she curled her lips in a silent snarl of disgust as she stalked slowly toward the ae'Magi. She crouched behind him and twitched her stub of a tail, waiting for just the right moment before she sprang.

Her front claws dug into his shoulders for purchase while her hind legs raked his back, scoring him deeply. But that was all that she had time for before the ae'Magi's staff caught her in the side of the head with enough force to toss her against a wall. As she lay dazed, her eyes focused on Wolf.

On his knees, Wolf carefully retraced the circle of power. Reaching out almost casually, he snagged his staff where it apparently had been waiting for him in the darkness.

"Father," he said, getting to his feet.

The ae'Magi turned and, seeing Wolf, brought his staff up and took up a fighting stance. It was quiet for a moment, then Wolf struck. Some of the fighting was physical, some of it was magical, most of it was both— accompanied by a very impressive light show.

Aralorn watched from her corner and got slowly to her feet. Anything that she could do as an icelynx was likely to do as much harm as good with so much magic flying around. She took back her human shape, from habit as much as anything else. She had started to lean against the wall to watch when she caught a glimpse of the sword, half-buried in the filthy rushes on the floor. On impulse she picked it up; the heat that had made her drop it was gone.

Atryx Iblis the Old Man had called it in an archaic dialect. *Atryx* was easy, it meant "devourer." *Iblis* took her a while longer, but when she understood it, she smiled and held it at ready, waiting for a chance to use it again.

Healing himself had weakened Wolf, and he was showing it. His blocks were less sure, and he lashed out in fewer and fewer attacks. The ae'Magi was also tiring; the blood he was losing to the deep slashes that Aralorn had made on his back was bothering him, but it was Wolf who slipped in the muck on the floor and fell to one knee, losing his staff in the process.

For a second time Aralorn attacked the ae'Magi's back with the sword, but this time she stabbed him with it instead of cutting him, and released the grip. The sword Ambris hung grotesquely from his chest, though it was doing no apparent harm. Without taking his eyes off Wolf, the ae'Magi swung the tip of his staff at Aralorn and said a quiet phrase.

Nothing happened, but the Smith's sword was glowing brighter than either of the staves, bathing the dungeon with pink. Wolf got to his feet and retrieved his staff, but made no move to attack. Frantically, the ae'Magi grabbed the blade and pushed the sword out, cutting his fingers in the process, although the blade slid out easily enough and fell, shimmering, to the floor.

Aralorn grabbed it, heedless of the heat, and sheathed it, as she said conversationally, "The Old Man says that it's one of the Smith's weapons. *Atryx Iblis*, he calls it—Magic Eater."

The ae'Magi's staff was dark, just an elaborately carved stick to his touch. The ae'Magi's hands formed the simple gestures to call forth light, and nothing happened. Turning to his son, he said, "Kill me, then."

Passionlessly, the predator the ae'Magi had created looked at him with glittering yellow eyes, then said in his macabre voice, "No."

Wolf turned to Aralorn and, gripping her arm tightly, transported them to the meadow where they'd faced the ae'Magi's illusion, leaving the Archmage in the darkness, alone.

Wolf stepped back from Aralorn almost immediately and stood looking at the magician's castle. Aralorn looked at his brooding face and wondered what he was thinking.

He spoke softly. "I am still what he made me, it seems."

"No," said Aralorn in a positive voice.

"Do you know what I just did? I left him bleeding, to face a castle full of Uriah that he no longer controls."

"A kinder fate than he had in mind for you," Aralorn reminded him, examining the burns the sword had left on her hand. "He has as much chance of escaping from the Uriah as Astrid did. More of a chance than Talor or Kai did." There was nothing wrong with her that wouldn't heal up in a few days.

"You also eliminated the threat that his faithful followers would attack us after we killed the ae'Magi," she told him. "He'll be found, mostly eaten by his former pets."

Wolf caught her hand, and the burns disappeared from it, along with much of the dirt. Aralorn laughed softly and wiped her other hand on his cheek, showing him the smudge on it. "This time, you are almost as dirty as I am."

"He's dead," Wolf said.

"Dead," she agreed.

He closed his eyes and shuddered. She took his hand and he gripped it tightly.

"I think," he told her, "that I have just enough magic to take us back to the library."

"Let's go find Myr and let him know what's happened. Then I have to get back to Sianim and let Ren know that there is going to be a plaguing awful mess of Uriah running around that someone's got to clean up. If he works it right, Sianim stands to make a lot of gold off this."

"Not that you care," Wolf said. "Since you gave up Sianim to follow Myr."

"To follow you," she said. "And I've had time to think a bit. Don't you think it was a coincidence that Ren sent me to an inn not twenty miles from where the King of Reth was hiding? And you know what Ren says about coincidence."

"Usually, coincidences aren't," said Wolf.

FINIS

The fifth baron of Tryfahr, Seneschal of the Royal Palace (also known as Haris the Smith) stepped into the kitchen to examine the food being prepared for the feast celebrating King Myr's formal coronation. Seeing the Seneschal slip into the kitchen, the Lyon of Lambshold, who currently held the title of Minister of Defense, decided to join him.

In the main kitchen, the cook who ruled sprawled asleep in her rocking chair near the dessert trays, a nasty-looking wooden spatula in one hand. The new court taster stood silently near the stove.

The new cook was a marvel; the fowl had never been so moist, the beef so tender, and her sweets were beyond comparison. More wondrous still was that she was able to maneuver her bulk around (though no one but the hulking taster who lurked in the corner had ever witnessed it) and cook.

"So," commented Haris, "the mercenaries have offered to help clean up the Uriah."

"Aye," snorted the Defense Minister, "for a discounted rate, since their troops will be in the vicinity clearing the Uriah out of Darran as well. They've already cleared out the ae'Magi's castle." His hand crept out involuntarily to hover over one of the lacy sugar cakes.

"I wouldn't," muttered the Seneschal to the Lyon, nodding at the massive hand that was tightening around the spatula's handle though the cook's eyes had remained closed. He cleared his throat and remarked in a louder tone, "Likely they were hoping to find the ae'Magi in a state to pay them, but I heard that they couldn't find a trace of him anywhere." There was a note of satisfaction in his tone.

The Lyon snatched his hand back, and said absently, "Eaten, most likely, poor man. Sianim'll probably make the next ae'Magi pay them before they turn the castle over to—" He was interrupted by a shout from one of the pages, who seemed to be taking over the castle lately.

"Haris! . . . Uhm, excuse me . . . I mean, my lord. Myr . . . uh, King Myr wants to know if the delegation from Ynstrah is here yet? He can't find them anywhere, though the gatekeeper says that they came in last night." The page stood at the top of the stairs pulling at the velvet surcoat he wore.

"Tell him I'm coming, Stanis," grunted the Seneschal.

The Lyon gave a last look at the cakes as he followed Haris up the stairs.

When they were safely gone, the small, bright sea-green eyes of the cook opened, almost concealed in the folds of her face. She shifted her amazing mass out of the chair and waddled to the bakery trays. Taking a cake in her pudgy hand, she threw it to the guardsman who served as taster. He caught it easily despite the eye patch he wore.

"I told Ren that we wouldn't learn anything at an event this size," she said. "There isn't enough privacy for any good plotting. The only thing that ever happens at a state occasion is an assassination attempt, but Myr has already hired Sianim guards to stop that."

The guard nodded—he'd heard her complaint more than once. He examined the little delicacy with his good eye before biting into it, saying, "You could have let him have the cake, Aralorn. They're easy enough to make." Another cake appeared in his hand as he spoke, and he tossed it to Aralorn.

"I couldn't undermine the authority of the castle cook," said Aralorn in a shocked voice, while catching the treat with a dexterity that was out of character. "Besides," she added, taking a bite of her cake, "this way they'll enjoy the two that Haris snitched even more."

Wolf sauntered to the dessert trays and saw that there were indeed three delicacies missing. "Should we tell Myr that his Seneschal is light-fingered?"

"Not unless he wants to pay for the information. We're mercenaries, after all, Wolf." Aralorn licked her fingers. "By the way, where did you learn to cook like this?"

Wolf bared his teeth at her, and said, his voice as macabre as always, "A magician needs must keep some secrets, Lady."

WOLFSBANE

AUTHOR'S NOTE

WHICH, NOT BEING A PART OF THE STORY, MAY BE SKIPPED

I WROTE *WOLFSBANE* IN BETWEEN *WHEN DEMONS WALK* AND *THE HOB'S Bargain*.

Careerwise, it was a dumb thing to do, and I knew it. *Masques* had been out of print for a couple of years by that point, and I was aware that its sales figures were abysmal and no one in his right mind would reprint it. My editor, Laura Anne Gilman, had left Ace for Roc (which at the time was owned by a different publishing company). After she left, Ace politely declined publishing *When Demons Walk*, for several very good reasons. First, the editor who had liked my work was gone. Second, my sales record was not good. *Masques* had failed. *Steal the Dragon* had done all right, but it'd had a terrific cover by Royo. I was pretty sure that, at least for the time being, my career as a writer was over. So I wrote the book I wanted to write.

I had lived with Wolf in my head since I was in fifth or sixth grade . . . maybe since I first read *The Black Stallion* by Walter Farley and recognized the pull of the powerful, dangerous creature who loves only one person. By the time I'd written three books, I knew that I had a lot to learn—and that I had learned a lot about writing since I wrote *Masques*. I still consider *The Hob's Bargain* my first professional work. It was the first book I wrote that turned out exactly as I'd envisioned it, the first one that I wrote from craft rather than instinct. I wanted to take those new skills and turn my hand to giving Wolf and Aralorn a story more worthy of them.

Wolfsbane was the result. Eventually, somewhat to our mutual surprise, Ace bought *When Demons Walk*, *The Hob's Bargain*, and the first book that really sold well for us, *Dragon Bones. Wolfsbane* stayed on my shelves, and every once in a while I thought a little wistfully about it. I admit, believing that this day of publication would never come, I borrowed things from *Wolfsbane* for other stories—you might see them. You might even pick up on a few that I haven't noticed.

So here, for your enjoyment, is a book from early in my career that has never seen the light of day—and without you, dear readers, would still be moldering on a floppy disk somewhere. I hope you have as much fun with it as I have.

BEST WISHES,
PATRICIA BRIGGS
SOMEWHERE IN THE DESERT OF EASTERN WASHINGTON

ONE

A WINTERWILL CRIED OUT TWICE.

There was nothing untoward about that. The winterwill—a smallish, gray-gold lark—was one of the few birds that did not migrate south in the winter.

Aralorn didn't shift her gaze from the snow-laden trail before her, but she watched her mount's ears flicker as he broke through a drift of snow.

Winterwills were both common and loud . . . but it had called out just at the moment when she took the left-hand fork in the path she followed. The snow thinned for a bit, so she nudged Sheen off the trail on the uphill side. Sure enough, a winterwill called out three times and twice more when she returned to the trail again. Sheen snorted and shook his head, jangling his bit.

"Plague it," muttered Aralorn.

The path broke through the trees and leveled a little as the trees cleared away on either side. She shifted her weight, and her horses stopped. On a lead line, the roan, her secondary mount, stood docilely, but Sheen threw up his head and pitched his ears forward.

"Good lords of the forest," called Aralorn, "I have urgent business to attend. I beg leave to pay toll that I might pass unmolested through here."

She could almost feel the chagrin that descended upon the brigands still under the cover of the trees around her. At long last, a man stepped out. His clothing was neatly patched, and Aralorn was reminded in some indefinable way of the carefully mended cottage where she'd purchased her cheese not a half-hour ride from here. The hood of his undyed cloak was pulled up, and his face was further disguised by a winter scarf wound about his chin and nose.

"You don't have the appearance of a Trader," commented the man gruffly. "How is it you presume to take advantage of their pact with us?"

Before she'd seen the man, she'd had a story ready. Aralorn always had a story ready. But the man's appearance changed her plans.

Though his clothes were worn, his boots were good-quality royal issue, and there was confidence in the manner in which he rested his hand on his short sword. He'd been an army man at some time. If he'd been in the Rethian army, he'd know her father. Truth would have a better chance with him than any falsehood.

"I have several close friends among the Traders," she said. "But as you say, there is no treaty between you and me; you have no reason to grant me passage."

"The treaty's existence is a closely guarded secret," he said. "One that many would kill to protect."

She smiled at him gently, ignoring his threat. "I've passed for Trader before, and I could have this time as well. But when I saw you for an army man, I thought the truth would work as well—I only lie when I have to."

She surprised a laugh out of him though his hand didn't move from his sword hilt. "All right then, Mistress, tell me this *truth* of yours."

"I am Aralorn, mercenary of Sianim. My father is dead," she said. Her voice wobbled unexpectedly—disconcerting her momentarily. She wasn't used to its doing anything she hadn't intended. "The Lyon of Lambshold. If you delay me more than a few hours, I will miss his funeral."

"I haven't heard any such news. I know the Lyon," stated the bandit with suspicion. "You don't look like him."

Aralorn rolled her eyes. "I *know* that. I am his eldest daughter by a peasant woman." At the growing tension in her voice, Sheen began fretting.

His attention drawn to the horse, the bandit leader stiffened and drew in his breath, holding up a hand to silence her. He walked slowly around him, then nodded abruptly. "I believe you. Your stallion could be the double of the one cut down under the Lyon at the battle of Valner Pass."

"His sire died at Valner Pass," agreed Aralorn, "fourteen years ago."

The bandit produced a faded strip of green ribbon and caught Sheen's bit, tying the thin cloth to the shank of the curb. "This will get you past my men. Don't remove it until you come to the Wayfarer's Inn—do you know it?"

Aralorn nodded, started to turn her horses, and then stopped. "Tell your wife she makes excellent cheese—and take my advice: Don't let her patch your thieving clothes with the same cloth as her apron. I might not be the only one to notice it."

Startled, the bandit looked at the yellow-and-green weave that covered his right knee.

Softly, Aralorn continued. "It is a hard thing for a woman alone to raise children to adulthood."

She could tell that he was reconsidering his decision not to kill her, something he wouldn't have done if she'd kept her mouth closed; but she could clearly remember the walnut brown eyes of the toddler who held on to his mother's brightly colored apron. He wouldn't fare well in the world without a father to protect him from harm, and Aralorn had a weakness for children.

"You are a smart man, sir," she said. "If I had wanted to have you caught, it would have made more sense for me to go to Lord Larmouth, whose province this is, and tell him what I saw—than for me to warn you."

Slowly, his hand moved away from the small sword, but Aralorn could hear a nearby creaking that told her that someone held a nocked bow. "I will tell her."

She nudged Sheen with her knees and left the bandit behind.

SHE CROSSED THE first mountain pass late that night, and the second and last pass before Lambshold the following afternoon.

The snow was heavier as she traveled northward. Aralorn switched horses often, but Sheen still took the brunt of the work since he was better suited for breaking through the crusted, knee-deep drifts. Gradually, as new light dawned over the edge of the pass, the mountain trail began to move downward, and the snow lessened. Aralorn swayed wearily in the saddle. It was less than a two-hour ride to Lambshold, but she and the horses were going to need rest before then.

The road passed by another small village with an inn. Aralorn dismounted and led her exhausted horses to the stableyard.

If the hostler was surprised at the arrival of a guest in the morning, he gave no sign of it. Nor did he argue when Aralorn gave him the lead to the roan and began the task of grooming Sheen on her own. The warhorse was not so fierce that a stableboy could not have groomed him, but it was her habit to perform the task herself when she was troubled. Before she stored her tack, she untied the scrap of ribbon from Sheen's bit. She left the horses dozing comfortably and entered the inn through the stable door.

The innkeeper, whom she found in the kitchen, was a different man from the one she remembered, but the room he led her to was familiar and clean. She closed the door behind him, stripped off her boots and breeches, then climbed between the sweet-smelling sheets. Too tired, too numb, to dread sleeping as she'd learned to do in the past few weeks, she let oblivion take her.

The dream, when it came, started gently. Aralorn found herself wandering through a corridor in the ae'Magi's castle. It looked much the same as the last time she had seen it, the night the ae'Magi died.

THE FORBIDDING STAIRWAY loomed out of the darkness. Aralorn set her hand to the wall and took the downward steps, though it was so dark that she could barely see where to put her feet. Dread coated the back of her throat like sour honey, and she knew that something terrible awaited her. She took another step down and found herself unexpectedly in a small stone room that smelled of offal and ammonia.

A woman lay on a wooden table, her face frozen in death. Despite the pallor that clung to her skin and the fine lines of suffering, she was beautiful; her fiery hair seemed out of place in the presence of death. Arcanely etched iron manacles, thicker than the pale wrists they enclosed, had left scars testifying to the years they'd remained in place.

At the foot of the table stood a raven-haired boy regarding the dead woman. He paid no attention to Aralorn or anything else. His face still had that unformed look of childhood. His yellow eyes were oddly remote as he looked at the body, ancient eyes that revealed his identity to Aralorn.

Wolf, thought Aralorn. This was her Wolf as a child.

"She was my mother?" the boy who would be Wolf said at last.

His voice was unexpected, soft rather than the hoarse rasp that she associated with Wolf.

"Yes."

Aralorn looked for the owner of the second voice, but she couldn't see him. Only his words echoed in her ears, without inflection or tone. It could have been anyone who spoke. "I thought you might like to see her before I disposed of her."

The boy shrugged. "I cannot imagine why you thought that. May I return to my studies now, Father?"

The vision faded, and Aralorn found herself taking another step down.

"Even as a child he was cold. Impersonal. Unnatural. Evil," whispered something out of the darkness of the stairwell.

Aralorn shook her head, denying the words. She knew better than anyone the emotions Wolf could conceal equally well behind a blank face or the silver mask he usually wore. If anything, he was more emotional than most people. She opened her mouth to argue, when a scream distracted her. She stepped down, toward the sound, into blackness that swallowed her.

She came to herself naked and cold; her breath rose above her in a puff of mist. She tried to move to conserve her warmth, but iron chains bound her where she was. Cool metal touched her throat, and Wolf pressed the blade down until her flesh parted.

He smiled sweetly as the knife cut slowly deeper. "Hush now, this won't hurt."

She screamed, and his smile widened incongruously, catching her attention.

It wasn't Wolf's smile. She knew his smile: It was as rare as green diamonds, not practiced as this was. Fiercely, she denied what she saw.

Under her hot stare, her tormentor's yellow eyes darkened to blue. When he spoke a second time, it was in the ae'Magi's dulcet tones. "Come, my son, it is time for you to learn more."

"No."

Something shifted painfully in Aralorn's head with rude suddenness and jerked her from the table to somewhere behind the ae'Magi, whose knife pressed against the neck of a pale woman who was too frightened even to moan.

Truth, thought Aralorn, feeling the rightness in this dream.

The boy stood apart from his father, no longer so young as her earlier vision of him. Already, his face had begun to show signs of matching the Archmage's, feature for feature—except for his eyes.

"Come," repeated the ae'Magi. "The death you deal her will be much easier than the one I will give her. It will also be easier for you, Cain, if you do as I ask."

"No." The boy who had been Cain before he was her Wolf spoke softly, without defiance or deference.

The ae'Magi smiled and walked to his son, caressing his face with the hand that still held the bloody knife. Some part of Aralorn tensed as she saw the Archmage's caressing hand. Bits and pieces of things Wolf had told her coalesced with the sexuality of the ae'Magi's gesture.

"As you will," said the sorcerer softly. "I, at least, will enjoy it more."

Rage suffused her with hatred of a man she knew to be dead. She stepped forward, as if she could alter events long past, and the scene changed again.

The boy stood on the tower parapet; a violent storm raged overhead. He was older now, with a man's height, though his shoulders were still narrow with youth. Cold rain poured down, and Wolf shivered.

"It's power, Cain. Don't you want it?"

Slowly, the boy lifted his arms to embrace the storm.

But that taint of wrongness had returned, and Aralorn called upon her magic, girded in the truth of natural order, to pull it right. She had no more magic than the average hedgewitch, but it seemed to be enough for the job. Once more, the scene shifted subtly, as if a farseeing glass were twisted into focus.

"It's power, Cain. Don't you want it?"

"It comes too fast, Father. I can't control it." Wolf spoke the words without the inflection that would have added urgency to them.

"I will control the magic." When Wolf appeared unmoved, the ae'Magi's voice softened to an ugly whisper. "I can assure you, you won't like the alternative."

Even in the storm-darkened night, Aralorn could see Wolf's face blanch, though his expression never altered. "Very well, then." There was something quiet and purposeful in his voice that Aralorn wondered at. Something that only someone who knew him well would have heard.

Wolf bent his head, and Aralorn was aware of the currents of magic he drew. The Archmage closed his hands on his son's shoulders; Wolf flinched slightly at the touch, then resumed passing his power on to his father. Lightning flashed, and the magic he held doubled, then trebled, in an instant. Slowly, Wolf lifted his arms, and lightning flashed a second time, hitting him squarely in the chest.

He called it to him on purpose, thought Aralorn, stunned. If he had been wholly human, he would have died there, and his father with him. For a green mage, whose blood comes from an older race, lightning contains magic rather than death—but he would have had no way of knowing that. He didn't know what his mother had been, not then.

For an instant, the two stood utterly still, except for the soundless, formless force Wolf had assembled; then a stone exploded into rubble, followed by another and another. The broken bits of granite began to glow with the heat of wild magic released without control. Aralorn couldn't tell if Wolf was trying to control the magic at all, though the ae'Magi had stepped back and was gesturing wildly in an attempt to stem the tide. Shadow was banished by the heat of the flames. Aralorn saw Wolf smile . . .

"No!" cried the ae'Magi, as molten rock splattered across Wolf's face, from a stone that burst in front of him. Wolf screamed, a sound lost in the crack of shattering stone.

The ae'Magi cast a spell, drawing on the very magic that wreaked such havoc.

A warding, thought Aralorn, as a rock fell from a parapet and bounced off an invisible barrier that surrounded the ae'Magi as he knelt over his unconscious son.

"I will not lose the power. You shall not escape me today."

The scene faded, and Aralorn found herself back in the corridor, but she was not alone.

The ae'Magi stepped to her, frowning. "How did you . . ." His voice trailed off, and his face twisted in a spasm of an emotion so strong she wasn't able to tell what it was. "You love him?"

Though his voice wasn't loud, it cracked and twisted until it was no longer the ae'Magi's voice. It was familiar, though; Aralorn struggled to remember to whom it belonged. "Who are you?" she asked.

The figure of the ae'Magi melted away, as did the corridor, fading into an ancient darkness that began to reach for her. She screamed and . . .

AWAKE, ARALORN LISTENED to the muffled sounds of the inn. Hearing no urgent footsteps, she decided that she must not have screamed out loud. This was not the kind of place where such a sound would have been dismissed. She sat up to shake off the effects of the nightmare, but the terror of the eerie, hungry emptiness lingered. She might as well get up.

She'd begun having nightmares when Wolf disappeared a few weeks ago. Nightmares weren't an unexpected part of being a mercenary, but these had been relentless. Dreams of being trapped in the ae'Magi's dungeon, unable to escape the pain or the voice that asked over and over again, "Where is Cain? Where is my son?" But this dream had been different . . . it had been more than a dream.

She pulled on her clothes. Her acceptance of what she had seen had been born of the peculiar acceptance that was the gift of a dreamer. Awake now, she wondered.

It had felt like truth. If the ae'Magi were still alive, she would have cheerfully attributed it to an attack by him—a little nasty designed to make her doubt Wolf and make his life a little more miserable. An attack that had failed only because she had a little magic of her own to call upon.

But the ae'Magi was dead, and she could think of no one else who would know the intimate details of Wolf's childhood—things that even she had not known for certain.

It was a dream, she decided as she headed out to the stables. Only a dream.

TWO

———— ⟋⟍ ————

THE PATH TO LAMBSHOLD WAS ALL BUT OBSCURED BY THE SNOW, BUT Aralorn could have followed it blindfolded even though she hadn't been here in ten years.

As Sheen crested the final rise, Aralorn sat back in the saddle. Responsively, the stallion tucked his convex nose and slid to a halt. The roan gelding threw up his head indignantly as his lead line pulled him to an equally abrupt stop.

From the top of the keep, the yellow banner emblazoned with her father's red lion, which signaled the presence of the lord at the keep, flew at half mast, with a smaller, red flag above.

Aralorn swallowed and patted Sheen's thick gray neck. "You're getting old, love. Maybe I should leave you here for breeding and see if I can talk someone out of a replacement."

Sheen's ear swiveled back to listen to her, and she smiled absently.

"There's the tree I found you tied to down there, near the wall."

She'd thought she was so clever, sneaking out in the dead of night when no one would stop her. She'd just made it safely over the wall—no mean feat—and there was Sheen, her father's pride and joy, tied to a tree. She still had the note she'd found in the saddlebags with travel rations and some coins. In her father's narrow handwriting the short note had informed her that a decent mount was sometimes useful, and that if she didn't find what she was looking for, she would always be welcome in her father's home.

The dark evergreen trees blurred in her sight as Aralorn thought about the last night she'd lived at Lambshold. She swallowed, the grief she'd suppressed through the journey home making itself felt.

"Father." She whispered her plea to the quiet woods, but no one answered.

At last, she urged Sheen forward again, and they walked the perimeter of the wall until they reached the gate.

"Hullo the gate," she called briskly.

"Who?" called a half-familiar voice from the top.

Aralorn squinted, but the man stood with his back to the sun, throwing his face into shadow.

"Aralorn, daughter to Henrick, the Lyon of Lambshold," she answered.

He gestured, and the gates groaned and protested as they opened, and the iron portcullis was raised. Sheen snorted and started forward without urging, the roan following behind. She glanced around the courtyard, noting the differences a decade had made. The "new" storage sheds were weathered and had multiplied in her absence. Several old buildings were no longer standing. She remembered Lambshold bustling with busy people, but the courtyard was mostly empty of activity.

"May I take your horses, Lady?"

The stableman, wise to the ways of warhorses, had approached cautiously.

Aralorn swung off and removed her saddlebags, throwing them over one shoulder before she turned over the reins for both horses to the groom. "The roan's a bit skittish."

"Thanks, Lady."

Not by word or expression did the stableman seem taken aback at a "Lady" dressed in ragged clothes chosen more for their warmth than their looks. By then, both the clothes and Aralorn had acquired a distinct aroma from the journey.

Knowing the animals would be well cared for, she started toward the keep.

"Hold a moment, Aralorn."

It was the man from the wall. She turned and got a clear look at his face.

The years had filled out his height and breadth until he was even bigger than their father. His voice had deepened and hoarsened like a man who commanded others in battle, changed just enough that she hadn't recognized it immediately. Falhart was several years older than she was, the Lyon's only other illegitimate offspring. It was he who had begun her weapons training—because, as he'd told her at the time, his little sister was a good practice target.

"Falhart," she said, her vision blurring as she took a quick step forward.

Falhart grunted and folded his arms across his chest.

Hurt, Aralorn stopped and adopted his pose, waiting for him to speak.

"Ten years is a long time, Aralorn. Is Sianim so far that you could not visit?"

Aralorn met his eyes. "I wrote nearly every month." She stopped to clear the defensiveness out of her voice. "I don't belong here, Hart. Not anymore."

His black eyebrows rose to meet his brick red hair. "This is your home—of course you belong here. Irrenna has kept your room just the way you left it, hoping you'd visit. Allyn's toadflax, you'd think we were Darranians the way you—" He stopped abruptly, having been watching her face closely. His jaw dropped for a moment, then he said in a completely different voice, "That is it, isn't it? Nevyn got to you. Father said he thought it was something of the sort, but I thought you knew better than to listen to the half-crazed prejudices of a Darranian lordling."

Aralorn smiled ruefully, hurt assuaged by the realization that it was anger, not rejection, that had caused his restraint. "It was more complicated than that, but Nevyn is certainly the main reason I haven't been back."

"You'd think that a wizard would be more tolerant," growled Hart, "and that you would show a little more intelligence."

That turned her smile into a grin. "He's not all that happy about being a wizard—he just didn't have any choice in the matter."

"You could have won him over if you had wanted to, Aralorn." He had not yet decided to forgive her. "The man's not as stupid as he acts sometimes."

"Maybe," she conceded. "But, as I said, he wasn't the only reason I left. I was never cut out to be a Rethian noblewoman, any more than Nevyn could have lived in Darran as a wizard. Sianim is my home now."

"Do they know you're a shapeshifter?" he inquired coolly.

"No." She grinned at him. "You know that the only people who would believe such a story are barbarians of the Rethian mountains. Besides, it's much more useful being a shapeshifter if no one knows about it but me."

"Home is where they know all of your secrets, Featherweight, and love you anyway."

Aralorn laughed, and the tears that had been threatening since she heard about her father fell at last. When Falhart opened his arms, she took two steps forward and hugged him, kissing his cheek when he bent down. "I missed you, Fuzzhead."

He picked her up and hugged her, stiffening when he looked over her shoulder. He set her down carefully, his eyes trained on whatever he had seen behind her. "That wolf have something to do with you?"

She turned to see a large, very black wolf crouched several paces behind her. The hair along his spine and the ruff around his neck was raised, his muzzle fixed in an ivory-fanged snarl directed at Falhart.

"Wolf!" Aralorn exclaimed, surprise making her voice louder than she meant it to be.

"*Wolf!*" echoed an archer on the walls, whose gaze was drawn by Aralorn's unfortunate exclamation. The astonishment in his voice didn't slow his speed in drawing his bow.

Lambshold had acquired its name from the fine sheep raised here, making wolves highly unpopular in her father's keep.

Aralorn threw herself on top of him, keeping herself between him and the archer, knocking Wolf off his feet in the process.

"Aralorn!" called Falhart behind her. "Get out of the way."

She envisioned the large knife her brother had tucked in his belt sheath.

"Hart, don't let them . . . *ooff*—Damn it, Wolf, stop it, that hurt—don't let them shoot him."

"Hold your arrows! He's my sister's pet," Falhart bellowed. In a much quieter voice, he added, "I think."

"Do you hear that, Wolf?" said Aralorn, an involuntary grin pulling at the corners of her mouth. "You're my pet. Now, don't forget it."

With a lithe twist, Wolf managed to get all four legs under him and threw her to one side, flat on her back. Placing one heavy paw on her shoulder to hold her in place, he began to industriously clean her face.

"All right, all right, I surrender—ish . . . Wolf, stop it." She covered her face with her arms. Sometimes he took too much joy in fulfilling his role as a wolf.

"Aralorn?"

"Irrenna." Aralorn turned to look up at the woman who approached. Wolf stepped aside, letting Aralorn get to her feet to greet her father's wife.

Irrenna was elegant more than beautiful, but it would take a keen eye to tell the difference. There was more gray in her hair than there had been when Aralorn left. If Irrenna wasn't as tall as her children, she was still a full head taller than Aralorn. Her laughing blue eyes and glorious smile were dulled by grief, but her welcome was warm, and her arms closed tightly around Aralorn. "Welcome home, daughter. Peace be with you."

"And you," replied Aralorn, hugging her back. "I could wish it were happier news that brought me here."

"As do I. Come up now. I ordered a bath to be prepared in your room. Hart, carry your sister's bags."

Futilely, Aralorn tried to keep her saddlebags on her shoulder, but Falhart twisted them out of her hands as he said in prissy tones, "A Lady never carries her own baggage."

She rolled her eyes at him before starting up the stairs into the keep.

"Dogs stay out of the keep," reminded Irrenna firmly when Wolf followed close on Aralorn's heels.

"He's not a dog, Irrenna," replied Aralorn. "He's a wolf. If he stays out, someone's going to shoot him."

Irrenna stopped and took a better look at the animal at Aralorn's side. He gazed mutely back, wagging his tail gently and trying to look harmless. He didn't quite make it in Aralorn's estimation, but apparently Irrenna wasn't so discerning because she hesitated.

"If you shut him out now, he'll only find a way in later." Aralorn let a note of apology creep into her voice.

Irrenna shook her head. "You get to explain to your brothers why your pet gets to come in while theirs have to stay in the kennels."

Aralorn smiled. "I'll tell them he eats people when I'm not around to stop him."

Irrenna looked at Wolf, who tilted his head winsomely and wagged his tail. "You might have to come up with a better story than that," Irrenna said.

Hart frowned; but then, her brother had seen Wolf when he wasn't acting like a lapdog.

Having heard the acceptance in Irrenna's voice, Wolf ignored Hart and leapt silently up the stairs to wait for them at the door to the keep.

Aralorn stepped into the great hall and closed her eyes, taking a deep breath. She could pick out the earthy smell impregnating the old stone walls that no amount of cleaning could eradicate entirely, wood smoke from the fires, rushes sweetened with dried herbs and flowers, and some ineffable smell that no place else had.

"Aralorn?" asked her brother softly.

She opened her eyes and smiled at him, shaking her head. "Sorry. I'm just a bit tired."

Falhart frowned, but followed Irrenna through the main hall, leaving Aralorn to fall in behind.

The cream-colored stone walls were hung with tapestries to keep out the chill. Most of the hangings were generations old, but several new ones hung in prominent places. Someone, she noticed, had a fine hand at the loom—she wondered if it was one of her sisters.

She tried to ignore the red carnations strewn through the hall: spots of bright color like drops of fresh blood. Red and black ribbons and drapes were hung carefully from hooks set in the walls, silently reminding her of the reason she had returned to Lambshold. The joy of seeing Hart and Irrenna again faded.

This was not her home. Her big, laughing, cunning, larger-than-life father was dead, and she had no place here anymore. Wolf's mouth closed gently around her palm. A gesture of affection on the part of the wolf, he said, when she asked him about it once. She closed her fingers on his lower jaw, comforted by the familiar pressure of his teeth on her hand.

The hall, like the courtyard, was subdued, with only a minimal number of servants scurrying about. On the far end of the room, the black curtains were drawn across the alcove where her father's body would be lying. Wolf's teeth briefly applied heavier pressure, and she relaxed her hand, realizing she'd tightened her grip too much.

At the bottom of the stairs, Irrenna stopped. "You go on up. I'll let the rest of the family know that you're here. Your old dresses are still in good condition, but if they don't fit, send a maid to me, and I'll see what can be done. Falhart, when you have taken Aralorn's bags up, please attend me in the mourning room."

"Of course, thank you." Aralorn continued up the stairs as if she had never refused to wear the dresses fashion dictated a Rethian lady confine herself to—but she couldn't resist adding dryly, "Close your mouth, Hart. You look like a fish out of water."

He laughed and caught her easily, ruffling her hair as he passed. He drew his hand back quickly. "Ish, Aralorn, you need to wash your hair while you're at it."

"What?" she exclaimed, opening the door to her old room. "And kill off all the lice I've been growing for so long?"

Hart handed her bags to her with a grin. "Still smart-mouthed, I see." When Aralorn tossed her bags into a heap on the floor, he added, "And tidy as well."

She bowed, as if accepting his praise.

He laughed softly. "Irrenna will probably be sending something up for lunch, in case you don't want to eat with the crowd that will be gathering shortly in the great hall. I'll see that someone carries hot water up here as well."

"Falhart," said Aralorn, as he started to turn away. "Thank you."

He grinned and flipped her a studied gesture of acknowledgment (general to sublieutenant or lower), then strode lightly down the hall.

Aralorn stepped into the room and, with a grand sweep of her arm, invited Wolf to follow. As she closed the door, she glanced around the bedchamber and saw that Falhart was closer to the mark than she'd expected. Her room wasn't exactly as she'd left it—the coverlet was drawn neatly across the bed, and the hearth rug was new—but it was obvious that it had been left largely as it had been the last time she'd slept here. Given the size of Lambshold and the number of people in her family, it was quite a statement.

"So," commented the distinctive gravel-on-velvet voice that was Wolf's legacy from the night he destroyed a tower of the ae'Magi's keep, "tell me. Why haven't you come here in ten years?"

Aralorn turned to find that Wolf had assumed his human shape. He was taller than average, though not as tall as Falhart. There was some of the wolf's leanness to his natural form, but his identity was more apparent in the balanced power of his movements. He was dressed in black silk and linen, a color he affected because it was one his father had not worn. His yellow eyes were a startling contrast to the silver player's mask he wore over his scarred face.

It wasn't actually a player's mask, of course: No acting troupe would have used a material as costly as silver. The finely wrought lips on its exaggerated, elegant features were curled into a grimace of rage. She frowned; the mask was a bad sign.

Aralorn wasn't certain if he'd chosen the mask out of irony or if there was a deeper meaning behind it, and she hadn't thought it important enough to ask. He used the mask to hide the scars he'd gotten when he'd damaged his voice—and to put a barrier between himself and the real world.

It was her vexation with his mask rather than a reluctance to answer his question that prompted her to ignore his query and ask one of her own. "Why did you leave me again?"

She knew why; she just wondered if he did. Ever since he'd first come to stay with her, even back when she'd thought he really was a wolf, whenever they grew too close, he would leave. Sometimes it was for a day or two, sometimes for a month or a season. But this time it had hurt more, because she thought they had worked past all of that—until she awoke alone one morning in the bed she'd shared with him.

She might not need him to tell her why he'd left, but she did intend to discuss it with him. She needed to tell him, if he didn't already know, that the change in their relationship meant that some other things would also have to change. No more disappearing without a word. Anger would distract her from the bleak knowledge that her father was gone, so she waited for Wolf to explain himself. *Then* she would yell at him.

He caught up her bags in a graceful motion and took them to the wardrobe without speaking. He closed the door, and, with his back to her, said softly, "I—"

He was interrupted by a brisk knock at the door.

"Later," he said, then with a subtle flare of shape and color, he flowed into his lupine form. She thought he sounded relieved.

Aralorn opened the door to four sturdy men bringing in steaming buckets of water and a woman bearing a tray laden with food.

Watching them pour water into her old copper tub in the corner of the room, she rethought the wisdom of pushing Wolf. He was a secretive person, and she didn't want to push him away or make him feel that there was a price to pay for staying. She didn't want to lose him just because she needed to yell at someone before she collapsed in a puddle of grief. She stuffed both anger and grief down to pull out later. She wasn't entirely successful, judging by the lump in the pit of her stomach—but the tub offered an opportunity to find another way to relieve her emotions.

When the heavy screen had been placed in front of the tub to reduce the cold drafts, she dismissed the servants.

She stepped behind the screen and began stripping rapidly out of her travel-stained clothing. Perhaps it would be best if she answered his question; it would give him a graceful way out of answering hers. Now, what had he asked?

"It seemed best," she said with playful obscurity, stepping into the tub.

"What seemed best?" From the sound of his voice, Wolf had moved from where she'd last seen him, curled before the fire with his eyes closed—a pose that seemed to reassure the servants, who had eyed him uneasily.

"That I leave here and not come back."

"Best for whom?" *He is closer now,* she thought, smiling to herself.

Sinking farther down in the luxuriously large bathing tub, she rested her head on the wide rim. Should she give him the short answer or the long one? She laughed soundlessly, then schooled her voice to a bland tone. "Let me tell you a story."

"Of course," he replied dryly.

This time Aralorn laughed aloud, a great deal of her usual equanimity restored by the hot water and the macabre voice of her love. She chose to forget, if only for a while, the reason that she was here, in her old bed-chamber. "Once," she began in her best storyteller manner, "and not so long ago, there was a lord's son who, for all that he was still but a young man, had already won a reputation for unusual cunning in war. Additional notoriety came to him from a source no one had reckoned upon."

She waited.

At last, with a bare touch of amusement, he said, "Which was?"

"'Twas a night in midwinter with a full moon in the air when a servant heard a thunderous knocking on the keep door. A man clothed in a close-woven wool cloak stood before him, carrying a covered basket. 'Take this to the lord's son,' he said, thrusting the basket at the servant. As the servant closed his hand on the handle, the man in the cloak stepped away from the door and leapt into the air, shaping himself into a hawk." She splashed her toes, enjoying the feeling of the water washing away dried sweat. Bathing in a tub wasn't quite as good as the Sianim bathhouses, but it was a lot more private. "The servant took it to the lord's son and described the unusual messenger who had delivered it. The young man removed the cover from the basket, revealing a girl-child with the peculiar gray-green eyes common to the race of shapeshifters. Next to her, tucked between a blanket and the rough weave of the basket, was a note. He read it, then threw it into the fire.

"Taking the baby into his own hands, he held her up until she was at a height with him. 'This,' he announced, 'is my daughter.'

"He introduced the baby to her three-year-old brother and her grandfather. Her grandfather was not pleased to find out his son had been meeting a woman in the woods; but then, her grandfather was not best pleased with anything and, as it happened, died of apoplexy when he was served watered wine at a neighbor's banquet only a few months later, and so had little influence in his granddaughter's life.

"The young man, now lord, decided he needed a wife to care for his children and to bear heirs for the estate. Presently, he found one, several years younger than himself. She looked at the trembling waifs and promptly took them under her wing. The children were delighted, and so was the lord—so much so that in due time there were twelve additional siblings to play with."

Aralorn ignored Wolf's choked-off laugh and explained blandly, "In most households, the life of a bastard child is miserable at best. I can't remember not knowing that I was illegitimate, but I never minded it much. As for being half shapeshifter . . . I've already told you that my father did his best to make sure that I was aware of my mother's people. Other than that, it was no more than an unusual talent I had. The people in the Rethian mountains are used to magic—most of them can work at least some of the simpler spells. Since the Wizard Wars, seven ae'Magi have come from these mountains. If anyone had ever felt I was odd, they'd grown used to it by the time I was grown. The worst problem I had was convincing Irrenna that I didn't want to be a Lady. Falhart taught me swordplay and riding, real riding, and by the time my parents found out, it was too late. Father said I might as well know what I was about and had the weaponsmaster teach me, too."

"Idiot," commented Wolf, sounding much more like his normal sardonic self. "He should have beaten you and sent you to bed without supper. Ten years in Sianim, and you still can't use a sword."

"Not his fault," replied Aralorn easily. "A sword never felt right in my hands, not even Ambris, and she's an enchanted blade. Hmm . . . now that's a thought."

"What?"

"I wonder if it has to do with the iron in the steel. Green magic doesn't work well with iron, while it has an affinity for wooden things . . . Maybe that's why I'm so good with the staff. But it doesn't seem to affect my ability with knives."

"I have always found modesty becoming in a woman."

"Best staffsman or -woman in Sianim," she said, unruffled. "Including longstaff, quarterstaff, or double staves. Now hush, you've interrupted."

"I shall sit quietly and contemplate my misconduct," he replied.

"That should take a while." Aralorn sank down until the warm water touched her chin. A benefit of having large people in one's family was that all of the tubs were big enough to stretch out in. "I guess I can wait that long—but the water will get cold."

There was a long pause. Aralorn stifled a giggle.

"Your story?"

"Finished so soon? I would have thought such a grave task would have taken longer."

"Aralorn," he said gently, "please continue. You were telling me of your wonderful childhood and why that meant that you had to stay away from your family for so long."

"My story," she continued grandly. "Where was I? It doesn't matter. When I was eighteen, my oldest legitimate sister, Freya—mind you she's still younger than I am—was betrothed in one of those complex treaties Reth and Darran spend months drawing up every few years or so and break within hours of the signing. It seems that a rather powerful Darranian noble had a mageborn second son who needed a bride."

Aralorn took a moment to rub soap into her mouse brown hair, hoping to evict the fleas that had taken up residence during her travels. Despite her joking with Falhart, she didn't think she had lice. "So Nevyn came to live at Lambshold. He was shy at first, but he and Freya turned out to be soul mates and fell quietly in love several months after they were married."

She ducked under the water to rinse the soap out of her hair. She didn't particularly want to continue, but some things would become obvious—and it generally wasn't a good thing to take Wolf by surprise. As soon as she was above water again, she continued. "I liked him, too. He was quiet and willing to listen to my stories. He had this air of . . . sadness, I suppose, that made us all treat him gently. He was the only one who defied Irrenna's edict about animals in the castle. He didn't keep pets, but anyone who found a hurt animal brought it to him. At times his suite looked more like a barnyard than the barnyard did." Aralorn hesitated, and said in a considering tone, "At the time, I was afraid I liked him too much. In retrospect, being older and wiser now, I think I wanted what Freya and Nevyn had together rather than Nevyn himself."

She soaped a cloth and began scrubbing at the ingrained dirt in her hands. "Now, I had long since gotten out of the habit of using my shape-shifting abilities at Lambshold. Father was very good at spotting little mice where they didn't belong. Irrenna was very clear on what was polite and impolite: Turning into animals in public wasn't polite. It never occurred to me that Nevyn didn't know what I was."

She examined her hands and decided they were as good as they were going to get. "I did know that he wouldn't think it proper for a Lady to fight, so I talked Falhart into practicing with me in the woods. It wasn't too difficult because he was starting to get teased when I beat him."

Her hair still felt soapy, so she dipped her head underwater again. She cleared her face with her hands and continued. "Nevyn didn't like girls who ran around in boys' clothing and would have been horrified to know that his wife's sister could best him in a fair fight—even with a sword. If you think I'm bad . . ." She let her voice trail off suggestively.

"Swordsman or not, I thought Nevyn was the epitome of what a young hero ought to be." She smiled to herself. "I admired his manner of seeing things in black and white—which was very different than the way my father saw things."

Aralorn paused. "About half a year after Nevyn came, Father drew me aside and told me that Freya was concerned with the amount of time her husband spent with me. When you see Freya, you'll understand why I didn't take that warning too seriously. Even if I had a crush on Nevyn, I knew he couldn't possibly look at me when he had Freya. But my younger sister is a wise woman."

Aralorn waved her hand in the top of the cooling water and watched the swell dash against her knee. "It seems that Freya was not mistaken in her apprehension. Nevyn had been flattered by my worship-from-afar, something that Freya was too pragmatic ever to do. I think he was a little intimidated by Freya, too."

"He attempted you?"

Aralorn snorted. "You make it sound like I'm a horse. But that's the general idea. He was teaching me to speak Darranian in Father's library. I was too stupid—"

"Young," corrected Wolf softly.

"—young *and* stupid to read his earlier manner correctly. It wasn't until I examined the incident later that I realized he could have misinterpreted my response to several things he said. He could very well have thought that I was eager for him."

Wolf growled, and she hurried on. "At any rate, he tried to kiss me. I stepped on his foot and elbowed him in the stomach. About that time, I heard my sister's voice in the corridor. Knowing that no good could come from Freya's finding me with Nevyn—even though nothing happened—I turned into a mouse and escaped out the window and into the gardens."

"And how did your Darranian take that?" asked Wolf.

"Not very well," admitted Aralorn, smiling wryly. "Obviously, I wasn't there for the initial shock, but when I came in to dinner, Nevyn left the table. Freya apologized to me for his behavior—all of it. From what she said, I understand that he confessed all to her, which is admirable. He also claimed that it was my evil nature that caused his 'anomalous' behavior. She didn't believe that—although Nevyn probably did—but Freya wasn't too happy with me anyway." She smiled wryly. "But Freya wasn't why I left. I'd seen Nevyn's face when he saw me: He was afraid of me."

Wolf walked around the screen. He wore his human form, but the mask was gone, and his scars with it. It could have been illusion—human magic—but Aralorn sometimes thought that it was the green magic that he drew upon when he chose to look as he had before he'd burned himself. Surely a mere illusion would not seem so real; but then, maybe she was prejudiced in favor of green magic.

The unscarred face he wore was almost too beautiful for a man, without being unmasculine in the least. High cheekbones, square jaw, night-dark hair: His father had left his mark upon his son's face as surely as he had his soul.

She would never let him see the touch of revulsion that she felt for that face, so close to the one his father wore. She knew that he wore it now in an attempt to be vulnerable before her, so that she could read his emotions better, for the scars that usually covered his face were too extensive to allow for much expression.

"It hurt you," he said. "I am sorry."

Aralorn shook her head. "I've grown up since then and learned a thing or two along the way. I've stayed away from Lambshold for my sister's sake, and, I think, for my father's as well. He loves—loved—Nevyn like another son. My presence could only have divided this family. And Nevyn . . . Nevyn came to us broken. One of us had to leave, and it was easier for me." She thought a moment. "Actually, looking back, it's rather amusing to think that someone thought I was an evil seductress. It's not a role often taken by folks who look like I do."

Although his lips never moved, his smile warmed his habitually cold eyes. "Evil, no," he commented, his gaze drifting from her face.

"Are you implying something?" she asked archly, not at all displeased. She knew she was plain, and her feminine attractions were not enhanced by the muscles and scars of mercenary life—but it didn't seem to bother Wolf.

"Who, me?" he murmured, kneeling beside the bath. He pressed a soft kiss on her forehead, then allowed his lips to trail a path along her eyebrow and over her cheekbone. Pausing at the corner of her mouth, he nibbled gently.

"You could seduce a glacier," commented Aralorn, somewhat unsteadily. She shivered when the puff of air released by his hushed laugh brushed her passion-sensitive lips.

"Why, thank you," he replied. "But I've never tried that."

"I missed you," she said softly.

He touched her forehead with his own and closed his eyes. Under her hand, his neck knotted with tension that had nothing, she thought, to do with the passion of a moment before.

"Help me here, love," she said, scooting up in the tub until she was sitting upright. "What's wrong?"

He pulled back, his eyes twin golden jewels that sparkled with the lights of the candles that lit the room. She couldn't read the emotion that roiled behind the glittering amber, and she doubted Wolf could tell her what it was if he wanted to. He reacted to the unknown the same way a wild animal would—safety lay in knowledge and control; the unknown held only destruction. Falling in love had been much harder on him than it had been on her.

"I wasn't going to ask you again," she said. "But I think I had better. Why did you leave?"

Wolf drew in a breath and looked at the privacy screen as if it were a detailed work of art rather than the mundane piece of furniture it was. One of his hands was still on Aralorn's shoulder, but he seemed to have forgotten about it.

"It's all right," said Aralorn finally, sitting up and pulling her legs until she could link her arms around them. "You don't—"

"It is not *all right*," he bit out hoarsely, tightening his grip on her shoulder with bruising force. He twisted back to face her, and his kneeling posture became the crouch of a cornered beast. "I . . . *Plague it!*"

Aralorn scarcely had time to realize that her cooling bathwater had become scalding hot before Wolf pulled her out dripping like a fish onto the cold stone floor. She took the time to snatch the bath sheet and wrap it around her twice before joining Wolf near the tub, watching as the water erupted into clouds of billowing steam. After a moment, she opened the window shutters to disperse the fog in the room.

"I could have burned you," he said, looking away from the empty tub, his voice too quiet.

"So you could have." Aralorn pursed her lips, and wondered how to handle this new twist in their relationship.

She knew him well enough to know that heating the water hadn't been a bizarre practical joke: He had a sense of humor, but it didn't lend itself to endangering people. It meant that his magic was acting without his knowledge—sternly, she repressed the tingle of fear that trickled over her. Unlike Aralorn, his magic, human or green, was *much* better than the average hedgewitch's: But her fear would hurt him more surely than a knife in his throat.

"I should have told you before," he said without looking at her. "I thought it was just my imagination when things first started happening around me. They were little things. A vase falling off a table or a candle lighting itself." He stopped speaking and drew in his breath.

When he spoke again, his ruined voice crackled with the effort of his suppressed emotion. "I wish I had never discovered I could work green magic as well as the human variety. It was bad enough before, when I was some sort of freak who couldn't control the power of the magic I could summon. At least then it only came when I called. Ever since I started using green magic, I've been losing control. It tugs me around as if I were a dog, and it held my leash. It would be better for you if I left and never came back."

As he spoke the last words, he made a swift gesture, and the steam clouds disappeared from the room. Aralorn stepped in front of him, so he had to look at her.

Smiling sweetly, she reached up to touch his face with both hands. "You leave, and I'll follow you to Deathsgate and back," she said pleasantly. "Don't think I can't."

His hands covered hers rather fiercely.

"Gods," he said, closing his eyes. Aralorn couldn't tell if it was a curse or a prayer.

"Green magic has a personality of its own," she said softly. "One of the elders who taught me likened it to a willful child. It responds better to coaxing than force."

Yellow eyes slitted open. "Do you not have to call your magic? Just as any human mage would do?"

"Yes," agreed Aralorn, though reluctantly. She hated it when he shot down her attempts to make him feel better.

Wolf grunted. "A human mage is limited by the amount of pure, unformed magic he can summon and the time he can hold it to his spell. The magic you call is already a part of the pattern of the world, so you have to respect that limit. I tell you that this *magic*"—he spat the word out—"comes when it wills. If you are not frightened by that, you should be. Remember that *my* magic is not limited except by my will. This does not heed my will at all. I cannot control it, I cannot stop it."

Aralorn thought about that for a moment before a cat-in-the-milk-barn smile crossed her face. "I do *so* hate being bored. You always manage to have the most *interesting* problems."

She caught him off guard and surprised a rusty laugh out of him.

"Come," she said briskly, "help me dry off, and we'll eat. My mother's people live near here—maybe they can help. We'll stop there before we go back to Sianim."

THREE

—⁓—

ARALORN WALKED TO THE GREAT HALL, WITH WOLF GHOSTING BESIDE her, once more in lupine form. When she'd told him he didn't have to accompany her, he had merely given her a look and waited for her to open the door. When he wanted to, the man could say more with a look than most people managed with a whole speech.

She'd searched through the clothing still in her closet, trying to find a long-sleeved dress that would cover the scars on her arms. The dresses were all in beautiful condition (many having never been worn), but the fashions of ten years ago had tight sleeves that she could no longer fit into thanks to a decade of weapons drills. She'd settled for a narrow-skirted, short-sleeved dress and ignored the scars.

The room was crowded, and for a moment she didn't recognize anyone there. Ten years had made changes. Some of the crowd were tenant farmers and gentry who held their manors in fief to her father; but from the number of very tall, blond people in the room, Aralorn thought most of them were her family, grown up now from the ragtag bunch of children she remembered.

Wolf received some odd looks, but no one asked about him. It seemed that mercenaries would be allowed their eccentricities.

She smiled and nodded as she waded through the crowd, knowing from experience that the names would sort themselves out eventually. Usually, she was better at mingling and chatting, but this wasn't just work, and the black curtain that hung in the far corner of the room held too much of her attention.

In the alcove behind the curtain, her father's body was laid out in state—awaiting the customary solitary visits of his mourners. Visits where the departed spirit could be wished peacefully on his way, old quarrels could be put aside, and daughters could greet their fathers for the first time in a decade.

She'd seen him now and again, the last time at the coronation of the new Rethian king. *But I was working, and he never recognized me under the guises I wore.*

"Aralorn!" exclaimed a man's voice somewhere behind her.

Aralorn gave herself an instant to collect her scattered thoughts before she turned.

The young man slipping rapidly through the crowd wasn't immediately identifiable, though his height and his golden hair proclaimed him one of her brothers. She hesitated for a moment, but realized from his age and the walnut-stained color of his eyes who he had to be—the only other boy near his age had blue eyes. When she searched his features she could see the twelve-year-old boy she'd known.

"Correy," she said warmly, as he came up to her.

Wordlessly, he opened his arms. She wrapped her arms around him and returned his hug. The top of her head was well short of his shoulders in spite of the torturously high heels on her shoes.

"You shrank," he commented, pulling away to reveal a twinkle in his dark brown eyes.

She stepped back so she wouldn't strain her neck looking at him. "Back less than a day, and already I've been insulted twice for my size. You should have more respect for your elders, boy."

"Correy—" A female voice broke into the conversation from somewhere over Aralorn's left shoulder. "Mother's looking for you. She says you forgot to get something that she needed for something else, I forget what. I can't believe that you are wearing a sword; Mother will pitch a fit when she sees that you're wearing a weapon to Father's wake." A tall, exquisitely groomed woman of somewhere around thirteen or so tripped past Aralorn without so much as a glance and stopped at Correy's side.

Correy rolled his eyes, looking for a moment much more like a boy of twelve than a grown man. With a smile for Aralorn, he reached out a brotherly arm and snagged the immaculately clad girl around the neck and pulled her to his side. "You won't recognize this one, Aralorn, as she was only four when you left. Lin has set herself up as the mistress of propriety at Lambshold. She wants to go to court and meet the king. I think she envisions him falling desperately in love with her."

The girl, only inches shorter than her brother, struggled out of his hold and glared at him. "You think you're so smart, Correy—but you don't even know that you shouldn't wear swords at a formal gathering. Mother's going to skin you alive."

Correy smiled, ignoring her wrath. "I meant to tell you that black looks exceptionally well with your hair."

"You really think so?" Lin asked anxiously, suddenly willing to listen to her brother's previously dismissed judgment.

"I wouldn't say so else, Lin," he said with obvious affection.

She kissed his cheek and drifted off, taking little notice of her long-lost sister.

"I apologize for her rudeness . . ." began Correy, but Aralorn smiled and shook her head.

"I was fourteen once, myself."

He smiled and glanced down casually at Wolf, but when he met the solemn yellow gaze, he started. "*Allyn's toadflax*, Aralorn, Mother said you'd brought your pet, but she didn't say he was a wolf."

He knelt to get a better view, careful not to crowd too close. "I haven't seen many black wolves."

"I found him in the Northlands," said Aralorn. "He was caught in an old trap. By the time he was healed, he'd gotten used to me. He still comes and goes as he pleases. I didn't know he'd accompanied me here until he showed up in the courtyard."

"Hey, lad," crooned Correy, cautiously extending his hand until he touched the thick ruff around the wolf's throat.

"You don't have to be quite so careful. He's never bitten anyone yet . . . at least not for petting him."

There were too many people in the room for her to worry about the purposeful steps that approached her from behind, but she did anyway. Hostility always had that effect on her.

The man striding toward them was dark-haired and dark-eyed, the epitome of a Darranian lord. Not as handsome as Wolf—who was half Darranian and looked it—and less dangerous-looking, though he had something of Wolf's grace when he moved. *Nevyn,* she thought with a touch of resignation accompanying her nervousness.

He stopped in front of her, close enough that he was looking down, forcing her to look up to meet his eyes. "You profane this gathering by your presence, shapeshifter."

"Nevyn," she greeted him courteously.

From the corner of her eye, she noticed Wolf pull away from Correy and slink toward Nevyn, his lips curled back from his fangs.

"Wolf, *no,*" she said firmly, hoping he would listen.

Yellow eyes gleamed at her, but the snarl disappeared as he trotted back to her side.

When she was certain Wolf was not going to do anything rash, Aralorn turned her attention back to Nevyn; but the distraction had done her good—and that might have been Wolf's intention all along. He was a subtle beast. Prepared now, she examined the Darranian sorcerer. The years had been kind to him, broadening his shoulders and softening his mouth. The shy anxiety that had plagued him had faded, leaving behind an intense, handsome man who looked prepared to defend his family from her.

"I am truly sorry you feel that way," she said. "But the Lyon is my father, and I will stay for his burial. For his sake, I bid you peace. If you feel it necessary, perhaps we could discuss this in a less public forum."

"She's right, husband," said a firm voice, and a woman, slightly taller than Nevyn, materialized to Aralorn's left. In Freya, Lin's promise of beauty was fulfilled. Thick red-gold hair hung in glorious splendor to her slender hips. Her belly was gently rounded with pregnancy, but that robbed her figure of none of its grace. The dark blue eyes that glanced a quick apology at Aralorn were large and tilted. "This is neither the time nor the place for this conversation."

"Freya," said Aralorn, smiling, "it's good to see you again."

Mischievousness lit the younger woman's smile as she patted her husband's arm before she left him to hug Aralorn. "Don't stay away so long next time, Featherweight. I missed you."

Aralorn laughed, grateful for the change of topic. "I missed you, too, Puff."

Correy gave a crack of laughter. "I'd forgotten that name. None of the youngsters got nicknames once you'd gone."

"Maybe," said Freya, her eyes twinkling as she folded her arms and puffed out her cheeks in the manner that had given her the once-hated appellation, "I didn't miss everything about your absence."

"If I remember Irrenna's letters correctly, your child is due this spring, right?" asked Aralorn.

Freya nodded and started to say more, but Irrenna, emerging from whatever social emergency had been keeping her at a distant corner of the room, called Aralorn's name.

Hurrying forward, Irrenna pressed a kiss on Aralorn's cheek. "Come, dear, the alcove is empty, so you can pay your respects to your father."

Although she knew the smile on her face didn't change, Aralorn felt a cold chill of grief. "Yes, Irrenna. Thank you."

She followed her stepmother's graceful form through the crowd. They paused here and there for introductions—Irrenna had taken refuge from her grief in the social amenities called for at any large gathering.

Wolf ventured ahead and found a corner near the black curtain where he was unlikely to be stepped on and settled quietly. Aralorn murmured something polite, squeezed Irrenna's hand, and continued to the curtained alcove on her own.

The black velvet was heavy, and it shut out a great deal of the sound from the outer room. Incense burned from plates set at the head and foot of the bier, leaving the room smelling incongruously exotic. She let the curtain settle behind her before stepping farther into the little chamber.

It was unadorned except for three torches that were ensconced on the stone walls, sending flickering light to touch all but the narrowest shadows. On the opposite side of the round room was a thick wooden door that was used to take the body to the burial grounds outside the keep. It was a small chamber, with space for only eight or ten mourners to cluster around the gray stone bier that held sway here, a private place.

The man on the stone slab didn't look like her father, though he wore the same state robes she had seen him in at the Rethian king's coronation. Aralorn's lips twitched when she remembered he'd been thieving sweet cakes out of the kitchens. *Green and brown velvet embroidered with gold.* She touched the rich cloth lightly with her fingertips. He had been an earthy man; it was fitting that his burial clothing reflected that.

"You should have died in battle, Father," she whispered. "Sickness is such an inglorious way to die. The minstrels are already singing ballads of your ferocity and cunning in battle, did you know that? They'll make up a suitably nasty foe to have dealt your mortal wound just to satisfy their artistic souls."

The stone of the raised bier was cold on her hips, surprising her because she hadn't realized she had stepped closer. "I should have come sooner—or stopped you at court when I saw you there. I'm a spy, did you know that? What would you have done if the scullery maid, or the groom who held your horse, shifted into me? Would you have had me tried as a traitor to Reth? Sianim's mercenaries aren't Reth's enemies until they are paid to be. You know I would never betray Reth's interests for my adopted home."

To Aralorn, touch was as much a part of talking as the words themselves. Almost without conscious thought, she bent forward, cupping her hand on his flaccid cheek . . . and stilled.

She had touched dead people before—a lot of them. She had even touched a Uriah or two, who were dead-but-alive. Her shapeshifter blood did more than allow her to change shape and light fires; it made her sensitive to the patterns of life and death, decay and rebirth.

Beneath her fingertips, the pulse of life was still present— and it didn't have the fragility of someone near death. Despite his appearance, her father seemed to be merely sleeping, though he did so without breath or color in his face.

"Father?" she said softly, her pulse beginning to race with possibilities. "What is this that you have gotten yourself into?"

She searched for sorcery, human or green, but her magic found nothing. She began to sing softly in her mother's tongue. Singing allowed her to focus her magic, letting her see more than just the Lyon's still form.

She had never been hungry for the power that magic could bring, so she'd never done much besides learn how to reshape her face, change into a few animal forms, and open locked doors. This was entirely different, but she had to try something.

She struggled for a while before she was able to discern the pulses and rhythms of his life; more difficult still was finding the underlying organization that was at the heart of all life. Just as she thought she found the Lyon's pattern, something dark bled through. She sought it, but it faded before her searching, as if it had never been. Deciding it might have been a fluke of her inexperience, Aralorn returned to her original search. As soon as her concentration was elsewhere, the darkness returned.

This time it caught at her magic as if it were a living thing. Startled but not alarmed, Aralorn stopped singing. But the connection between her magic and the shadow didn't dissolve. Creeping up through her magic, the darkness touched her. As it did, pain swept through her, raking her with acid claws.

"Wolf," she croaked, meaning to call out, but her voice was only a hoarse whisper as she fell to her knees.

LYING JUST OUTSIDE the curtained alcove, Wolf listened to Aralorn's singing and wished he couldn't feel the stirring of green magic at her call. He didn't know what she was doing, but he sent a thread of silence around the curtain, hiding the sound of her music from everyone except him.

No one needed to know that she called magic, not when so many here disapproved of her. He'd seen the looks that Aralorn had ignored. She chose to believe that they did not hurt her, but he knew better.

The pads of his feet tingled, and the air thickened with the sharp, clear presence of Aralorn's magic. He shifted irritably but stilled when the singing stopped. Abruptly, Wolf surged to his feet, trying to put a name to the change he sensed. Then, faintly, he heard her call his name.

He bolted under the curtain to find Aralorn curled on her side, and the magic in the air so strong it almost choked him—not Aralorn's magic; hers never stank of evil.

"Eavakin nua Sovanish ven," he spat, straddling Aralorn as if his physical presence could ward off the attack of magic. At the end of his speaking, the dark magic reluctantly faded back from Aralorn. He shaped himself into his human form: He could work magic whatever shape he took, but there were some spells that he needed his hands for.

"Kevribeh von!" he commanded as he gestured. Rage twisted his voice as it could not touch his fire-scored face. "She is mine. You will not have her."

As suddenly as it had come, all trace of the magic that had attacked her disappeared. The chamber should have retained a residue of it—he could detect the traces of his own spellwork—but the shadow magic was gone as if it had never been.

Wolf moved aside as Aralorn began to push herself up.

"Wolf," she said urgently, "look at him. Look at my father and tell me what you see."

"Are you all right?" he asked, crouching down beside her.

"Fine," she said dismissively, though at the moment she seemed to be having trouble sitting up. He helped her. "Please, Wolf. Look at my father."

With a curt nod, Wolf turned and approached the bier.

ARALORN WRAPPED HER arms around herself and waited for his answer. When Wolf stiffened in surprise, she clenched her hands into fists. He set his right hand over the Lyon's chest as he made a delicate motion with his left.

Remembering what had happened to her when she had used magic, Aralorn said, "Careful."

It was too late. Even without her magic, she saw the unnatural shadow slipping from under the Lyon's still form to touch Wolf's hand.

"Plague it!" Wolf exclaimed, using Aralorn's favorite oath as he stumbled back from the bier, shaking his hand as if it hurt.

The shadow vanished from sight as quickly as it had come.

"Are you all right?" asked Aralorn, staggering to her feet. "What is it?"

Wolf walked slowly around the stone pedestal, careful not to touch it. He frowned in frustration. "I don't know. I can see it, though, when it moves. It seems to have a limited range."

"Is it a spell of some sort?"

Almost reluctantly, Wolf shook his head.

"It's alive then," said Aralorn. "I thought it might be." The hope she'd been clinging to left her. The life that she'd sensed had been the shadow-creature and not her father at all.

Of course the Lyon was dead. She sucked in a deep breath as if air could assuage the hurt of departing hope.

The sound brought Wolf's gaze to her, his amber eyes glittering oddly in the flickering light. "So is your father."

"Wolf?" she whispered.

The rattle of the brass rings that held the heavy curtain over the door gave brief warning before both Correy and Irrenna burst in. Wolf dropped his human form for the wolf more swiftly than thought. If one of the intruders had looked sharp, they would have caught the final touches of his transformation, but their attention was on Aralorn, still sitting on the floor.

"Are you all right?" asked Irrenna anxiously, surveying the dust on Aralorn's dress and the dazed expression on her face.

"Actually, yes," replied Aralorn, still absorbing the certainty that Wolf had given her. "Much better than I was." Then she smiled, accepting the improbable. She might have been mistaken, but Wolf would not have been.

"I apologize then," said Correy, clearly taken aback at her cheerfulness. "I saw your wolf scramble under the drapery, and I thought something might be wrong. That door"—he gestured to the oaken door that led to a small courtyard—"is usually kept barred, but I could have sworn I just heard a man's voice." Though his words were an explanation for the discourtesy of interrupting a mourner, his voice held a dozen questions.

Aralorn shook her head. "No one came in from the courtyard. I have noticed this room can distort sound—it might be the high ceiling and the narrowness of the room."

Wolf gave her a glance filled with amusement at her storytelling. She patted him on the head and climbed laboriously to her feet.

"You look as if your visit with Henrick did you some good," commented Irrenna after a moment. "I'm glad you are more at peace."

Aralorn smiled even wider at that. Trust Irrenna to be too polite for bluntness.

"Well"—Aralorn paused, almost bouncing with excitement—"I'm not certain 'peace' is quite the right word. I would say joyous, exuberant, and maybe exultant—though that might be pushing it a bit. I wouldn't be too hasty about burying Father tomorrow—he might not be best pleased."

Her brother stiffened, drawing himself up indignantly, but Irrenna, who knew her better, caught his arm before he could say anything.

"What do you know?" Irrenna's voice was hushed but taut with eagerness for all that.

Aralorn spread her arms wide. "He's not dead."

"What?" said Correy, his voice betraying his shock.

Irrenna took a step forward and peered closely into Aralorn's face. "What magic have you wrought?" she asked hoarsely.

At the same time, Correy shook his head with obvious anger. "Father is dead. His flesh is cold, and there is no pulse. I don't remember that your humor lent you toward cruelty."

The smile dropped from Aralorn's face as if it had never been. "You've been listening to Nevyn."

Irrenna stepped between them, shaking her head. "Don't be absurd,

Correy. If Aralorn says that he lives, then he lives. She wouldn't make up a story about this." She drew in a tremulous breath and turned back to Aralorn. "If he is not dead, why does he lie so still?"

Aralorn shook her head. "I'm not certain exactly, except that there's magic involved. Has Father annoyed any wizards lately?"

Irrenna looked thoughtful for a moment. "None that I know of."

"You think Father's ensorcelled? Who do you think did it? Nevyn?" asked Correy. "I know death when I see it, Aralorn. Father is dead."

Aralorn looked at him, but she couldn't read his face. "I don't know Nevyn anymore. But the man I knew would never have put everyone through all of this."

"You are certain it was a human mage?" asked Irrenna. She'd reached out to touch the Lyon's hand.

"Have you been having difficulty with the shapeshifters?" asked Aralorn.

"Father's been working with them to improve the livestock." Correy was still stiff with distrust. "But last month, something burned out a crofter's farms on the northern borders of the estate, one of the places where they'd been conducting their experiments. All that's left are the stone walls of the cottage, not even the timbers of the barn. Father said he didn't think it was the shapeshifters, but I know that they've been nervous about dealing with humans."

Aralorn nodded her understanding. "I haven't had time to look very closely at the spell holding the Lyon. I can check if it was a shapeshifter's doing or a human mage's."

She took a step forward to do just that, but Wolf placed himself four-square before her.

"I can do it without using magic," Aralorn said, exasperated. She'd momentarily forgotten, in her excitement, that her family would think it odd that she explained herself to her wolf. Ah well, she could hope that they would chalk it up to the stress of the moment. She needed to see the Lyon. "All I want to do is *look*. The shadow-thing only came out before when magic was being patterned."

"What shadow-thing?" asked Correy.

"I don't know," Aralorn said. "Something odd happened when I was using magic."

Reluctantly, Wolf stepped aside. Aralorn managed another half step before Wolf again stepped between her and the bier; this time his attention was all for the shadows under the silent form laid out on the stone table. He growled a soft warning.

"What is it?" asked Irrenna.

Aralorn narrowed her eyes, catching a flicker of movement in the shadow under the Lyon's still form. She moved around Wolf and reached out, watching the shadow stretch away from her father's fingertips and slide toward hers.

Wolf took a mouthful of the hem of her dress and jerked his head. If she'd been wearing her normal clothes, Aralorn would have caught her balance. As it was, the narrow skirt kept her legs too close together, and she fell backward on the cold floor again. This time she bruised her elbow.

"Plague it, Wolf—" she started, then she heard Correy's exclamation. "What *is* that?"

Irrenna gasped soundlessly, and Aralorn turned to look. The shadow was back, rising over the top of the bier as if it had form and substance. Wolf crouched between her and the thing, his muzzle curled in a soundless snarl.

Aralorn pushed herself away from the shadow to give him more room. As she distanced herself, the shadow shrank, until it was nothing more than a small area under her father where the torchlight could not reach.

"I think," said Aralorn thoughtfully, getting to her feet, "that we need to seal this room so no one comes in. There must be some plausible explanation we can give them. It's a little late to start talking about quarantine for an unknown disease, but . . ."

"Why didn't that happen before?" asked Correy. "There have been any number of people who have been around Father's . . ." He hesitated a moment, staring at the bier, then he smiled, a great joyous smile. ". . . around Father after he was ensorcelled."

"That's a good question," said Aralorn briskly, with a nod that acknowledged his capitulation without gloating over it. "It was dormant until I worked some magic when I first noticed Father wasn't as dead as he appeared. The magic might have triggered it. Regardless of what it is and why it didn't act sooner, it certainly seems to be active now."

"I propose that we tell everyone as much as we know," suggested Correy in a reasonable tone of voice. "We're not Darranians to be frightened of a little magic—but wariness comes with the territory."

Aralorn was nonplussed for an instant, then a slow smile lit her face. "I've gotten used to fabricating stories for everything—I'd forgotten that sometimes it is possible to tell everyone what's really going on—it *is* good to be home."

THE ACTIVITY AROUND the bier room had attracted the attention of several people in the great hall. When Correy drew back the curtain, Aralorn saw that Falhart was standing near the opening with a slender woman who could only be his wife, Jenna. Nevyn and Freya were there, too.

Correy glanced around the room with an assessing eye. Impatiently, he grabbed a pewter pitcher from a surprised servant and dumped the liquid it contained onto the floor. With a boyish grin, he took the empty vessel and flung it against a nearby stone pillar. The resultant clamor had the effect of silencing the room momentarily.

"Good people," bellowed Correy, though the effect was somewhat marred by the silly grin on his face. "I am here to announce that my father's interment has been indefinitely postponed because of a slight misconception on our part. It seems that the Lyon lives." He had to wait a moment before the noise level dropped to where he could be heard. "My sister, Aralorn, has determined that it is some ensorcellment that holds Father in thrall. I will send to the ae'Magi at once for his aid. Until he arrives, I would ask that no one enter the chamber."

"You say the shapeshifter wishes no one to enter?" Nevyn's face was pale. Freya touched his arm, but he shook himself free of her hand.

"*I* say no one enters," snapped Correy.

"There is a trap of some sort," said Aralorn before matters between the two men worsened. "I have neither the skill nor the knowledge to deal with it. I fear that anyone without safeguards would be in danger of ending up in the same state as my father." She bowed her head formally at Nevyn. "As you are far better trained than I, you are free to enter or not as you wish."

Nevyn gave a shallow nod but didn't move his eyes from Correy. "I would like to verify her opinion."

"Fine," said Correy.

"Have a care," murmured Aralorn, as Nevyn brushed past her to enter the smaller room.

Aralorn looked at Wolf and gestured after Nevyn. He sighed loudly and ducked through the curtain behind the human mage.

While Irrenna dealt with the questions thrown at her, Falhart picked up the dented pitcher and handed it to Correy with a brotherly grin. "Never thought to see the day that my courtly brother dumped good ale on the floor in a formal gathering."

Correy took the pitcher with a sheepish smile and shrugged. "It seemed . . . appropriate."

Falhart turned to Aralorn. "Well, Featherweight, you did it again."

She raised her brows. "Did what?"

"Managed to put the whole household in an uproar. You even turned Correy into a barbarian like ourselves. Look at all the work you caused the servants: This room will smell like a brewery for a se'night."

Aralorn drew in her breath and puffed out her chest and prepared to defend herself. Before she could open her mouth, she was engulfed in Falhart's arms.

"Thanks," he said.

When Falhart set her down, Correy picked her up in a similar fashion, then gave her to an older man she recognized as one of the Lyon's fighting comrades—and she wasn't the only woman passed from one embrace to the next. From there the gathering took on the festiveness of Springfair.

Out of the corner of her eye, Aralorn saw Wolf find a place under one of the food-laden tables. Knowing from his actions that Nevyn was safely out of the curtained alcove, she relaxed and enjoyed herself.

NEVYN HAD NO intention of working magic while under the watchful eye of Aralorn's companion, who had inexplicably followed him.

He usually loved four-footed beasts of all kinds, but the cold yellow eyes of the wolf gave him chills. Would it have followed him if it were only a pet wolf as she claimed? Was it some relative of hers? He couldn't tell the shapeshifters from any of the other creatures of the forest.

After completing a brief inspection of the room, Nevyn rejoined the guests. He would return to the Lyon when everyone was gone.

The tenor of the evening had changed during the short time he'd been gone. The quiet, hushed crowd had grown boisterous and loud, forgetting, in their joy at Aralorn's news, that the Lyon still was in danger.

Nevyn watched his wife dance with Correy for a moment, but he was uncomfortable with the noisy crowd. He disliked strangers and gatherings of people. Not even eleven years in Lambshold had managed to change that. Without so much as a touch of envy, he watched the others celebrate: He liked knowing that so many people cared for the man who'd been a much better father to him than his own.

Smiling faintly, he turned and left the room, taking care to leave unseen. If Freya knew he'd gone, she would follow him—not understanding that he wanted her to enjoy herself. He loved her more because they were different, and had no desire to change her.

The smile grew more comfortable on his face as he took the servants' stairs to reach the suite he shared with his wife. He felt better than he had for a long time. Aralorn's discovery took a large portion of the weight of responsibility off his shoulders. He'd dreaded the thought that he would have to stop the burial himself despite the assurances he'd received to the contrary.

He felt guilty for what had been done to the man he loved as a father. But that would soon be over as well. He also hadn't wanted to hurt Aralorn, and she would be hurt when she realized that she was responsible for her father's condition: She was too smart not to make the connection. At least she wasn't in any danger, not now.

He truly believed that she was something unnatural—even evil—but part of him still had a tender spot for the funny, teasing girl who had welcomed him to Lambshold. For that child's sake, he hoped this would soon be over. He'd hurt her tonight. He hadn't meant to, but he had to remind himself what she was lest he begin to forget the terrible things that magic could do no matter how good the man wielding it.

He entered his bedroom with a sigh of relief. One of his cats jumped down from the chair it had been sitting on to strop itself against his leg.

Nevyn stripped off his formal dress, leaving it where it fell. The cat mewed imperatively, and he picked it up before lying down in the bed he shared with Freya.

"Problems, Nevyn?" whispered an accentless voice in Darranian from the shadow-laden window alcove.

Nevyn jumped, still unused to the way the mage could appear out of nowhere. "My lord," he greeted him. "I was just thinking. It happened as you said it would. Aralorn discovered the spell, though she managed to stay out of the trap as you feared she might." He was glad of it, he thought with unusual defiance.

The sorcerer emerged from the alcove and stood in the light of the single candle Nevyn had left burning. He was taller than Nevyn and moved like a warrior despite the wizard's robes he wore. His hair was the same color as the black cat that rested on Nevyn's lap. His eyes were cobalt blue.

"Don't fret," he said, his voice matching the perfection of his face. "She could only escape because *he* was there."

Nevyn shook his head. "I saw no one enter the room but Aralorn, Irrenna, and Correy."

"Nonetheless," said the other man again, "it was *his* magic that stopped the *banishan* from completing its work. That you did not see him enter is hardly surprising. My son is capable of great magics. There is a door into the bier room—a lock would be no barrier to a mage of his caliber." He paused, then snapped his fingers. "Of course," he said softly. "I should have thought . . . The girl, Aralorn, has been known to travel quite often with a large black wolf. Was he there?"

"Yes," answered Nevyn. "What does that have to do with her escape from the trap, my lord ae'Magi?"

The other man looked thoughtfully at Nevyn. Then he smiled. "Since my son's attempt on my life, I no longer hold that title—it belongs to Lord Kisrah, who holds the Master Spells. You may address me as Geoffrey, if you like."

"Thank you," said Nevyn.

"My son is the wolf," said Geoffrey. "It is some effect of the combination of my magic and his mother's that allows him to take that shape as if it were his own. Be careful when he is about."

Nevyn nodded. "I'll do that."

"Thank you." Geoffrey smiled. "You look tired now. Why don't you sleep. Nothing more will happen tonight."

Nevyn found that he was more tired than he remembered. He was asleep before Geoffrey left the room.

In her bedchamber, Aralorn stepped behind the screen to remove the torn dress and the shoes as well. Pulling her toes up to stretch her protesting calf muscles, she listened to the sounds of Wolf stirring the coals in the grate.

"Did you get a good enough feel for the spelling to tell if it was a human mage who attacked my father?" she asked, pulling a bedrobe off the screen and examining it, curious. It was the shade of old gold embroidered with red, and the needlework was far finer than any she had ever done. "I couldn't get close enough to tell."

"I don't know," replied Wolf after a moment. "The magic in that room didn't feel like human magic—at least not always. Nor did it feel the way green magic does." There was a pause, then he continued in a softer voice. "There's black magic aplenty, though. It might be some effect of the corruption that makes it difficult to say whether it is a human or one of your kinsmen responsible."

"Most everyone here is a kinsman of mine," she said, and wrapped the robe around herself.

She sighed. The robe was unfamiliar because it quite obviously belonged to one of her sisters. The sleeves drooped several inches past her hands, and the silk pooled untidily at her feet. She felt like a child playing dress-up.

"If it is human magic, Nevyn is the most obvious culprit."

Reading her tone, Wolf said, "You find that so far-fetched?"

"Let's just say that I'd suspect the shapeshifters—I'd suspect *myself*—before I'd believe that Nevyn harmed my father," she said, standing on her toes without appreciably affecting the length of fabric left on the ground. "Me, yes—but not my father. When Nevyn came here . . . something in him was broken. My father accepted him as one of us. He bellowed at him and hugged him, and Nevyn didn't know what to make of him." Aralorn smiled, remembering the bewildered young man who'd waited to be rejected by the Lyon as he'd been rejected by everyone else. "Nevyn wouldn't hurt my father."

"So what are we going to do?"

"Tomorrow," she said, "I'd like to find my mother's brother and see what he has to say. If he did this, he'll tell me so—my uncle is like that. If not, I'd like him to take a look at the shadow-thing. He's familiar with most of the uncanny things that live here in the mountains."

She tried rolling up the sleeves. "By the way, did you ward the alcove to keep curiosity seekers out, or are we relying on Irrenna's guards?" The soft fabric slid out of the roll as easily as water flowed down a hillside.

"I set wards."

Deciding there was nothing to be done about the robe, Aralorn stepped around the screen. Unmasked and scarred, Wolf set the poker aside and turned to face her. He stopped and raised an eyebrow at her, his eyes glinting with unholy amusement.

"You look about ten years old," he said, then paused and looked at her chest. "Except, of course, for certain attributes seldom found in ten-year-olds."

"Very funny," replied Aralorn with all the dignity she could muster. "Some of us can't magically zap our clothing from wherever we put it last. Some of us have to make do with what clothing is offered us."

"Some of us can do nothing but complain," added Wolf, waving his hand at her.

Aralorn felt the familiar tingle of human magic, and her robe shrank to manageable size. "Thanks, Wolf. I knew there was a good reason to keep you around."

He bowed with a courtier's flair, his teeth white in the dim light of the room. "Proper lady's maid."

Aralorn snorted. "Somehow," she said dryly, "I don't think you convey the right air. Any Lady worthy of her title would not let you close enough to tie her laces . . . untie perhaps, but not tie."

Wolf walked by her on the way to the bed and ruffled her hair. "I prefer mercenaries."

She nodded seriously. "I've heard that about you wizards."

SHE WAS DRIFTING contentedly off to sleep snuggled against Wolf's side when he said, "I've been assuming this was a spell, but it could be something the shadow-creature is doing to him."

She moaned. "Sleep."

He didn't say anything more, but she could all but feel him thinking.

"All right, all right," she groused, and rolled over onto her back with a flop. "Why do you think it is the shadow-thing holding my father?"

"I didn't say that," he corrected. "But we know nothing about it, or about the spell holding your father. You're the story collector. Have you heard any stories about a creature who holds its victims in an imitation of death?"

"Spiders," she answered promptly. She was very awake now. For some reason she'd assumed that since the Lyon was still alive, he'd stay that way until she and Wolf figured out how to rescue him.

"You know what I mean," Wolf said. "Is there something that uses magic to bind prey as large as a human?"

"No," she said, then continued reluctantly, "not explicitly—but there are a lot of strange creatures I don't know much about. The North Rethian mountains were one of the last places settled. Many of the old things were driven here from other places as humans moved in. Supposedly, the Wizard Wars destroyed most of the really dangerous ones—but if the dragon survived, other things might have made it as well. That leaves a lot of candidates, from monsters to gods."

"Gods?" he asked.

She tapped his chest in objection to the sneer in his voice. Wolf, she had long ago realized, was a hopeless cynic. "If the Smith built weapons to kill the gods, there must have been gods to kill. I'll have you know that this very keep was cursed once. Family legend has it that one of the Great Masters who began the Wizard Wars razed a temple dedicated to Ridane, the goddess of death, before erecting his own keep here." She lowered her voice and continued in a whisper. "It is said that *Her* laughter when he died was so terrible that all who heard it perished."

"Then how did anyone know that *She* laughed?" Wolf asked.

She poked him harder. "Don't ruin the mood."

His shoulder shook suspiciously, but he was quiet. She settled back against him, slipping her hand under his arm.

"My uncle," she said, "told me that the shapeshifters lived in these mountains before humans ever came this far north. They were driven into hiding here by a creature they called the *safarent*—which translates into something like big, yellow, magic perverter." She waited for his reaction.

"Big, yellow, magic perverter?" he said, his voice very steady, making the name even more ridiculous.

"Sort of the way your name, in several Anthran dialects, would translate into hairy wild carnivore which howls," she replied. "Would you prefer the Great Golden Tainter of Magic?"

"No," he said dryly.

"Anyway," she said, happy to have her attempt to amuse him succeed, "the shapeshifters were already hiding when humans came. It's probably why they survived here and nowhere else."

"So what happened to the . . . *safarent*?" asked Wolf, when Aralorn didn't continue.

"Probably the Wizard Wars," she said. "But the stories are pretty vague." She closed her eyes and hugged his arm to still her fears. "I'll get my uncle to look at the Lyon tomorrow."

Wolf grunted and began nibbling at the soft place behind her ear, but she was too worried about her father to follow his mood.

"Wolf," she said, "do you think I should try my sword? It might be able to rid us of that shadowy thing, or even break the spell that holds my father."

Carrying an enchanted sword wasn't the most comforting thing to do. It intimidated her to the point where she tried to ignore it most of the time. Since she'd used it on Wolf's father, she hadn't even practiced with it—though she carried it with her always so that no one else picked it up.

Wolf nipped her ear sharply and rolled her on top of him, shifting her until he could see her face.

"Ambris, once called the *Atryx Iblis*," he said thoughtfully.

"Magic eater," she translated.

"Devourer sounds much more impressive," he said, "if we're still debating translations. That name is the only thing we really know about it, right?"

"What do you mean? There are lots of stories, not about the sword, I grant you, but the Smith's weapons—"

"—cannot be used against humankind," he broke in. "They were built to defeat the gods themselves: the black mace, the bronze lance, and the rose sword. 'Only a human hand dare wield them—'"

"'—against the monsters of the night,'" she said completing the quotation. "I know that." Then she thought about what he'd said. "Oh, I see what you mean. You think the stories might be wrong."

"My father was a monster, but he was a human monster. You, my sweet, are not human."

"Half," she corrected absently, "and I'm not so certain about your father. Other than your Geoffrey and a few Uriah, I don't think I've ever actually ever so much as wounded anyone with it. I seldom use it except for training, where the idea is *not* to cut up your opponent. For real fighting, I use weapons I'm more competent with. Wolf, if your father was human, Ambris shouldn't have worked against him."

Wolf tapped his fingers absently on her rump with the rhythms of his thoughts. "Perhaps the Smith's interpretation of human was broader than ours. He might have included half-breed shapeshifters as human. My father was trying to become immortal like the gods—maybe he succeeded far enough that the sword could be used against him."

"For the spell holding my father, it doesn't matter what its capabilities, does it? I'm not going to try and kill anyone with it—just break a spell. It did break through the ae'Magi's wards—"

"No, it didn't."

She sat up then so she could look at him. "What do you mean?"

"Ah," he said. "You wouldn't know. My father's wards protected him by preventing any weapon from doing physical damage. Magical damage is more difficult to guard against by warding, and he believed that he was more than capable of protecting himself from magical attack. Your sword never did draw blood. The wards stayed there until his magic died."

He threw back the covers, set her off him, and arose. "There's an easy way to see if it can break spells as well."

He pulled a small bench to a clear spot in the room and made a few signs in the air over it. Stepping back, he shook his head. "We might as well test it against a more powerful spell, since that is what we will be facing." He made a few more gestures. "Now nothing should be able to touch this bench."

Still tucked warmly under the covers, Aralorn snickered. "The Bench No Axe Could Touch Nor Rump Rest Upon," she intoned, as if it were the title of some minstrel's song.

"At least not until the magic wears off in a week or two," said Wolf. "I've worked a series of spells on this bench. Do you want to try your sword on it?"

Aralorn left the warmth of her bed and found Ambris where she'd tucked it under the mattress before attending the gathering. Unsheathing it, she watched the reflected glow from the fire shine on the rose-colored blade.

It was small for a sword, made for a young boy or woman rather than a full-grown man. Except for the metal hilt, it could have been newly forged—but no one made swords with metal grips anymore. After the Wizard Wars, when most of the mages were dead, metal hilts hadn't been much of a problem. Being connected to a dying magician by metal was a *very* bad idea. Now hilts were made of wood or bone, and had been for the past few centuries as the mageborn slowly became more numerous again.

The metal hilt hadn't worried Aralorn when she'd chosen it from the armory before she'd left Lambshold. She'd always been able to tell mageborn from mundane. The sword had been the right size and well balanced, so she'd taken it. For years, she'd carried it, never realizing that she held anything other than an odd-colored, undersized sword fit for an undersized fighter.

She approached the bench and examined it thoughtfully.

"It won't attack back," said Wolf, apparently amused at her caution. "You can just hit it."

She gave him a nasty look. She always felt awkward with the blasted weapon even though years of practice had made her almost competent. The recent change in their relationship had made her, to her surprise, a bit shy around him. She wanted to impress him, not remind him just how poor a swordswoman she was.

Experimentally, she swung the sword at the bench. It bounced off as if propelled, the force of it almost making Aralorn lose her grip. Shifting her stance, Aralorn tried simply setting the sword against the warding. The repelling force was still there, but by locking her forearms and leaning into the sword, she managed to keep it touching the spell. She held it there for a while, before she gave up and let the sword fall away.

"You need to follow through better," said Wolf with such earnestness that she knew he was teasing.

Aralorn turned and braced both hands on her hips and glared at him, but not seriously. "If I required your opinion, I'd give you over to my father's Questioner and be done with it."

He raised his eyebrows innocently. "I was only trying to help."

She snorted and spun, delivering a blow to the bench that should have reduced it to kindling, but it did no damage at all.

"I don't think it works this way," she said. "It's not heating up at all, and when I used it on the ae'Magi, it was so hot I couldn't hold it."

"All right," said Wolf. "Let's try this. I'll try to work a spell on you while you hold the sword up between us."

Aralorn frowned. "Correct me if I'm wrong, but aren't you being a little rash? If that's why it killed your father, then it could do the same to you."

He didn't say anything.

She had a sudden remembrance of the look on his face as he'd called lightning down upon himself in her dream. *It was only a dream*, she told herself fiercely.

"Plague take you, Wolf," she said as mildly as she could. "It's not important enough to risk your life over. If it won't work on the spells, it can't help us here."

"It might work against the shadow-thing we both saw," he said. "Then perhaps you and I could examine the spells holding your father more closely."

"Fine," she said. "Then we'll try it on that. Do you want to go down now?

Wolf shook his head. "Wait until morning. There are a lot of creatures who are weakened by the rising of the sun—and I'm tired."

Aralorn nodded and slid Ambris back into the sheath before storing her in the wardrobe. She watched Wolf release the spells he'd laid on the bench, creating quite a light show in the process. Reaching out with the sixth sense that allowed her to find and work magic, she could feel the shifting forces but not touch them—what he was using was wholly human in origin.

Later, when the banked fire was the only light in the room, Aralorn snuggled deeper into Wolf's arms.

It will be all right, she thought fiercely.

LATE IN THE night, long after the inhabitants of the castle had gone to sleep, a man emerged from the shadows of the mourning room and stepped to the curtained alcove that contained the slumbering Lyon, his path lit by a few torches left burning in their wall sconces. He pulled back the curtains and started to step into the room but found himself unable to do so.

He placed a hand on the barrier of air and earth that Wolf had erected.

"Yes," he said softly, "he is here."

The warding would keep out human visitors, but he was something more. The tall, robed figure dissolved into the darkness and reappeared inside the room. Before he materialized completely, a shadow slipped from the side of the man on the bier.

"Ah, my beauty," crooned the intruder. "It's all right. I know, you were never meant to face *his* powers. I forget things now. I had forgotten that he could take the form of a wolf, or we would have been ready for him." The shadow stroked against his legs like a cat, emitting squeaks and hisses as it did so. "Hold the Lyon fast, little one. We will force them to come to us."

FOUR

—⁓—

THE CHILL WIND WEAVED ITS WAY THROUGH ARALORN'S HEAVY WOOLEN cloak with the ease of a skilled lover, and she shivered in spite of the layers of clothing she wore. Although the keep was barely out of sight, the bones of her hands ached from the bitter chill. It always took weeks for her to acclimate to the cold northern winter.

Wolf, warm under his thick pelt, observed her attempts to tame her cloak, and asked, "Why did you decide to walk? Sheen would be much faster, not to mention warmer."

"The shapeshifters' village is difficult to reach by horse—sometimes impossible—and that area of Lambshold is too dangerous to leave him tied for any length of time." Aralorn winced at the sharpness of her voice. His question had been reasonable; there was no need to give him the edge of her tongue because she was disappointed.

Before first light, they had visited the bier room and attempted to use the sword to slay the creature. Neither she nor Wolf, who, plague take the man, was a much better swordsman, had been able to even touch the shadow-thing with Ambris. The shadow had melted away from the sword with laughable ease.

Wolf hadn't been able to tell anything more about the spells that held her father than he had before. Black magic had been used, but the pattern of the spelling was too complex to decipher while distracted by the creature who lurked in the bier room.

The only good thing to come out of the visit was that, as far as Wolf could determine, her father was no worse off this morning than he'd been last night. Scant comfort when his condition was so close to death that most people could not tell he was alive.

Wolf gave the clear skies a skeptical glance. "No clouds—I suspect it will be colder than sin. Why don't you shapechange? Your mouse and goose aren't much good here, but the icelynx is adapted for this area."

The wind gusted, blowing snow into Aralorn's face.

"Good idea" said Aralorn. "Then the shepherds will attack me, too." She took a deep breath and reined in her temper. Snapping at Wolf was not going to free her father any faster, and for all that Wolf appeared so impassive, she knew better than most how easy it was to wound him. "Sorry. It's all right. I'll warm up as we walk."

"I would not fret much about a bunch of sheepherders."

Aralorn slanted a glance at him, unable to tell if he was serious or teasing. "They are my father's men. No use stirring them up unduly if we don't have to—besides, I'd just as soon talk to anyone we see. You never know what kernels of information might prove useful."

They followed one of the main paths for several miles; this close to the keep, it was usually well traveled even in the dead of winter. They didn't meet anyone, but it surprised her how much livestock had been left in the high pastures. Usually, they'd have been brought down to the lower, warmer valleys before any snow fell.

The first few herds they passed were distant, but she could tell they were not sheep from their color. When she had lived in Lambshold, there had been few herds of cattle; they were better suited for more temperate climates.

By chance, they came upon a herd unexpectedly close, and she caught a good look at the short, stout animals with long red hair that would have done credit to one of the mountain bears.

She stopped where she was and frowned at them a moment. Softly, so the animals wouldn't be alarmed and charge, she said, "Ryefox."

"Crossbred, by those horns," Wolf replied. "I saw a ryefox drive away a bear once. Good eating, though."

"If they're only half as nasty as their full-blooded relatives, I'd rather face a half dozen Uriah," commented Aralorn. "Naked," she added, as one of the animals took a step toward them.

"They're almost as sweet-tempered as you are this morning," observed Wolf.

"Hah," she said, forgetting that she'd been trying to keep quiet so as not to arouse the ryefox crossbreeds. "Look who's talking, old gloom and doom."

Wolf wagged his tail to acknowledge the justice of her comment, but only said, "I wonder that he found a cow or bull willing to go near enough to a ryefox to breed."

"This must be the livestock experiment that Correy was talking about last night. The one my uncle was helping my father with."

She kept a wary eye on the herd as they walked, but the ryefox appeared to be satisfied that their territory wasn't being threatened and stayed where they were.

A chest-high rock wall marked the boundary where the grazing ended and the northern croplands began. Aralorn caught the top of the wooden gate barring the path and swung over without bothering to open it. Wolf bounded lightly over the fence a few feet away and landed chest deep in a drift of snow. He eyed her narrowly as he climbed back onto the path. Aralorn kept her face scrupulously blank.

She cleared her throat. "Yes, uhm, I was just going to advise you that this area gets windy from time to time—the mountains, you see. And . . . uh, you might want to watch out for drifts."

"Thank you," replied Wolf gravely, then he shook, taking great care to get as much of the snow on Aralorn as he could.

As they continued their journey, the path began to branch off, and the one that they followed got narrower and less well-defined with each division.

"Why farm this?" asked Wolf, eyeing the rough terrain. "The land we just traveled through is better farmland."

"Father doesn't do anything with this land. His farms are along the southern border, several thousand feet lower in altitude, where the climate is milder. But there is good fertile soil here in the small valleys between the ridges—the largest maybe twenty acres or so. The crofters farm it and pay Father a tithe of their produce for the use of the land and protection from bandits. He could get more gold by running animals here instead—but this makes good defensive sense. The lower fields are easily burned and trampled by armies, but up here it's too much trouble."

"Speaking of burning," said Wolf, "something has burned here recently. Can you smell it?"

She tried, but her nose caught nothing more than the dry-sweet smell of winter. "No, but Correy said that one of the crofts had been burned. Can you tell where the smell is coming from?"

"Somewhere a mile or so in that direction." He motioned vaguely south of the trail they were following.

"Let's head that way then," she said. "I'd like to take a look."

They broke with the main path to follow a trail that twisted here and there, up and down, through the stone ridges. It had been well traveled lately, more so than the other such trails they had passed, although a thin layer of snow covered even the most recent tracks. As they neared the farm, Aralorn could smell the sourness of old char, but it didn't prepare her for the sight that met her eyes.

Scorched earth followed the shape of the fields exactly, stopping just inside the fence line. The wooden fence itself was unmarked by the blaze, which had burned the house so thoroughly that only the base stones allowed Aralorn to see where the house had been. All around the croft, the fields lay pristine under the snow.

Wolf slipped through the fence and examined the narrow line that marked the end of the burn.

"Magic," he said. He hesitated briefly, his nostrils flaring as he tested the air. "Black magic with the same odd flavor of the spells holding the Lyon. Look here, on the stone by the corner of the fence."

She stepped over the fence and knelt on the blackened ground. Just inside the corner post, there was a fist-sized gray rock smudged with a rust-colored substance.

"Is it human blood?" she asked.

Wolf shook his head. "I can't tell. Someone used this fire and the deaths here to gather power."

"Enough power to set a spell on my father?"

Before he could answer, the wind shifted a little, and he stiffened and twisted until he could look back down their path.

Aralorn followed his gaze to see a man coming up the trail they had taken here. By his gray beard, she judged him to be an older man, though his steps were quick and firm. In ten years a child might become a man, but a man only grayed a bit more: She matched his features with a memory and smiled a welcome.

"Whatcha be doing there, missy?" he asked as soon as he was near enough to speak, oblivious to Aralorn's smile.

"I'm trying to discover what kind of magic has been at work, Kurmun. What are you doing here? I thought your farm was some distance away."

He frowned at her, then a smile broke over his face, breaking the craggy planes as if it were not something he did often. "Aralorn, as I live and breathe. I'd not thought to see tha face again. I told old Jervon that I'd have a look at his place, he's still that shook. Commet tha then for tha father's passing?"

She smiled. "Yes, I did. But as it turns out, Father's not dead—only ensorcelled."

Kurmun grunted, showing no hint of surprise. "Is what happens when tha lives in a place consecrated to the Lady. Bad thing, that."

She shook her head. "Now, that was taken care of long since. You know the family's not been cursed by the Lady since the new temple was built. This is something quite different, and it may take a few days to discover what. I thought the burning of the farm might have something to do with it."

The old man nodded slowly. "Hadn't thought there was a connection, but there might, there might at that. Have a care here, then. Tha father, he took ill here."

"I didn't know that." But she could have guessed.

Black magic had long carried a death penalty. A mage would avoid it as much as possible. It only made sense that the black magic Wolf felt here would belong to the spell on the Lyon.

"Aye, he come here tha day after it burned. Walked the fence line, he did. Got to the twisted pole over there and collapsed."

"Now, that's interesting," said Aralorn thoughtfully. "Why didn't anyone at the hold mention it?"

"Well," replied Kurmun, though she hadn't expected him to answer her question, "reckon they didn't know. Just he and I here, and I tossed him on his horse and took him to the hold. They was in such a state that no one asked where it'd happened. Only asked what, so that's all I told they. This is some young men's mischief, thought I then." He made a sweeping gesture that encompassed the burnt farm. "Tha father was felled by magic. Didn't rightly think one had much to do with t'other myself. But if tha thinks it so, then so think I now."

"I think it does," she said. "Thank you. Did we lose any people?"

He shook his head. "Nary a one. Jervon's oldest daughter come into her time. The missus and Jervon gathered they children and went up to attend the birth. Lost a brace of oxen, but they sheep was in lower pastures."

"Lucky," said Aralorn. "Or someone knew that they were gone."

Kurmun grunted and scratched his nose. "The Lady's new temple ha' been cleaned and set to rights. Word is that there's a priestess there now; I be thinking tha might want to be stopping in and talking to her. Happens she may help tha father. Happens not." He shrugged.

"Ridane's temple is being used?" There had been a lot more activity in the gods' temples lately. She didn't see how that could have any bearing on the Lyon's condition, but she intended to check out anything unusual that had happened recently. "I'll make certain to visit."

"I'll be on my way then," he said, tipping his head. "Told my son's wife I'd find a bit of salt for her out of the hold stores." As he turned to go, his gaze met Wolf's eyes. "By the Lady," he exclaimed. "Tha beast's a wolf."

"Yes," agreed Aralorn, adding hastily, "He doesn't eat sheep."

"Well," said the old man, frowning, "see that he don't. I'd keep him near tha so some shepherd doesn't get too quick with his sling afore he has a chance to garner that tha wolf doesna eat sheep."

"I intend to."

"Right." Kurmun nodded, and, with a last suspicious look at Wolf, he was on his way.

As soon as he was out of sight, Wolf said, "He called the death goddess the Lady?"

Aralorn smiled briefly. "Lest speaking her name call her attention to him, yes. The new temple is nearly five centuries old. 'New,' you understand, differentiates it from the 'old' temple that my long-dead ancestor had razed to build a hold. There wasn't much left of the new temple when I last saw it; it's been deserted for centuries. I wouldn't think it would be possible to resurrect anything from the piles of stones. In any case, the temple is on the other side of the estate, so we'll have to go there another day."

She tapped her finger on a fence post. "This burned down before my father came here. Wouldn't it have to happen at the same time?"

"There are ways to store power or even set spells to complete when certain conditions are met—like having your father come to this place."

"It was a trap," said Aralorn, "set for my father. The burning of the croft served both as bait and bane. Anyone who knew my father would know that he'd investigate if one of his people's houses burned." She shuffled snow around. "This farm is not too far from the shapeshifters' territory. Other than knowing that it is possible for them to use blood magic, I don't know what they would do with it or how. My uncle will know."

"It could be a human mage," said Wolf. "But any mage who came by here could tell that there was black magic done here. Why would they risk that? My father's reign excepted, the ae'Magi's job is to keep things like this from happening. They kill black mages, Aralorn. Only my father's assurances and his power kept them from killing me—and they had no proof such as this. When we discover who did this, he will die. Why risk that merely to imprison the Lyon when killing would have been easier? What did he accomplish that was worth that?"

Silence gathered as Aralorn stared at the blood-splattered rock.

"Nevyn could do this," said Wolf. "As long as no one knows I'm here, he will be the first one Kisrah ae'Magi will suspect. Nevyn first trained under old Santik."

Aralorn frowned. She'd forgotten that as the ae'Magi's son, Wolf would know a lot of the politics and doings of the mageborn. "Santik is someone Kisrah would associate with black magic?"

Wolf sighed. "His reputation wasn't much better than mine—it wouldn't surprise me or anyone else to find that he'd slipped into dark ways. Certainly, his library would have had the right books; nearly all the great mages have books they aren't supposed to."

"Nevyn's first master was a great mage, too? Was that because of his family's station?" Aralorn asked. "I thought the reason they married him off to my sister was that he wasn't good enough to be a wizard proper. I've never seen him use magic at all."

"He can work magic," Wolf said. "They'd never have wasted Kisrah— or Santik, for that matter—on just any apprentice. But between Santik and being a Darranian-born mage, Nevyn learned to hate being a wizard. When Kisrah was satisfied that Nevyn could control his magic, he let him choose his own path."

"You knew Nevyn," said Aralorn slowly. It wasn't in the details; those were something any wizard might know of another. It was the sympathy in Wolf's voice. "Why didn't you say something to me before?"

"We weren't friends," he said. "Not even acquaintances, really. Kisrah was a particular favorite of my father's—"

"Because your father enjoyed playing games with honorable men," muttered Aralorn.

"—*whatever* his reason," continued Wolf, "and Kisrah brought Nevyn to the ae'Magi's castle several times. Nevyn was quiet, as I remember him, always trying to disappear into the background. He had plenty of courage, though. I think I frightened him to death, but he never gave ground."

"Ten years ago you were just a boy," said Aralorn. "Nevyn's a couple of years older than me—which makes him more than five years older than you."

"I frightened a lot of people, Aralorn," Wolf said.

She ruffled the fur behind his ears. "Not me. Come, let's go visit my uncle so you can frighten him, too."

As THEY CLIMBED higher in the mountains, the area became heavily wooded, and they left behind all signs of cultivation. Here and there great boulders were scattered, some the size of an ox and others as big as a cottage. The narrow path they followed was obviously traveled by humans and game alike, and few enough of either. The dense growth, steep slopes, and snow made it difficult to find a place to leave the path. At last, Aralorn found a shallow, frozen creek to walk on.

"It must be uncomfortable to do this in the spring," commented Wolf, stepping onto the snow-covered ice.

"It's not easy anytime," replied Aralorn, momentarily busy keeping her footing. After a moment, she realized his comment had more to do with the streambed they followed than the difficulty of the trail. "You don't have to come this way exactly. All that's necessary is to find someplace in this part of Lambshold that is not often traveled. Then you can find the maze."

"The maze?" Wolf sounded intrigued.

She smiled, stopping to knock the snow that had packed itself around the short nails that kept the leather soles of her walking boots from slipping on the ice and snow. "You'll see when we find it. But if you'd care to help, keep your eye out for a bit of quartz. I need it to work some magic. There should be quite a bit of it in the steep areas, where there's no snow to cover it."

They came to a small clearing bordered on two sides by the sharp sides of a mountain. Aralorn crossed the clearing and began searching for rocks on the steep areas where the sun and wind had left large sections bare.

"It doesn't have to be quartz," she said finally. "Sandstone would work as well."

Wolf lifted his snow-covered nose from a promising nook under a clump of dead brush. "You could have said so earlier and saved yourself a case of frostbite. There is sandstone all over here."

Aralorn tucked her cold, wet hands underneath her sweaters and warmed them against her middle as Wolf searched back and forth over the area they'd just covered. She'd taken her gloves off to push aside the snow that the afternoon sun had begun to thaw. They had too far to travel to risk getting her gloves wet. When she could feel her fingers again, she pulled the gloves out of her belt and slipped them over her hands.

"You know," she said, as he seemed to be having no success finding the sandstone, "aren't the crystals on your staff quartz?"

"I ought to let you try casting a spell using one of them," said Wolf, not lifting his gaze from the ground, "but I find that I have become more squeamish of late. Ah, yes, here it is."

Aralorn bent to pick up the smooth yellowish brown stone Wolf had unearthed and polish it free of dirt on her cloak.

"Sandstone is for perseverance," she said, "quartz for luck. Which is why I started out looking for quartz: I suspect we'll be spending the night up here."

Wolf lowered his eyelids in amusement. "If you want luck, I have some opal you could use."

"Thanks, but I'll pass," Aralorn demurred. "Ill luck I don't need."

She held the stone in her closed hand and raised her arm to shoulder height. Closing her eyes, she began singing. The song she chose was a children's song in her mother's tongue—though the words didn't matter for the magic, just the pattern of the music, which would be their key to entering her mother's world.

Slowly, almost shyly, awareness of the forest crept upon her. She could feel the winter sleep encasing the plants: wary curiosity peering at them from a rotted-out cedar in the form of a martin; the brook waiting for spring to allow it to run to the ocean far away. Finally, she found what she had been searching for and brushed lightly against the current of magic threaded throughout the forest. When she was certain it had perceived her, she stopped singing and allowed the awareness to pass from her. She looked down at the rock in her hands and, just for a moment, could see an arrow.

"Now, why doesn't it surprise me that we have to travel up the side of the mountain?" she grumbled. She showed the arrow to Wolf, then tossed the stone back on the ground since it had served its purpose. "I should have brought some quartz from home. Irrenna won't have disturbed my stashes of spell starters."

"The maze would have been different?" asked Wolf, pacing beside her as she started up the mountain.

"It's always different," replied Aralorn. "The magic I worked to find the start of the maze will only work with sandstone or quartz—someone's idea of a joke, I suspect. You know—'Only with luck or persistence will you find the sanctuary hidden in the heart of the mountains.' The kinds of words storytellers are fond of. I prefer to start with luck."

The mountainside looked rougher from the bottom than it actually was, an unusual occurrence in Aralorn's experience. All the same, she almost missed the stone altogether, hidden in plain sight as it was in the midst of a dozen other large boulders.

"Good," she said, turning abruptly off her chosen path upward and taking a steep downward route that brought her skidding and sliding to the cluster of granite boulders. "The maze remembers me."

"Ah?"

Aralorn nodded, touching a stone half again as tall as she was and twice as wide. "This stone is the first. The identity stone—for me that has always been granite."

"Granite for compromise," rumbled Wolf, "or blending."

"Right." She smiled. "Blending—that's me. You'll have to touch it, too."

Wolf pawed it gently, drawing back quickly as if he had touched a candle flame. "That's not magic," he said, startled.

"No," agreed Aralorn, waiting.

"It's alive."

"That's the secret of the maze," she agreed.

She drew a simple rune on the granite boulder with a light touch of her finger. As with the sandstone, a directional arrow appeared, outlined in shimmering bits of mica. It pointed across the mountain.

As they started on the indicated route, Wolf was silent. Aralorn left him to his thoughts and concentrated on staying aware of their surroundings. The stones could be difficult to find. She was so busy peering under bushes that she almost missed the waist-high rock standing directly in her path, as out of place in its environment as a wolf in a fold.

"Obsidian," observed Aralorn soberly, touching the black, glasslike surface. The second stone would be Wolf's. The maze's choice surprised her at first; she'd half expected hematite, for war and anger. But the stones of the maze had read deeper than that, identifying Wolf's nature as clearly as they had seen hers. He wore the mask of anger on his face, but his heart was enclosed in sorrow.

"This one's yours," she told him, in case he'd missed its significance. "Obsidian for sorrow. The rest we find will be something about both of us."

"Sorrow?" commented Wolf.

"Yes," said Aralorn. "Like the maze as a whole, the first stones can tell you more than that. They'll show you a bit about yourself and the pattern you're living now—if you interpret what they're saying correctly. I've always mostly ignored what the maze had to say about me, but you can try it if you'd like. Touch the stone for a minute or two, and it will tell you something."

He hesitated, then took a step sideways and leaned against it, saying as he did so, "I'm not certain this is wise. I've never been fond of prophecy."

"Mmm. Remember, it's not a prediction of things to come: It's an assessment of who you are now. And they're not infallible."

After a bit, he stepped away. He didn't say anything, so she didn't ask him what he'd seen. She drew the rune she'd used before, and the arrow appeared on the top of the stone, sending them at a shallow angle downward.

"The next stones are less personal and intended to help predict the near future—some of the time. The language of stones is pretty limited. Mostly it will just present attributes we have or will need."

"Not very helpful," said Wolf, and Aralorn grinned at him.

"Not that I've ever noticed."

During the next several hours, they wandered from stone to stone, finding serpentine for wit, quartz for luck, and malachite for lust (she snickered a bit at that one). They ate the salted meat and cheese Aralorn had brought with them. As the sun reached its zenith, they started down the path the malachite had chosen for them. The stone they found was amethyst, protection against evil. When they came to a second, then yet a third amethyst, Aralorn grew concerned.

"I wonder if the stones will let us through," she said, crouching in the snow beside the melon-sized crystal. "They might not if they think that harm will enter with us."

"Do you want me to wait here?" Wolf asked softly. "You might find this easier on your own."

Realizing he'd taken the message incorrectly, she raised her eyebrow. "Amethyst may be protection from evil, but the stones have already appraised you and have named you sorrowful. If they had judged you as harshly as you judge yourself, we would never have come this far."

"Then you took quite a chance not coming here alone."

She braced both hands on her hips. "I took no chances."

"Stubborn as a pack mule," he said.

Since she'd heard a number of people claim that, she couldn't disagree.

She drew another rune and saw that their path led upward, as it had for the past few stones.

"I hope this ends soon," she grumbled. "I really don't want to spend the night outside. It's cold, it's getting late, and we still have to make the trip back."

Waiting at the top of the climb was a wolf-sized chunk of white marble.

"Judgment," said Aralorn in satisfaction. She thought it would be the last one, but found another maze stone at the top of a twisting bramble-and-brush-filled gorge.

"Rose quartz," murmured Wolf. "It seems we are welcome here."

Even so, Aralorn was unsurprised when the stone pointed them down the gorge.

"I knew I should have held out for luck," she said. "Sometimes, there are ways around the gorge."

There was no trail. Aralorn tore the knee out of her pants and almost lost her cloak before they arrived safely at the bottom. Wolf, of course, had no difficulty at all.

They emerged from the deep undergrowth into a small grotto. From the cliffs overhead, a solidly frozen waterfall plunged into an ice-covered pool. The transformation from the dense gray vegetation to the pristine little valley was shockingly abrupt, as if they had stepped into someone's neatly kept castle garden. Even the snow that covered the ground was evenly dispersed, unmarred by footprints.

"This is it," announced Aralorn with satisfaction. After a moment, she nodded toward the waterfall. "I spent one summer trailing streams in this part of Lambshold, trying to find every stream anywhere near here, and never found one that came through this grotto. I even tried to backtrack this one, but I never managed it. I'd look away for a moment, and the stream would be gone."

"I could do that with a variation of the *lost* spell." Wolf eyed the rushing water speculatively.

"If you say so." She heaved a theatrical sigh. " 'Frustrating' is what I called it."

He laughed. "I'll bet you did. Isn't there supposed to be someone here?"

"No, this is just the end of the maze. There's a trail over by the waterfall," Aralorn said, and began picking her way up the path that edged the pond.

A thin layer of snow turned to a sheet of ice as they approached the waterfall. Aralorn set her feet carefully and kept moving. Wolf drew to a halt and growled.

"I know," said Aralorn quietly, stepping behind the shimmering veil of the frozen waterfall. "Someone's watching us. I had expected them earlier."

The difference between the bright daylight and the shadow of the falls caused her to stop to allow her eyes to adjust. Wolf bumped into her, then slipped past, examining the stone surface of the cliff face behind the waterfall. Behind a thin sheet of ice over the rock where a few last trickles of water had frozen, there was a small tunnel in the rock.

"That goes in about ten feet and ends," said Aralorn. "I stayed there overnight once, but it was summer."

The far end of the narrow path behind the falls was frozen over, but a few hits with the haft of one of her knives broke a small hole, and her booted foot cleared a space large enough to climb through.

Once out from under the waterfall, their way twisted up the side of the mountain. The path was cobbled, and the smooth stones were slicker than the natural ground. Aralorn tried to walk beside the path as much as she could. The climb was thankfully short, only to the top of the falls.

Over the years, the stream that formed the waterfall had cut a deep channel between the two mountains that fed it with the runoff from the snowy peaks. The path was cut into the side of one mountain several feet above the stream, winding and twisting with the course of the water.

After walking a mile or so, the path turned abruptly away from the mountain, through a thicket of brush and into a wide valley.

WOLF COULD STILL feel the eyes watching them, though he couldn't tell where the spy was. It was not magic that told him so much, but the keen senses of the wolf. Not scent, nor sight, nor hearing, but faint impressions gathered from all three. It distracted him as he examined the place to which Aralorn had brought them.

The valley was surrounded by steep-sided hills that reminded him of the valley in the Northlands where he'd spent the past winter, although that had been far smaller. Someone had taken a lot of time to find a place this sheltered. The stone path, now half-buried in the snow, led up a slight incline to a pair of gateposts. Other than those, the valley appeared empty. Perhaps, he thought as he followed Aralorn, the village was located over the next rise.

Then, between one step and the next, magic rose over him from the ground, momentarily paralyzing him with its strength. Defensively, he analyzed it: a blending illusion that utilized the lay of the land to hide something in the valley.

Without conscious act, he found himself holding the magic to break the spell, magic that had nothing to do with the familiar, violent forces he normally worked. This was a surge of power that took its direction from the brief alarm he'd felt at the sudden wall of magic. It flared in an attempt to twist out of his fragile hold and attack the ensorcellment before him. The effort it took to restrain it challenged his training and power both.

"Wolf?"

Even wrapped as he was in the grip of his power, her voice reached him. Fear of what his magic would do to her gave him the strength to contain it, just barely.

"Wolf?" Aralorn said again, kneeling beside him.

She didn't dare touch him as he swayed and shook with rhythmic spasms. Gradually, the spasms slowed and stopped. He took a deep, shuddering breath and looked up at Aralorn.

"Problems?" she asked.

"Yes."

"Do you want to wait for me back by the waterfall?"

"No," he said. "It's all right now. It just took me by surprise."

She looked at him narrowly for a moment before deciding to accept his word on the matter.

"Fine, then. There is some kind of protective illusion over the village. I don't think we ought to tamper with it, but if we approach, I suspect we'll be met."

"Such an illusion is not the usual practice?" He sounded as controlled as he usually did, though he was so tense she could see the fine trembling of his muscles.

Aralorn shook her head in answer. "Not when I lived here."

Though the village was hidden, the gateposts that marked the entrance were still there. Wolf, the ruff on his neck still raised from his battle for control of his magic, ranged in random patterns to either side.

"Stay on the path," she warned him. "They wouldn't have left the gateposts here if they didn't have something nasty protecting the village from people who aren't polite enough to enter by the proper way."

When she tried to walk between the gateposts, a barrier of magic stopped her. It wasn't painful, just solid.

Aralorn drew the rune she'd used in the maze on the left-hand pillar, but the barrier remained. She frowned but didn't try to force her way through the gate.

Instead, she spoke to the watcher who'd accompanied them from the waterfall. "I have come to speak with Halven, my uncle." Her tongue fought her a little as she curled it around the shapeshifter language that she hadn't used since she'd last been here.

Beyond the posts, the wind stirred the snow into random swirls. The quiet was oppressive and uncomfortable.

Turning to Wolf, Aralorn said, "They may make us wait for a long time. Sometimes, the oddest things strike them as humorous."

Without reply, Wolf made himself comfortable though he fairly vibrated with tension. Aralorn shivered as a cold breeze ran under her cloak.

"It is cold here," said a man behind her in the same tongue she'd used. "You must want to talk to this uncle very badly."

Wolf came to his feet with a growl; he hadn't heard the man approach.

She put a hand on his head, then turned to face the stranger.

Shapeshifters were hard to identify: They could assume any features they chose. Nothing in the beautiful face and artfully swept-back bronze hair was familiar. Voices, though, were more difficult to change, and given a moment to recover, she knew who it was. She smiled.

"Badly," she agreed, switching to Rethian for Wolf's sake. "I would have waited a lot longer than this, Uncle Halven."

"You might have indeed," he replied without altering his language, "had I not seen you myself. I am not high in favor at this moment, and you never were."

"You flatter me," Aralorn replied. She continued to speak Rethian. If he was going to be rude, she'd follow his lead. "As I recall, I was too insignificant to warrant animosity."

Halven smiled like a cat—with fangs and cold eyes. "Aralorn the half-breed certainly was, but the Sianim spy is a different matter altogether."

She raised her eyebrows. "Spy? Who says I am a spy?"

"If you would talk," said Halven mildly, "it would best be done here."

"That's fine," she said. "I apologize in advance for keeping you out in the cold."

"Not at all." Halven was suddenly all gracious host, though he'd yet to switch to Rethian, which he would have if he'd really been in an accommodating mood. "What brings you and your dog here on this chilly morning?"

Wolf was sometimes mistaken for a dog by people who hadn't seen him move because he lacked the usual gray coat. It surprised her that Halven would mistake him, though, and she almost turned to look at Wolf. But she didn't want to draw her uncle's attention to him.

Assuming the shapeshifters were as resistant to the ae'Magi's magic as she had been, there was no reason they would be upset about his death; but she would rather they didn't know any more about Wolf than was necessary. Unlike the people at Lambshold, if Halven looked closely, he might be able to tell that Wolf was a shapeshifter—and a both green and human mage of great power. With that much information, it was only a step to identify him as Cain ae'Magison, who killed the ae'Magi. The shapeshifters didn't talk much to people in the outside world, but that was one thing she would rather no one knew. The ae'Magi's spells ensured that almost everyone loved him—and if they knew where Cain was, they would try to kill him.

The maze stones knew what, and who, Wolf was already, but they seldom spoke anymore.

"Have you heard that my father's been taken ill?" she asked.

"I'd heard he was dead," replied Halven flatly.

"Yes, well these things do get exaggerated upon occasion, don't they?"

Aralorn said. "I'm pleased to tell you that he's alive, but there is some sort of magic binding keeping him in a deathlike trance. I wondered if you might know something about it."

For a moment, her uncle's expression changed, too quickly for her to catch what it was he felt; she hoped he was glad the Lyon wasn't dead.

Seeing her face, Halven laughed with real humor that pierced the armor of his outward charm like a ray of sunlight through a stained-glass window. "You want to know if I did it, eh?"

"That was the general idea," she replied.

"No, child, I haven't done anything to him. As a matter of fact, we have begun to exchange favors." He shook his head in bemusement. "I never thought I would deal with a human, but the Lyon is nothing if not persistent—much like his daughter."

Relief swept through her. Halven prided himself on being truthful in all things. If he'd hurt her father, he'd have told her or found some clever way of not admitting one way or the other.

"Would you be willing to come and look at him? I've never seen anything like the spell that holds him—I can't even tell if it is green magic or human."

Halven was shaking his head before she finished speaking. "No. Call down one of the human mages. My position in the quorum of elders is touchy enough without risking a visit to the human stronghold. They feel I have compromised our safety, though they agreed before I helped your father with his breeding project."

"The ryefox," said Aralorn thoughtfully. "That's the reason for the new glamour and protection for the village. Too many people know you're here. What did my father give you for your help?"

"The Lyon has deeded this section of Lambshold to me and my kindred by special dispensation of the new king. We also have a treaty calling for the protection of our land by the Lord of Lambshold in perpetuity."

"If the Lyon said it, it is true," said Aralorn. Then she raised an eyebrow. "*If* he had time to tell my brother Correy about it. You can't expect Correy to take *your* word on the matter, given the suspicion that you yourself might have caused my father's strange condition."

The Lyon wouldn't have left it to chance, she knew. He would have recorded it immediately—but Halven might not know that.

"Your manipulation is heavy-handed, Aralorn," he said.

She shrugged. "I only tell you what you have been telling yourself. The Lyon probably told my brother. *Probably* my brother will hold to my father's word—even with the suspicion that will be aimed toward the shapeshifters. But it would be better for you if the Lyon was returned to health. Irrenna has sent word to the ae'Magi, but the spells are black magic. Kisrah may be quite brilliant, but his reputation does not make him an expert in the dark arts."

"And I am?" he asked.

"How old are you?" asked Aralorn. "Kisrah is only a few years above forty. How many more centuries have you spent learning? Don't tell me that you have nothing more to offer us than a human mage."

"Persistent," he said chidingly. "I told you his affliction was none of my doing, child. Making an agreement with the Lyon is one thing; going to the keep is an entirely different matter. I will not endanger my people further."

Aralorn met his gaze. "Come. Because I ask it of you. Because my mother would have done so if she had lived."

His eyelids fell to cover the expression in his eyes as he thought. She wasn't certain her appeal would be enough, especially because she had no idea if her mother cared enough for the Lyon to come to his aid.

It might just be possible that he would want to come. No one could resist the Lyon's charm when it was directed at them, not even, she hoped, Halven. If he liked her father enough . . .

WOLF WATCHED ARALORN's uncle with sympathy—Aralorn could talk a cat into giving up its mouse. He could only understand her half of the conversation, but he could tell quite a bit from Halven's gestures and Aralorn's speech.

Wolf wondered, for a moment, why Aralorn had told him once that her uncle was indifferent to her. The poor man hadn't even taken his eyes off her long enough to notice that her pet was a wolf. The shapeshifters had few children—Halven, Wolf knew, had none at all.

"LEAVE THE HUMANS to their own trials, my dear," said a lark as it landed on Halven's shoulder. Her voice was light and high-pitched, making it difficult to understand her.

He shrugged irritably, sending the small bird to perch on top of a gatepost. "Does this concern you, Kessenih? Tend to your own business."

Aralorn could have cheered. Nothing was as likely to persuade her uncle to go to the hold as his wife's opposition.

"Very well, Aralorn," he said, "I'll accompany you to see your father. Is that silly goose still the only bird you do?" He stopped abruptly and frowned. "That dog"—he paused, frowning at Wolf—"wolf of yours is going to slow us down."

Halven had looked at Wolf but hadn't been able to detect his nature. Shapeshifters always knew their own—but Halven hadn't seen Wolf for what he was any more than Aralorn had at first.

"Why don't you meet me there?" she suggested. "I'll walk back with Wolf. Maybe the stones will aid our travel."

Halven frowned. "All right. I will ask the stones to speed you to Lambshold. Sometimes that helps." In a flutter of hawk feathers, he was gone.

FIVE

—⁂—

"SO, YOU'VE GROWN UP, HALFLING," OBSERVED THE LARK, HAVING FLUT-
tered to one of the gateposts after Halven made his abrupt switch.

Aralorn bowed shallowly to the yellow-and-black-banded bird. Not
certain how much Rethian her aunt understood, she switched back to
the shapeshifters' tongue Kessenih had used. "As you see, Aunt."

"No good will come of this." The lark's beady eyes focused malevo-
lently on Aralorn. "If it is known he is gone to the castle again, he will
be cast out. They came close to doing it when he helped the Lyon with
his cattle breeding. He was told not to contact the humans again without
the approval of the quorum."

Aralorn looked at the snowy ground for a moment. She didn't know
how far to trust Kessenih. Her aunt hated her husband almost as much
as she despised Aralorn herself.

"It is his decision to make," Aralorn said at last, a little fiercely. "I have
no choice but to ask him to make it."

"Selfish child," her aunt decreed.

"Perhaps so," agreed Aralorn, "but the fact remains that the shapeshifters benefit as much from my father's continued existence as I do, if
not more. It is in your best interest to keep Halven's activities a secret, as
you will share his fate if he is exiled."

"Then you'd best be gone from here before someone notices," snapped
Kessenih as she exploded into flight.

Wolf waited until she was gone before speaking. "She said something
that upset you?"

Aralorn nodded, switching back to Rethian. "My uncle is risking a lot to help us."

"He's going to help? I couldn't tell."

"He's meeting us at the castle." She shrugged, feeling discouraged as well as guilty for asking Halven to risk so much.

"He says he didn't have anything to do with Father's current problem. There appears to be opposition to the aid Halven gave Father in breeding the ryefox. Judging from my aunt Kessenih's attitude, I think that there could be enough opposition to having humans know of their presence that they might be willing to kill to stop the association with humans." Aralorn gave him her best smile. "It would be simpler if the shapeshifters didn't have a hand in this. If the people here are convinced that my father's affliction came at the hands of the shapeshifters, it would mean war."

"We'll have to see to it that doesn't happen." He paused. "If necessary, we could provide them with a villain."

She glanced at him, and said sharply, "Oh, no, you don't. You've been maligned quite enough as it is. Let the late ae'Magi's evil son disappear from view after his father's death."

She started hiking back toward the waterfall. "My uncle might be able to do something about the creature that is guarding the Lyon. He's a lot older than he looks—and powerful. If nothing else, he should be able to tell us what the shadow-thing is."

As THEY EXITED the waterfall, Wolf glanced over his shoulder, then froze, pricking his ears. Aralorn followed his gaze and saw that the smooth surface of snow behind them was unmarred by any sign of their passage.

"It's always that way," murmured Aralorn. "There are never any trails—not even of casual wildlife. I don't know why the stones extend the effort since no one can come here without first going through the maze. They are very old, though, and have their own ideas of what's important."

She headed for the place they'd entered the grotto, where the undergrowth was thinner. Ascending the gorge was worse than climbing down had been—at least while they'd been going downhill, when she slipped it was in the right direction. It didn't help that Wolf seemed to have no trouble at all and spent most of his time waiting for her to struggle through the underbrush.

They emerged finally into a level meadow, where frozen strands of grass poked gracefully through the snow at the bases of fifteen gray monoliths set in a circle, each one the height of a man. It looked nothing at all like the place that had been at the start of their descent earlier that day.

"The maze stones as they are from this side of the maze," said Aralorn. "Do you want to take a closer look?"

Without replying, Wolf stepped into the circle.

"The story is that each of the stones was once a shapeshifter. They gave their lives to protect the remnants of their people," she said.

High above them, a red-tailed hawk called out.

Aralorn looked up. "That's my uncle. We'd best be on our way."

"You know where we are?" asked Wolf, leaving the circle after a last thoughtful look.

She shook her head. "After we pass through the center of the maze stones, there is a barrier to cross outside the circle—here it is, do you feel it?"

The wolf shivered briefly as he started through it. Quickly, Aralorn grabbed a handful of fur and followed.

"Sorry," she said, releasing his pelt. "If you cross separately, we'll end up in two different places."

"Ah?" Wolf turned to look behind him. There was no clearing, no monolithic stones, only dense forest. "A translocation spell? It didn't feel like it."

Aralorn frowned, smoothing the fur she'd ruffled on his back. "I don't know how like your translocation spell it is. With green magic it is possible to build . . . pathways from one area strong with magic to another. The stones direct the paths and work magic constantly to keep the valley safe." She smiled. "If they listened to Halven, it shouldn't take us long to get home."

The woods closed in upon them, and the path they trod became a knee-high growth of evergreens amid the older trees. Here and there, it became so choked with brush that they had to leave it altogether and look for a better way around. It was in the middle of one such detour that they came upon an old abandoned stone hut in a small clearing.

"The hermit's cottage," exclaimed Aralorn in surprise. She looked around the forest and shook her head. It was funny how familiar everything suddenly looked when she knew where she was. "I should have figured it out earlier: This is the only part of Lambshold that has so much forest. We're not as close to the keep as we could be, but if we head due south from here, we should make it before dinner."

As she turned to look at Wolf, something crashed through the trees half a dozen yards away. She turned to see an animal as tall as Sheen and even more massive emerge from the forest. It let out a hoarse moaning sound that started deep in its chest and rose to a high-pitched mewl.

The terrible cold of its breath touched her face though she shouldn't have been close enough to feel it. The animal was covered with a thick white coat that darkened to a dirty yellow in the heavy mane that ringed its neck. Its blunt-featured face was similar to a bear's, but the intelligence in the eyes above the yellow-fanged mouth made it much more threatening.

"Howlaa," murmured Aralorn in disbelief as she stumbled back.

The creatures were rare, even in the Northlands, where they hunted with the winter winds. She'd never heard of one this far south, but, she recalled abruptly, the trappers had been whispering about an increase in the magical creatures of the Northlands for the past few years. Frightening as the beast was, the storyteller in her captured images of the creature.

Her fascinated gaze traveled from the howlaa's fangs to its glittering diamond eyes and stopped. Awareness of anything but the howlaa faded to insignificance. Distantly, she felt an odd dizziness that rapidly increased to nausea. Though she knew she stood firmly planted on the ground, she could feel nothing solid under her feet. As she swayed, torn adrift from her moorings, the wind touched her—gently at first.

Sadness, despair. It is out of place here and dying from the warmth.
Aralorn winced away from the alien deluge but could not escape the net
the howlaa had caught her in.

THERE WERE SOME *things a human mind was never meant to understand . . . the color of warmth and the voices that rode the winter winds.
How to ride the blue currents of biting ice. The many textures of evil and
its seductive, icy grip. Evil gave generously to those who knew ITS call . . .
IT had sent this one to look for a shapechanger. IT wanted the wolf
dead and promised a return to icy sheets that went on forever in all directions.*

A pained whine added itself to the growing cacophony surrounding
her. Ice-colored eyes turned from her.

Without the grip of the colorless gaze, Aralorn fell to her hands and
knees, unable to feel the bite of the snow, for she'd been touched by
something even colder. The wind blew past her. Gathering its chill
thoughts and whispering to her in a thousand thousand voices, voices
that murmured and shrieked of death, of evil and all its incarnates. She
couldn't pull any one thing out of the deluge, only flinch from it and
cower in terror.

A muffled grunt sounded from nearby, this time as human as the
howlaa's whine was not.

Wolf, she thought. The thought of him allowed her to pull her hands
to her ears, and the voices ceased with blessed suddenness. Awareness
returned, and she looked up at Wolf in human guise, his back to her,
confronting the howlaa.

Despite the blood that dripped from his shirt to melt the snow, Wolf
wielded his black staff with cool grace. The crystals that grew from one
end of the staff glittered like the eyes of the howlaa, while the finger-long,
sharp metal talons on the other end dripped blood.

The talons were a weapon of a sort. Against a human opponent, they
could be deadly—but against the howlaa's thick hide and inner layer of

fat, the short blades were virtually useless. It was unlike him to choose such an inept method of attack—unless he hadn't known the things were immune to magic. His education in such matters was a bit haphazard—gleaned from books rather than teachers. His magic would have been an excellent weapon against a natural creature like a bear or wild boar, but it would help him not at all against the howlaa.

Stumbling to her feet without using her hands (as they were covering her ears against a cacophony of voices that couldn't possibly be there), Aralorn noticed there was something wrong with her vision as well. Some things were blurry, while others were incredibly detailed.

Focusing on the fight, she drew her hands away from her ears and frantically stripped away her hampering cloak before the voices could claim her again. She had left her sword at Lambshold, worried that such a powerful weapon would antagonize the shapeshifters; now she wished she'd brought it along.

Aralorn drew her knives, one in each hand, and watched the rhythm of the fight to see where she could best attack.

Come on, concentrate, she thought. The effort of ignoring the muttering tones caused her to break out in a light sweat in spite of the ice and wind.

Wolf struck with the clawed end of his staff, and the howlaa turned away, bawling angrily as the sharp points scored its side. With a growl, it snapped at the staff and received another slash. Had the talons on Wolf's staff moved, or was it merely an effect of whatever the howlaa's gaze had done to her?

Aralorn shook her head in an attempt to drive away thoughts and voices alike. She needed to know where the battle would move, not what Wolf's staff was doing. It was hard to read the purpose of Wolf's pattern of attack. He wasn't looking for a possible fatal hit, just using his staff to poke and prod the creature in the sides. He wasn't trying to back away to the woods, where the howlaa's size would work against it. It was as if . . . of course, Wolf was trying to pull the howlaa away from her—just like one of the idiotic, plaguingly foolish heroes in a bard's tale. He probably could have backed off and conjured something more useful than his pox-eaten staff if he hadn't been worried about her.

Wolf's next attack should come *there*, and the howlaa would close from the right. Just as it had kept away pain, cold, and terror over the years, the taste of battle forced the voices into the background at last.

As silent as Wolf himself, Aralorn edged around the battle until she was behind the howlaa. When all of its attention was on Wolf, she ran and sprang into the air, leaping on the howlaa's back as if it were a horse and she a youngster trying to show off. She clamped her legs beneath its shoulder blades and plunged her sharp steel knives into either side of its neck, where the fat was not as thick.

Rising on its haunches, the howlaa sang, a high, piercing death-song that the wind answered and echoed. Aralorn clung to its back as it rose, her face against the coarse, musky-smelling fur while the creature's blood warmed her cold hands and made the hafts of her knives slick.

The howlaa jerked again as Wolf hit it in the throat with his staff, sinking the talons deep into flesh. He shifted his grip on the staff and braced his weight against it to force the dying animal sideways.

If not for Wolf's quick action, the howlaa would have fallen backward on top of Aralorn. As it was, she loosed her hold on her knives, jumped off the animal, and ran out of the reach of the powerful claws, which were flailing about wildly.

From opposite sides, she and Wolf watched the creature's death throes. It struggled for a moment more, then lay still. Aralorn shivered and retrieved her cloak from the snow where she'd tossed it.

"One of your relatives?" asked Wolf, cleaning the end of his staff in the snow.

Aralorn shook her head, pulling the enveloping folds of wool around her, trying to still the shudders of cold and battle fever. "No, it's a howlaa."

The fight done, the murmuring voices fought for her attention, though they were quieter than before. She knew she should do something, but she couldn't remember what.

Wolf finished cleaning the ends of his staff, then buried it in the snow so he could tuck his hands under his arms to warm them. He walked over to the dead animal and nudged it gently with a foot. "What is a howlaa doing so far south?"

"Hunting," replied Aralorn softly. She noticed that the wind was dying down.

Wolf left off examining the dead beast. "Aralorn?"

"It was sent to get you, I think. I . . ." The wind died down to nothing, taking the voices with it. Cautiously, she relaxed.

"Are you all right, Lady?"

She smiled at him, trying for reassurance. "Ask me tomorrow. What about your shoulder?"

He shook his head. "A scratch. It'll need cleaning when we get to the keep, but it's nothing to worry about."

She insisted on seeing it anyway, but he was right. She'd held on to the rush of battle until she was certain he was all right. Her worry satisfied, she relaxed.

Taking the edge of his black velvet cloak, Wolf wiped the smudges of tree sap and howlaa blood off her face. Finishing her nose, he pulled a few sticks out of her hair and pushed it back from her eyes.

"I don't know why you bother," said Aralorn. "Ten steps through the trees, and it will look just as bad."

Wolf's amber eyes glittered with amusement. He made a motion toward his mask as if he were going to take it off, when his gaze passed by her, and he stopped. Aralorn turned to see the red-tailed hawk perched on the dead howlaa.

"Where did you find a shapeshifter powerful enough that I could not tell he was anything other than a wolf who followed at your heels?" Her uncle spoke in his native tongue.

Without replying, Aralorn translated his speech into Rethian for Wolf. She was too tired for verbal battles—though translating wasn't much better.

"She found me, and I followed her home," said Wolf dryly.

"So why do you need me, child?" Halven switched to Rethian, though his tone lost none of its hostility. "I felt the force of the magic he called when you were imperiled; your shapeshifter is surely as capable as I."

"No," said Wolf.

"He only knows human magic," said Aralorn, when it became obvious that Wolf had said all that he would on the matter.

Her uncle let out a coughing sound and ruffled his feathers. "I am not stupid. No human mage could hold the shape of a wolf for so long without being trapped in his own spelling."

"His father, who raised him, was a human mage," she said cautiously, not wanting to give too much away. "We think his mother was a shapeshifter or some other kind of green mage. His ability to work green magic . . . fluctuates." She wouldn't tell her uncle how badly it fluctuated, not now. Perhaps later, when he was in a better mood. "In green magic, he has only the little training that I've been able to give him, and you know how poorly trained I am."

"Your own fault," he snapped.

"Of course," she said, happy to have distracted him to a more familiar frustration. "Wolf has already looked at the spells holding Father. Perhaps you might be able to tell how they were cast, but neither of us could figure it out. There is this also: Father is guarded by some sort of creature that I have never even heard stories about. We thought you might be able to identify it."

"Why didn't you tell me about all this before?" asked Halven in a dangerously soft voice.

Tired as she was, Aralorn found the energy to grin.

"What?" she said. "And use my best ammunition first? I thought that you would be much harder to convince, and I'd have to pull out the shadow-thing to draw you to the keep out of curiosity. I wasn't counting on Kessenih doing half the work for me."

She couldn't be sure, but she thought she saw an answering amusement rising in her uncle's eyes.

"We think," said Wolf slowly, "that your people have nothing to do with this. If you can banish the creature who guards him, or tell us how to do it, then with luck we can unwork the spell and identify the caster."

Halven raised his eyebrows. "I hadn't heard that you could trace a black spell back to the wizard."

"If it is human cast, I can," said Wolf.

The shapeshifter cocked his head. "So if I can help you rid the Lyon of this creature, you can deal with the black magic binding him?"

"If it is black magic, worked by human hands—yes."

"I thought," said Halven with soft intent, "that human mages proscribed black magic. A mage caught using it is killed."

"Working black magic is," replied Wolf. "But unworking it usually requires no blood or death."

"You are very familiar with something that is supposed to have been forbidden for so long."

"Yes, and you are not the first to note it," agreed Wolf, without apparent worry, though Aralorn curled her hands into fists. He took such a risk. Her uncle would figure out who he was, and she no longer knew him well enough to predict what Halven would do. If he told any of the humans about it, Wolf would become a target for anyone. The Spymaster, Ren, liked to say that anyone could be killed, given enough time, money, and interest in accomplishing that person's death.

"If I am seen by a human mage," Wolf continued, "he will most certainly attempt to see that I am killed. It is to spare myself needless effort defending myself that I spend so much time as a wolf."

The wind had been teasing the treetops, but as the sun moved down and removed that slight source of warmth, it began to blow in earnest once more. Aralorn lost track of the conversation, unable to tell one voice among many. Keeping her face impassive, she slipped her hand onto the curve of Wolf's elbow and kept her mouth closed for fear of echoing the shrieks reverberating in her head.

Wolf glanced at her face, then said something to Halven.

The hawk cocked its head and gave a jerky nod. With a leap and a thrust of wings, it took flight.

Wolf waited until the hawk was out of sight before turning back to Aralorn. The wind howled through the trees, making Wolf's cloak snap and crackle around her as he drew her under its shelter.

"What is it, Lady?" he asked, the rough velvet of his voice penetrating the chaos that rang in her head.

"The wind," she whispered. "It's the wind. I can *hear* them."

"'Them'?" He frowned at her. "Who do you hear?"

"Voices." She saw the worry in his eyes and tried to explain better. "An effect of the howlaa's gaze, I think."

He didn't speak again; she drew comfort from the warmth of his body and the strength of his arms. Her hands weren't sufficient to block out the noise, but they helped. She wasn't aware of time's passing, but when the wind finally died down, the sky was noticeably darker, and a light skiff of snow had begun to fall.

She pulled away slowly, meeting Wolf's worried gaze with one of her own. "In the Trader Clans, when a man goes insane, they say that he is listening to the wind. I have always wondered what the wind said."

Wolf nodded slowly. "I have heard that the Traders have another saying—may your road be clear, your belly full, and may you never get what you wish for."

Aralorn summoned a grin. "Just think of the legends I can spawn now . . . the woman who could hear the wind—it has a certain rhythm to it, don't you think?"

"More likely it would be the woman who died in the winter because she couldn't quit talking long enough to get out of the cold," replied Wolf repressively.

Her smile warmed into something more genuine. "By all means, let us avoid such an ignominious fate." She gestured grandly to the underbrush that covered the old trail. "Away, then, to the Lyon's keep."

He bowed low. "Allow me to retrieve your knives first?"

"Of course," she said, as if she hadn't forgotten them. She slipped the knives, cleaned by Wolf, back into their sheaths and strode into the woods.

Her heroic stride was shortened somewhat by the waist-high aspen seedlings and drifts of snow nearly as high, but her spirits lifted all the same—how many people could claim to have met a howlaa and survived? Her optimism was greatly helped by the wind's continued absence.

BY THE TIME they reached the keep, the snowfall was no longer so light, and Aralorn was grateful to have Wolf's eyes to depend upon rather than her own feebler senses—he had shifted back to lupine form as soon as the keep was in view. The sentries allowed her entrance through the gates without challenge.

She took the time to shake out her cloak and dust the worst of the snow off Wolf before she opened the door into the keep. As the warmth of the hall fire touched her cheek, a red-tailed hawk landed lightly on her shoulder. Ignoring the surprised expressions of the servants, she transferred the bird to one of her arms, which were protected by the layers of clothing she wore, and handed off her cloak. The hawk climbed her arm and perched once more on her shoulder. Her sweaters had slipped to one side, leaving only a single layer of clothing between her skin and the hawk's sharp talons.

"You be careful," she admonished her uncle. "I don't want any more scars. I look odd enough in an evening gown as it is."

Halven flexed his talons lightly without gripping hard enough to hurt.

"All right," she said.

The hawk unfurled his wings slightly to keep his balance as she strode through the keep. Wolf trailed silently behind. With the funeral preparations on indefinite hold, most of the visitors had left, and the servants were busy with dinner, so the back ways through the keep were empty—at least until they passed by a turret staircase near the mourning room.

"Why does Mother let you bring your pets into the keep when we can't even bring in our dogs? Is she frightened of you? Or do you have her bewitched like Nevyn says?" asked a young voice coolly.

Aralorn took two steps back until she could see the area under the stairs clearly. In her hurry, she hadn't seen the dim light cast by the oil lamp, but now that her attention had been drawn to it, she could see that a small study had been neatly tucked into the cramped space beneath the stairs. The keep was not overly large, and with a family the size of the Lyon's brood, it took cleverness to find a place unclaimed by anyone else.

The boy who'd spoken sat perched on a stool with a large book on his lap. He was on his way to gaining the height of the rest of the family—already he was taller than Aralorn—but he was painfully thin. His wrists were bare for several inches where he had outgrown his shirt, an oddly vulnerable touch for such a self-possessed young man. It took a moment for her to see the toddler she knew in the man he was becoming.

"No coercion," replied Aralorn lightly. "I doubt a . . . howlaa could frighten Irrenna. I've seen her face down Father a time or two, and he's much more scary than I could ever be. Nor sorcery either—I don't have the kind of power that can influence people's thoughts." Once she would have said that no one did, but recent history had proven otherwise. "The wolf would worry the shepherds if he wandered freely about, Gerem. It's safer for everyone if he stays with me."

Gerem was a year younger than Lin. Aralorn remembered him as a quiet little person with an unexpected stubborn streak. The icy blue eyes that glittered with dislike and fear were something new. This kind of moment was why she'd left Lambshold. Bad enough that Nevyn felt that way about her; to have her family fear her was more than she could bear. She felt a sudden empathy with Wolf.

"And the hawk?"

"Hmm," said Aralorn, trying not to let his coldness hurt—she had, after all, left when he was a toddler; he couldn't know her. "Lady Irrenna doesn't know about the hawk yet."

"If the Lady Irrenna objects, I will shift back to human," said the hawk softly. "But I prefer to stay as I am."

"Shapeshifter," Gerem whispered, his eyes widening.

Aralorn nodded. "Yes. I told Irrenna . . ."

"Is he the one who did it?"

Aralorn gave him an assessing look. There was something in his voice that led her to think that he was attempting offense rather than speaking out of belief.

"You overstep yourself, accusing a guest of this house." She dropped the friendly tone she'd been using and replaced it with ice. "He did nothing but volunteer to look at the workings of the spell."

The hawk tilted its head to the side. "I will answer the boy, Aralorn Sister's Daughter. You need not come to my defense. I have not ensorcelled the Lyon at any time, Master Gerem. If I were inclined to use my magic in such a fashion, I would certainly have done it decades ago, when it might have done me some good. As it is, his incapacity has inconvenienced me greatly."

Gerem looked embarrassed. His rudeness, thought Aralorn, had been directed at her.

Recalled to his manners, the boy bowed graciously, if briefly. "My apologies, sir. My words were ill directed."

The hawk bent to preen his wing. Aralorn nodded formally and proceeded on her way.

"I think we just saw Nevyn's influence," commented Wolf, once they were out of earshot.

"Ah yes, Nevyn—the wizard who dislikes magic." Halven sounded amused.

Aralorn smiled without humor. "Something tells me I'm going to have a long talk with Nevyn before I leave. Speaking of people who do stupid things, why did you announce your presence to my brother? Kessenih informed me that you've taken a serious risk coming here."

"As if no one would have thought 'shapeshifter' when you came into the keep with a hawk on your shoulder," murmured Wolf. "A hawk like the one that brought you here as a baby."

"Plague take it," said Aralorn. "I didn't think of that. The howlaa must have stolen all that was left of my wits."

"Peace, child," replied the hawk with amusement. "Kessenih worries overmuch. I have dealt with the quorum before, and I will again. They need me more than I need them."

SIX

THERE WAS A GUARD SEATED JUST OUTSIDE THE ENTRANCE TO THE BIER room. She'd told Irrenna the room was warded, but apparently someone thought that Aralorn's wards would be insufficient to keep people away. Since they might have been right—if *Aralorn* had set the wards—she was amused rather than offended.

The guard rose to his feet as they entered. "Lady Aralorn."

"It might be wise if you leave for a candlemark or two," she said. "My uncle has agreed to look at the Lyon, and he might work some magic. If anyone asks you, tell them it is on my authority."

He probably wouldn't be in any danger, but the shadow that guarded the Lyon worried her. There was no way to tell what it was capable of until they knew more about it. If Wolf and Halven were going to be prodding it with magic, she'd prefer to keep the defenseless away.

The guardsman glanced at the hawk riding her shoulders and blanched a bit, letting his gaze slide to the safety of her human face. "As you say, Lady. I'll report to the captain, then return in two candlemarks." So saying, he started off with suspiciously brisk steps.

But she must have been wrong about how much her uncle frightened him because he stopped abruptly and turned back. "The Lyon gave me my first sword and taught me to use it."

"Me, too," she said.

"Luck and the Lady be with you," he said, then executed an about-face and continued on his way.

As soon as the guard was out of sight, Wolf trotted to the entrance to the alcove where the Lyon lay in state. He sniffed at it suspiciously.

"What is it?" asked Aralorn.

Wolf shifted abruptly to human form, wearing his usual mask to hide his face from her uncle. He ran his fingers carefully over the edge of the entrance.

"Someone's attempted the warding," he said.

"What?" asked Aralorn. She touched the stone where he had, but she could only feel the power of his wards. The human magic was beyond her ability to decipher for subtleties.

"Someone started to unwork the wards I set this morning. He left off halfway, as if something interrupted him, or he decided not to go on with it."

"Maybe he couldn't get through," she suggested.

He shook his head. "No, he knew what he was doing—he could have dispelled it."

"Nevyn?" she suggested.

He shrugged, then touched the air just in front of the curtain, letting his hands rest on the surface of the warding. "I can't tell, but it must have been him. Unless there are other mages who live in Lambshold. I wonder if he recognized my work."

"Could he?"

"Maybe."

"Irrenna said she was calling on Kisrah for help—though I wouldn't have thought she could get a message to him so soon," Aralorn said. "Nevyn is the more likely candidate. As far as I know, there are no other trained mages on my father's lands right now. I'll ask around, though." What if Nevyn figured out Wolf was here?

"If the wards were not breached, what does it matter?" asked Halven.

"Wolf is not very popular among the wizards right now," said Aralorn. Though Geoffrey ae'Magi had disappeared without a trace in a keep filled with hungry Uriah, rumor had attributed his death to his son Cain—who was also her Wolf.

"Oh Mistress of the Understatement," murmured Wolf, "I salute you."

Her uncle clacked his beak in an irritated fashion and launched off her shoulder, taking human shape as he landed.

"I know of a human mage that many of the mages are searching for," he said.

Aralorn raised her chin, and Halven laughed. "No need to look daggers at me, child. I can hold my tongue. What need have I to please a scruffy lot of bungling human mages?"

She stared at him, but Wolf, either easier to appease or not as worried, released the warding with a quick gesture of his left hand, saying, "Past time we attended to our immediate business." He threw back the curtain and exposed the Lyon's dark chamber to the light from lamps in the mourning room.

Aralorn's father lay unchanged upon the bier. Wolf reached into a shadowed area and pulled out his staff from wherever it had been since he left it in the woods. As he took it up, the crystals that grew out of the top flared brightly before settling into a blue-white glow that chased the darkness from the room where the Lyon rested.

Halven strode through the entrance and Aralorn followed him, leaving Wolf to close the curtains and hide their activities from prying eyes.

Halven looked closely at the bier for a moment before turning to Aralorn. "I thought you said there was a creature guarding him. I see— *by faith!*"

Aralorn twisted around to look toward Wolf also. Against the wall, where there should have been no shadows at all, there was a subtle dimness that oozed slowly down the stone. It was only a little darker than the room itself, almost as if it were her imagination painting monsters. She turned back to Halven and opened her mouth to speak, when her uncle's rough grip pulled her aside and behind him.

Wolf, too, had turned to see what caused Halven's exclamation. The shadow caught his eye just as it touched the floor and abruptly shot forward. It rippled swiftly over the stones, flowing around Wolf on both sides, like a stream of water around a rock—though no part of the shadow touched him. It drew to a halt in front of Halven, stopped by the barrier of the shapeshifter's magic.

SHIELDING, THOUGHT WOLF, recognizing the patterning though the magic Halven used was different. Even as he thought it, the shadow-thing oozed through a hole in the shield spell that hadn't been there an instant before. Halven responded with another shield, but that obviously wouldn't answer for long.

The power of Halven's magic called answering force from Wolf. He could feel magic seeping in from the old stones that surrounded him, enticing him with its nearness, but he feared its ability to do more than its designated task. With an effort so fierce that it left him with a head-ache, he forced the green magic away.

Instead, he reached for the more familiar forces he had always worked with. Though outwardly more destructive than green magic, the raw magic that was the stuff human mages could weave responded to his control as a harp to an old bard.

With careful dispatch, he created an adaptation of the magelight spell, seeking to cancel shadow with light. His spell should have flared with white light as it touched the shadow, but nothing happened. The creature might have expanded a little, but he wasn't certain. It paused, then threw the light spell at Halven.

Wolf felt the surge of force Halven called upon to block both the light and the creature, felt it as if it were coming from his own hands. The brilliant light was swallowed by Halven's open palm, and once more, the creature was turned away.

Wolf knew the other mage had begun to tire; the flow of Halven's magic had become erratic though no less powerful. The shapeshifter was doing all he could to keep the creature back; it was up to Wolf to stop it from getting Aralorn. Oh, it might have been trying to get her uncle, but bone-deep instinct told him that was not true.

Something about the way the thing absorbed his spell reminded him of demons—which reminded him of a spell.

Before he started to gather magic, he found himself abruptly filled with more than he could use. Startled, he paused, and the magic began to form its own spell. It wasn't until that moment that he realized the magic he held was green magic.

He controlled his frustration and ruthlessly broke the weaving already begun, stripping the natural magic of its essence and turning it back to the chaotic energy of the wild, but less willful, magic human wizards used. This he wove and focused, ignoring the pain that backlashed through him from his struggles.

The spell he chose was only to be found among the books of the black mages, for it had one use: to hold demons safely when they were summoned unbound. However, the spell required neither death nor blood, so he patterned it—hoping anything that could hold a demon would hold the shadow-creature as well.

The spell finished, he threw it at the creature, careful that it did not touch Halven. To his relief, it fell as it should have, a glowing circle of light containing everything in the room between Halven and Wolf. He held his breath as the shadow touched the light and drew back from the binding, prowling restlessly within the circle's confines.

Wolf shrank the boundaries until the shadow was enclosed in a circle the size of a foot soldier's shield. The creature cowered in the small area in the center of the spell, where it shivered, small and dark, like a slug exposed to open air.

The green magic he had not used continued to fight him, struggling for the freedom to complete the pattern it had begun. He wasn't sure what he was going to do with it when he got it under control. Human mages were very careful to draw only as much power as they needed, since magic left unformed was dangerous. He had no idea what a similar situation with green magic would do.

The magic fought against his dominance like a wild stallion bridled for the first time, and he found himself losing his grip on it. Reaching for a firmer hold, he found that he was grasping nothing; the green magic had faded, dissipating like fog in the sun.

He would have felt more reassured if he thought it was gone rather than merely biding its time. Sweating beneath his mask, he turned his attention to his companions. As he did so, he realized he hadn't struggled with the magic for as long as he thought: Halven and Aralorn had just closed in on his prisoner, apparently unaware of the battle he'd just barely won. Grateful for the mask that hid his features, he turned his attention to the shadow-creature.

"Baneshade," said Halven, looking at the creature. "Interesting."

"What's a baneshade?" asked Aralorn.

Wolf stepped to the edge of the binding and examined the thing himself, saying, "I hadn't thought of that. They used to be quite common, I understand. The wizards before the Wizard Wars used them. They were nasty little creatures who lived in dark places, usually where magic had been performed—deserted temples and the like. On their own, they're said to be harmless enough, but they can work like a sigil—keeping a human spell going for an indefinite length of time." He paused. "Or they can store power. They were supposed to have the ability to alter some spells a little, too. I had assumed they were long gone." He was pleased that his voice came out as controlled as it usually was.

"It didn't act like something that was harmless," said Aralorn.

"I saw another one once," commented Halven. "When I was younger, I sometimes wandered from place to place. There was a deserted building—not much larger than a hut, really. I was told it was haunted by the ghost of one of the great wizards from the time of the Wizard Wars. The building didn't feel that old to me, but it did have a baneshade. It took me a while to find a name for the thing." He turned his attention to Wolf. "Why didn't you try capturing it that way before?"

"I didn't even think of it." It was black magic, and he tried not to use it. He didn't have to use blood to call enough power to build the spell, but most other human mages would have.

Halven raised his eyebrows but didn't comment. Instead, he turned to the bier. "Now that that's taken care of, I suppose I should look at this spell."

He laid his hand on the Lyon's head and began humming in a rich baritone. After a moment he pulled back and looked at Wolf. "I think it's human magic. But there is something else as well. Perhaps you ought to look."

Wolf looked at the shadow his magic held. "Hold a moment. I need to fix the spell so I can work other magic."

He drew a sign on the stone floor with his finger, then touched the glowing circlet. The symbol he'd drawn flared orange before disappearing. "That should hold it."

He released the spell, knowing that the rune would maintain the spell for the time he needed. Stepping past it, he approached the bier. Like Halven, Wolf laid his palm on the Lyon's forehead. With his free hand, he gestured in a controlled motion as he closed his eyes.

"Black magic," he said finally, pulling away. "I still can't tell if it is human or not, but I'll take your assessment. I don't recognize the patterning, but it's been muddled enough it could be anyone—maybe the baneshade's work. It almost has the feel of a collective effort, but it is hard to tell. There is a second spell as well, but it doesn't seem to have been activated. Hopefully, Lord Kisrah can unravel it."

Halven nodded in satisfaction. "I thought it felt as if there was more than one hand involved."

"Can you break the spell that holds him?" asked Aralorn.

"Not this one," said Halven.

Wolf shook his head. "Lady, I could try. I would rather wait until I find out just what the spell is, though. I've never seen its like. It will be far less dangerous to your father if I know what I'm working with."

Halven tapped his finger idly on the stone bier. "Why didn't anyone else notice he wasn't dead? Surely someone should have noticed his body didn't behave properly?"

"He's not breathing, has no pulse, and is as cold as stone," answered Aralorn. "What was there to notice?"

Halven's brows rose. "His body didn't stiffen as a corpse would."

"Well," said Aralorn, looking for an explanation, "Kurmun rode here with Father from the croft—that would not have been long enough for a corpse to rigor. It is traditional to leave a body in the cellar for a full day before dressing it out—to give the spirit time to depart. There was no reason for anyone to notice."

"A useful tradition," observed Wolf. "It is so much easier to work with a pliable corpse."

Halven smiled grimly. "So if you had not come, he would have been buried?"

Aralorn nodded, but Wolf said, "There's no way to tell, is there? I think perhaps someone would have conveniently discovered it at the last moment—and would have seen to it that word was sent to Aralorn, as the family's own green mage. Perhaps it would have been suggested that shapeshifter magic had done this."

"You think this was set to draw me here?" asked Aralorn.

He shrugged. "I don't know. But it is significant that the Lyon is held by black magic when his daughter is"—he paused—"has a friend who has the reputation of being the last black mage—the rest being controlled by the ae'Magi's power over them. I think that it is further interesting that the baneshade was inactive until you walked in—and it has been after you ever since."

"What would it want with me?" asked Aralorn.

"I believe the spell that it attempted to place on you when we first discovered it is the same one that binds your father. Perhaps the person who engineered all of this decided he wanted more certain bait."

"Bait for you." She considered it.

"Someone would have to want you very badly to go to this much trouble," commented Halven.

"Yes," admitted Wolf. "Quite a few people do."

Despite the seriousness of the subject, Aralorn grinned. "Every woman wants to find herself a man who is desired by so many others."

"Why were they so careful to make certain the Lyon lives?" asked Halven, ignoring Aralorn. "It would have been just as easy to kill him. Aralorn would have come to pay her last respects."

"Perhaps the one who set the spell likes him," replied Wolf, and Aralorn knew he was thinking of Nevyn. "Sometimes, Aralorn, the most obvious answer—"

His speech stopped as he felt the ripple of his hold spell dissolving. He shifted his gaze to see what had happened just in time to observe the last of the daylight fade and the shadow flow across the stone floor. Wolf didn't have a chance to gather magic, or even call out a warning—the baneshade was moving too fast . . .

A surge of green magic, his own magic, flared suddenly. There was so much of it that the whole room glowed with the unearthly midnight blue light that flowed down his staff like wax from a candle.

The room looked sinister and nightmarish, full of darkness and deep shadows. At Aralorn's feet, a bare handspan from her heel, the baneshade hissed, glowing ice blue—lighter by far than anything in the room—held in place by Wolf's magic.

Aralorn, quick acting and quicker witted, jumped away from it, stopping only when she touched the wall. Wolf began belatedly seeking dominion of the magic before it could do anything more. Although its initial action was beneficial, Wolf didn't want to chance harming Aralorn or Halven.

As he reached for it, he discovered it was already weaving itself into a pattern of destruction that allowed him no room to gain control. The light began to concentrate around the baneshade, flowing from the corners of the room until the cool white illumination from the staff dominated once more.

Glowing a deep indigo, his magic appeared viscous as it surrounded the creature, consolidating in a thick mass near the floor. There was a moment of stasis, then a fog began to rise from the blue-black base, a fog that had the odd effect of illumination and concealment at the same time.

By the curious radiance of the fog, the baneshade appeared to have a solid form, but it didn't last long enough to be certain. Wolf caught a glimpse of fine downy fur before the outer surface began to bubble and dissolve with a terrible stench that reminded him of something long dead at the first touch of the fog. Flesh and bones were revealed in turn, each dissolving with a speed that testified to the power of the magic that consumed it. In the end, there was nothing left but the vaporous mist of darkness at Wolf's feet and a malodorous scent that permeated the room.

In that moment, when the destruction was complete, Wolf tried again to dominate his magic. Cold sweat ran down his back, and for a moment, all he could see were *flames melting stone, destructive magic only he could call tearing apart everything in its path.* He blinked and set the memory aside with the conviction that someone was about to die. His magic was good at killing. He needed coolness that fear would interfere with if he was going to keep everyone safe, keep Aralorn safe.

Frantically, he fought for control, barely aware of the pain when he fell to his knees. He had to stop it before it hurt Aralorn; he felt certain that if it touched—

Aralorn's firm hands locked on his shoulder as the cloud whipped violently out of his control, sweeping around the room. Aralorn dodged, but it touched her anyway, ruffling her hair.

Wolf cried out hoarsely, but the magic left her unharmed and came for him.

Yes, he thought, *let it be me.*

The swirling mist slid aside as it touched a barrier spell that Wolf had not called, and it turned the destructive force without ever quite meeting it. Again, Wolf grappled with it, fighting to bring it under control before it had another chance at Aralorn.

Words drifted by his ears, Halven's words. He ignored them.

"No, plague you, listen to me. *Wolf.*" Aralorn was less easily disregarded. "My uncle says let it go. Don't hold it. Release it. It's done what you asked; if you release it, it will go."

Fear gnawed at his control, giving the magic more room to act, and the mist concentrated on the barrier the shapeshifter had set.

"I can't!" He gritted out the words. The damaged vocal cords made speech more difficult than usual. "Aralorn."

"It won't hurt her." Halven's voice was low and soft, as if he were soothing a wild beast. "Let it go."

At last, because he had no better plan, Wolf did as the shapeshifter suggested. For a long moment, he thought it had done no good. The magic continued to rage, pushing hard at a warding Halven had thrown up around them. Then it faded, until only a faint trace lingered in the air, evidence that magic had been worked there.

"Fluctuates," muttered Halven in a voice of great disgust. "As the gods gave us life, your control *fluctuates*, she said."

Wolf hung his head in exhaustion, sitting on the ground because he didn't have the energy to stand. With a gesture, he dissolved the mask, letting the cool air touch his scarred face.

Aralorn knelt behind him, her hands still on his shoulders. "It was attacking you, Wolf. What happened?"

HE DIDN'T REPLY to her question. Looking at him, she wasn't sure he'd heard her. Eyes closed, he was breathing in great gulps of air like a race-horse after the meet of its life. Without the mask, his face was pale and covered in sweat.

Halven examined the massive burn scars that covered Wolf's ruined face. Her uncle's eyes widened a bit as he took in the extent of the damage. He shared a thoughtful look with Aralorn.

Her uncle waited until a little color had returned to Wolf's face and his breathing had settled before he spoke. "Has anyone ever told you it's unhealthy to work green magic when you have a death wish?"

Aralorn took in a breath so deep it hurt. Though Wolf's self-destructive tendencies were nothing new to her, she'd thought he was getting better, thought she'd been helping him to heal.

"If I had been a tad less powerful," Halven continued, "it would have killed you. If you don't ask anything of the magic you gather, it strives to do what your inmost self desires—regardless of your awareness of those desires. I would have thought that even a human-trained mage would know better than that."

"I didn't gather it." Wolf's voice was hoarser than usual, but he opened his eyes and managed a respectable glare.

"I have to disagree," replied Halven, not visibly intimidated, "though you certainly shouldn't have been able to. Usually, green magic only responds to the call of a mage who is in tune with the world around him—and from the demonstration we've just had, I would say that you are not even in tune with yourself."

Wolf reached up and gripped Aralorn's hand hard with his own. "I almost killed you—again," he said without taking his eyes from Halven. "The baneshade broke through the demon-imprisoning ring. I saw it come after you, and there was no time to do anything."

"In your moment of need, you were served," said Halven, sounding as if he were quoting something.

Aralorn glanced at her uncle and nodded. "I've heard of green magic doing that—but only in stories."

"That's because only an uneducated *human* mage wouldn't know how to control his magic."

Wolf came to his feet, swaying. Aralorn was hampered by his tight grip on her hand, but Halven grabbed his shoulder to steady him.

"Easy there," he said. "Give yourself a minute."

Wolf stepped away from the unaccustomed touch and looked at Aralorn. "Are you hurt?"

She shook her head. "Not at all." If she'd broken every bone she had, she would have said the same. But, as it happened, the thick flow of Wolf's magic had been a caress rather than a strike.

"You weren't attacking *her*," said Halven impatiently. "The only one who had anything to worry about in this room was you."

Wolf looked away from them both. He reached up to touch his mask, something he did when he was uncomfortable. But his mask wasn't there, and when his fingers touched the scars, he flinched. Aralorn wasn't the only one who saw it.

"When you want to be rid of that reminder," said Halven, "come to me, and I'll teach you how to heal yourself. You've the power, and I can teach you the skill." He looked at the floor, where the baneshade had been. "It was best to destroy the baneshade anyway. It seemed to be focused on Aralorn, and the things can be dangerous in a place as old as this."

"Plague it," said Aralorn softly, as a sudden thought occurred to her. "Kisrah is coming here. We might have a problem."

"What is it?" Wolf tightened like a predator scenting prey; even his body seemed to lose the fatigue that had made his moves less fluid than usual.

"The night your father died, when I came back after you, Lord Kisrah was there."

"He would know you?" asked Wolf intently. "As the daughter of the Lyon?"

"Although I have absented myself as much as possible from human affairs," broke in Halven mildly, "I do know that this has become a dangerous conversation. I wish to know nothing about Geoffrey ae'Magi's death." He hesitated. "If you survive all of this, *Wolf* . . . come to me, and we will talk about your recalcitrant magic. Good luck to you both." He heaved up the bar on the door to the outside and left by that way.

Aralorn shut the door behind him and settled the bar back in place. "Kisrah saw me quite clearly, as a matter of fact—I wasn't expecting to run into anyone at the time, so I was wearing my own face. I don't think he connected me with my father—we would have heard something. Kisrah was caught well and good by the last ae'Magi's spells. If he knew, he'd have come after me before this. But he can hardly miss me when he comes here."

"I can handle Kisrah if he becomes a problem," Wolf said mildly enough to frighten Aralorn.

"Thank you," she said. "But I don't think that we would survive killing a second ae'Magi."

"We could do it every year on the anniversary of my father's death," suggested Wolf. "Though technically Kisrah would be our first, as my father was killed by the Uriah after you stole his magic."

He was joking, she thought, though sometimes it was difficult to tell. He liked it that way.

"I saved Kisrah's life," she said, returning to the matter at hand. "The lady he was sleeping with had a tendency to eat her lovers. Sadly, he was unconscious, so he won't know he owes me." She ran her fingers over her father's hand. It was cool to the touch. She continued thoughtfully. "You know, he obviously didn't recognize me at the time, but he has the right contacts. If he wanted to find out badly enough who I was, he could. As ae'Magi, he would have access to all the knowledge of black magic he wished."

"Especially with most of my father's library at his disposal," agreed Wolf as he took a step back and leaned against the wall. Not to relax, noticed Aralorn worriedly, but to keep himself upright. His consonants softened with fatigue, leaving his voice difficult to understand. "It is true that he was very close to my father, certainly close enough to thirst for revenge. But I know Kisrah; he would never touch the black arts."

"Neither would Nevyn," said Aralorn somberly.

Wolf sighed. "I don't want it to be him. I like him, Aralorn." Wolf didn't like many people. Aralorn suspected that he could count them on the fingers of one hand, with fingers left over. "Shortly before I left, when I was at my most vicious, he cornered me. He told me he was concerned about rumors he'd been hearing. Things that might get a man killed if the wrong person heard about them. He suggested that the rumors might die down without more sparks to fuel them."

"What did you tell him?"

Wolf's scarred lips quirked in an attempt at a smile. "I invited him to meet me at the next full moon and find out if they were true."

"Not overly intelligent on your part, my love," observed Aralorn dryly. "If he'd gone to the council, they'd have been able to pull you in for questioning."

"I was young." He shrugged.

"It amazes me," she said thoughtfully, "how many people knew you were working black magic and never stopped to ask how you learned such things on your own—or wondered why the ae'Magi didn't stop you."

"Everyone knows that there are books if you know where to look for them." He sighed softly and returned to the original topic. "It could be Kisrah, I suppose. Hatred and vengeance are corrupting emotions. Perhaps they could have caused him to use black magic. I would hate to see him caught in a web spun by my father."

"It could be Nevyn," she offered. "He might have found the connections between you and me, and between us and the ae'Magi's death. He knows that I am a spy in Sianim, and he knows Kisrah. Kisrah could have told him about seeing me at the ae'Magi's castle the night he died, described me well enough that Nevyn identified me. Nevyn loved your father—he used to tell me stories about him—and he certainly loves my father. Since he distrusts magic of any kind, black magic might not bother him as much as it would Kisrah."

Wolf thought a moment—or else he dozed; Aralorn couldn't tell which—then he shook his head. "The croft, perhaps, might have been possible for Nevyn. It wouldn't have called for much skill, but the spell binding your father was done with both power and craft. Poor Nevyn had more teaching than he wanted, but he fought it. I heard Kisrah fussing over him to my father—all that talent and too scared of magic to use it." He gave Aralorn a bleak look. "My father would pat him on the back and commiserate with him. Told him that a Darranian mage was bound to be a mess." Geoffrey ae'Magi, Wolf's father, had been Darranian. "They would laugh and then my father would tell his good friend how worried he was about me, about how I was fascinated by the darker magics." He closed his eyes for a deep breath. When he opened them again, he said, "My father was afraid to teach me, I think, for fear that the monster he created would be too powerful for him to control. Kisrah tried his best with Nevyn, but I doubt that he knows much more than I do."

He turned to her, a mockery of his usual graceful movements, and made a negating gesture. "He was given to Kisrah to apprentice partially because of Kisrah's easy nature but also because Kisrah had the power to control a rogue sorcerer. When he was first apprenticed to Santik, Nevyn had the potential to become a master, maybe even ae'Magi. By the time he went to Kisrah, he was capable of little more than lighting candles. Santik was brought up on charges of abuse and neglect, his powers sealed away from him by the ae'Magi. Ironic isn't it, that my father convicted another mage of abuse? Kisrah worked with Nevyn, but finally gave in to Nevyn's own wishes once he was certain that Nevyn knew enough for safety. So Nevyn is much like me—a powerful mage who doesn't know what he's doing. Which is why I don't think he's our villain. He simply does not have the skill to create something like the spell that holds your father. He's a good man, Aralorn. I don't think he did this."

Aralorn looked at Wolf, surprised at his long speech.

It made her suspicious.

She thought about what had happened that night and realized why Wolf was painting such a clear picture for her. Poor Nevyn indeed. A decade of spying and influencing the thoughts of others without attracting their attention had honed her instincts: She knew when someone was trying to manipulate her in return.

So Nevyn was a powerful mage, was he? Hurt by someone who should have protected him. A good man.

Wolf, on the other hand, was a devious man, her lover: She had a weakness for devious men.

"I am certain," she said slowly, "that you believe Nevyn had nothing to do with this." Or he wouldn't have offered the man to her on a platter.

Sometimes, she thought, you had to tell someone that you loved them; sometimes you had to beat them over the head with it.

"I don't love you for your powers, Wolf. Nor for the beauty of your body." His hand twitched toward his scarred face. "I certainly don't love you because you were abused by your father." Her voice began to take on the bite of her anger, not all of which was feigned. "I *certainly* don't love you because you are a powerful mage. Nevyn's powers or lack of same may have made a half-grown child look at him twice, where one look at you would have sent her running—but I'm grown now and have been for some time. So tell me"—she was snarling at him now—"*why* are you trying to turn my attention to Nevyn with the skill of a village matchmaker?" She changed her voice, giving it an elderly quaver and a Lambshold crofter's accent. "'Look at this wonderful man, wounded, yet noble—a powerful mage in need of tender care. So he's married to tha sister, so he hates shapeshifters—what's a little challenge?'"

She needed him to talk about what was bothering him in order to address it. She needed to goad him; perhaps a shift to gentleness would work—he hadn't experienced enough to be entirely comfortable with it. "I don't need Nevyn, dear heart. I have you."

"Of course," he snapped. She was glad to see anger because sadness in his eyes tore her soul. "Oh, *I* am any maiden's dream. A master wizard—except the only magic I know, other than a few basic spells, is black magic, and it will, at some future time, ensure my death at the hands of any mage who can back me into a corner. Without my conscious will, green magic randomly chooses to use me to call itself into being and do whatever the"—he paused and drew in a deep breath and deliberately relaxed his shoulders—"and do whatever seems fit at the time. You are better off without me."

The prudent thing, Aralorn considered, would be to allow him to work it out on his own. *She* knew he'd never hurt her, not even with magic he couldn't control; she was even fairly certain he wouldn't hurt anyone else who didn't deserve it—and she thought that when he had a chance to reason it through, he would come to the same conclusions.

What *really* bothered him was the nature of green magic. You coaxed it, you asked it, but you couldn't always force it to do exactly what you wanted—but he'd dealt with much worse than that. She was confident he would again; she would just have to be patient until he worked it out.

The prudent thing, she told herself, would be to leave him alone. He had a nasty temper when he was pushed.

Since prudence wasn't one of her attributes, she said, "Self-pity never accomplishes much, but sometimes it's nice to wallow in it for a while. Do hurry up though—I'm getting hungry." She tilted her head to indicate the sounds of people gathering on the other side of the curtain for their meal. "I'm tired of eating cold food."

Wolf closed both eyes. He stretched his neck to the left, then to the right. Only then did he open his eyes. Baleful lights glittered in their amber depths as he closed his hands ever so gently around her neck and pulled her forward until she had to tilt her chin up to look at him.

"Someday," he whispered, bending down until his lips were next to her ears, "you're going to step into the fire and find out that it really is hot."

"Burn me," she said in equally soft tones, and for a few moments he did—without a single spell.

When he released her, there was a measure of peace in his eyes. "Shall we go eat?"

She turned to go, and her eyes touched her father. Smile fading, Aralorn approached him and put her hand on his face.

"Got rid of the creepy crawly, but no luck yet, sir, on your entrapment," she murmured. "But tomorrow's another day."

Wolf's warm hand came down to rest on her shoulder. "Come."

SEVEN

WOLF CHANGED BACK INTO HIS FOUR-FOOTED FORM, THEN STAGGERED. Aralorn put a hand on his shoulder to steady him, and he leaned against her with a sigh and an apologetic look.

"Sorry," he said.

"You need food," she replied, and pulled back the curtain, only to find that not only was the great hall filled with people dining, but every head was turned to her. By the intentness of their gazes, she figured that the guard told them all that she'd brought her uncle to look at the Lyon.

She bowed, and said, "We've made some progress, but the Lyon still sleeps."

She closed the curtain and set her own wards against casual interlopers since Wolf was in no condition to be working magic. By the time she was through, most of the diners had turned their attention back to their plates.

Aralorn snagged a clean trencher from a passing kitchen servant and sat at the nearest table, Wolf collapsing at her feet. She took one of her knives and cut a bit of this and that from the platters arrayed on the table and tossed a large piece of roasted goose breast at Wolf, who caught it easily and ate it with more haste than manners.

She took a hunk of bread from her trencher and put a piece of sliced meat on top of it. This she kept, placing the plate and its remaining contents on the floor for Wolf.

"There she is! I see her."

A loud voice drew her attention away from her meal as she saw two towheaded children running toward her.

"Aunt Aralorn. Hey, Aunt Aralorn, Father said you would tell us a story if we cornered you."

Putting their ages roughly at eight and five, Aralorn quickly came up with the identity of "Father." Falhart was the only one of her brothers old enough to have sired them.

"All right," she said, hiding her pleasure—as tired as she was, storytelling opportunities were not to be lost. "Tell Falhart you cornered me. I'll do some tale-telling in front of the fireplace after I'm finished eating."

The two scurried off in search of their father, and Aralorn finished the last of her bread. Wolf yawned as she picked the empty trencher off the floor and got to her feet.

"Come on, we'll take this to the kitchen and . . ." Her voice trailed off as she saw Irrenna making her way toward her.

It wasn't Irrenna that made her lose her train of thought, but the man who walked beside her. Flamboyantly clothed in amber and ruby, Lord Kisrah looked more like a court dandy than the holder of age-old power.

It was too soon for Irrenna's message to have reached him; he must have come for the Lyon's funeral.

Well, Aralorn thought, *if he didn't know who it was that he met in the ae'Magi's castle the night Geoffrey died, he will now.* Even if he wasn't involved with her father's collapse, he was not going to be friendly. If he was responsible for her father's condition . . . well, she wasn't always friendly either.

She let none of her worries appear on her face, nor did she allow herself to hesitate as she approached them, dirty trencher in hand.

"You said that you weren't able to wake him?" asked Irrenna.

Kisrah, Aralorn noted warily, was intent, but not surprised at all at seeing her face in this hall. He had known who she was before coming here. He moved to the top of her suspects.

"That's right," said Aralorn. "My uncle agreed to come and look. He didn't know the spell that holds Father, but he was able to dispose of the baneshade—"

"Baneshade?" Kisrah broke in, frowning.

She nodded. "Apparently the one who did this has a whole arsenal of black arts—"

"*Black* arts?" he interrupted.

"You must not have looked in on him yet," she said. "Whoever laid the spell holding the Lyon used black magic. I'm not certain if you'd call the baneshade black magic precisely, but it attacked me the first time I worked magic in the room—the mage must have set it to guard my father. My uncle—my mother's brother, who is a shapechanger—is the one who identified it and rid us of it as well."

"My apologies," Irrenna broke in. "Allow me to present the Lady Aralorn, my husband's oldest daughter, to you, Lord Kisrah. Aralorn, this is Lord Kisrah, the ae'Magi. He came here as soon as he heard what happened to Henrick."

"It took me a while to connect Henrick's daughter with the Sianim mercenary the ae'Magi had me fetch for him," replied the Archmage, bowing over Aralorn's hand. "I suppose I had expected someone more like your sisters."

At her side, Wolf stiffened and stared at Kisrah with an interest that was definitely predatory. She took a firm grip on a handful of fur. She'd never told him of Kisrah's role in her capture and subsequent torture by the ae'Magi because she'd worried about his reaction.

"How did you make the connection?" asked Irrenna, unaware of the coercive nature of Kisrah's "fetching" of Aralorn. "She has very little contact with us; she says she is afraid her work will draw us into jeopardy."

Sadness crept across his features, an odd contrast to the rose-colored wig he wore—like an emerald among a pile of glass jewels. "The council appointed me to investigate Geoffrey's death even before they called me to assume his role. I looked into the backgrounds of anyone who had anything to do with him in his last days. You"—he directed his speech to Aralorn—"provided me with a particularly odd puzzle and kept the investigation going much longer than it otherwise would have. It was especially difficult until I discovered that the Lyon's eldest daughter was of shapeshifter blood." He was almost as good with a significant pause as she herself was. After a moment, he turned back to Irrenna. "It was the Uriah that were his downfall. He was looking for a way to make them less harmful and lost control of the ones he had with him. There was not even a body left."

"It was an accident, then?" asked Irrenna. "I had heard that it was— though there were all of those rumors about his son."

"The council declared it an accident," confirmed Kisrah. "A tragedy for us all."

Aralorn noted how carefully he avoided saying that he believed the council's decision that his predecessor's death had been an accident. Surely he didn't—he'd *been* there.

"Would you care to look at my father? Or would you prefer to rest from your travels?" she asked.

Lord Kisrah turned back to her. "Perhaps I will eat first. After that, would you consider accompanying me to your father? I tried to open the wards when I arrived, but I couldn't get through."

It had been Kisrah, then, who'd tried the wards. Did he know Wolf's magic well enough to tell that he'd set the spells? *Stinking wards,* she thought. If she'd had the sense of a goose, she'd have set them herself in the first place.

". . . at first it might have been Nevyn's work, but I know his magic." He looked at her inquiringly, and Aralorn wondered what she'd missed while she was cursing herself.

"No, not Nevyn's, nor mine either—my mother's gift of magic is green magic. I can set wardings, of course, but the baneshade's presence called for a stronger magic. I did a favor for a wizard once, and he gave me an amulet . . ." Wizards were always giving tokens with spells on them, weren't they? At least in the stories she told they were. At her feet, Wolf moaned softly, so maybe she was wrong.

Kisrah's eyebrows raised in surprise. "An amulet? How odd. I've never heard of a warding set on an amulet. Do you have it with you?"

Yep, I was wrong.

Aralorn shook her head and boldly elaborated on her lie. "It wasn't that big a favor. The amulet itself was the main component of the spell—so it could only be activated once. I thought the baneshade warranted using it. But my uncle killed the creature, so it's safer now. I'll come with you to take them off."

He stared at her a moment, his pale blue eyes seeming blander than ever. But she had been a spy for ten years; she knew he saw only what she intended him to see. Innocently, she gazed back.

She was lying. He knew she was lying. He wasn't going to call her on it, though—which made her wonder what he was up to.

"I see," he said after a moment. "With the baneshade gone, did you look at the spell holding Henrick?"

She nodded. "I'm not an expert, though I can tell black magic. My uncle said that it feels as if there was more than one mage involved in the spelling."

"Black magic," he said softly, and she had the impression that it was the real man speaking and not his public face. For an instant, she saw both shame and fear in his eyes. Interesting.

"Why don't you get some food, Lord Kisrah," said Irrenna.

"That would be good," agreed Aralorn. She wanted to give Wolf time to recover a little before they went back to the bier room with Kisrah. "My brother sent a pair of his hellions to force me into telling a story or two, and I gave them my word of honor I would entertain them after I'd eaten."

Irrenna laughed. "You'll have to stay for it, Lord Kisrah. Aralorn is a first-rate storyteller."

"So I have heard," agreed the mage, smiling.

ARALORN SAT CROSS-LEGGED on the old bench near the fireplace where she'd spent many long winter hours telling stories. The children gathered around were different from the ones she remembered, but there was a large number of her original audience present, too. Falhart sat on the floor with the rest, a couple of toddlers on his lap. Correy leaned against a wall beside Irrenna and Kisrah, who stood with his food so that he could be close enough to hear.

"Now then," Aralorn said, "what kind of story would you like?"

"Something about the Wizard Wars," said one of the children instantly.

"Yes," said Gerem softly, as he approached the group from the shadows. "Tell us a story about the Wizard Wars."

Startled, Aralorn looked up to meet Gerem's eyes. They were no more welcoming than they had been earlier that day.

"Tell us," he continued, taking a seat on the floor and lifting one of the youngsters onto his lap, "the story of the Tear of Hornsmar, who died at the hands of the shapechangers in the mountains just north of here."

She was going to have to teach her brother some subtlety, but she could work with his suggestion. She needed a long story, to give Wolf as much time to recover as possible. One came to mind as if it had been waiting for her to recognize it.

"A story of the Wizard Wars, then, but the story of the Tear is overtold. I have instead a different tale for you. Listen well, for it contains a warning for your children's children's children."

Having caught their attention, Aralorn took a breath and sought the beginning of her tale. It took her a moment, for it wasn't one of the ones she told often.

"Long and long ago, a miller's son was born. At the time, this hardly seemed an auspicious or important event, for as long as there have been millers, they have been having children. It was not even an unusual occurrence for this miller, because he'd had three other sons and a daughter born in a similar fashion—but not a son like this. No one in the village had ever had a son like this." She saw a few smiles, and the hall quieted.

She continued, punctuating her story with extravagant gestures. "When Tam laughed, the flowers bloomed, and the chairs danced; when he cried, the earth shook, and fires sprang up with disconcerting suddenness. Concerned that the child would set fire to the mill itself and ruin his family, the miller took his problem to the village priest.

"In those days, the old gods still walked the earth, and their priests were able to work miracles at the gods' discretion, so the miller's action was probably the wisest one he could have taken.

"And so the boy was raised by the village priest, who became used to the fires and the earthquakes and quite approved of the blooming flowers. The miller was so relieved that when the temple burned down because of a toddler temper tantrum, he didn't even grumble about paying his share to rebuild it—and he grumbled about everything.

"Now, in those days, there was trouble brewing outside the village. Mages, as you all know, are temperamental at best, and at their worst . . ." Aralorn shuddered and was pleased to see several members of her audience shiver in sympathy. At her feet, Wolf made a soft noise that might have been laughter. Kisrah smiled, but in the dim light of the great hall, she couldn't tell if it was genuine or not.

"Kingdoms then were smaller even than Lambshold, and each and every king had a mage who worked for him. Usually, the most powerful mages worked only for themselves, for none of the small countries could afford to hire them for longer than it took to win a battle or two. The strongest mages of them all were the black mages, who worked magic with blood and death."

Gerem straightened, and said, "I never knew black magic was more powerful than the rest."

Aralorn nodded. "With black magic, the sorcerer has only to control the magic released; with other magics, he must gather the power as well. Collecting magic released in death takes nothing out of the mage . . . except a piece of his soul."

"You sound as if you've had personal experience," said Gerem challengingly.

Aralorn shook her head. "Not I."

When Gerem looked away from her, she continued the tale. "This balance of power had worked for centuries—until the coming of the great warrior, Fargus, and the discovery of gold in the mountains of Berronay."

She rolled out the names with great ceremony, like the court crier, but added, much less formally, "No one knows, now, where Berronay or its mines were. No one knows much more about Fargus than his name. But it was his deeds that came close to destroying the world. For he ruled Berronay shortly after its rich mines were discovered and before anyone else knew how rich that discovery was. He amassed a great army with the intent of conquering the world—and he hired the fourteen most powerful mages in the world to ensure that he would do so.

"Tam's village was the smallest of three in the kingdom of Hallenvale—that's 'green valley' in the old tongue. It was located in the lush farmland in the rolling hills just northwest of the Great Swamp." Aralorn paused, sipping out of a pewter mug of water someone had snagged for her.

"But there isn't any farmland there," broke in a tawny-headed girl of ten or eleven summers.

"No," agreed Aralorn softly, pleased that the child had added to the drama of her story. "Not anymore. There's just an endless sea of black glass where the farmland used to be."

She paused and let them think about that for a little while. "As I said, Tam was raised in the small farming village by the priest. When the boy was twelve—the age of apprenticing—he was sent to the king's wizard for training. By the time he was eighteen, Tam was the most powerful wizard around—except for those using black magic."

Aralorn surveyed her audience. "There were a lot of black mages, though. Black magic was common then, and most people saw nothing wrong with it."

"Nothing?" asked Gerem.

"Nothing." Aralorn nodded. "Most of the mages used the blood and death of animals—if they used human deaths, they kept it quiet. If you kill a pig for eating, its death releases magic. Isn't it a waste if you take the animal's hindquarters and throw them in the midden? Why then is it not a waste to leave the magic of its death to dissipate unused?" She waited. "They thought so. But our Tam, you see, was different. He'd been raised by a priest of the springtime goddess—a goddess of life. Out of respect to her, he didn't sully himself with death."

Satisfied that she'd given them something to think about, she continued the story. "Fargus, with the wealth of the gold mines of Berronay behind him, bade his mages ease the way for his armies, and he took over land after land. As each new country added to his wealth, he hired more mages. Even the Great Swamp was no barrier to Fargus's mages, whose powers only grew as the number of the dead and dying mounted.

"Now, Fargus was not the first warlord to conquer others using the power of the black mages. A score of years earlier, the battles between Kenred the Younger and Agenhall the Foolish had raged wildly until the backlash of magic had sunk the whole country of Faen beneath the waves of the sea. A hundred years before that, the ravages of the Tear of Hornsmar destroyed the great forest of Idreth with the magic of his sorceress mistress, Jandrethan." Aralorn looked up and saw several members of her audience nodding at the familiar names. "But it was Fargus's war that changed everything.

"Hallenvale," she went on, "came at last to Fargus's notice, and he sent his magic-backed army to fight there. But it was not an easy conquest. The king of Hallenvale was a warrior and strategist without equal—called Firebird for his temperament and the color of his hair. Ah, I see several of you have heard of him. Hallenvale was a prosperous little country, as it had been ruled wisely for generations. The Firebird used his wealth to gather together wizards of his own, including Tam. The small unconquered countries all around, knowing that if Hallenvale fell, their lands would be next, aided him any way they could.

"A battle was fought on the Plains of Torrence. The armies were equally matched: Thirty-two black mages fought for Fargus, a hundred and seven wizards stood beneath the Firebird's banner—though these were mostly lesser mages."

She let her voice speed up and drop in pitch as she fed them details of the fight. ". . . Spells were launched and countered until magic permeated the very earth. After three days, a pall hung over the plain, an unnaturally thick fog, a fog so dense they could not see twenty paces through it. To the mages, whichever side they fought upon, the air was so heavy with magic that it took more power to force yet more magic into the area. *Fortunately*"—she let her tongue linger on the word and call it to her audience's attention—"there were so many dead and dying on the field that there was power enough to work more and greater magics.

"Tam, his power exhausted, was sent to the top of a nearby hill that he might get a better view of the battlefield. He did so. What he saw sent him galloping for the Firebird's personal mage, Nastriut."

"Wasn't the mage who escaped the sinking of Faen on a boat called *Nastriut*?" Falhart asked.

She nodded. "The very same. He was an old man by then, and tired from the battle. Tam coaxed him onto a horse and hauled him up to the top of the hill."

She sipped water and let the suspense build.

"Only a very great mage could have seen what Tam had, but Nastriut was one of the most powerful wizards of his generation. From the vantage point of the hill, Nastriut and Tam could see that the fog that had grown from the first day of the battle was not what either had thought. It was not a spell cast by one of Fargus's wizards or some side effect of the sheer volume of magic.

"'Just before Faen fell into the sea,' Tam said, 'you saw a dark fog engulf the whole island.'

"'There was magic so thick it hurt to breathe,' said Nastriut. 'Death, more death, and dreams of the power of blood. From the sea I saw it like a great hungry beast.' The old man shuddered and swallowed hard. 'Have you been dreaming of power, Tam? I have. Dreams of the power death brings and the lust that rises through my blood. It promises me youth that has not been my state for a century or more.'

"'If I use black magic,' whispered Tam, 'my dreams tell me that I can end all the fighting and go back to my home. Are you saying this thing is in my dreams?'

"'Such dreams we all had before Faen died,' the old man said. 'I dreamed that we created this with the taint of death magic, but I had no proof. When this beast killed the island, it was half the size it is now. But it is the same, the same.'"

The great hall was deathly quiet, and Aralorn was able to drop her voice to a whisper that echoed—a trick of tone and architecture she'd discovered a long time ago.

"Tam could not have done it, but Nastriut's reputation was such that Fargus's mages left the battlefield to help. Over a hundred mages pooled their magic to create a desert of obsidian glass to contain the Dreamer their blood magic had brought into being. Nastriut died in the doing— and he was not alone. The rest of the wizards vowed never to use black magic again upon pain of death. To ensure that this promise was kept, they placed upon themselves a spell that allowed their magic to be controlled by one man—the first ae'Magi, Tam of Hallenvale."

"A pretty tale to cover the wizards' stupidity," said Gerem abruptly. "It was abuse of magic that created the glass desert, not some heroic effort to save the world."

Aralorn smiled at him. "I only tell the tale as it was told to me. You can judge it true or false if you wish. It won't change the results."

"The destruction of a dozen kingdoms," he said.

"You've been listening to your teachers." Aralorn smiled her approval. "But there were other results as well. The wizards were vulnerable, most of them trained to use magic in a way that was forbidden them. Now the people feared them and killed them wherever they found them. For generations, a mageborn child was killed as soon as it was recognized. Only in Reth or Southwood could wizards find sanctuary."

Aralorn surveyed her audience, child and adult alike. "If you wonder if this story is true, ask the Archmage what the first words of the wizard's oath are, the oath every apprentice must make to his master since the ae'Magi was set over the mages at the end of the Wizard Wars."

"*Ab earum satimon*," said Kisrah. He frowned thoughtfully at Aralorn, then translated softly, "To protect our dreams. Where did you hear this story? I have never heard it before. I thought the glass desert was a mistake caused by a clash of magic gone wild and out of control."

"I told it to her," said Nevyn, stepping out from a doorway. "It's an old tale I heard somewhere—though Aralorn has improved upon it."

Aralorn nodded gravely in acknowledgment of the compliment as she rose from her seat. "I have heard several variations of the story since. Lord Kisrah, you wanted to see my father?"

"One more story, before you go?" asked Falhart. "Something less . . . dark, if you would? I don't know about anyone else, but I'd rather not spend the night trying to convince my children that there is nothing lurking in the shadows."

Aralorn glanced down at Wolf, who was lying on his side being patted by small hands, his eyes closed. It was unusually tolerant of him. In his human form, he avoided people's hands, other than her own, altogether. The wolf was less shy, but she wondered if he was really asleep. If so, a few minutes more could only help him.

She gave Falhart a challenging look. "No more comments about my height?"

He raised his right hand. "I swear."

She glanced at Kisrah.

"I can wait," he said.

Aralorn resumed her seat. "All right, let's see what I can come up with. Hmm. Yes."

She waited for it to quiet down, then began. "Not so very long ago, and not so far away, there lived a sorcerer's apprentice named Pudge. As you might expect from his name, he enjoyed nothing so much as a nice soft pudding, except perhaps a piece of cake. He especially liked it when the sorcerer's cook would try to cover up the fact that his cake had fallen by filling in the hole with sugary frosting this thick." Aralorn held up two fingers together and watched a smile cross the face of one of Falhart's brood at the thought of such a delicacy.

"Now, Pudge's master had several apprentices who teased him about his eating. They might have meant it kindly—but you and I know that doesn't matter. It got so that Pudge would take whatever sweet he happened to thieve from the kitchen and eat it in secret places where the others wouldn't find him.

"His favorite was a little cubby he'd found in the library. The passage was so small and insignificant that even if the sorcerer had remembered it, he would never have used it. It was, in fact, so narrow that only a child could squeeze though the long tunnel that led to a comfortably cozy ledge on the side of the sorcerer's castle several stories above the ground.

"As the months passed, and the cook's sugary treats took their toll, the passage grew tighter and tighter, until Pudge began to wonder if there wasn't some kind of shrinking spell laid upon it.

"'Perhaps,' he thought, 'perhaps, it once was a normal sort of hall and every day it gets smaller and smaller.'

"It was an idea he found pleasing, though he found no mention of such a spell in any of the books he was allowed to delve into. I might mention here that Pudge was quite an adept little sorcerer in his own right. Had he been of a different temperament, the other apprentices might have truly regretted their teasing.

"One bright and sunny morning, the cook made little cherry tarts, each just large enough to fit into one of Pudge's hands. Nobody makes a better thief than a boy—just ask the Traders, if you don't believe me. Nobody, that is, except a sorcerer. Pudge came out of the kitchen with twelve cherry tarts, and he scrambled to the library before the cook realized they were gone.

"He opened the passage and managed to squeeze in, though he had to push the pies, stored in a knapsack he used for such nefarious missions, ahead of him in order to fit. It was really only the thought of the cook's ire that made him fight and struggle through the passage. The cook was a man after Pudge's own heart, but he had a terrible temper and was best avoided for a while after a successful raid.

"At last, Pudge was safely through the passage and out on his ledge. He ate eleven of the tarts and shared the twelfth with a few passing birds. Then he decided it was time to go back." Aralorn paused.

"He couldn't get back," said a young boy seated near the back of the group.

"Why not?" asked Aralorn, raising her brows.

"Because he was too big!" chorused a series of voices (some of which were bass or baritone).

Aralorn smiled and nodded. "You're right, of course. It took several days before Pudge was thin enough to get back through the passage, and by that time, his master was getting really worried. Upon hearing of Pudge's adventures, the sorcerer taught Pudge a spell or two to help him get out of tight places." She waited for a moment to let the chuckles die down. "Over the years Pudge grew in both girth and power. You might know him better by his real name—Tenneten the Large, own mage to King Myr, current ruler of Reth." She stood up briskly and made a shooing motion. "All right, that's all for the night. Correy, if you could spare a moment?"

Correy approached her, with Kisrah somewhat behind him, as the children shuffled off to their respective parents.

"What did you need?" asked her brother.

"Hmm, well, you know that old vacant cottage where the hermit used to live? In the clearing, not too far from here?"

"The one Hart fell through the roof of when he was pretending he was a dragon?"

Surprised, she nodded. "That was well before your time."

"Some things become family legends," he replied. "Besides, the knowledge he gained reroofing the cottage came in useful when Father sent us to build a house for Ridane's priestess to live in."

"Ah," she said, wondering why her father was building houses for the death goddess's priestess. Guessing why he sent his sons to do it was easier—the Lyon liked to make certain his children knew as many skills as possible. He also liked to keep them humble. "Well, in any case, you need to send someone there to take care of a rather large carcass we left. It might attract some predators, and it's near some good winter pasture."

Correy nodded. "I saw that your wolf is missing some hide. Run into a bear?"

Aralorn coughed, glanced at Kisrah, who was listening in, and said, "Something of the sort, yes." There is nothing more disastrous than allowing your opponents to overestimate your abilities: Killing legendary monsters almost always led to that very thing.

"I'll see to it," he said. "Good night, Featherweight."

She reached way up and managed to ruffle his hair. "Good night, Blue-eyes."

Correy laughed and kissed her cheek.

"Good night, sir," he told Kisrah with a friendly nod.

Kisrah waited until Correy had gone. "Blue-eyes?" he asked.

If they'd been friends, she would have laughed; she satisfied herself with lifting an eyebrow instead. "Because they are not, of course."

He nodded seriously. "Of course. I compliment you on your storytelling."

She shrugged, rubbing her fingers into the soft fur behind Wolf's ears. "It's a hobby of mine to collect odd tales. Some of them have even come in handy a time or two. Come, I'll take you to the bier room."

She set off across the great hall, which had largely emptied of people. She didn't look behind her, but she could hear the rustle of the Archmage's cloak and the click of Wolf's nails on the hard floor.

Before they reached the curtain, Kisrah stopped walking. Aralorn stopped and looked at him inquiringly.

"Do you think that the only reason black magic was abandoned was this beast in your story?"

"The Dreamer? I'm not certain that the Dreamer ever existed," replied Aralorn. "There's a less dramatic version of the story in which Tam himself creates the Dreamer in order to stop the general use of black magic. I am a green mage, my lord ae'Magi: I don't need to eat rotten meat to know that it is tainted. Blood magic . . . is as foul-smelling as a raw roast left out for a couple of days in the sun."

"Ah," said Kisrah. He frowned at her intently and changed the subject smoothly. "Did you kill the ae'Magi?"

"Geoffrey?" she asked, as if there had been a dozen Archmages killed in the last few years.

"Yes."

Aralorn folded her arms and leaned against the cold stone wall. Wolf settled at her feet with a sigh, though he kept a steady eye on Kisrah. The Archmage ignored him.

"The Uriah killed Geoffrey," she said softly. "Poor tormented creatures he, himself, created." Then she forced herself to relax and continue lightly. "At least that's what the mercenaries who were hired to clean up the castle reported."

"He had no trouble controlling them before," said Kisrah. "I've used the spells myself—they were neither difficult nor draining. And, Aralorn, despite what your friend, the wizard who gave you that *amulet*"—not one of her better stories, she admitted—"told you, Geoffrey didn't create the Uriah, just summoned them to do his bidding. I think that you have been misled."

She shrugged. She'd learned her lesson; she didn't argue with someone who might still be under the influence of the late ae'Magi's spells.

"You *were* there that night," he said. "I saw you."

"And if I say I killed him," asked Aralorn in a reasonable tone, "what then? You will kill me as well to even the score?"

"No," he said hoarsely. "My word of honor that I will not. Nor will I tell anyone else what you say to me. I believe I know who did the killing, but I need . . . I need to be certain."

Why? she thought to herself. *So you can justify the black magic used to hold my father as bait to trap Wolf?*

"How could I, a second-rate swordswoman and a third-rate green mage, do such a thing to the ae'Magi?" She indulged herself a bit more than was strictly safe, though she was careful that he would not hear the sarcasm in her voice. "Everyone knows how powerful a sorcerer he was—and a swordsman of the highest ability. Why would I want to kill him? He was the kindest, most tenderhearted—not to mention amusing—sorcerer I have ever met. His death was a great tragedy."

Second-rate swordswoman, but first-rate actress; Aralorn knew that Kisrah could only hear the sincerity in her voice. It was the sort of addlepated garbage everyone said about the last ae'Magi and meant in its absurd, simplistic whole—thanks to the ae'Magi's charisma spell, which lingered even now. If she hadn't accused Geoffrey of creating the Uriah, she thought, she might have persuaded Kisrah of her innocence in the Archmage's death.

Kisrah frowned at her. "You were there that night. Wielding a mage's staff . . ." He hesitated a bare instant, but obviously decided he might as well push all the way. "Wielding Cain's staff—it is very distinctive."

She wouldn't help him convict Wolf. Aralorn gave Kisrah a puzzled look. "I was there that night, but I don't recall any staff. I sometimes run messages for the Spymaster. When the Uriah started acting strangely, I left as soon as I could. I'm not a coward, but those things scare me. Look what they did to the ae'Magi."

Kisrah stared at her; she could almost taste his frustration. "The Uriah captured you for him. He had me translocate you to his castle. What did he want from you?"

Aralorn shrugged and modified her story without a pause. "A misunderstanding, I'm afraid. He thought that I had some knowledge of the whereabouts of King Myr. You remember that was about the time Myr, distraught over his parents' deaths, left without telling anyone where he had gone. It turns out that King Myr visited a healer, who lives quietly in the mountains near the king's summer residence." Without a qualm, she stuck to the official story. If it became widely known that Myr and the ae'Magi were enemies . . . it might confuse a lot of Myr's followers who were still under the influence of the previous ae'Magi. Perhaps time would solve that—perhaps not. "I actually did know where he was, but was told not to tell anyone—you know how the Spymaster is. The ae'Magi didn't intend any harm to him, obviously, but orders are orders. The ae'Magi eventually accepted that I couldn't tell him anything."

Storytelling did come in handy sometimes, Aralorn reflected. Take a grain of truth and embellish it with nonsense, and it was more believable than what had actually happened. It wasn't as if she really expected Kisrah to believe her anyway; she just wanted to keep him from deciding what had happened with any certainty.

Wolf whined, and it echoed weirdly in the stone-enclosed corridor. Maybe he was worried about how much storytelling she was doing this night. Probably he was right.

"Shall we go, Lord Kisrah? Or would you like to put me to the question? I'm certain Father has some old thumbscrews around here somewhere."

The Archmage stared at her as if the intensity of his gaze alone would be enough to pick through the tale she'd woven. His expression was as far removed from the charming man of his public image as Wolf was from a sheep. The pink wig looked like the absurd camouflage it was. He looked very tired, she thought suddenly—as if he had spent more than one sleepless night lately.

"No doubt," he said tautly, "torture would get another answer out of you, equally plausible and equally false."

Aralorn smiled pleasantly at him; it wasn't difficult—few things gave her greater pleasure than frustrating someone else's attempt to gain information. "No doubt," she agreed congenially.

"Sometimes," he said with absolute conviction, "I wish there were a truth spell that really worked. Lead on, then, by all means," he said with a sigh, abruptly shifting back to the harmless dandy. "I would take a look at this spell that holds your father."

The guard had returned to his duty.

"Lord Kisrah is here to take a look at Father," she told him.

"Of course, Lady. Should I remain here, or would you like more privacy?"

Aralorn looked to the Archmage, who shrugged his indifference.

"Stay here," she said to the guard. "I'd rather not have any curious souls wander in while the ae'Magi is here."

"Yes, Lady." The guard smiled.

"The wardings are different," said Lord Kisrah, examining the curtains.

Aralorn shrugged and dispelled her wards. "It was a onetime warding amulet. These wards are mine."

He opened the curtain and passed through, murmuring without looking at her. "The wardings were Cain's work—I know it well. I've never heard of talismans of warding."

She was not so easily won from her chosen story. She merely raised her eyebrow at him. "I had not heard of baneshades before today. Isn't it wonderful that we may learn throughout our lifetimes. I assure you that the only ones here when the wardings were drawn were my wolf and I. You have your choice of mages." She gestured to Wolf, who whined and wagged his tail gently. No human mage could manage to stay in an animal form as long as Wolf had tonight. That Cain ae'Magison was something other than purely human was something his father had kept quiet.

Kisrah spared her a brief glare before continuing into the room. She lit a magelight as she followed him in, but he lit his own as well. Obviously, she thought with amusement, he didn't trust her. Smart man.

She tugged the curtain shut behind her, stopping just inside the alcove, where she could see the sorcerer without interfering with his magic.

Like Wolf, he placed a hand on her father's forehead and made a gesture that looked somewhat similar. Watching him closely, Aralorn saw the Archmage's full lips tighten with some emotion or perhaps just the effort he put into the spell. When he was done, he stepped back for a moment, then began another spell.

At Aralorn's side, Wolf stiffened and took a swift step forward, crouching slightly. Aralorn felt a swift rush of fear; had she trusted too much to her knowledge of this man?

In spite of her suspicions, she really didn't believe he would actually harm her father. His reputation aside, Aralorn had access to more rumors than a cat had kittens, and she'd never heard a word to indicate he was dishonorable; and *someone* had taken great care to keep from harming her father. She knew too much about magic to make the mistake of interrupting Kisrah, but she watched him narrowly and trusted Wolf to stop it if need be.

Whatever the spell the Archmage wrought, Aralorn could tell by the force of the magic gathering at his touch and the beads of sweat on his forehead that it was a powerful one. When he was through, Kisrah leaned against the bier for support.

"Cursed be," he swore softly, wiping his face with impatience. He turned to Aralorn. "Quickly, tell me the names of the magic-users who live within a day's ride of here."

"Human mages?"

"Yes."

Aralorn pursed her lips but could think of no reason to lie to him. "Nevyn, for one. I think Falhart's wife Jenna might be a hedgewitch— someone said something like that once—but you'd have to talk to them to be sure. I know she's the local midwife. Old Anasel retired to a cottage on the big farm over on the bluffs about a league to the south. I believe that he's senile now. That's it as far as I know—though there are probably a half dozen hedgewitches."

Kisrah shook his head. "Wouldn't be a hedgewitch. Anasel . . . Anasel might have been able to do it. I'll speak to Lady Irrenna about him. It is certainly not Nevyn. I know his work."

Aralorn tapped her fingers lightly on her thigh. Hedgewitches aside, Kisrah should have been able to answer the question about wizards for himself. He was, after all, the ae'Magi. All the trained human wizards, except for Wolf, were bound to him.

"Ask Irrenna about other mages as well—she might know something I don't, but after you do that, you might see if you can contact one of the Spymaster's wizards in Sianim. Tell them you're asking for me, and they won't charge you. If there is another wizard here, Ren will know."

Kisrah looked startled for a moment at her helpfulness, but he nodded warily. "I'll do that."

THAT NIGHT, COMFORTABLY ensconced in the bed, Aralorn watched as Wolf, in human form, scrubbed his face with a damp cloth.

"Wolf, what do you know about howlaas?"

He held the cloth and shook his head. "Something less than a story collector like you, I imagine."

She shrugged. "I was just wondering how long I'll be listening to the wind."

"Is it bothering you now?"

"Not as long as I stay away from windows."

"Give it a few days," he said finally. "If it doesn't stop soon, I'll see what I can find out."

She nodded. The thought that it might never fade was something she didn't want to dwell on. She came up with a change of topic.

"What was the second spell Lord Kisrah tried to work?" she asked. "The one you were worried about."

Wolf shrugged off his shirt and set it aside so he could wash more thoroughly. "I believe it was an attempt to unwork the spell holding your father."

Admiring the view, she said, "I thought that was what he was doing with his first spell?"

Wolf shook his head. "No. He was checking to make certain your father was still alive."

She thought about that, frowning. "Why did his second spell bother you?"

He wiped dry and took off his loose-fitting pants. "Because he didn't examine the spell before he tried to unwork it."

"Which means?"

"He knew what the spell was already."

She pulled back the cover from Wolf's side of the bed and patted it in invitation. "You think that Kisrah cast it?"

He joined her and spent a moment settling in. "Yes. I think that's exactly what it means."

"Then why couldn't he remove it?" she asked, scooting over until her head rested on his shoulder. "And why was he surprised by the bane-shade's presence?"

"I think that another wizard has his hands in the brew. Remember, Kisrah asked about other wizards in the area."

Aralorn nodded. "So he can't release the spell until he finds the other mage?"

"Right."

"If he cast the spell with this other wizard, then why doesn't he know who it is?"

"Perhaps he set the spell in an amulet," said Wolf, grunting even before she poked him. "Seriously, I don't know."

"Nevyn," she said with a sigh. "It must have been Nevyn. I've heard that poor Anasel can hardly feed himself."

But Wolf shook his head. "If it was Nevyn, I'd expect that Kisrah would know it. Kisrah was telling the truth when he said it wasn't Nevyn—he's a terrible liar."

She wriggled her toe in the covers for a minute, then she twisted around and braced her chin on Wolf's chest. "So Kisrah decided that you and I had a hand in the former ae'Magi's death. In a fit of vengeance, he uses black magic on Father to draw me, and therefore you, into coming here, where he could exact vengeance. Then another wizard steps in to add his two bits' worth—I don't buy it."

"That's because you are trying to make whole cloth from unspun wool."

She grinned in the darkness. "You've been hanging around Lambshold too long. 'Sheepish' comments aside, I suppose, you're probably right. Do you have a better idea?"

"I have a suspicion, but I'll wait until I've had a little more time to think on it."

She yawned and shifted into a more comfortable position. "I think I'll sleep on it, too."

She really didn't expect to gain any insight while she lay dreaming, but it was several hours before morning when she awoke with her heart pounding.

"Wolf," she said urgently.

"Umpf," he said inelegantly.

She sat up, letting the chilly night air seep under the warm blankets. "I mean it, Wolf, wake up. I need your opinion."

"All right. I'm awake." He pulled the covers snug around his neck.

Almost hesitantly, she asked, "Did Kisrah look tired to you? I thought so, but I don't know him very well."

"Yes. There are a lot of people around here who haven't gotten enough sleep." Sleep-roughened as it was, his voice was almost difficult to understand.

Aralorn smoothed the covers as they lay over her lap, not at all certain her next question was important enough for the pain it would cause him. "When you saw her, the one time you saw her, did your mother have red hair?"

He withdrew instantly without moving at all.

"It's not an idle question," she told him. "I thought of something while I was telling stories tonight. I thought it was silly then, but now . . ."

"Yes," he said shortly, "she had red hair."

"Was it long or short?"

"Long," he bit out after a short pause. "Long and filthy. It smelled of excrement and death."

"Wolf," said Aralorn in a very small voice, looking at the bump her toes made under the quilts, "when you destroyed the tower, were you trying to kill yourself?"

She felt the bed move as he shifted his weight.

This question seemed to bother him less than the one about his mother. The biting tone was missing from his rough voice, and he sounded . . . intrigued. "Yes. Why do you ask?"

She ran her hands through her hair. "I'm not sure how to tell you this without sounding like a madwoman. Just bear with me."

"Always." There was a bit of long-suffering in his tone.

She leaned back against him and smiled wryly. "Ever since you left this last time, I've been having nightmares. At first they weren't too different from the ones I had after you rescued me from the ae'Magi's dungeons, and I didn't think much more about them. About a week ago, they became more pointed."

She thought about them, trying to pick out the first that had been different. "The first set seemed to have a common theme. I dreamed that I was a child, looking for something I had lost—you. In another dream, I was back in the dungeon, blinded, and the ae'Magi asked me where you were—just as he did when he had me at the castle. It was so real I could feel the scratches on my arms and the congestion in my lungs. I've never had a dream that real."

She reached out a hand to rest on Wolf's arm for her own comfort. "I saw Talor again, and his twin. They were both Uriah this time, though Kai died before he could be changed."

She paused to steady her voice and wasn't too successful. "They asked me where you were."

"You think they were more than dreams?" She couldn't tell what he thought from his voice.

"I didn't at first, though I thought it was strange that in my dreams they never asked where 'Wolf' was—I don't think of you as 'Cain' very often. That's what my father asked me. He said, 'Don't tell me you've forgotten where you put Cain.'" She laughed softly, shaking her head. "As if you were a toy I'd misplaced." She grinned at him. "I thought that one was just worry because you'd left so abruptly."

She lost her smile. "That's where the color of your mother's hair comes in. The last dream, the one I had in the inn on the way here, was even odder than the others. At least they seemed to come from my experiences: This one wasn't about anything I'd ever seen."

"It concerned my mother?"

Aralorn nodded. "Partially, yes. It was more a series of dreams. They all concerned you—things you had done."

"What sorts of things?"

"Unpleasant ones. Like when your mother died. Someone who didn't know you as well as I do might have thought you didn't feel anything."

"I didn't."

Aralorn shot him a look of disbelief, remembering the boy's frozen face, then shook her head at him. "Right," she said dryly. "At any rate, that was the first part. In another, I was tied down, and you were going to kill me. But I knew there was something wrong, and I fought it. When I did, it . . . altered. I was watching again, and it was the ae'Magi who held the knife. He offered it to you, and you refused."

"I didn't always," commented Wolf softly—he had stiffened again.

Aralorn tightened her grip briefly on his arm. "I know. But you wouldn't smile while you killed—or talk either, for that matter. At any rate, the last part was when you destroyed the tower. What I saw at first presented you as a power-mad mage, but this time it was easier to shift the dream back to what really happened. I can picture you motivated by rage, hurt, or cold-blooded anger, but greed just doesn't fit."

"The story you told tonight made you think that something was sending you dreams like the Dreamer?" repeated Wolf carefully.

"It sounds even stupider when you say it than when I think it," she commented, but she slid back under the covers and huddled near his warmth just the same. How to explain the alien feel of the dreams without sounding even stupider? "I didn't know the color of your mother's hair, or that you were trying to destroy yourself with the tower. We are living in odd times." Times made odder by the last ae'Magi's foray into forbidden magics—she didn't need to say it. Wolf knew his father was in some part responsible for the changes taking place. "Dragons fly the Northland skies, and howlaas venture into Reth."

She continued without pause. "There has even been a resurgence in the followers of the old gods for the past several years. Look at the temple here. It's been centuries since there was a priest in residence, but there's one here now. The trappers have been decimated by nasty critters like the howlaa and other things that haven't been seen in generations. Is it so impossible that . . . that something else was awakened?"

Wolf broke in. "You mean that the black magic my father worked might have fed the Dreamer you told us about tonight?"

"Yes." She swallowed. "That howlaa today. It was sent, Wolf."

"Sent?" asked Wolf.

"Uhm." She nodded. "When I met its gaze, it spoke to me. Something evil sent it searching for us—it was meant to kill you." She hesitated, then continued. "Then there was the wind . . . Wolf, I believe that there is something evil here."

Silence lingered for a while as Wolf thought of what she'd said.

"Well," he said finally, "as long as we are throwing out odd theories,

I have developed one of my own, just for you. It even has to do with dreaming."

"You didn't laugh at mine, so I won't laugh at yours," she promised.

"Right," he replied. "When it became obvious to me that Kisrah had worked the spell, I thought about just what it would have taken to persuade him to do so. I could only think of one thing—and tonight I realized that it was even possible. Let me tell you a little something you may not have known about human magic."

"That doesn't limit the topic much," she quipped.

He ruffled her hair. "Quiet, little mouse, and listen. Human mages have different talents; one of them—though it is very rare—is a form of farseeing. The mage's spirit leaves his body and can travel over vast distances in a matter of moments. In that state, he can speak to others in their dreams or merely watch them. Usually, they are invisible in that form—but occasionally they can be seen as a ghostly mist."

"All right," agreed Aralorn. "I think I've heard of that. It's called spirit travel or something of the sort—but I thought it was rare."

"Like shapeshifters," agreed Wolf.

"Your point," she acquiesced, grinning a little in the darkness of the chilly old castle room. "So you think that maybe my dreams might be coming from a human mage? Someone deliberately trying to get information from me?"

"My father could do it," said Wolf softly. "I heard him talking about it once with another wizard. They were discussing another mage, I think. I don't know which one. He said, 'Of course I'm certain he's a dreamwalker. I have some talent in that direction myself.' I think he used his talent to influence his rise to power—by speaking to the other mages as they slept." He hesitated a moment, then added, "I remember, because I marked a rune on my staff that kept him from doing the same to me as soon as I overheard him."

Aralorn tightened her arms around him, wondering how he was still sane after all his father had done to him. He squeezed her in return—to comfort her, she thought—and continued to speak without a pause.

"If the body of a dreamwalker is killed while the spirit is outside, the spirit remains alive for a time. He probably would not be able to work magic as a spirit, but he can persuade others to act on his behalf."

"A ghost?" she asked.

He grunted. "No. Ghosts are . . . bits of memory trapped in place. A spirit is—it's too late at night for lessons in magic theory, my Lady. Let me get back to the subject at hand. It is possible that my father managed to leave his body before the Uriah killed him. In that state, he could have visited Kisrah—as well as the other mage who appears to have had his hands in the pie—and persuaded them to act in his stead."

"You think the only reason Kisrah would use black magic . . ."

"Was if my father asked him to do so," said Wolf. "Yes."

"To use Father as bait for us."

"Perhaps."

Aralorn stiffened at his cautious tone, which usually meant things had gone from bad to worse. "What do you mean?"

"My father wanted to live forever, Lady. Do you think that he would be content with mere vengeance?"

"You think he's trying to use Father's body?"

"Your father can't work magic; but your father is connected intimately with three mages. Attack him with magic, and my father has a whole selection to choose among."

"He would prefer yours since you are the most powerful of the three." Aralorn shivered and settled closer. "I think I prefer the Dreamer."

"Perhaps," suggested Wolf mildly, "we'll be lucky, and it is only Kisrah trying to kill me."

She snickered into his shoulder. "Not everyone would look at that as lucky."

"Not everyone is looking at our list of alternatives."

"True." She yawned.

They fell silent, and she thought Wolf had drifted off to sleep. She patted him gently.

Her uncle had said that Wolf had a death wish.

She'd known that he had a tendency to be reckless, thought that it was something they shared. In her dreams (and she was convinced that the memories of Wolf's experiences were true dreams, however they'd been sent), she'd seen that he'd expected death when he'd destroyed the tower. He'd hoped for death. Apparently, he still did.

She took in a deep breath of his familiar scent and held it to her heart. She would not lose him.

"Tomorrow, I think we might visit the priestess of the death goddess," she said. He *had* been asleep, because her voice jerked him awake. "If there's a ghost or a Dreamer out there, the death goddess ought to know—don't you think?"

"Could be," Wolf muttered groggily. "Go to sleep, Aralorn."

EIGHT

———ɷ———

"I HADN'T EXPECTED THIS TO BECOME AN EXPEDITION," MUTTERED ARA-
lorn softly to Sheen as she rocked back and forth with his exuberant
stride. He was feeling frisky after his rest, and his steps were animated
and quick. Wolf, gliding soundlessly beside the gray warhorse, gave her
a sardonic look before turning his attention to the snowy path.

She shook her head, and said in a tone meant to carry to her escort,
"It's not as if Lambshold is riddled with outlaws. Even if it were, I am
fully capable of taking care of myself."

"See, Correy," boomed Falhart from behind her and somewhat to the
left, "I told you she'd like to have some company."

"She's been gone a long time. She's probably forgotten where the
temple is," said Correy solemnly, behind her and to the right. "Dead howlaas aside, an itty-bitty runt like her needs her big brothers to protect her."

Aralorn spun Sheen around on his hocks with enough speed to leave
the stallion snorting and looking for the enemy. If she'd known what an
overprotective streak the howlaa was going to stir up, she would never
have let Correy know it was there. Let his stupid sheep get eaten by wolves.
Protection she might have to put up with while she was here, but . . .

She pointed accusingly at Correy. "You promised no more jokes about
my size."

"Or lack thereof," added Falhart smugly.

"No," said Correy. "Falhart is the one who promised. Besides, I just
commented on *our* size, right, Gerem? Just because your thirteen-year-
old brother is a hand and a half taller than you doesn't mean you're small.
We just happen to be taller than most people."

"Especially itty-bitty runts like you," added Falhart helpfully.

She shook her head at the three of them. Hart had come because he wanted to get out and ride. Correy, she thought, had come out of an honest desire to protect her. Gerem, she strongly suspected, had come to save her hulking brothers from their nasty, shapeshifting sister, itty-bitty runt or not.

"Men," she snorted with mock disgust.

She pivoted Sheen until he faced their original direction and sent him off racing across the sun-sparkled snow, smiling when her brothers called out in protest at her head start as they picked up the race.

RIDANE'S TEMPLE WAS a large structure nestled in an isolated valley. Aralorn remembered the "new" temple as a ruin heavily overgrown with ivy, but even under the snow, she could see that was no longer the case. Someone had been doing quite a lot of work, and the result was elegant and impressive. The snug little house built unobtrusively on one side was a new addition to the site as well.

Correy pointed to it. "When Father heard there was a priestess at the temple, he rode here by himself to talk with her. When he got back, he sent me out with a score of workmen to build her a house to live in."

Falhart grinned at Aralorn. "Correy's been really helpful around here. He took several days to clear the ivy and a week to scrub the lichen off the stone. He even got the old well working again."

Before Correy could reply, a cheery "Who comes?" rang out from the cottage, and the door opened to reveal a woman bundled in a wool cloak dyed cherry red. She shut the door behind her and came out to greet them.

"My lords! And isn't it a cold day to be out visiting, I'm thinking." The priestess, for she could be no other, was close enough for Aralorn to see that her face matched the promise of her voice. A warm smile lit eyes the color of dark-stained oak, and it was aimed particularly at Correy.

Correy jumped lightly off his horse and took one of her hands in his, bringing it to his lips. "Any day with you in it, Lady, is as warm as midsummer's eve."

Hmm, thought Aralorn. *Maybe Correy didn't come to protect me after all.*

Falhart shook his head as he dismounted also. In tones of apologetic despair, he addressed the priestess. "Smooth-tongued demon, isn't he? I'm sorry, Tilda. It's my fault. I taught him all I knew."

"That took the better part of supper," confided Correy without releasing the priestess's hand. "And only that long because he was eating most of the time. It's amazing the man ever managed to get married in the first place."

Aralorn slipped off Sheen and dropped his reins to the ground.

"It's obvious that he wasn't teaching you manners," Aralorn muttered in a voice loud enough for everyone to hear, "or you would have introduced me by now."

"Forgive me, O Small-but-Sharp-Tongued-One," said Falhart, taking Aralorn's hand gallantly. "I have neglected my duties as older brother. Tilda, allow me to present my sister Aralorn. Aralorn, this is Tilda, priestess of the death goddess."

"The shapeshifter," murmured Tilda thoughtfully.

"The mercenary," Aralorn murmured back.

They exchanged cheerful grins. Then the priestess turned to Gerem, standing quietly beside his mount.

"Gerem," said the priestess, "well come. I haven't seen you since last summer."

Aralorn watched Gerem's face closely, but apparently Nevyn had no objection to the death goddess, for Gerem's smile was genuine, lighting his eyes as it touched his lips. "I'm sorry, Lady, but Correy made us stay home so he could have you to himself."

"To what do I owe this visit? Would you like to come in?" Tilda gestured to her house.

Correy shook his head. "Today's an official visit to the priestess, I'm afraid. Aralorn thinks Ridane might be able to shed some light on the matter with Father."

The priestess lost none of her warmth but nodded understandingly. "I was not surprised when I was told he was not dead—Ridane had said nothing of his death to me. I don't know if She knows any more than you do, but you may certainly ask. Would you go into the temple? I will meet you inside."

Aralorn followed her brothers to the main entrance of the temple. Correy started to open the rough-hewn, obviously temporary door, then hesitated.

"Aralorn, I think it might be best if you leave your wolf outside," he said.

"The wolf is one of the death goddess's creatures," said Gerem unexpectedly. "I doubt the goddess will object—though her priestess might."

Wolf settled the matter by slipping through the narrow opening and into the temple.

Aralorn shrugged. "I suspect this temple has been infested by everything from rats to cows over the last hundred years. One animal more or less will make little difference."

Correy shook his head but opened the door farther and allowed the rest of them to pass. As Aralorn moved by him, he caught her arm.

"Don't be fooled by Tilda's friendliness. The death goddess has a very real presence here. Be careful how far you choose to push Her."

Aralorn patted him gently on the top of his head—she had to stand on her toes to do it. "Go teach Lord Kisrah how to cast a light spell, baby brother. I'm not as uncivilized as it sometimes appears."

Brushing by him, she walked into the entrance hall. It was not very impressive as such things go. Although it was large enough for twoscore people to stand without feeling crowded, there was still a multitude of evidence of the temple's long spell of neglect. High above, the vaulted ceiling showed white plaster and gaping holes where frescoed wolves and owls once frolicked. The floor had been pulled up and the usable flagstone piled to one side. On the other side, several large and crudely made benches lined the wall.

Though there was no sign of a fire, the room was remarkably warm. When the men began to toss their cloaks and gloves on the benches, Aralorn did the same.

As she dropped her gloves on top of her cloak, the creak of door hinges drew her attention to the far end of the room. The doors set in the wall were neither makeshift nor temporary; only years produced such a fine patina in bronze. They swung slowly open with a ponderousness in keeping with their hoary age.

Dressed in robes of black and red, Tilda stepped through the doorway onto the narrow platform set between the doors and the three stairs down to where Aralorn and her brothers waited. They approached the priestess with varying degrees of wariness, reverence, and enthusiasm. When Correy stopped several feet from the stairs, the rest of them did as well, leaving the priestess above them.

"You are come to ask about the Lyon." The priestess's voice had lost the hills accent and the warmth. Her earthy beauty was in no way faded, but it seemed out of place.

Aralorn thought it wasn't Tilda speaking at all. A shiver ran through her. She could never have stood for such a thing; the last ae'Magi had come close to controlling her thoughts. Even as part of her shuddered in distaste, she felt a flash of awe—and satisfaction. This priestess was a priestess in truth; even her small store of green magic told her that much. She might really be able to help the Lyon.

"My father lies with the seeming of death," said Correy, when no one else spoke. "Can you free him?"

She seemed to consider it a moment, and Aralorn held her breath. Finally, the priestess shook her head. "No. There are limits on the things that I control. This is no death curse, though he may die of it, and I can do little but speed his death. That I will not do without reason."

"How long—" Aralorn's voice cracked, and she had to try again. "How long before he dies of the magic?"

"A fortnight more will the spell hold stable. Until that time, he comes not unto me."

"Two weeks," said Aralorn softly to herself.

"As I said," replied the priestess.

"Do you know of the Dreamer?" asked Aralorn, drawing surprised looks from her brothers.

The priestess turned her head to the side, considering.

"The creature that sleeps in the glass desert," Aralorn clarified further.

"Ah," said the priestess. "Yes . . . I had forgotten that name . . ."

"Has it awakened?"

The priestess hesitated. "I would not know of it, unless it killed—and that was not its way. It incited others to do its killing."

Falhart spoke for the first time. "Do you know anything about the farm that was burned to the ground?"

"Yes. Death visited there and was caught to pay the price of the Lyon's sleep."

"You mean," said Gerem, with a tension that was strong enough to attract Aralorn's interest, "something was killed there. That death was used in the magic that ensorcelled my father."

The priestess nodded. "As I said."

"Is Geoffrey ae'Magi dead, or does his spirit attend the living?" asked Aralorn.

"He is dead," said Tilda. "But in the way of such men, much of him lives on in the hearts of those who loved him."

She swayed alarmingly. Disregarding his wariness for the goddess in concern for the woman, Correy jumped up the short flight of stairs and wrapped an arm around her waist.

"Here, now," he said, helping her sit on the floor.

"Did you get the answers you needed?" she asked. "She left without warning me. Usually, I can tell when She's ready to leave, and I can give notice of the last question. Otherwise, you are left with the most important thing unanswered."

"It was fine," said Aralorn thoughtfully. She would rather have had a simple yes or no to her last question, but she hadn't really expected as much help as they'd gotten. Usually priests and priestesses were much less forthcoming and a lot more obscure when they did tell you something.

"Aralorn"—Tilda got to her feet and shook out her robes briskly, obviously putting off whatever weakness the goddess's visit had left her with—"I wonder if you would mind speaking with me in private for a bit."

Since Aralorn had been debating how to phrase the same request, she nodded immediately. "Of course." Last night she'd thought of another thing that Ridane could help her with.

Tilda walked down the stairs and, with a shooing motion, said, "Go along now and wait for us in the cottage. There are some fresh scones on the table, help yourselves."

Aralorn's brothers left without a protest. As he turned to close the door behind them, Gerem shot a calculating look at Aralorn. When she smiled and waved, he frowned and pulled the door shut with a bang that reverberated in the large, mostly empty room.

"He doesn't trust me," commented Aralorn, shaking her head.

"With Nevyn around, you're lucky anyone does," said Tilda in reply.

"For someone who lives several hours from the hold, you know an awful lot about my family." Aralorn rubbed the itchy place behind Wolf's ears.

The death goddess's priestess grinned companionably and answered Aralorn's observation. "My news travels fast—Correy's new horse has a rare turn of speed."

Aralorn returned her smile. "You wanted to talk to me about something?"

"Hmm." Tilda looked down and tapped her foot. "The goddess told me to ask you if you would change shape for me."

Of all the things she could have asked, that was something Aralorn had not expected.

"Why?"

"You are a shapeshifter," Tilda said. "A few weeks ago, I saw an animal that had no business being in the woods. A shapeshifter was the only explanation I could come up with, though, other than the fact that there hasn't been a report of a howlaa around here for generations, the animal didn't seem unnatural. I asked Ridane if I'd be able to tell the difference between a shapeshifter and a natural animal; She told me to ask you." The priestess smiled. "Since you hadn't been here in a long time, I did wonder. When you came here today, She reminded me again to ask you."

"There was a howlaa," said Aralorn. "It was killed yesterday, not far from the keep. But I don't see any reason to refuse to change in front of you: a favor for a favor."

"What is it you need of me?" asked Tilda warily.

Aralorn threaded her fingers through the hair on Wolf's neck and cleared her throat. "I have this friend who needs to get married."

Tilda's jaw dropped for a moment. "No one's ever asked me that before."

Not surprising, thought Aralorn. There hadn't been a priestess of Ridane here for generations, and even when there had been, few people chose to be married in Her temple. Marriage bonds set by the goddess of death had odd consequences: Two people so bound could not live if one died.

Aralorn was counting on three things: that no one would see the marriage lines written in Tilda's recording book and use them to trace Cain ae'Magison to Aralorn and her wolf; that Wolf and his unbalanced education wouldn't know about the quirk of Ridane's marriages; and that, afterward, when she told him, he'd want her life more than his own death.

"You can perform a marriage ceremony?" Aralorn asked.

"Yes," Tilda said slowly. "I know the rites."

Aralorn inclined her head formally. "Thank you."

She turned to Wolf, who had been staring at her incredulously since she'd begun speaking.

"Well?" she said.

He glanced at Tilda for a moment, then swung his yellow gaze back to Aralorn.

Evidently deciding that Aralorn had already spoiled any chance to maintain his secrecy, he asked, "Why?"

Because I don't want to lose you, she thought. That sounded right to her, so she said, "Because I don't want to lose you, not ever. I love you."

Her declaration seemed to mean something to him though he'd heard it before. He stood so still that she could barely see him breathe.

"It is too dangerous," he said finally. "Someone will see the records."

His voice was so sterile she could read nothing from it. A good sign, she thought. If he'd known what the marriage would mean, he'd have refused her outright. "Too dangerous" was no refusal, and he knew her too well to think that it was.

"Who would ask a temple of the death goddess for a record of marriage lines?" asked Aralorn reasonably. "And an avatar of a goddess surely won't be caught up in the residue of your father's spells." She turned to Tilda, who was watching them with some fascination. "Would you agree to keep this marriage secret?"

Slowly, she nodded. "Barring that it violates any request of Ridane, yes."

"I know you, Aralorn," Wolf said in a low growl. "You do not fight in the regular forces because you don't like the ties that bind such folk to each other. You work alone, and prefer it. You have many people who like you and some people you like, but no one who is truly a friend. You protect yourself with a shield of friendliness and humor."

"I have friends," she said, taken aback by his assessment; it had come from nowhere—and she thought he was wrong. She wasn't the loner; he was.

"No," Wolf said. "Whom did you tell when you came here?"

"I left a note for the Mouse."

"Work," he said. "You believed your father had died, and you told no one. What did the note to Ren say? That you'd been called home on family business? Did you tell him the Lyon was dead or leave it for his other spies?"

He was right. How odd, she thought, to see yourself through someone else's view and discover a stranger.

"You fight to have no bonds to anyone," he continued, an odd hesitation in his rough voice. "You don't even come to visit your family because you fear the pain of those ties. But you would tie yourself to me anyway. Because you love me."

She felt stripped naked and bewildered. "Yes," she said, when he seemed to be waiting for some response.

"If you wish to marry me," he said, "I am most honored."

Tilda cleared her throat awkwardly. "Uhm. I'm not actually certain that I can marry someone to a wolf."

Aralorn gathered her tattered defenses together and managed a grin. "I agree. Wolf?"

Wolf could no more have resisted putting on a show for the priestess than a child could resist a sweet.

Black mist swirled up to engulf him until he was merely a darker shadow in the blackness. Gradually, the mist rose to the height of a man before falling away to reveal Wolf's human shape, complete with his usual silver mask.

Aralorn turned to Tilda, who had recovered from her initial surprise, and indicated Wolf. "May I introduce you to Cain, son of Geoffrey ae'Magi. But I call him Wolf, for obvious reasons."

"Cain the Black," whispered Tilda, horrified. She drew a sign in the air that glowed silver and green.

Wolf shook his head in disgust. "You can hardly think, whatever tales you have heard, that I would attack a priestess in her own temple. Not the brightest of moves."

"Don't mind him," offered Aralorn. "He always responds to other people's fear this way—not that the fear is always unwarranted, mind you, but, generally speaking, he's harmless enough."

"You want me to wed you to Cain the Black?" asked Tilda, sounding like she'd had one too many shocks.

"Look," said Aralorn, stifling her impatience. "I'm not asking *you* to marry him. Do this for me . . . ask the goddess what She thinks of Wolf . . . Cain. Then decide what you would do."

Tilda spared Wolf another wary glance. "I'll do that. Wait a moment."

She sat on the middle stair and bowed her head—without removing the sign she'd drawn. It hung in the air, powered by human magic rather than anything of the goddess's. Tilda was mageborn. Aralorn wondered if she should add the priestess's name to the list of mages Kisrah had requested.

"You've taken quite a risk," murmured Wolf in a voice that went no farther than Aralorn's ears. "What if the goddess decides I am so tainted by my early deeds that I should die to pay for them?"

Aralorn shook her head, not bothering to lower her voice. "I know my stories. The goddess has always had a weakness for rogues and reprobates—just like me."

"You're right," agreed Tilda quietly, visibly calmer. Her sign faded quickly, without a motion on Tilda's part. "She likes you—very much. If you would like to stand before me, the goddess of death will bind you tighter than the threads of life."

"Take off the mask, please," Aralorn asked him.

He slanted a glance at the priestess and flicked his fingers toward his face. The mask disappeared and left his face bare of scars. Aralorn touched his cheek.

The priestess stood on the middle step, and Wolf took Aralorn's hand formally on his forearm. They faced Tilda together: Aralorn in her riding leathers, doubtless, she thought, smelling of horses; Wolf in his customary sartorial splendor, not a hair out of place.

"Who stands before me?" asked Tilda formally.

"Wolf of Sianim, who once was Cain ae'Magison."

"Aralorn of Sianim, once of Lambshold."

"To what purpose would you come?"

"To wed." They answered together.

"For all things to come, either good or evil? Desiring no other mate?"

"Yes," said Wolf.

"Yes," agreed Aralorn.

Tilda took out a small copper knife and pricked her thumb so that a drop of blood formed. She pressed it to the hollow of Aralorn's throat, then to Wolf's.

"Life to life entwined as the goddess wills, so be it. Kiss now, and by this shall the deed be sealed."

Wolf bent and touched his lips to Aralorn's.

"Done!" The priestess's word rang with a power that had nothing to do with magic.

"It shall be recorded," said Tilda, "that Wolf of Sianim married Aralorn of Sianim on this date before Tilda, priestess of Ridane."

"Thank you." Wolf bowed his head.

From her perch on the stairs, Tilda leaned forward and kissed the top of his head. "We wish you nothing but the best."

Wolf drew back, startled at the gesture. He started to say something, but shook his head instead. Without a word or an excess bit of magic, he shifted to his lupine form.

Aralorn looked at the priestess with full approval. "Now, do you still want me to shift for you?"

Tilda shook her head with a sigh. "It's not necessary. I had no idea that he was anything other than a wolf."

Aralorn laughed. "Neither did my uncle the shapeshifter—and we can usually tell our kind. Hold a moment." She knew her change wasn't as graceful or impressive as Wolf's, but it was swift. She chose the icelynx because she'd been working on it and because someday she might have to spend some time at the temple: She didn't want Tilda to be looking too hard at strange mice.

She arched her back to rid herself of the final tingles of the change. The shadows held fewer secrets in this form, but there were fewer colors as well. Staring at the priestess's face, Aralorn could see a hint of satisfaction in Tilda's eyes.

No, Aralorn thought, *this should be a fair exchange of favors.* She lay down on the floor and began tentatively to hide herself within the icelynx's instincts. She was better with the mouse—and it was less dangerous that way, but she trusted that Wolf would stop her if she lost control of her creation. When she had done what she could to disguise herself, she waited for ten heartbeats, then allowed herself to reemerge.

Hiding so deeply always left her with a headache to remind her why she seldom went to such extremes. She stood up, shook herself briskly, then shifted back to human form.

"Well," asked Aralorn, rubbing her arms briskly, "could you tell I was not the real thing?"

Tilda took a deep breath and loosened her shoulders with a rolling motion. "When you first changed, yes, but for a moment while you lay still, no."

"I think then you should be all right. Most of the shapeshifters don't care to get that deep into their creations," said Aralorn. "There's always the chance that the shaper might get lost in his shape."

"Thank you," said Tilda. "I found that to be most . . . enlightening."

Me, too, thought Aralorn, who had learned that a cleric mage was going to be harder to get her mouse shape past than human mages were—but not impossible.

CORREY EDGED HIS horse even with Sheen, but waited until Aralorn made eye contact before speaking. "We only have two weeks to break this spell."

Aralorn nodded. "I think it's time to really talk with the ae'Magi. I may know some things he doesn't. Perhaps together we might think of something."

"Why did you ask the question about the Dreamer?" queried Gerem, pushing forward until he was on Falhart's off side. "It is just a story."

Though her other brothers rode coursers, bred for speed and ease of gait, Gerem's horse, like Sheen, was bred for war. Younger than Sheen, with a rich sorrel coat, there was something in the horse's carriage that reminded Aralorn strongly of her own stallion. His nostrils were flared, and his crest bowed, though Gerem rode with a light hand—Sheen did the same when she was upset.

There was something about the deliberately casual tone combined with his horse's agitation that planted an odd thought in her head. She sat back, and Sheen halted abruptly, forcing the men to stop also for politeness's sake. Gerem appeared surprised at her reaction to his question, but she didn't allow that to speed her tongue. *Thirteen,* she thought, *Gerem is thirteen.*

"How," she said finally, "have you been sleeping at night lately? Have you been having bad dreams?"

A muscle twitched in his cheek. "And if I have?"

"Are they dreams of our father?" she speculated softly. "Perhaps you dreamed of his death before he actually fell?"

Gerem paled.

"Aralorn," said Falhart sharply, "pick on someone up to your fighting weight. Anyone can have seemings."

"Not seemings," said Aralorn firmly, not removing her eyes from Gerem's face. "They felt like reality, didn't they?"

Without warning, Gerem slipped his feet out of his stirrups and dropped to the ground. He made it into the bushes before they all heard the sounds of his being violently ill.

Guilt caused Aralorn more than a twinge of discomfort as she dismounted as well.

Gerem reappeared looking, if anything, paler than before. "I thought it was a dream," he said hollowly. "It had to have been—I don't know anything about magic or how it works. But I dreamed of lighting a fire and making a great magic. It burned until I thought the flesh was coming off my hands. I thought it was a dream, but when I awoke, the farm had been torched, and there were ashes on my boots. I . . . think"—he stopped and swallowed heavily, then said it all in a rush—"I think I must have put the spell on Father."

"Nonsense," said Falhart bracingly.

"Don't be an idiot," snapped Correy.

"I think you might be right," murmured Aralorn thoughtfully if unkindly. Then she continued quickly. "No, now don't look at me like that. It certainly wasn't his fault if he did. You asked me why I inquired about the Dreamer. This is the kind of thing it was supposed to be able to do. It seduced its victims into doing what it wanted, either by promising them something they wanted or by making them think they were doing something else." She looked at their solemn faces. "It is said that the Tear of Hornsmar had a dream one night. A serpent attacked him in his bed. When he awoke, he turned to tell his mistress, Jandrethan, of his nightmare—which was still vivid in his mind. He found that she had been beheaded by his own sword, which he still clutched in his right hand."

"But the Dreamer is just a story," said Gerem. "Like—like—dragons."

"Ah," said Aralorn, swinging lightly back into the saddle. "But so are shapeshifters, my lad. And I am living proof that sometimes the stories have facts behind them." She crossed her arms over the saddlebow and shook her head at him, but when she spoke, her voice was gentle. "Don't take it to heart so, Gerem. Like enough there was nothing you could have done about it anyway."

Though he remounted, Correy made no move to push on. "We have two weeks before Father dies. Kisrah will try his best . . . but there has to be something we can do. Aralorn, do you know any sorcerers who might be of help? If it is black magic that holds Father, perhaps a mage who has worked with such things can help."

"You do know that it is a death sentence for any mage who admits to working such magic," commented Aralorn without glancing at Wolf.

"Yes." Correy hesitated. "I spoke with Lord Kisrah before we left this morning. He told me to ask you . . . He said that he thought you might know Geoffrey ae'Magi's son, Cain."

"He thought what?" asked Aralorn, as she damned the Archmage for voicing his suspicions out loud. If it became common knowledge she knew Wolf, they were in deep trouble.

"He thought you might know Cain the Black," repeated Correy obligingly. "It is well-known that Cain worked with the darker aspects of magic, as Lord Kisrah has not. He suggested that we might be well-advised to call upon someone with more experience in these matters."

"Been keeping bad company, little sister?" asked Falhart in deceptively gentle tones.

"Never worse than now," she agreed lightly. Sheen snorted, impatient with the long stop, and she patted him on the neck, giving herself some time to pick her reply. "I have been communicating with someone who knows something about the dark arts. He assures me that he is doing all that he can."

"Who—"

"Well enough," said Correy, over the top of Gerem's impatient question. "That's all that we can ask."

"Is it?" asked Gerem hotly. "I've been having other dreams too, dreams of Geoffrey ae'Magi's son. Isn't it in the least suspicious that the only mage known to work the black magic of old happens to associate with our sister when such magic strikes the Lyon of Lambshold? Doesn't that bother anyone but me?"

Abruptly, Aralorn kneed Sheen, and the warhorse jumped forward until she could turn him to face Gerem with only inches between them, tapping the stallion's neck when he nipped at the sorrel's rump. "Yes, plague it, it does. And worries me as well, if you want to know the truth of the matter. Only one man knew that . . . Cain and I know each other—and as far as I know, he died before he could tell anyone." *I hope he's dead,* thought Aralorn. *I hope so.* "If he's not dead, then we have a greater evil to face than some storytime creature."

She drew in a deep breath, and the war stallion shifted beneath her—every muscle ready to fight at her command. "Plague it," she said.

She took Sheen a safe distance from the other horses and tried to get a handle on her temper. "I'm sorry for that," she said finally. "I know that we are all under a great deal of strain. It absolutely was not Cain who ensorcelled Father. He does not work with black magic any longer."

"The ae'Magi," said Correy in hushed tones. "That's the evil man you're talking about. He just died a couple of months ago."

"Don't be an ass, Correy," said Falhart with a laugh. "He was the kindest of men . . . warmhearted and generous to a fault."

Correy started to say something further when Aralorn caught his eye and shook her head strongly at him.

"You're right, Falhart," she said quietly. "He was a most unusual man."

"A man of sterling character," said Gerem. *Unlike you,* he meant. "I never met him, but I never heard anyone say a word against him."

"Never," agreed Aralorn solemnly.

"Never," said Correy on an indrawn breath. "Not once. No complaints—everyone loved him."

"Absolutely," said Falhart seriously.

"I wonder," said Correy thoughtfully, to no one in particular, "where his son picked up all the knowledge of black magic."

Aralorn smiled at him approvingly before sending Sheen down the trail to Lambshold.

She took her time grooming Sheen, as did Correy his own horse. Falhart and Gerem left for their own business, and as soon as they were gone, Correy turned his horse out into its run and leaned against the wall near where Aralorn was running a soft cloth over Sheen's dappled hindquarters.

"Tell me about the last ae'Magi," he said, kneeling to pet Wolf.

Before she answered, she glanced casually around the stables, but there were no grooms around near enough to overhear. "Why do you ask?"

"Because you're right. I've never heard anyone say a word against him. That's just not natural." With a last pat, he stood up. "I met him several times at court, and I liked him very much. I never talked to him—but I had this feeling he was a wonderful person even though I didn't know him at all. It didn't even strike me as odd until I thought about it today. And Hart . . ."

"Yes?" asked Aralorn with a smile.

"He *despises* courtiers of any type—except those of us related to him by blood. He only tolerates Myr because the king is a wonderful swordsman. There is this as well: Falhart makes an exception for you and his wife, but he really doesn't like magic. He prefers things he can face with his broadsword or quarterstaff. That attitude tends to carry over to sorcerers. Oh, he's not as bad as say, Nevyn, about it—but, I've never heard him approve of any of them. Yet he considers the last ae'Magi a paragon among men? Hart has never mentioned anything in particular that Geoffrey did to inspire the kind of enthusiasm he showed today."

"Geoffrey," said Aralorn quietly, "was a Darranian. Did you know that?"

"No," said Correy, with the same disbelief she had felt the first time she'd heard it.

"It twisted him, I think. You've seen what being a Darranian wizard did to Nevyn. Nevyn pretends he is not a mage; Geoffrey had to be the greatest. So he looked farther for his power than a less driven man might have."

Wolf growled at her.

She smiled at him. "All right, so perhaps he was just evil." Turning back to Correy, she said, "It doesn't matter why he was the way he was, only that he was a black mage such as the world has not seen since the Wizard Wars."

"The ae'Magi was a black mage? Why didn't someone notice?" asked Correy.

"Hmm." Aralorn began brushing Sheen again. "One of the first things we all learn about magic is that a mage cannot take over a man's mind, that free will is stronger. That may be true of green magic, like mine, and all other forms of human magic—but it is not true of black magic. I saw the ae'Magi whip the skin off a man's back while the man begged for more. The ae'Magi created a spell that made everyone his adoring slave. It protected him and gave him easy access to his victims. As he amassed more power, he extended the spell. Even now, his magic hasn't faded entirely—as you saw with Falhart."

"Why aren't you or I afflicted?"

She shook her head. "About you, I don't know for certain. Some people seemed a little immune to it, though most of them were mageborn. You have a priestess of Ridane for a lover, and that might help. Or it could simply be the fading of the spell."

"So your shapeshifter blood protected you?"

She nodded. "Yes." She hesitated, but decided the more people with as much information as was safe, the more likely it was that someone would figure out how to save the Lyon. "I suspect it might also have had something to do with my close association with another mage."

"His son."

She shrugged, then nodded.

"You said that you're afraid Geoffrey is not dead?"

"All that was found in the ae'Magi's castle were bits and pieces of Uriah leavings. It was impossible to know for certain that the ae'Magi's remains were there. The bindings between the Archmage and the other sorcerers were broken, and the wizard's council assumed that meant Geoffrey was dead. But who can say for certain?"

"If he was not killed," said Correy slowly, "would he have any reason to look for you?"

Aralorn nodded. "He wanted to conquer death, and he thought he could do it through his son. He knows I am . . . a friend of his son—I, Aralorn of Lambshold, not just of Sianim. He might also have a touch of vengeance in his motivation. We—ah—had something to do with his untimely demise."

Correy gave her a small smile. "If he's not dead, it would be his *almost* demise."

"Point to you," she agreed.

"You think he is responsible for what happened to Father," said Correy slowly. "That he set Father up as bait, knowing you would go to Cain for help."

"I think that if he were alive, that is what he would do, yes."

"Do you think he is alive?"

"No." She sighed, rolling her shoulders to relieve the strain of reaching Sheen's back. Short people should have short horses. "I hope not."

"Kisrah knew," said Correy slowly. "He knows about you. Did the last ae'Magi tell him?"

"I don't know," she said. "Probably. Or he scryed it somehow."

"Was it Kisrah who ensorcelled Father?" he asked.

"I think . . . I think it was Kisrah and Gerem. I think someone used both of them to set a trap that neither was responsible for." That sounded right and fit with Kisrah's actions.

"Someone like Geoffrey ae'Magi."

She nodded. "He's not the only possibility." But he was—unless a legendary, possibly fictitious, creature had begun to stir again. Unfortunately, the ae'Magi's surviving a Uriah attack without use of his magic was more likely than the emergence of a creature who'd been trapped under a sea of glass for ten centuries.

"Have you really asked for Cain's help?" asked Correy. "Knowing it could be a trap set for him?" He hesitated. "Knowing what he is?"

She decided that defending Wolf to her brother could be put off for another time, so she simply said, "He's doing what he can."

She set the cloth down on a rough bench, took up a comb, and began to work on Sheen's tail. The stallion jerked his tail irritably, twitching it halfway out of her hand before resigning himself to his fate with a sigh.

Aralorn had been going back through the information she'd given her brother and regretted some of it.

"Correy, for your own safety, don't talk to anyone about the ae'Magi. His spell is waning, but it is by no means gone—most especially in connection with people he associated closely with, like Lord Kisrah. And I would appreciate it if you would try to keep Hart and Gerem from bandying Cain's name about, for my safety. There are any number of mages who would like to have something to use against him, someone he cares about—like me."

"You care about him, too," said Correy.

"Yes," she agreed without looking at Wolf. "I do."

"I will try to keep the others quiet," Correy promised. He patted her on the shoulder and walked down the wide aisle between stalls. As he left, the wind, which had been still all day, flitted through the open stable doors in a ragged gust.

Death is coming . . . Death and madness dreaming . . .

"Aralorn," said Wolf sharply, coming to his feet.

She shivered, and, knowing he couldn't hear the screaming shrieks, gave him a half smile. "I'm all right. It's just the wind. Wolf, do you still think that talking to Kisrah is a good idea?"

"I don't know that we have any other option," he replied. "If he can tell me what spell was used to bind your father, I may be able to unweave it. It's obvious Gerem, if he's had any training at all, barely knows how to call a light spell; he couldn't tell me what he did even if you could persuade him to talk to me. Kisrah will know what his part in the spell was. Otherwise, two weeks doesn't give me a lot of time to prowl through old books for an answer. Whether Kisrah knew it before your father was ensorcelled or not, he obviously knows that I am involved with you. Talking with him won't make matters any worse."

"You don't think that he's the impetus behind this?"

"He could be," he said. "But he has information we need—and now that I'm rested, I can handle Kisrah if he tries anything."

"Then I'll go look for him as soon as I finish with Sheen," she said, and went back to work.

Grooming was soothing and required just enough thought that she could distract herself from the worry that the Lyon would gradually fade into death no matter what they could do, and that the possibility the ae'Magi (and no other man held that title in her heart of hearts for all that it now belonged to Kisrah) was still alive lingered. Most of all, she could allow the work to keep her from the confession she was beginning to dread more than all the other evils the future could hold: How was she going to tell Wolf that she'd married him to keep him alive? It had seemed a good idea at the time. However, she'd had a chance to think it over. Would he see it as another betrayal?

Sheen stamped and snorted, and Aralorn coaxed her hands to soften the strokes of the comb.

"Shh," she said. "Be easy."

NINE

It wasn't as hard to find Kisrah as she had thought it might be. He was seated on a bench in the main hall, talking to Irrenna.

"Truthfully, I don't know what can be done, Irrenna. I have to find the wizard who initiated the spell—and it's no one I've ever dealt with before." He yawned.

"We kept you up half the night with our problems," said Irrenna apologetically.

He took her hand and kissed it. "Not at all, Lady. I have been having troubled dreams lately. Perhaps I'll go up and rest."

His words stopped Aralorn where she was, and an icy chill crept over her.

Aralorn had been sleeping just fine. Her own dreams had stopped when Wolf had come back to guard her sleep.

She'd been assuming that the dreaming had stopped because the one giving all of them dreams had either given up on her, changed his mind, or been kept out by some stray effect of Wolf's power. What if it was something simpler than that? What if the dream sender was detectable in some way? Maybe he had stopped because he was worried Wolf would notice what he was doing.

Perhaps, she thought, perhaps it might be better to watch what happened when Kisrah was asleep before she spoke to him. She turned on her heels and left before anyone saw her.

"Why aren't we chasing down Kisrah?" asked Wolf mildly.

She glanced around hurriedly, though she knew Wolf wouldn't have said anything if anyone could have overheard.

"Tomorrow," she said. "We'll talk tomorrow. I want to go spend some time with Father."

ARALORN CROUCHED ON the rosewood wardrobe behind a green vase in the room Kisrah had been given. She'd spent most of the day avoiding the Archmage. She didn't want to talk to him until after she'd done a little bit of spying.

When she told Wolf what she planned, he'd paid her the compliment of not arguing: Or at least he restrained himself to a few pithy comments about certain people's rashness leading them into hot water. She'd left him to stew in her room, wolves being somewhat more unexpected guests than mice were. And, although he'd tried other shapes, the only one he could hold on to reliably was the wolf. If she didn't see anything in Kisrah's room, then she and Wolf could hide Wolf from her brother Gerem while he slept. Not even Wolf could conceal himself from the Archmage with magic.

She still hadn't told him what she'd done by marrying him. She didn't fear his anger—but she found that the thought of hurting him was painful. She'd have to do it soon, though. The whole thing would be worse than useless if he managed to get himself killed before she told him that his death would mean hers, too: There was one more reason than the obvious one that people didn't lightly ask Ridane's priests to officiate in weddings.

Her hiding place wasn't ideal. It gave her a clear view of the bed while leaving her well concealed behind the vase, but there was nothing else to hide behind. If Kisrah saw her, she would be forced to run in the open.

The distance wouldn't have been a problem if he hadn't been a mage. Wizards had rather abrupt methods of dealing with mice, methods that could leave her no time to run.

It was as Aralorn's vivid imagination came up with unusual and painful ways in which a wizard could dispose of a mouse that Kisrah came into the room. And, of course, if she managed to get herself killed—Wolf would die, too. The irony of that situation didn't escape her. She sat very still in the shadow of the vase, not even allowing her itchy whiskers to twitch.

Kisrah seemed to be taking longer to get to bed than he needed to: tidying up the already painfully neat room, refolding an extra quilt at the end of his bed, and messing around in the wardrobe. As if, thought Aralorn hopefully as she cowered behind her vase, he was dreading facing his dreams.

Without his public mask, he looked even more tired than he had earlier. In the harsh illumination of the light spell he'd summoned rather than lighting the candles, he looked ten years older than he was.

"Gods, what a mess," he said tiredly. As he was staring at the perfectly tidy bed when he spoke, Aralorn assumed he wasn't talking about the room.

He stared at the bed a moment longer, then ran a hand through his artfully styled hair. With a sigh, he stripped out of his flamboyant clothes, leaving on only a pair of purple cotton half trousers.

Clothing in hand, he approached Aralorn's chosen hiding place. The wardrobe swayed slightly as he opened the doors and hung his garments, and Aralorn wished that it were summer so there would at least have been some flowers in the vase to offer more cover. A taller wardrobe would have been nice, one that didn't leave the top level with Kisrah's gaze. She didn't so much as twitch a whisker until he turned away.

A fire had been lit shortly after Aralorn had arrived in the room, and some of the winter dampness that plagued old stone buildings had left the air. Kisrah pulled a chair near the fireplace in front of the merry flames.

She gave a relieved sigh and tried not to stare at him; some people, most of the mageborn, could feel it when they were the center of attention. He gazed deeply into the rose-and-orange light of the burning pine and never turned his head toward the vase with the mouse settled behind it.

In spite of her precarious position, the warmth of the fire had Aralorn half-asleep herself before Kisrah finally pulled back the bedclothes, climbed between the muslin sheets, and put out his magelight. She shook herself gingerly, careful that her claws made no sound on the polished wood.

The lack of Kisrah's magelight was no handicap to her rodent eyes—the dying embers of the fire provided more than enough light to see with. The rhythms of Kisrah's breathing slipped slowly into sleep. Aralorn waited intently.

She couldn't have pinpointed exactly what first alerted her to the second presence in the room. It could have been a slight sound or the fur on her back ruffling as if a chill wind had blown into the room, though the air remained still and comfortable.

She took her eyes from the bed in time to see a pale mist settle before the fire. Slowly, it condensed into a familiar form. The voice was so soft she wouldn't have heard it if she hadn't been so close . . . perhaps she wouldn't have heard it if she hadn't met the howlaa. It felt like that, sounds heard without her ears.

You were not to come here, Kisrah. Someone will connect you with the deed, then where will you be? Aralorn trembled with utter terror as she watched Wolf's presumably dead father. His lips did not move, though she heard his voice clearly.

What have you done, my old friend? You said the spell was for Cain, to hold him without harm. It was Kisrah who spoke. She dared a glance at the bed, but Kisrah lay unmoving; to all appearances he was sleeping deeply.

And who would have used it on him? I was the most powerful mage in the world, and he destroyed me. Which of my friends should I have sent against him? You would have done it had I asked—but you would not have succeeded. Geoffrey's voice was soft. *Should I have let him kill you, too? I did what I had to. This way, no one is harmed.*

There was a short pause, then Kisrah said, *Why black magic? And why bring others into it, to blacken their souls as well?*

If it were not black, any mage could unwork the spell. As for the others— Geoffrey's voice softened with understanding—*did you not try and unwork the spell? If it had been only one, anyone could have freed the Lyon. The time is not yet met for him to awaken. Have patience, all will be well.*

Aralorn tried to make herself even smaller without moving so much as a hair. She very much would rather that neither of the participants in this bizarre conversation realized that there was a mouse listening to every word.

The Lyon will die if something is not done soon. She has no intention of bringing Cain into this, or she would have done it long since. No good can come of this, Geoffrey. Evil begets only evil. The magic that I, and whatever other poor benighted fools you chose to aid you, wrought here is evil. I should not have done it.

Geoffrey's voice was harsh. *You think my son is so stupid that you could snare him any other way? I searched for him fruitlessly for years without catching him—because I could not find the right bait. Now I have it. Don't fret yourself, he's here with her. Cain's mother was a shapeshifter. She gave him the ability to use green magic, something I failed to recognize until it was too late because of his talent with human magic. The mixture proved volatile—too volatile for his sanity. At least I hope he is insane . . . that is easier to accept than flesh of my flesh being so given to evil.*

Geoffrey paused as if putting aside an old grief. Aralorn's face twisted into a snarl, an expression that sat oddly on the mouse's face as she traded terror for rage at last. She put aside all thoughts of an ancient evil, satisfied that her enemy was Geoffrey ae'Magi. She and Wolf must have failed. *This is Geoffrey ae'Magi. He twists and manipulates with a skill I might envy if he did not use it as he does.*

Kisrah did not respond, and at last the phantom continued. *Don't be so impatient. I told you he would come. He might even be here already. I've seen him take the shape of animals before. Have you looked closely at Aralorn's wolf?*

With those words, Geoffrey's form dissolved. As it left the room, Lord Kisrah drew in a deep breath that was more of a gasp and sat up, clutching his head and grimacing in pain. He got up slowly, like an old man, and stirred the coals in the fire before setting a log in the grate. It was a very long time before he went back to sleep, and Aralorn didn't move until he did.

A very cautious mouse crept out of the room at last, shivering and wary.

WOLF, IN HUMAN form and wearing his mask, opened the door and let Aralorn into her room before she had a chance to knock. Startled, she looked quickly around to make certain there was no one to see him before stepping through the door and pushing it closed behind her.

"What's wrong?" he asked after a brief look at her face. "What frightened you?"

She stepped closer to him and pressed against his warm chest. She felt him stiffen momentarily, as he still did at unexpected touches, then he relaxed and pulled her more tightly to him. She took a deep breath, feeling her panic abate.

She stepped back to see his face.

"Thanks, I needed that." She hesitated. "I saw . . . Wolf, it was your father. I was watching Kisrah sleep when your father materialized in the room."

He didn't appear surprised, just tugged her closer again and bent to rest his head on top of hers as she told him the whole of what she had seen.

"He has to be dead," she whispered. "He has to be, but I swear to you this was him."

"Are you certain it was he?"

An illusion? Aralorn examined her memory. Illusionists could not create an actual double any more than a shapeshifter could take on the appearance of a specific person. There were too many fine details to be missed—a mole behind the earlobe, the slant of a smile, the swing of a walk.

"Not unless it was created by an illusion master who knew your father very well," she said finally. "Every nuance of speech or expression was Geoffrey's." She frowned. "Though he didn't really speak. I would say that it was mindspeaking, but I've never been able to send or receive by mind. I understood everything he said—*they* said—quite clearly."

"Dreamspeaking is different," replied Wolf. "If Kisrah was asleep, probably it was a dreamspeaker—which was one of my father's odder talents."

"Dreamspeaking as in dreamwalking?" asked Aralorn.

"It can be part of the same gift. Did my father have a scent?"

"What do you mean?" she asked, shocked at the inane . . . Wait, not such an inane question after all. "Allyn's toadflax, I never thought of that. I don't remember . . ." A mouse's sense of smell was not as good as a wolf's, but it was better than a human's.

"Father had a scent that he always wore: cloves and—"

"—cinnamon," she broke in. "I remember. I would have noticed that. I don't think he had any scent at all."

"Dreamwalker then," said Wolf. She couldn't tell what he thought about it. "Though it's a rare talent, my father was not the only dreamspeaker among the wizards. Whatever you saw was not a real person but a similitude. Any dreamwalker who knew my father well could produce it."

"So it isn't your father," she said with a rush of relief.

"I didn't say that." Wolf sighed and tightened his hold. "Dreamwalking is one of the two or three things that wizards are supposed to be able to do for a while after they die."

"There are a lot of dead wizards around?" Aralorn asked.

Wolf shrugged. "I've never seen any. There are stories, but no one really believes them." He hesitated. "It's just that if any wizard would come back from the dead, it would be my father."

"So this is either your father or another wizard who knows a lot about your father."

"If Kisrah were a little better at self-deception," said Wolf, loosening his hold, "it could even have been him. I never heard that dreamwalking was one of his abilities, but most of the great mages have several."

"Kisrah thought your father was a good man," she returned.

"My father's magic was powerful enough to reach Sianim," he said.

"Certainly he'd have put stronger spells on any wizard close enough to smell black magic. On his own, Kisrah is pretty observant: He'd know if he was causing my father's appearances in his dreams."

"I was hoping for the Dreamer." Aralorn stepped away and began undressing.

"You just think the Dreamer would make a better story," he said.

She frowned at him. "What's the use of going to all this work if you can't brag about it when you're through? If it is your father, we have to be quiet about it." She took a step nearer to him, then said suspiciously, "If I didn't know you better, I would say that you're cheerful. You are never cheerful around the subject of your father."

"My father isn't a cheery topic," he said. "But whether we are dealing with him, some other wizard, or a creature out of one of your stories is something that can wait. I think I have a solution to our more immediate problem. I've been doing some thinking while you were gone, and I've remembered a few things. If we can get Kisrah and Gerem's cooperation, I think I can break the spell on your father."

She stilled. "Are you sure?"

"My dear Lady, nothing's certain in this life, but it should work."

"What about the possibility of Geoffrey's attacking you?"

"*If* Kisrah and Gerem are willing to cooperate, it shouldn't be a problem."

He sounded very certain, but so had Geoffrey.

"Kisrah's not very happy with what's been done to my father, or his own part in it," she said. "But convincing him that Geoffrey is . . . was . . . is—*Plague it!*—that Geoffrey *was-and-is* not a good man won't be easy."

"Hmm," Wolf said. "I think I might have an idea or two on that score."

He was, she noticed, dividing their problem into two: save her father and deal with his. That he believed her father's ensorcellment was solvable was beyond good. She could feel herself relax into belief in his ability. That he was ignoring his father was less good. She worried that it was less confidence in his own skills than it was indifference to danger to his life. It was time to let him know what she had done.

"Wolf," she said, "I—"

"I know," he said with a wicked smile glinting in his eyes. "We've done enough work for now." The smile left his eyes, and his hands traced her face.

"I've never had a family before," he said in wonder. "Not really. It feels so strange to belong to you and have you belong to me."

She looked up at him and opened her lips, but she couldn't do it. Couldn't tell him that she'd married him to force him to take care of himself, not when it obviously meant so much more to him than that. Come to think of it, it meant a lot more than that to her as well. It was just that . . . Wolf had belonged to her for a long time in a way that tied them far more than any goddess could.

She reached up and tugged at his mask, and he let it fall into her hands.

"Don't hide from me," she said.

Dropping the cold silver false face on the floor, she pulled his head down so she could kiss him fully.

WOLF HELD HER while she slept, and smiled. His wife was a manipulative minx; but then, he'd known that for a long time. The difference between her and his father was that she manipulated people for their own good—or at least what she perceived to be the greater good. He wondered when she'd break down and tell him.

How could she think that he wouldn't know what she'd done? As soon as the priestess placed the blood-bond between them, he'd realized what it was, had known what Aralorn had tried to do. He was not a well-trained mage in most areas, but black magic he knew well. A blood-bond was well within his area of expertise.

He sent a caress through the tie the death goddess had placed between them, and Aralorn sighed, shifting against him.

He could sever it when he needed to. He'd tell her that after she managed to confess her deed—he couldn't resist the urge to tease her a little and teach her a lesson about trying to manipulate him as she did the rest of the world.

"If you had known how to find me, you would have come to me when you were told your father had died," he said softly, and, remembering her face when he'd shown up at Lambshold, he knew it was true. How odd that someone loved *him*. That *Aralorn* loved him.

He pulled her closer and relished the light feeling that had come over him, softening the edge of the inner core of rage that was always with him. He was happy, he thought with some surprise.

If she thought so much of him, it might be worth the risk of the potential for disaster that clung to him through his magic. Maybe—he kissed the top of her head—maybe they could discover a way to control his magic rather than destroy it with his death.

ARALORN AWOKE EARLY and began planning what was best to do. She didn't know if Kisrah would take his nighttime visitor's information at face value or if he could tell that Wolf was Cain by some arcane human magic. Wolf said that he needed Kisrah's help. There was a chance that Kisrah would attack Wolf the first time he saw him. She couldn't risk it. She needed to talk to the Archmage first.

She liked Kisrah, but if he reacted badly, she would kill him before he got a chance at Wolf—if she could. She certainly would hate to do something like that in front of witnesses. So she needed a meeting without Wolf and outside of Lambshold.

Aralorn sat up and waited for Wolf to awaken. She wiggled a little. Nothing. She stared at him. Nothing. She reached her hands toward his side.

He rolled over and caught them. "If you tickle me this early in the morning, I'll see to it that you regret it."

She laughed. "How long have you been awake?"

"Long enough," he growled, completing his roll.

SOMETIME LATER, HE said, "Now, what was so important that you woke your husband up before the birds?"

He liked that word, she'd noticed, liked being her husband and the formalization of their bonds to each other. Given how hard he'd tried to keep a distance from her from the beginning of their association, she found it unexpectedly touching.

"Wasn't this enough?" she asked, trying for a sultry tone. It wasn't a role that she'd ever tried as a spy.

He bit one of her fingers gently. "Yes. So let us go back to sleep."

She bit him back, harder.

"Ouch," he said obligingly, but without any real emphasis, so she didn't feel that she had to apologize.

"That's what you get for trying to be funny. We need to go talk to Kisrah."

Wolf grunted, then said, "So, what have you plotted for the poor man?"

Aralorn decided to overlook his attitude. "We'll need to be careful—don't you snort at me; I can be cautious when I have to be. I think I will take him on a ride along the trail to Ridane's temple. Whoever visited him last night told him that you were Cain. I think that until I get a chance to talk to Kisrah, you need to stay out of sight."

"Ah," he said. "You meant *I* need to be cautious."

She grinned. "You're the one under the death sentence. Is Kisrah still under the influence of Geoffrey's charisma spell?"

"Probably," he replied. "If I were my father, I certainly would take no chances as far as Kisrah or any other high-ranking mage was concerned."

"Can you break it?"

She felt him shrug. "I don't know, but that was my thought as well. *If* my father is truly dead and can work no more magic, and if he chose to ensure that Kisrah never be a problem as I believe he would have—I might be able to."

"It would be easier to get his cooperation if he didn't attack me every time I said something nasty about his predecessor—and I don't know how else to proceed."

"I'll do what I can," he promised.

ARALORN FINALLY FOUND Kisrah in the bier room with her father. He'd arisen earlier than she'd expected, and she'd missed him at breakfast. A few questions to scattered servants had sent her to her father's bier.

He looked up at the sound the curtain made as she entered and watched her with a hooded glance from his seat on one of the tables meant for gifts and flowers. He looked a bit like a gaudy bouquet in a combination of mauve and emerald that offended even Aralorn's indifferent sense of style, but the bright array made the little room less somber.

"Lady Aralorn," he said, acknowledging her entrance after he'd returned her stare for several seconds.

She bent and kissed her father's slack face, taking a moment to reassure herself that he still lived, before turning back to the Archmage. "I visited the death goddess's temple yesterday," she said without preamble.

"I know," said Kisrah. "Correy told me."

She toyed with the front of the Lyon's shirt, straightening it carefully where it had been pulled askew. Finished, she turned to the Archmage. "I owe you my apologies, sir. I have been rude. I know that you have come to help my father, and I'm sorry to be so secretive. My only excuse is that the last few days have been nerve-racking at best, and I've been a spy for long enough that questions make me nervous."

"You sought me out to apologize?" asked the Archmage with a touch of wariness.

Although she noted that he hadn't accepted her apology, Aralorn smiled and shook her head. "Not primarily, though it needed to be done. There are things that we should speak of, but outside of the keep walls. Would you ride with me?"

Kisrah gazed at the stone floor. "Where is your wolf? I was under the impression that he went everywhere with you."

She pursed her lips thoughtfully and added a little bait. "That's one of the things I need to speak with you about."

The Archmage leaned back against the wall. When he spoke, it seemed off the topic of discussion. "I fought a campaign against the Darranians with your father once, did you know?"

"Yes," she answered.

"Battles are odd things," he said in musing tones. "Sometimes it seems as if you do nothing but hack and slash; at other times it seems as if you do nothing at all for weeks at a time. During the former, you learn a lot about your comrades by their actions; during the latter, you learn about them from their speech."

His gaze rested on the Lyon's quiet figure. "Your father is ferocious, tireless, and absolutely honorable. But more than that, he is cunning, always thinking—especially in the thick of battle, when everyone else is lost in bloodlust. He taught me a lot about how to judge men, to choose leaders and followers. He knew every man in our group and used them according to their strengths, and he tried to know as much about the men we fought as he did our own." He reached out and touched the Lyon's still face. "I learned to love him as much as I ever did my own father—as I expect every man to fight under him felt."

While he spoke, Aralorn half sat, half leaned against the bier. When he paused to make sure she was listening, she nodded.

"While we waited for battle, we talked, your father and I. He told me something of you. He told me you'd fought with him against brigands here at Lambshold and said he'd rather have had you beside him than any three men. He'd have brought you to fight by his side as he did Falhart if it hadn't been for his lady wife. He said you were clever, devious, and deadly—said you could outthink and outride any man he had with him, including himself."

"You have a reason for all this praise, I trust," said Aralorn.

Kisrah nodded, and a sudden grin lit his face. "Absolutely. First, let me say that I do not accept your apology, as I'm certain that you intended every frustrating minute of our last meeting—and enjoyed it as well. Devious and manipulative, your father said."

He sobered, and Aralorn thought it might be sadness that crossed his face. "But—despite what I have been told, having the father you do, you could not be without honor and decency. I hope that a productive talk might shed some light on a few things. I think that I, too, have some things to tell you that it were better to talk of outside these walls." He paused, and continued softly. "You might bring your wolf."

Aralorn nodded. "I'm sure Wolf will join us at some point in our journey. Father's got enough animals around here that you shouldn't have a problem finding a mount: I assume by the speed of your arrival that you chose to translocate yourself—"

She didn't know why she'd brought that up until she realized she was watching his face for guilt. There was none, of course; he hadn't realized what Geoffrey had done to her after Kisrah had used his magic to transport her into the ae'Magi's care.

Instead, Kisrah nodded, with a faint grimace of distaste. "Not my favorite spell, but it was important that I get here as soon as possible."

"You're a braver man than I am," murmured Aralorn. "I'll meet you in the stables. Ask Falhart if you need help finding warm clothing."

ARALORN HAD INTENDED to take him only a short distance before stopping to talk, but she hadn't counted on the wind. It kicked up when they were just out of sight of the keep.

The voices screamed through her ears: screams that brought visions of Geoffrey's dungeons and dying children, the cries of the Uriah—shambling, rotting things that had once been human but now only hungered. Sheen picked up on her agitation and began snorting and dancing in the snow, mouthing his bit uncertainly as he waited for an ambush to leap from the nearest bush.

Hoping that the wind would settle down, she kept going. At this rate, they'd be at the temple before she could talk. She tried to ignore the wind for as long as she could, but at last she tucked the reins under her knees and tugged a woolen scarf from around her neck and wrapped it tightly around her ears.

"Are you all right?" asked Kisrah.

"I seem to have developed a bit of a problem with the wind," she said truthfully: She tried to limit her lies when she could, especially when she was talking to wizards.

"Earache?" said Kisrah with some sympathy.

"I'm looking for someplace less windy," she told him. "I hadn't planned on riding all the way to the goddess's temple for a little private conversation."

He smiled. "I could do with a little exercise anyway. But if you can find a sheltered place I might be able to do something about the wind."

She frowned at him. "You human mages," she said. "Always so ready to impose your will where it doesn't belong. There's a small valley not too far from here; we'll be free from the wind without any magic at all."

He looked startled for a moment. "I've never been referred to in quite those terms. Do you not think of yourself as human, then?"

She smiled tightly, her tension owing more to the wind than any irritation with him. "No. But I won't use the terms my shapeshifter cousins use for mageborn who use unformed magic. They aren't flattering. Human will have to do."

As she'd thought it might, the steep sides of the valley—well, gully, really—provided some relief from the wind. Aralorn stopped Sheen and cautiously removed the scarf from her ears. The roar had died to a dull whisper she could safely ignore.

"Why don't you start, as you still owe me for your rudeness yesterday?" said Kisrah after he'd stopped and turned his horse so he faced her directly.

"All right," agreed Aralorn readily. "How much do you know about charismatic spells?"

"What?" he asked in some surprise, but he answered her question without waiting for her to repeat herself. "I've never heard of one that was not black magic."

"Yes," said Wolf from behind them, "they are. Of the blackest kind."

Aralorn turned to frown at Wolf. He was supposed to wait until she'd made certain that Kisrah wouldn't attack him on sight. She supposed that it said something about Kisrah's state of mind that he did not.

Wolf was in human form, clothed as always in black—an affectation Aralorn was determined to change. It wasn't that he didn't look good in it, just that it was a bit morbid at times. The silver mask was nowhere evident, and the magic-scarred face looked worse than usual in the bright winter sunlight.

"Cain," said Kisrah softly, as if he hadn't really believed what the specter had told him.

Wolf bowed shallowly without letting his eyes drop from the Archmage's. "Lord Kisrah."

"You are here to tell me the importance of . . . these charismatic spells, I assume?"

Wolf shook his head. "I wouldn't have mentioned them myself, but as Aralorn has seen fit to do so, I will explain—better yet, I'll cast one." He made an economical motion with his hand.

Aralorn sucked in a breath at his recklessness. She would have thought the battle with his father would have cured him of seeking battle with another powerful mage. Couldn't he have just told Kisrah how the spell worked?

Kisrah looked white and strained, but he gestured with equal rapidity— a counterspell, thought Aralorn—or rather a breaking spell of some sort, because it wasn't possible to directly counter an unknown spell.

"Here," said Wolf softly. "I'll give you more magic to work with."

Aralorn didn't see anything happen, but a moment later Kisrah swore and pulled a thick gold-and-ruby ring off his finger, tossing it into the snow. It must have been quite warm, as it fell quickly through to the ground, then melted a fair-sized hole around it that exposed the yellowed grass beneath.

For Aralorn's benefit, Wolf said, "He just broke the charisma spells— both of them."

Aralorn looked at the ring, seeing the magic imbued in it. "Both of them?"

"Mine and my father's."

Kisrah nodded, looking stunned as he stared at the ring. "Geoffrey gave me that ring. I can't believe I didn't see that it was runescribed. Why would he do that?"

"My father," observed Wolf, his hoarse voice sounding even dryer than usual, "was very good at making people overlook things when he chose."

"The ring was runescribed?" asked Aralorn. She put her hands on her hips and glared at Wolf. "So mages do use rings and amulets for spells."

"*Not* for warding spells," said Wolf repressively. "The runes are too complex to fit on an amulet—at least a warding that would keep out much more than errant mice."

"Ensorcelled," said the Archmage, ignoring their byplay. "A charm spell, indeed, but to what purpose?"

"What indeed?" said Wolf.

"The ae'Magi spread his charisma spell over a fair bit of territory before he met his untimely end," said Aralorn. "Why do you think everyone loved him so? Even people who'd barely heard of him."

Kisrah stared at her.

"Who would ever think that the reason there were so few children in the villages around the ae'Magi's castle was because the ae'Magi was killing them for the power he could get from untrained mages?" she said.

"He . . ." Kisrah's voice trailed off, then became firmer. "He wouldn't do that. He couldn't. A rune set in a ring—maybe. But I felt the power you had to use, Cain. No one could keep a spell like that running for long over more than a few people."

"No one worries about charisma spells," agreed Wolf. "They require too much power to be of use, and the control of the ae'Magi bars black magic anyway. Unless, of course, you are the ae'Magi and are perfectly willing to turn elsewhere for your power. There are a lot of spells that require too much power without death magic, sex magic, or, at the very least, blood, aren't there? Some spells that haven't been worked since the Wizard Wars."

Kisrah flinched.

"He gave you such a spell to work, didn't he?" asked Aralorn softly.

"He gave you the proof, himself, that he knew . . . that he knows black magic."

She wasn't going to tell Kisrah that they weren't sure that it was Geoffrey who had been visiting his dreams.

The Archmage looked up sharply.

"I've had a few dreams, too," she said. "Dreams of blood and magic."

"Yes." His voice crackled like the ice under the horses' hooves. "I set up part of the spell that holds the Lyon, plague take you both. I had to use black magic to do it."

"Why?" asked Wolf.

"Shortly after Geoffrey disappeared, before anyone knew what might have happened to him, I awoke one night, and there he was, standing beside my bed. I was overjoyed at first, thinking that he was found—but then he told me he was one of the dreamwalking dead. He told me that you and your"—he glanced at Aralorn and changed the word he was going to use—"that you and Aralorn had killed him."

"Did he tell you how it was done?" asked Aralorn. Had Kisrah been given true dreams or false?

"He said that you used one of the Smith's weapons to destroy his magic and left him in the castle, which was full of Uriah, without defense." Kisrah paused. "He asked me why I hadn't helped him." The wizard took in a deep breath, but his voice was unsteady when he continued. "I was there that night. I woke alone in the bedchamber with the body of the woman"—he glanced at Aralorn, his eyes hot with remembered fury—"the woman you killed with Cain's staff. It was nigh on a quarter of an hour later when I felt Geoffrey's grip on the Master Spells break. I could have saved him had I acted sooner."

The Archmage's voice was taut with sorrow and rage. He was lost in his habitual opinion of Geoffrey ae'Magi, forgetting for the moment that he'd had any doubts about Geoffrey's virtue.

"Better that you didn't," said Aralorn, hoping to jolt him out of the remnant of the spell's effect before he goaded himself into attacking them. It didn't work.

Kisrah's eyes flashed with anger. "He was my friend, and you killed him." He turned abruptly toward Wolf, his horse snorting at the sudden jerk on its bit. "I know you, Cain, I know what you have done. I've seen the color of the magic you wield, and it stinks of evil. Should I take your word about his character?"

"Yet you worked black magic for Geoffrey ae'Magi yourself, didn't you?" said Aralorn coldly, provoked by Kisrah's verbal strike at Wolf. "Just as Cain did. Was it a goat you killed or a hen? Do you think that you are the purer for not having touched human blood? You know, of course, that Cain has done that, and you suspect he's done more. You suspect that he's killed, raped, tortured, and maimed. But don't feel too superior—if we can't break this spell within the next two weeks, my father will die. He will die because of your decision to play with black magic, because Geoffrey's ghost taught you how to use death to gain power, more power than you might have had without resorting to black magic. When you wanted revenge, it was easy to overcome the scruples of a lifetime, wasn't it? And you are a grown man who was taught right from wrong by people who loved you; not—"

"Enough, Aralorn," Wolf broke in gently.

She bit back the words that might have wounded Wolf more than they hurt Kisrah. "Sorry," she said.

"No," said Kisrah, mistakenly believing her apology was to him. "You're right. About what I have done, and why." He looked at Wolf. "That doesn't mean that what *you* have done is right, only that I am guilty of similar actions."

Wolf shrugged when it became apparent that Kisrah was not going to speak further. "I have used no black magic since I left him; if you look, you will not find its touch on me. What I have done, I am responsible for—but for no more than that. As for accepting our word on the ae'Magi's intentions, don't be a fool." Wolf bent down and picked up the ruby ring. "My father gave this to you. You know the spell it contained as well as I do—you broke it yourself. Why would my father need such a thing unless he was as we say?"

"I would be a fool," said Kisrah softly, ignoring the ring Wolf held for him, "if, having found my judgment questionable once, I leap without thought a second time. Give me time to think over what we have talked about. I knew Geoffrey for most of my life. He was more than just a mentor to me." He flexed his hands on the reins. "The girl Aralorn killed the night you destroyed Geoffrey—her name was Amethyst, and she was not yet twenty years old."

"Do you remember"—Wolf's rasp was so low that Aralorn could barely hear it over the wind—"that thing you came upon in the dungeons?"

Kisrah shivered, but Aralorn thought it might have been from the cold; they had been standing for a while.

"Yes," said the Archmage. "I couldn't sleep. It was dark, and I heard someone moving around in the cells, so I called a magelight and looked inside."

He swallowed heavily at the memory of what he'd seen. "The next thing I remember is you standing in front of me and my face hurt where you slapped me. 'Screams only agitate it,' you said. 'It can't get out.'"

Kisrah's lips twitched in something that might have been a faint smile. "Then you said, 'It doesn't like to eat sorcerers anyway—especially those without half the sense of a cooped chicken.'"

Wolf said, "Two days before, that thing had been my father's whore. I believe she was fifteen. A peasant, of course, and so of little account except for her beauty. Father liked beautiful things. He also liked to experiment. He showed you some of them. I believe you referred to them as my father's 'unfortunate hobbies.'"

A myriad of expressions flittered across Kisrah's face. Anger, disbelief . . . then dawning horror.

"The night I met you in the ae'Magi's castle," said Aralorn quietly, "after you were unconscious, the girl you'd slept with sprouted fangs and claws. I suppose I could have just left rather than killing her: She was far more interested in eating you than me."

Kisrah didn't say anything.

Aralorn spread her hands to show they were empty, the universal sign of truce. "If you want to ride by yourself a bit—the horse knows the way back to the keep. We can leave you."

Kisrah hesitated, then nodded. "If you would, please. That might be best."

"WELL?" ASKED ARALORN.

Wolf, who'd shifted in front of Kisrah into his four-footed form for travel, shook his head. "I don't know. It depends upon which he loves best, my father or the truth."

He put on a brief burst of speed that precluded talk. Like Kisrah, she thought, he wanted a moment to himself.

The wind had picked up again as they'd ridden back onto less sheltered ground. It was not enough to send her shrieking for cover, but it was a near thing. It spoke to her in a hundred whispers that touched her ears with bits and scraps of information directly out of her imagination.

"Wolf?" she asked, when the sound grew too much.

"Ump?"

"Wizards have their specialties, right? Like the farseer who works for Ren."

"Ump."

A conversation takes two people, one of whom says something other than "Ump." She thought about letting him be. His past was a sensitive topic, and she and Kisrah, between them, had all but beaten him over the head with it. The wind carried the sobs of a young child, bringing with the sound a hopeless loneliness that chilled her to the bone in an echo of her dreams of Wolf's childhood. She tried again. She remembered a story about the gaze of the howlaa driving a man mad; too bad she hadn't recalled that before she looked into its eyes.

"What is Kisrah's specialty?"

"By the time a mage becomes a master, he has more than one area of expertise."

"You knew him before that," she persisted. "What was his field?"

"Moving things."

"Like translocation?" asked Aralorn.

"Yes." Wolf sighed heavily and slowed. "But he worked more with objects and delicate things—like picking locks or unbuckling saddle girths."

"No wonder Father likes him," she observed, relieved that he'd decided to talk. "Saddle girths and horseshoes have lost as many battles as courage and skill have won. What was Nevyn's specialty?"

"Nevyn?" said Wolf. "I don't know that I remember. By the time he got to Kisrah, he was in pretty rough shape—and the two of them didn't really spend a lot of time with my father, in any case. He is fortunate he went to Kisrah; if he'd come to my father, he'd have been a babbling idiot for the rest of his life—I thought at the time that it looked like it might go either way." His voice reflected the indifference he'd felt at the time, showing Aralorn how badly he'd closed down because she'd reminded him of what he'd once been.

"I hadn't realized it had been so bad for him." Aralorn pulled her scarf from the pocket she'd stashed it in and wrapped it around her ears. This conversation hadn't helped either of them as much as she'd hoped it would. It hadn't distracted her from the voices, nor had it restored Wolf's mood. "I guess he was lucky to come out of all that with only a few quirks about shapeshifters."

The wind swayed the larger branches now and sent odd bits of snow to swirl in place.

"Come on," said Wolf. "See if that old fleatrap can move out a little; no sense wasting what's left of the day playing in the snow."

TEN

ARALORN WAS SLIPPING CHOICE BITS OF MUTTON TO WOLF WHEN FAL-hart came up behind her.

"If Irrenna catches you feeding that wolf at the table, she's likely to banish him outside," he said.

She shook her head, holding down another piece. "As long as we're discreet, she'll leave him in peace. She doesn't want a hungry wolf roaming the castle. He'll just go into the kitchens to be fed—and there she'll be, without a spit boy. It might take the cook several days to replace whomever he ate, not to mention the fuss."

Falhart gave Wolf a wary glance, then began to laugh. "Scourge on you, Aralorn, if you didn't have me believing it. Which brings me to my mission. I have a half dozen youngsters and a few not so young who've been approaching me all dinner to see if you would give us another story."

"An audience," said Aralorn, scraping the last of her dinner onto a small bit of bread and popping it into her mouth. "See, Wolf, *some* people appreciate me."

He didn't seem to hear her, lost in thought as he'd been since they'd gotten back. If she could take back what she'd said to Kisrah, she would have—not that Kisrah didn't need to hear it. She would have bitten her tongue off, leaving Kisrah believing his version of Geoffrey ae'Magi the rest of his life, rather than hurt Wolf.

Despite his apparent disinterest, Wolf trailed her as she left to greet her audience and made himself comfortable at her feet.

Kisrah was not there, though she knew he'd returned from their ride.

She didn't see Gerem, either, but Freya and Nevyn were seated on a bench against the wall, just close enough to hear.

She chose her story primarily for Wolf, something light and happy that should appeal to the rest of her audience as well. As laughter warmed the room better than any winter fire, Wolf rested his head on her lap with a sigh.

WHEN ARALORN awoke the following morning, she found a red-tailed hawk perched on the back of a chair near the fireplace, preening its feathers. Wolf was gone.

"For a man who was worried about showing himself among humans, you certainly are volunteering your time generously," she said severely.

The hawk fluttered his feathers noisily into place. "He said you'd probably be grumpy when you woke up. I can't say I approve of your choice of mates, niece."

"Your own choice being superior," she said.

The hawk bobbed its head and squawked with laughter, and the chair rocked dangerously beneath him. "True, true," Halven chortled as he settled back down.

"Wolf told you we were married?" asked Aralorn.

"Yes, child," said the hawk. "And he asked me to tell you to amuse yourself. He's off to find the ae'Magi."

"Did he say which one?" Aralorn stretched. It had taken Wolf a long time to get to sleep last night even though she'd done her best to tire him.

"Which one?" Her uncle cocked his head at her. "There is only one ae'Magi."

Aralorn pursed her lips. "We're not certain that's true." She told Halven the things that Wolf had told her about his father and the dreams that she, Gerem, and Kisrah had experienced. After a brief hesitation, she told him of Wolf's relationship to Geoffrey ae'Magi and exactly how the last ae'Magi had died. She didn't easily give up information—except when that information might be vital. She had a feeling that they might need help before this was over, and her uncle would be a lot of help if he so chose.

Halven made an odd little sound that Aralorn couldn't decipher, but the incredulity in his voice when he spoke was clear enough. "So you think that a *human* mage who is dead is walking in the dreams of a shapeshifter and the newest human Archmage, and they are not able to stop it? The dead have very little power over the living unless the living grant that power to them. I can think of a half dozen more likely things— including the return of the Dreamer."

"I was able to take control of my dreams," said Aralorn. "And Kisrah loved Geoffrey and welcomed him. I don't think Gerem has any defenses against magical attacks." Someone—Nevyn—should have seen to it that Gerem had started training a long time ago.

She looked away from the hawk as she worked out some things she'd never put together before. "The dreams I was given were true dreams, Uncle. At first, whoever sent them to me had tried to alter them, but I was able to see through to the true memories. The dreams concerned things that only the ae'Magi and Wolf knew about."

"How do you know Wolf didn't send the dreams?"

"It was *not* Wolf," she said.

"Where was he when your father was enspelled?" Her uncle's voice was somber. "If his father was a dreamwalker, can you say for certain he is not? He wouldn't necessarily even know he was doing it. You've seen how his magic escapes him."

Aralorn snorted. "If you knew Wolf, you would understand just how stupid it is to accuse him."

She tried to think how to put into words something that was so clear to her that it was almost instinctive. "First, he would never involve other wizards in his spellcasting. He doesn't trust anyone except maybe me that much. He would never—*not ever*—voluntarily share as much of his past as I saw in that dream. I knew him for years before he would admit to being anything but a wolf."

"I think that it is a better possibility than a dead wizard," said Halven.

"Humans just don't interact with the natural world well enough to do anything after they are dead."

Aralorn digested that comment for a minute. "You mean shapeshifters do?"

The hawk gave its version of a laugh. "Not to worry. Most people who die don't linger to torment the living."

"The only other explanation that we've come up with is that the Dreamer has awakened," she told him.

Halven made a derisive sound.

"Do you have another explanation?" she asked.

"What about another dreamwalking wizard? A living dreamwalker might be able to do what you have described," he said.

"I'm told it's a rare talent," said Aralorn.

"Not rarer than a dead human mage who is making everyone tap to his tune," said Halven. "Have you figured out why someone decided to attack the Lyon?"

She shrugged. "As we discussed earlier, it is probably to get me here. There are any number of people after Wolf, and some of them know that where I go, Wolf is not far behind."

"To get Wolf here and do what?" asked Halven. "What do they want?"

She frowned at him. "To kill him."

"You don't know that," Halven said. "Maybe they only need you."

She laughed ruefully. "I don't die easily. And other than as bait for Wolf, I can't think of a reason any wizard would want me."

"If they kill you, they kill him," he reminded her.

"Only since day before yesterday," she said. "And how did you know about that?"

"After I objected to finding my niece in a man's bed, Wolf told me Ridane's priestess married you."

"You couldn't care less if I was sleeping with the sheep," she said tartly.

"He didn't know that. You didn't invite me to the wedding."

"I didn't know for certain that I was going to go through with it until we were there. I had to do something," she told him, trying to stem the defensive tone that wanted to ease into her words. She'd known that she was making him more vulnerable—she was certainly more easily killed than he. But her reasoning still stood. "You said he had a death wish, and I believe you."

"So you tricked him into the death goddess's binding?" asked her uncle. There was, she thought, a certain admiration in his tone. "That's the reason for your sudden marriage. He'll take more care of himself now."

"Uhm," she said. "I haven't told him about the side effect of being married by Ridane."

"He doesn't know?"

"He wasn't raised next to Ridane's temple," she answered. "She's not worshipped many places anymore. The gods have been quiet for a long time."

Two beady eyes stared at her unblinkingly. "What good is marrying him going to do if he doesn't know that his death will kill you also? You've undercut the very reason for the marriage."

She started to defend herself, but a slow smile caught her unexpectedly. "Not really."

The marriage itself, she thought, had accomplished what she had sought to enforce with the bond the priestess had set between them. From the awed tone in Wolf's voice when she'd asked him if he'd marry her to last night when, after they'd retired to this room, he'd brought his pain to her and allowed her to help him forget. She was still a little stiff from the methods they'd employed.

Her uncle waited for a moment, and when she didn't continue, he said, "Just make sure you don't die before you tell him."

She grinned. "I'll try to keep that from happening." She threw back the bedcovers, restless with prebattle nerves. She knew how to deal with those. "Rather than wait around for Wolf, I'm going to visit Falhart and persuade him to fight with me. You're welcome to come if you'd like."

SHE FOUND FALHART, finally, in the accounting room, slaving over the books. As she walked into the little room, she heard him swear, and he began to scratch out what he'd written.

"Why don't you find someone who likes those things?" asked Aralorn with a certain amount of fellow feeling. Give her a scroll of stories or a five-volume history, and she'd devour them, but account books were a whole different kettle of fish. Somewhere in the volumes stacked neatly against the walls was a large number of accounting sheets in her own poorly scribed hand.

Falhart looked up and scraped the hair from his eyes. "No one, but no one, likes to keep the accounts. Father, Correy, and I switch off, and this is my month." He eyed the hawk on her shoulder, nodded at it, then focused on the pair of staves she carried in one hand.

She grinned. "Want to play, big brother? Bet you a copper I can take you two times out of three."

"Make it a silver, and I'll do it," he said, pushing back his chair. "But I get to use my staff."

She shook her head at him. "Your staff is fine, but someone has given you an inflated idea of what they pay us mercenaries, Hart. I'll go three coppers and not a bit more."

"Three coppers isn't enough to make it worth my time," he said.

"I guess you'll just have to stay here and do the books then," replied Aralorn with a commiserating pat on his arm. "Come on, Halven, let's see who else we can find."

"All right, all right, three coppers it is," grumbled Falhart, then he brightened. "Maybe I can find someone else to lay a bet with."

Aralorn examined his bearlike form and shook her head as she started for the training grounds. "And who are you going to find who will bet on a woman against a brute like you?"

"You did," he pointed out.

"Yes, but I've fought you before."

They faced off in the old practice ground. It was cold, and the sand was packed hard, though the snow had been swept away. Once they started fighting, the cold wouldn't matter. Aralorn wielded one of her staves while Falhart held a quarterstaff half again as large and twice as thick as hers. Halven had opted for a better perch on the corner of the stable roof.

"You're sure you don't want to use a quarterstaff as well?" Falhart asked, watching her warily.

"Only a brute like you gains an advantage wielding a tree," she replied. "It's all right, though; you'll need all the advantages you can find, big brother."

Falhart laughed and tossed his staff lightly in the air. "You may have learned something in the past ten years, Featherweight. But so have I. What are the rules for this bout?"

"Three points," said Aralorn. "Any hit between the shoulders and waist is good. Arms, head, and below the waist doesn't count."

"Right," said Falhart, and he struck.

His swing had more speed than a man of his size had any right to have. Aralorn stepped respectfully out of its path and tapped him gently on the temple.

"Zap," she murmured as she darted away, "you're dead."

"No point," grunted Falhart, sweeping at her knees.

Rather than avoiding the sweep, Aralorn stepped lightly on the center of the quarterstaff between his hands and vaulted over his back. She touched her staff to his back twice in rapid succession before he had time to turn, and quickly bounced away.

"Two points," called one of the onlookers in a gleeful voice.

She didn't get away free though; as she jumped back, one end of his staff caught her in the diaphragm.

"Oof." Though the blow was light, Aralorn expelled a breath of air unexpectedly.

Falhart backed away quickly, clearly worried. "Are you all right?"

She shot him a mock-disgusted look. "I said 'oaf,' you ox. You're going to lose this round if you treat me like your little sister."

"Just like to make certain my prey is feeling all right before I destroy it." Falhart gave her a gentle smile as he circled her warily. "It's more sporting that way. My point."

Aralorn shook her head. "Poor babbling fool, I think I must have hit his head harder than I meant to."

The two combatants exchanged merry grins before they went at it again. Falhart gained another point with a feint that he pulled back after she thought he was committed to the blow past the point he could alter it. In revenge she stuck her staff between his legs and toppled him to the ground.

"'Ware, down it comes," she deadpanned in the carrying cry of an axeman felling a tree.

He caught her in the ribs as he came rolling to his feet. "Too busy being funny, Featherweight. Lost you the game."

She shook her head in mock despair. "Beaten by a man . . . I'll never live it down."

Falhart patted her gently. "Poor little girl—oof."

Aralorn removed her elbow from his midsection. "Don't patronize me after you've beaten me. Losing puts me in a foul temper."

"I'll remember that," said Lord Kisrah cordially, stepping onto the training grounds, Wolf at his heels. "Lady, if you would walk with me a bit? In private?"

She'd barely had a chance to warm up and had been planning on a few more rounds with Falhart before she was done. But she preferred the real battle to sparring bouts.

"Certainly, Lord Kisrah. I will leave the scene of my defeat, and my opponent can go back to accounts."

The triumphant look faded from Falhart's face. "Thanks for the reminder—but remember, you owe me three coppers." He waited until she started fumbling with her purse, then he said, "Double or nothing this time tomorrow?"

He was planning something; she could hear it in his voice. "Five coppers altogether. No more," she said.

"You've got it, Featherweight." He gave in much too easily. He was planning some mischief or other.

She frowned at him, and he grinned unrepentantly. "I'd better get back to the accounts," he said, and took his leave.

Kisrah extended his arm, and Aralorn set her staves against the stable wall before shaking her head at him. "You don't want to touch me right now," she said, pulling on her overtunic, sweater, and cape. "Save good manners for when I'm not sweaty."

He gave a half bow, sending the long ribbons in his hair a-fluttering as he let his arm fall gracefully to his side. "As you wish, Lady Aralorn."

"We could go to the gardens," she suggested, trailing her fingers over Wolf's ears.

Kisrah and Wolf fell in step on either side of her as she led the way to Irrenna's pride and joy.

In the summer, the gardens were beautiful, but the winter left nothing more than frost-covered barren branches and gray stalks pressing up through the snow. The walks were swept, though, so they didn't have to wade through the drifts.

"I know it's chilly," apologized Aralorn, "but no one much comes here in the winter."

He raised an eyebrow. "So why didn't we come here yesterday instead of riding out in the cold?"

"Because now you know who Wolf is," she said. "I was worried how you would react. A body is much easier to hide outside the keep walls."

He stopped walking. "I'd laugh if I didn't think you were serious."

"Maybe a bit," she said. "Come, let's move while we talk; it'll keep us warm." She was aware without actually looking at him that her uncle had followed them and was making lazy circles around them.

"Did you see Falhart's face?" asked Wolf. "He thinks you threw the fight."

"What do you think?" she asked blandly.

"I think you got cocky and lost."

"You know me so well," she admitted.

Kisrah gave Wolf a baffled frown. "Are you sure you're Cain?"

Wolf tilted his head considering, then said, "I am."

They walked for a while between sleeping flower beds. Aralorn turned her sweaty face into the cold air and paced beside the Archmage and felt grateful that there was no wind this morning.

"I have thought upon yesterday's conversation," Kisrah said finally.

"In the end, there is only one answer. Black magic is evil. Good never breeds from evil—and I can see no good in this in any case. But I cannot remove the spell. If you are able to do so, I'll help in any way I can. I know that Nevyn is one of the mages who added to the spell, but there is another."

"We know the other," said Aralorn. "My brother Gerem."

"Gerem?"

"Sometimes magic ability doesn't show until adolescence," commented Wolf, answering Kisrah's surprise.

"But Nevyn would have seen it," said Kisrah. "He would have told me."

Aralorn pursed her lips, and said, "Nevyn is very fond of my brother. Do you think that he would encourage anyone he cared for to go through the same abuse he suffered?"

"That's a very serious charge," observed Kisrah softly. "Untrained wizards are a danger to themselves and everyone around them."

"So are trained wizards," said Aralorn. Before the wizards she strolled with could comment, she continued blandly. "My brother cast a spell in his sleep. He didn't have a chance to resist. My understanding, from the stories I've heard, is that a formal apprenticing would have protected him from such use."

"Yes," agreed Kisrah. "There are not many mages who can control the minds of others in such a fashion, anyway—even with black magic at their call. But given that the consequences of such control are dire, precautions are always taken. Apprentices are safeguarded."

"You'll have problems with my brother," predicted Aralorn. "Nevyn is convinced that magic, any magic, is evil. I think he's managed to persuade my brother. Most especially, shapeshifters are abominations."

"Magic isn't evil," said Kisrah.

"All Darranians believe magic is evil," said Aralorn. "Geoffrey ae'Magi believed that and embraced it. Nevyn believes it, and he's trying his best to protect my brother. We need Gerem's cooperation to save my father. We need you to get Nevyn to ask him to help."

"I can get Nevyn to help," agreed Kisrah, a bit more optimistically than Aralorn felt was warranted, but maybe he knew Nevyn better than she. "Shall we meet tonight in the bier room?"

Wolf shook his head. "This kind of black magic doesn't require the night. You all will be more comfortable in the daylight."

"Black magic?" questioned Kisrah sharply. "It shouldn't be necessary to unwork the spell with black magic."

"This spell was set with blood and death by three wizards. It will require sacrifice to unwork," Wolf said.

"I thought that black magic couldn't be worked in the day," said Aralorn.

"It can be worked anytime," answered Kisrah.

"Sometimes it works better at night," corrected Wolf. In the shadows of the hedge, his pale golden eyes glittered with light reflected from the snow on the ground. The harsh macabre voice somehow made the barren garden something strange and frightening. "Terror can add power to a spell, and fear is easier to inspire in the night."

Aralorn noticed that Kisrah's even pace had faltered. Wolf only did things like this when he was in a particularly dark mood. She hoped that it was nothing more than talking about black magic that had brought it on and not something about unworking the spell to free the Lyon.

She hid her worry, and said dryly, "You sound like a ghoul, Wolf." Her words cut through the mood Wolf had established, and the garden was merely a collection of plants awaiting spring again. "Is there something you haven't told me about yourself?"

He flattened his ears in mock irritation, and said direly, "Much. But if the thought of my late sire's ghost has failed to touch your undeveloped sense of prudence, nothing I have done will accomplish that either."

Aralorn watched Kisrah's expression out of the corner of her eye and was satisfied when humor replaced the unease that had been in his face earlier. The gods knew that Wolf was not a soothing man to associate with, but there was no need to worry Kisrah at this point.

"Tomorrow morning, then?" said Kisrah. "At first dawn?"

Aralorn nodded. "Tomorrow."

"Kisrah," said Wolf. "What did you kill to work your spell?"

"A Uriah," he said uncomfortably. "I had intended to use my own blood—it should have been enough. I was working the spell in the basement workroom when a passageway door opened, and the Uriah came stumbling in. It must have escaped the Sianim mercenaries who took care of cleaning up the Uriah Geoffrey left scattered about. I killed it, and the spell slipped my control and used the creature's death instead of my blood."

"Ah," said Wolf. "Thank you."

Kisrah nodded and turned on his heel with every sign of a man escaping.

"Uriah," said the hawk after Kisrah was gone, settling on the top of a trellis that bore the thorny gray vines of a climbing rose. "Human sacrifice. Aralorn, I begin to believe what you told me this morning. Maybe I have been underestimating human mages." He stared coldly down at Wolf.

"How did you know what the Uriah are?" asked Aralorn.

"Human mages are very good at warping things unnaturally," said Halven. "Any shapeshifter looking at a Uriah can see the true nature that human magic has perverted. Only a human mage could be so blind as to not understand his own work. Why didn't you tell him that he'd made your task more difficult?"

"I would rather the secret of their making die with my father," Wolf said. "I do not expect that Kisrah would be anything but repelled—but he might tell others or write it down for someone to discover."

"Ah," said Halven. "Sometimes it is a good thing that human mages are so blind, and some knowledge is best lost. But Kisrah's ignorance has caused you trouble." Halven sighed. "I had better help you control your magic, Nephew. So much of your magics require balance—of which Kisrah has some, you have little, Gerem has none, and Nevyn has less than that."

"He's in worse shape than I am?" asked Wolf, sounding surprised, but Aralorn thought it was more because Halven named him nephew than her uncle's assessment of Nevyn.

Halven laughed. "Nevyn has been broken and badly mended. Your spirit is strong as an oak, wolf-wizard. It may be a bit battered, but as long as you don't misdirect it, you'll be fine." He cocked his head at Aralorn. "There is something different since your marriage. You may be right."

"She's right about what?" asked Wolf.

"You keep out of this, Uncle," snapped Aralorn. "Wolf, can we talk of this later?"

She could have sworn that there was laughter in Wolf's eyes, but it was gone almost before she saw it. She couldn't think of anything they'd said that he would find funny.

"If you'd like," Wolf said.

"I can't do anything about the nature of the sacrifice," said Halven. "I can't do anything about Nevyn. But I think I can help you with your magic problem. Aralorn, haven't you taught him to center?"

"*I* can't center," she said, exasperated. "Just how do you expect me to teach someone else? Besides, centering is more of an exercise in . . ." Her voice trailed off as she realized what she was going to say.

"Control." Her uncle's voice was smug. "We need someplace warm and private."

"We can work in my room," suggested Aralorn. "That would allow us some privacy and warmth as well."

"I'll meet you there," said the hawk, taking flight.

"Wolf," said Aralorn, once they were alone.

"Yes?"

"You haven't worked black magic since you left your father's home, have you?"

"No."

Aralorn tilted her face into the sun, though she felt no warmth on her skin. "I don't know a lot about human magic, but I do know that good seldom comes from evil. I don't want you to hurt yourself to save my father."

"Aralorn," said Wolf, "you worry too much. I have worked such magic before."

"And chose not to do it again, until now." She turned a rock over with the toe of her boot and kicked it into the snow.

"This is not your doing, Lady. It is my father's work."

"Would you work black magic if it were not my father?" she asked.

"Would he be ensorcelled if he weren't your father?" he returned. "We'd best not keep your uncle waiting. I'll be all right, Aralorn."

Wolf is the only expert I have, thought Aralorn. *If he says there will be no harm in it for him . . .* He'd never tell her if there was.

Frowning unhappily, she started back for the castle, with Wolf padding by her side.

ARALORN LAY ON the bare floor of her room and reconsidered calling her room warm—without the rugs to cover it, the floor was icy. Halven was taking Wolf through some basic meditation exercises, things she'd learned the first summer she'd spent with him.

In honor of the lesson, her uncle had taken on the shape of a venerable old man, with a rounded face and belly—someone to inspire confidence, she supposed.

Wolf, to Aralorn's surprise, had left the mask off. Halven had already seen the scars, of course—but Wolf used the mask as much for a shield as he did to cover his scars.

"Now, stop that," her uncle admonished Wolf, in tones Aralorn would bet tomorrow's winnings against Falhart that no one had used on Wolf in a very long time, if ever. "I don't want you to do anything to the wood—just feel it. See the growth patterns, the years where water was hard to come by and the years where it was abundant. Feel the difference between the old oak of the original floor and the plank of maple that someone used to replace an old board—yes, that's the one. Let yourself feel how much easier magic slides through the oak than it does through the maple. Aralorn, an exercise does no good unless you do it."

"Yes, sir." She grinned, obediently losing herself in the pitted surface of the wooden floorboards.

There was almost a sensuous pleasure in working with the wood. Oak had a sparkle to it that always made her feel as if she ought to glow with joy while she worked with it. Not that she could do much more with it than look. A few shapes, some basic spells, and a little inventive lock picking—that was about as far as her command of magic went. That didn't mean that she couldn't enjoy it for its own sake.

"Now that you know the wood beneath you, children, I want you to concentrate on yourselves. Feel the texture of the floor against your skin, the fabric that separates you from the support of the wood. Ideally, of course, there would be no fabric, but I understand that you humans are sensitive about exposing your bodies. As I discovered in training Aralorn, the distraction of the clothing is less by far than the distraction of not wearing any at all."

"Not to mention it's warmer this way," murmured Aralorn, her eyes still closed.

"Enough, child. I am the teacher here. You will merely listen and absorb my wisdom."

"Of course. I shiver at your feet in humble awe at the—"

"Kessenih"—he interrupted—"would be happy to take over the training of you; I believe that she offered to do it the last summer you came to us."

Kessenih, as Aralorn recalled, had wanted to peel the skin from her feet and make her walk back to Lambshold—who'd have thought she'd have gotten so upset over a chicken egg in her shoe?

"Yes, sir. Sorry, sir."

Halven had changed, she thought. He'd always been cold to her, though he'd sponsored her training. After a moment she decided it could be that she, herself, had changed. As a child, she'd always been too much in awe of Halven to tease him. She'd never been able to relax around him, but now . . . everything crystallized, like a wooden puzzle that suddenly slid into shape.

It felt odd seeing herself in the way she had always been able to look into wood, to feel her heart beat and *know* why it did. Like an outsider, she could see into the fears and petty angers, touch the bond that tied her to her mate.

"I've *got* it . . ." It startled her so much that she sat up and lost it again, but she laughed anyway.

"So you did," said Halven, sounding pleasantly surprised. "See if you can explain it to Wolf. Sometimes two talk better than one."

"What did you find?" asked Wolf.

"My center," she said, sounding as shocked, as elated as she felt. "I've always been able to sense it well enough that I can use magic, but it was never clear. Like being in a boat and knowing that there's water under me, but not being in the lake myself."

"So this time you fell in?" Wolf sounded amused.

Aralorn grinned at him. "And the water was superb, thank you."

"You," said Halven to Wolf, "have no sense of center at all, that I can see. Without centering, it is impossible to be grounded—to be aware of yourself and your surroundings at a level where it is safe to work green magic. If we can get you there, then having your magic run amok should no longer be a problem."

He ran a hand down his beard. "For human magic, this is not necessary—you control the magic with your thinking self. Like working a logic problem, with just a touch of artistry to give it form. Green magic is just the opposite. Your . . . emotions, your *needs*, generate the magic with just a touch of conscious control. Aralorn has been working half-blind for most of her life, and *you* are wiggling puppet strings without knowing which string is connected to which puppet." He looked pleased with his analogy, savoring it for a moment before turning back to Aralorn. "You found it once—do it again."

It took her a while before she could do it reliably, but once she had it, Halven went back to work on Wolf.

IF IT HAD been difficult for Aralorn to relax into her center, it was night-marish for Wolf. Control had been his bulwark for most of his life, a defense against the things he had done and what was done to him. Unless he could give it up, he would never be able to control his magic: a paradox he understood in his head, but not in his heart, where it mattered.

It made for a long afternoon. By the end of it, he was sweating, Halven was sweating, and Aralorn was exhausted, but Wolf came out of it with a better sense of self, if not precisely his center. An achievement that left Halven nodding grudgingly.

"At least," he said, helping Wolf to his feet, "you know that there are strings on your fingers now. If you don't know what they do, you can elect not to tug on them." He sounded almost as tired as he looked.

"Thank you," said Wolf.

Halven smiled slyly. "Couldn't do less for my sister's daughter's mate, now could I?" He slid from old man to bird shape. "I expect you to keep her in line."

"How?" asked Wolf, amused.

Halven let out a bark of laughter. "Don't know. I've never seen it done. Open the shutters now, and I leave you children to your rest."

"Well," Aralorn said after Halven had left, "I don't know about you, but I'm hungry."

Wolf gave her what might have been a wolfish smile without his scars, looking more relaxed than she'd ever seen him. "I could eat a sheep."

"You think so?" she said thoughtfully, pulling on her boots. "I'm not so sure; the local shepherds are awfully quick with their arrows."

He laughed, changing gracefully into wolf shape.

Most of the family was already eating when they made it to the great hall. Aralorn slipped into her old place between Falhart and Correy. Nevyn, sitting directly across from her, pointedly didn't look up when she sat down. Freya shrugged apologetically once and otherwise ignored her husband's distress.

". . . when I came out of the village smithy, there was my meek and ladylike wife screaming at the top of her lungs." Falhart stopped to eat a bite of food, giving Aralorn a quick view of his wife on his other side with her head bowed and a flush creeping up her cheekbones.

"I thought something was wrong and was charging to the rescue when I realized what she was saying." He cleared his throat and raised his bass rumble to a squeaky soprano. "Three geese, I tell you! I need three. I don't want four or two—I need three. I don't care if they are mated pairs. I am going to eat them, not breed them!" Falhart laughed.

Aralorn was too tired to join in the usual family chatter and picked at her food. The familiar scents and voices, some deeper now than they had been, were soothing.

She let her eyes trail across her siblings with the magic she'd been working all day. She'd occasionally been able to use her magic to look deeply into a person, but never for more than a moment or two.

It was an odd experience, her senses interpreting what her magic told her sometimes as color—Falhart radiated a rich brown that warmed those around him. Irrenna was musical chimes, clear and beautiful. Even though he sat at the far end of the table, Aralorn could feel Gerem's magic flickering eagerly, vibrating on her skin like the wings of a moth. One of the little children, a toddler, had it, too. She'd have to remember to tell her father . . . She turned abruptly and caught Nevyn staring at her.

Wide-eyed, she saw what Halven had meant when he'd said that Nevyn was broken and poorly mended. She had no experience to interpret what she saw, but it was like looking at a tree split by lightning. As the thought occurred to her, that's what she saw, as if an illusionist had superimposed the image over Nevyn's human form. One side of the tree struggled to recover, but the branches were gnarled, and the leaves were edged with an unhealthy gray. The other side was black and burnt.

Nevyn pulled his eyes away, but that didn't release Aralorn from the vision. Sharp teeth closed on her hand, and she dropped her eyes to see Wolf beneath the table, glowing like lightning. Dazed, she blinked her eyes rapidly, only to see the bright wolf imposed on her eyelids.

Wolf growled, and Aralorn took in a deep breath and set her magic aside.

"You are quiet tonight," said Correy in her ear. "Have you found out anything more about Father?"

His tone was conversational, so he hadn't noticed her doing anything unusual.

"Enough to be hopeful," she said, striving for a normal tone.

"Do you know who might have done it?" asked Freya.

Warily, Aralorn looked at her, but she saw only the face that Freya had always shown her.

Aralorn shrugged and, because she was thinking about what had just happened rather than paying attention to the conversation, she said more than she should have. "I think so, but he is dead now—so knowing who he is doesn't do us much good."

"Who?" asked Irrenna from the head of the table, her voice sharp.

Aralorn put down her knife and fork. "No one it would be healthy to accuse at this point. When I'm more certain of my facts, I'll tell you. I promise."

Irrenna looked at her narrowly for a moment, then nodded. "I'll hold you to your promise."

ELEVEN

———∿∿———

THE CASTLE WAS QUIET IN THE EARLY-MORNING HOUR THEY'D CHOSEN for their meeting. She and Wolf got to the bier room before dawn, more because she was too nervous to sleep longer than anything else. The guards had gotten used to her coming and going at odd hours, though this morning's portal defender had given an odd look to the hen she'd stolen from the kitchen coop.

Wolf told her that he might need it if he decided to break the spell right then. Wolf hadn't had to catch the blasted thing, of course.

She paced restlessly in the little room, taking a twisted path around the bier and the woven chicken basket, stopping now and again to touch her father.

Wolf lay with his nose tucked between his forepaws, watching her pace. "They'll be here soon enough. Stop that."

"Sorry"—she sat on her heels next to him and leaned against the wall—"I'm just anxious."

"More anxious than the hen," he commented shortly, "and with less reason, too."

As if to emphasize his point, the hen clucked contentedly in its nest of hay. Aralorn stuck a sore finger in her mouth—the chicken had been upset when she grabbed it. "Nasty critter, anyhow."

"Who's a nasty critter?" asked Gerem suspiciously, pulling the curtain aside so he could enter.

"The hen," said Aralorn, pointing at the villain with her chin.

Gerem peered at the battered crate. "What'd you bring a hen here for? Mother's going to pitch a fit!"

"To free your father," replied Wolf.

Gerem came as close to jumping out of his skin as anyone Aralorn had ever seen. Three shades whiter than he'd been when he came in, he stared at Wolf.

"I see Kisrah informed him completely," murmured Wolf sarcastically, wagging his tail gently as he returned the stare. "How much do you want to bet we get to inform him what method we're using as well."

"We needed him here," warned Aralorn. "I don't think that we can complain how it was done." She stood up and turned to her brother. "Gerem, I'd like to introduce you to my—to my Wolf. At one point in time, he went by the name of Cain—son of Geoffrey ae'Magi. I'd suggest you be polite to him; at present, he appears to be the best chance we have of resurrecting Father."

"The old ae'Magi's son is a shapechanger?"

Aralorn blinked at him. One of the things her brother didn't know, apparently, was Cain ae'Magison's reputation. She supposed that made a certain amount of sense. Gerem had been a young boy when Cain dropped out of public view.

"Sometimes," agreed Aralorn. "I find it a good thing that he takes after his mother's side of the family."

"Dead?" asked Wolf. "Of course, Father's dead as well."

She rolled her eyes at him. "Do you *have* to go out of your way to intimidate everyone? Wouldn't it be nice if we could all work together this morning?"

"Ah," said Kisrah, entering the room rather languidly.

He had to duck around the curtain to make certain it didn't bend the pale pink feather that was set jauntily into his elaborate hairstyle. Wearing a three-foot-long feather was not something *Aralorn* would have done in his place; but then, she wouldn't have worn pink with scarlet and emerald either. The brass bells on the heels of his shoes were nice, though—if impractical.

"I thought I would be the first one here. I see you brought the chicken. Marvelous. I thought I might have to do it."

"We ought to make you do it," said Wolf thoughtfully, "if only to see what the chickens would do when they heard those bells."

"Unkind," admonished Kisrah. "To intimate that I would risk scuffing these boots chasing chickens—what do you think I studied magic for, dear man?"

"They are joking," said Aralorn, watching Gerem's face. There were some benefits to Kisrah's three-foot-long feather—it was hard to be frightened in the presence of such a creation.

Unexpectedly, Gerem grinned. "I'd place bets on Lord Kisrah. Nevyn told me about the time you chased a pickpocket into the heart of the infamous slums of Hathendoe and came back unscathed. A chicken should be child's play."

"Stole my best gloves," agreed Kisrah solemnly. "Purple with green spots, just the color and shape of spring peas."

Gerem laughed but stopped when he saw Kisrah's mournful face.

"Don't worry about hurting his feelings," rumbled Wolf. "He knows what the rest of the world thinks about his clothes."

Reassurance was not exactly Wolf's strong point, so Aralorn was pleasantly surprised that he'd gone out of his way to smooth the waters.

The Archmage grinned, looking Gerem's age despite his wrinkles. "Faugh, Cain, you ruined it. He would have begged my pardon in another moment."

"I like the bells," commented Aralorn, leaning a shoulder against the wall. "Perhaps I'll get myself a pair."

Kisrah looked superior. "Spies don't wear bells."

She snorted. "Fat lot you know about spies. I was in your household for three months, and you never even knew my name."

He frowned, staring at her intently. "The maidservant . . . Lura—"

"Not even close." She shook her head mournfully.

"She's a shapeshifter," said Gerem. "She wouldn't look like herself."

"Even if you did manage to guess what part she played, she'd never admit it," added Wolf, coming to his feet.

He took on human form, leaving off the mask and the scars—for Gerem's sake, Aralorn thought. She glanced at her brother, who was looking nervous again. Yes, she was definitely going to have to do something about the black clothing. It was hard to look intimidating in . . . say, yellow. She grinned at the thought of Wolf dressed in yellow, with a bow to hold his hair back in its queue.

Kisrah drew in his breath at seeing Geoffrey's face on Wolf.

"You need to wear a different color," she said out loud, to distract both Wolf and Kisrah from something neither cared to think about. "Black is so . . . so—"

"Conservative," chided Kisrah, recovering from his initial shock.

Gerem looked from Kisrah in pink, red, and green to Aralorn in her muddy-colored tunic and trousers, then advised dryly, "Keep the black."

Wolf, bless his soul, smiled—a small smile that bore little resemblance to the charm of his father's. "I intend to."

The curtain rattled again, and Nevyn shut it carefully behind him. He surveyed the room, his eyes stopping on Wolf.

"Cain," he said, in a tone that was more of an acknowledgment than a greeting.

At his entrance, Wolf had gone still, almost, thought Aralorn, apprehensive.

"Nevyn."

"It's been a long time. I—I—I had forgotten how much you look like him." The stutter irritated Nevyn, and he stiffened further.

Rather than make things worse, as was his general reaction to people who feared him, Wolf merely nodded. "Shall we begin?"

"Yes," agreed Kisrah. "We're all here now." He looked around, and for lack of a better place, he pulled himself up on the bier to sit beside the Lyon. "What do you need from us?"

"I need to know what you have wrought," said Wolf. "So I can unmake it."

"Then I'll tell my part first." The ae'Magi wiggled his feet, and the bells chimed softly in response.

"Tell us all of it," suggested Aralorn. "Not just the spell—not everyone here knows what has been going on. I suspect that Gerem, for one, has no idea what happened to him, and we still only have guesses about who is responsible for this mess."

"The whole story?" asked Kisrah. "There are parts that should remain secret."

"Everyone here knows how my father died, or should," said Wolf. "We might as well tell our version, too—after you are through with your story, Kisrah."

"Very well, then," agreed the ae'Magi. "I'm no storyteller, but I'll tell you as much as I remember. Shortly after Geoffrey—the ae'Magi—died . . . I had a dream."

Aralorn saw Gerem stiffen, like a good hound on a scent: Gerem had dreamed, too.

Kisrah continued. "Geoffrey came to me as I slept and sat upon the end of my bed—just as he used to.

"'My friend,' he said. 'I have nowhere else to turn. I need your magic to come to my touch.'

"This surprised me greatly, for he was the greatest mage I ever saw.

"'A spell?' I asked. 'Can't you work it yourself?'

"He shook his head chidingly, and said, with that grin he used when I was being particularly obstinate, 'Dead men cannot use magic, child.'

"I woke up, sweating like a frightened horse, but there was nothing in my room that hadn't been there when I went to sleep. I thought at first that it had simply been a dream. But I'd forgotten what Geoffrey was."

"A dreamwalker," said Nevyn softly.

Kisrah nodded. "Exactly." He looked at Gerem. "Do you know what dreamwalking is?"

"Yes," replied Gerem. "Nevyn does it."

Nevyn is a dreamwalker? thought Aralorn.

"Right," agreed Kisrah. "There are a number of mages who can dreamwalk at the most basic level—fardreaming, it's called. While fardreaming, a mage can send his spirit outside his body, usually no farther than a mile or two. Dreamwalking, though, is much more powerful and unusual. Nevyn and Geoffrey are the only living mages I've heard of who can send their spirits anywhere they want to. Generally speaking, a dreamwalker cannot affect the physical world—like moving chairs or tables. I say 'generally' because one or two of the better dreamwalkers were said to have tossed a chair or two."

"Or a knife," added Wolf dryly.

Kisrah nodded. "I stand corrected. A dreamwalker also cannot work magic in his spirit form. What he *can* do is look and listen without people suspecting they are being watched. And, though he can't talk in a normal manner, he can communicate in a fashion called dreamspeaking."

"Like a mindspeaker?" asked Gerem.

Kisrah nodded, "Only better. It takes one mindspeaker to hear another. A dreamspeaker can make himself heard by anyone he wants."

Aralorn thought about the conversation she'd overheard and wondered if the dreamwalker who'd been Geoffrey had known that she was there listening.

"Anyone?" asked Gerem. "I thought that when a wizard becomes an apprentice, his dreams are protected by the Master Spells."

"That's right," said Kisrah, though his mouth tightened just a little. "Smart lad. Yes, the Master Spells protect young wizards to a certain extent. There are other ways to ward yourself, too. It is possible for a dreamwalker to manipulate an unprotected person through dreams. Unethical, but there you are. But dreamspeaking isn't any more manipulative than normal speech."

Yes, thought Aralorn, watching Gerem as relief touched his face. *No need to feel so guilty. You were not protected from the dreamwalker's manipulations.* Kisrah and Nevyn had known what they were doing.

Aloud, she asked, "Is magic necessary for dreamwalking, or are there dreamwalkers who are not mages?"

"Dreamwalking is a magic talent, like transporting things or illusions. Geoffrey said"—Kisrah hesitated—"if a dreamwalker's body is killed while he is walking, his spirit can remain behind. Like a ghost, but with the full consciousness of the living person. He told me that the second time he came. And then he told me how he died." Kisrah looked at Wolf, who looked back without any expression at all.

"He told me that you came back because you'd heard that he was looking for you, and you were tired of it. He said that you argued about your use of black magic. He finally tried to use the Master Spells to limit your ability to work magic." Without dropping his gaze from Wolf's, Kisrah said, "That's one of the ways that an ae'Magi can control rogue wizards, Gerem—as a last resort."

He seemed to be waiting for a response from Wolf, but after a fruitless pause, Kisrah continued. "In any case, he said he underestimated your power and the strength that black magic had given you; the spell was reversed. There came a point when you could have stopped it. He said you held the power for long enough to say something ironic—I've forgotten exactly what—and then you killed him."

He believes it, thought Aralorn, *at least at this moment.*

"As a point of fact," said Aralorn mildly, "it didn't happen like that. I was there. Wolf did not kill Geoffrey; nor did I." She started to tell them more about the last ae'Magi but caught the subtle shake of Wolf's head in the corner of her eye. He was right. She had to be careful not to trigger whatever was left of the charisma spells. "He was killed by the Uriah."

Kisrah stared at her, but she didn't drop her gaze.

"Only the ae'Magi, Wolf, and I were there the night he died," she continued mildly. "If your visitor was Geoffrey, then he put my father in danger—without Wolf's cooperation, you three would not be able to remove the ensorcellment from my father. You have the word of a goddess that if it is not removed soon, the Lyon will die. Your dreamwalker asked you to work black magic upon an innocent man—is this something a good man would do? If it was not Geoffrey, then he doesn't know what happened any more than you do."

Kisrah rubbed his eyes. "At any rate, Geoffrey's story is the one I believed when he asked me to work some magic for him. It was supposed to be for you, Cain. It would not kill you, just hold you for the wizard's council's justice. I agreed. He told me that he needed me to find a secret room in his bedroom. So I found the room and the sword he'd hidden there. With his directions fresh in my mind, I inscribed on the sword the rune he told me. Runes are not my strong point, and the one he used was unfamiliar and complex. It required all of my concentration to get it right. Just as I finished the last line, something grabbed my shoulder."

He took a deep breath. "There was a Uriah standing just behind me, reflex took over, and I beheaded it with the sword—only then did magic pour into the rune I'd just finished." Kisrah closed his eyes. "I didn't know it needed blood magic. I don't think I did. At the time, I told myself it was an accident that turned the spell black. I wanted to destroy the sword, offered to spell something else for him—anything else."

The Archmage sighed. "He said that the sword was the only sure bait, that perhaps the black magic would work in our favor. Even the Master Spells had failed to hold Cain; maybe it would take black magic to counter black magic. Geoffrey was always good at getting his own way by fair means or foul." He paused, as if surprised by what he'd said. "By the time I realized that he'd intended to use black magic all along, I was already resigned to it. Maybe I'd have done it for him anyway."

"Did Geoffrey tell you to send the sword here, or did you suggest it?" asked Aralorn. When the Archmage had died, he knew that she and Wolf were together—but she was certain that he hadn't made the connection between her and Lambshold. She took great care that most people didn't know.

"Geoffrey," he said. "The night after I brought the sword back with me, he told me he wanted me to send it to Nevyn. He told me that Nevyn's sister by marriage was Cain's lover. I sent the sword. Only afterward did I begin to question what I had done."

The hen clucked in its crate, reminding everyone in the room (except perhaps for Gerem and Nevyn, who Aralorn was not certain knew what they'd been planning) that black magic was needed to release the Lyon. Aralorn looked at the bird thoughtfully for a moment.

"Perhaps a more noble motive might have allowed me to shut my eyes longer to what I had done." Kisrah smiled grimly at Wolf. "I didn't work the spell to capture Cain and save the world from dark magic—I worked it for revenge. I hated you for taking my friend from me. I knew that the end result of Geoffrey's plan was your death."

"I would have expected no less," agreed Wolf softly. "I know what he was to you. What was the rune he had you draw?"

From an inner pocket, Kisrah produced a sheet of paper with two neat drawings he gave to Wolf. Since drawing the rune itself would activate it, rune patterns were split into two drawings that, when laid one over the other, formed the rune. Aralorn had never been able to put the patterns together in her head without getting a headache, but Wolf nodded, as if it made sense to him.

"What did he have you add to it?" he asked Nevyn.

Nevyn had taken a seat on the floor where he could lean against the wall, as far from where Wolf stood as he could get. He had listened to Kisrah's story with his eyes closed; dark shadows and lines of weariness touched his face. At Wolf's question, he dug into the pouch attached to his belt and mutely handed him two sheets of paper.

Wolf took them and held them up separately, frowning. "Where did you place it? On the blade as well?"

Nevyn nodded. "Farther down on the blade, near the point."

"Another binding spell of some sort," said Kisrah after a moment of staring over Wolf's shoulder. "Had you seen it before, Nevyn?"

He shook his head. "No."

"Cain?"

Wolf shook his head as well, but slowly. "Not exactly, no."

"Did he ask you to kill anything?" asked Kisrah.

"No," said Nevyn. "But what I did was worse." He turned slightly to address everyone. "I knew that the spell was intended for the Lyon and that he was to be the bait that drew Aralorn and . . . Cain here." His voice grew quieter. "I—I—I suggested it to him. Aralorn hadn't come here for ten years. When he asked me what would make her return, I told her that I thought the only thing that would work was if someone died—if Henrick died."

He looked at Wolf, and his voice became guttural. "So he put a spell on the Lyon that only you could break. Black magic, he said, so that Kisrah would not know how to unwork the spell. I told him that you might not come, might not expose yourself for someone you didn't know. So he decided to see if we could trap Aralorn in it as well. I called the baneshade here and set it to extend the spell to Aralorn."

"Do you know what he intended to do to Wolf—sorry, Cain—once he was here?" asked Aralorn, interested in what Geoffrey had told Nevyn. "After all, here he is . . . and no one has moved against him."

Nevyn shrugged. "Kisrah was to come upon Cain working black magic, and then he'd have to face justice at the ae'Magi's hands."

Kisrah's bells rang as he started in surprise. "My dear Nevyn, I don't think I have the power to constrain or kill Cain—you haven't seen what he can do."

"After unworking the spell on the Lyon, he would be in no shape to resist you." He sat forward suddenly, a bitter twist to his mouth. "You can rot, Cain, for all I care. But Henrick has been more of a father to me than my own ever thought of being, and *I* helped to trap him. Any magic that binds a person as tightly as he is bound will be tricky to unwork at best. It has become increasingly obvious that Geoffrey doesn't care if Henrick lives or dies—but *I* do. If I can help you, I will—if you die in the process, so much the better."

"All right," said Wolf, and Aralorn eyed him sharply.

"What did you do with the sword after you worked the spell?" asked Kisrah.

Nevyn drew in a breath. "I gave it to Henrick the day he was enspelled; I met him at the stables as he was leaving to inspect the burnt-out croft. I told him a messenger brought it from Aralorn." He lowered his eyes. "Henrick gave me his old campaign sword, told me to put it in the armory, and carried the one I'd given him."

With a casualness that spoke of more practice than Aralorn had suspected, he gestured with both hands, and a sword appeared on the floor in front of them. "This sword. You see why we knew that he would carry this one."

It wasn't a ceremonial sword, nor was it ornate. But even Aralorn, who was admittedly not the best of sword judges, could see the care that had gone into its making. The pommel was wood, soft finished—nothing spectacular, but high quality nonetheless. It was the blade that attested to the care that had gone into the sword's making. Countless folds of a repeating pattern marked the blade: a masterwork of a talented swordsmith.

Wolf knelt and ran a hand over it without touching. "There's no magic to it now other than the power of a sharp blade." He smiled. "It belonged to my father's predecessor. I suspect that means it is yours now, Kisrah."

"No," said the Archmage, sounding revolted. "If there's no more harm in it, then it should be the Lyon's, assuming you can fix this. He's paid enough for it."

Once he'd called the blade, Nevyn had ignored it completely. Rising to his feet, he walked around Wolf to the bier.

"He'll hate me when he knows what I have done." Nevyn stared at the Lyon's body.

"No," said Aralorn gently. "He never expected any of his children to be perfect. Tell him what you have told us; he'll understand. He liked Geoffrey, too."

Nevyn shook his head.

"My turn," said Gerem, flushing when his voice cracked.

"Your turn," agreed Aralorn.

"I've been having strange dreams for a long time. Nightmares mostly." He swallowed heavily. "I don't really know where to start."

They waited patiently, giving him a chance to get his thoughts in order.

Finally, he looked at Aralorn. "I don't know what life here was like when you were a child, but to me it always seemed as if I was lost in a crowd. I'm clumsy with a blade and have no interest in hunting some poor fox or wolf. The only thing I *can* do is ride, but in this family even Freya and Lin do that well. The week . . . the week that Father was ensorcelled, he talked to me once—and *that* was to ask me if I had any clothes that fit." Self-consciously, he pulled a sleeve down so it briefly covered the bones in his wrist before sliding back up.

"One night I dreamed that I saddled my horse and rode up to the old croft. There was a rabbit hiding under a bush that I killed with an arrow. Something happened then . . . when it died I felt a rush of power that filled me until I could hold no more. I walked the fence line of the croft, chanting as the rabbit's blood dripped to the ground."

There was a grim factuality to his story that Aralorn could not help but approve. To a boy who disliked hunting, the realization of what he had done must be sickening.

"When I was through, I dipped my finger into the rabbit's death wound, and I was thinking of Father, on how much this would impress him, how proud he would be to have a son who was a mage. I made a mark on the corner post of the fence."

"What did the mark look like?" asked Wolf.

"Two half circles, one above the other—connected bottom to top."

Wolf frowned. "Open to the left or right or one each way?"

"To the left."

Wolf closed his eyes as if it allowed him to better visualize the spell. Still looking at the drawings, he asked, "You said you were chanting. Do you remember what you said?"

Gerem frowned. "No. It was in Rethian, though, because I knew what I was saying at the time. I remember thinking that it was strange. I remember that it rhymed." He was silent for a moment. "Something about feeding, I think. Death, magic, and dreaming, but that's all I can remember."

"And then you burned the croft," said Wolf.

Gerem nodded. "They said later there were animals in the barn." He sounded sick.

"Be glad there weren't people," commented Aralorn.

"Thanks," he said sourly, but with a touch of humor. "Now I can have nightmares about that every night, too."

"You thought this was a dream?" asked Kisrah.

Gerem nodded. "Until we received news of the burning of the croft. Even then I didn't really believe I'd been the one to burn the croft until

Father collapsed." He paused and looked at Aralorn. "I am *really* glad he isn't dead. After he was brought back to the keep, I took out my hunting knife—there was dried blood on the blade just beneath the handle where my cleaning cloth might have missed."

"Gerem," said Kisrah, "of all of us here, you hold the least guilt. Without the protection of the spells binding master to apprentice, a dreamwalker of Geoffrey's caliber could make you do anything he wanted you to. You are no more guilty of killing that rabbit, burning the animals in the barn, or entrapping the Lyon than a sword is guilty of the wounds it opens."

Aralorn could have kissed him.

Gerem's lips twitched up just a little. "You're saying that I was just a hatchet that happened to be in the right place at the right time."

The Archmage smiled and nodded. "After we free your father, I'll speak to him about setting up a real apprenticeship." He turned to Nevyn. "I'll make certain he doesn't have your experiences, Nevyn. You should have told—" He stopped when Nevyn flinched and shook his head. "It doesn't matter now."

Wolf folded the drawings and put them into a pouch he carried on his belt.

"Do you know enough to release him?" asked Aralorn.

Wolf hesitated. "I will only get one chance at this. I'd like to think about it a little more. I know where Father kept his favorite spell books: Let me take a day or so to look through them before I try this."

"In my library," said Kisrah dryly.

"Not exactly," said Wolf. "Remind me sometime to show you some of the secrets you ought to know about the ae'Magi's castle. In the meantime, I need to look a few things up."

"That sounds like a good idea to me," said Kisrah. "Do you need any help?"

Wolf shook his head. "No. There are only two rune books he used—it wasn't Father's forte either."

Kisrah bit his lip. "May I talk to you in private before you go, Cain?"

Wolf raised one eyebrow in surprise. "Certainly." He took Aralorn's hand and raised it to his lips. "I'll be back this evening."

She smiled and kissed his cheek. "Fine."

He turned back to the Archmage. "Shall we walk?"

KISRAH LED THE way to the frozen gardens, making no attempt to talk until they were out in the cold.

"Cain, the Master Spells are missing—or rather half of them are."

"What?" Shock broke through Wolf's preoccupation with the spell he would have to perform in order to free Aralorn's father.

"Haven't you noticed?"

Wolf shook his head, still feeling disbelief—the Master Spells held the fabric of wizardry together. "They haven't had any effect on me for a long time."

"Without the spells, the position of ae'Magi is no more than a courtesy title. I have no way of controlling a rogue wizard, no way of detecting black magic unless I am in the proximity of whoever is working it. When I found them in Geoffrey's library, the pages that contained the ae'Magi's half of the rune spells were missing."

Ah, thought Wolf, as he said, "I don't know where they are."

"I believe you," said Kisrah, leaving Wolf feeling odd—as if he'd braced himself for an attack that hadn't come. "You had no motive to take them. If anyone could have controlled you with them, Geoffrey would have done so a long time ago. Do you know where he would have hidden them?"

"The only time that I saw them, they were in the ae'Magi's grimoire in the vault in the library."

"They are no longer there. If you find them—"

"I'll bring them to you. It's not rogue wizards that bother me; it's what will happen if everyone realizes you no longer control them."

"Witch hunts," agreed Kisrah grimly.

Wolf nodded. "I'll look out for them, but don't be surprised if I don't find them. Father wasn't the only wizard who dabbled in the black arts—I know there were at least two others. It would be worth their lives to keep them from you."

Kisrah swore heatedly. "I hadn't thought of that. Who are they?"

Wolf shrugged. "I don't know their names, and they kept their faces hidden. Do you still have the other half of the spells?"

Kisrah nodded. "We hid them as soon as it was clear that something had happened to Geoffrey's."

"I'll look," promised Wolf again, then turned away from the ae'Magi.

"Cain," Kisrah said.

"Yes?"

"Thank you."

Wolf swept him a low bow before heading briskly out of the gardens. He would look, but he suspected the spells were long gone, maybe destroyed. Not entirely a bad thing, he decided after a while. Geoffrey ae'Magi could not have been the only ae'Magi who used them for other than their intended purposes, otherwise there wouldn't be so many black grimoires left after ten centuries.

He had a library to visit with more urgent business. More than he needed his father's books, he needed a quiet place.

ARALORN WAITED UNTIL Gerem and Nevyn followed the other mages out the door before turning to the chicken in the crate.

"Coming out, Halven?" she asked.

The hen let out a startled squawk.

She pulled the lid off the crate and shook her head. "Don't give me that. If you wanted to remain anonymous, you could have made your clucks less pointed. Otherwise, I'd never have thought to check to see if the chicken was really a chicken. I never have been able to switch from one sex to the other."

The hen jumped to the top of the crate and landed on the floor as her uncle—this time in the form of a tall redheaded man wearing the clothes of one of the Trader Clans. "Having you around makes spying much more interesting," he said, sounding pleased.

"What would you have done if he'd been ready to unwork the spell and tried to sacrifice you?" she asked.

He grinned. "I wouldn't have let him slit my throat, but I was pretty sure that he'd want to consider the spells for a while."

"Be that as it may, I for one am glad you're here. How much do you know about human magic?"

Halven raised his eyebrows. "Less than Wolf, I imagine."

"He's busy—and I'm not certain that it's something I want to discuss with him right now. Just how powerful would a dreamwalker have to be in order to control a howlaa?"

"Ah, dreamwalking is not just a human talent, and I do know a little something about it." He scratched his chin. "Howlaas are magical creatures, much more difficult to influence than a half-fledged boy like Gerem. Dreamwalking is more common among us than among the humans, but we don't tend to be nearly as powerful. I know two dream-walkers; only one of them can dreamspeak. We don't even have stories of dreamwalkers who can influence others the way Gerem was, except for the—what was it you called it? Ah yes, the Dreamer."

"Now you've heard the whole story of the spell on the Lyon. Do you still think that a dead dreamwalker couldn't do this?"

"Maybe one could," he said. "Kisrah and Nevyn's part, yes. I am less certain of whoever held your brother in thrall—I'd think that would take a fair bit of power. The howlaa? I just don't see how a dead man would have the power to do that. But I haven't talked to any dead dreamwalkers to be certain of it."

"Maybe," she said thoughtfully, "I should go talk to someone who knows more about dead people."

THE WIND WAS gusty as Aralorn took the path to the temple, but it didn't bother her as much today. Perhaps her lessons on centering helped her to block the voices more effectively, or else the ability was fading with time. She rather hoped for the latter.

The temple doors stood open, so she rode directly there, dismounted, and left Sheen standing outside.

"Tilda?" she called softly. The room appeared deserted, though by no means empty. In spite of the open door, it was warm inside, but there was no sign of a fire. She shivered and backed out of the temple, closing the doors carefully behind her.

Leading Sheen toward the little cottage, she told him, "I don't know why that should unnerve me when I run around with wizards and shapechangers, but it does."

There was a hitching post in front of the cottage, and Aralorn dropped Sheen's reins beside it.

"Be good," she said, and patted him on the shoulder before taking the shoveled path to the door of the cottage.

"Enter," bade a cheerful voice when she knocked. "I'm in the kitchen, baking."

Sure enough, when Aralorn opened the door, the smell of warm yeast billowed out.

"It's me, Aralorn." She followed the smell to find Tilda up to her elbows in bread dough. "I see I caught you working."

Tilda laughed. "Shh. Don't tell. A priestess is supposed to stand around and look mysterious."

"That's all right, I generally get plenty of mysterious. Speaking of which, the temple door was opened. I shut it before I came here."

Tilda smiled. "Well then, we both welcome you here."

"Thank you," said Aralorn with what aplomb she'd managed to develop running around with Wolf. "I came because I need to ask you a few questions."

"Me or the priestess?"

Aralorn shrugged. "Whichever one can answer my questions. Geoffrey ae'Magi is dead, right?"

"Yes," Tilda answered without hesitation. "Ridane sometimes tells me when significant people die."

Aralorn let out a harsh breath of relief. She'd been pretty sure of it, but hearing it was better. She could deal with him dead—it was the living Geoffrey who had scared the courage out of her. "A great many people, including the current ae'Magi, are convinced that his spirit is dreamwalking around Lambshold. Is that possible?"

"Dreamwalking?" Tilda stopped kneading her bread and looked thoughtful. "I don't know." She closed her eyes and took in a deep breath.

Something stirred in the air. It wasn't magic, but it was like enough to it that Aralorn could feel it drift through her and wrap itself about the priestess.

When Tilda opened her eyes, the pupil filled her iris, making her eyes appear almost black. "No," she said. "There are a few ghosts in the area, old things for the most part. But nothing strong enough to influence the living."

Aralorn nodded slowly. "That's what I needed to know. Thank you." She turned to go.

"Wait," said the priestess. "There is something . . ."

"Yes?"

Tilda stared at her bread for a moment before looking up. She was pale as milk, and her pupils were contracted as if she stood in the noonday sun rather than in a cozy but rather dim cottage. "If you are not very careful and very clever, there will be several more deaths soon."

"I am always clever," responded Aralorn, with more humor than she felt. "Careful, we may have to work around." Tilda still looked upset, so Aralorn added, "I know that there is danger. It should not take me long to discover what has been happening these last few weeks. Once I know that—I'll know what can be done."

"Ridane says that the web is spun, and one person at Lambshold will die no matter what you do."

Aralorn had not dealt with gods much, but she was a firm believer in writing her own future. She was not about to let Ridane decide the fate of her family and friends. "I'll do what I can. Thank you, Tilda. You've helped a great deal."

NEVYN, SHE THOUGHT as she mounted Sheen. *It is Nevyn.*

The stallion snorted and sidled and generally kept her attention until they were well on their way back to Lambshold. As she'd listened to Gerem's story, she had known it wasn't Geoffrey. If Geoffrey had known that there was a mage of Gerem's potential, untrained, at Lambshold, he would have moved mountains to get to him—untrained mages gave him so much more power than trained mages. So Geoffrey hadn't known about Gerem before he died. And, as a dead man seeking revenge, he would not have used Gerem to do his work—he'd have used Anasel. Surely a doddering old man who had been a great mage would have been a better target. But Nevyn avoided Anasel as he avoided most of the mageborn if he could. If he needed two other mages to help him, it would be Kisrah and Gerem. But Nevyn would never hurt her father.

One of Aralorn's greatest talents as a spy, other than being able to turn into a mouse, was her ability to take a few bits of knowledge and knit them into a whole story.

Kisrah told her that Nevyn was a dreamwalker.

Kisrah had long been a favorite of the ae'Magi's and spent a lot of time at the ae'Magi's castle.

Nevyn, who'd already suffered from being a mageborn Darranian, had been first apprenticed to a wizard who had abused him. That wizard, though powerful, had a bad enough reputation that the ae'Magi had never associated with him willingly.

Those were the facts she had. It was enough for an experienced storyteller to work out the probabilities.

She saw in her head that boy, wary and nervous, taken by his new master to the ae'Magi's castle. Abused children try to protect themselves any way they can. They hide, they try to please their abuser, they use their magic. Santik had not been a dreamwalker; certainly his apprentice would have used his talent to spy upon him to try to stay safe. Perhaps dreamwalking to watch his master had already been a habit when he'd gone into Kisrah's care.

Kisrah would certainly have taken his new apprentice to the ae'Magi to see if Geoffrey had suggestions on how to handle the boy. Like Kisrah himself, Nevyn had had the promise of power, and Geoffrey would never have let such a wizard in his presence without ensuring that he, too, was caught up in the charisma spell. Maybe Nevyn had a ring like Kisrah's or some other bit of jewelry, given to him by the ae'Magi.

She wondered how long it had been before Nevyn, dreamwalking, had first spied upon the ae'Magi. Because once he had been abused, he certainly would have had trouble believing in the goodness of those assigned to his care. Spying on Kisrah would have caused him no harm. But the ae'Magi . . . Even Kisrah, an adult, had been torn by the discrepancy between how he felt about Geoffrey because of the charisma spell and what he witnessed at the ae'Magi's castle. And Kisrah hadn't seen half of it. Wolf had—and Aralorn would have bet that Nevyn had as well.

Ah, gods, she thought. *The poor boy.*

Sheen guided himself for a bit while she dropped her reins to wipe at her eyes. He shook his head when she drew the reins taut again.

That first time, she thought, *how old was Nevyn the first time? What did he see?*

She'd seen Geoffrey kill children, had seen a man she knew in the face of a shambling Uriah, had seen a woman who turned into a flesh-eating thing—and she'd only been around the last ae'Magi for weeks, not years. Wolf had experienced worse—and so, she was certain, had Nevyn. All the while he'd been defenseless, caught up by the ae'Magi's spell that bound him to think that the Archmage was the best, most wonderful of good men.

Each thread of the story flowed worse than the last.

Spying on the ae'Magi would have allowed Nevyn access to black magic. Geoffrey was a dreamwalker, too. Had he known that Nevyn was spying?

Of course he had, she thought. How could he not? Geoffrey had been as powerful as only a black mage who was also the Archmage could be. Had he compared them, Wolf and Nevyn, as he taught them both things children should never have to know? Nausea curled in her belly. It would have given him great pleasure to have them both, she thought, one boy who fought him and one who had already been taught to please an abusive master and now had one he was forced to love.

Nevyn would have been fully under the influence of the ae'Magi's magic. *Knowing* that the ae'Magi was wonderful and seeing the horrors he committed. What had that done to Nevyn?

"Aralorn!" bellowed Falhart from the stable door as she rode up. "You missed our date."

"Date?" she raised her eyebrows.

"Rematch, double or nothing—don't you remember?"

"Ah," she said. "I wasn't certain you'd let me have another match since you won the first. Luck can't be with you all the time."

"Luck, she says!" He appealed to the interested spectators who'd begun gathering in the courtyard at his first bellow. Then he turned back to Aralorn. "Skill it was, and right well you know it, small one."

"Big people have farther to fall," she retorted. "Let me get my staves, and I'll meet you there." She'd tire her body, then see if she could piece together some way to save her father, Nevyn, and Wolf. Because, with Nevyn as the enemy, Wolf was still at risk.

TWELVE

FALHART WAS WAITING FOR ARALORN WHEN SHE GOT TO THE PRACTICE grounds. He'd stripped down to his trousers, which was gutsy of him, if not too smart. A leather shirt was fair protection against bruises—and the cold for that matter.

Shirtless, he appeared even larger than he did clothed, and if that flesh was tinged blue from the weather, it didn't detract from the whole. From the looks of him, he trained as hard as any new recruit, for there wasn't a spare bit of flesh anywhere.

If she'd been the kind of person who was easily intimidated, she'd have been getting nervous. As it was, she looked around but didn't see his wife or any other reason for the display—though there was a fair-sized crowd beginning to gather.

Aralorn generally preferred to keep as much clothing on as possible when fighting someone who didn't know her; the less anyone saw of her muscles, the more they underrated her abilities—not that she expected Falhart to underestimate her. Perhaps he fought stripped down to intimidate his opponent. If she were as large as he, she might try that tack, but she wouldn't expect it to be too effective against a small woman who was used to fighting musclebound men.

"Let you win once, and you get visions of invulnerability," she mourned, gesturing toward his discarded clothing. "Just think of the bruises you'll carry tomorrow."

"You talk pretty big for a little thing who got beaten soundly yesterday," he returned, working his big staff in a pattern that made it blur and sing.

His weapon was impressive: He was using his war staff rather than the practice one he'd had yesterday. It was half a foot taller than he was and as big around as he could comfortably hold—Aralorn doubted she could close her hand around it. It was stained almost black and shod with polished steel that caught the light as he made it dance. She shook her head at him—there were easier ways to warm up.

Watching the gathering crowd, Aralorn grinned at the looks of awe her brother was receiving from the young men. Obviously, he didn't put on a display like this every day.

In comparison, she knew that she made a pitiful showing. She'd picked the same single staff she'd fought with yesterday: Her staff looked like a child's toy in comparison to Falhart's. She set it aside as she warmed up, stretching her muscles but not using them appreciably.

She could hear active betting in the crowd, which meant that someone expected her to win, which surprised her given Hart's show of force.

"Got those five coppers handy?" she asked, as a way of announcing she was ready to fight. "I don't accept credit."

"I've got them," said Correy, pushing his way to the fore of the crowd and stepping over the low barrier that defined the ring. "Can't even buy a night's stay in a decent inn for that, Aralorn. Are you sure you don't want to up the bet?"

She shook her head. "I never bet more than ten—and then only if it is a bet I'm certain to win. Any more than that, and I might miss it. I'm just a poor mercenary, not heir to a landed noble like some people I know. And, Correy, anyone who spends five coppers for a night at the inn better be paying for more than room and board, or else he's getting rooked. Falhart, are you through wasting your strength yet?"

He looked at Correy, who nodded.

Which was odd—unless she tied it in with Falhart's bare chest and the active betting. "It's not kind to sucker people who can't afford it, Correy," she said softly.

"I'm not taking more than they can afford—Father pays his men well." He turned his back to the crowd so he wouldn't be overheard. "Besides,

Hart's not throwing the fight. He just told me that he'd be surprised if you let him win twice in a row."

"He owes me a gold for fighting without my shirt," murmured Hart. "I get that win or lose."

Aralorn grinned at him, "Does your wife know you take your shirt off for money?"

"Just don't tell Irrenna," he pleaded—only half joking.

"Oh-ho," she crowed. "This sounds like blackmail material."

Hart rolled his eyes, "Can we get on with this? It's blasted cold out here."

Aralorn straightened and shook her shoulders out. "Fine. I'll add a little black to your blue skin."

Correy stepped out of the ring, leaving it to the combatants.

The secret of fighting against a man using a tree was never to be where he thought you were going to be. Her staff could turn his, but if she was stupid enough to try to block his directly, it would snap.

For the first few minutes, they fought silently, trying to take each other by surprise before it turned into an endurance contest. Falhart had to move more bulk around than Aralorn, but she had to move hers faster because of the length of his reach, so they were both breathing heavily when they backed off.

"There's a story I once heard," she said, pacing around the ring without taking her eye off him, "about a thief-taker who worked for the king of Southwood several generations back. His name was Anslow."

"Never heard of him," grunted Falhart, moving at her in a rush. She dove under his blow, tucked her stick neatly between his knees, and twisted. He fell to the ground, rolling, and she jumped lightly back out of his reach. "Don't try that move on me again," he warned. "Twice is pushing it."

She shrugged, grinning. "Some moves bear repeating, if only for entertainment value. That's the trouble with your being so large—it's too much fun to watch you fall."

They circled warily for a moment. Without the protection of a shirt,

Falhart was more cautious than he'd been the day before. "Why don't you continue with your story?"

Aralorn nodded, walking backward as he stalked her. "Anslow solved crimes that had stumped many before him, winning a reputation as the best of his kind. There are stories of cases he solved with nothing but a bit of thread or a single footprint."

Falhart closed, taking a swing at her middle. Aralorn didn't even pause in her story as she avoided the blow. "He was a legend in his own time, and lawbreakers walked in fear of his shadow. But there was one criminal who did not fear him."

"Stay put, you runt," he snapped, as she dodged past him, catching him a glancing hit on his ribs.

"Point," she crowed. "This criminal was a killer who chose women for victims."

"I can see his—*point*," muttered Falhart as he caught her squarely in the back, knocking the breath out of her.

Chivalrously, he stepped back and waited for her to breathe again. It took her a moment before she came to her feet.

"Allyn's toadflax, Hart, that's going to hurt tomorrow."

He grinned, showing not the least hint of remorse. "That's the point of the whole thing."

"Right," she said dryly, though she couldn't help smiling.

This was *fun*. She hadn't been able to really cut loose since her last good sparring partner had been killed. If you didn't trust the skills of your opponent, you couldn't use your best moves against him unless you wanted to kill him. With a wild yell, she launched an attack designed to do nothing more than tire Falhart out.

"You were telling me about the thief-taker," he said, matching her blow for blow and adding a few moves of his own to show her she wasn't in control of the fight.

"Ah," she said, slipping nimbly out of the path of his quarterstaff. "So I was. The killer took his prey only once a year, on the first day of spring. He laid his victims out in some public place in the dark of the night. As the years passed, the killer taunted Anslow, sending him notes and clues that did the thief-taker no good."

While he was extended in a thrust that she'd turned aside, she slipped the end of her staff sideways and hit him squarely in the breastbone, where it left a bruise to match the one on his ribs. "Two."

He growled and circled. She stuck her tongue out at him; he made a face.

"The night before the killer would take his fifteenth victim," she continued, "Anslow took every note the killer had sent him and set them before him, trying to find a pattern. He thought it was someone he knew, for the notes contained a few private references—things that only Anslow should have known."

She broke off speaking, for Falhart moved in with a barrage of blows that required all of her concentration to counter. At last, he managed to hit her staff directly, snapping it in two. The blow continued more gently, but she came out of the encounter with sore ribs.

"Two," he said.

She snapped in with the remnants of the staff and poked him in the belly—gently. "Three—my match."

There were loud groans from the audience as they sorted out who owed what to whom. Falhart grinned and leaned on his staff.

"So, tell me the rest of the story," he said, breathing heavily.

She sat down briefly on the ground, but the cold drove her to her feet. "About Anslow? Where was I?"

"He had the notes from the killer in front of him."

"Ah, yes. Those notes. He set them out on his desk, oldest to newest. He had noticed early on that the killer's handwriting bore a strong resemblance to his own—but it was the last letter he stared at. The killer's hand had developed a tremor; the letters were no longer formed with a smooth, dark flow of ink. Just recently, Anslow had noticed that his hands shook when he wrote. He himself was the killer."

She touched the broken end of one of the sections of her staff in the dirt and dragged it back and forth gently in random patterns.

Falhart frowned. "How could he be the killer and not know it?"

Aralorn contemplated her broken staff as if it might hold the secrets of the universe. "There is a rare illness of the spirit in which a person can become two separate beings occupying the same body. There is a shadow that forms, watching everything the primary person does, knowing what he knows—but the real person may have no knowledge of what the shadow does when he controls the body." She flipped the piece into the air and caught it.

"Strange," observed Falhart, shaking his head.

Correy came up to them and took Aralorn's hand in his, turned her palm upright, and placed six copper coins in it, talking to Falhart all the while. "Thanks for the tip, Hart. I got ten-to-one odds. It was only six to one before they had a chance to compare your manly figure with the midget here—you can put your shirt back on now."

WOLF STARED AT the rows of books in his shelves, caressing the bindings gently. He didn't pull any out—that could wait. He knew which ones held the information he needed. But he already knew what the spell would cost, had known, really, since Kisrah had told him that he'd killed a Uriah to set his spell, though he'd held out some hope until he'd heard everything that had been put into the binding magic holding the Lyon. He had known that his father had at last succeeded in destroying him.

A human had died to power the spell created by three mages. A human death was needed to unmake it. A Uriah counted as a person, ensorcelled and altered though he was—he had been a man once. If Kisrah had known the nature of the Uriah, he would have known such a sacrifice was necessary. He might have told Aralorn, then she would believe it was her decision to make. Wolf knew that it was his, and he had made it as soon as he realized what would be needed.

How ironic that when he finally decided that he might actually deserve to live, he discovered that he was going to have to die. How had his father known that he would love Aralorn enough to sacrifice himself for her? Except that it wasn't really for her, he realized, though that was part of it.

He touched the backs of a half dozen of his favorite books, not rare grimoires but heroes' tales. It was his father who had caused this, and only Geoffrey ae'Magi's son could put an end to his father's evil once and for all—if Cain ae'Magison could stiffen his will to it.

He had always come to his books for the strength he needed to resist his father. So he had come here, to his collection of books that rested deep in the heart of a mountain in the Northlands, to find the strength to do the right thing.

He walked on through the rows of books, pausing here and there to set one straight until he reached his worktable. Not bothering with the chairs, he sat on the table itself, right next to the pair of books he'd retrieved from the ae'Magi's castle. He touched a splatter of ink, remembering days not long past that he and Aralorn had worked there, searching through the books for just the right spell. He remembered the ink that stained her hand and the table as she scratched out notes in handwriting that was just short of illegible.

He remembered bringing her from his father's dungeons more dead than alive, laying her still form on the couch, worrying that what he'd done for her wouldn't be enough—that she would die and leave him alone again.

He remembered and wept where there was no one to see.

ARALORN FRETTED THROUGH dinner. Her theory was a fishing net with holes a sailing ship could get through.

She knew the story about Anslow was true. She'd had it from Ren the Mouse, who'd been a personal friend of the thief-taker. Was she wrong in thinking that the odd vision she'd had of Nevyn as a tree split down the middle meant he had no idea of what his darker half had done?

For that matter, why was she certain it was Nevyn? Kisrah might have depths she'd never seen. Why couldn't he be the one who was dreamwalking? It was he who said that Geoffrey and Nevyn were the only ones who could dreamwalk. He might have lied. Maybe he and Nevyn were in it together.

Aralorn stared at the ceiling. Matters that had seemed so clear riding back from Ridane's temple now seemed muddled. She really did not have enough evidence to know who was behind the Lyon's bespelling—only that it was not Geoffrey.

"Aralorn, are you all right?" asked Irrenna.

Aralorn glanced up and realized that everyone was looking at her—obviously she'd missed something. Or maybe she'd been staring at the pickled eel on the flat of her knife for too long.

"Yes, sorry," she answered. "Just tired."

She set the black stuff back on her plate. Snake she could take or leave, but freshwater eel was beyond horrible—especially pickled. She vowed not to let herself get so distracted at mealtime again if the results could be so hazardous.

"I was asking you when you needed to be back at Sianim," said Irrenna.

"Uhm." She smiled. "I didn't exactly take a formal leave of absence. Just left them a note. If they need me, they know where to find me."

She would tell Wolf that she knew that it wasn't Geoffrey, so he could take what precautions he could. When her father was back on his feet, they'd figure out the rest.

WOLF CAME BACK while she was getting ready for bed, surprising her by teleporting himself right into the room. She knew that he preferred to find somewhere private because the first few moments after he translocated, he was disoriented. He looked pale, but she thought it might just be the result of the spell.

"Any luck?" she asked.

"I have what I need," he responded, swaying slightly where he stood. He closed his eyes, and she ran to offer a supportive arm.

"Sorry," he said. "Just dizzy."

She was near enough to him to smell the familiar scent of the cave.

"My nose tells me you've been to the Northlands. I thought you were going to check your father's library."

"My dear Aralorn," he said, without opening his eyes, "a fair portion of my father's library is in the cave."

She laughed and hugged him, tucking her head against him in a manner that had become familiar.

"Did you find what you needed?" she asked.

"Yes," he said, tightening his arms until she squeaked.

"I figured out something, too," she said.

"Oh?" He nuzzled at her neck, scratching her a little with the faint roughness of beard that was new-grown since that morning.

"Wolf, stop that—it tickles. It isn't your father."

"How did you come to that conclusion?"

He switched his attentions to her ear, and she shivered at the effect of his warm breath against her sensitive skin.

"He would—Wolf . . ." She couldn't speak for a moment.

"Hmm?"

"I asked Ridane's priestess. She says he's dead and not influencing anyone here."

He stilled, then kissed the top of her head. "Smart."

"Always," she said smugly.

"I love you," he said.

"Of course you do," she said, to make him laugh—which it did. "I love you, too. Now you can kiss me."

He bent down to her ear again, and whispered, "How long were you going to take before you told me that the priestess bound us together unto death?"

Now it was her turn to still. She felt guilty for half a breath, then she realized what his words really meant.

"How long have you known? Plague take you, Wolf."

She tried to take a step away, but he held her too tightly. His breath seemed to be behaving oddly—then she realized he was laughing. She hit him—not hard enough to hurt, just enough to express her displeasure.

"Aralorn, Aralorn," he tried to croon between laughs and pretending her halfhearted blows were hurting him. "Did you think I wouldn't feel it when the priestess set a blood-bond between us? I am a black mage, my love. I understand about blood-bonds—and I can break them if I wish."

"This one was set by a goddess," she informed him.

"Maybe she could set a bond between us I could not break," he told her. "But this one I could. If I wanted to."

He lifted her off the floor to allow himself better access to her mouth—as well as various and sundry other sensitive areas. Aralorn caught her breath and braced her hands on his shoulders.

"I know you love me," he told her, the laughter dying from his eyes.

She found herself blinking back tears as she heard how profoundly that knowledge had affected him.

"I know you love me, too," she said, before her mouth was occupied by things other than speech.

AFTERWARD, HE SLEPT. Snuggled tightly against him, Aralorn closed her eyes and wished she didn't have to ask him to use the dark arts. He had tried to kill himself once rather than use them, but for her he would take the part he had been given. She didn't know that she was worth it.

No good comes from black magic, Kisrah had said. Ridane's priestess had told her that someone would die before long. Aralorn shivered and shifted closer to Wolf as if she could protect him by her presence.

It hadn't been said, but the assumption Wolf had led them all to was that he would remove the spell tomorrow. Surely that would give the dreamwalker something to fret about.

Maybe he'd be walking again tonight.

She decided the best place to keep watch would be in Nevyn's room. It might already be too late, but there was still a fair portion of the night left—and it had been about this time that she'd seen "Geoffrey" talking to Kisrah.

She started to slide out of bed.

"Aralorn?" Wolf sounded sleepy.

"I'm going spying for a couple of hours," she said quietly, though he was already awake. She should have known that she couldn't sneak out on him. "I have a few questions to clean up, and this might be my only chance to do it."

He cupped her face in the darkness and pulled her until she rested her forehead on his for a moment. "All right," he said. "Be careful."

She tilted her face until her lips met his. "I will."

She dressed in the dark, not bothering with shoes. Though, after a brief moment of thought, she grabbed her sword to go along with her knives. If she ended up facing an enraged sorcerer, she'd just as soon have Ambris's help as not.

In the darkness, Wolf said softly, "I love you."

Aralorn looked back, but the bed was too shadowed. She could distinguish nothing more than the shape of him in it. "I love you, too. See you in a few hours."

"Yes," he said.

He waited in the darkness and counted slowly to a hundred before getting to his feet. He dressed with care. He'd done many hard things in his life; in some ways this was not the worst. At least this time it was clearly the best answer for everyone.

He wished that he could postpone it, but he was unlikely to get another such opportunity soon. He'd been cudgeling his brain for a way to keep her away from him for long enough. Trust Aralorn to make things easy for him. He took his knife from his belt and tested it lightly against the ball of his thumb. A drop of dark liquid ran down the edge of his hand, and he licked it clean.

ARALORN WAS MAKING her way up the stairs when a soft sound alerted her to someone else's presence. She froze where she was, searching the darkness above her for any hint of movement. At last she saw a flash of lighter color where the minimal light touched the railing to the right of the stairway.

She darted up the stairs, blessing the stone under her feet for its silence—it was far more difficult to sneak up a wooden stairway. If she had been in a hall, she would have found a dark corner to hide in, but the stairway was too narrow for that. The best that she could hope for was to meet them at the top of the stairs.

She told herself that there was no reason to feel nervous about meeting someone walking the halls here, but she had been a spy for too long. Her instincts kept her on edge.

As she rounded the last stair, she came face-to-face with Gerem. He couldn't have heard her, but he gave no evidence of surprise.

"Gerem?" she asked.

He frowned at her, but vaguely, as if he were concentrating on something else. "What are you doing here?" he asked, but without real interest.

"I was just going to ask you that." There was something wrong with him, she thought. His words were soft and slurred as if he'd been drinking, though she smelled no alcohol when she leaned closer to him.

"Death walks here tonight," he said, not at all dramatically, rather as if he were talking about grooming his horse.

An ice-cold chill swept up her spine, as much from his tone as from what he said. "Gerem, why don't I take you to your room. Wouldn't you like to go back to sleep?"

He nodded slowly. "I have to sleep."

He took a step forward, forcing Aralorn down a step from the landing, giving him as much of an advantage in height as Falhart had over her.

Gently she took his arm and tried to turn him, stepping up as she did so. It was a move she often used on stubborn pack animals that refused to go where she wanted them; turning worked much better than pushing or pulling. "Your room is this way, brother mine. You can sleep there."

He shook his head earnestly. "You don't understand. I *have* to go to the stables."

"The stables? What's in the stables?"

He stopped tugging against her hold and bent down until his face was level with hers. "I killed Father," he whispered.

"Stuff and nonsense, Gerem. Father is not dead." She looked around for the nearest source of help. This wasn't near anyone's sleeping chambers—

those were a floor above them. No one would hear her . . . But then she remembered that Irrenna had given Kisrah the Lyon's library to sleep in.

"Kisrah!" she shouted, hoping her voice would penetrate the thick oak door.

"Let me go. I don't want to hurt you."

"No more do I," she muttered.

Gerem pulled a knife with a slow and awkward movement. Once he had it out, he held it as if he didn't know what to do with it now that it was in his hand.

Misled by that and by his earlier claim of clumsiness, Aralorn tried a simple grab to relieve him of the weapon. She should have realized that the Lyon wouldn't let any of his sons go without training. As smoothly as he must have done it a hundred times in practice, he caught her hand in his free one and used leverage to twist her around until her back was against him, her arms caught firmly by his off hand, and the cool edge of his knife laid against her throat.

Without the knife, she'd have gotten out of it easily enough—a former thief of the Trader Clans had taught her a number of interesting tricks— but the knife made any movement on her part highly stupid. Half-grown though he was, he was still stronger and bigger than she was—and better trained than she'd thought. She didn't want him to grow to adulthood knowing that he'd killed his sister, so she remained very still.

"What are you going to do in the stables, Gerem?" she asked as un-aggressively as possible. *Give him some time to break the hold the dream-walker has woven,* she thought. *Keep him talking.*

"Sleep." His arms relaxed a shade but not enough.

"Why do you need to sleep in the stables?" She kept her voice in big-sister-to-little-brother tones, not frightened-victim-with-knife-at-throat. If you reminded someone you were at their mercy too often, they just might decide to kill you and get it over with.

He tightened his grip. "I *killed* Father. Don't you understand?"

Abruptly, he twisted, thrusting her at someone who'd been approaching from behind. She knocked the man flat and heard Gerem running down the stairs.

She swore like any guttersnipe and leapt to her feet, noting only peripherally that it was Kisrah she'd landed on.

Though instincts would have sent her tearing off after Gerem, she took the time to change. The goose would be faster gliding down the stairs than the icelynx would be since the stone offered no grip to claws.

"What the—" croaked Kisrah as he sat up in time to witness the last part of the change.

"After him," she said, and took flight.

By now, Gerem was already down the stairs. He didn't bother with the more polite methods of getting to the stables but threw the bolts on the shutters of a window and jumped through.

He's going to break a leg doing that, thought Aralorn. The window might be waist high inside the keep, but it was better than half a story higher on the outside. Closing her wings, she darted through the open window after him.

Hurry, said the wind's unwelcome voice. *Death is waiting.*

Let it wait, then, she thought.

She'd overshot Gerem and was close to the stables before she could turn around. Goose wings were meant for great sweeping turns, not falcon-quick maneuvering. Especially a domestic goose that had to work far too hard to fly. She started to turn back when she saw the howlaa.

It waited in front of the stables in the moonlit courtyard, the wind carrying its scent away from the sensitive noses of the horses in the stables. She thought about how unexpectedly the last howlaa had come upon her and wondered if it could control the wind and keep its scent from prey.

The dead one's mate, said the wind, as clearly as if someone were whispering into her ears. *Dream-called and hungry for blood.*

Closer, she could see differences between this one and the one she'd killed before. Its mane was longer and darker, with red as well as yellow tints. Its eyes, though, were the same, crystal so deep she could drown in its depths.

Spelled, she thought. It had magic to compel its victims to meet its eyes. It wasn't just stupidity on her part that had let her be caught by the first howlaa.

Called by the howlaa, she let herself get too close. Only when it moved was she able to break the hold of its eyes. It rose to its hind legs with lethal swiftness and struck. Aralorn tucked her wings and dove to the ground, avoiding the crushing blow by a margin so slim as to be nonexistent.

The wind laughed alternately in thunderous then high tones that hurt her ears. *Wind-touched,* it said. *Howlaa bait. How could you think to approach it unnoticed?*

Gerem ran into the courtyard. He dropped his knife and looked at the howlaa. It returned his look, freezing him where he stood. Ignoring Aralorn, it took a step forward, then cried out in the chilling, whining tones she'd heard before.

ALONE, SO ALONE without the harmonies its mate provided. She wanted to find the one who brought them to this cursed place and rip his mind away, but the caller was too strong and could not be disobeyed. This child must die first.

Aralorn launched herself from the ground, changing in midflight to her own human form. When she dropped, she landed on the howlaa, much as she had its mate—and this time she had Ambris instead of her knives.

But the howlaa dropped as soon as Aralorn touched her, rolling agilely on the cold ground, making Aralorn scramble to get off it in time without coming within reach of the creature's talons. She wasn't wholly successful.

Blood poured down her arm as she backed away rapidly, and she'd lost Ambris; the sword lay on the ground behind the howlaa. It was easily within Gerem's reach, but her brother hadn't moved since he'd come to the courtyard. The howlaa stood between Aralorn and her brother—between Aralorn and the sword.

Well, she thought wryly, at least she had its attention. Without a weapon, she wasn't going to hold its attention long—not unless it was hungry. But—there was help in the stables. She gave a long, shrill whistle as she backed up one slow step, then another.

She was grateful for every second she'd shaved off the time it took to change to icelynx form, for as soon as the howlaa realized what she was doing, it charged.

Aralorn's vision was still trying to adjust to the difference between human and cat when the howlaa was upon her. She barely managed to avoid the howlaa's swipe by running underneath it and out the other side. This put her on the right side of the howlaa to retrieve her sword if she wanted to take human form. She hesitated and decided not to risk changing again. It was just possible that the icelynx would have a better chance than a human bearing a sword. As soon as the thought occurred to her, she changed.

She shook her head and tried to ignore the lingering itches and tingles the shift had left her. Tension caused her to yowl irritably at her bulky foe—between its noise and hers, they were going to have the entire keep out here soon. Not that it would be a bad thing to have a few more people to help with the howlaa.

She and the wind demon paced back and forth, Aralorn keeping between the howlaa and its intended prey. That the howlaa didn't just attack was a hopeful sign. She hadn't been absolutely certain that howlaas were vulnerable to the poison of an icelynx bite, but the larger animal's caution gave her hope. She was careful to avoid looking the howlaa in the eye, watching instead for the slight tensing of muscles that would presage a charge.

She had no illusions about her chances for survival. *Thank the gods,* she thought, *that Wolf can break Ridane's bond if I happen to get my stupid self killed.*

Kisrah, who must have taken a safer route through a door, entered the courtyard wearing only a pair of light-colored sleeping pants. When he saw the howlaa, he stopped.

"Aralorn. Which one are you?" he asked urgently.

The sound of his voice seemed to release Gerem from the howlaa's hold, but instead of running, he took two steps forward.

Sensing Aralorn's distraction, the howlaa chose that moment to close. It mewled as it ran, somehow a much more chilling sound than the roar of a bear or lion. Aralorn was forced to engage to keep it away from the two unarmed men.

She tried to leap on the howlaa's back again, but her weakened shoulder betrayed her, and she stumbled at the last minute, rolling frantically under the beast. She thought later that the stumble had saved her life, for the great jaws just missed closing on her back.

Instead, the howlaa caught her with its paw instead, but it hadn't had room to put much force behind the blow. It hurt, though, landing right on top of the bruises Falhart had left on her back that afternoon. The blow, relatively light as it was, sent her rolling farther under the howlaa.

While the howlaa scrambled to back away, where its size and power better offset her speed, Aralorn used her claws on the icy ground to gain her feet, then launched herself at the nearest vulnerable place she could find. Her fangs sank through the heavy coat that protected its ribs and into the howlaa's side.

The howlaa shook itself wildly, trying to dislodge her, but it only succeeded in driving her teeth in deeper. Aralorn felt the throbbing of the glands beneath her eyeteeth as they pumped poison deep into the howlaa's flesh. Unfortunately, it was too far from any major artery to kill swiftly.

The howlaa was almost as fast as the icelynx, and ten times its weight; it was only luck that had allowed her to last this long against it.

Even as the thought crossed her mind, the howlaa dropped to its side, crushing her beneath it. The weight of the howlaa kept her from breathing properly, and she grew dizzy with lack of air. A dull thud sounded in Aralorn's ears, and the howlaa's body heaved at the same time.

With a shriek of rage, the howlaa came to its feet, but it didn't move as swiftly as it had before—neither did Aralorn, for that matter. The wind demon's cry was answered with a stallion's high-pitched scream as Sheen, called by Aralorn's whistle, attacked the howlaa again, teeth bared and front feet flying. Relentless and fearless, the stallion drove the creature away from Aralorn.

On her feet again, Aralorn ran—or rather, hobbled—for her sword. She was glad that she'd been working with Halven, because she wasn't altogether certain she could have shifted back to human form in the shape she was in without the extra potency that being better centered gave her. She'd done all the damage the lynx could manage; her right arm was too weak to maintain a four-footed attack. She hadn't had time to take a close look at the damage the howlaa had done to her shoulder, and battle heat kept her from noticing the pain—but, considering the speed with which she had lost strength, she was afraid that it was worse than she had thought.

Exhaustion washed over her in waves as she completed her fourth shift. She noticed, almost absently, that Kisrah was struggling with Gerem and that there were other people in the stableyard now. She took Ambris in her good left hand and turned back to the fight.

A normal horse wouldn't have stood a chance against such an opponent, but Sheen was war-trained and iron shod. His winter shoes were rough-bottomed like a file for better grip on ice and snow, and the damage they inflicted when propelled by a ton of battle-maddened stallion was not inconsiderable. He was canny, too, taking care to avoid the front end of the howlaa when he could.

Aralorn found the energy somewhere to run, keeping clear of Sheen's line of attack. The horse sported a dark slash down his ribs, but in the darkness she couldn't see how bad it was. Squealing, he spun and kicked with his hind legs, but missed because the howlaa collapsed abruptly. Both Aralorn and Sheen drew to a halt, watching the creature warily. Its ribs rose once, twice, then stopped.

The icelynx's poison, thought Aralorn in relief, allowing her sword tip to drop.

"It's all right, Sheen," she crooned to the snorting stallion, knowing her voice would calm him faster than anything else. "It's dead now."

THIRTEEN

WOLF STOOD JUST INSIDE THE CURTAIN OF THE BIER ROOM AND WOVE a thin layer of darkness so that a casual observer would not see the light around the edges of the heavy fabric and realize that there was someone in the room with the Lyon. Green magic rose to his desire, if not his call, and the spell thickened with other magics to conceal his presence.

Wolf waited, but when the lingering magic dissipated and did not return, he took on human form, called his staff, and used it to light the room. He walked to the Lyon and ran his fingers lightly over the still face.

Aralorn had always laughed about how little she resembled the rest of the family, but Wolf could see the strong line of her jaw and the arrangement of her features in her father's face. Take away the coloring and the size difference, and it was easy to tell that the Lyon was her sire. His skin was cool under Wolf's touch.

"This is your last night of rest, my lord," Wolf murmured aloud. "I hope your dreaming was pleasant."

He took off his belt pouch and emptied the contents, mostly chalks, ink, and quills, on the bier next to the Lyon. It would take some time to set the spells that would undo the Lyon's binding.

ARALORN WALKED AROUND the howlaa's body, murmuring a soft reassurance to her stallion. After a long moment, Sheen lost his battle stance and nuzzled her hard enough to knock her back several steps. She examined the cuts in his side and sighed with relief. They were shallow, and the bleeding was already slowing. He wouldn't be carrying a saddle for several days, but she thought if the cuts were cleaned and doctored, that would be the worst of it.

Aralorn was torn between the dictates of a lifetime of training—tend to your horse first—and the knowledge that Gerem was still in danger. She compromised by turning Sheen into a small empty pen beside the stables and promising him better care as soon as she was done.

The wind had shifted direction, bringing the scent of the dead howlaa through the stables. Horses thumped and whinnied, bringing grooms running to stand gawking over the body of the howlaa.

Aralorn avoided them all and hurried to where Kisrah had Gerem pinned, picking up Ambris along the way and sheathing her.

"He's been trying for his knife," said Kisrah, as soon as she was within conversation range. "Seeing how anxious he was to go for the howlaa, I thought the knife might be an equally bad idea."

"Can you hold him for a bit more?" she asked. "I'll go for Nevyn."

Kisrah looked relieved. "Good thought. Nevyn's a dreamwalker. He will know how to help your brother. I'll enlist one of the stableboys—who seem to be finally figuring out something is going on out here—and take him up to Nevyn's rooms if you'll go ahead of us and tell him what to expect."

"Right," said Aralorn, not bothering to address Kisrah's assumption that Nevyn was the cure rather than the cause for Gerem's condition. Kisrah had, by saving her brother, provided her satisfactory proof that he wasn't involved any deeper than he had claimed. Gerem would be safe with Kisrah.

She left them there, pushing herself to run though her shoulder protested the pounding gait. She had to go the long way around on her own human feet; she couldn't jump back through the window in human form, and she wasn't up to any more shapeshifting for a while.

As she had hoped, Kisrah had come out the nearest side door—one that was usually kept bolted, so at least she didn't have to run halfway around the keep. She heard a few people stirring, awakened by the commotion by the stable, but she didn't see anyone as she came upon the door to her rooms.

She should stop and get Wolf for backup. She stopped before the door and put a hand on it. Wolf could handle Nevyn if Aralorn couldn't persuade him with her words.

Unfortunately, she was under no illusion about what Wolf would do to anyone who tried to hurt her. If she gave him some time to cool down, to understand—if there was something to understand—then he would act as reason dictated. But in the heat of the initial discovery . . . it was safer for everyone if she went at this alone.

She took her hand off the door and continued on.

Nevyn and Freya had rooms a floor above the hall where she'd found Gerem. Aralorn didn't bother to knock as she walked in.

The first thing she saw was Freya sleeping soundly on the bed, her peaceful features revealed by the flickering light of the fireplace.

The sound of the door opening hadn't disturbed Nevyn either: He was waiting for her in a chair on the opposite side of the fireplace from the bed. The firelight illuminated one side of his face clearly, while the other lay in shadows.

"I thought you might come," he said softly. Then, seeing her glance at her sleeping sister, he said, "Don't worry, she's sleeping until morning."

The sound of his voice sent a chill of unease coursing through her veins. Nevyn spoke Rethian with a thick Darranian accent she'd never heard him use.

"Let Gerem go, Nevyn," she said.

"You aren't beautiful," he said, as if she had never spoken at all. "What magic do you work that holds a man to you like that? Ten years, and the thought of seeing you was more important than punishing *him* for killing Geoffrey. Geoffrey, who was my teacher, my creator—giving me life and understanding when Nevyn would have seen me dead."

"Punishing Wolf?" she asked.

He nodded jerkily. Even in the dimly lit room, Aralorn could see the flush that swept up his cheeks as he abruptly leaned forward, every muscle in his body tightening. His voice, in stark contrast to his posture, was soft and slow. "How could you take up with *him*? We waited and waited for you to come home. Then Geoffrey died, and I found out you'd taken his killer as your lover."

"How did you find out?" she asked.

Nevyn took a deep breath in through his nose. "Geoffrey told me when he told me that Cain killed him. Cain is evil, don't you understand?"

He could have found out about her relationship with Cain while he was dreamwalking, she thought.

"Cain did not kill Geoffrey," Aralorn told him. "What he knows about black magic, Geoffrey taught him—as he taught you."

Nevyn shook his head. "No. Geoffrey was *good*. He helped me. It was Cain . . . in the night while Nevyn slept. I saw—I saw it all. Night after night, he called me to perform for me and to teach me . . . I showed you it all, I gave you dreams so that you would know what he was. What I did." His voice dropped to a whisper. "What he forced me to do."

"I don't remember," she said. "I only dreamed of Wolf." But after she said it, she wondered if it was really true. The story, Nevyn's story, had come to her so completely while she was riding back from Ridane's temple—could she have come up with it from some half-remembered dreams?

"You only kept dreams of *him*," said Nevyn, his voice dark and ugly. "You're just a shapeshifting, magic-tainted whore. I've told him and told him, but he loves you. *Loves* you when he hates his magic, hates *me* because he can't quit using his magic, can't give me up altogether."

He laughed slyly. "But you ruined it the first time he saw the two of you together. It took him a long time to realize that your wolf was Cain—but then, Nevyn was always a little slow."

"You *are* Nevyn," she said, but he ignored her.

"He sent the howlaa then, on impulse. Then he worried and worried until it was killed. Stupid sod forgot that he needs Cain to free the Lyon. If the Lyon is harmed, he'll never believe it wasn't his fault."

"You knew enough about black magic to set the spell," she said, changing the subject, because it didn't seem helpful to try to argue with this shade of Nevyn about Nevyn's guilt or innocence. "Why can't you unwork it yourself?"

"If he'd succeeded in killing Cain, I could *tell* Nevyn enough about it to work the spell—but he'd never be able to do it. No stomach for it, I'm afraid. Kisrah might do it, but he doesn't love the Lyon enough." He sounded both amused and exasperated.

"Why try to kill Gerem?" asked Aralorn.

"The spell needs a human death," he said. "Gerem is already tainted by magic, and I needed someone whom Nevyn could see dead. I couldn't leave the choice to Cain. But I don't need Gerem anymore." As he spoke the last word, he came up out of the chair and struck with the sword that he'd held in the shadows.

She saw his intention in his face an instant before he moved, so she threw herself backward, and his blade missed.

Swords, she thought as she stumbled to catch her balance. *Plague it, why does it always have to be swords?* She dodged another slice as she pulled Ambris.

It was obvious from the first blow who the better swordsman was, and it wasn't Aralorn. He had been good when she left, and he obviously hadn't quit practicing. He might even give Wolf a run for his money. She caught the edge of his blade on Ambris and let it slide off.

Even if she'd been able to use her good arm, she wouldn't have stood a chance. Even if she'd been an excellent swordswoman, she would have had a problem: She was using Ambris. She didn't want to hurt Nevyn at all—she certainly didn't want to steal his magic. She wasn't certain that was what would happen—Nevyn wasn't trying for godhood as Geoffrey had been. But that was the trouble with ancient artifacts—no one really knew what they did.

There was a game she knew, one her uncle taught her, called *Taefil Ma Deogh*, Steal the Dragon. Strategy and skill were necessary, but it was deviousness that determined who won and who lost. The last time Aralorn stayed with her mother's people, she had beaten her uncle eight times out of ten.

Devious, she thought, parrying furiously. *Do the unexpected.*

She turned and ran—out the door, down the hall to the nearest empty room, and through the doorway. The room was dark, which suited Aralorn just fine. She slid Ambris into a tall, narrow vase, where she wouldn't be immediately obvious.

Nevyn's sprinting footsteps were almost at the door as she gathered herself together for another shapechange. She was too weak, too many changes with too little rest between.

Gasping a little, she centered herself and tried again. Pain seared her from toes to fingertips, but as his form appeared in the doorway, she slipped into the shape of a mouse. She huddled just behind the door as he came into the room, called a magelight, and looked briefly around. She waited until he left, then scampered out the door and back to his bedroom.

WOLF FINISHED THE last of the painstakingly drawn ink lines on the Lyon's face. When he was through, he looked over all of his work carefully, for he wouldn't get a second chance. Satisfied that all was in order, he took out his knife. He should sever the bond he shared with Aralorn before he started, but the chances were too great that she'd find him before he was done. He had to wait until the last moment.

He slid the sharp blade sideways across one wrist. Touching the tip of a fresh quill pen into the dark liquid that pooled in his wound, he began painstakingly retracing the inked lines with blood.

IN NEVYN'S ROOM, Aralorn shifted once more to human shape, shaking and shuddering when she was done. If she survived this night, it would be days before she could do so much as light a candle with magic.

She could hear him searching for her, quick footsteps, doors opening quietly. Her heart settled; the sweat dried; and, after a few moments, the pain of overusing her magic receded except for a nagging headache.

She found a likely ambush spot, just inside his door. She was counting on him to believe she would have gone for help rather than come back to face him on her own.

He neared the door, making no attempt at stealth, and Aralorn breathed as silently as she could. He walked in confidently; his first glance fell to the bed. That was all the opening she needed.

With a war cry designed to make him start, she leapt to his back and wrapped one arm around his neck and grabbed the elbow of her opposite arm. This locked the bones of her forearms against the arteries that carried blood to his brain. The mercenaries called it a "nighty-night," and, if she could hold it for a count of fifteen, Nevyn should drop unconscious. The first five counts would be the telling ground because after that, he would get weaker fast. Surprise counted for two, then he slammed her against the edge of the door.

She held on, ignoring the pain for the moment, though she knew that she was going to have a vertical bruise to go with the horizontal one Falhart had given her with his quarterstaff. The second time Nevyn slammed her back, it hurt worse because he managed to catch her howlaa-wounded shoulder on the door, so she bit his ear to distract him. He tried to twist away and stumbled, which would have been all right except that it gave him an idea that she would rather he not have thought of.

He threw himself backward on the floor, and the air left her lungs with a faint hint of protest.

Twelve, she thought.

He managed to bring his shoulders up and smash her head onto the floor.

Fourteen, plague it, go to sleep.

He repeated his previous move with such success that Aralorn was starting to feel woozy herself. Luckily, it was the last one he made.

Lying under him, she waited to catch her breath before sending Nevyn into a more lasting sleep with the dregs of her magic. She'd never have been able to do it with him awake.

Should have just hit him over the head, she thought when she was finished, and touched her bottom lip gently with her tongue to inspect that damage he'd wrought with the back of his head, *so there's a chance I'd have killed him. I could have lived with that.*

"Aralorn?"

Nevyn's body blocked her view of the door, but she knew Kisrah's voice.

"I suspect she's under him somewhere, but she's small enough that it might take us a while to find her," observed Gerem a bit shakily.

"Ha-ha," she said coldly. "Never tease a person who knows enough about you for blackmail."

"Never get grumpy with someone you need to help drag bodies off you," replied her brother, sounding somewhat calmer after ascertaining that Nevyn was still alive. "What have you done to Nevyn—and why hasn't Freya woken up?"

"Sleep spell—not mine. I did Nevyn, though," she replied, then allowed a touch of whine to her voice. "Want to lever Nevyn off before we have a long conversation? I need to find Wolf and see if he can get a message to my uncle and get him here before Nevyn wakes up. It might also be nice to breathe."

"Aralorn?" asked a third voice, right on cue. "You were looking for me?"

Kisrah and Gerem between them managed to drag poor Nevyn off to the side.

"I should have known that you couldn't resist sticking around when things were about to get interesting, Uncle," said Aralorn, sitting up gingerly: Her head hurt, her back hurt, and her shoulder felt as if she'd been clawed by a howlaa and beaten against the door a couple of times.

"Actually," he replied, "I was looking for you. I've talked to a few of our elders, and they say that there is no way a dead dreamwalker could do the kinds of things you think Geoffrey ae'Magi has done. I stopped by your room first, but no one was there, so I came here instead."

"It wasn't Geoffrey; it was Nevyn," said Aralorn.

"Nevyn?" asked Gerem, sounding hostile. "Nevyn would never hurt Father."

"Who are you?" asked Kisrah.

"Kisrah, meet my uncle Halven—he's a shapeshifter who's been trying to help. Uncle Halven, this is Kisrah, the current ae'Magi." Introductions done, she continued without taking a breath. "Nevyn has a problem," she said, then stopped. There had to be a way to explain without sounding like a madwoman. Her weak sleep spell wasn't going to keep him under much longer. She had to make them believe her before he awoke.

"Nevyn is ill," said Kisrah, kneeling beside Aralorn. He patted the sleeping man's shoulder gently. "If I'd thought that he would have harmed anyone but himself, I never would have sent him here. He was half-mad when we took him from Santik. I'd hoped he'd settle down with me, but he was too damaged. I thought that this was the perfect place for him; he's seemed happy since he came here."

"Part of him is," said Aralorn. "But there is a part of him that is not."

"There is an unusual separation of his spirit," observed her uncle.

"I think that the part of him that dreamwalks has separated itself almost completely," Aralorn said. "He was talking about himself as if he were two different people."

"I've heard that green mages are great healers," said Kisrah diffidently. "Is there anything that you can do to help him?"

He'd taken the right tone; Halven preened before the respect in the Archmage's voice. "Since I can see the damage, I might be able to do something," he said. Graciously, he half bowed to Aralorn. "I think you're right. It's the dreamwalking part of him that has split off from his spirit. What is broken can be mended together again—as long as the cause for the break is gone."

"Santik is dead, and so is Geoffrey," said Aralorn in answer.

She got to her feet and backed away so that Halven and Kisrah could have free access to Nevyn.

It was over, she thought. Nevyn had been certain that Wolf could free her father. But as his words came back to her, the relief she'd been feeling stopped.

"Human death," she said.

The two mages were involved in their discussion over Nevyn, but Gerem said, "What?"

Halven had said Wolf hadn't been in her room.

"Gods," she said. And she'd been so grateful there were no more secrets between them while she was fighting the howlaa because after her probable demise, Wolf would know exactly how she had felt about him. She could see now how careful he'd been to clear up any misunderstanding that might lie between them, any regrets or doubts that she might have.

If Nevyn knew that it would take a human sacrifice, Wolf did as well.

"Aralorn?" Gerem touched her arm. "What is it?"

Wolf knew, and, like Nevyn, he'd chosen a sacrifice. If Nevyn had realized just who Wolf had picked, he wouldn't have tried to kill Gerem.

"He told me three times," she said softly. "He said he loved me, three times."

"Aralorn?" asked Gerem again.

She didn't bother to answer but bolted out the door and sprinted down the hall. She took the stairs in leaping strides, ignoring the danger of falling, ignoring the pain in her shoulder, which throbbed in time with her steps.

The great hall was dark, and there was no sign of light behind the alcove curtain, but Aralorn felt the richness of magic at work.

She threw back the curtains and stepped into the darkness, only then feeling the wrongness of the power. It slid across her skin like thick, filthy oil. A moment later, the full effect of the tainted magic hit her as strongly as any fear spell she'd ever felt, leaving her unable to take a step forward for the sheer terror of what lay ahead.

It didn't feel like a fear spell, though, so she had no antidote for its effects. Perhaps it was a side effect of the magic Wolf was working. As she hesitated in the darkness, fighting the urge to turn tail and run, she could feel the surge of power, and the corruption of the magic grew stronger.

"Deathsgate and back, Wolf," she said, managing to put one foot in front of the other once, then again, until she stood on the far side of the darkness. "I warned you."

He stood behind her father, who was covered with markings. Wolf's scarred face was almost as masklike as the silver one. He touched the side of the Lyon's face with the first finger of each hand as his macabre voice chanted words in a language she'd never heard. His staff, balanced upright on the claws on its base, glowed radiantly from just behind his right shoulder. Lights and shadows fought for his face so it was unevenly illuminated.

The scent of blood and herbs was neither unpleasant nor pleasurable. It was much hotter than it should have been in a stone room in the winter, and the heat and strong scent combined to make her almost dizzy.

He hadn't noticed her come in, but she wasn't surprised. The worst thing a human wizard can do is lose control of a spell, so most of them had incredible powers of concentration—she would have expected no less of Wolf.

Relief swept her briefly at the sight of him still standing, breaking the hold of terror. Her thoughts clear for the first time since she entered the room, she saw the runes that covered the bier and the floor around it. Runes in herbs and chalk and char, but too many of them were drawn in blood.

She looked up swiftly to note how pale his skin was where it was not scarred, and she knew where the blood had come from. His voice rose hoarsely, and the magic surged as he called; it was so strong, her skin tingled, and so foul, she wanted to vomit.

Wolf pulled his hands away from her father, and she saw the dark wound on his wrist. The slowness of the bleeding told its own story, though Wolf should have been unconscious before he lost so much blood. Or dead.

"*No!* Plague take you, Wolf!" she said, and ran, ignoring the runes she destroyed on her way, ignoring the knowledge that by breaking his concentration, she could destroy herself and her father as well.

She broke his focus, and he looked up. For a moment, she had a clear view of his scarred face, then the light from his staff went out. She caught him as he fell—as they fell—cushioning his head against her. She grabbed his sticky wrist and wrapped her hand around it, sealing the wound with her own flesh, but his skin was colder than it should be in a room this warm.

In her heightened state, she could feel the wild magic he'd called reach for him, could feel his life fading. She had no time for panic; instead, she drew in a deep, calming breath and centered herself . . .

KISRAH WATCHED GEREM follow Aralorn out of the room. He'd overheard enough to have a pretty good idea of where they were going—especially since, once he looked for it, he could feel magic taking shape somewhere in the keep.

Kisrah wasn't certain that it wouldn't be better if Wolf didn't survive. No matter that Kisrah was virtually convinced that Aralorn was right to claim that Geoffrey was a villain. It did not take away the fact that Wolf knew black magic and carried its taint. By Wolf's own admission, the Master Spells had not allowed Geoffrey to control him—and even if they had, the Master Spells were gone.

If he followed her, he would be forced to choose—to help Wolf or to kill him; so he chose to stay with Nevyn while Aralorn's uncle tried to heal him.

"This damage had been mostly scarred over once," the shapechanger said, finally looking up from Nevyn. "And only recently torn asunder. Violently."

"Can you heal him?"

But Halven was looking around the room. "Where is Aralorn?"

"Rescuing Wolf," Kisrah said.

Halven gave him a sharp glance but turned back to Nevyn. "I can mend the surface," he said. "That ought to give Nevyn control over his dreamwalking self—probably return him to where he was before this most recent damage. True healing of such an old hurt will take a very long time, but it can be done."

"If he'll let you try," said Kisrah. "He's stubborn, and his life has not made him fond of magic."

Halven's eyes grew cold. "After the damage he's done here, he'll accept my healing, or I'll kill him myself. Henrick is a friend of mine."

"Nevyn is my friend," said Kisrah in warning.

The shapeshifter's mouth turned up, but his eyes did not warm. "Let me do what I can for him now, then. You go help Aralorn—there's something going on in the bier room. Can you feel it?"

Caught, Kisrah hesitated. "Yes."

"Go," said Halven. "This will be easier without you here."

But not easier for me, Kisrah thought. He would have to choose.

HALVEN WAITED FOR the door to swing shut behind the Archmage before turning again to his patient. The quiet was helpful but not necessary. Once he knew what had to be done, it was not difficult: A spirit was not meant to be divided. All he had to do was provide the magic to assist the weaving.

It did not take long before it was done as well as magic could make it. Only time would completely heal the rift. When he was finished, he waved his hand, and Nevyn's eyelids fluttered.

Nevyn opened his eyes.

"Welcome back, sir," said Halven, not unkindly. "I think we may have much to discuss."

Nevyn rolled to a sitting position and buried his face in both hands. "It was me," he said. "It was me all along."

ARALORN HELD WOLF'S wrist tightly in one hand, sealing the wound, though she feared it was too late. With her free hand, she touched the artery in his neck. For a horrible moment, she thought that he had no pulse, but then she felt the faint beat beneath her fingertips.

He'd been holding to consciousness with magic, she thought. When she'd distracted him, he'd lost control of the power sustaining him and fainted.

They should both be dead. She'd broken the cardinal rule of magic and interrupted Wolf. His spell should have turned this corner of Lambshold into a melted slag like the tower in the ae'Magi's castle.

It had not.

She was so weary. If she'd been a human mage, she would have had to watch Wolf die. But there was so much power in the room that the warmth of it strengthened her.

Most of the power was in the spell that awaited some missing component to act: Wolf's death. Aralorn could feel the magic coerced and caged into some shape of Wolf's devising, but it was human born, and she could not touch it. But flickering around the spell like a candle flame in the wind was other power, a latticework of green magic that held the spell at bay: Wolf's magic protecting her still.

Someone came into the room, and a last vestige of caution made her look up for an instant and see Gerem stagger through the spell of darkness and silence that covered the curtain to the bier room. In that moment of inattention, when she strayed from her center, Ridane's bond stretched tight.

Aralorn cried out at the pain and drove her fingers into Wolf's shoulder and wounded wrist.

"Don't you leave me, you bastard." She gritted out the words, and called his green magic to her.

Even though she was careful to leave enough magic to hold Wolf's spell, power flooded her, filling her veins with icy fire and making it difficult to breathe. She couldn't tell where the pain was coming from now, from the too-great magic that had answered her call or from the death goddess's binding that stretched taut and thin between them.

She had no idea what she was doing.

She bowed down and pressed her forehead against his too-cool flesh. She fed him magic at first, but it flowed through him and back into her without leaving any virtue behind. It was his magic, and he'd called it to save her, not himself.

She growled deep in her throat. "Not yet," she said. "I'll not lose you to your own stubbornness."

She took the magic and twisted it until it was attached to her, then thrust it back into him like a needle pulling her life force through him.

"Wolf," she murmured, touching his unresponsive lips, "don't you die on me."

She could feel that his pulse had steadied with the force she'd added, but she could feel, too, that it wasn't going to be enough. Remembering how she had touched her father's life, she began singing to aid her work. She hadn't consciously chosen the song, and was almost amused when she realized it was a rather lewd drinking song—so be it. If anyone knew how to fight off the cold thought of death, it was a bunch of drunken mercenaries.

The music soon soothed her into a trance that allowed her to seep into the pattern of Wolf's death. With more need than skill, she followed Wolf's spirit where it lingered, held by thin traces of life.

Recklessly, she threw energy to his fading spirit, to anchor him to his body, using his own magic to do it. She found the bond the death goddess had drawn between them and gripped it like a rope to pull him to her, only to find it gripped in return as Wolf, free from reason and memory, helped her at last.

She came out of her trance slowly, gradually becoming aware of Wolf's head in her lap, the unusual warmth of the stones beneath her, and the wild, surging magic that filled the room.

"Crap," she said. She'd called upon too much magic and released the power that had been bound in Wolf's spell.

She swung her gaze around to look for the reason that the walls were still standing. Kisrah stood before the darkness that was the entrance to the room. His feet were braced and his arms held wide. Gerem stood just behind him, gripping his shoulder with one hand in a position that even Aralorn recognized as "feeding."

"Wolf?" she said, shaking him with her good arm. "Wolf, wake up."

"Good idea," muttered Kisrah. "We're not going to be able to hold this back much longer."

Aralorn took the hint and quit being so gentle. *"Wolf,"* she barked with force enough to please a drill sergeant. "You've got to wake up, love. We need you."

He stirred this time and opened his eyes, frowning at her in puzzlement. He started to speak, and his eyes widened as his senses told him what was going on.

"Gods," he growled, sitting up a little too abruptly.

She caught him before he could fall back and held him while he closed his eyes against the dizzying weakness of extreme blood loss. Since his weight hit her bad arm with a certain amount of force, she was feeling a bit dizzy herself.

"What did you think you were doing?" he rasped. "You know better than to interrupt a spell in progress."

"Hmm," she agreed. "Deathsgate and back, remember? You shouldn't have tried this."

"Excuse me," interrupted Kisrah politely, though his voice sounded a little strained. "Not to break in on a personal moment or anything, but do you suppose you could give me a little advice, Wolf?"

"Hmm," said Wolf. "I suppose 'run' won't work?"

Kisrah laughed, which was a mistake.

Power lit the room with a faint red haze, and the temperature went from warm to hot in an instant. Aralorn felt the surge in magic so strong that it hurt. The smell of scorching cloth filled the room, and the stones gave off an odd grumbling noise. Sweat gathered on Kisrah's face, and Gerem was looking almost as drained as Kisrah.

"Your magic held it in check while you were unconscious," said Aralorn urgently. "Green magic, Wolf. Can you call it again?"

In answer, green magic slid over her skin in a caress, then spilled over the imminent spell like oil over boiling water. Gently, it worked its way between the spell and Kisrah's magic.

Wolf vibrated in her arms, shaking with the control that it took not to fight for domination over the green magic.

"What in the name of . . ." murmured Kisrah, relaxing his stance. "I've never seen anything like this."

"Green magic," replied Wolf in a strained voice. "It scares me, too. But I *think* it will work."

"'Think'?"

Wolf's scarred lips writhed into a semblance of a smile. "Would you rather I said 'hope'?"

As Wolf took up the reins of the magic, Kisrah relaxed and ran his hands through his hair, leaving it an untidy mess. Actually, thought Aralorn with exhaustion-born whimsy, he looked quite different from his usual self, his lemon-colored sleeping trousers setting off pale skin stretched over a swordsman's muscles, his feet bare.

"Now what do we do?" he asked.

"Well," said Wolf, "at this stage the spell can't be banished, for it has already been given a taste of that which was promised. Can you feel the hunger? So what we do is bring it into completion." He turned to Aralorn, who was already shaking her head, but she was too weak to do anything more. "I love you, dear heart. If you love me as well, you'll allow me this. Someone must die tonight—I won't allow my father to kill again and not do something about it."

He held her gaze with his own until tears slid down her cheeks.

"Ridane said someone had to die," said Aralorn. "This is what she meant, wasn't it? The nature of the spell laid on Father is such that either he dies, or someone else does. I didn't bring you back for this, Wolf."

His eyes warmed, and he touched her face. "If you hadn't brought me back, my love, Ridane's bond would have taken you with me. I should have severed it before I started the spell—I waited too late. I didn't want to lose you."

He dropped his hands, leaving her cold and alone. "This was laid upon your father because of me; should he die for my sins?"

"Not your sins," returned Aralorn heatedly. "Your father's sins."

"No," said Nevyn from the doorway. "My sins."

The darkness that had blocked the door was gone, banished by Nevyn, or perhaps her uncle, who stood behind him. Nevyn's face was grim and pale.

"I have allowed myself to be used," he said. "I allowed Geoffrey to twist my thoughts until I have become what my father thought I was."

He stepped forward until he stood before Wolf, facing him. "I thought that it was you who was corrupt, who needed destroying—instead, I find that you are willing to sacrifice yourself for a man you barely know. Evil corrupted me; it has tempered you."

He turned to Aralorn and crouched in front of her.

"Sister," he said softly, so quietly that she knew that no one else in the room heard exactly what he said. "Story-Spinner, weave a good one for Freya when she wakes—that she will honor the father of the child she carries, for its sake."

Exhaustion made Aralorn's thoughts slow. She was preoccupied with keeping Wolf alive, and it made her slow.

When Nevyn surged to his feet, and told Wolf, "Use this," she finally caught on. "Nevyn, *wait.*" But it was already too late.

Nevyn called upon his magic and was engulfed in flames so hot that his flesh melted from his bones like water.

"Wolf?" said Aralorn in a voice she hardly recognized, so thickened was it from grief. But there was a real possibility, given Wolf's reluctance to use black magic, that he would refuse Nevyn's sacrifice.

But it was Kisrah who said, "Don't let him die in vain, Wolf."

WOLF HESITATED, TORN between the horror of using yet another person's death to fuel his magic and the desires of the man who had given his life for his convictions.

"Please," whispered Aralorn, tears of grief sliding down her face.

He dropped his knife and lifted his arms, drawing the power of Nevyn's death to him. He waited for the filth to settle on his soul, but the death magic rested quietly within his grasp, as if a dead man's blessing had the ability to wipe clean the foul work to which Wolf had been put.

The respite was brief, for as he willed it, the hold that had kept the spell in abeyance began to fade slowly, allowing Wolf to take control of one part before releasing another. No benediction could wash away the evil of the black art that comprised the spell, and Wolf shook under the force of it even as he threaded death magic through it in completion.

The spell pulsed wildly for a moment before concentrating upon the still form of the Lyon, then, as swiftly as the flight of a hawk, it was gone, leaving the room reeking with the stench of evil.

Wolf dropped to his knees.

Aralorn slid across the floor to the small mess of charred bones, where Kisrah and Gerem already knelt.

"What is happening? Who is that man?"

Aralorn looked up to see Irrenna standing in the entranceway, clad only in her nightrobes. The lady's gaze traveled around the room, pausing at the silent form of her husband before halting on Aralorn's tear-streaked face.

"There is a dead howlaa by the stables," Irrenna said. "We were trying to find out how it got there when there was a terrible noise, as if the stones of the keep were shifting."

"Oh, Mother," croaked Aralorn, as Correy and Falhart, who must have been drawn by the same sound, came into the room as well. "Irrenna," she tried again. "Nevyn saved Father, but he died in the doing of it."

"The Lyon's waking now," said Kisrah.

Gerem jumped up and ran to the bier. Kisrah lingered a moment. He murmured something that Aralorn couldn't hear and conjured a white rose, which he set just inside the charred area. Then he, too, left the dead for the living.

Irrenna froze for an instant before she, Falhart, and Correy all ran to the Lyon's side.

Bound by weakness and inclination, Aralorn stayed by Nevyn's remains. She touched the blackened skull gently, as if a stronger touch would have hurt him. "Rest in peace, Nevyn."

A cold nose touched her hand, and she turned to Wolf, who wore his wolf form once more.

His golden eyes were dim with sorrow, and Aralorn drew him close, pressing her face into Wolf's shoulder. "I know," she said. "I know."

FINIS

—⁓—

FAR TO THE EAST, THE DREAMER STIRRED. IT HAD BEEN FOR NAUGHT—all the manipulation, all the work, and its own tool had betrayed it.

It had known the dreamwalker was not stable, but it had not expected him to choose to die so that the Lyon would live. By that choice, he had rendered the magic useless for the Dreamer to feed upon. Cain's death would not have been useless, for the Archmage's son had been used by the Dreamer before; not even the purity of Cain's willing self-sacrifice would have stopped the Dreamer from feeding.

It would sleep now, but its sleep would not be as long, or as deep. It would not have to wait another millennium for a corrupt Archmage to awaken it. When Geoffrey ae'Magi had died, it had seen to it that the Master Spells would not be used again.

The Dreamer stirred, then settled beneath the weight of the ancient bindings. It would wait.

ARALORN EXAMINED THE healing cut on Sheen's side. It looked as if it had been healing a week rather than three days; she was going to have to talk to the stablemaster and find out what he used for ointment.

She wouldn't need it for her shoulder. Halven had taken care of the cuts left by the howlaa's claws, though it still ached a bit when she over-worked her arm. She heard someone enter the stables and stuck her head over Sheen's door.

"You're leaving today." Her father moved a little stiffly, but otherwise showed little sign of any aftereffects of the spell.

Aralorn smiled. "Yes, sir, as soon as Kisrah comes back with my wolf. They went hunting with the boys—I include Falhart in that category."

He reached up and rubbed Sheen's forehead. "I understand you've been making quite a reputation for yourself."

"Me or the horse?"

He grinned. "You."

She raised her eyebrows, and said, "Let's just say that having a shapeshifter for a spy, whether they know it or not, hasn't hurt Sianim any."

"I've missed you," he said softly.

"I've missed you, too. I'll be back, though. If you let me know, I'll come after Freya's babe is born."

The Lyon's hand stilled on the horse's forehead. "I wish Nevyn would be alive to see it. They waited so long for this child."

She nodded. She'd told him the truth about Nevyn, knowing that he would not judge his son-in-law for it.

Freya deserved the truth as well, if she wanted it. Aralorn had left that for her father to decide. Freya hadn't spoken to her since she'd awakened to the news that her husband was dead. Maybe she already knew at least part of what had been going on.

"This friend of yours, the one Nevyn was after when he set the spell on me. He is safe?"

"I think so," she said. "With Geoffrey well and truly dead, no one but Kisrah and the family know that I was ever involved with him."

Neither Gerem nor Kisrah had challenged the story she'd told Irrenna and repeated often since—that the last ae'Magi hadn't been the man he'd appeared to be. He'd made an attempt on King Myr's life, and, in response, she and his son had moved against him. They had thought he died, a victim of the Uriah—but he was a dreamwalker, and survived long enough to set up his son's death. It had been Nevyn, she explained, who had figured out how to break the spell, but in doing so, had brought about his own death. Nevyn deserved to be a hero—and Geoffrey, who had hurt Nevyn so badly, deserved whatever blame fell to him.

With Kisrah's corroborating testimony regarding the character of the previous ae'Magi, almost everyone seemed to accept the tale. Aralorn suspected that Kisrah had done something to the hold the previous ae'Magi's spells had continued to have—because no one challenged him or seemed unnaturally sure of Geoffrey's goodness.

The Lyon rubbed his beard. "I knew Geoffrey, but I met Cain a time or two as well—when he was younger than Gerem by a few years."

"I didn't know that."

"Up until that point, I'd been favorably impressed by the ae'Magi. I was curious about his son though, mostly because of the stories that were circulating about him even then."

"What did you think of him when you met him?" she asked, curious.

"He . . . Something that Correy said leads me to believe that the relationship that you have with Cain is somewhat more than friendship."

She smiled slowly. "You might say that, yes."

"Then bring him with you the next time you come down—tell him he doesn't have to come and go mysteriously as he did this time. Irrenna and I would be pleased to have him as a guest."

Her smile widened, and tears threatened as she slipped out the door, so she could give him a hug. "I love you, Da."

No matter what her father said, it still wasn't safe for too many people to know where the Archmage's infamous son was, but she'd tell Wolf what her father said. It would matter to him.

He bent down, and whispered, "Especially if one of you teaches my cook how to make those little cakes that you had at the king's coronation. I know you were playing cook, so the nasty-looking guard must have been Cain."

Her mouth dropped open, and she took two steps back and kinked her neck so she could look him in the eyes. "How did you know?"

He shook his head. "I'm not really certain, to tell you the truth. But I've always been able to tell who you are, no matter what shape you wear."

"You DIDN'T TELL him we were married," Wolf said with neutrality he didn't feel as he paced by Sheen's side. Had she been ashamed of him?

She shook her head. "He'd have been hurt that he missed the ceremony," she told him. "We can do it up properly later, when it won't be tied up with Nevyn's deal, don't you think? You have his approval, though, if that helps."

That bewildered him. How could he approve of Cain, the ae'Magi's despised son, for his daughter? "He doesn't know me."

"He's met you," she told him. "He knows what you did here and why. That was apparently enough for him—oh, and he really wants to know how you made those little cakes you fixed for Myr's coronation."

Wolf stopped. Sheen halted beside him, and Aralorn waited with unusual (for her) patience for him to speak. He didn't know what to say.

"You married me so I would not seek death for fear of causing yours," he said.

She got that mysterious smile that usually meant she knew more than she should about something, but all she said was "Yes."

He didn't know why that bothered him so much. And if he couldn't explain it to himself, how could he explain it to her?

She took pity on him eventually.

"Wolf," she said. "Married is wonderful, married is lovely. But I loved you before that, and you were mine before that. Only you for me—only me for you. That's how it was before our marriage." The smile fell away and left her pale and determined. "That's how it was when I found you in that pit trap all those years ago—I knew as soon as I first saw your eyes. But then, I've known all my life what love is. It took you, who had nothing to compare it to, rather longer to figure it out, to understand what is between us. But even when you did not understand or recognize it—it was always love."

Sheen sighed and shifted his weight, but Aralorn didn't turn her attention from Wolf as he took her words and warmed himself on them.

"Yes," he said, and started out for the inn where they would spend the night. "Yes. That is how it is."

She rode beside him, and he didn't need to turn his head to know that she was there.